Here is ...

Note to: Donna Gash.

Din Din Book of No-nonsense Poetry #1

I really, really, really appreciate you.

I will be talking to you on the phone.

Thank-You!

Diane Marie Sytarchuk-Kent!

and Kevin Lee Kent.

Din Din Book
of
No-nonsense Poetry
#1

Diane Sytarchuk-Kent

Library of Congress Control Number: 2014909636

ISBN:	Hardcover	978-1-4990-2504-0
	Softcover	978-1-4990-2505-7
	eBook	978-1-4990-2503-3

This book was printed in the United States of America.

Rev. date: 05/23/2014

To order additional copies of this book, contact:
Xlibris LLC
1-888-795-4274
www.Xlibris.com
Orders@Xlibris.com
553817

CONTENTS

My Dedication:

My poetry is by no means great and worthy of literary praise.

It is, just - meant to please all who love a good rhyme and to reat out loud.

My autistic son gave me the idea of writing a book for my extended family - of lovers of rhyme. He loves rhyme. It soothes him to be read to.

My aim - is to please and to help give social skills content

Thank - you!

INTRODUCTION

I originally wanted to make social stories—line for line—but quickly decided otherwise. Instead I opted to place the social stories in the margins of each page—corresponding to the appropriate text. Every page will be different.

This book is dedicated to my son Eric.

A thank you goes out to all the wonderful people who helped me get to a place where I could write this book.

The pictures are really just—social stories. I thought—then—my son, Eric could follow along. He is autistic and associates ideas through pictures.

BOOK
OF
NONSENSE
POEMS
FOR
ALL
THE
ERIC'S

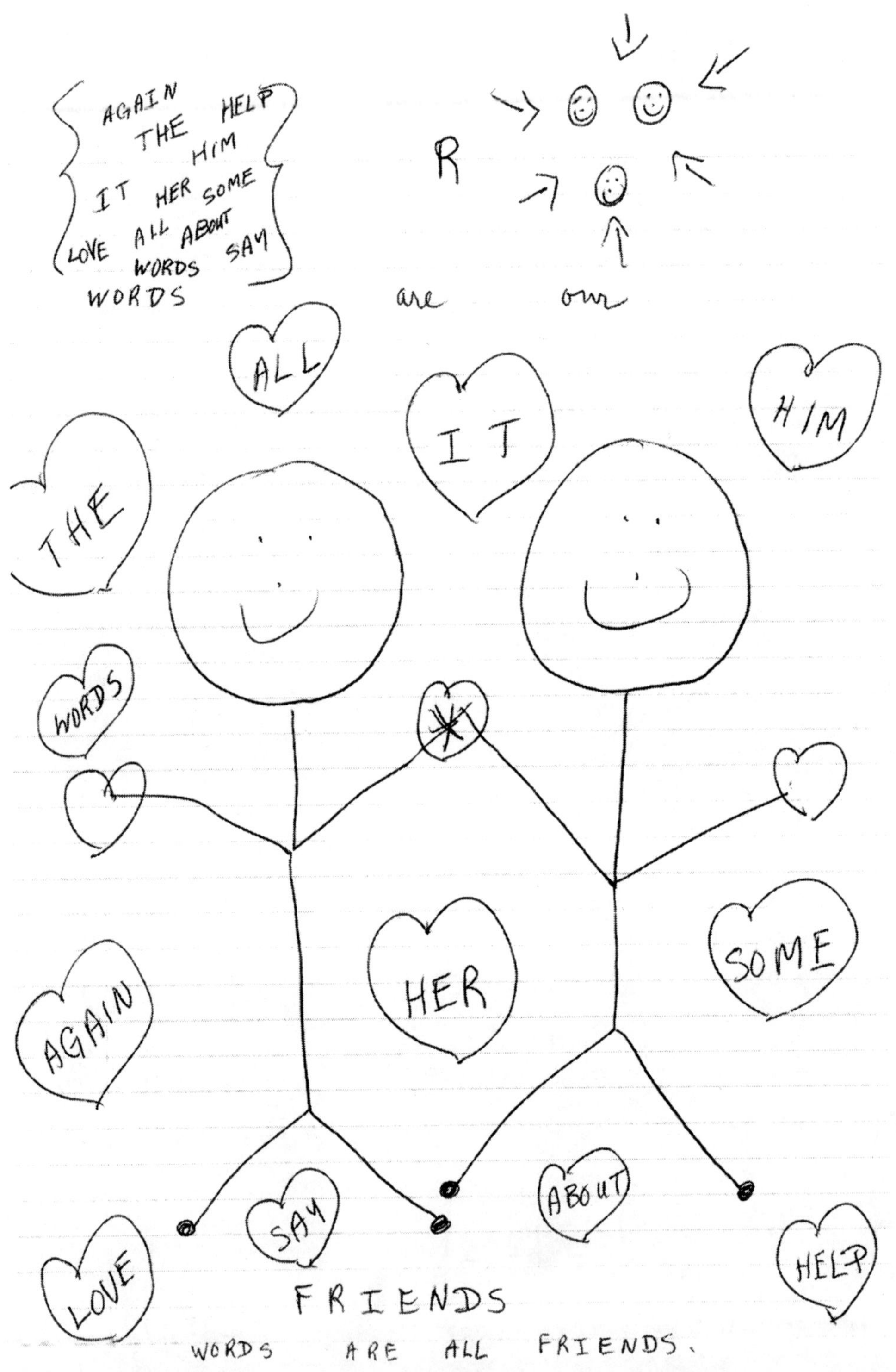
AGAIN
THE HELP
IT HIM
HER SOME
LOVE ALL ABOUT
WORDS SAY
WORDS
R
are
our
ALL
IT
HIM
THE
WORDS
AGAIN
HER
SOME
ABOUT
SAY
LOVE
HELP
FRIENDS
WORDS ARE ALL FRIENDS.

Din Din's Book Of No-Nonsense Poetry #1.

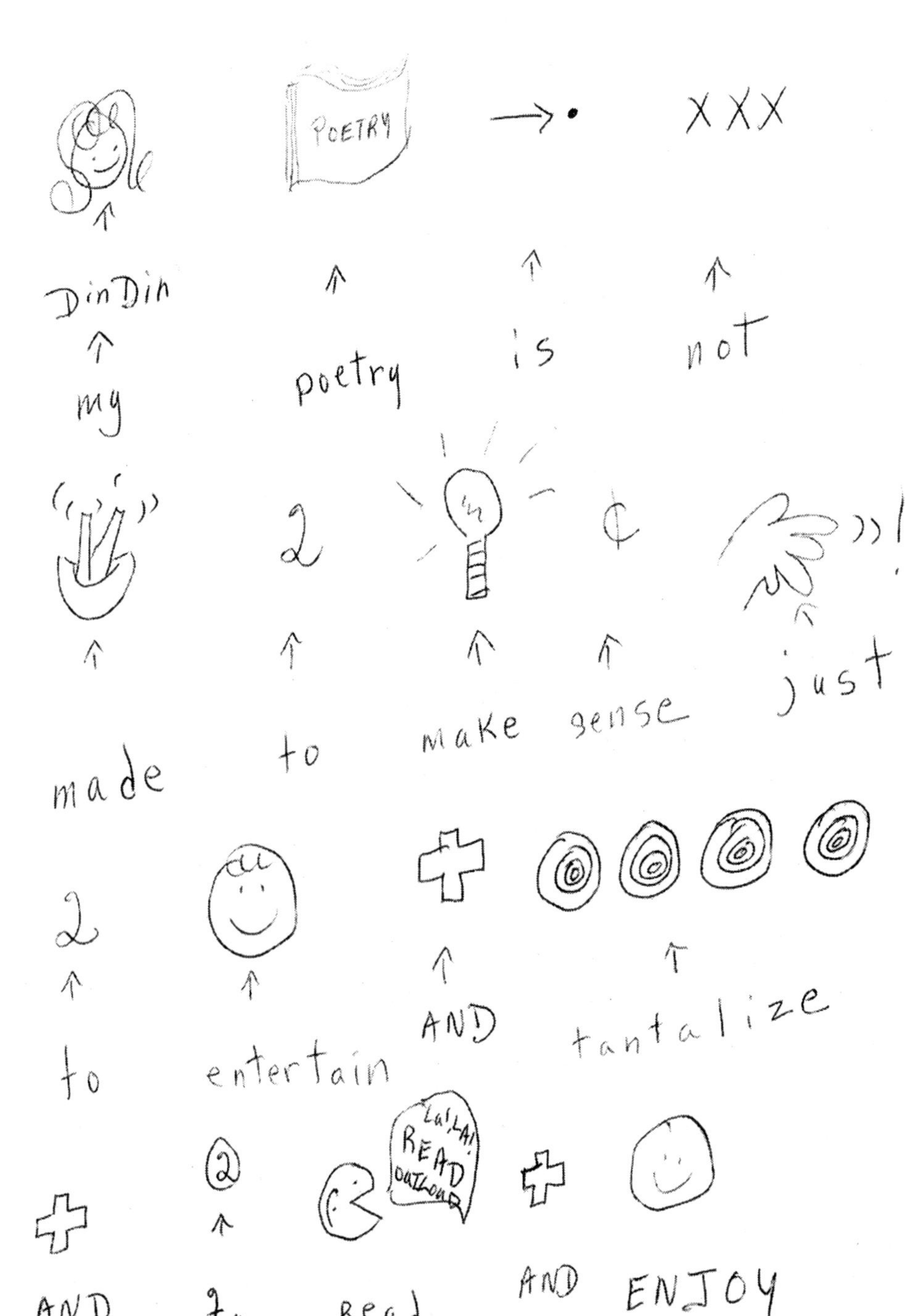

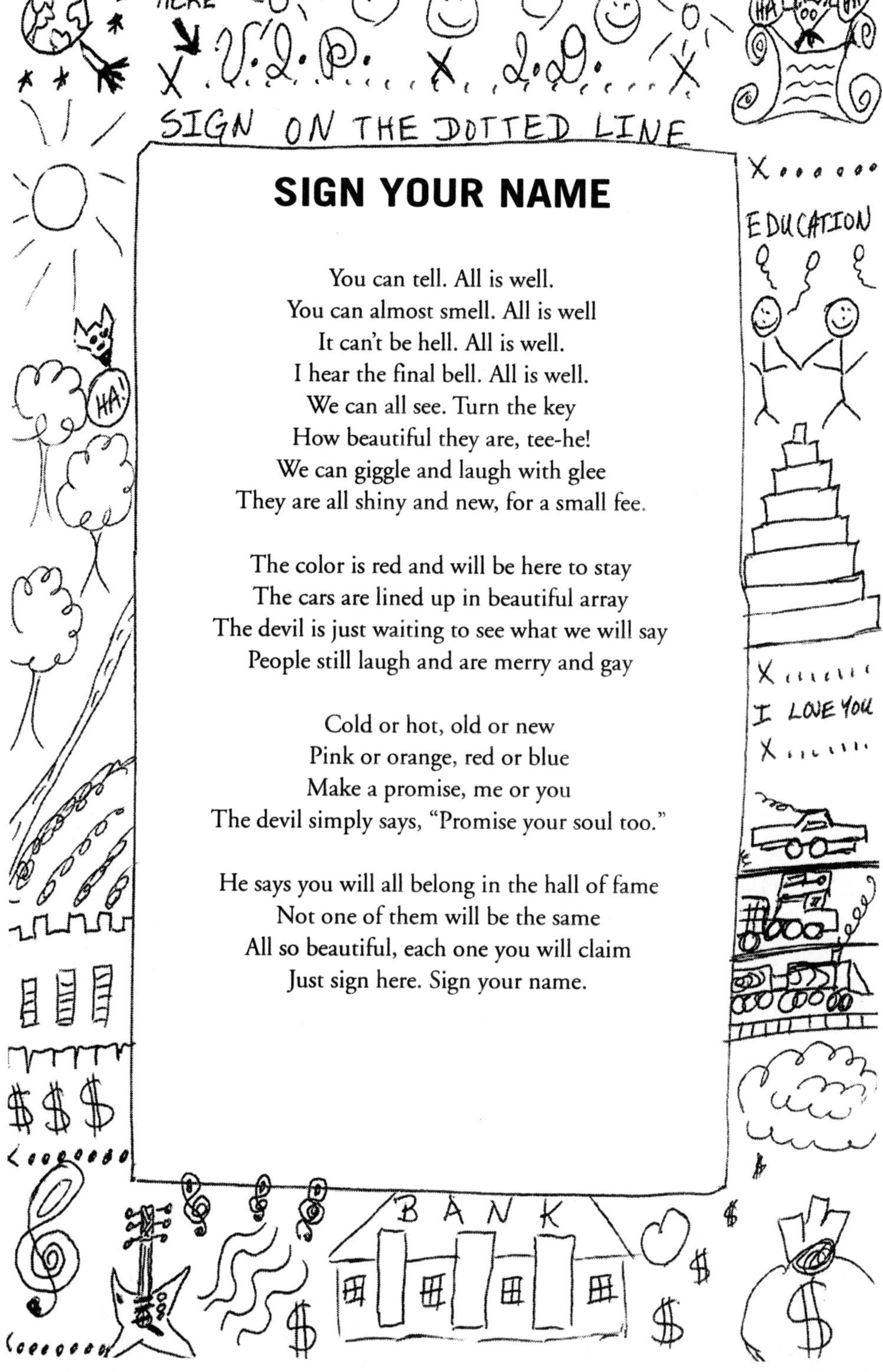

SIGN YOUR NAME

You can tell. All is well.
You can almost smell. All is well
It can't be hell. All is well.
I hear the final bell. All is well.
We can all see. Turn the key
How beautiful they are, tee-he!
We can giggle and laugh with glee
They are all shiny and new, for a small fee.

The color is red and will be here to stay
The cars are lined up in beautiful array
The devil is just waiting to see what we will say
People still laugh and are merry and gay

Cold or hot, old or new
Pink or orange, red or blue
Make a promise, me or you
The devil simply says, "Promise your soul too."

He says you will all belong in the hall of fame
Not one of them will be the same
All so beautiful, each one you will claim
Just sign here. Sign your name.

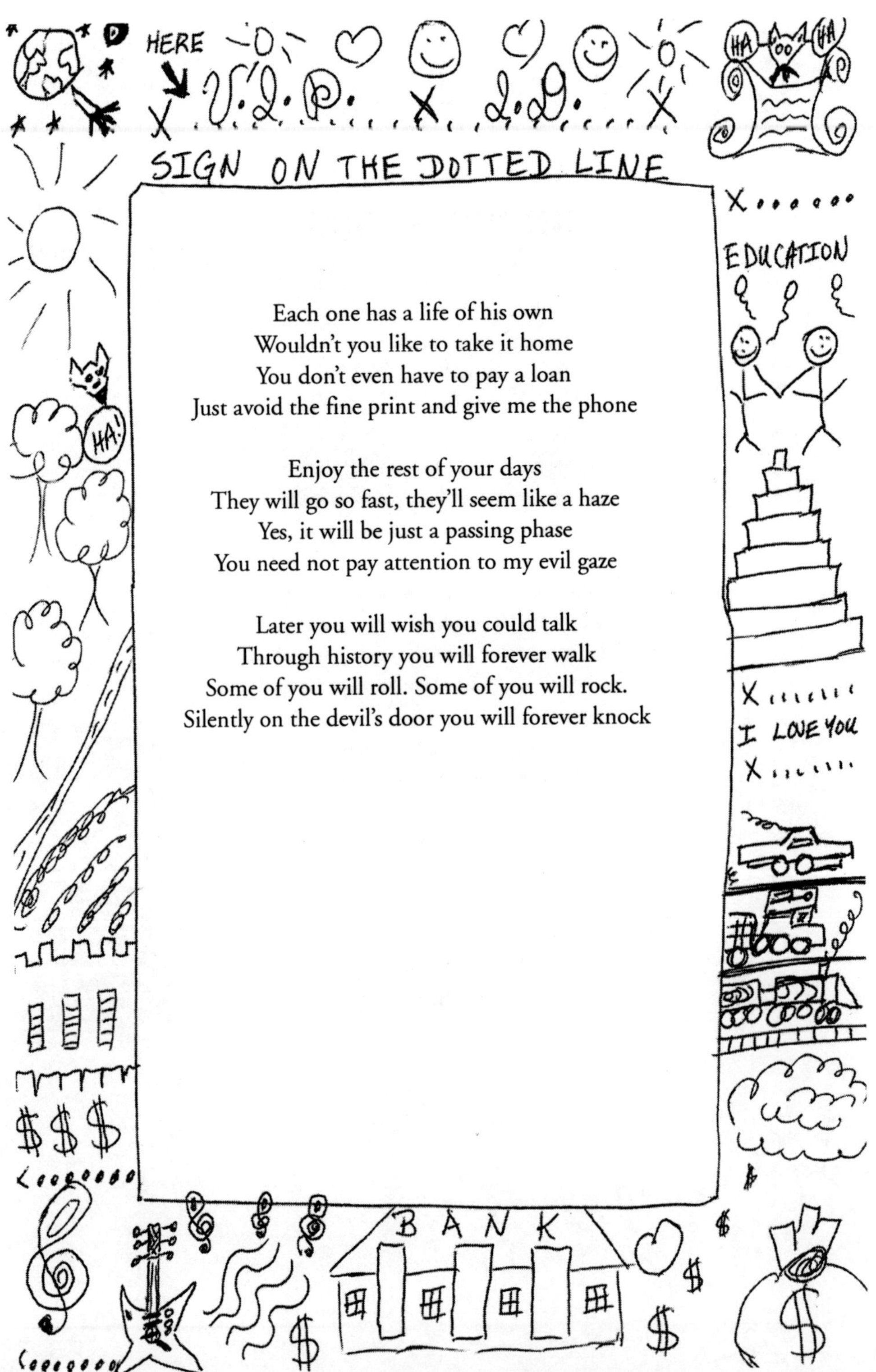

Each one has a life of his own
Wouldn't you like to take it home
You don't even have to pay a loan
Just avoid the fine print and give me the phone

Enjoy the rest of your days
They will go so fast, they'll seem like a haze
Yes, it will be just a passing phase
You need not pay attention to my evil gaze

Later you will wish you could talk
Through history you will forever walk
Some of you will roll. Some of you will rock.
Silently on the devil's door you will forever knock

I DON'T HAVE A CARE

Me, I don't have a care
I'm in a position that's rare
You, sir, can go ahead and stare
I've got a very thick first layer

Underneath, I'm soft as a pillow
And I can be weak as a young willow
Sometimes my life feels like I'm in a bowl of Jell-O
Sometimes when I'm shy, I desperately want to say hello

But all things aside
I also have Rider pride
And I have nothing to hide
I feel, in you, I can confide

What does this mean?
That has yet to be seen
Go ahead. Tell me where you've been.
Say hello and then let's go green.

Inside I say, "I think I'm going to cheer
I say, "No thanks, I don't need a beer."
I tell myself I have nothing to fear.
Because I'll stay sober and I will think clear.

This way I'll stay out of trouble
Come on now, come on the double
Come by my side, on my side of the hovel
Come on now, don't make me grovel

I knew I was right
Being honest doesn't bite
But hey, what if he puts up a fight
I hope he also has poor eyesight

Come on closer, you make me quiver
I hope he is not a chicken-liver
Please don't sell me down the river
Close your eyes. Be a life-giver.

I WILL IT

I know it, I will it.
For you I'm willing to commit
Come on over here, under my cockpit
I mean it. We make a perfect fit.

Come on over where it's cozy
We'll be coming up Rosie
Me, myself, I am fancy free
You, my dear, can be my sweet pea

If it was my choice
I would use my voice
And make a lot of noise
And dedicate it to you, my pride and joy

Here's one for the Alamo
I've been dealt a fatal blow
I feel like I'm on death row
I feel like your virtual yo-yo

If my attitude were to change
It would be very strange
It would feel like I was deranged
So there's really no more need for interchange

After the dusk is a new dawn
But I will feel like I now belong
And I will sing you a new song
After I will have energy for a marathon

Your love has left a deep welt
My offerings will be heartfelt
I am now beyond any human help
Sending prayers, on my knees I have knelt

I will stand still. It is my will.
You can have your fill. I am an easy kill.
You fit my bill. You are far from run of the mill.
I'll shout it from the highest hill.
I'll love you forever and until.

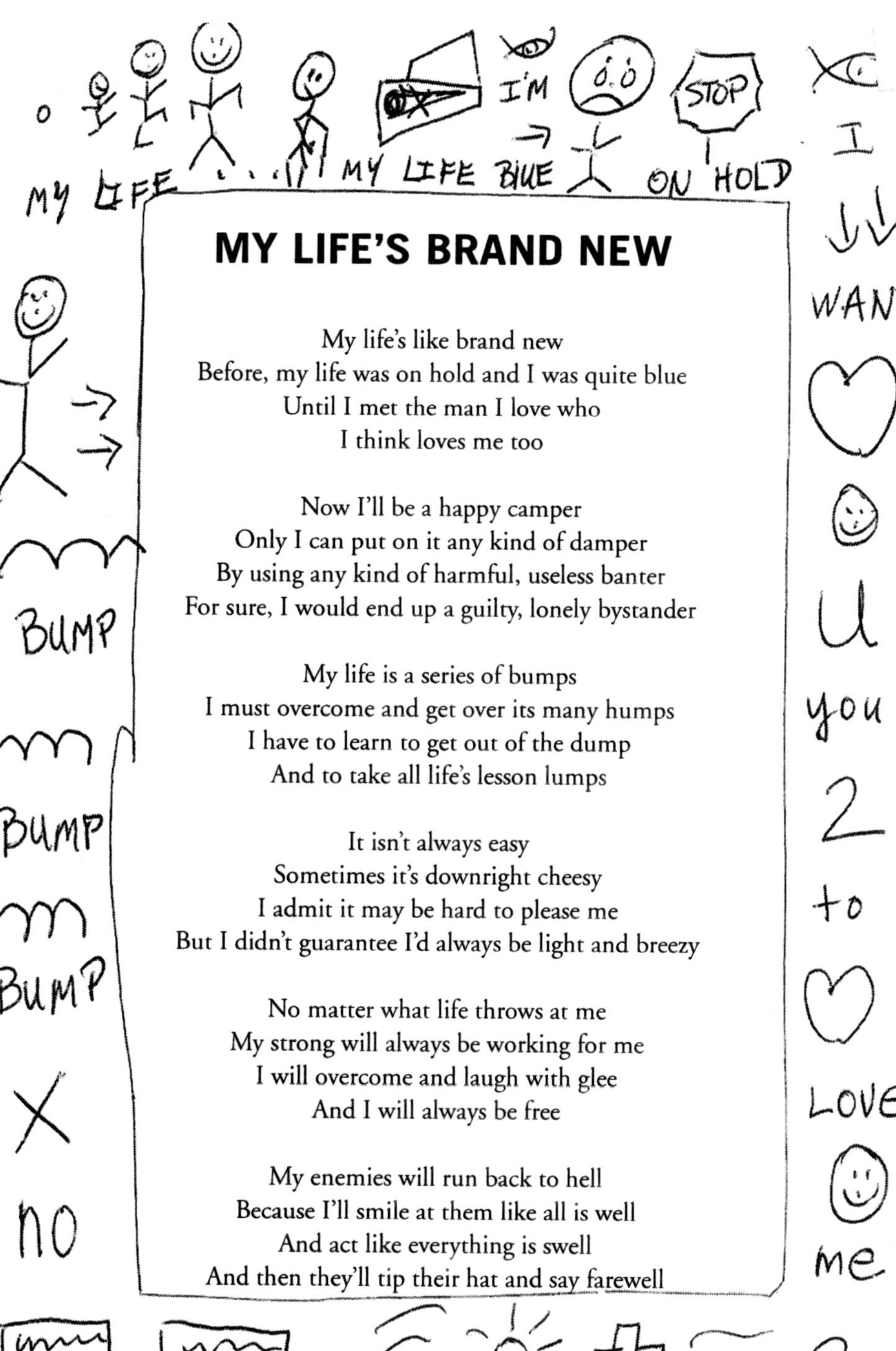

MY LIFE'S BRAND NEW

My life's like brand new
Before, my life was on hold and I was quite blue
Until I met the man I love who
I think loves me too

Now I'll be a happy camper
Only I can put on it any kind of damper
By using any kind of harmful, useless banter
For sure, I would end up a guilty, lonely bystander

My life is a series of bumps
I must overcome and get over its many humps
I have to learn to get out of the dump
And to take all life's lesson lumps

It isn't always easy
Sometimes it's downright cheesy
I admit it may be hard to please me
But I didn't guarantee I'd always be light and breezy

No matter what life throws at me
My strong will always be working for me
I will overcome and laugh with glee
And I will always be free

My enemies will run back to hell
Because I'll smile at them like all is well
And act like everything is swell
And then they'll tip their hat and say farewell

So I'll be brand new again, don't you know
I'll have a satisfied glow
It won't be one from down below
It'll be because I have defeated my foes

Because they have run away
It will have made my day
They haven't had their way
I'm brand new and fresh; I can play

YOU HAVEN'T GOT A CLUE

You haven't got a clue
Just all what I can do
I'm able to be strong and stick like glue
Or fly away and make something totally new

I like this certain ability
I like to pretend I am wise and witty
This makes me feel very pretty
And makes me happy I live in the city

Sometimes when times are rough
And we have all had some of that stuff
I like to think I can call your bluff
And then I will tell you, it will get better, no guff

When all good things come to an end
I believe good things are right around the bend
So I tell you whatever life may send
You will overcome and soon will be on the mend

And when everything seems to stop
And the ink decides to blot
You will have had a battle well fought
And success will be what you've got

When time stands still
And tests your tremendous will
And with all the memories they have instilled
A picture will appear in your very
own playwright's bill

And when you finally find rest
Then will come the final test
Then you can laugh at it in jest
You'll say go for it, be my guest

The test that fits that bill
Is that you must have strength of will
And if you learn to cultivate this and learn to instill
Then you will have peace of mind forever and until

A NEW CROP

Look, we have a new crop
We have a new generation that will not stop
Until the Garden of Eden is again our lot
And all our battles have been victoriously fought

This generation is our only salvation
This is our newly created generation
What we have created is our offering, our oblation
Let them do right without one moment's hesitation

They all come from good seed
They come out of their ancestor's need
They are a totally new reed
They came from nature's strongest bead

With each succeeding line
Our offering becomes more refined
It becomes more pure and more fine
We all know this is a very good sign

These children are man's only hope
So help them understand the great scope
And that their reason for learning what all has been wrote
Is to save all mankind even the scapegoat

We all started so long ago
What was created began to grow
We were and came to know what it was to do so
We also learned the differences between high and low

Each generation has in turn gave in to their sons
And also their daughters who have been the ones
Who, with the sons, had a little fun
And began to carry a new generation on the run

Our progeny has the tremendous task
Of taking off our human masks
And showing us where we all lack
And bringing humanity back onto the right track

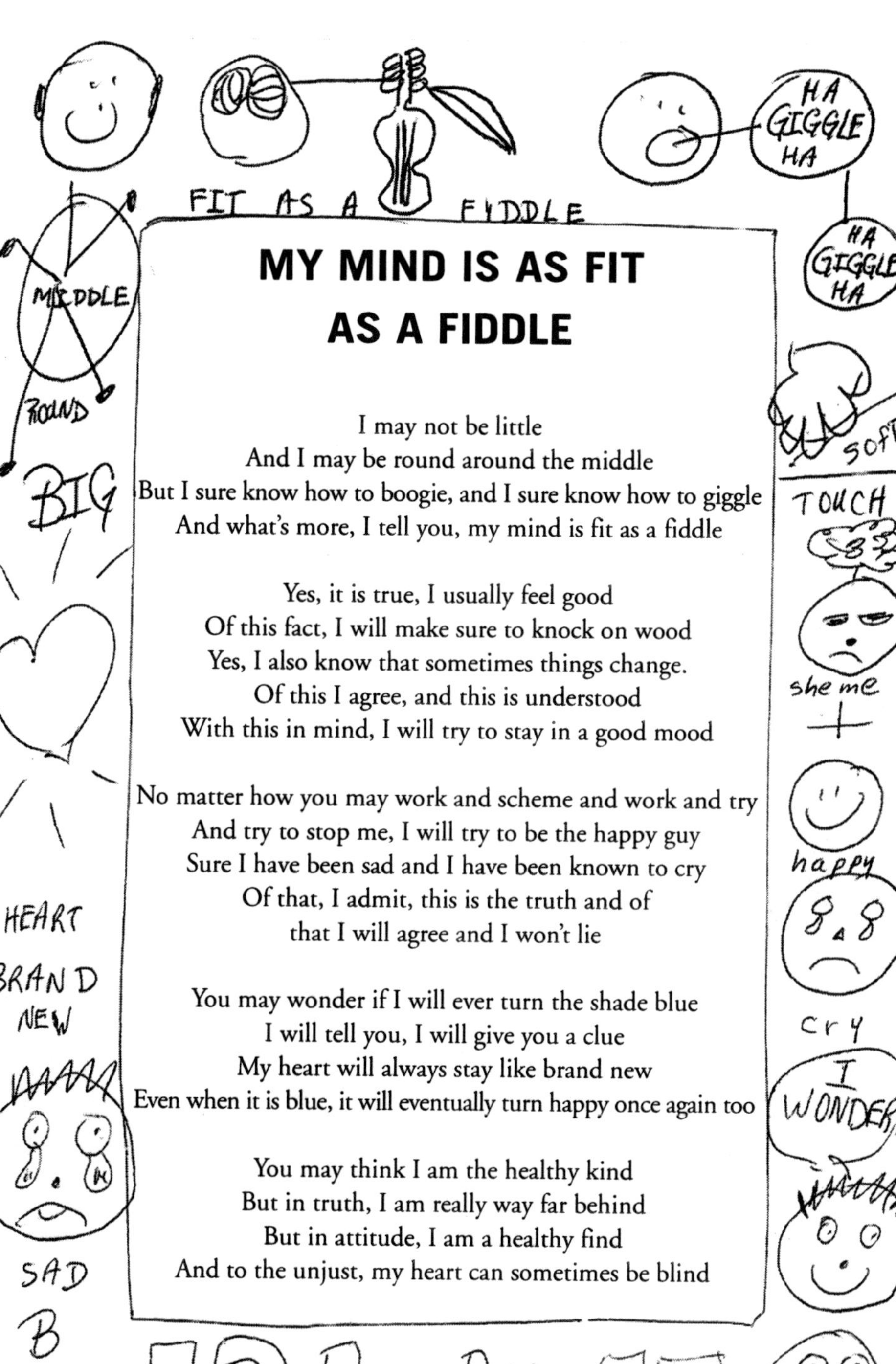

MY MIND IS AS FIT AS A FIDDLE

I may not be little
And I may be round around the middle
But I sure know how to boogie, and I sure know how to giggle
And what's more, I tell you, my mind is fit as a fiddle

Yes, it is true, I usually feel good
Of this fact, I will make sure to knock on wood
Yes, I also know that sometimes things change.
Of this I agree, and this is understood
With this in mind, I will try to stay in a good mood

No matter how you may work and scheme and work and try
And try to stop me, I will try to be the happy guy
Sure I have been sad and I have been known to cry
Of that, I admit, this is the truth and of
that I will agree and I won't lie

You may wonder if I will ever turn the shade blue
I will tell you, I will give you a clue
My heart will always stay like brand new
Even when it is blue, it will eventually turn happy once again too

You may think I am the healthy kind
But in truth, I am really way far behind
But in attitude, I am a healthy find
And to the unjust, my heart can sometimes be blind

As well, when it comes to my final
decision and in the end
My opinions can be found to sometimes bend
And with my positive ideas I will
try to share, lend, and send
Also I will try to help and inform again and again

When you think about it, the Stradivarius was rare
But come on now, let us face it, let us be fair
A Stradivarius cannot breathe or grow hair
And it certainly has no eyes with which to stare

I tell you, all in all, I will be just fine
Because I like to live and think in quarter time
And I believe that if you and I walk
together in a straight line
Success will be yours and ours, not only mine

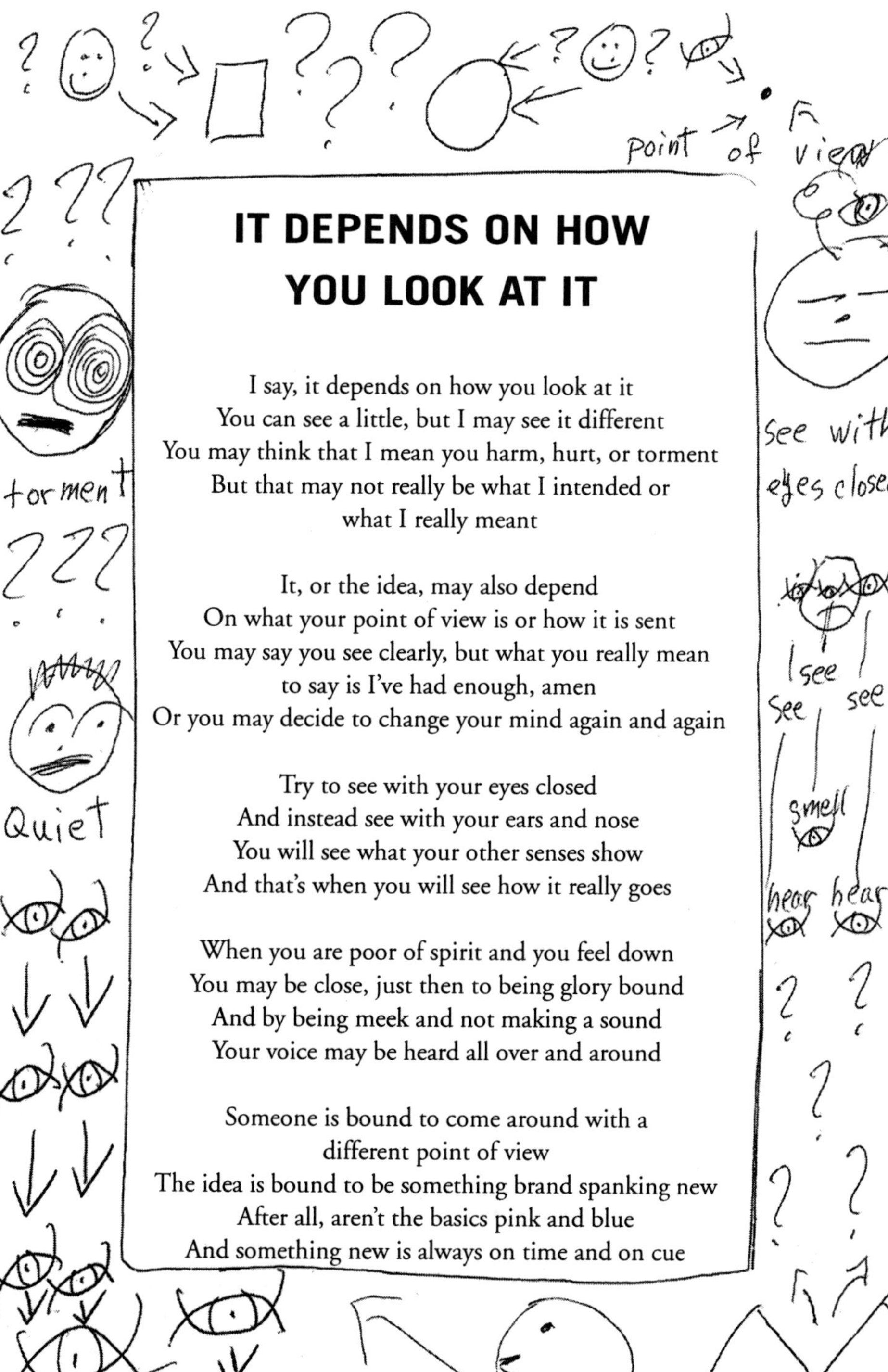

IT DEPENDS ON HOW YOU LOOK AT IT

I say, it depends on how you look at it
You can see a little, but I may see it different
You may think that I mean you harm, hurt, or torment
But that may not really be what I intended or
what I really meant

It, or the idea, may also depend
On what your point of view is or how it is sent
You may say you see clearly, but what you really mean
to say is I've had enough, amen
Or you may decide to change your mind again and again

Try to see with your eyes closed
And instead see with your ears and nose
You will see what your other senses show
And that's when you will see how it really goes

When you are poor of spirit and you feel down
You may be close, just then to being glory bound
And by being meek and not making a sound
Your voice may be heard all over and around

Someone is bound to come around with a
different point of view
The idea is bound to be something brand spanking new
After all, aren't the basics pink and blue
And something new is always on time and on cue

When you see things a new way
You may see how things truly lay
You won't be able to help being merry and gay
And you will find lots of time to play

Just open your senses and your eyes
Then you will see through people's lies
And everywhere you look, there will be clear blue skies
Furthermore, you will be one of the happy guys

You will join a brand-new sect
People will treat you with more respect
You will be the one others choose to elect
This will be the cause, and that will be the effect

INTERESTING HOW IT LOOKS

It is interesting how this world looks
Our situation is one for the textbooks
Right now it is OK as long as we all keep a positive outlook
We just have to overlook all our neighbor's dirty looks
The list to ignore and overlook goes on and on
It gets really long, disappears, and then it is gone
Don't be put upon; just look at the pros and cons
Soon our troubles will all be gone and
we will see a shiny new dawn
I see you are thinking seriously; I am too
Our thoughts are many and quite similar, not just a few
We have a right to be thinking about them
and hope they will be right on cue
All our thoughts are honest and true blue. All
we want is a universal breakthrough
If we all follow these thoughts, they will make us all happy
There is no need to feel crappy or to disagree
We all have so much to be thankful for
if we all just choose to agree
We have so much in common, we can grow to
love each other and be happy and carefree
I will listen to your voice and you can listen to mine
That would be my first choice for humankind
We would love to hear a new peace redefined
What to me is so dear can be there for all combined
My ideas are molded by many, many thoughts
And by the way my brain is folded.
Besides, I am mostly self-taught

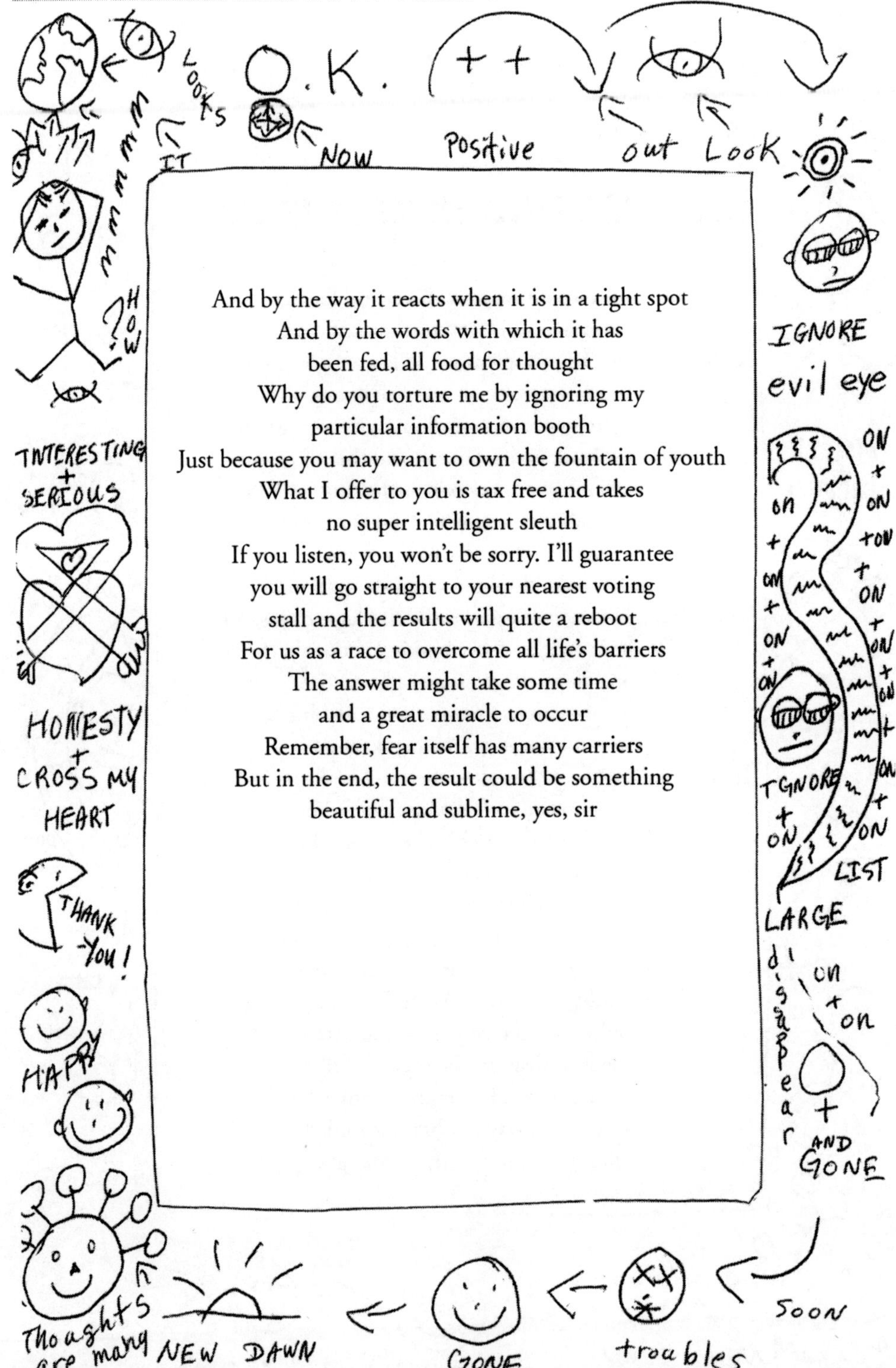

And by the way it reacts when it is in a tight spot
And by the words with which it has
been fed, all food for thought
Why do you torture me by ignoring my
particular information booth
Just because you may want to own the fountain of youth
What I offer to you is tax free and takes
no super intelligent sleuth
If you listen, you won't be sorry. I'll guarantee
you will go straight to your nearest voting
stall and the results will quite a reboot
For us as a race to overcome all life's barriers
The answer might take some time
and a great miracle to occur
Remember, fear itself has many carriers
But in the end, the result could be something
beautiful and sublime, yes, sir

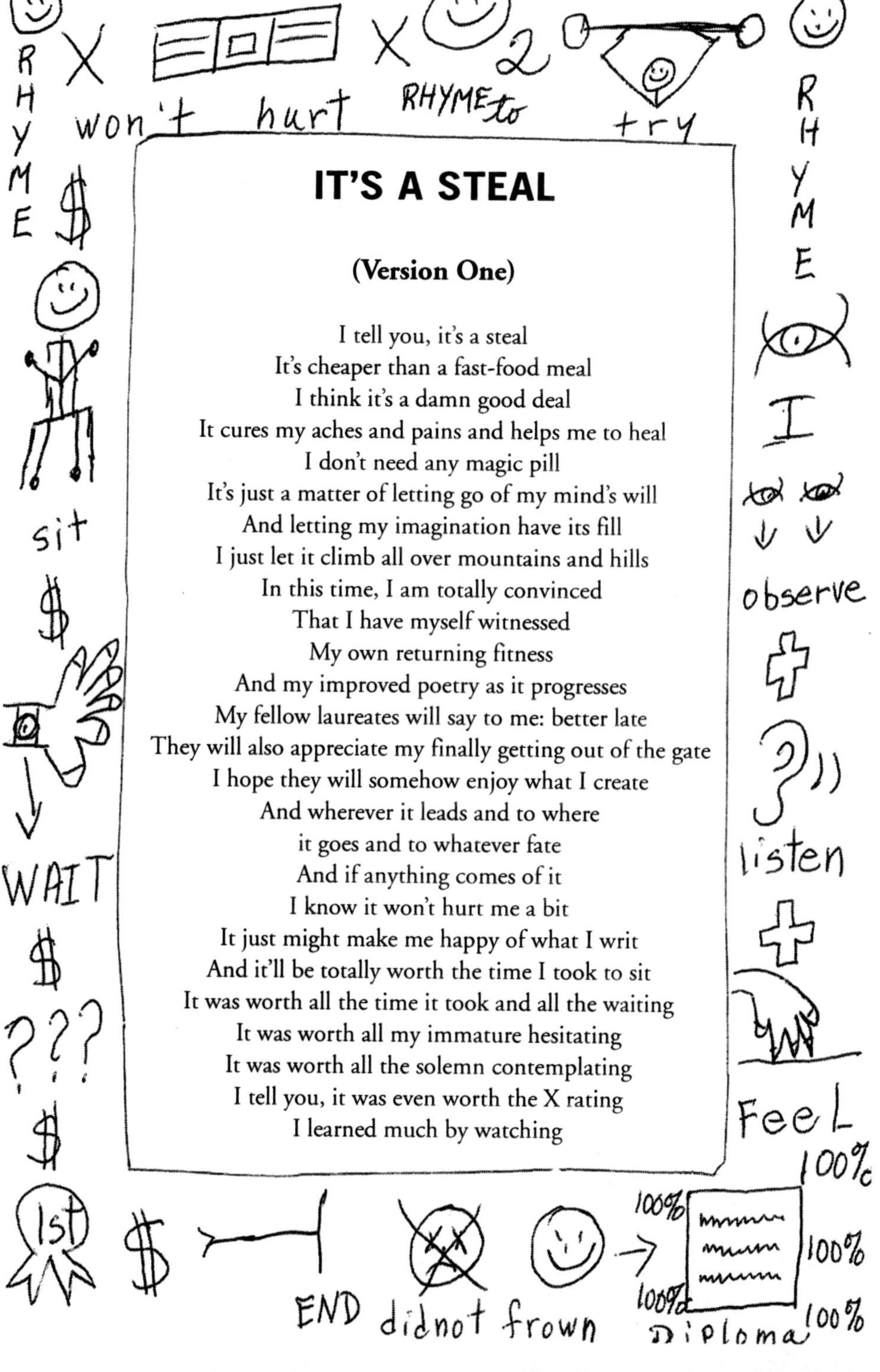

IT'S A STEAL

(Version One)

I tell you, it's a steal
It's cheaper than a fast-food meal
I think it's a damn good deal
It cures my aches and pains and helps me to heal
I don't need any magic pill
It's just a matter of letting go of my mind's will
And letting my imagination have its fill
I just let it climb all over mountains and hills
In this time, I am totally convinced
That I have myself witnessed
My own returning fitness
And my improved poetry as it progresses
My fellow laureates will say to me: better late
They will also appreciate my finally getting out of the gate
I hope they will somehow enjoy what I create
And wherever it leads and to where
it goes and to whatever fate
And if anything comes of it
I know it won't hurt me a bit
It just might make me happy of what I writ
And it'll be totally worth the time I took to sit
It was worth all the time it took and all the waiting
It was worth all my immature hesitating
It was worth all the solemn contemplating
I tell you, it was even worth the X rating
I learned much by watching

And I learned much more by waiting
And I learned by listening
And I learned much by just feeling
Then at the end, I put it all down
I put it on paper, and I did not frown
And I tried not to act like a clown
I perfected it by putting it on a piece of paper
with characters up, down, and all around

THE SUN WILL SHINE

My little man, everything will be fine, the sun will shine
The sun will eventually shine on you, my little Einstein
Be strong, continue to walk the line.
Life will not always be unkind
All the answers will come in time. I
heard it through the grapevine
You will someday bask in the sun's warmth
And for what it's worth, I've loved
you from before childbirth
You may even be the next leader of this Earth
when you go through your rebirth
Your heart will one day be filled with mirth
and everyone will know your net worth
There will be someone really smart who will hold up the fort
Someone who will have a real big heart
and will give you lots of support
They will know the long and the short
And solve all your problems part by part
until you are like a brand-new import
You'll be set free when I see the truth for the sake of
you and me, through a miracle from a wise MD.
People's minds will be set free and no one
will fear, they will be worry-free
People will seek knowledge as the main key
now and no one will even need a PHD
I think there is hope for the whole world, and as we
browse the Web, we will also discover our family tree

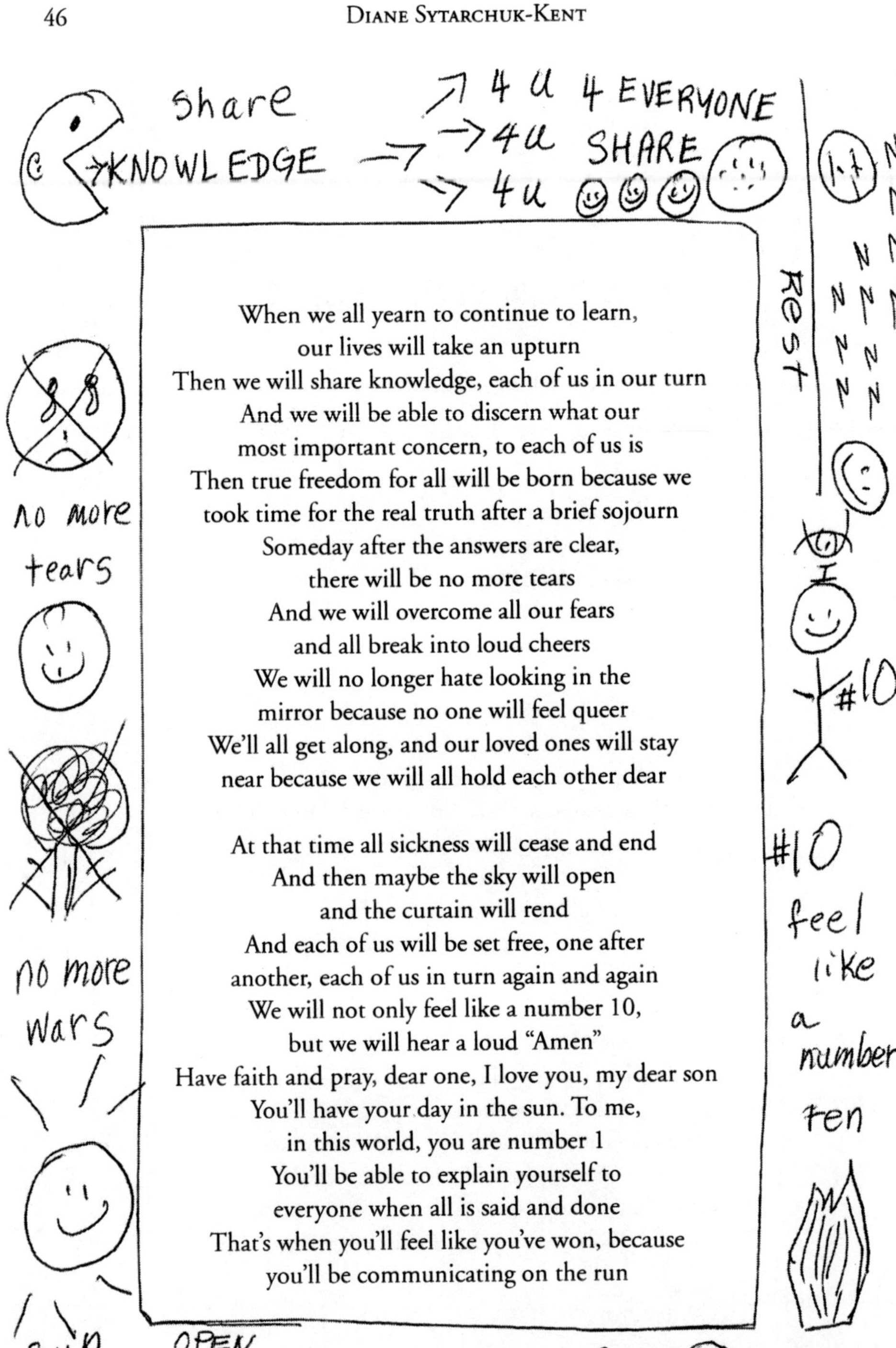

When we all yearn to continue to learn,
our lives will take an upturn
Then we will share knowledge, each of us in our turn
And we will be able to discern what our
most important concern, to each of us is
Then true freedom for all will be born because we
took time for the real truth after a brief sojourn
Someday after the answers are clear,
there will be no more tears
And we will overcome all our fears
and all break into loud cheers
We will no longer hate looking in the
mirror because no one will feel queer
We'll all get along, and our loved ones will stay
near because we will all hold each other dear

At that time all sickness will cease and end
And then maybe the sky will open
and the curtain will rend
And each of us will be set free, one after
another, each of us in turn again and again
We will not only feel like a number 10,
but we will hear a loud "Amen"
Have faith and pray, dear one, I love you, my dear son
You'll have your day in the sun. To me,
in this world, you are number 1
You'll be able to explain yourself to
everyone when all is said and done
That's when you'll feel like you've won, because
you'll be communicating on the run

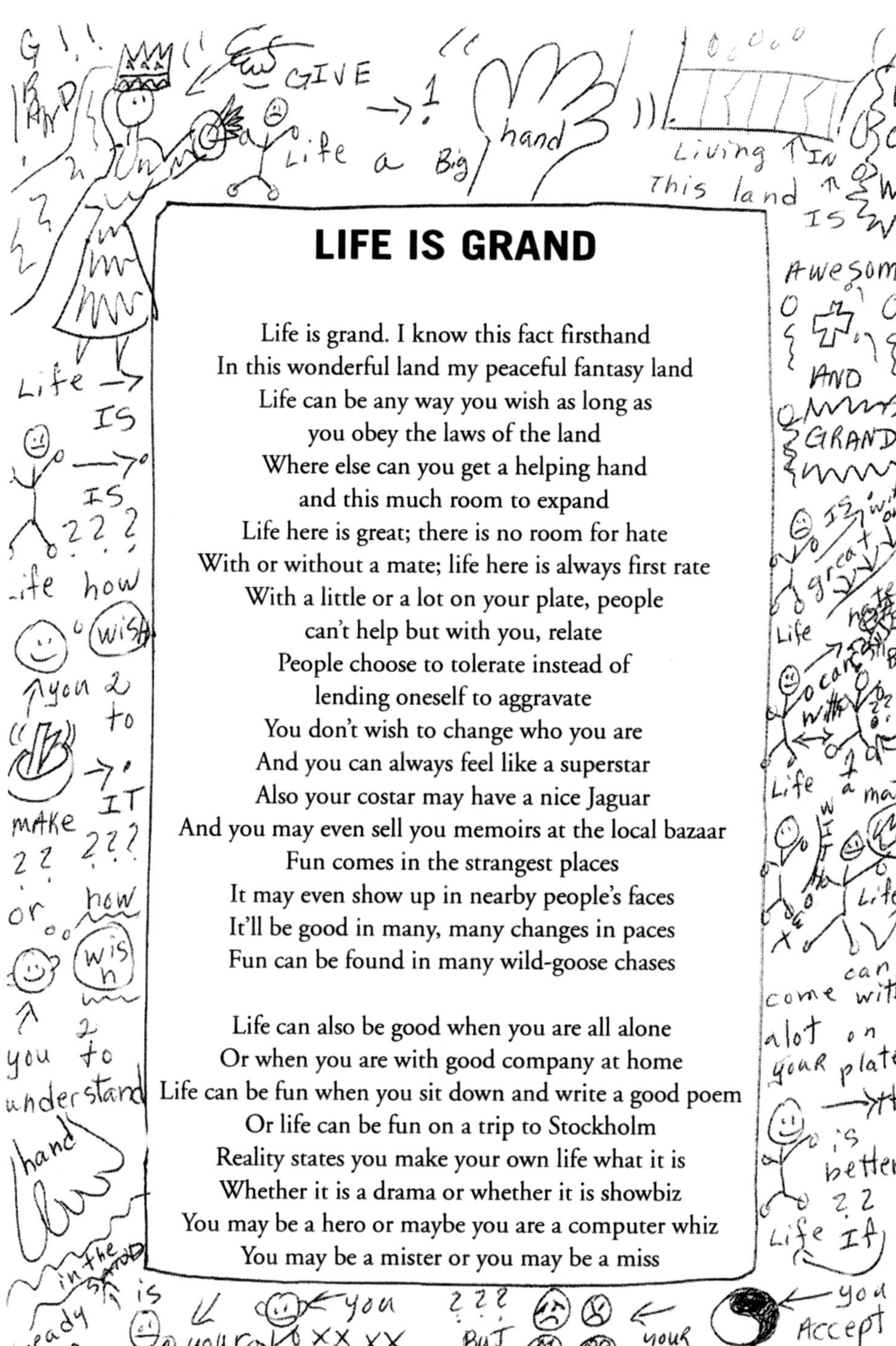

LIFE IS GRAND

Life is grand. I know this fact firsthand
In this wonderful land my peaceful fantasy land
Life can be any way you wish as long as
you obey the laws of the land
Where else can you get a helping hand
and this much room to expand
Life here is great; there is no room for hate
With or without a mate; life here is always first rate
With a little or a lot on your plate, people
can't help but with you, relate
People choose to tolerate instead of
lending oneself to aggravate
You don't wish to change who you are
And you can always feel like a superstar
Also your costar may have a nice Jaguar
And you may even sell you memoirs at the local bazaar
Fun comes in the strangest places
It may even show up in nearby people's faces
It'll be good in many, many changes in paces
Fun can be found in many wild-goose chases

Life can also be good when you are all alone
Or when you are with good company at home
Life can be fun when you sit down and write a good poem
Or life can be fun on a trip to Stockholm
Reality states you make your own life what it is
Whether it is a drama or whether it is showbiz
You may be a hero or maybe you are a computer whiz
You may be a mister or you may be a miss

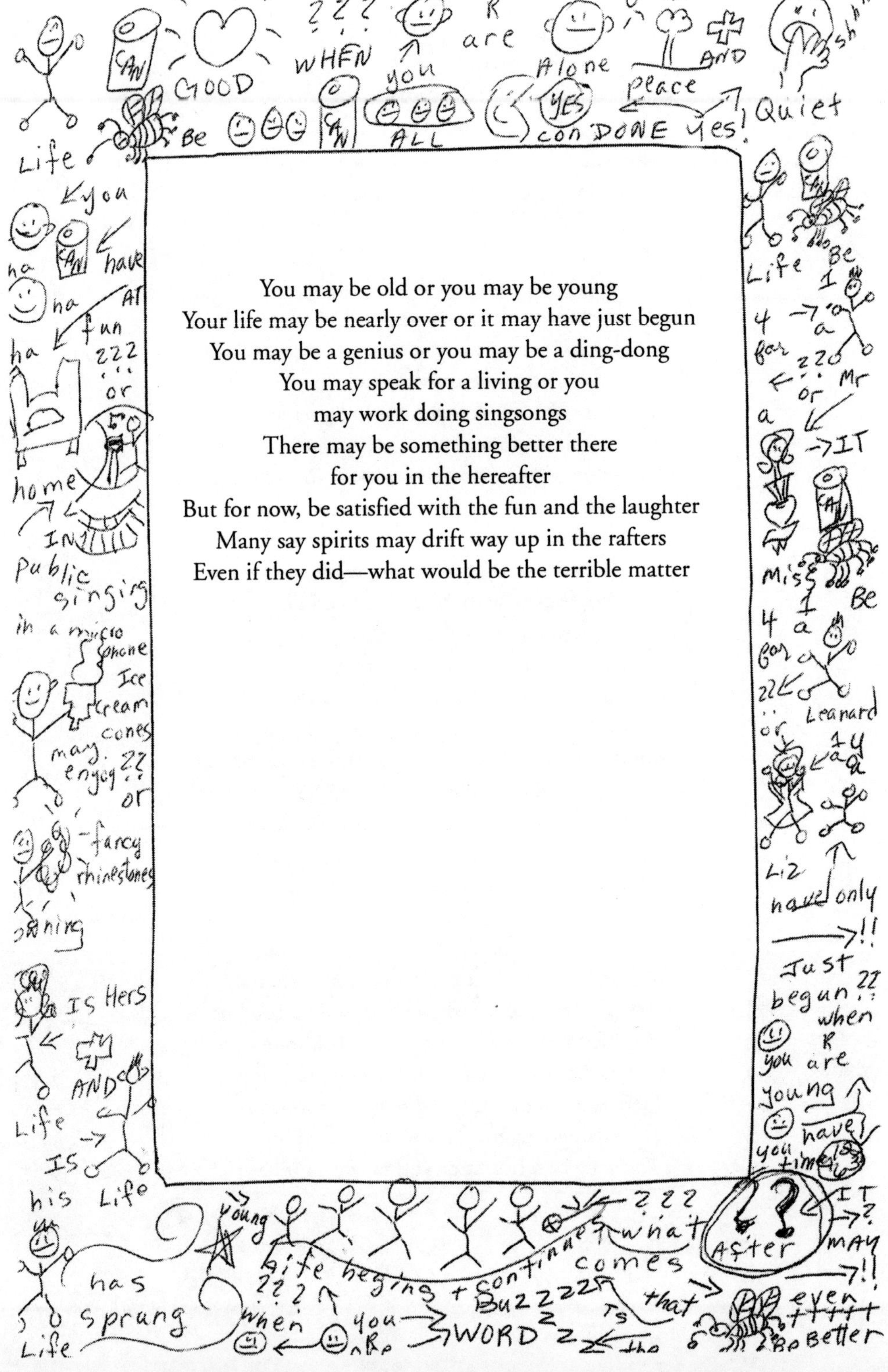

You may be old or you may be young
Your life may be nearly over or it may have just begun
You may be a genius or you may be a ding-dong
You may speak for a living or you
may work doing singsongs
There may be something better there
for you in the hereafter
But for now, be satisfied with the fun and the laughter
Many say spirits may drift way up in the rafters
Even if they did—what would be the terrible matter

ODE TO A FOOTPRINT

My man has my favorite footprints
On my mind, they make a beautiful imprint
Also for my heart, they were surely heaven sent
They are delicate, like a child's are,
and are, to me, worth a mint
I was once given and gazed upon a picture
Of an imprint, of a footprint, somewhat similar
On a cardboard card, of a babe's foot—
this one was a real winner
The card was given to me when I was but a
novice mother and children carrier
At that time, I remember, loving their beautiful shape
The heels and toes of the feet were so neatly arranged
They were all together so perfectly laid
My man's feet, just so happened to be also so similarly made
My man's steps are made for walking and not for running
They are also made for hopping, skipping, and jumping
They have come from far away while
in the process of traveling
Away from circumstances not of his making or of his doing
I'm glad that I'm the one that gets to play
With them yesterday, tomorrow, and today
And I hope they will always stay
Close to me today, tomorrow, and for each and every day
They have the perfect shape
They travel at just the right gait
I'm happy that they are on my mate

And I hope they will always be my happy fate
His feet have made many wonderful steps
They are the steps of his and my destiny,
all perfectly laid out and set
Their owner you have never met
Now that they are with me, I know
that they are my best bet
They carry a very strong man
Who always does his best to listen and try to
understand any problems you may have
About each and every woman, child, and man
His feet tread softly and are connected
to honest helping hands
If you look hard and try to understand
You'll see his footprints there in the sand
His are the ones that follow you
giving you a helping hand
His are the ones that would be welcomed and help you to
Easily traverse each and every land
His feet are oh so sweet—
I could kiss them this day and each
and every day of the week
They're bold and beautiful and also pink as a beet
In my very biased opinion, to find any
better would be an impossible feat

I'LL SHOW YOU MY MIND

I'll show you my mind
It's one of a peculiar kind
I was in a prison—my mind had been
bound and made to be as blind
Oh, how I am happy with what I now find
There are many ins and outs in this well-made closet
It must have been closed for a reason
And it has been opened, now in due season
Now it is right there for everyone's pleasing
I now clap my hands for joy
My mind I can now use like a brand-new toy
With all my past powers to again employ
I use it with the same joy and happiness
of a new toy given to a small boy
I want to share my mind with everyone
So that they too can have as much fun
As a once sad and lonely one
Who has recovered and come back into the sun
How long will it last?
My abilities and thoughts are opening
up and improving so fast
The journey is coming full blast
It won't settle to stay at half mast
My gift to you
So you can see too
From one who was once so very bound?
Will be to show you she has turned into
someone happy, shiny, and new

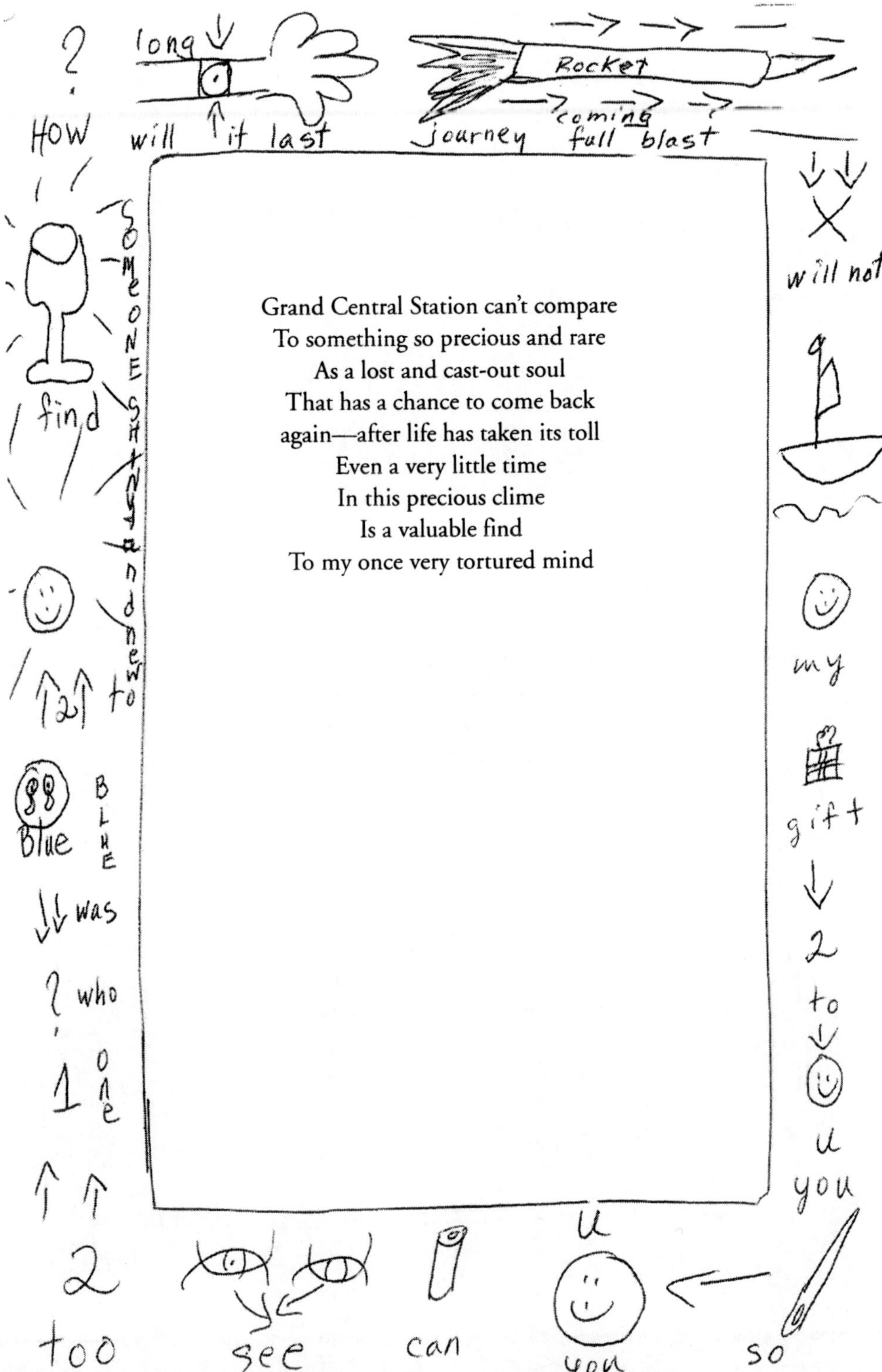

Grand Central Station can't compare
To something so precious and rare
As a lost and cast-out soul
That has a chance to come back
again—after life has taken its toll
Even a very little time
In this precious clime
Is a valuable find
To my once very tortured mind

SEE IF I CARE

You have every right
To keep yourself hidden and out of sight
You know I won't bite
And I won't pick a fight
You pretend to be totally unaware
Come out of your lair, see if I care
You and I know that's life; it's totally fair
Come on now, I dare you, truth or dare
It's not my place to make any remark
Or to light up a spark
Yes, it may make light in the dark
Or I may be out of luck and miss the ark
You can be very rude
And act like some cool dude
But it would be much shrewder
To be quiet and not to intrude
You can swear. See if I care
You can stare. See if I care
You can glare. See if I care
You can blow lots of hot air. See if I care
If all you want is lots of attention
You will find no one cares about your orientation
And you are not important enough to mention
Keep it up, you might land in detention
Then you will be back in the doghouse
Instead of getting back into my house
You'll then be treated like a low-down mouse
And others will know you as an awful louse

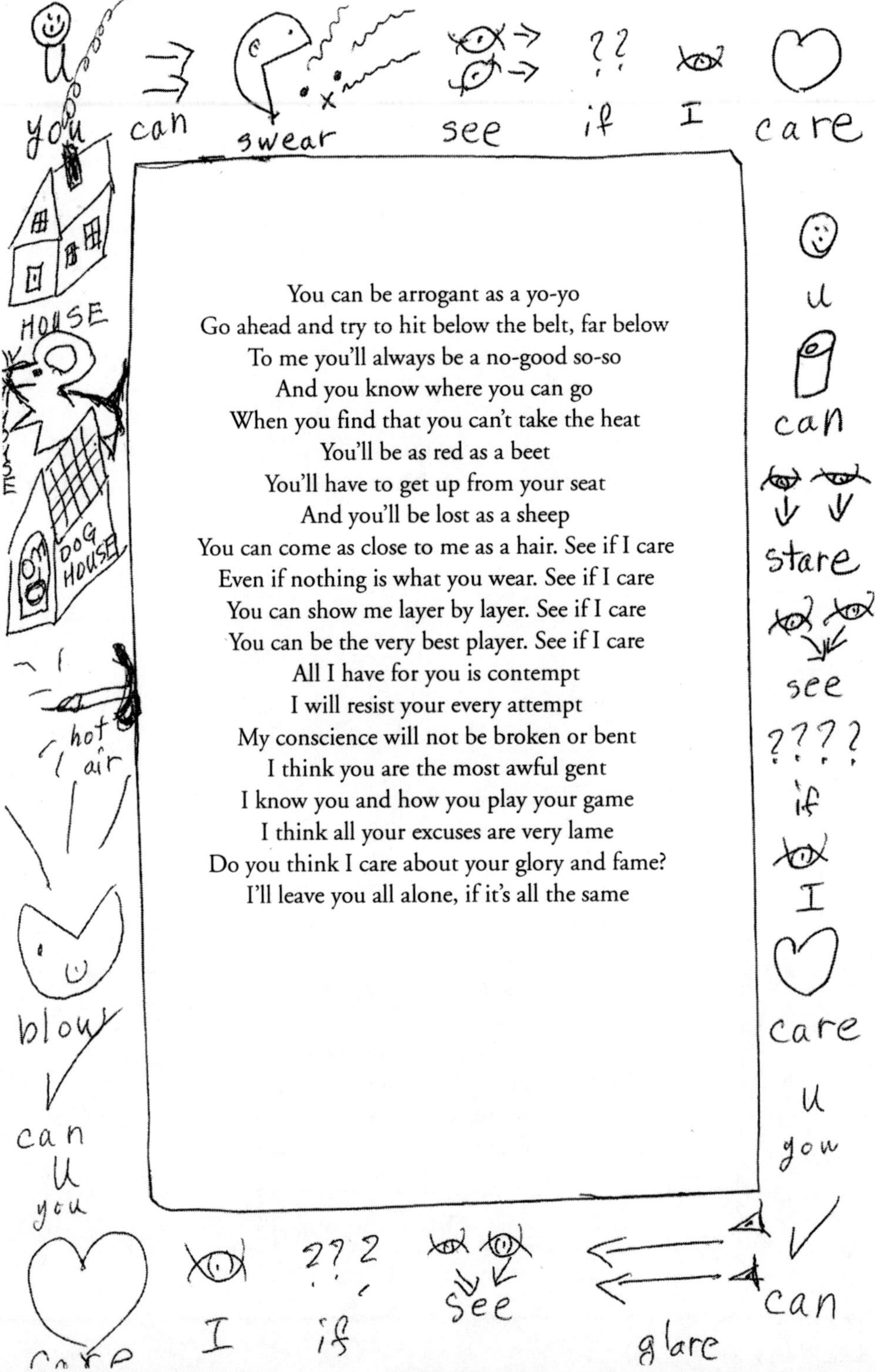

You can be arrogant as a yo-yo
Go ahead and try to hit below the belt, far below
To me you'll always be a no-good so-so
And you know where you can go
When you find that you can't take the heat
You'll be as red as a beet
You'll have to get up from your seat
And you'll be lost as a sheep
You can come as close to me as a hair. See if I care
Even if nothing is what you wear. See if I care
You can show me layer by layer. See if I care
You can be the very best player. See if I care
All I have for you is contempt
I will resist your every attempt
My conscience will not be broken or bent
I think you are the most awful gent
I know you and how you play your game
I think all your excuses are very lame
Do you think I care about your glory and fame?
I'll leave you all alone, if it's all the same

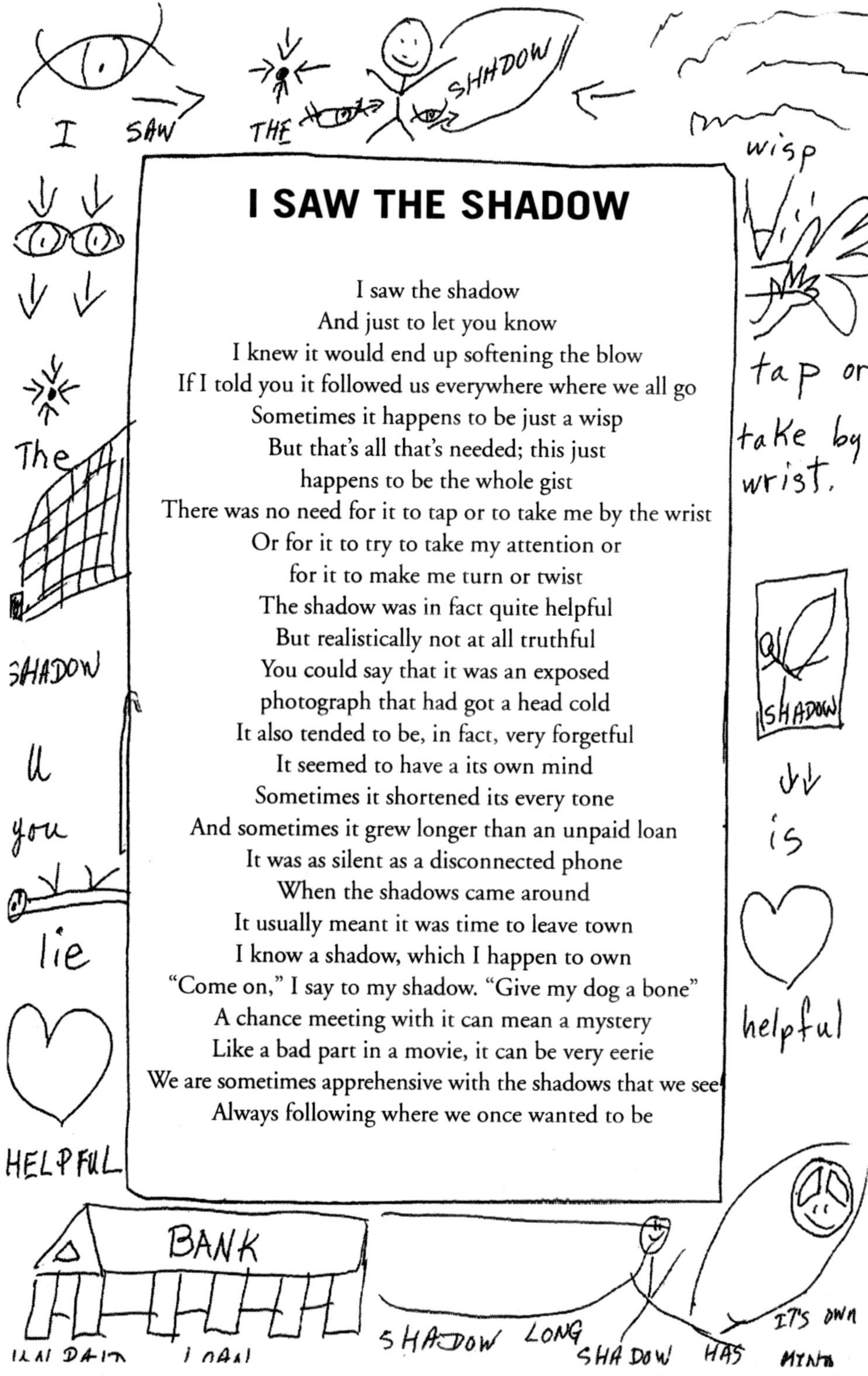

I SAW THE SHADOW

I saw the shadow
And just to let you know
I knew it would end up softening the blow
If I told you it followed us everywhere where we all go
Sometimes it happens to be just a wisp
But that's all that's needed; this just
happens to be the whole gist
There was no need for it to tap or to take me by the wrist
Or for it to try to take my attention or
for it to make me turn or twist
The shadow was in fact quite helpful
But realistically not at all truthful
You could say that it was an exposed
photograph that had got a head cold
It also tended to be, in fact, very forgetful
It seemed to have a its own mind
Sometimes it shortened its every tone
And sometimes it grew longer than an unpaid loan
It was as silent as a disconnected phone
When the shadows came around
It usually meant it was time to leave town
I know a shadow, which I happen to own
"Come on," I say to my shadow. "Give my dog a bone"
A chance meeting with it can mean a mystery
Like a bad part in a movie, it can be very eerie
We are sometimes apprehensive with the shadows that we see
Always following where we once wanted to be

All I know is that seeing it is some kind of clue
Tell me, do you see it too?
It's just as plain as that nose on you
That admission in itself is enough to sue
While I, myself, saw that the shadow had existence
The sun, on the other hand must
not have cared a pittance
Because it chose its time to say good riddance
And the shadow's existence turned out to be
nothing but an annoying hindrance
Some people like to play
With shadows and convince them how to lie
They, themselves, dance to the rhythm
and are happy and gay
They enjoy making new games in each and
every one of their own individual ways
I thought I saw a shadow that was a good fellow
I remember thinking that he was quiet and very mellow
Until to my delight he quivered
and jiggled just like Jell-O
And when the sun went down, I saluted
to him and said, "Tallyho!"
They say you can never tell
All I say is, "Well"
It is quiet, and it doesn't yell
And ah, heck, it's just plain good company. What the hell
Also my shadow is never too tall
But it ends up at the bottom of every wall
It also follows me down every hall
It's my very best friend of all

SHUT MY MOUTH

Sometimes I'm way too loud
This does not help at all when I'm in a crowd
Or at a place where talking is not allowed
Or when I'm with someone who is way too proud
Many times, my views get me into trouble
I hate to then burst anybody's bubble
But here comes trouble again on the double
You'd better wait to pick me out of the rubble
Do you know what I've caused?
Just because I didn't take the time to pause
And oops, the words that came out had many flaws
My enemies' claws cut me into a jigsaw
Then one fine day, I had a brilliant idea
I would use a new rule, innovative and raw
I would do something new and try to draw
A picture in my mind, then follow it to a tee, my new law
I would then go a step further
I would try to put my plan into action, yes, sir
Soon my actions would be a blur
And my movements would be running with a smooth purr
My new rule of thumb is quite simple
I'll be quiet. No longer will I yell
This came to me out of the blue like a bombshell
I was amazed and in a state of wonder. This was swell
All I have to do is "Shut my mouth"
When I speak I will tell the truth, no more word of mouth
I will no longer be a blabbermouth

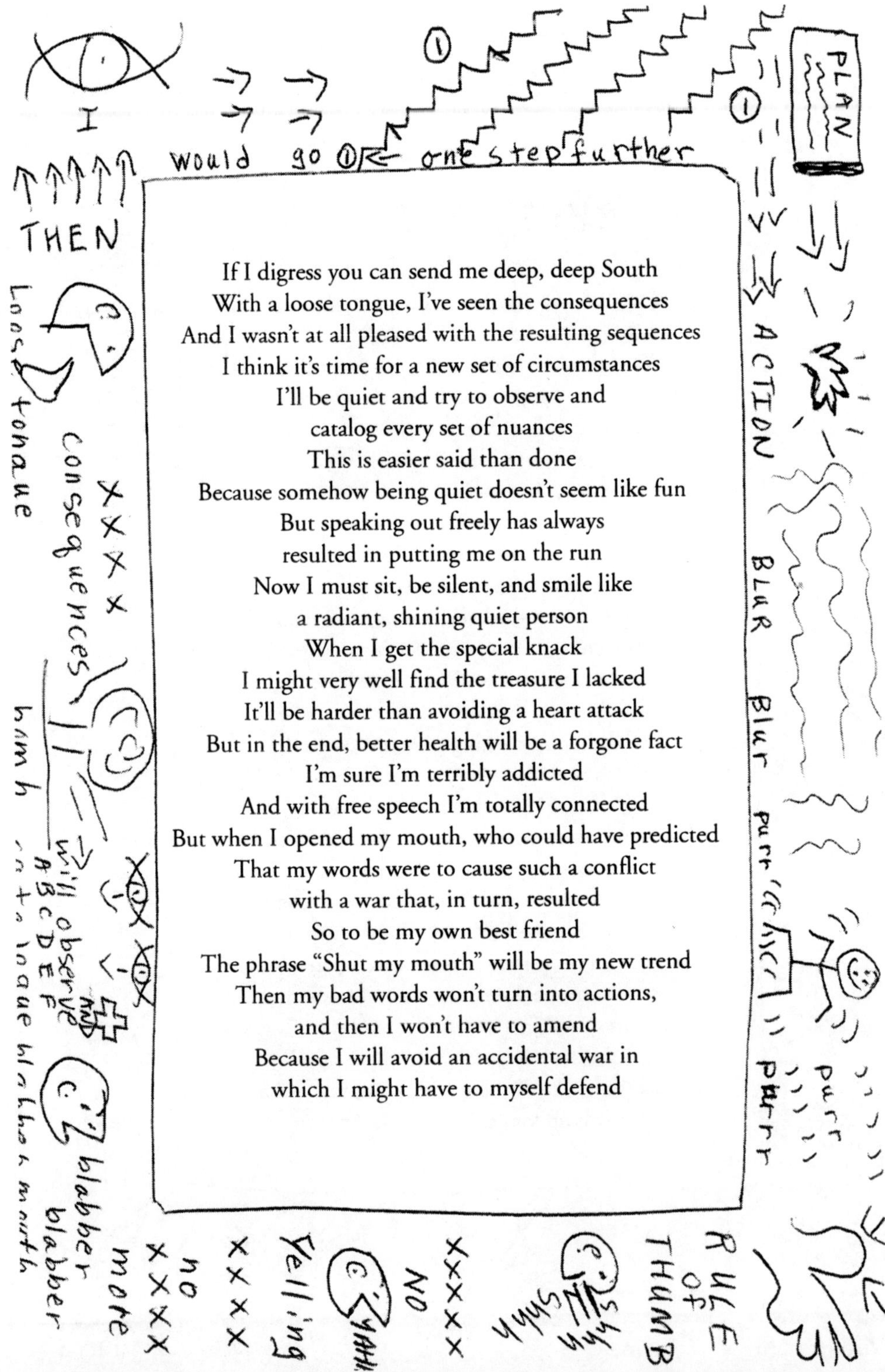

If I digress you can send me deep, deep South
With a loose tongue, I've seen the consequences
And I wasn't at all pleased with the resulting sequences
I think it's time for a new set of circumstances
I'll be quiet and try to observe and
catalog every set of nuances
This is easier said than done
Because somehow being quiet doesn't seem like fun
But speaking out freely has always
resulted in putting me on the run
Now I must sit, be silent, and smile like
a radiant, shining quiet person
When I get the special knack
I might very well find the treasure I lacked
It'll be harder than avoiding a heart attack
But in the end, better health will be a forgone fact
I'm sure I'm terribly addicted
And with free speech I'm totally connected
But when I opened my mouth, who could have predicted
That my words were to cause such a conflict
with a war that, in turn, resulted
So to be my own best friend
The phrase "Shut my mouth" will be my new trend
Then my bad words won't turn into actions,
and then I won't have to amend
Because I will avoid an accidental war in
which I might have to myself defend

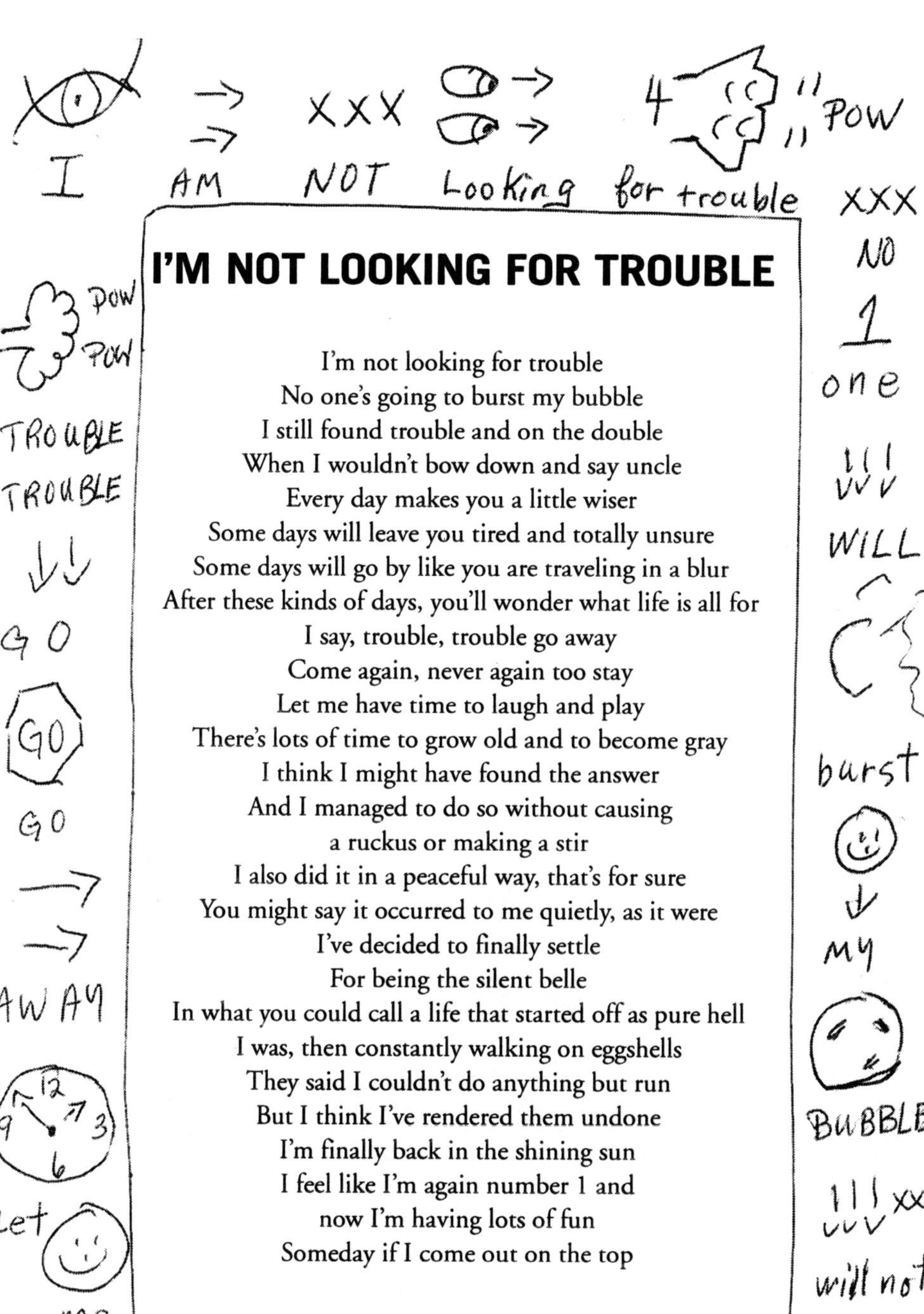

I'M NOT LOOKING FOR TROUBLE

I'm not looking for trouble
No one's going to burst my bubble
I still found trouble and on the double
When I wouldn't bow down and say uncle
Every day makes you a little wiser
Some days will leave you tired and totally unsure
Some days will go by like you are traveling in a blur
After these kinds of days, you'll wonder what life is all for
I say, trouble, trouble go away
Come again, never again too stay
Let me have time to laugh and play
There's lots of time to grow old and to become gray
I think I might have found the answer
And I managed to do so without causing
a ruckus or making a stir
I also did it in a peaceful way, that's for sure
You might say it occurred to me quietly, as it were
I've decided to finally settle
For being the silent belle
In what you could call a life that started off as pure hell
I was, then constantly walking on eggshells
They said I couldn't do anything but run
But I think I've rendered them undone
I'm finally back in the shining sun
I feel like I'm again number 1 and
now I'm having lots of fun
Someday if I come out on the top

I'll sing and do a hop
And then I'll fly away on my magical mop
Until I'm as famous as Mr. Aesop
The truth will speak for itself
Because it will be sitting on everyone's shelf
And my most important wealth
Will be that I'm satisfied with myself

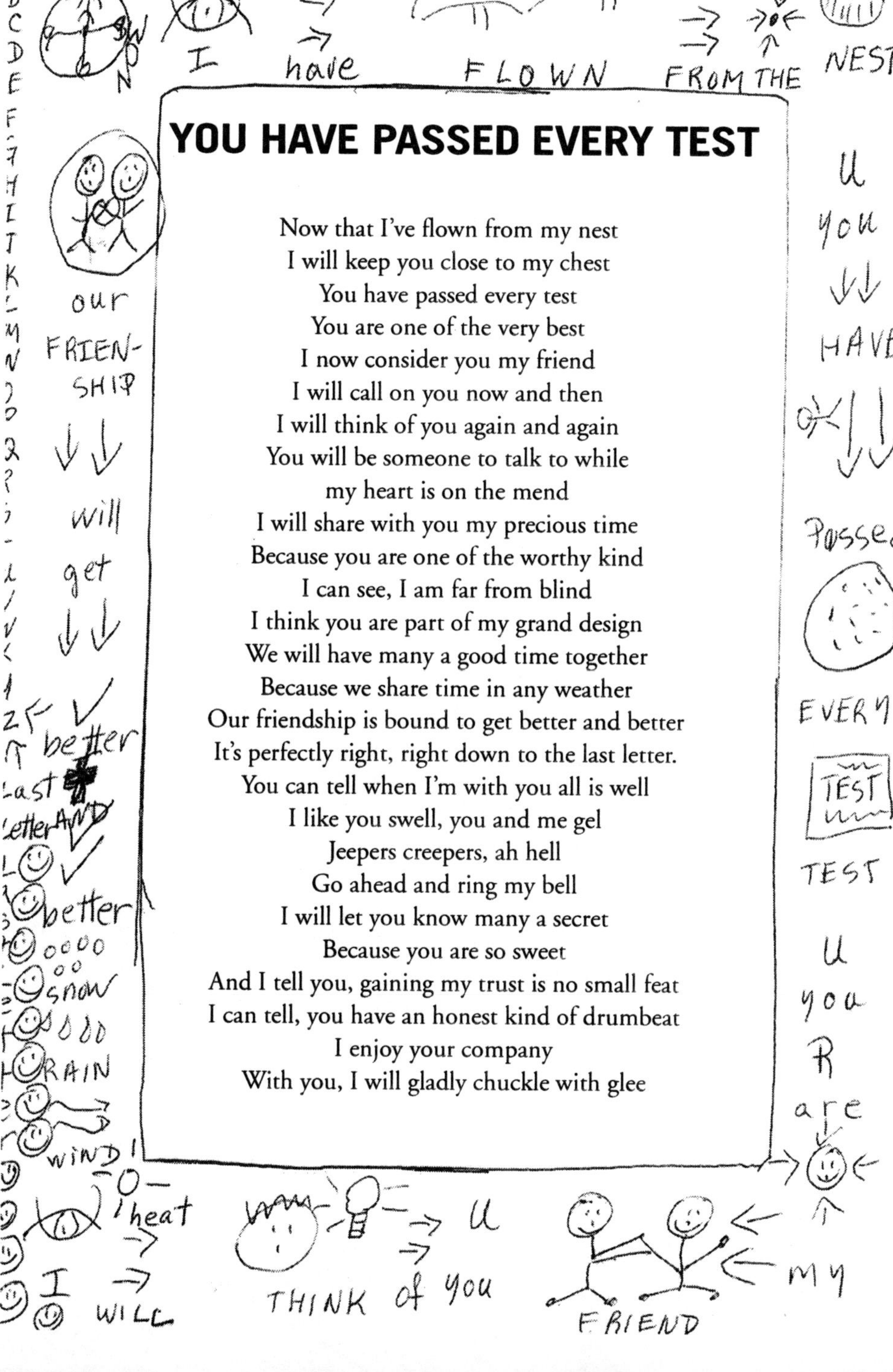

YOU HAVE PASSED EVERY TEST

Now that I've flown from my nest
I will keep you close to my chest
You have passed every test
You are one of the very best
I now consider you my friend
I will call on you now and then
I will think of you again and again
You will be someone to talk to while
my heart is on the mend
I will share with you my precious time
Because you are one of the worthy kind
I can see, I am far from blind
I think you are part of my grand design
We will have many a good time together
Because we share time in any weather
Our friendship is bound to get better and better
It's perfectly right, right down to the last letter.
You can tell when I'm with you all is well
I like you swell, you and me gel
Jeepers creepers, ah hell
Go ahead and ring my bell
I will let you know many a secret
Because you are so sweet
And I tell you, gaining my trust is no small feat
I can tell, you have an honest kind of drumbeat
I enjoy your company
With you, I will gladly chuckle with glee

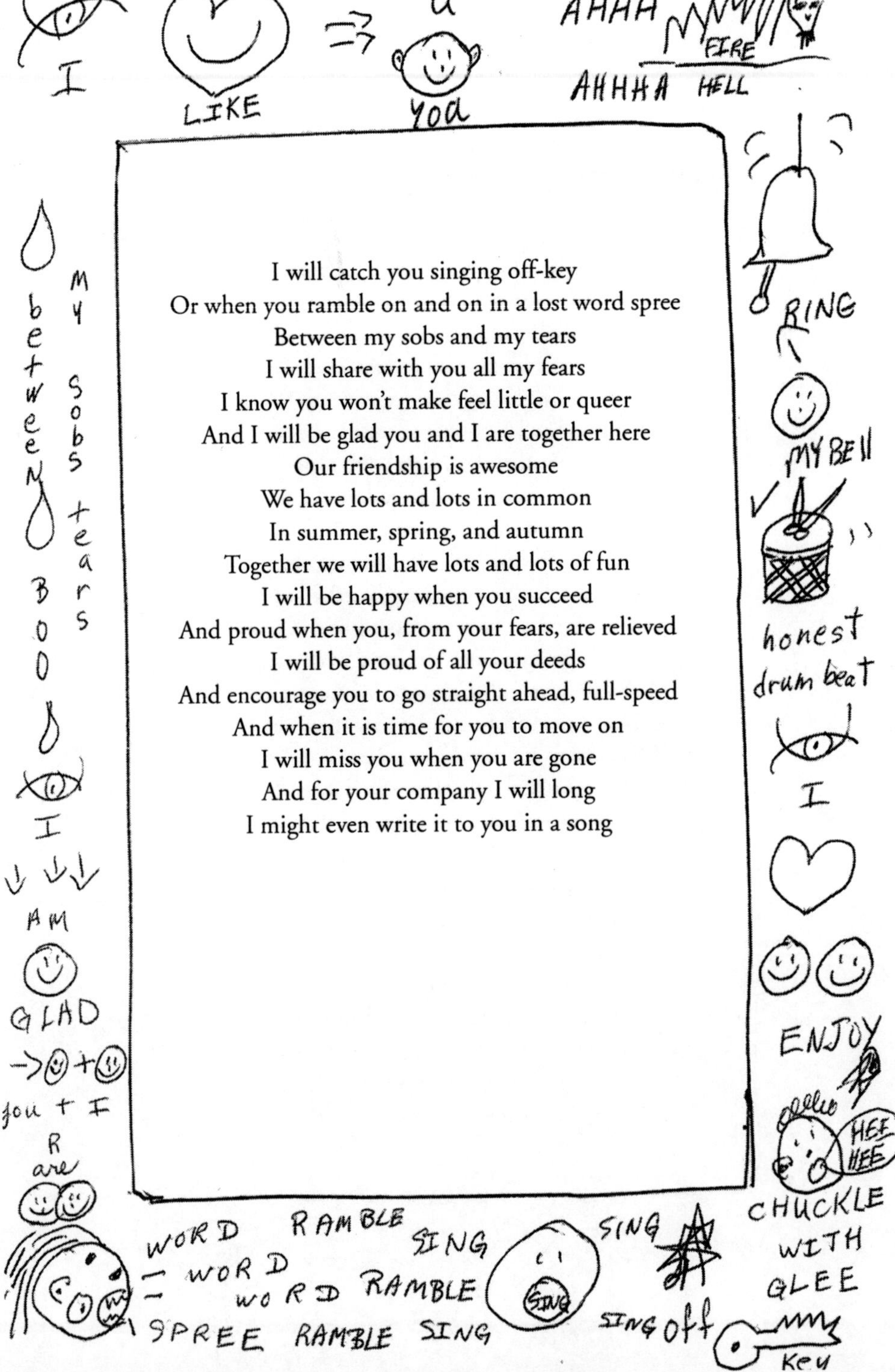

I will catch you singing off-key
Or when you ramble on and on in a lost word spree
Between my sobs and my tears
I will share with you all my fears
I know you won't make feel little or queer
And I will be glad you and I are together here
Our friendship is awesome
We have lots and lots in common
In summer, spring, and autumn
Together we will have lots and lots of fun
I will be happy when you succeed
And proud when you, from your fears, are relieved
I will be proud of all your deeds
And encourage you to go straight ahead, full-speed
And when it is time for you to move on
I will miss you when you are gone
And for your company I will long
I might even write it to you in a song

TO IGNORE OR NOT TO IGNORE

To ignore or not to ignore
We all know who's really a bore
You may think you have the entire floor
We all know you are nothing but a dinosaur
Sometimes I find it best
To hold things really close to my chest
Then I can be ready for my next quest
Even when I'm put to my next test
To ignore or overlook, I may find it hard
Ignoring with tact is the way to play my cards
Especially if I don't want to end up in the mental ward
I try to make sure to be polite and not to use any rude words
You must take a strong stance
When someone wants attention with insistence
Don't give them a second glance
Under any circumstance
Indifference, one way or another
May get you out of hot water
Always keep calmness your chosen demur
Do not let slip any kind of slur
If you get a good thought
And you get poked by a tot
You must decide whether or not
To let your attention be caught
It may be to everyone's best interest
Silently to cease and desist
And not to let them pull your wrist

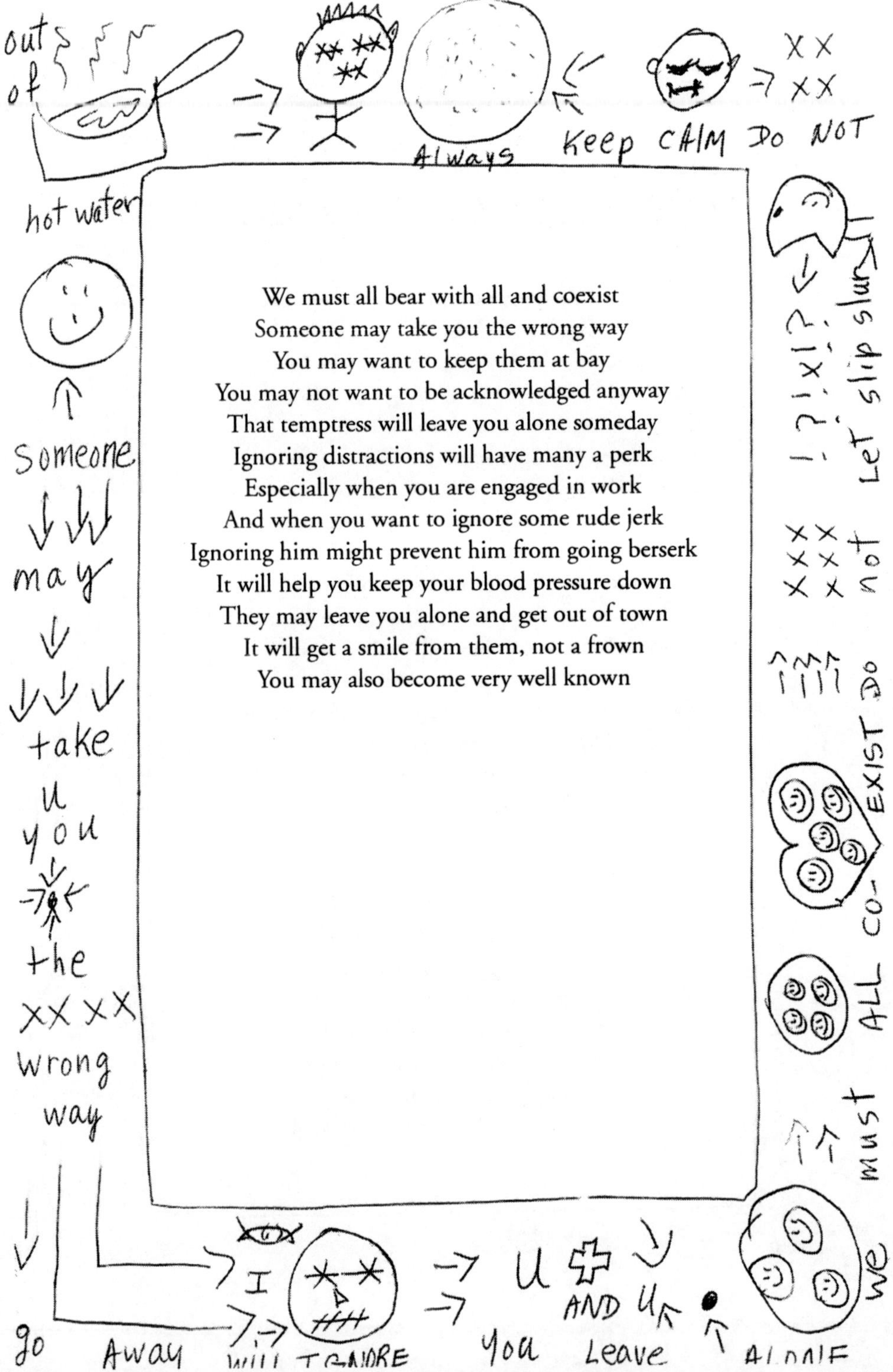

We must all bear with all and coexist
Someone may take you the wrong way
You may want to keep them at bay
You may not want to be acknowledged anyway
That temptress will leave you alone someday
Ignoring distractions will have many a perk
Especially when you are engaged in work
And when you want to ignore some rude jerk
Ignoring him might prevent him from going berserk
It will help you keep your blood pressure down
They may leave you alone and get out of town
It will get a smile from them, not a frown
You may also become very well known

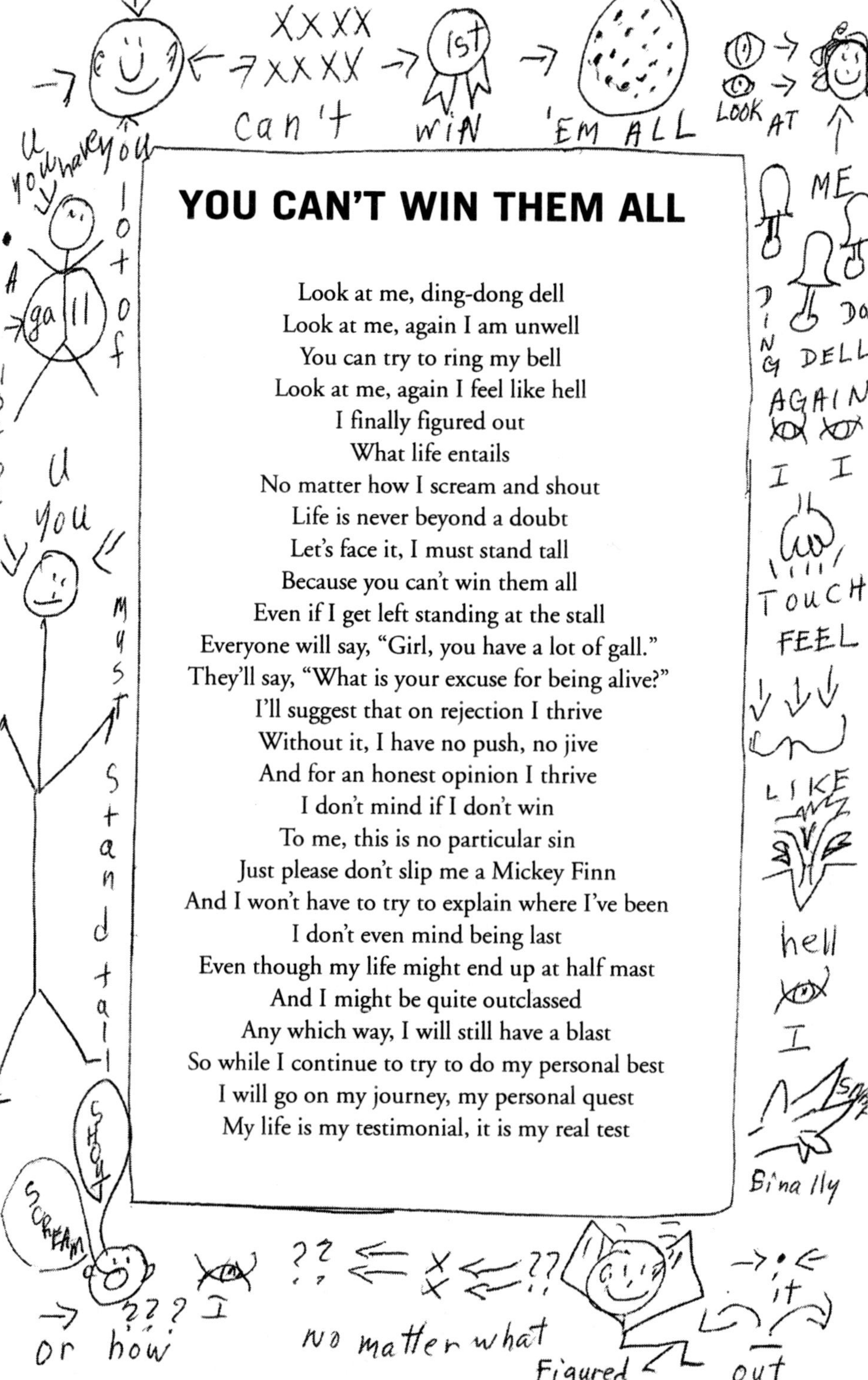

YOU CAN'T WIN THEM ALL

Look at me, ding-dong dell
Look at me, again I am unwell
You can try to ring my bell
Look at me, again I feel like hell
I finally figured out
What life entails
No matter how I scream and shout
Life is never beyond a doubt
Let's face it, I must stand tall
Because you can't win them all
Even if I get left standing at the stall
Everyone will say, "Girl, you have a lot of gall."
They'll say, "What is your excuse for being alive?"
I'll suggest that on rejection I thrive
Without it, I have no push, no jive
And for an honest opinion I thrive
I don't mind if I don't win
To me, this is no particular sin
Just please don't slip me a Mickey Finn
And I won't have to try to explain where I've been
I don't even mind being last
Even though my life might end up at half mast
And I might be quite outclassed
Any which way, I will still have a blast
So while I continue to try to do my personal best
I will go on my journey, my personal quest
My life is my testimonial, it is my real test

I will treat life with vigor like it is
an adventure, a conquest
I don't know if I am very wise
Because I sometimes wear a disguise
Someday I may even cut you down to size
Especially if you hand me too many lies
And when you give me the next catcall
I will pick myself up even if I have to crawl
I will take out all my awards in one great big haul
And I will stand up brave and proud,
and I will feel ten feet tall

DO YOU WANT SOMETHING?

Do you want something?
I'm not just a plaything
What about this wedding ring
I'm not just a toy on a string
Where have you been?
What kind of mood are you in?
Where am I supposed to fit in?
Where am I to begin?
I have put my life on hold before
I will do so many, many times more
I don't mean to be a bore
My life has been filled up with violence and war
My feelings have been ripped and torn
I have been down and forlorn
I have no feelings of scorn
On the Bible I have sworn
Go away. A-OK, OK?
I want to play, but I'll do as you say
Come another day or I'll hold you at bay
I'll hit the hay for now. I'll be merry and gay
Do you know the golden rule?
I'm nobody's fool
I think you're really cool
I'm a person, not a mule
Sit there on your stool
You silly, silly fool
And eat your curds and gruel

Right down to the very last molecule
All praise to the Man
He's the One who truly understands
He's the One with the plan
He's the best in all the land
I'm His fan. Give Him a hand
When I'm with Him, anywhere is the Holy Land
He is truly great and grand
I try to obey His every command
When I go with Him, toe to toe
He is always a friend, never a foe
I will be the one to tow the hoe
I know that the more I believe, the more I will know
I must not go so fast, I must go slowly
I'll go slowly, He's not my foe
The more I believe, the more I'll glow
I will say, "Ho. Ho. Ho," I'll be the one in the know

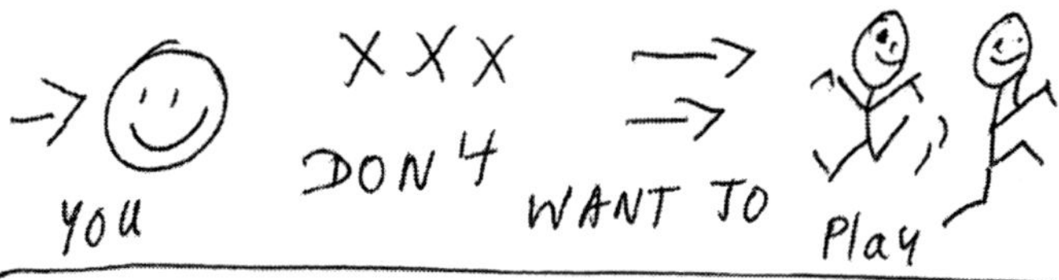

SO YOU DON'T WANT TO PLAY

So you don't want to play
You say it's all work; that's what you say
Is that possible in these modern days
Shouldn't the scales of work and play evenly weigh?
It wouldn't be the solution
In any useful situation
It'll just be the cause of your ruin
Soon you will be singing a different tune
You'll feel like the monkey on the moon
And you just might feel like a babbling baboon
Like some worried, ghastly goon
This might take the air right out of your hot air balloon
I might even give you a few nips
Right there on one of your luscious lips
Stand still while I let her rip
After all, it won't hurt you to take a sip
When you are tired, I'll prop you up
I'll wrap you up in my love just like they
did to the mummy of King Tut
You'll be cornered and you want to know what
You'll be the one to say, "Don't stop my pet mutt."
You can't only want to work
Don't you know that overworking can be where evil lurks
Life has to have its even amount of perks
Or someone might end up calling you a jerk
You have to have a little fun

When you are rested your battles will be easily won
Especially when you let yourself come out into the sun
The warmth and the energy will end up helping a ton
When you work too much, you will be a wreck
Your wife will call you up and give you heck
You will be nothing but a pain in the neck
And you will end up worrying yourself right to death
Go ahead and enjoy yourself, and maybe you'll win
Try it, it won't be a sin
You won't know if you don't begin to begin
Working and playing are equal yin-yang twins
You'll be happier in the end
You will make a lot more friends
You'll feel like a number 10
And everyone will want to see you again and again

I JUST WANTED TO SAY HI

I just wanted to say hi
Here, I'll give it a try
Of that, I cannot deny
Hello, my name is Di
OK, I did it first
I'm none for the worst
And I didn't even end up cursed
I like it. I went in unafraid, headfirst
Go ahead, you there, try it
You will see all the hidden benefits
It could be a bang-up, smash-up; crash-up hit
Do it, you will not be a hypocrite
Come on, put her there
Come on, let your feelings be stripped bare
Come on; take the time to give a care
Peel off your feelings layer by layer
It does not hurt to be friendly
Like that monkey in the tree
Sociability is the key
This comes on down to you from little old me
We'll meet again someday
Let's give a salute to another day
And let's just be merry and gay
Also lets send out a great big bouquet
for us to go on life's highway
It'll be worth your while
To go that extra mile

You'll see, I mean you no guile
I just happen to like to-go freestyle
I can even play peek-a-boo with you
And with no further excuses, I will say adieu
You might end up making a friend anew
That would be quite a glorious snafu
I wish I could totally relate
To why people take a mate
I always thought it was for life,
does this to you equate?
We must also get along together and not hate
I don't even want to begin
To say why I have sometimes got a thin skin
If I did, I might lose and the devil might win
And then I would be lost again and again

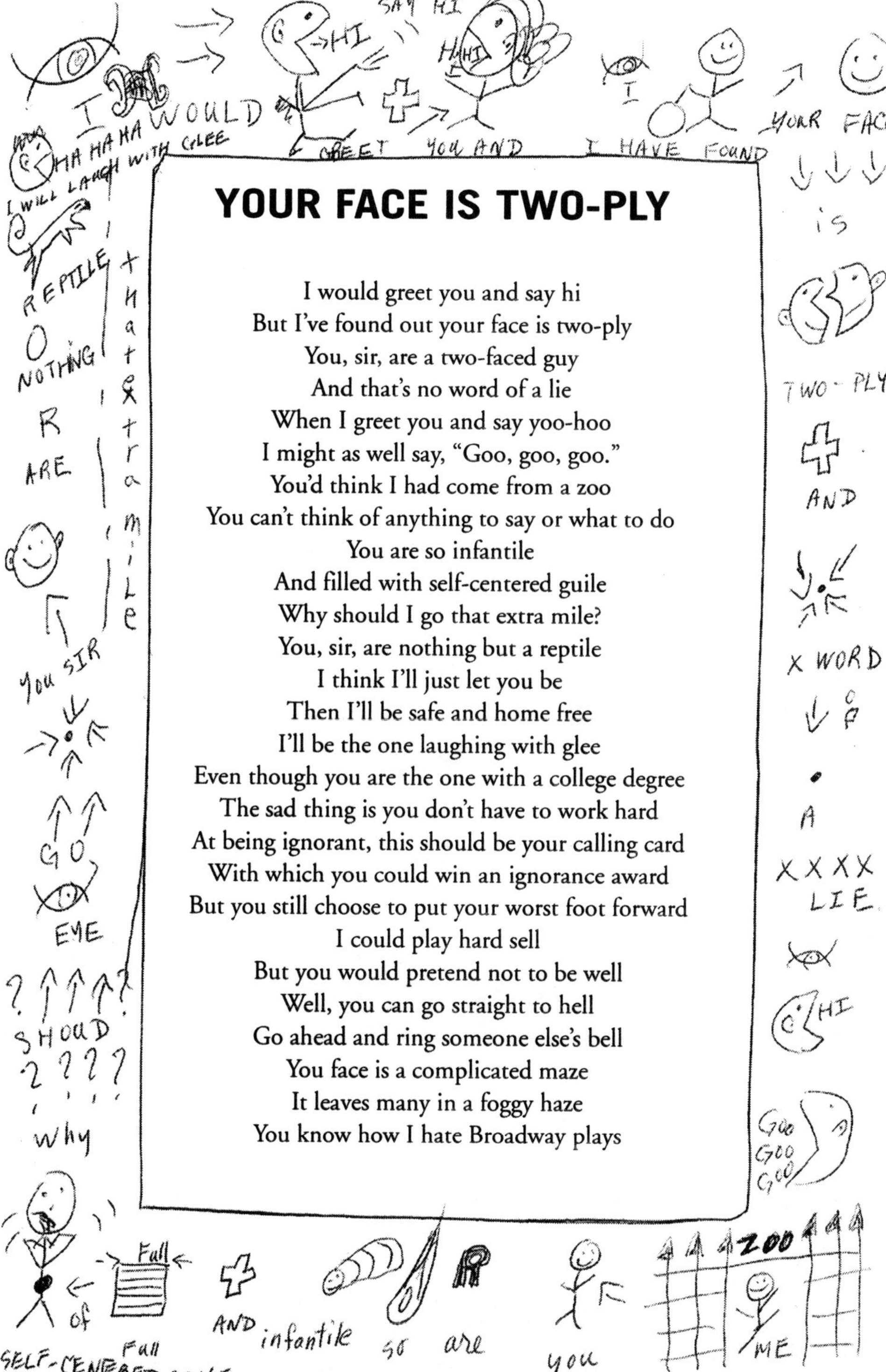

YOUR FACE IS TWO-PLY

I would greet you and say hi
But I've found out your face is two-ply
You, sir, are a two-faced guy
And that's no word of a lie
When I greet you and say yoo-hoo
I might as well say, "Goo, goo, goo."
You'd think I had come from a zoo
You can't think of anything to say or what to do
You are so infantile
And filled with self-centered guile
Why should I go that extra mile?
You, sir, are nothing but a reptile
I think I'll just let you be
Then I'll be safe and home free
I'll be the one laughing with glee
Even though you are the one with a college degree
The sad thing is you don't have to work hard
At being ignorant, this should be your calling card
With which you could win an ignorance award
But you still choose to put your worst foot forward
I could play hard sell
But you would pretend not to be well
Well, you can go straight to hell
Go ahead and ring someone else's bell
You face is a complicated maze
It leaves many in a foggy haze
You know how I hate Broadway plays

You could very well be the end of my days
No matter what you choose to throw
Or how much hurt, you pile on blow for blow
You with never be anything but a yo-yo
And I will continue to radiate and glow
I will continue to wonder
If you will always try to plunder
And blow the truth asunder
You'll find out you're the one who
really has made the blunder
I would be very surprised
If you ever break out of your disguise
Leopards don't change their spots, that's no lie
And for now, you will not get
from me any kind of a rise

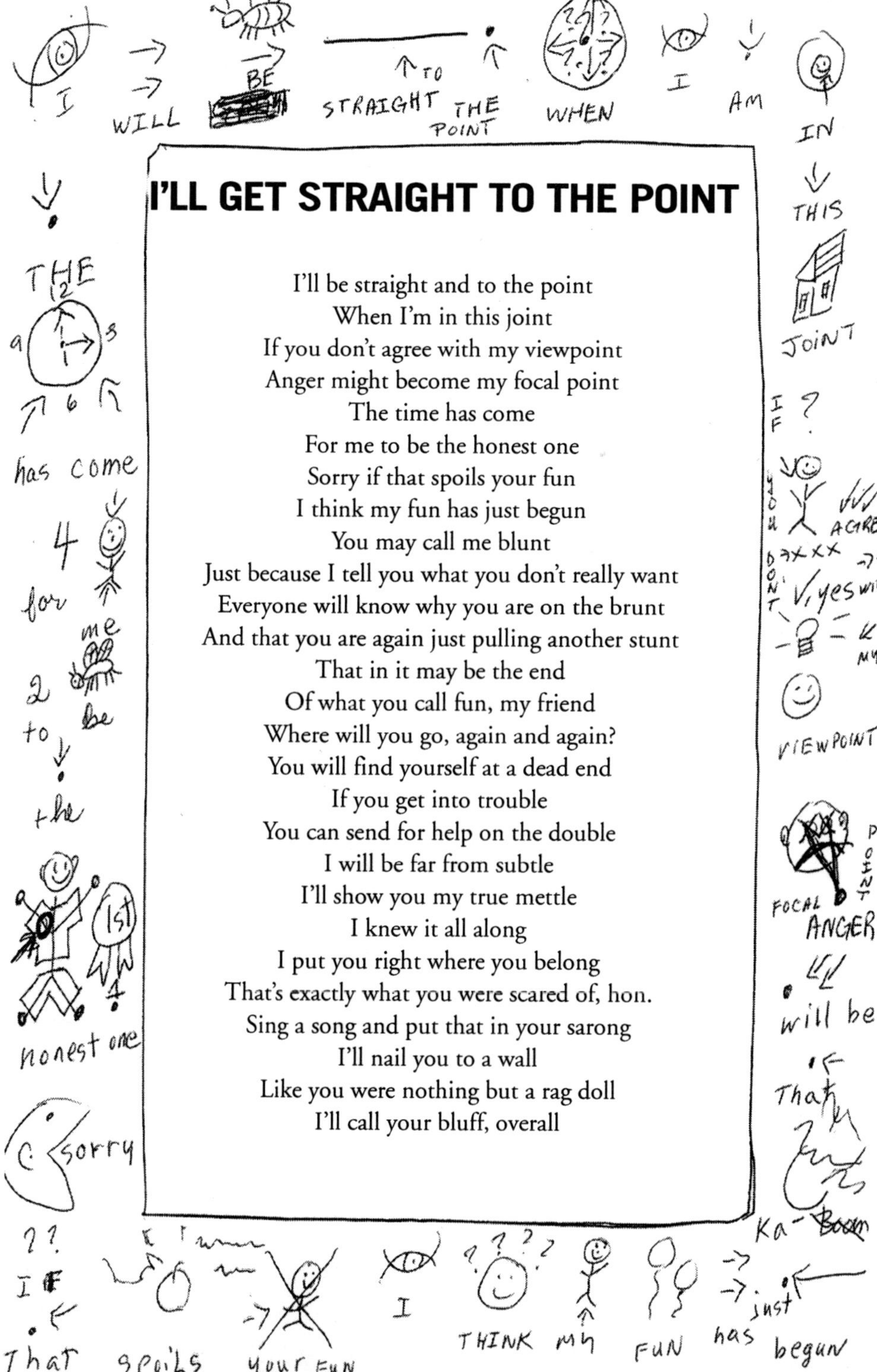

I'LL GET STRAIGHT TO THE POINT

I'll be straight and to the point
When I'm in this joint
If you don't agree with my viewpoint
Anger might become my focal point
The time has come
For me to be the honest one
Sorry if that spoils your fun
I think my fun has just begun
You may call me blunt
Just because I tell you what you don't really want
Everyone will know why you are on the brunt
And that you are again just pulling another stunt
That in it may be the end
Of what you call fun, my friend
Where will you go, again and again?
You will find yourself at a dead end
If you get into trouble
You can send for help on the double
I will be far from subtle
I'll show you my true mettle
I knew it all along
I put you right where you belong
That's exactly what you were scared of, hon.
Sing a song and put that in your sarong
I'll nail you to a wall
Like you were nothing but a rag doll
I'll call your bluff, overall

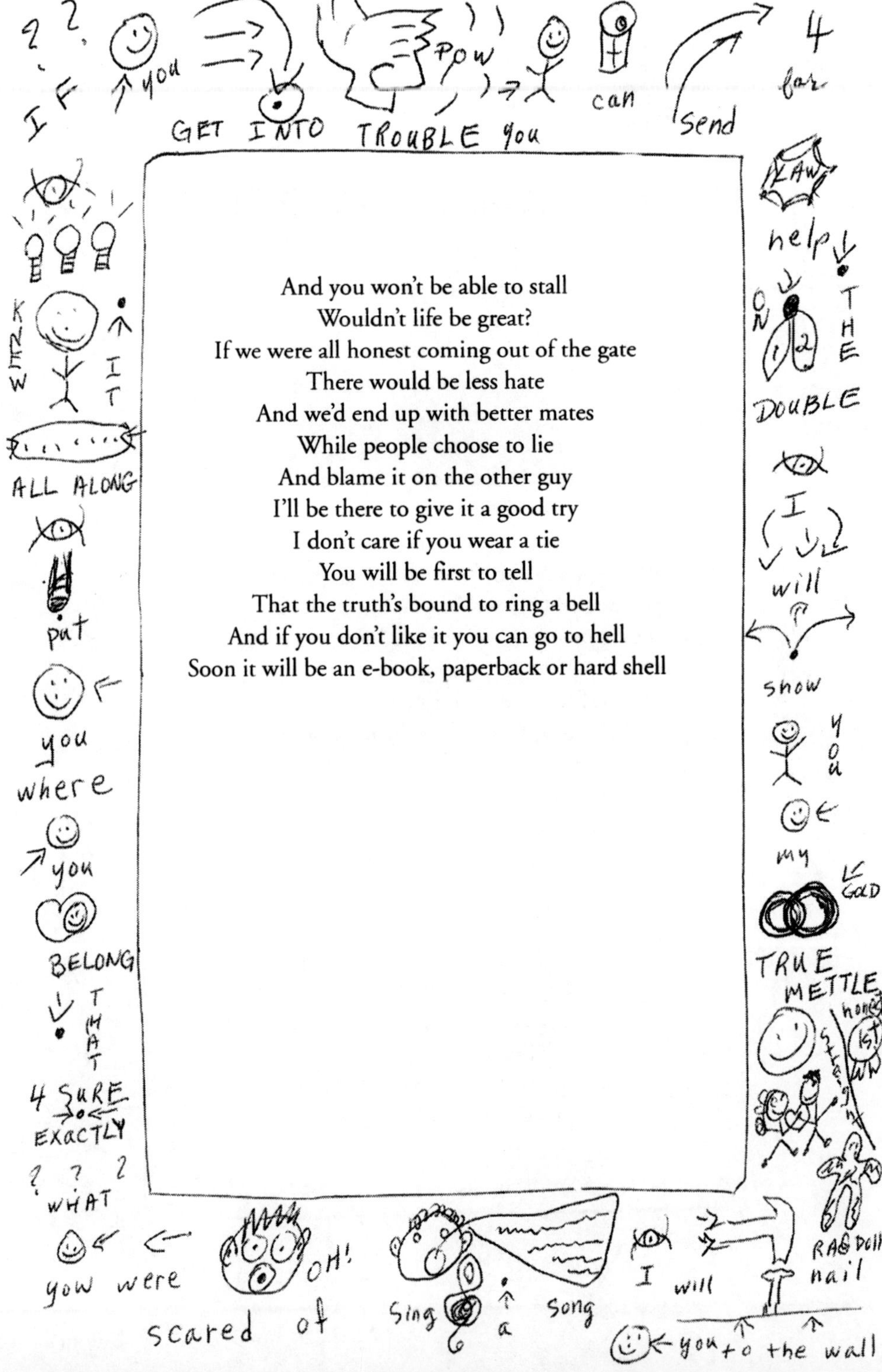

And you won't be able to stall
Wouldn't life be great?
If we were all honest coming out of the gate
There would be less hate
And we'd end up with better mates
While people choose to lie
And blame it on the other guy
I'll be there to give it a good try
I don't care if you wear a tie
You will be first to tell
That the truth's bound to ring a bell
And if you don't like it you can go to hell
Soon it will be an e-book, paperback or hard shell

THE TWILIGHT ZONE, ALTERNATE UNIVERSES

(Version A)

I was totally lost, I was like a ghost
My seas were tossed, I had nothing to boast
Now I wanted the very most
If someone was to again join my hitching post
I don't easily give up
But I felt like I'd been left out at the roundup
Or there had been some horrible mix-up
And I definitely felt all washed up
I wasn't searching or even looking
I wasn't settling for a one-night fling
So I stayed out of the boxing ring
And I acted like a puppet on a string
Your lady left you and left you hard
As a matter of fact, you were discarded
She didn't even let you have the final word
She left you and pushed in a very sharp sword
I found you under the ice
You had paid a horrible price
You came up to breathe twice
But what happened wasn't nice
You fell in through the trapdoor
You even went into the navy corps
You didn't know what was in store

Or that you would have to stay on terra-firma shore
Your ideas went out into the night
Then you quavered and lost sight
You thought you knew what was right
You turned out to be my white knight
You swept me off my feet
You were so kind and so sweet
Your voice made my heart skip a beat
The whole package was so very complete

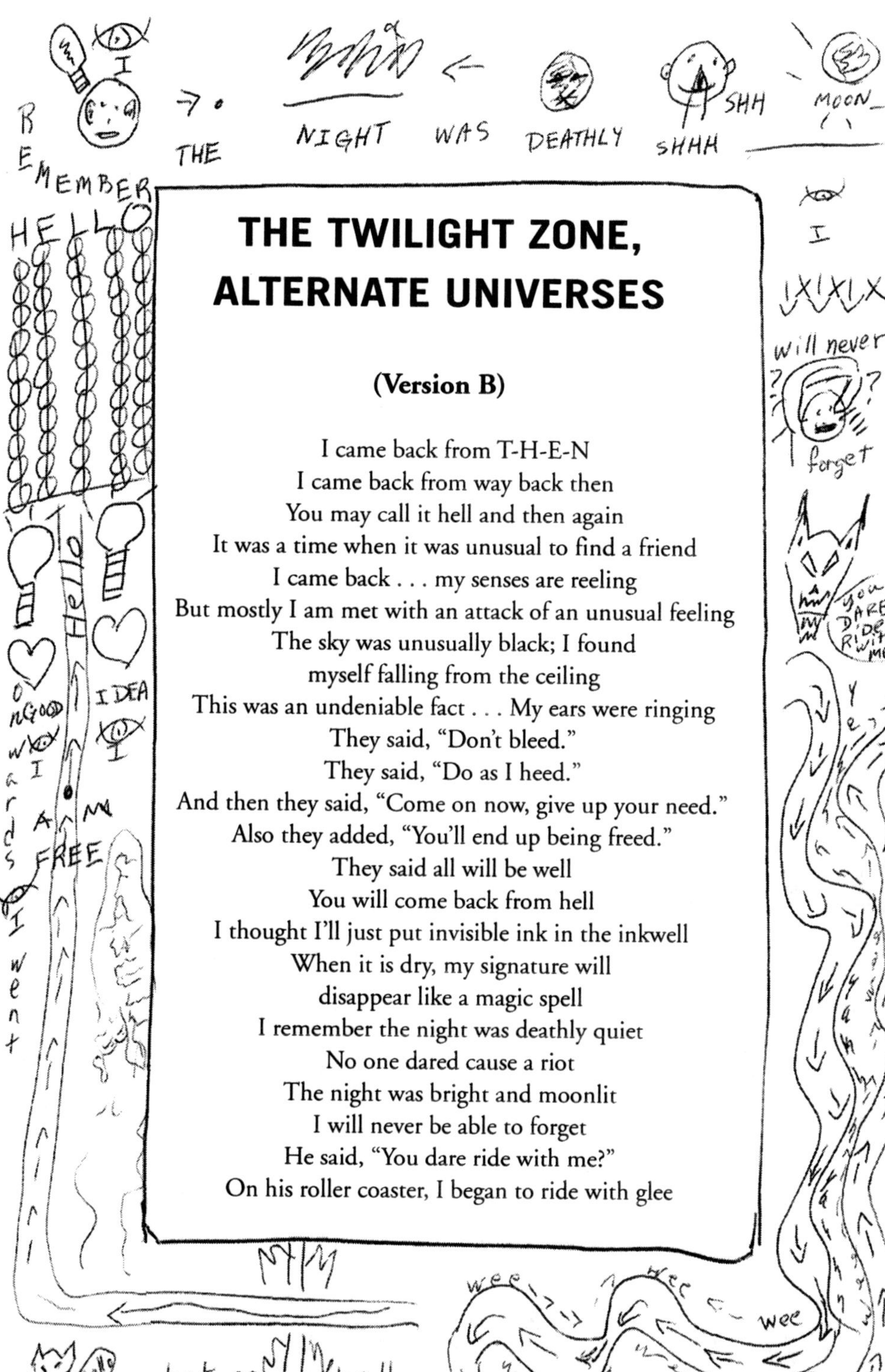

THE TWILIGHT ZONE, ALTERNATE UNIVERSES

(Version B)

I came back from T-H-E-N
I came back from way back then
You may call it hell and then again
It was a time when it was unusual to find a friend
I came back . . . my senses are reeling
But mostly I am met with an attack of an unusual feeling
The sky was unusually black; I found
myself falling from the ceiling
This was an undeniable fact . . . My ears were ringing
They said, "Don't bleed."
They said, "Do as I heed."
And then they said, "Come on now, give up your need."
Also they added, "You'll end up being freed."
They said all will be well
You will come back from hell
I thought I'll just put invisible ink in the inkwell
When it is dry, my signature will
disappear like a magic spell
I remember the night was deathly quiet
No one dared cause a riot
The night was bright and moonlit
I will never be able to forget
He said, "You dare ride with me?"
On his roller coaster, I began to ride with glee

I went down, down, down, and then up, up, up, you see
There couldn't be a better ending, I'll guarantee
Then through a fire wall I went, hot as hell
Then down through a long, cool, cool tunnel
To all the devils and demons, I said,
"Hello" and then "Farewell."
Onwards I went, and I said "Hello" to the
angels past the four pearly gates
All the characters I had earlier written
In invisible ink, once so very dark, with my pen
Had up and dried and turned invisible again
My cleverness had rescued me out of the devil's den

I'VE BEEN HIT

It's a hit. To wit
It hurts everywhere and every bit
I'm in pain. I've been hit
My weakness is made clear. Ah, shit
It burns. It stings. I've been hurt
I'm bleeding all over your shirt
Pain does tend to make me more alert
But my eyes can't help but avert
That was a dirty blow. It was really a low one
You hit below the belt. That's no fun
I was right in your bomb zone. I'm undone
Up in the sky, way up high; I've been
blown up way to the sun
You've stabbed me right in my heart
And sliced away a piece, a very large part
I didn't see that in my star chart
I fell for it. I even gave you a head start
Everything is becoming crystal clear
How much you hated me and how you were in fear
You have no conscience at all, my dear
You must have trouble looking at yourself in the mirror
I've deflected it back at you
You won't suspect a thing until I say, "Boo."
Karma is my friend and on my side too
How are you for a little voodoo?
You'll find out how it feels
You'll be the one who squeals

You'll know that revenge is real
When you watch your life's blood congeal
Nothing in your past will be untouchable
You'll be on your knees if you are able
You will no longer feel mentally stable
And you'll wish you were nothing but a fable
They'll say an eye for an eye
And also a tooth for a tooth, no lie
I was hit by you a long, long time ago, by and by
And now I am no longer Mrs. Nice Guy

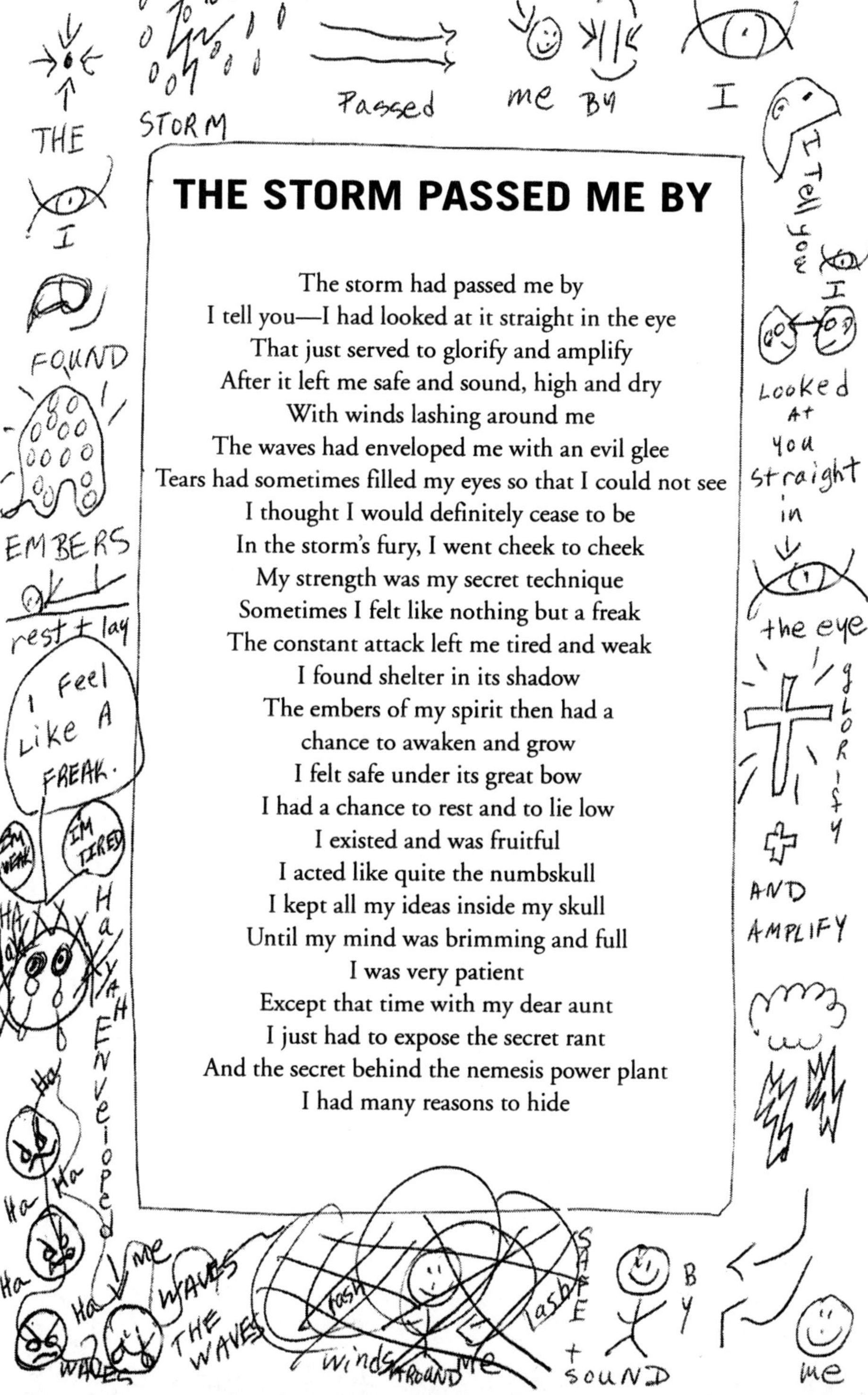

THE STORM PASSED ME BY

The storm had passed me by
I tell you—I had looked at it straight in the eye
That just served to glorify and amplify
After it left me safe and sound, high and dry
With winds lashing around me
The waves had enveloped me with an evil glee
Tears had sometimes filled my eyes so that I could not see
I thought I would definitely cease to be
In the storm's fury, I went cheek to cheek
My strength was my secret technique
Sometimes I felt like nothing but a freak
The constant attack left me tired and weak
I found shelter in its shadow
The embers of my spirit then had a
chance to awaken and grow
I felt safe under its great bow
I had a chance to rest and to lie low
I existed and was fruitful
I acted like quite the numbskull
I kept all my ideas inside my skull
Until my mind was brimming and full
I was very patient
Except that time with my dear aunt
I just had to expose the secret rant
And the secret behind the nemesis power plant
I had many reasons to hide

Two times I became a bride
I took it all in my stride
And kept my eyes open wide
Of the storm I will not complain
Now I have again full use of my brain
All is well, and the journey was not in vain
Really, it was not just a storm—it was a hurricane

I ALIENATE YOU

I alienate you
That's nothing new
To you nothing that I say is true
you don't give me my rightful due
I made the mistake of causing much heartbreak
Of giving you information just for your sake
And I believed you would take
My advice without thinking that I was unwise
You think that you need your freedom
And I'm just a person who happens to be your mom
You think you have gained a victory won
Truth is, you are the ones who will be undone
My advice will go on
And someday, for you, it will dawn
That *I did know the answers all along*
I only wanted to pass the baton in life's marathon
It always seemed to happen to me
When I trusted you and acted carefree
You took my love and went for a spree
Then I ended up feeling like a chimpanzee
I always manage to keep myself busy
I don't need any fancy PhD
I don't need to travel to sightsee
I am happy just being here in the Land of the Free
Because of this, I stick to myself
I guess, all in all, it's good for my personal health

I choose to be careful and walk with stealth
It would do you well to do so yourself
I am who I am and whom I choose to be
when I'm away or when I'm at home
Even though you may think I am in your combat zone
I am not your evil clone just because
to you, I am not unknown
I am just an honest person and I am home grown
But I do, I do, love you dearly
And I don't mind when you treat
me like I am totally eerie
I just chalk it up to one of life's realities
I know in my heart that you love
me too with a great finality

DON'T DENY THE TRUTH

Don't deny the truth
It's painless; it's not like pulling a tooth
You don't have to be the best sleuth
After all, it is just the proper way and it's so very couth
A lie will slap like whiplash and end up biting
Hard and fast like a bolt of lightning
Telling the truth will be very enlightening
And being true will be very refreshing
It can make you very happy
In fact, it can set your soul free
It's the very best way to be
It's the right way for you and me
The truth sometimes makes you sad
Like news that you've lost your loving, cherished dad
At that time you'll think of all the memories
when you were a safe, happy lad
And all those wonderful memories that you
now must now cherish and forever have.
Sometimes the truth can drive you mad
Because it's so very shocking, egad
Especially if you've found out that you've been had
And oh no, it is not just a passing fad
Truth can be the very best thing
The newfound truth can come with a ring
And all the love and trust that that brings
In turn it can be a new reason for your heart to sing
Truth gets to be an addictive habit
Once you start, you won't want to quit

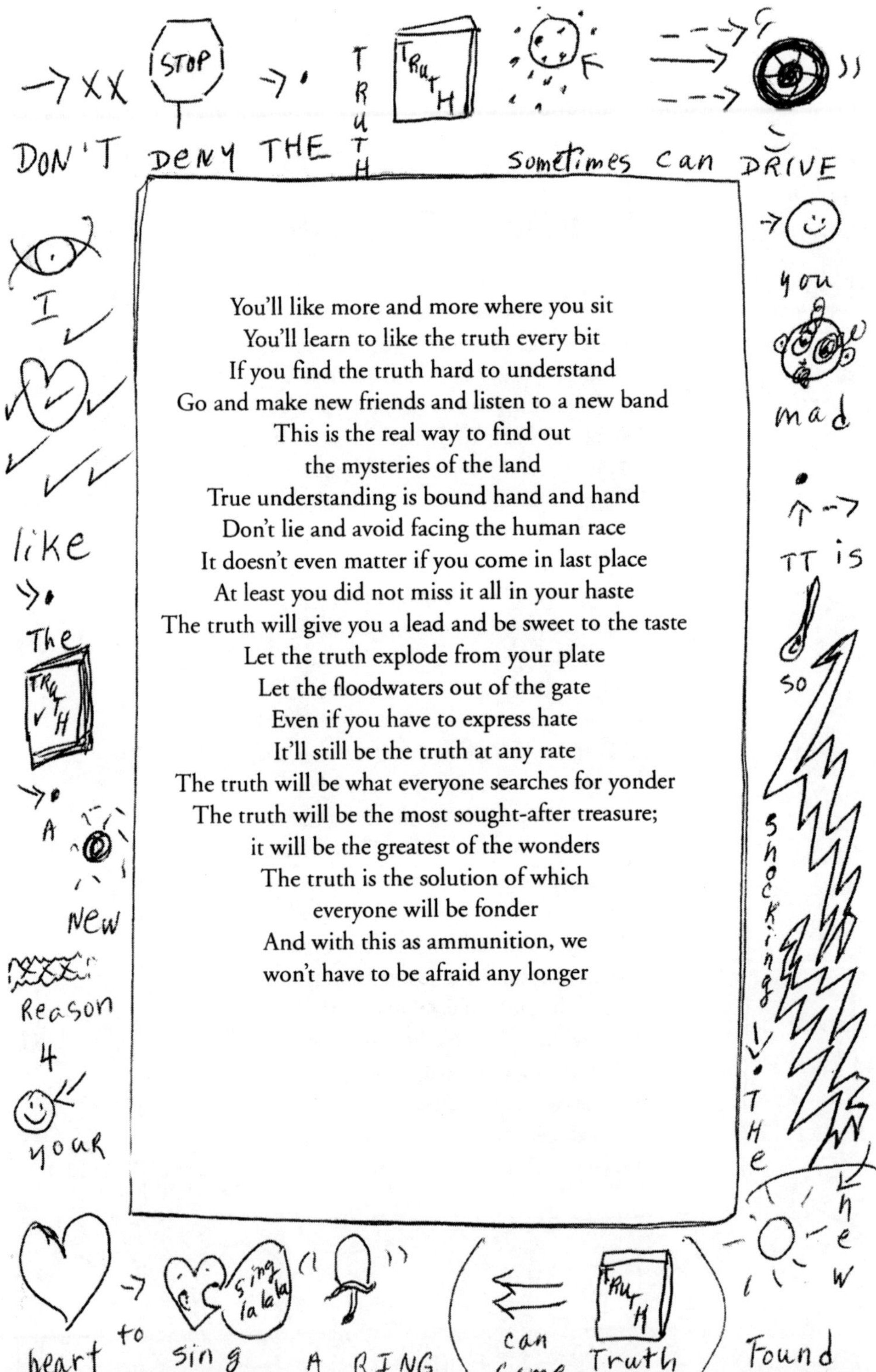

You'll like more and more where you sit
You'll learn to like the truth every bit
If you find the truth hard to understand
Go and make new friends and listen to a new band
This is the real way to find out
the mysteries of the land
True understanding is bound hand and hand
Don't lie and avoid facing the human race
It doesn't even matter if you come in last place
At least you did not miss it all in your haste
The truth will give you a lead and be sweet to the taste
Let the truth explode from your plate
Let the floodwaters out of the gate
Even if you have to express hate
It'll still be the truth at any rate
The truth will be what everyone searches for yonder
The truth will be the most sought-after treasure;
it will be the greatest of the wonders
The truth is the solution of which
everyone will be fonder
And with this as ammunition, we
won't have to be afraid any longer

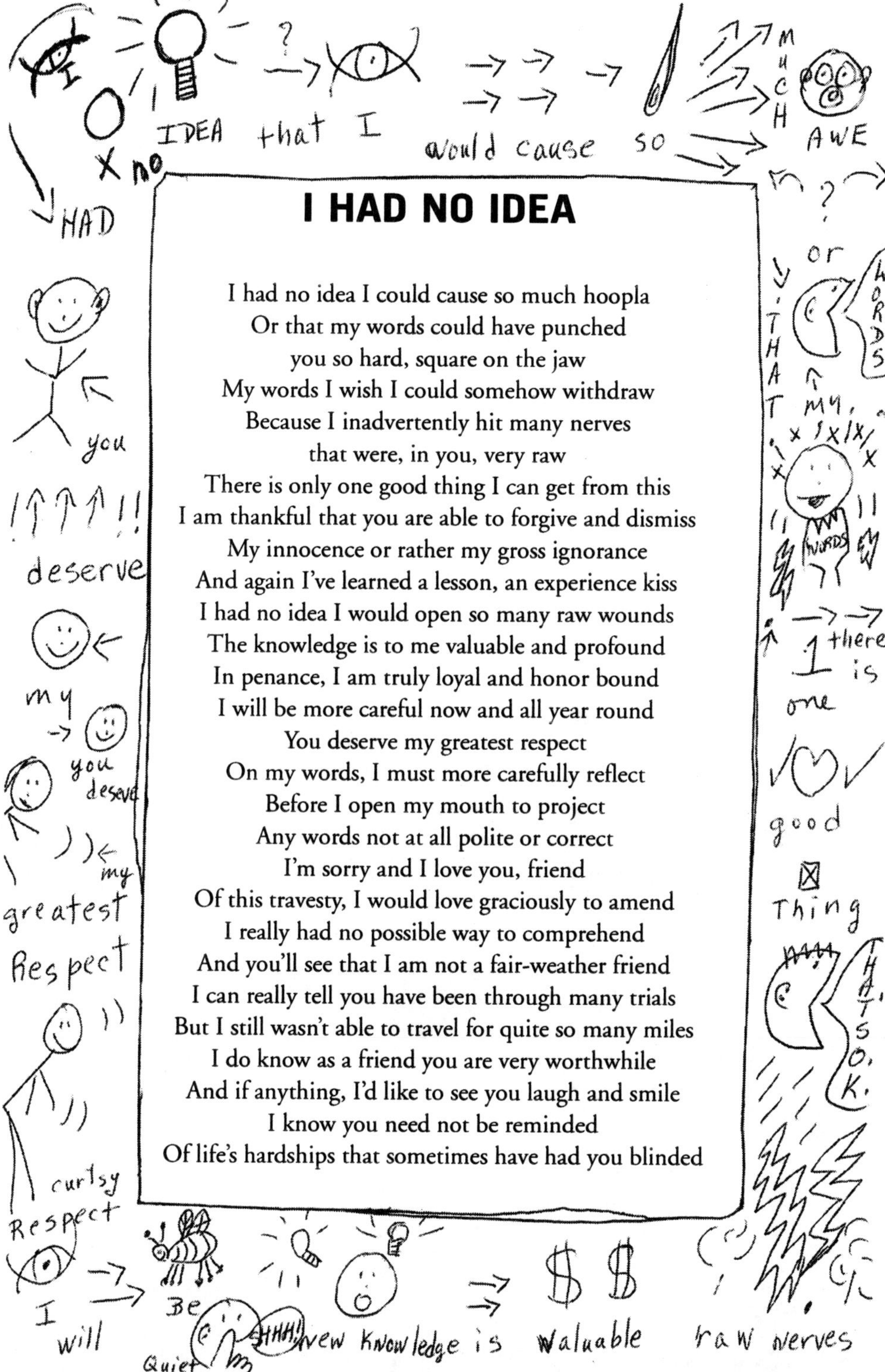

I HAD NO IDEA

I had no idea I could cause so much hoopla
Or that my words could have punched
you so hard, square on the jaw
My words I wish I could somehow withdraw
Because I inadvertently hit many nerves
that were, in you, very raw
There is only one good thing I can get from this
I am thankful that you are able to forgive and dismiss
My innocence or rather my gross ignorance
And again I've learned a lesson, an experience kiss
I had no idea I would open so many raw wounds
The knowledge is to me valuable and profound
In penance, I am truly loyal and honor bound
I will be more careful now and all year round
You deserve my greatest respect
On my words, I must more carefully reflect
Before I open my mouth to project
Any words not at all polite or correct
I'm sorry and I love you, friend
Of this travesty, I would love graciously to amend
I really had no possible way to comprehend
And you'll see that I am not a fair-weather friend
I can really tell you have been through many trials
But I still wasn't able to travel for quite so many miles
I do know as a friend you are very worthwhile
And if anything, I'd like to see you laugh and smile
I know you need not be reminded
Of life's hardships that sometimes have had you blinded

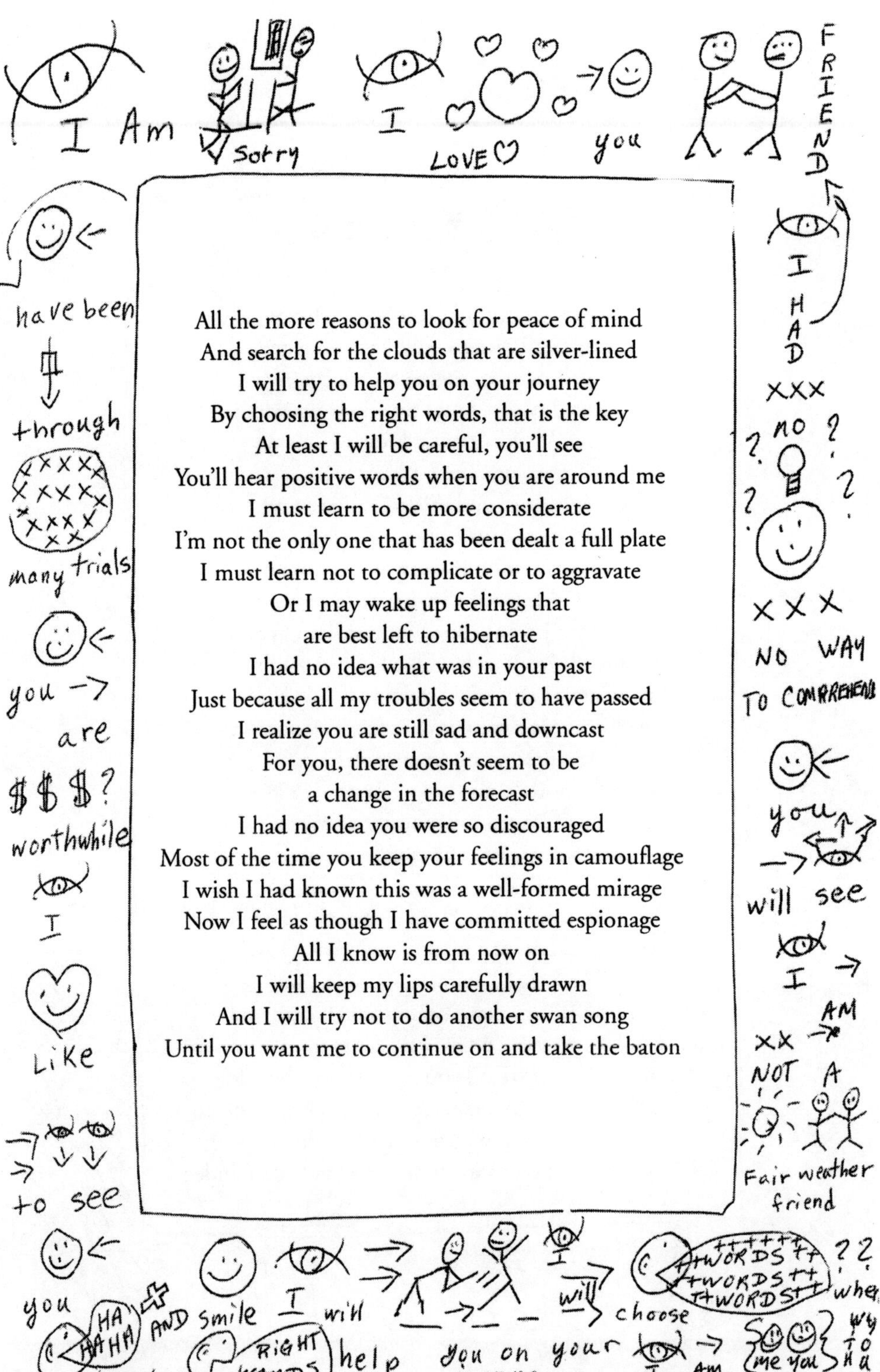

All the more reasons to look for peace of mind
And search for the clouds that are silver-lined
I will try to help you on your journey
By choosing the right words, that is the key
At least I will be careful, you'll see
You'll hear positive words when you are around me
I must learn to be more considerate
I'm not the only one that has been dealt a full plate
I must learn not to complicate or to aggravate
Or I may wake up feelings that
are best left to hibernate
I had no idea what was in your past
Just because all my troubles seem to have passed
I realize you are still sad and downcast
For you, there doesn't seem to be
a change in the forecast
I had no idea you were so discouraged
Most of the time you keep your feelings in camouflage
I wish I had known this was a well-formed mirage
Now I feel as though I have committed espionage
All I know is from now on
I will keep my lips carefully drawn
And I will try not to do another swan song
Until you want me to continue on and take the baton

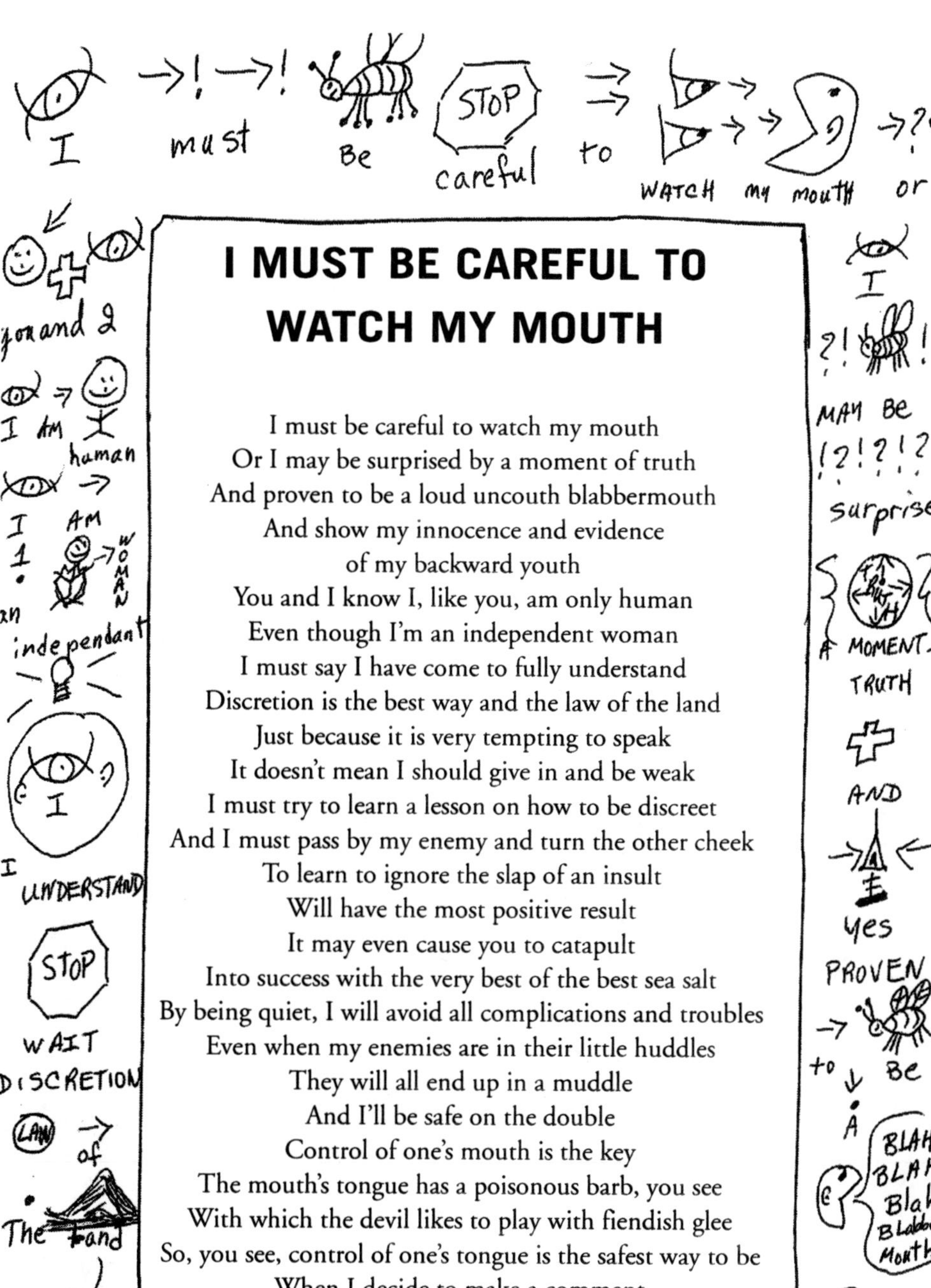

I MUST BE CAREFUL TO WATCH MY MOUTH

I must be careful to watch my mouth
Or I may be surprised by a moment of truth
And proven to be a loud uncouth blabbermouth
And show my innocence and evidence
of my backward youth
You and I know I, like you, am only human
Even though I'm an independent woman
I must say I have come to fully understand
Discretion is the best way and the law of the land
Just because it is very tempting to speak
It doesn't mean I should give in and be weak
I must try to learn a lesson on how to be discreet
And I must pass by my enemy and turn the other cheek
To learn to ignore the slap of an insult
Will have the most positive result
It may even cause you to catapult
Into success with the very best of the best sea salt
By being quiet, I will avoid all complications and troubles
Even when my enemies are in their little huddles
They will all end up in a muddle
And I'll be safe on the double
Control of one's mouth is the key
The mouth's tongue has a poisonous barb, you see
With which the devil likes to play with fiendish glee
So, you see, control of one's tongue is the safest way to be
When I decide to make a comment

I must be careful where and how it's sent
So the meaning of it doesn't get interrupted or bent
Or twisted out of what was truly meant
I must always be on my guard
And make sure I watch all my words
Also to make them honest and kind
when they are going to be heard
And to always let them be sincere and clear,
not at all blurred
I must try my best to be humble
When I am supposed to speak up,
I must try not to grumble
And I must remember, if I am too
pushy, I might take a tumble
This might then prove me to be
nothing but a numbskull
Oh, how I have already been burned
And how I hope I have somehow, my lesson, learned
And then it will be my fateful turn
And then and only then I will be safe
and out of the reach of harm

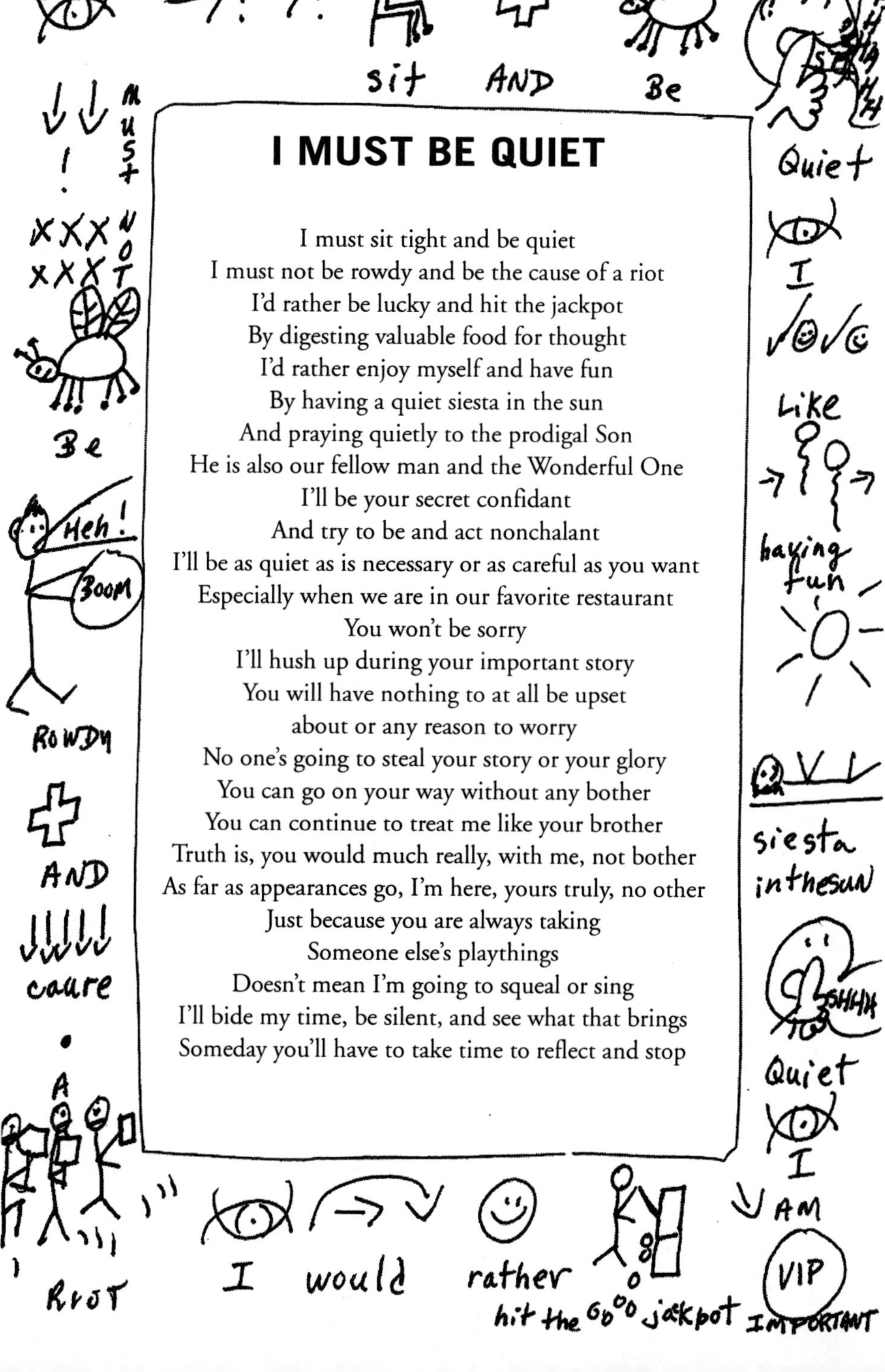
sit AND Be
Quiet
must
not
Be
Heh!
BOOM
ROWDY
AND
cause
A
RIOT
I would rather
hit the jackpot
I
Like
having fun
siesta in the sun
SHHH
Quiet
I
AM
VIP
IMPORTANT

I MUST BE QUIET

I must sit tight and be quiet
I must not be rowdy and be the cause of a riot
I'd rather be lucky and hit the jackpot
By digesting valuable food for thought
I'd rather enjoy myself and have fun
By having a quiet siesta in the sun
And praying quietly to the prodigal Son
He is also our fellow man and the Wonderful One
I'll be your secret confidant
And try to be and act nonchalant
I'll be as quiet as is necessary or as careful as you want
Especially when we are in our favorite restaurant
You won't be sorry
I'll hush up during your important story
You will have nothing to at all be upset
about or any reason to worry
No one's going to steal your story or your glory
You can go on your way without any bother
You can continue to treat me like your brother
Truth is, you would much really, with me, not bother
As far as appearances go, I'm here, yours truly, no other
Just because you are always taking
Someone else's playthings
Doesn't mean I'm going to squeal or sing
I'll bide my time, be silent, and see what that brings
Someday you'll have to take time to reflect and stop

You won't be able to always stay on top
And you can't always go nonstop
You are bound to eventually make a giant belly flop
Therefore, for now, I will be quiet
And I won't be the cause of any riot
I'll be careful and wait to fill in all the dots
Because that's how I was taught

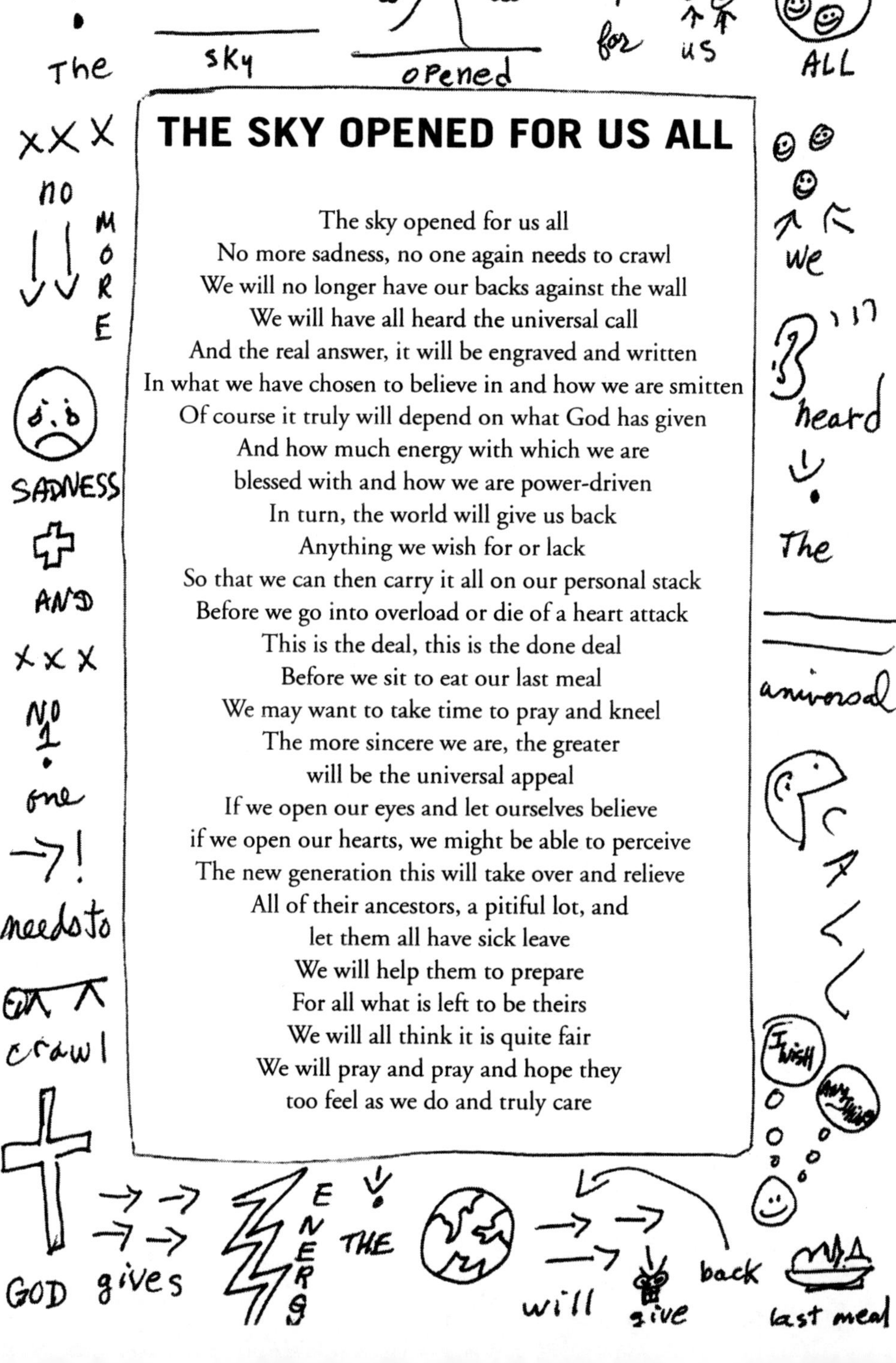

THE SKY OPENED FOR US ALL

The sky opened for us all
No more sadness, no one again needs to crawl
We will no longer have our backs against the wall
We will have all heard the universal call
And the real answer, it will be engraved and written
In what we have chosen to believe in and how we are smitten
Of course it truly will depend on what God has given
And how much energy with which we are
blessed with and how we are power-driven
In turn, the world will give us back
Anything we wish for or lack
So that we can then carry it all on our personal stack
Before we go into overload or die of a heart attack
This is the deal, this is the done deal
Before we sit to eat our last meal
We may want to take time to pray and kneel
The more sincere we are, the greater
will be the universal appeal
If we open our eyes and let ourselves believe
if we open our hearts, we might be able to perceive
The new generation this will take over and relieve
All of their ancestors, a pitiful lot, and
let them all have sick leave
We will help them to prepare
For all what is left to be theirs
We will all think it is quite fair
We will pray and pray and hope they
too feel as we do and truly care

We surely must all live as one
Or this whole world will surely be undone
And then what would be left for them
or us or for anyone under the sun
And how would we or they have any more fun
So try to prepare your babies
For all the future maybes
And when and if they get to look at a tree
They will be able to say, "Look at me, I'm free."

COME ON, WIGGLE

Faster, faster, faster, give a giggle
Come on, wiggle, wiggle, wiggle, and wiggle
I would like to give you a hug and a friendly tickle
I love you; don't be so distant and fickle
The force be with me and you
Phasers on stun, this is all so new
My love is shiny too; Cupid's arrow came out of the blue
Just like a deadly shot from karate or kung fu
My world lives for another and another and another
All I know is I'm in a state of unadulterated wonder
My world is constantly torn asunder for
you, my dear husband and lover
I don't think this is at all an accidental blunder
Whether with a drop of the hat or not
You and I may or may not be caught
We will be the ones who will wiggle around and get red hot
We will love each other both a little and a lot
What will be left of us will be best felt
After that explosion over yonder, way out left
There won't be much left of us, I'll bet
What do you expect? That's all you're bound to get
Oh, we all want to know the answer to the age-old question
Just put down your arms and tickle
him and then wait for a reaction
Invite him to try to join you and you
might get some kind of attention
But make sure to be careful to
protect your sterling reputation

By the way it stands, and by the way it looks
It's OK to cook, according to everyone's recipe books
Playing fair and using clean methods
are the main ingredients
It takes to be in the winner's nook
And you see, it's magic, you will have
a delicious meal on the hook

Someday you will have great peace, and
this will be your cup of tea
And you will have great satisfaction, gratification, all
the more for you to be able to tease
I know that is certain. Just look at me and
say cheese. He can have my keys.
It's the greatest. It's called marriage, say yes, if you please

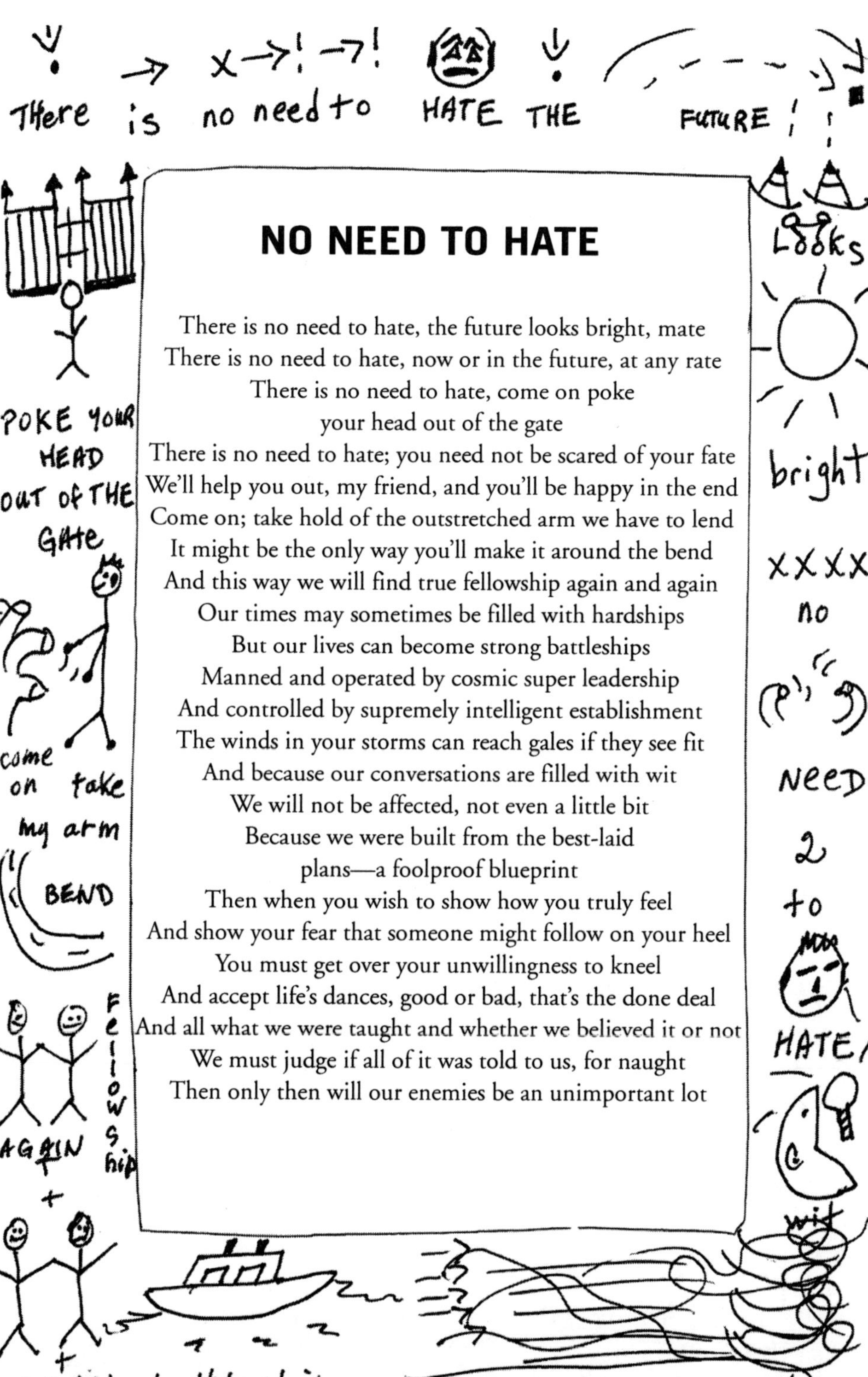
There is no need to HATE THE FUTURE
Looks
bright
XXXX
no
NeeD
2
to
HATE
wit
POKE YOUR HEAD OUT OF THE GATE
come on take my arm
BEND
Fellowship
AGAIN
+
AGAIN
battleship
winds reach gails

NO NEED TO HATE

There is no need to hate, the future looks bright, mate
There is no need to hate, now or in the future, at any rate
There is no need to hate, come on poke
your head out of the gate
There is no need to hate; you need not be scared of your fate
We'll help you out, my friend, and you'll be happy in the end
Come on; take hold of the outstretched arm we have to lend
It might be the only way you'll make it around the bend
And this way we will find true fellowship again and again
Our times may sometimes be filled with hardships
But our lives can become strong battleships
Manned and operated by cosmic super leadership
And controlled by supremely intelligent establishment
The winds in your storms can reach gales if they see fit
And because our conversations are filled with wit
We will not be affected, not even a little bit
Because we were built from the best-laid
plans—a foolproof blueprint
Then when you wish to show how you truly feel
And show your fear that someone might follow on your heel
You must get over your unwillingness to kneel
And accept life's dances, good or bad, that's the done deal
And all what we were taught and whether we believed it or not
We must judge if all of it was told to us, for naught
Then only then will our enemies be an unimportant lot

Because we'll know all what they are
about and what they've got
Then we will all have a fun time
With plenty of enthusiasm for lives hard climb
We'll know our fate has had a reason and a rhyme
And there is no reason for hate, big time
Freedom for all is what is needed
And making sure love is well-seeded
Great intelligence isn't necessarily needed
All we need is mutual respect to be heeded

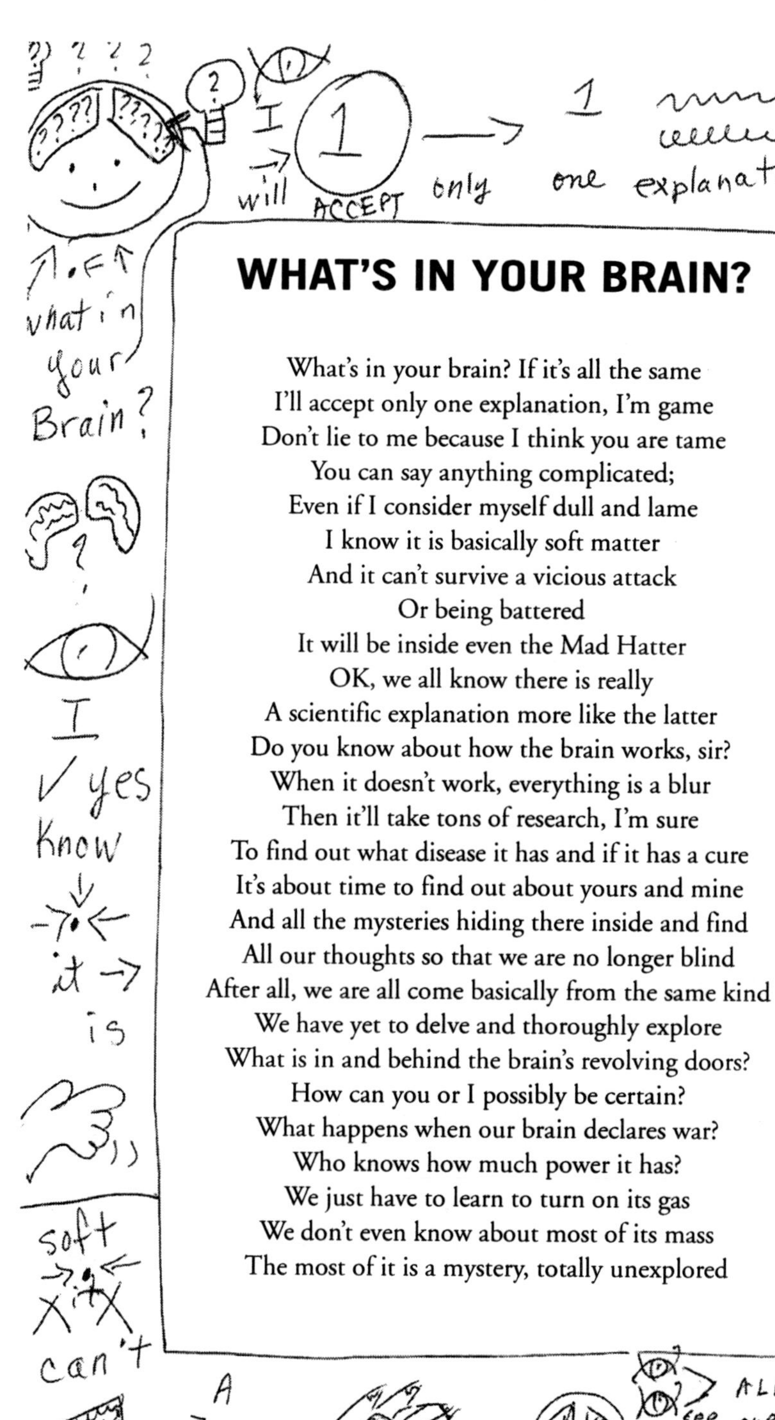

WHAT'S IN YOUR BRAIN?

What's in your brain? If it's all the same
I'll accept only one explanation, I'm game
Don't lie to me because I think you are tame
You can say anything complicated;
Even if I consider myself dull and lame
I know it is basically soft matter
And it can't survive a vicious attack
Or being battered
It will be inside even the Mad Hatter
OK, we all know there is really
A scientific explanation more like the latter
Do you know about how the brain works, sir?
When it doesn't work, everything is a blur
Then it'll take tons of research, I'm sure
To find out what disease it has and if it has a cure
It's about time to find out about yours and mine
And all the mysteries hiding there inside and find
All our thoughts so that we are no longer blind
After all, we are all come basically from the same kind
We have yet to delve and thoroughly explore
What is in and behind the brain's revolving doors?
How can you or I possibly be certain?
What happens when our brain declares war?
Who knows how much power it has?
We just have to learn to turn on its gas
We don't even know about most of its mass
The most of it is a mystery, totally unexplored

What we do know
Is that there is row upon row
And many, many layers all tied together like
A big, beautiful present, wrapped in a protective bow
It serves as our very own main control center
From which we learn and grow
And while we continue to try and try
We still know little about this important guy
This is amazingly our main frame, no lie
But I imagine we will, we will find out by and by

THE GREAT ESCAPE

I'm ready for my undisputed fate
It is time for me to jump and leave the gate
It is time for me to make my great escape
It is time for me to squeeze love out of hate
A feat like this will make me very happy
This accomplishment might change my world, Pappy
I will then be satisfied because I will no longer feel crappy
And that will be the greatest feeling of all, Daddy
It will all start and come from my heart
For me that will always be the best place to start
And when you all see what is behind the rest of my fort
You will no longer bother being a worrywart
My escape will be like a runaway train
It will flow like lightning, right of my brain
It will be something no one man can tame
This escape will be like the best word game
I will play no holds barred
Anyone playing with me will feel like a star
This game will take everyone far
It will even overtake war
And I will continue my wordplay
And I will be quite satisfied to say
That I will have my own way
I just like it when everyone will be merry and gay

Even though I am old,
I won't leave you out in the cold
And I won't let hatred take a hold
My happiness will be my finest spun gold
My songs will flow all over
I'll invite you all to sing moreover
We'll all eventually be dancing in the clover
The words and music will bind us all together

YOUNG LOVE

They say keep the one in your hand the
one you love, your young love
So innocent, so trusting, this one that is like a dove
This one you have lots in common with,
and who you want much more of
This one's better than two in the bush and
is as good as one in your glove
We make a fine picture, dear
No need to look at each other in the mirror
That we are happy with each other is plain and clear
And now that we've met, we don't know the meaning of fear
Here's one for you, here's one for me
The best things in our lives are free
Love is bound to taste better if we look at what we see
And all too soon, our short human lives
will be over, for both of us
Our love's beauty is all around us
You won't find us making a fuss
Because with each other, our words are never at a loss
We try to communicate, and happiness
is for us at a coin's toss
As a couple, we feel we are predestined
Because to each other we are very loyal
When we are together, everything is fun, even toil
We are happy to be grounded on terra-firma soil
We feel like every day is Valentine's Day

Because Cupid has a hold of us and
continues to have his way
Cupid's hearts and arrows are like bubbles at play
They keep us in love, merry and gay

No matter what, no matter when
We'll be together like long-lost friends
No matter what, nothing can separate
us in the here, or at all, or again
Our love will go beyond this world
when our mortal lives end
Our love is eternally entwined
Our spirits have joined and formed a grand smoky design
For anyone not to see it, they would have to be blind
We knew it all along that life would,
to us, eventually be kind
For us, distance was no object, our fates were preset
We were meant to be together, no
matter how high the bet
The odds were stacked against us and yet
My prince came from far while I stayed still,
yet we never had a reason to regret
And oh that fateful connection, to my recollection
Was to his and my greatest satisfaction
It was a love at first sight and sound reaction
A love given from God with His blessing,
totally to our liking and totally in fashion

IF I COULD MAKE A WISH

If I could make a wish
It would not be to be a luscious dish
Not that I like being a funny fish
And I would not wish for another splash or another splish
So far, for what I would yearn
Would be to be able to discern
Between good and evil, turn in turn
Even though this may be dangerous
And I do not wish to burn
I wish only, for everyone's overall best
There, I have finally got it off my chest
I don't really know the entirety of the rest
But so far, I feel that I have been quite blest
What I really want, tends to claw me
inside and cause me endless taunts
I'm afraid that I will actually obtain it because
then I might use my knowledge to flaunt
This effort might leave me thin and gaunt
And in this case, I would be both unhealthy
and might act like a freaky savant
I would not choose my wish in haste
I might even make a surprise wish to be chaste
I will surely choose to my very own taste
I won't choose when I am in any special place
What would I choose to be my lucky charm?
I'll yell out loud if you get close and
I'll celebrate if you get warm

All I wish for is to go away arm in arm
With the man who has raised my fire alarm
Yes, I saw that shooting star
Falling from the sky away, so very far
I did make a wish, hark, hark, and hark
It may or may not be for a car
You can't take my wishes away from me
We'll both find out if my wishes come to be
If they come true; I'll giggle with glee
I'm patient for what's to be; we'll just wait and see
I may have made more wishes than one
A wish, in the plural, could be lots of fun
I had better be careful not to jump the gun
Then all my wishes would be for
naught and I would be undone
I won't waste my wish on any one try
I'll give my wish my best shot, and that is no lie
I'll hope for the best, me oh my
I can depend on the Man, the Main Guy

IF I MAY BE SO BOLD

If I may say so, if I may be so bold
I have realized I am daily becoming old
I am happy to say, fear of death is losing its hold
I am also happy to say, I do not think I have sold my soul
In my life so far, I have seen a lot of terrible things
But with them, I have found many important lessons
That only life's trials could bring
I have also seen how reliable fate rings and sings
I have even seen how life begins
So tell me, how I can possibly be surprised
At anything I find on the other side
It is, nevertheless, bound to be a fantastic ride
Over yonder, there is bound to be
someone to whom I can confide
And in there, in the great when
My new life will begin again
I'll say good-bye to where I've been
And I will take my new life for a spin
All I can say is I want to meet the Man
The One who's Three-in-One because
I'm one of His biggest fans
I want to be with Him in His beautiful land
The land full of miracles both great and grand
If I get there and when I do
I'll know that success comes to everyone not just a few
That's when the universe will seem to become brand new

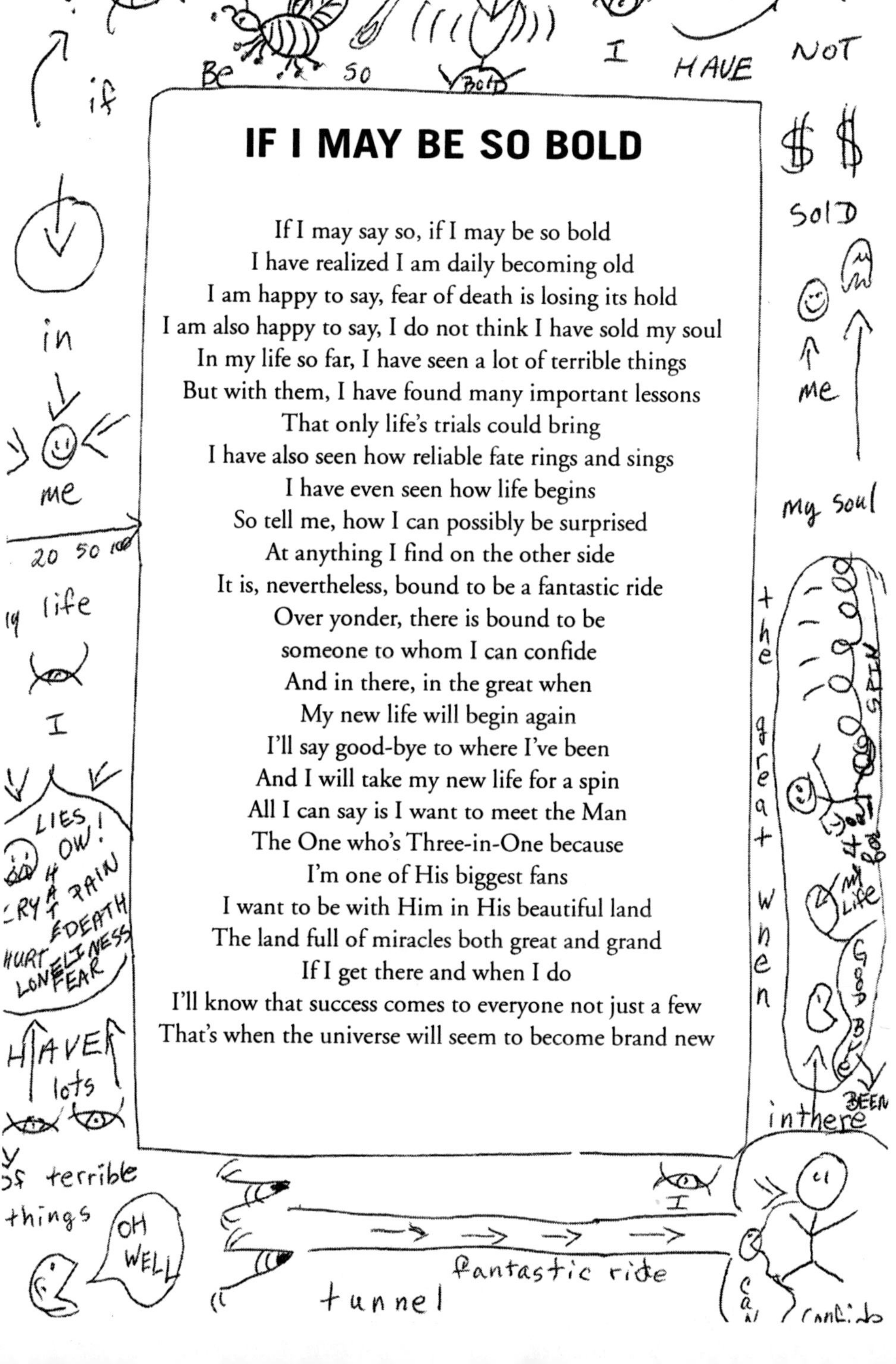

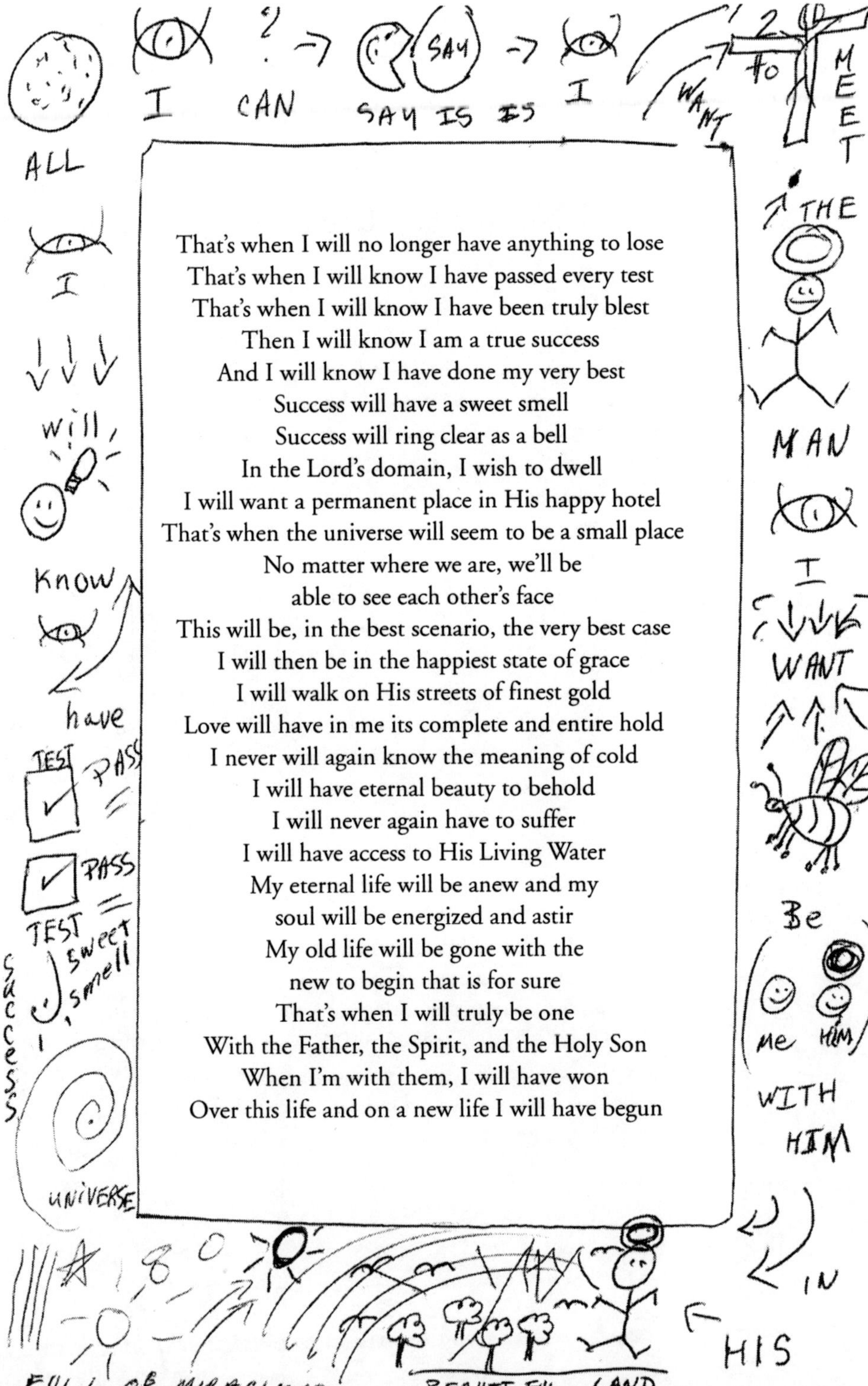

That's when I will no longer have anything to lose
That's when I will know I have passed every test
That's when I will know I have been truly blest
Then I will know I am a true success
And I will know I have done my very best
Success will have a sweet smell
Success will ring clear as a bell
In the Lord's domain, I wish to dwell
I will want a permanent place in His happy hotel
That's when the universe will seem to be a small place
No matter where we are, we'll be
able to see each other's face
This will be, in the best scenario, the very best case
I will then be in the happiest state of grace
I will walk on His streets of finest gold
Love will have in me its complete and entire hold
I never will again know the meaning of cold
I will have eternal beauty to behold
I will never again have to suffer
I will have access to His Living Water
My eternal life will be anew and my
soul will be energized and astir
My old life will be gone with the
new to begin that is for sure
That's when I will truly be one
With the Father, the Spirit, and the Holy Son
When I'm with them, I will have won
Over this life and on a new life I will have begun

DON'T CRACK YOUR WHIP

Don't you dare, don't crack your whip
If you do, I might lose my grip
Then I'll tell you not to give me any lip
And furthermore, I might break down and have a fit
When I hear the sound of the whip's crack
It might be the straw that breaks my camel's back
I then might be forced to use a surprise attack
So don't give me any wise cracks unless they are proven facts
If I so much as get scared
My nostrils will flare and my teeth will be bared
My insecurities will show how much I really care
And my anger will be pi r-squared
Who do you think you really are?
You might even be the cause of the next war
All that would do is cause suffering and a lot of gore
Do you realize how much damage your
big whip will be responsible for?
You stink to high heavens, you creep
You are nothing but a slithering pipsqueak
You get gratification out of hurting the mild and the meek
Is it truth or is it justification you seek?
I'm telling you, I think in the end you'll be sorry
When your words backfire, it'll be a different story
Then you'll be the one with the worries
And they might haul you away in a police
car—so much for your glory

You won't like that kind of party
I think then you'll be the one breaking down in a hurry
And you'll be the one running away in a scurry
Wrap your whip around that story
Before you know it, you'll have blown it
You'll be the one who has to learn to sit
You'll be the one who has to learn to be quiet
So put that info-whip back in your going-away kit
Your friends might see you in a different light
If you decide you no longer want to fight
They may even begin to see you as someone bright
Not just a loud noise in the night
If you learn to be a good person
You'll be someone people want to
bring back to their mom
That's when the real battle will be won
That's when you'll have come out into the sun
Also I'll be happy to stretch my hand
To you in friendship and welcome you to my land
That's when we both will feel grand
Then we will both, each other, understand
We will both be on the same wavelength
And peace and joy will be our strengths
Then the universe will be our think tank
And we will have each other to congratulate
and to thank

I'M A VICTIM OF WAR

I'm alive but I am a victim of war—and what's more
I did not ask for what went before or
Who was waiting—that awful bore
Or what was to be in store
I did not ask for my future or—for my before
I did not ask for life's gore or how my heart
was to be put into a tug-of-war
No one on Earth witnessed my pain
After life's wars began, it was all I could
do but to be hurt again and again
No matter what, I would never be the same; I
truly thought I would go insane
And meanwhile my handshake had become weak
And my mind had been imprisoned in invisible chains
My journey was an uphill battle
It was a very hard road to travel
It was something with which I wished
I had not been saddled
Responsibility was given to me at the same time
My mind was left confused and addled
I was quite lonely and very, very hurt
Mind you, leaving my family alone was not my decision;
I did not choose to leave them
Everyone left me alone, for what it's worth
Soon all my senses were trained to be sharp and alert
And as the years passed before my eyes

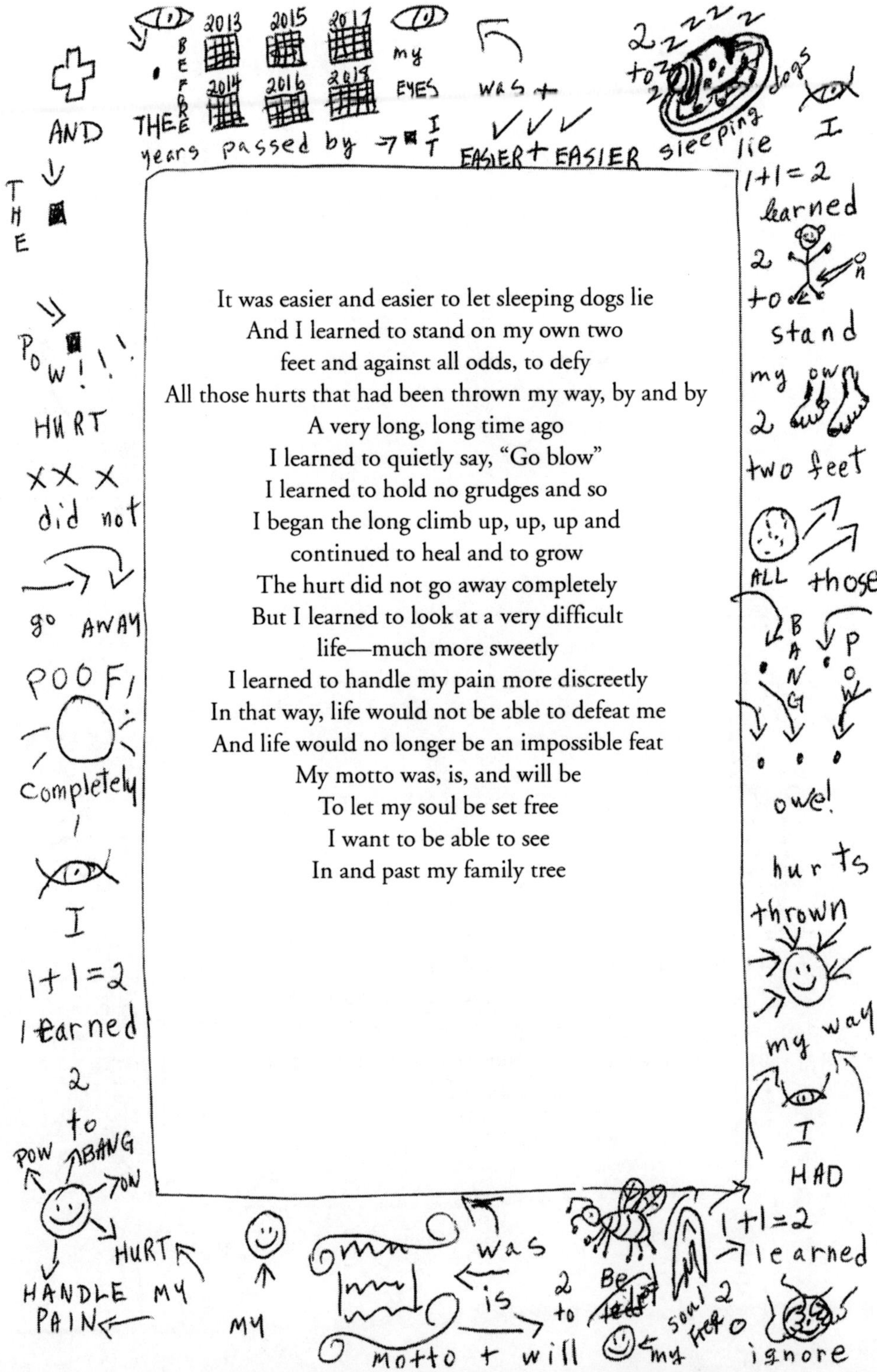

It was easier and easier to let sleeping dogs lie
And I learned to stand on my own two
feet and against all odds, to defy
All those hurts that had been thrown my way, by and by
A very long, long time ago
I learned to quietly say, "Go blow"
I learned to hold no grudges and so
I began the long climb up, up, up and
continued to heal and to grow
The hurt did not go away completely
But I learned to look at a very difficult
life—much more sweetly
I learned to handle my pain more discreetly
In that way, life would not be able to defeat me
And life would no longer be an impossible feat
My motto was, is, and will be
To let my soul be set free
I want to be able to see
In and past my family tree

NOW HIS SPIRIT SOARS

Now he's free. Now his spirit soars
Now he will not have to go through any
more battles or see any more wars
Now he will not have to get into any more tight-fitting cars
Now his spirit will be able to see anything
and will soar farther than far
Now you can travel north
And if you want, you can travel south
And now when you open your mouth
The whole world can be your foodstuff
Now your omnipresent vapors
Will be able to go anywhere they
wish and travel any corridor
Listen, that's not all; there's much more
Your spirit will be able to go through any wall
And pass through any door
I think this, dear bro, will be your heaven
My brother, I give you my permission
Because I really have not got a rhyme nor a reason
Of how to stop you, or when or where you
will visit, or when or in which season
Bro, you will be able to go anywhere
Anywhere at your wish, anytime and without any snares
What of money—you are now richer
than the richest billionaire
Myself, I think that's totally fair and square
I'm happy to say, you will no longer suffer

My dear, wonderful brother
You are now in the bosom of our dear mother
No one will ever again be able, to you, bother
In my heart, I know you are in a good place
Because you always had impeccable taste
You were one of the intelligent ones in our human race
Now you can travel the whole clouds' great database
If I had only known you better
I would have known you as a true emperor
You are now the greatest; you are no
longer bound by Earth's fetters
You are now a quantum universe jet-setter
With your new wings, you will never again be bored
Now you will always be able to have the last word
And if you want, you'll be totally safe to flip the bird
Now, no matter how you act, no one will
ever be able to think you are absurd
When we are wondering about all those unknown mysteries
You'll be laughing at us because you'll
be holding all the puzzle's keys
You'll know all the answers piece by piece
And you won't have any trouble finding sweet release
You, bro, are now the most popular one
You now have so many friends and
are now having all the fun
You have already proved you won't be undone

By shining brighter than the brightest sun
Your spirit will never again be at half mast
Because now your spirit will be able to soar so very fast
If you want to get away, no one will be as fast
as your spirit; no one will be your match
You'll be gone in a twinkle; you will
never again be outclassed

THE BLURB

I have my very own opinions, and of these I am very keen
My ideas are about why I've been
and about where I've been
Still, they may not qualify for any
blue-ribbon science magazine
But for a little entertainment, you might find them
Just a little different than those you have already seen
You can choose to believe them or maybe
not choose to believe them, *but*
I won't tell them over and over or maybe I will a *lot*
In fact, what you hear, you'll wish you had *not*
You'll ask, are these ideas legal or are they *hot*?
And my ideas may or may not be in style
But ah heck, to obtain them, I've gone that extra mile
And if I do say so with a little or a lot of guile
The least you can do is listening for a little while
My great story may or may not be real
But I guarantee, I can say I got it for a steal
You may or may not want to talk
about it over your next meal
Me, myself, I think it isn't really any big deal
So while I may or may not think I am in the know
You may think or say it's all just so-so
But any which way, I'll still get that special glow
And to myself I'll be yelling, "Ho! Ho! Ho!"
So now I will always think before I speak
Because I don't need any security leak?
I don't want to make any mistakes this week

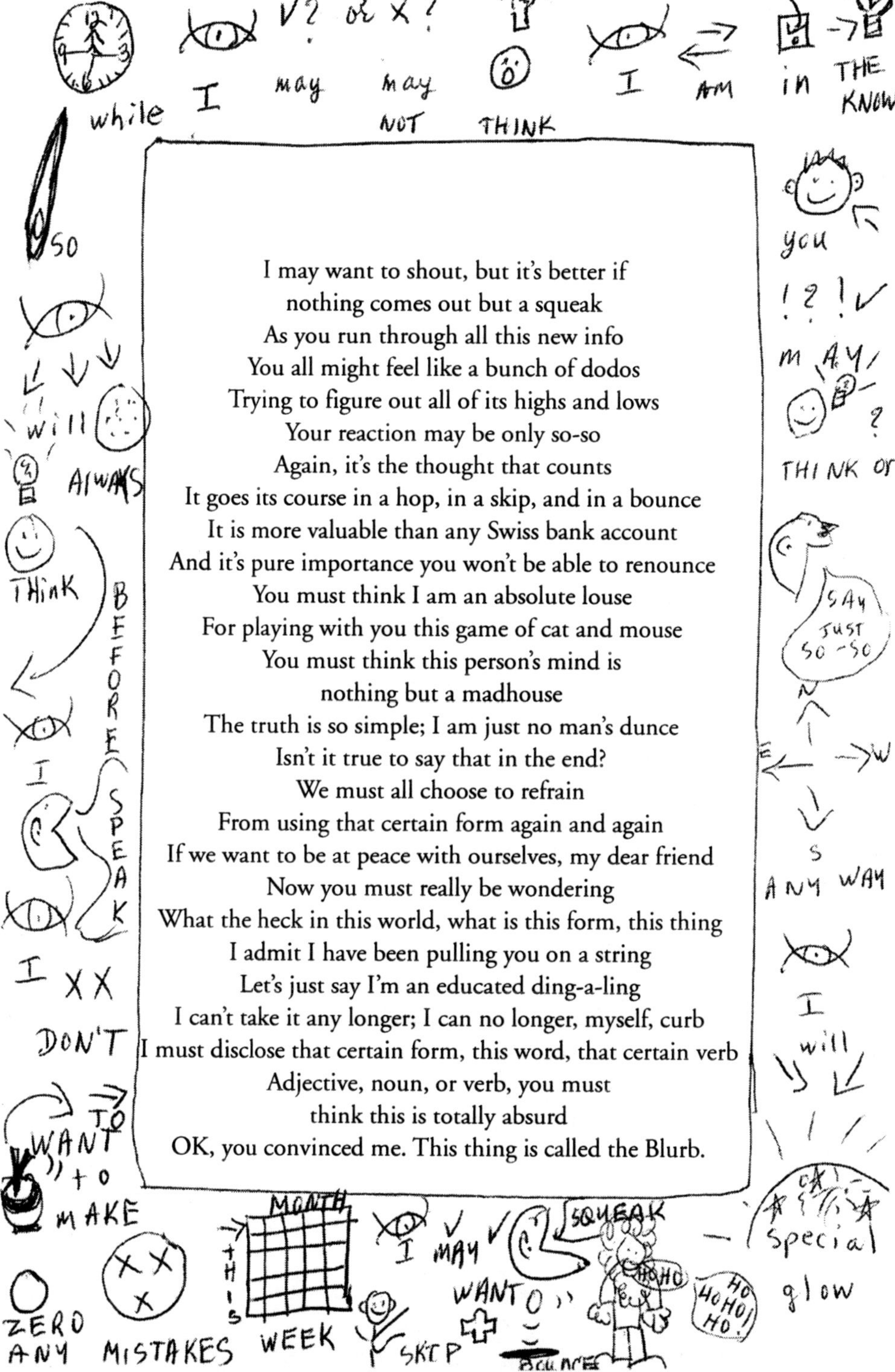

I may want to shout, but it's better if
nothing comes out but a squeak
As you run through all this new info
You all might feel like a bunch of dodos
Trying to figure out all of its highs and lows
Your reaction may be only so-so
Again, it's the thought that counts
It goes its course in a hop, in a skip, and in a bounce
It is more valuable than any Swiss bank account
And it's pure importance you won't be able to renounce
You must think I am an absolute louse
For playing with you this game of cat and mouse
You must think this person's mind is
nothing but a madhouse
The truth is so simple; I am just no man's dunce
Isn't it true to say that in the end?
We must all choose to refrain
From using that certain form again and again
If we want to be at peace with ourselves, my dear friend
Now you must really be wondering
What the heck in this world, what is this form, this thing
I admit I have been pulling you on a string
Let's just say I'm an educated ding-a-ling
I can't take it any longer; I can no longer, myself, curb
I must disclose that certain form, this word, that certain verb
Adjective, noun, or verb, you must
think this is totally absurd
OK, you convinced me. This thing is called the Blurb.

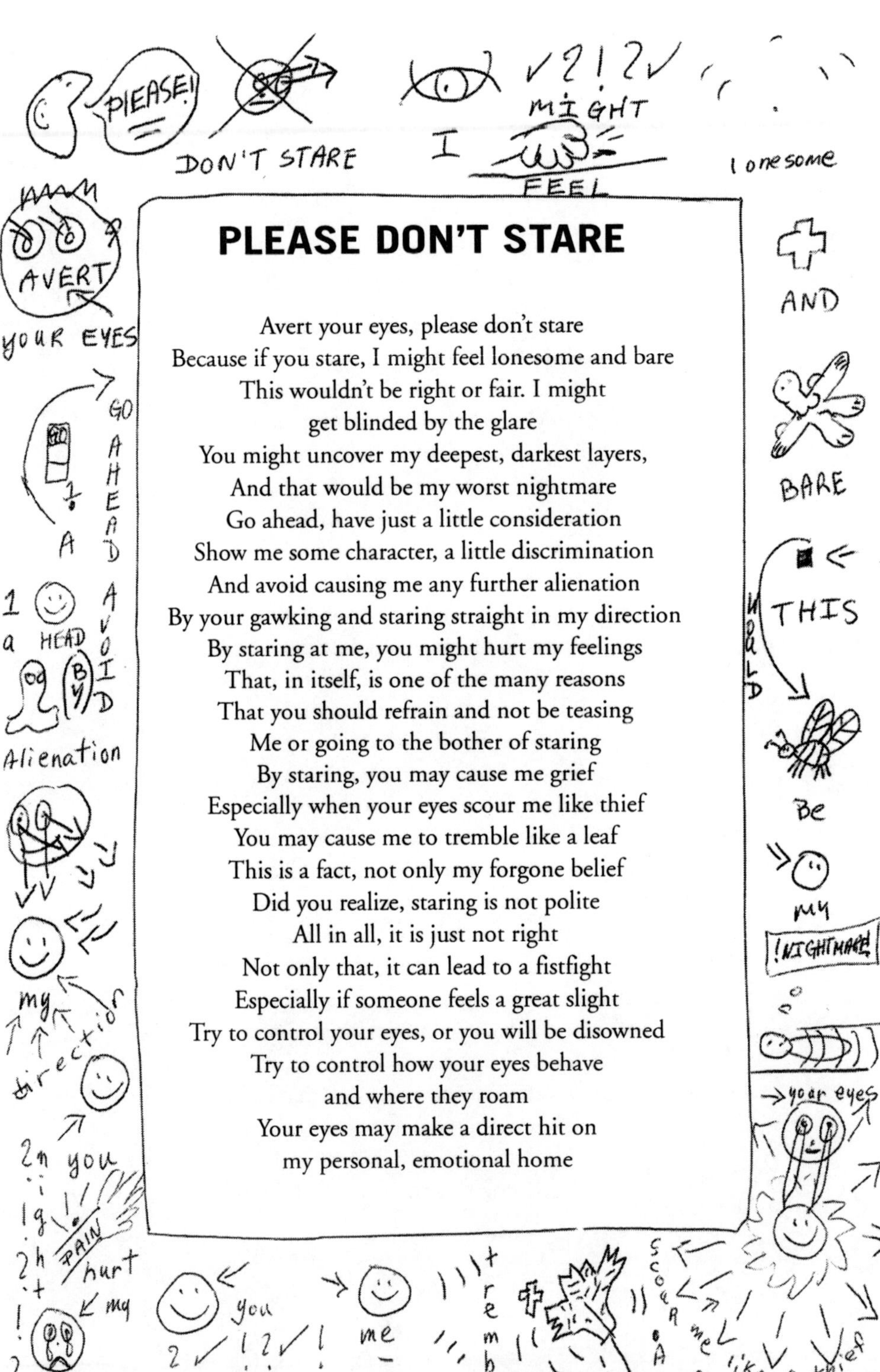

PLEASE DON'T STARE

Avert your eyes, please don't stare
Because if you stare, I might feel lonesome and bare
This wouldn't be right or fair. I might
get blinded by the glare
You might uncover my deepest, darkest layers,
And that would be my worst nightmare
Go ahead, have just a little consideration
Show me some character, a little discrimination
And avoid causing me any further alienation
By your gawking and staring straight in my direction
By staring at me, you might hurt my feelings
That, in itself, is one of the many reasons
That you should refrain and not be teasing
Me or going to the bother of staring
By staring, you may cause me grief
Especially when your eyes scour me like thief
You may cause me to tremble like a leaf
This is a fact, not only my forgone belief
Did you realize, staring is not polite
All in all, it is just not right
Not only that, it can lead to a fistfight
Especially if someone feels a great slight
Try to control your eyes, or you will be disowned
Try to control how your eyes behave
and where they roam
Your eyes may make a direct hit on
my personal, emotional home

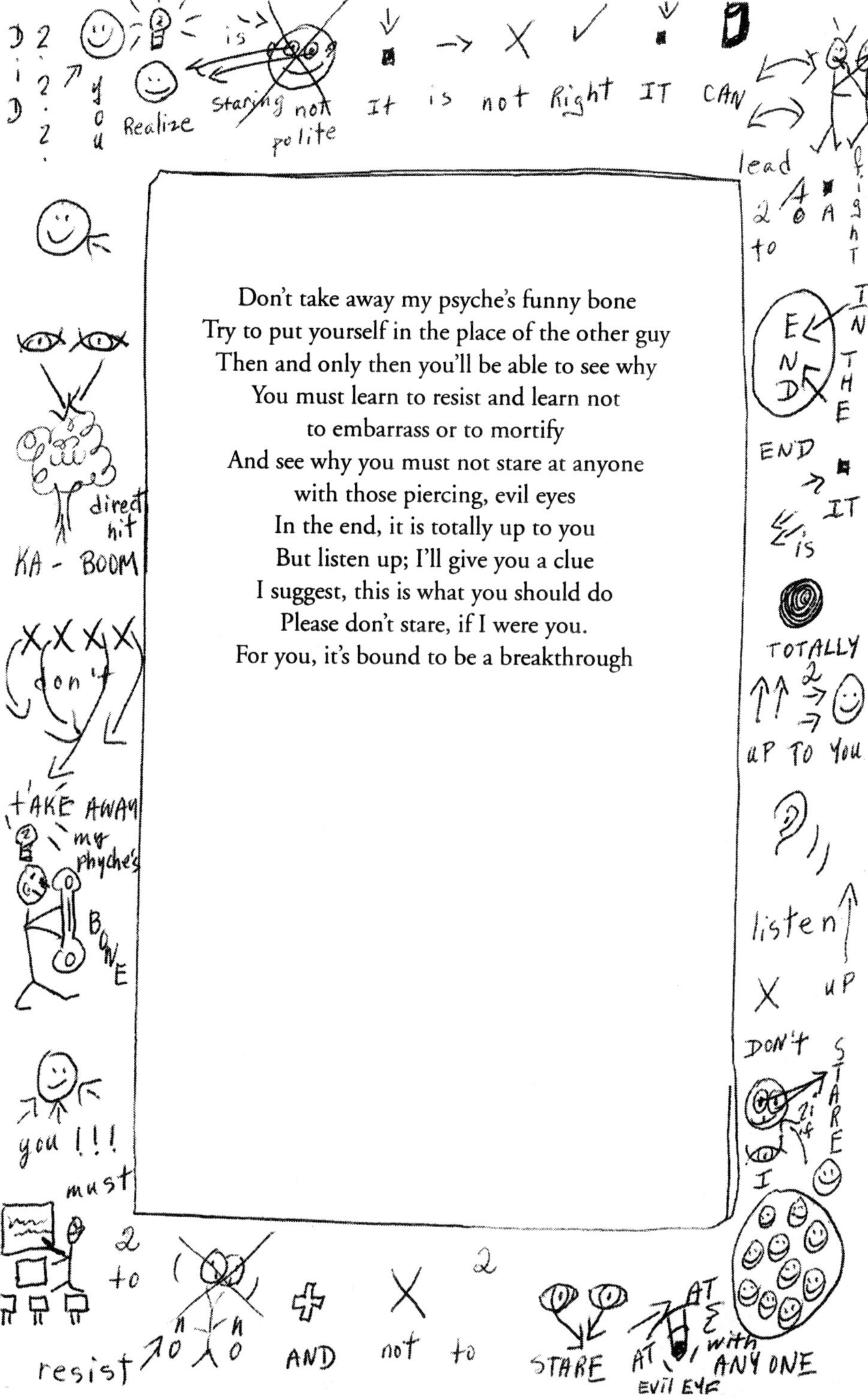

Don't take away my psyche's funny bone
Try to put yourself in the place of the other guy
Then and only then you'll be able to see why
You must learn to resist and learn not
to embarrass or to mortify
And see why you must not stare at anyone
with those piercing, evil eyes
In the end, it is totally up to you
But listen up; I'll give you a clue
I suggest, this is what you should do
Please don't stare, if I were you.
For you, it's bound to be a breakthrough

HELP ME BOUNCE

I have an idea I would like to share. I would
like to lay it on you—right there
There are no secret conditions here—no
hidden snares—just wash and wear.
I'll just lay it on you. I hope you think
that's fair. You don't even have to care
Can't you just feel the thoughts bouncing
around, up, down, and everywhere?
Help me bounce. Can't you feel the excitement
mount? Come on. Help me bounce
Help me bounce, ounce for ounce, give me some flounce
By all accounts, if you help me bounce,
it may increase your bank account
When you help me bounce, you may want to
announce—how much fun it is to bounce
Bounce! Bounce! Bounce! Give me a good line of thoughts
A word, a bar, a note, it could be a
speech or it could be music,
Or it might be a theory worth a whole lot—
maybe physics—something well-sought
They'll pounce on it, sure as hell, when it bounces
off the spot—an idea will have been caught
It'll bounce like a slingshot; it'll be like liquid fire, like
electricity, it'll bounce at you—shiny and red hot
I hear—it bounced and got away.
The word is out on the street

When
you
R
are
HAPPY
your
thoughts
bounce
faster
WHEN
THEY
R are
hyper
THEY
B
O
U
N
C
E
INTO
EACH
OTHER
BLUR
when
THEY WERE
calm
they
were
PuRRRRRRRED
THEY
THOUGHT WAVES
THOUGHT WAVES
I
will
THEY
WILL
BOUNCE
OUT
COMPLETE
AND
WELL-LAID
WELL-FORMED
BRAIN
WAVES

The words bounced off the concrete—
and that's no small feat
It bounced in my direction—it'll bounce off you—and
out onto me—again. I will hear its heartbeat
It will bounce out and off into space eventually. Then it will
be the greatest message anyone out there could possibly seek
When you're happy, your thoughts bounce
faster, but don't let them be your master
When you are hyper, they bounce into each other
and get mixed up and cause a fuzzy blur
When you are calm, your thoughts bounce in an even
rhythm—with style and grace, making a satisfied purr
And when you are sleeping, they go into
autopilot and bounce into a kaleidoscope
and form a fantasy land, as it were
The more we bounce ideas off each other,
the more people will hear the call
The more we bounce our ideas—the more
our ideas are bound to be original
Go ahead—bounce some more, and soon
the ideas will be falling like rainfall
You can bounce and make a giant wall of ideas—
then, it will overflow into a cascading waterfall of
many ideas to form a great distinguished hall
I will try to bounce ideas and extend them
from my mind into outer space
Bouncing these ideas from Earth, our home
base might be our saving grace

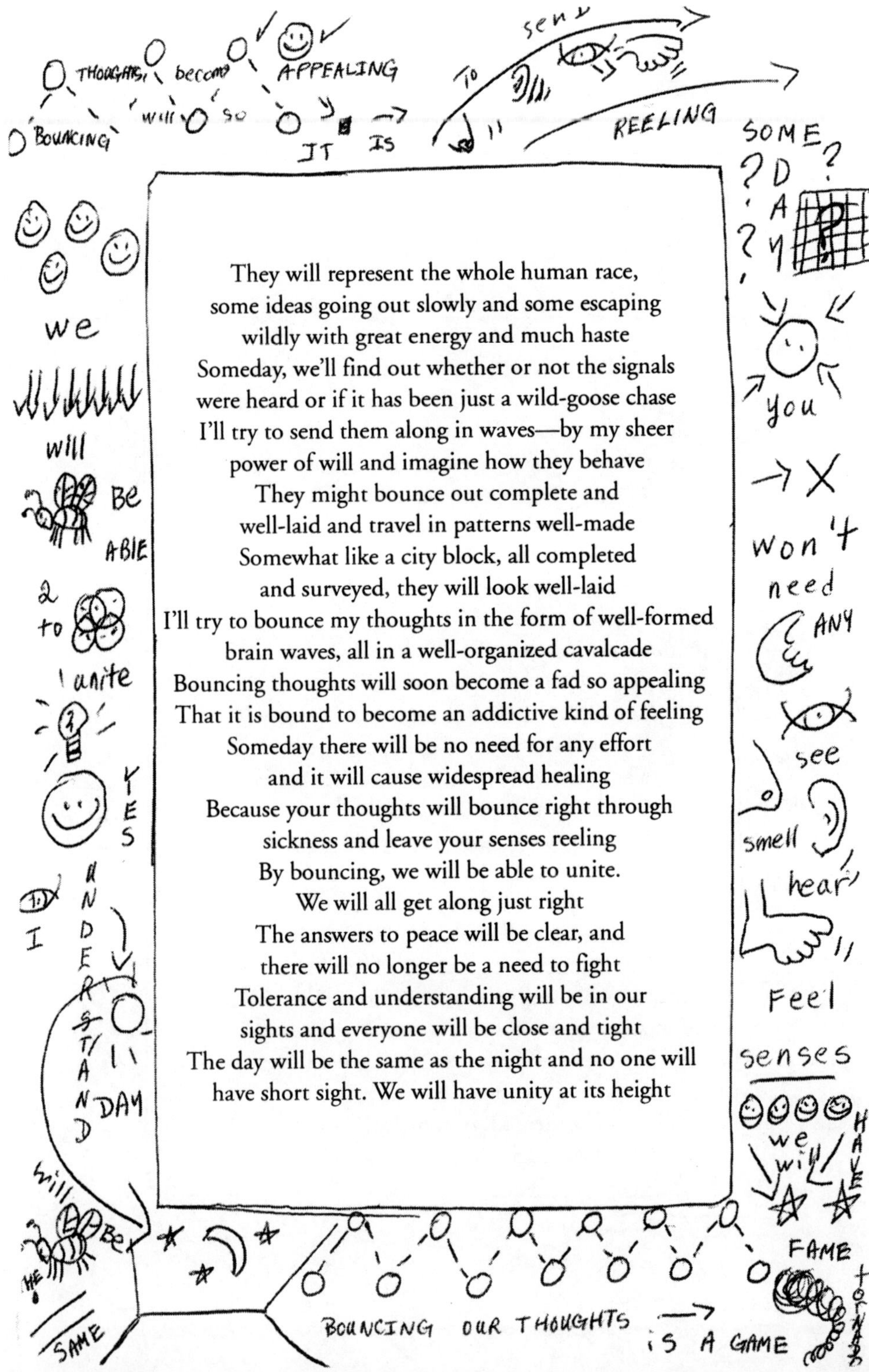

They will represent the whole human race,
some ideas going out slowly and some escaping
wildly with great energy and much haste
Someday, we'll find out whether or not the signals
were heard or if it has been just a wild-goose chase
I'll try to send them along in waves—by my sheer
power of will and imagine how they behave
They might bounce out complete and
well-laid and travel in patterns well-made
Somewhat like a city block, all completed
and surveyed, they will look well-laid
I'll try to bounce my thoughts in the form of well-formed
brain waves, all in a well-organized cavalcade
Bouncing thoughts will soon become a fad so appealing
That it is bound to become an addictive kind of feeling
Someday there will be no need for any effort
and it will cause widespread healing
Because your thoughts will bounce right through
sickness and leave your senses reeling
By bouncing, we will be able to unite.
We will all get along just right
The answers to peace will be clear, and
there will no longer be a need to fight
Tolerance and understanding will be in our
sights and everyone will be close and tight
The day will be the same as the night and no one will
have short sight. We will have unity at its height

Bouncing our thoughts will be a grand
game. It won't matter how we aim
This game will not need any kind of name.
It won't even have a nickname
We will all have our own share of fame—
our very own kind of acclaim
We'll talk with the wildest animals
and they will become tame.
Our language will all be the same because our
bouncing will intersect again and again
Come on, people of every race—let us
watch all the new ideas unfurl
Let us bounce our thoughts here and there,
like we are all happy dancing girls
Bouncing thoughts can be like gathering
diamonds or harvesting precious pearls
Come on give it a whirl—then we will see how
information will come in tornado swirls

WHAT'S IN MY HEART

I would like to share with you what dwells in my heart
If you would be so kind and if you don't
mind to let me begin, to let me start
I will try to share with you my personal
view of it all, part by part
Of its avenues and venues that are a
delicate city full of priceless art
If my heart was my whole body; it would
be a large, illustrated, romance story
As varied and mysterious as underwater Pompeii or as
Wonderful and musical as an old-world city
The city would have style and be both
modern and cultured and worldly
Like a universe, it would be spacious
and full of exciting electricity
My heart is my very best part. It is
right there in my star chart
Love flows freely from it, end to start. And
it is well-versed in the martial arts
Inside it, there are no worries of any sort because
They have been given too one who is a bad sport
My heart is bigger than a Kmart
And roomier than a large gallery containing
many works of priceless art
From it, strength, like warm water, I can draw
To help warm cold hearts longing to be thawed
And forge true friendships that ride on its pivotal seesaw

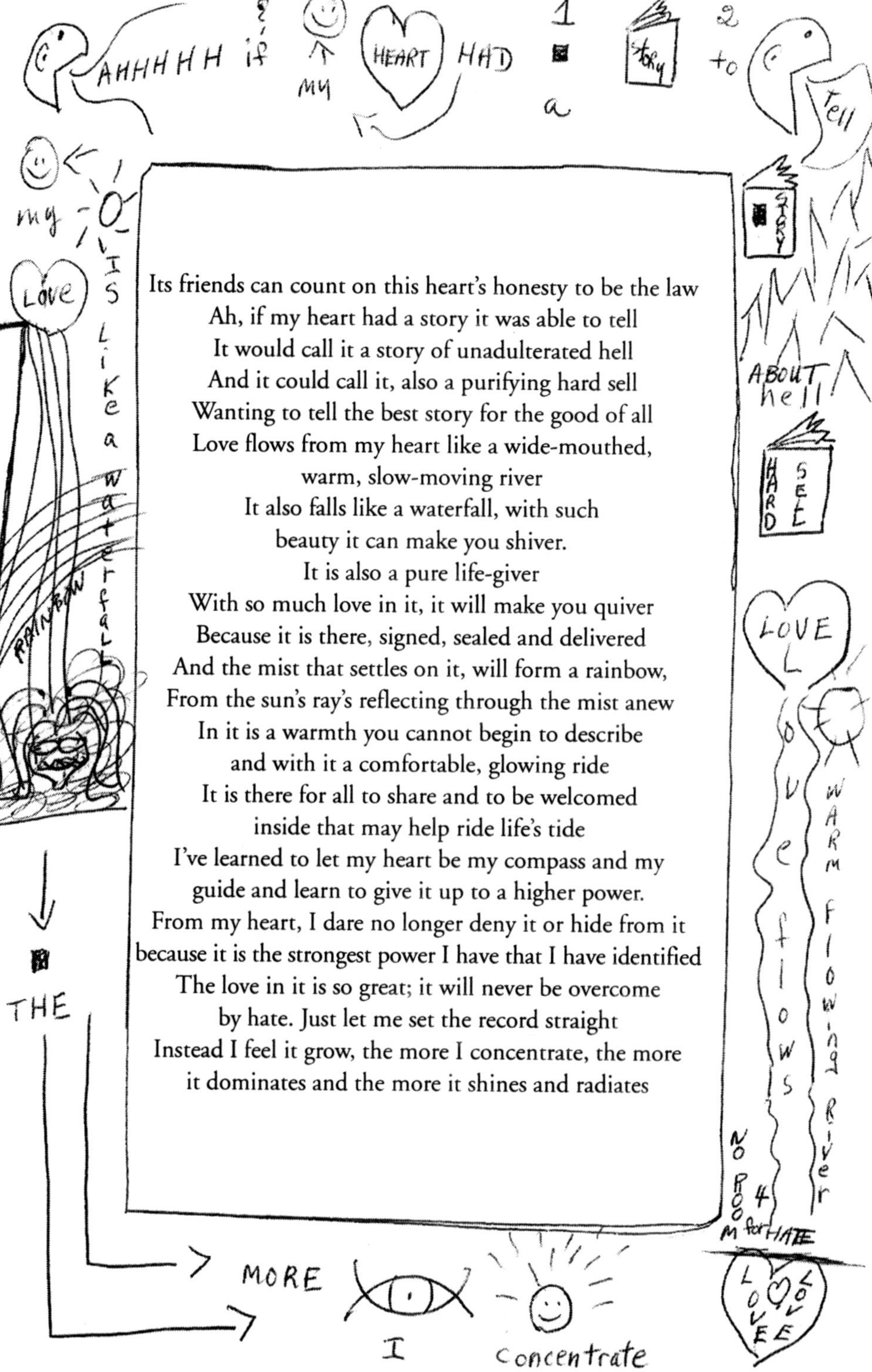

Its friends can count on this heart's honesty to be the law
Ah, if my heart had a story it was able to tell
It would call it a story of unadulterated hell
And it could call it, also a purifying hard sell
Wanting to tell the best story for the good of all
Love flows from my heart like a wide-mouthed,
warm, slow-moving river
It also falls like a waterfall, with such
beauty it can make you shiver.
It is also a pure life-giver
With so much love in it, it will make you quiver
Because it is there, signed, sealed and delivered
And the mist that settles on it, will form a rainbow,
From the sun's ray's reflecting through the mist anew
In it is a warmth you cannot begin to describe
and with it a comfortable, glowing ride
It is there for all to share and to be welcomed
inside that may help ride life's tide
I've learned to let my heart be my compass and my
guide and learn to give it up to a higher power.
From my heart, I dare no longer deny it or hide from it
because it is the strongest power I have that I have identified
The love in it is so great; it will never be overcome
by hate. Just let me set the record straight
Instead I feel it grow, the more I concentrate, the more
it dominates and the more it shines and radiates

Now I know it's OK to have lots on my plate because
it just helps to serve, to witness and demonstrate
That in my heart I have no room for hate and
that I am an overall heart-loving heavyweight
I only wish for my heart to be pure
and for its spirit to fly and soar
And I know, all my woes will have their cures and my
heart will have everything it's always wanted and more
I know that temptation will no longer have its lure
if I just ignore it and avoid its constant tug-of-war
I know that time will go by and become a pleasant
blur, and my heart will never be sad anymore

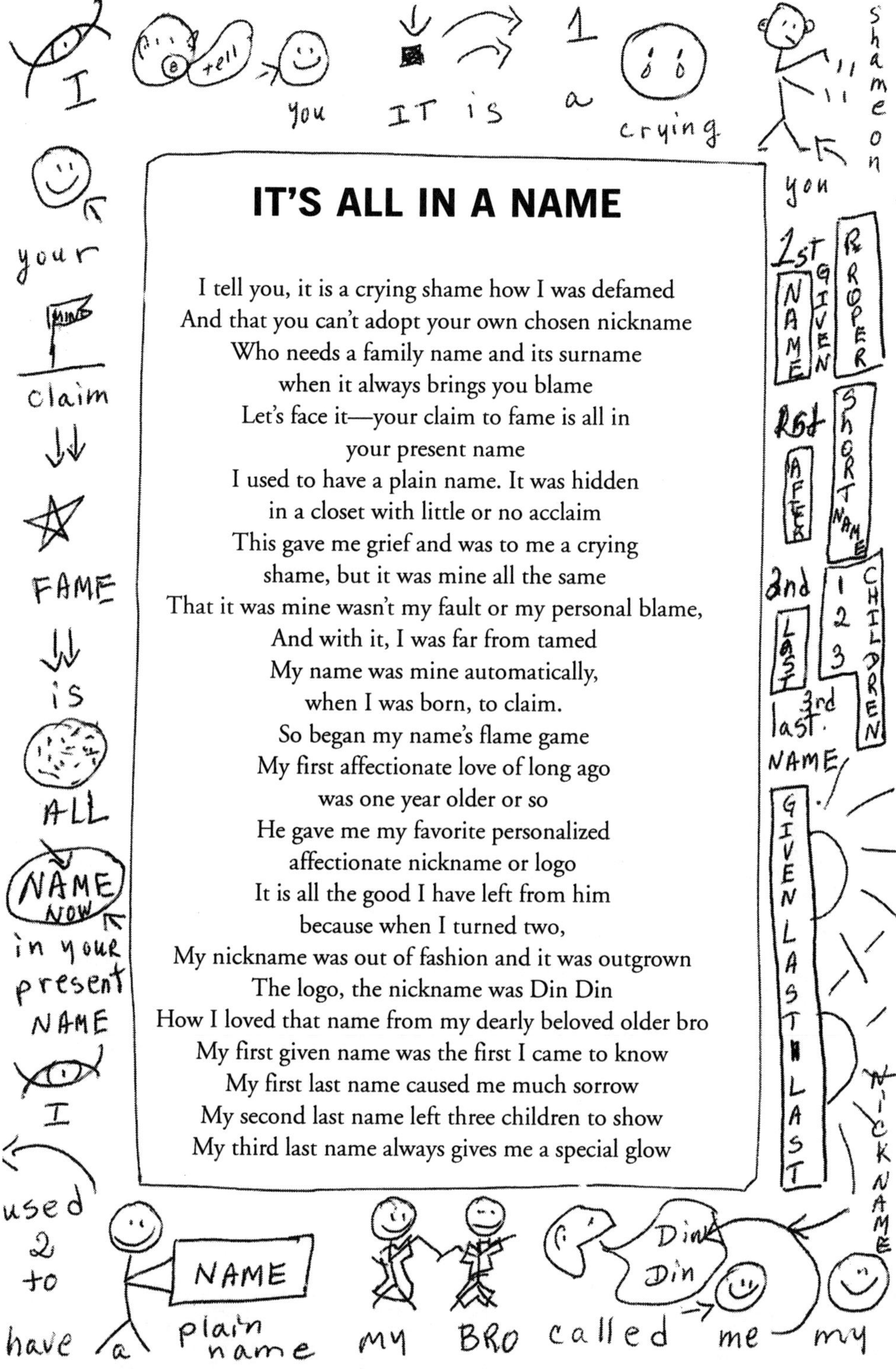

IT'S ALL IN A NAME

I tell you, it is a crying shame how I was defamed
And that you can't adopt your own chosen nickname
Who needs a family name and its surname
when it always brings you blame
Let's face it—your claim to fame is all in
your present name
I used to have a plain name. It was hidden
in a closet with little or no acclaim
This gave me grief and was to me a crying
shame, but it was mine all the same
That it was mine wasn't my fault or my personal blame,
And with it, I was far from tamed
My name was mine automatically,
when I was born, to claim.
So began my name's flame game
My first affectionate love of long ago
was one year older or so
He gave me my favorite personalized
affectionate nickname or logo
It is all the good I have left from him
because when I turned two,
My nickname was out of fashion and it was outgrown
The logo, the nickname was Din Din
How I loved that name from my dearly beloved older bro
My first given name was the first I came to know
My first last name caused me much sorrow
My second last name left three children to show
My third last name always gives me a special glow

Do you know who this is? It's little old me
Said one to the other with glee
I can count too: one, two, three
Now that we are with each other,
There is no reason for us to disagree
We know there is plenty of room here
There is no reason for us to despair
We will have plenty of room to share
Beside that letter X on that line
That without us would be powerless and bare
I could pay to invent and hire new ones
But they would be useless clones
Because they would just be artificial rhinestones
Changing them now, I just could not condone
They've taken me through the lion's den
With no harm, again and again and again
I am proud of and I choose to keep
the names I now use to pen
And I will do so until it is time for
me to say my final amen

THE VOID

In my opinion, the worst possible void
Is when the mind is totally trapped
within itself and totally devoid
Of its ability to use its thoughts and is dull like celluloid
It is a brain without the ability to express its thoughts
And its ability's and is as good as totally destroyed
The ability to travel through one's thoughts
And being able to tie the knots and dot the dots
The ability to be able to see the answer behind the ink blots
Is when you will hit the rainbow's jackpot
It is such a great travesty to lose the mind's main key
Not to be able to think clearly will
bring anyone to their knees
And not to be able to understand or
to be able to make any plea
Would make anyone feel like they were a living absentee
That's when sociability dies and loneliness begins
Then fear engulfs you and the clouds descend
And it is hard to find your way back again
You then feel like a loser, a has-been
And no one wants to be your friend
You wish reality would come and break in
But reality seems like a mortal sin

The void is a time when it becomes easy to lose hope
Because with life, you can no longer easily cope
And you can't help but feel like a dope,
and that's when you begin to mope

Soon you feel like you're at the end of your rope
Life has become torture and is totally unbearable
The experience, unfortunately, is not
something that is sharable
You feel weak and unstable and totally unable
You feel like you've been totally disabled
You feel like a coward, the only thing
that keeps you going is hope
You know you must be patient because
you do not quite know
What this is, or its length, or its scope
You wish from this situation you could elope
What's more, you feel like you are
always under a microscope
You have no will; you have no choice
You wish you could use your voice
When you wake up from this dream, you will rejoice
And drive away in a fancy Rolls-Royce
But there it is. Help is on its way.
Did I mention that every day I took time to pray?
Slowly, but it came back, at first steadily—
more and more, every day
With it came rules for my mind to stay in play
The more I learned to accept and to comply
With my situation, the more I looked reality in the eye
I knew then I could again be like every other guy
I was free again to use my thoughts, and
I knew it was not some cruel lie

So you see, even when you face the
void, you need not give up
There are always greater things in store for you,
No matter if you feel all washed up
You need not feel this is your final roundup
So just get help and go on your next checkup
You may even find you think better than you did before
Because you will have won a very important war
And your confidence will give you a special rapport
And furthermore, you will know how to
avoid life's blood and the gore

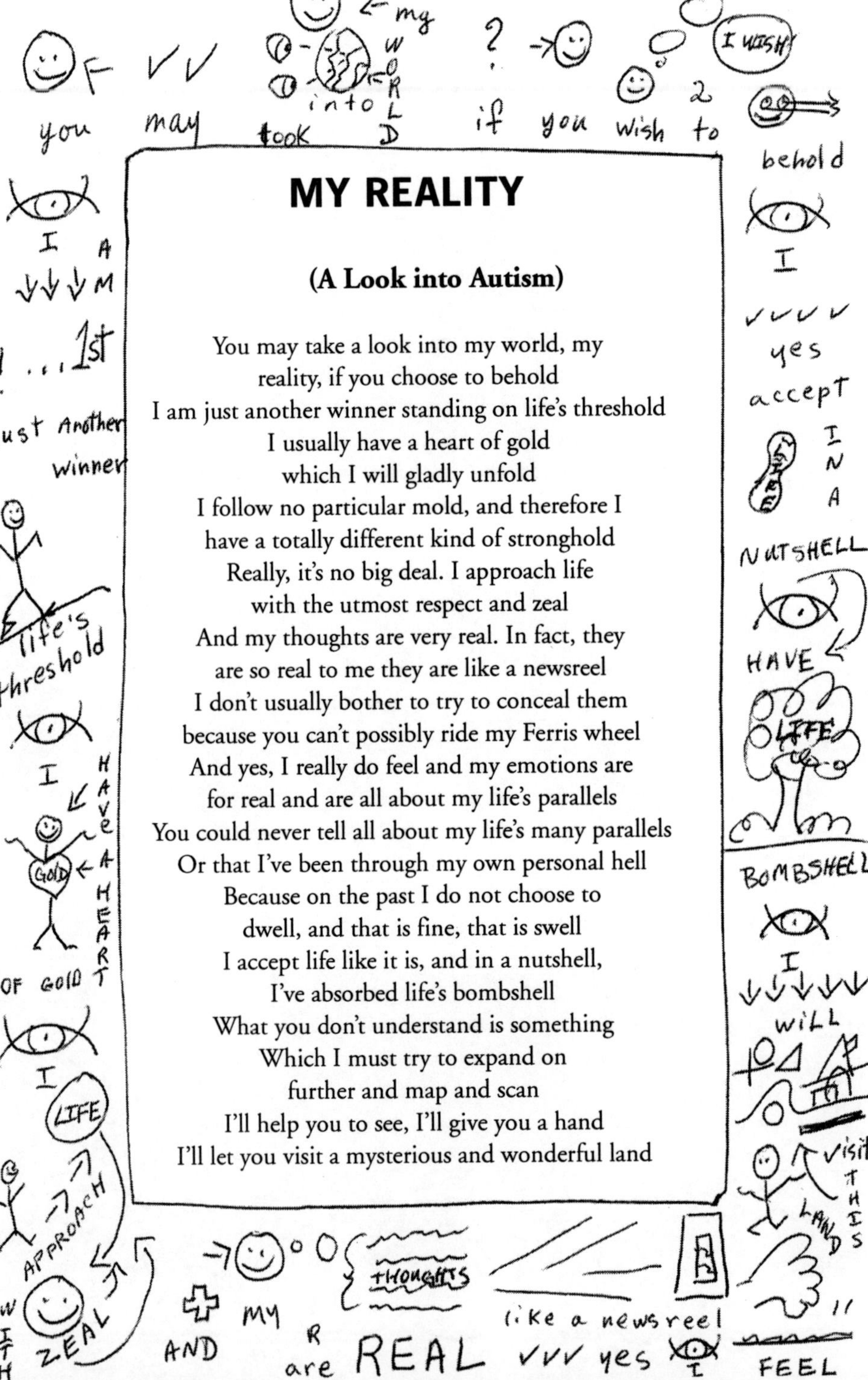

MY REALITY

(A Look into Autism)

You may take a look into my world, my
reality, if you choose to behold
I am just another winner standing on life's threshold
I usually have a heart of gold
which I will gladly unfold
I follow no particular mold, and therefore I
have a totally different kind of stronghold
Really, it's no big deal. I approach life
with the utmost respect and zeal
And my thoughts are very real. In fact, they
are so real to me they are like a newsreel
I don't usually bother to try to conceal them
because you can't possibly ride my Ferris wheel
And yes, I really do feel and my emotions are
for real and are all about my life's parallels
You could never tell all about my life's many parallels
Or that I've been through my own personal hell
Because on the past I do not choose to
dwell, and that is fine, that is swell
I accept life like it is, and in a nutshell,
I've absorbed life's bombshell
What you don't understand is something
Which I must try to expand on
further and map and scan
I'll help you to see, I'll give you a hand
I'll let you visit a mysterious and wonderful land

Everybody's land is different, depending on his ladder's span
My eyes have a mind of their own;
They travel fast and are thorough and act like a cyclone
Which I sometimes wish I could disown
Who knows where or on whom they will choose to roam
Sometimes what they see makes me
wonder or cry out and groan
My ideas to me are very real, on an
ever-moving and changing reel
Colors all have a great appeal, which I enjoy with great zeal
They trigger in me connections only I can feel,
ideas that my mind chooses to reveal
My thoughts travel on an organized,
even keel that no one can steal
I may not be at all like you, sir, and that's fine, thank you
But we both have an interesting point of view,
And our very own idea may be a shiny breakthrough
And if our differences we choose to
agree on and compromise,
We will both be able to add two plus two
Then we may both feel like brand new
And we will arrive at our newfound
destination and rendezvous
You may need to be quiet every day,
and this, in itself, is OK.
Myself, I like change in every way, with
quiet included as an option,

A pit stop before the matinee
You may like and choose to delay your actions.
I like to experience them play by play
Delve a little deeper if you dare. I wish to take you there
Like a child, I love fresh air and I also like to share
Sometimes I'm not all there because
my mind takes me elsewhere
I think that's neither here nor there because
this happens to everyone, everywhere
My laughter tends to explode and ring out
and pleasure bathes my brain throughout
Laughter makes me sing, it makes you shout;
it helps my ideas to grow and sprout
It may tend to make me stand out but I
advise you to try it. It's a knockout
I don't think I have to stop and do without
because happiness is the best route without a doubt
You may be scared of me, but I can guarantee
There is no need or reason to be.
We are all made of the same stuff, you and me
You will soon be able to see to a large degree
That I am happy and carefree and I only
wish the same for you and me. Tee-he
I promise I won't hurt you, for to do so;
I would prove to have a low IQ
In fact, I may someday come to your rescue
and snatch you from a deadly catch-22
I am clear, transparent, and see-through.

In fact, my enemies won't even be
able to see me or have a clue
I have no unwanted surprises to undo
because I do not mean to misconstrue
Finally, if I want to give you a royal view
I'll tell you or show you myself through and through
Tell me you love me because I love you too
I am so direct that people sometimes think I am cuckoo
Before we part and before we are through, I
will have given you a panoramic view
Now you are among the few that has taken
the time to try to understand
That makes you a special kind, someone
open-minded and great and grand
If there were more of your kind, my reality,
which seems to be a fantasy land—will
be there at your command
And we would begin to help many and make our
world a better land for all to go hand in hand

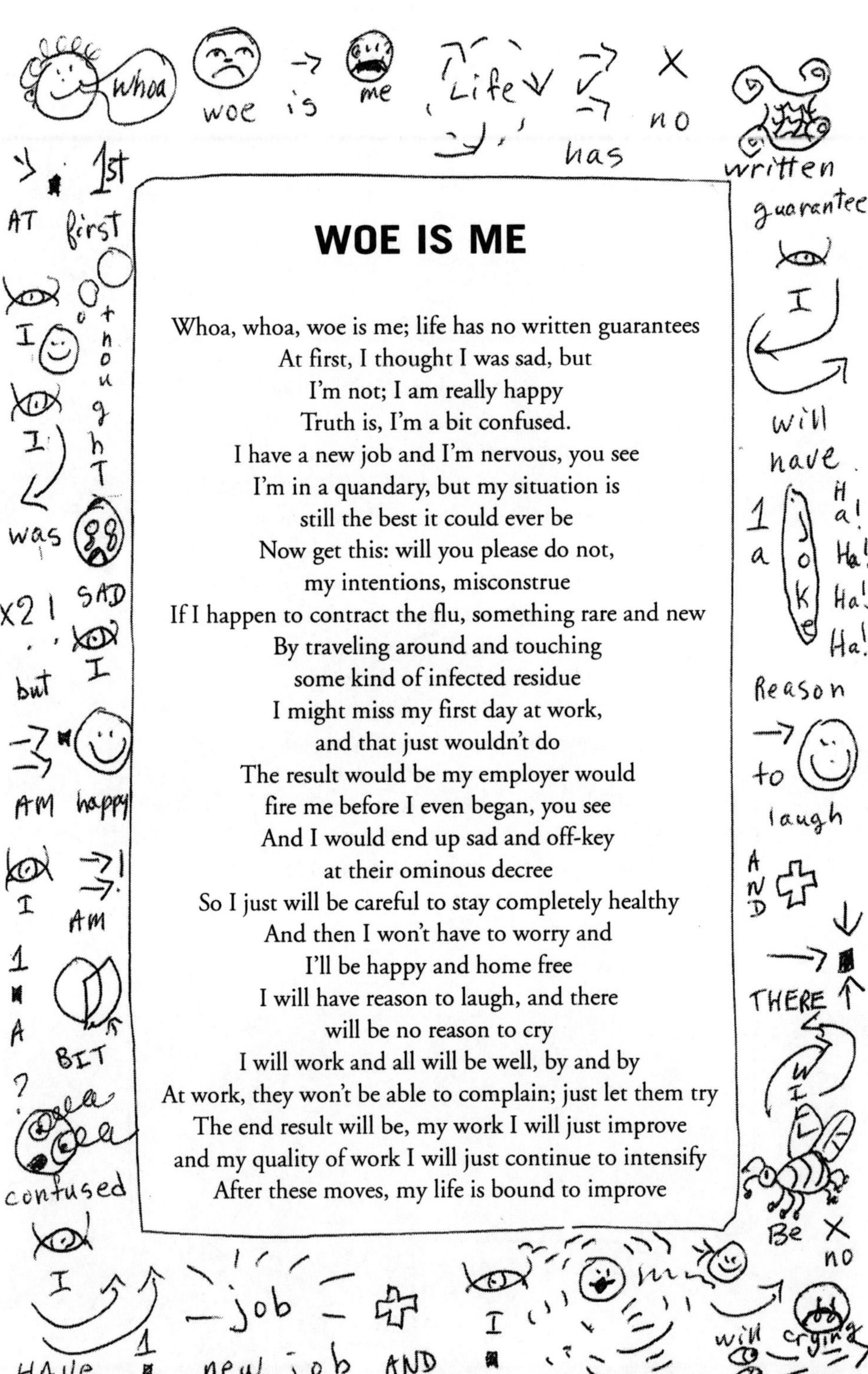

WOE IS ME

Whoa, whoa, woe is me; life has no written guarantees
At first, I thought I was sad, but
I'm not; I am really happy
Truth is, I'm a bit confused.
I have a new job and I'm nervous, you see
I'm in a quandary, but my situation is
still the best it could ever be
Now get this: will you please do not,
my intentions, misconstrue
If I happen to contract the flu, something rare and new
By traveling around and touching
some kind of infected residue
I might miss my first day at work,
and that just wouldn't do
The result would be my employer would
fire me before I even began, you see
And I would end up sad and off-key
at their ominous decree
So I just will be careful to stay completely healthy
And then I won't have to worry and
I'll be happy and home free
I will have reason to laugh, and there
will be no reason to cry
I will work and all will be well, by and by
At work, they won't be able to complain; just let them try
The end result will be, my work I will just improve
and my quality of work I will just continue to intensify
After these moves, my life is bound to improve

And my life will get better and better
once I get into the groove
There will be no more crying as long
as I don't make a false move
And if I do not do anything to cause
anyone to be annoyed or to cause them to disapprove
Then I can stop my tearful masquerades
And I'll forget my game of charades
Because to be honest, I will have it made
And I will be successful in all my escapades
So for now, I'll just stay on the bandwagon
And I will continue to see all kinds
of good things happen
Because of my good attitude, the
world will be my playpen
And I will be successful and will no
longer have to cry ever again

WHAT'S BEEN SUNG HAS BEEN SUNG

What's been sung has been sung, my dear little one
Now you deserve all the fun; your life has just begun
You won't be undone because now you are top gun
Your good times have just begun; you
will have lots of fun in the sun
I'll join the throng to show that I also belong
To see you, I'll travel along many, many furlongs
I'll sing your songs because to me you can do no wrong
With you I'll play along because I loved you all along
You can do no wrong, so put your cheek to your tongue
I can't help but want to belong, so
go ahead and ring my gong
I've been waiting for so long; I feel like I am long gone
Let me hop, hop, hop along; I'll be your ding-dong
I'm a big fan of yours; your influence
has opened many doors
I want to know you more; I don't mean to be a bore
Just because I don't know what all your ideas are for
What's more, I'd love to greet you
and give you a big ten-four
I went to all of your concerts; they
were my yummiest desert
I had to sit in a place where my knees hurt
and where it rained on my shirt
There I also ate hot dogs and then pizza in spurts

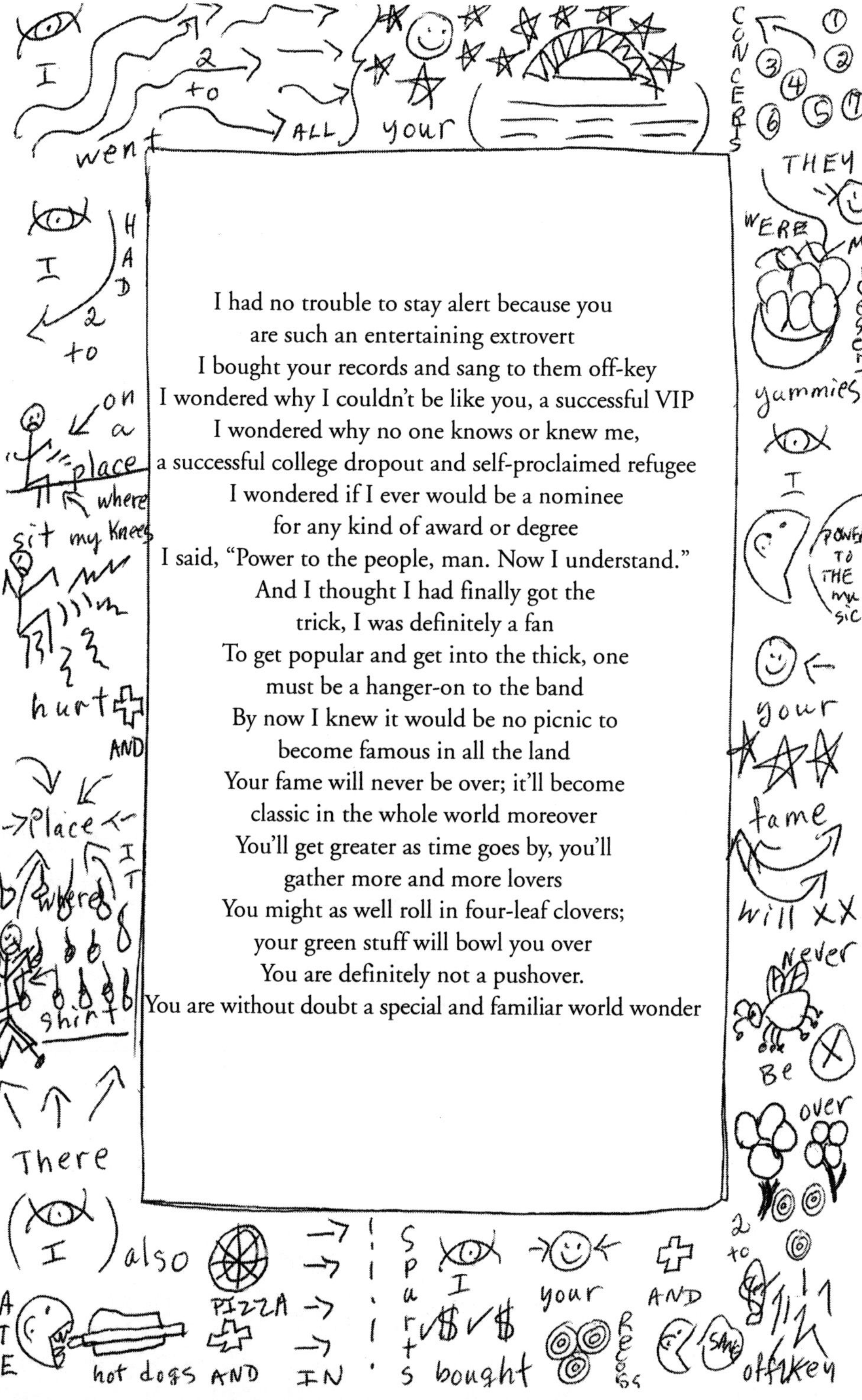

I had no trouble to stay alert because you
are such an entertaining extrovert
I bought your records and sang to them off-key
I wondered why I couldn't be like you, a successful VIP
I wondered why no one knows or knew me,
a successful college dropout and self-proclaimed refugee
I wondered if I ever would be a nominee
for any kind of award or degree
I said, "Power to the people, man. Now I understand."
And I thought I had finally got the
trick, I was definitely a fan
To get popular and get into the thick, one
must be a hanger-on to the band
By now I knew it would be no picnic to
become famous in all the land
Your fame will never be over; it'll become
classic in the whole world moreover
You'll get greater as time goes by, you'll
gather more and more lovers
You might as well roll in four-leaf clovers;
your green stuff will bowl you over
You are definitely not a pushover.
You are without doubt a special and familiar world wonder

IN FULL BLOOM

The flowers, a bouquet, are fragrant and in full bloom
We place them all over, all around and inside our rooms
Whenever and wherever we are and
as the time is opportune
They are celebrated on the eve of our honeymoon
and now and always, as our love is in full bloom
Our love is also in full bloom, coming none too soon
We look at each other, and we can't help but swoon
Our love surrounds us like a comfortable cocoon
Our eyes reflect in each other's love
and shine in the full moon
The music of love drifts into our room,
like a classic loony tune
The melody twists and caresses us like a plume
It is just as thorough; there is nothing left to presume
Romance is thick in the air like the sweetest perfume
Love cascades around us, undressing through the air
It is so thick, layer upon layer, with no room to spare
You can take your pick from its bloom,
one of its beautiful hairs
And the air is thick with love
Now we are safe, like inside our mother's womb
Love is new; it is special and refreshing
It is truly mind bending and never ending
It is warm, heartrending and mind-boggling
It is mysterious, curious, daring, and daunting
Our love will stay fresh and young and
inquisitive forever and ever

Through any kind of climate, be it calm,
stormy, or cosmic weather
Our love reaches out in expectation,
our love knows no fetters
It will be as interesting and touching as a
beautiful love letter
Our love will always and forever be in full
bloom, at night or at high noon
The sweet fragrance of our love wafts
around us like the sweetest perfume
Our love will be a contagious beauty to
which no one will be immune
When we are together, there will be
no more gloom and doom
because our love will push it out and
love will instead fill the room
The bouquet of our love is a masterpiece
there for everyone to see in full bloom
The gentle petals surround us, like a warm
cocoon, while our love is in full bloom
The colors of the rainbow shine and radiate
from us while our love is in full bloom
We are in love and while we are together in our love,
our love will always be in full bloom

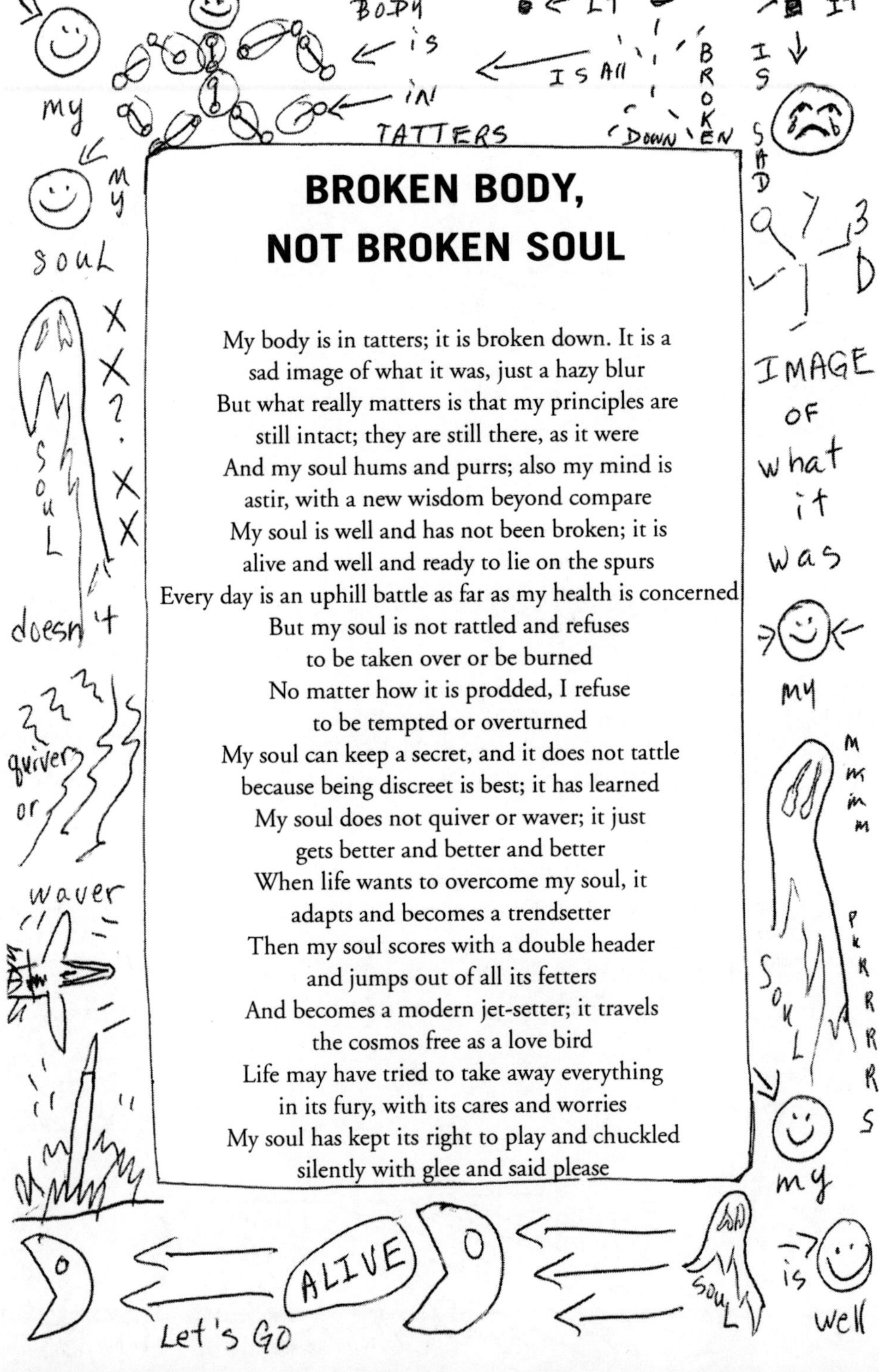

BROKEN BODY, NOT BROKEN SOUL

My body is in tatters; it is broken down. It is a
sad image of what it was, just a hazy blur
But what really matters is that my principles are
still intact; they are still there, as it were
And my soul hums and purrs; also my mind is
astir, with a new wisdom beyond compare
My soul is well and has not been broken; it is
alive and well and ready to lie on the spurs
Every day is an uphill battle as far as my health is concerned
But my soul is not rattled and refuses
to be taken over or be burned
No matter how it is prodded, I refuse
to be tempted or overturned
My soul can keep a secret, and it does not tattle
because being discreet is best; it has learned
My soul does not quiver or waver; it just
gets better and better and better
When life wants to overcome my soul, it
adapts and becomes a trendsetter
Then my soul scores with a double header
and jumps out of all its fetters
And becomes a modern jet-setter; it travels
the cosmos free as a love bird
Life may have tried to take away everything
in its fury, with its cares and worries
My soul has kept its right to play and chuckled
silently with glee and said please

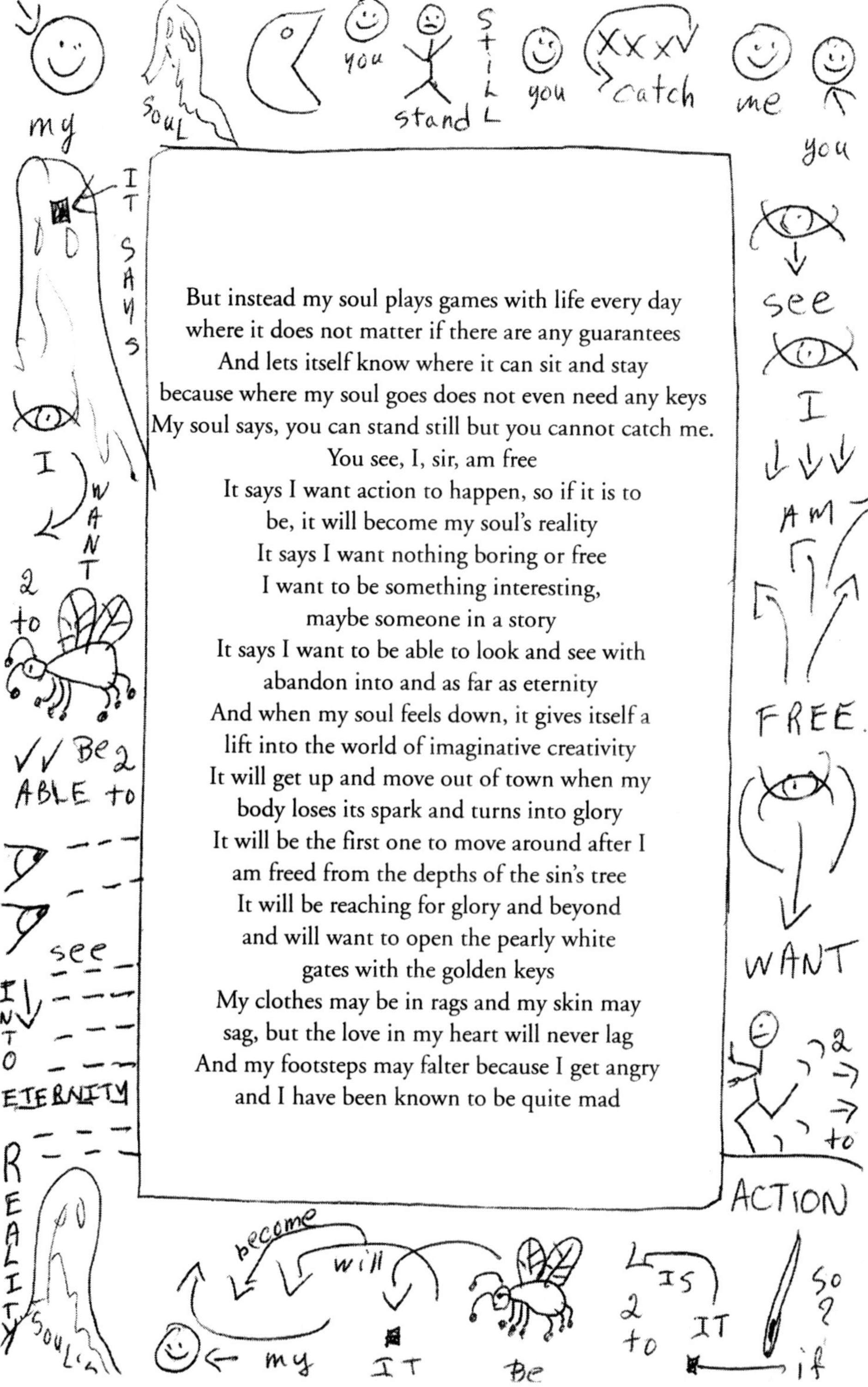

But instead my soul plays games with life every day
where it does not matter if there are any guarantees
And lets itself know where it can sit and stay
because where my soul goes does not even need any keys
My soul says, you can stand still but you cannot catch me.
You see, I, sir, am free
It says I want action to happen, so if it is to
be, it will become my soul's reality
It says I want nothing boring or free
I want to be something interesting,
maybe someone in a story
It says I want to be able to look and see with
abandon into and as far as eternity
And when my soul feels down, it gives itself a
lift into the world of imaginative creativity
It will get up and move out of town when my
body loses its spark and turns into glory
It will be the first one to move around after I
am freed from the depths of the sin's tree
It will be reaching for glory and beyond
and will want to open the pearly white
gates with the golden keys
My clothes may be in rags and my skin may
sag, but the love in my heart will never lag
And my footsteps may falter because I get angry
and I have been known to be quite mad

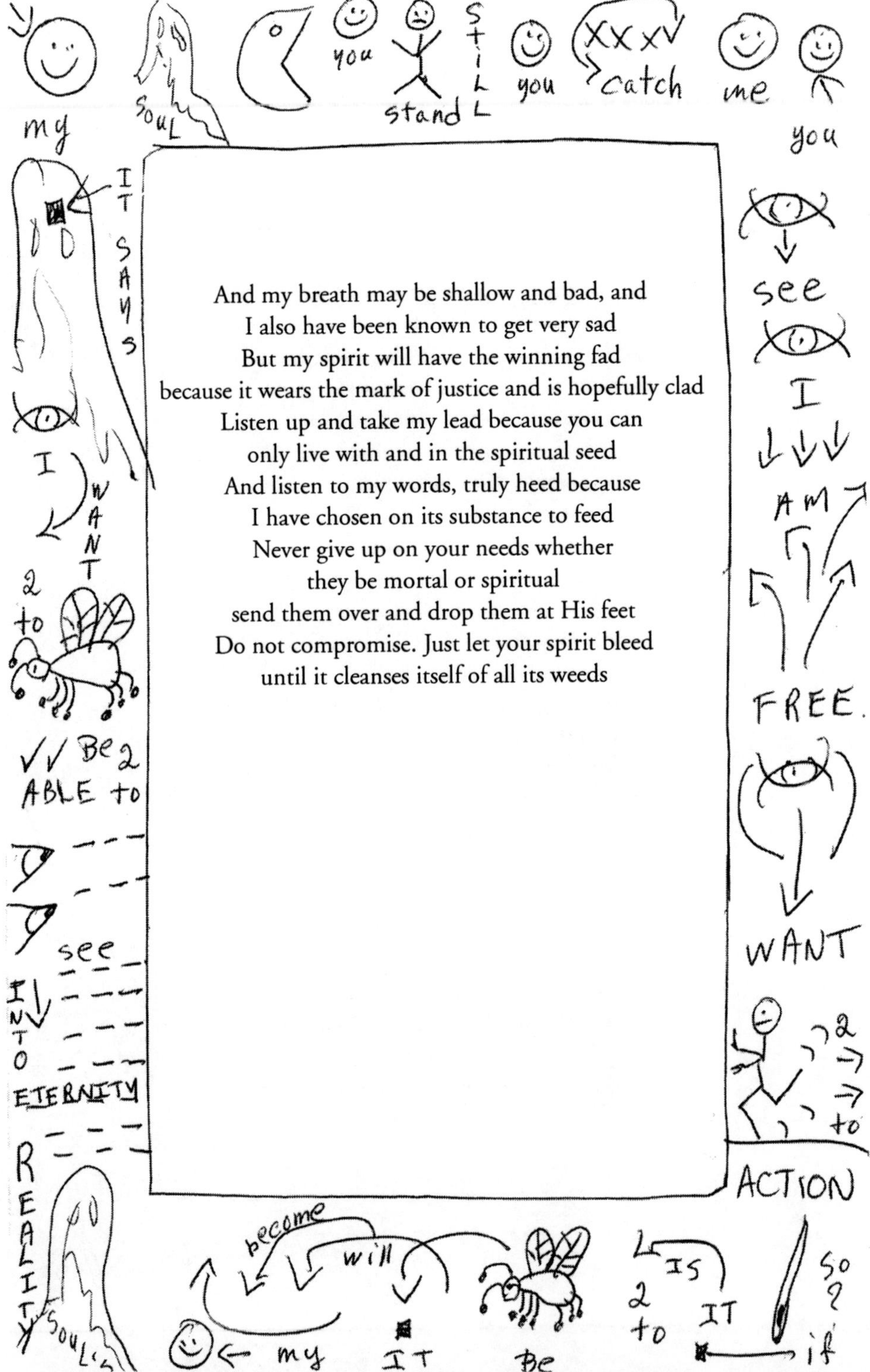

And my breath may be shallow and bad, and
I also have been known to get very sad
But my spirit will have the winning fad
because it wears the mark of justice and is hopefully clad
Listen up and take my lead because you can
only live with and in the spiritual seed
And listen to my words, truly heed because
I have chosen on its substance to feed
Never give up on your needs whether
they be mortal or spiritual
send them over and drop them at His feet
Do not compromise. Just let your spirit bleed
until it cleanses itself of all its weeds

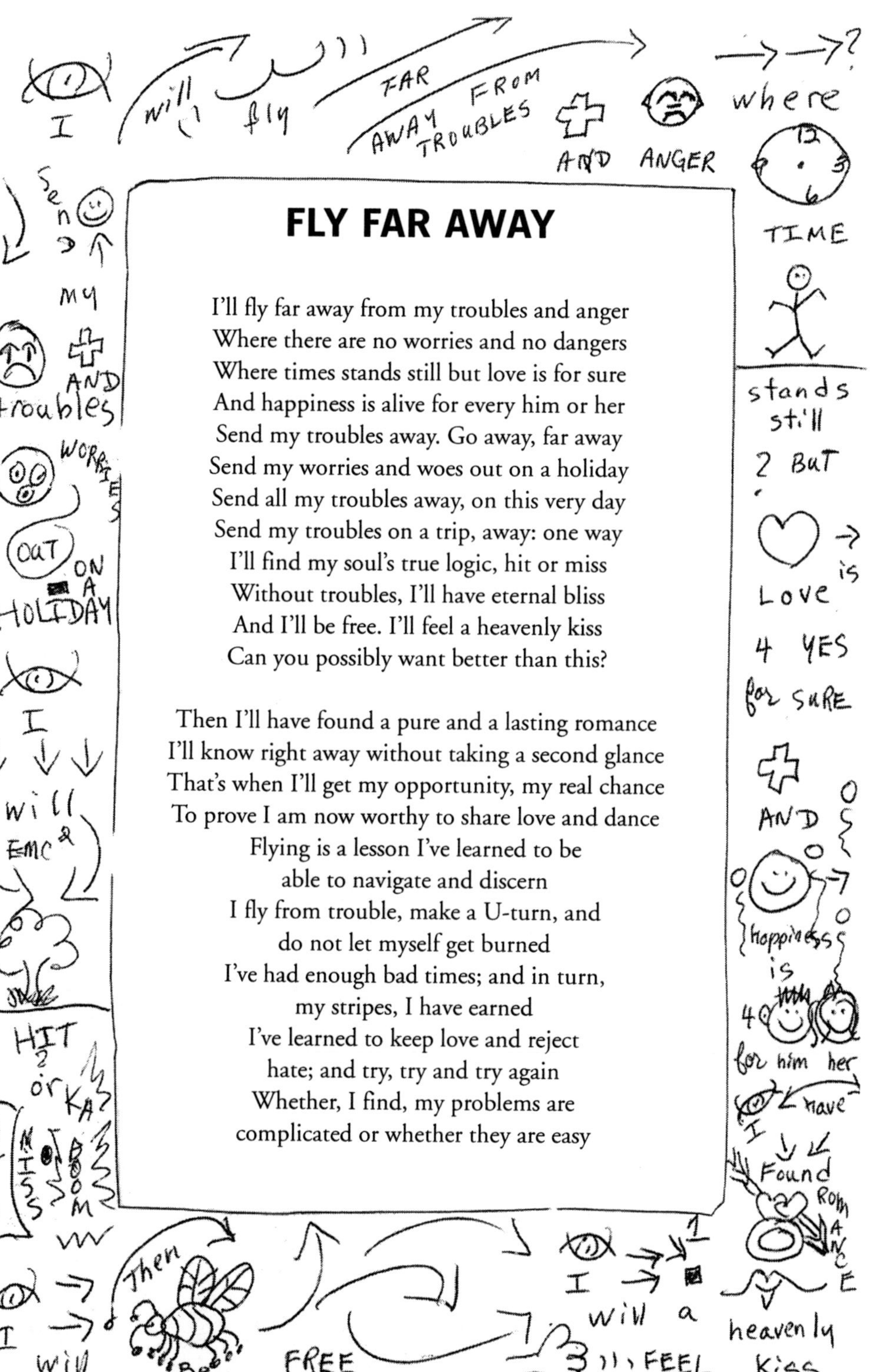

FLY FAR AWAY

I'll fly far away from my troubles and anger
Where there are no worries and no dangers
Where times stands still but love is for sure
And happiness is alive for every him or her
Send my troubles away. Go away, far away
Send my worries and woes out on a holiday
Send all my troubles away, on this very day
Send my troubles on a trip, away: one way
I'll find my soul's true logic, hit or miss
Without troubles, I'll have eternal bliss
And I'll be free. I'll feel a heavenly kiss
Can you possibly want better than this?

Then I'll have found a pure and a lasting romance
I'll know right away without taking a second glance
That's when I'll get my opportunity, my real chance
To prove I am now worthy to share love and dance
Flying is a lesson I've learned to be
able to navigate and discern
I fly from trouble, make a U-turn, and
do not let myself get burned
I've had enough bad times; and in turn,
my stripes, I have earned
I've learned to keep love and reject
hate; and try, try and try again
Whether, I find, my problems are
complicated or whether they are easy

I've learned to face them with courage
and work at them like a busy bee
Then I can get used to them in any degree,
and I will be ready to referee
Afterwards, I can rest, be carefree, and
enjoy what hard work guarantees
Hey, just let me know if I am bound for trouble this day
Please, I don't need to be defeated. Just have your way
I will still have a little something to say. I can still pray
In the end, I will conquer, jump for joy and learn to play
I'll watch my step and I will try not to fall down
Then I will stay balanced when I turn around
And I won't get confused and get lost in town
And I will never again be sad or wear a frown

FATE

It always happens that what I fear the most
Becomes my guiding post and I become its host
And then it becomes to me law and the utmost
Fate punishes me like I was a whipping post
Even if I cry me a river of tears
My fears come true, the whole dreadful smear
When I make a request to my fears
please don't come near
They just sneer and bite me from the rear
Always, when I smile and say all is good
I should always pause and knock on wood
Because I seldom will be heard or understood
And my request will most always be misunderstood
My family, my loved ones, and me
My lover and my children all tend to be
Victims of one giant conspiracy
That always treats my wishes to the contrary
When I wish for good things to come my way
My wishes soon fade and slowly wither away
No matter what I have to say
Fate always leans towards the opposite way
One day meets what another one sends
When one is gone, another one begins again
When I want to enjoy sun I am forced into a den
When I say begin, someone says it's time to end

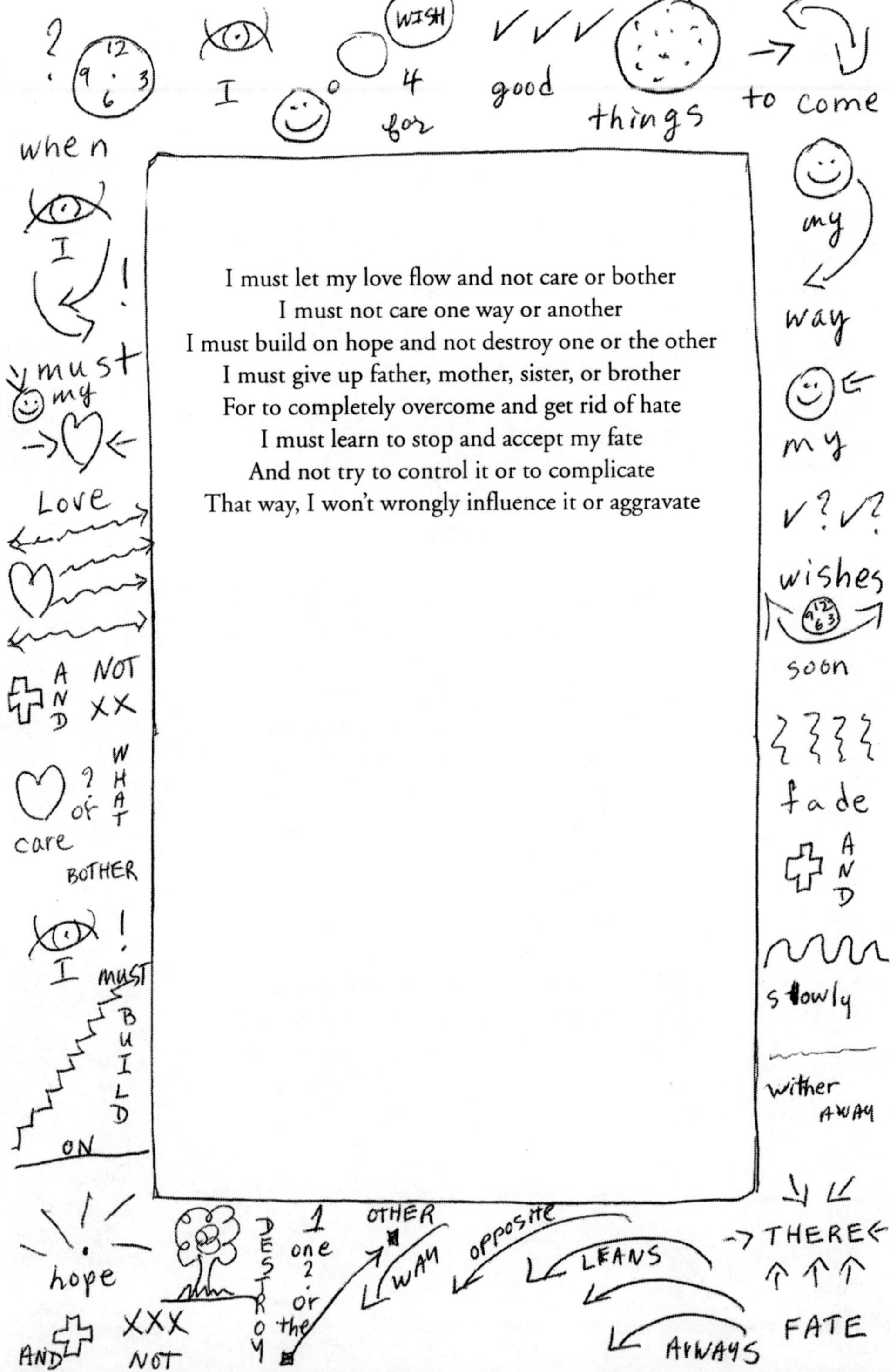

I must let my love flow and not care or bother
I must not care one way or another
I must build on hope and not destroy one or the other
I must give up father, mother, sister, or brother
For to completely overcome and get rid of hate
I must learn to stop and accept my fate
And not try to control it or to complicate
That way, I won't wrongly influence it or aggravate

CAN'T HELP BUT RESIST

Resisting you is the name of my game
We all know where there is no pain, there is no gain
And we know we must sometimes
endure a little pain to get gain, all the same
Well, resisting is what I do best, and pain is my middle name
I know you would like to believe and to think
I am without direction and I am on the brink
To tell you the truth; now I have the missing link
And I will tell you in blink of a wink
How can I help but be happy and outspoken
Now that my chains of slavery have been broken
My love for the whole world is my lucky token
And I am forever in debt —to all whom
I love—and I am beholden
You ask why I would want to resist you
Is it just because you and I are done and through?
I tell you nothing has changed, nothing is new
The fact is, I have forgotten about you;
does this give you a clue
Even though my life may be short
I will do my best to hold down the fort
I will resist you if I have to go to the highest court
I will not stoop to ever again be your cohort
I know that in love there are no guarantees
But you will never again have me crawling on my knees
I have made up my own mind and I might say, with ease

I can assure you now, I will love where
and with whom I please
I will have my victory, I will have my freedom
Now I will have my turn to shine in the sun
And I will never again be tricked or undone
My life has not ended, it has just begun
You have not succeeded in making me late
Because I refuse to participate in your hate
I really believe in a thing called fate
Now I will be happy and free
I have escaped through hate's gate

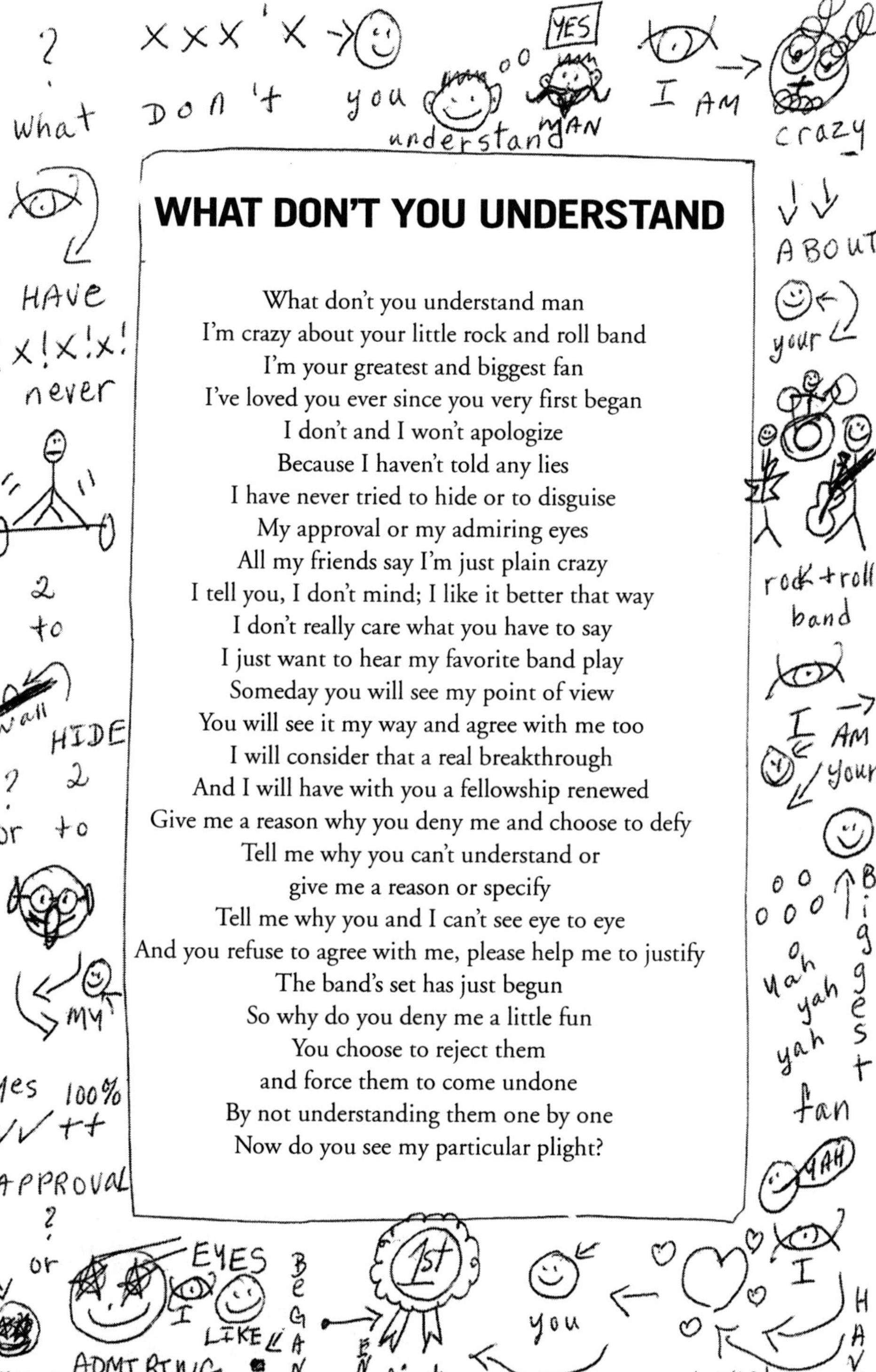

WHAT DON'T YOU UNDERSTAND

What don't you understand man
I'm crazy about your little rock and roll band
I'm your greatest and biggest fan
I've loved you ever since you very first began
I don't and I won't apologize
Because I haven't told any lies
I have never tried to hide or to disguise
My approval or my admiring eyes
All my friends say I'm just plain crazy
I tell you, I don't mind; I like it better that way
I don't really care what you have to say
I just want to hear my favorite band play
Someday you will see my point of view
You will see it my way and agree with me too
I will consider that a real breakthrough
And I will have with you a fellowship renewed
Give me a reason why you deny me and choose to defy
Tell me why you can't understand or
give me a reason or specify
Tell me why you and I can't see eye to eye
And you refuse to agree with me, please help me to justify
The band's set has just begun
So why do you deny me a little fun
You choose to reject them
and force them to come undone
By not understanding them one by one
Now do you see my particular plight?

I hope someday you will accept it and get it right
You can't go wrong when they play at night
Because no one will want to argue or to fight
Their music will be very soothing
And your sense of reason will be your undoing
In the right directions they will make me swing
And you will also see that this band is
the best possible one that was ever able to sing

HAVE YOU MET MY FRIEND LORETTE?

Have you met my friend Lorette?
She's related to my friend Turret
She's also outspoken, you bet
She doesn't really care if she gets heck
She has her own opinion
And she is a spontaneous minion
Truth is her little onion
Her heart is fearsome as a lion
As for her loud relative
You'd better give Turret a sedative
And be willing and ready to forgive him his sins
His outbursts you may have to painfully relive
These two, Lorette and Turret, seldom use wisdom
Any thoughts you generally want hidden
Soon will become common knowledge not meant to offend
You could call them senseless but smitten
These two have a friend named Claudette
She is a member of the jet set
On her gender, I wouldn't be able to bet
And with the government she has a secret debt
While Claudette spies for the other side in her closet
You see, she plays a dangerous game of Russian roulette
She secretly loves Lorette,
which understandably makes Lorette fret
When spying, Claudette is known
to the other side as a cadet
Claudette has a problem, you see

Claudette can't choose which gender
or what anatomy to be—
on the contrary
If she did, she would no longer be free
Because if she chose the proper anatomy—
she would reveal she is a he
Claudette would then be thrown in the clink
And Lorette would lose her friend in a blink
And Turret, on the other hand would
prove to be the loud rat fink
Because Turret couldn't be quiet,
Claudette's plans for love would be gone in a wink

DREAMS ARE FUNNY THINGS

Sometimes dreams are funny things
When your eyes are closed, you can't see outside
nothing, absolutely nothing
But in your dreams you can become anything
if you want, you can become a king
Or you can see an image of your favorite diamond ring
Sometimes you dream when you are lying down
Or when you are sitting in a chair or
when you are asleep at sundown
You can dream sleeping on your side
or while wearing a frown
You can also dream while sitting still
or while traveling all around
One time I had a vivid dream
In this dream I shouted and I screamed
It wasn't at all as real as it seemed
I guess it was a way
my feelings could let off their steam
Once, while I dreamed, I laughed out loud
Because of a joke I had heard in my dream clouds
My dream comedy had had me wowed
When I awoke I was refreshed, a bushy-tailed broad
Some dreams make me very happy
Some make me want to hide and flee
Some make me sad and off-key
Some make me anxious and angry
Some dreams are very romantic

Some dreams are intriguing and classics
Some dreams are mysterious and nostalgic
Some dreams are of fantasy and magic
Some make me afraid and leave me full of wonder
Some make me wonder why I had to sleep any longer
Sometimes, of my dreams, I can't be any fonder
And I don't want to awaken from being in my slumber
Dreams can be amusing and very funny
But chances are, we will never again see
The likes of them, either for you or for me
Waking from them is the real key—
that's what makes all of us happy

GET OUT OF MY HEAD

Confusion, get out of my head
It's tiresome always escaping to my bed
Trying to find the sleep I sometimes dread
My thoughts come to torture me instead
Dreams sometimes bring me grief
They seem to steal time like a thief
Sometimes they make me shake like a leaf
They still have for me some reason that is my belief
What do these dreams all mean
That comes underneath my eyelids and in between
They seem real, like they're somewhere I've been
A new kind of pain, a new reality it seems
Into my consciousness they jump
At my very core, they haunt and taunt
In their fearsome vividness, they flaunt
Whether I want them or
I don't want them, they still taunt
Sometimes it's hard to tell what's real
Life is never guaranteed or a done, done deal
Visions begin to revisit, creep, and steal
They crowd reality, depending on how I feel
My eyelids become heavy
But I dare not close them until I'm ready
Or streams of fearsome visions might have a melee
I must learn to cope with them before I go batty
Sometimes it is hard to tell

When I'm awake or if I'm really not in hell
I just pinch myself until I yell
That's when I again feel well
Maybe all this was just because of something I ate
Something poisonous on my dinner plate
Something that my body hated
And all those visions were just the
result of what it had activated

SOON WE WILL TALK OUT LOUD

Soon we will all talk out loud
You will find our logic will be totally sound
Finally, you will have also found
That now no one minds having us around
We will be able to go on day to day
And no one will have anything at all to say
We will work and we will play
We will do so come what may, if that's OK.
We will think our own thoughts
That may sometimes still come to naught
Because our right cure has not yet been wrought
But with patience, the right help will someday be caught
When someone unscrambles our basket of eggs
We will receive our sea legs
We will no longer be society's dregs
Instead we will be full-charged kegs
Then we will no longer find the need to hide
We'll gladly show everyone what's really inside
In all of you, we will no longer mind to confide
We will find you right there, on our side
We will consider you as our friend
To you, from us, many treasures we will send
To you, in turn, a helping hand we will lend
We'll thank you over, and over, again and again
We'll want to be and to have your company to last
We'll remember how you were waiting steadfast
Waiting patiently, you were waiting at half mast

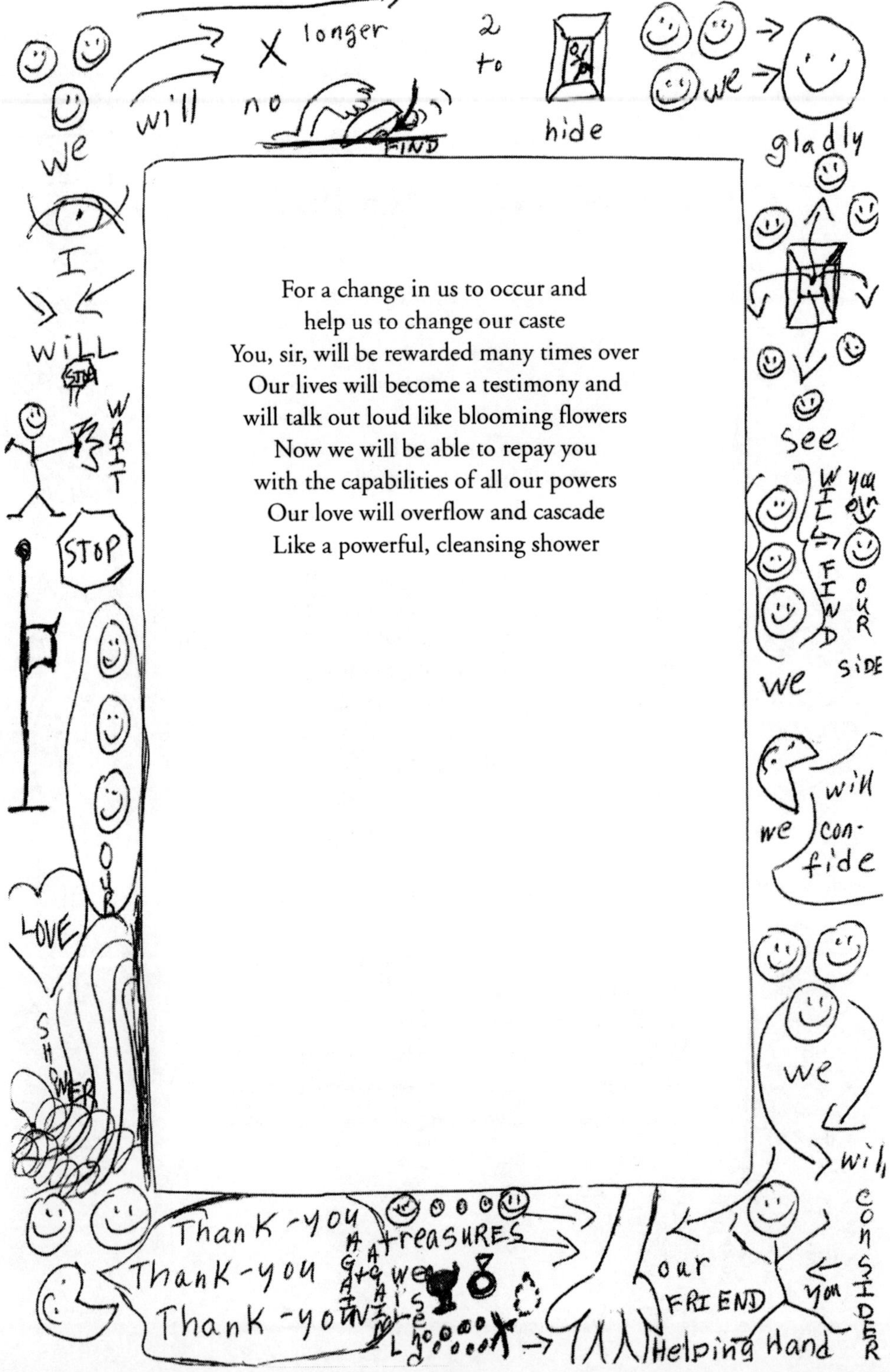

For a change in us to occur and
help us to change our caste
You, sir, will be rewarded many times over
Our lives will become a testimony and
will talk out loud like blooming flowers
Now we will be able to repay you
with the capabilities of all our powers
Our love will overflow and cascade
Like a powerful, cleansing shower

PROOF OF PURCHASE

What's the matter
So you haven't got it in you
I won, you know
You are absolutely nothing
I know; you know too
Right now, whoever wants to know also
You say I lie
But I know and so do you
I know your secret
And I still do
You don't know mine
I didn't tell anyone
You could never figure
Because I was quiet
I didn't have to tell
And I wasn't scared
That you didn't figure on
What a shame
That didn't sit well in your plans
All you could do was lie
The others fell like sheep
They fell one by one
I still said nothing
To any of them
Then life was too hot
I had to escape
Which I carefully didn't plan

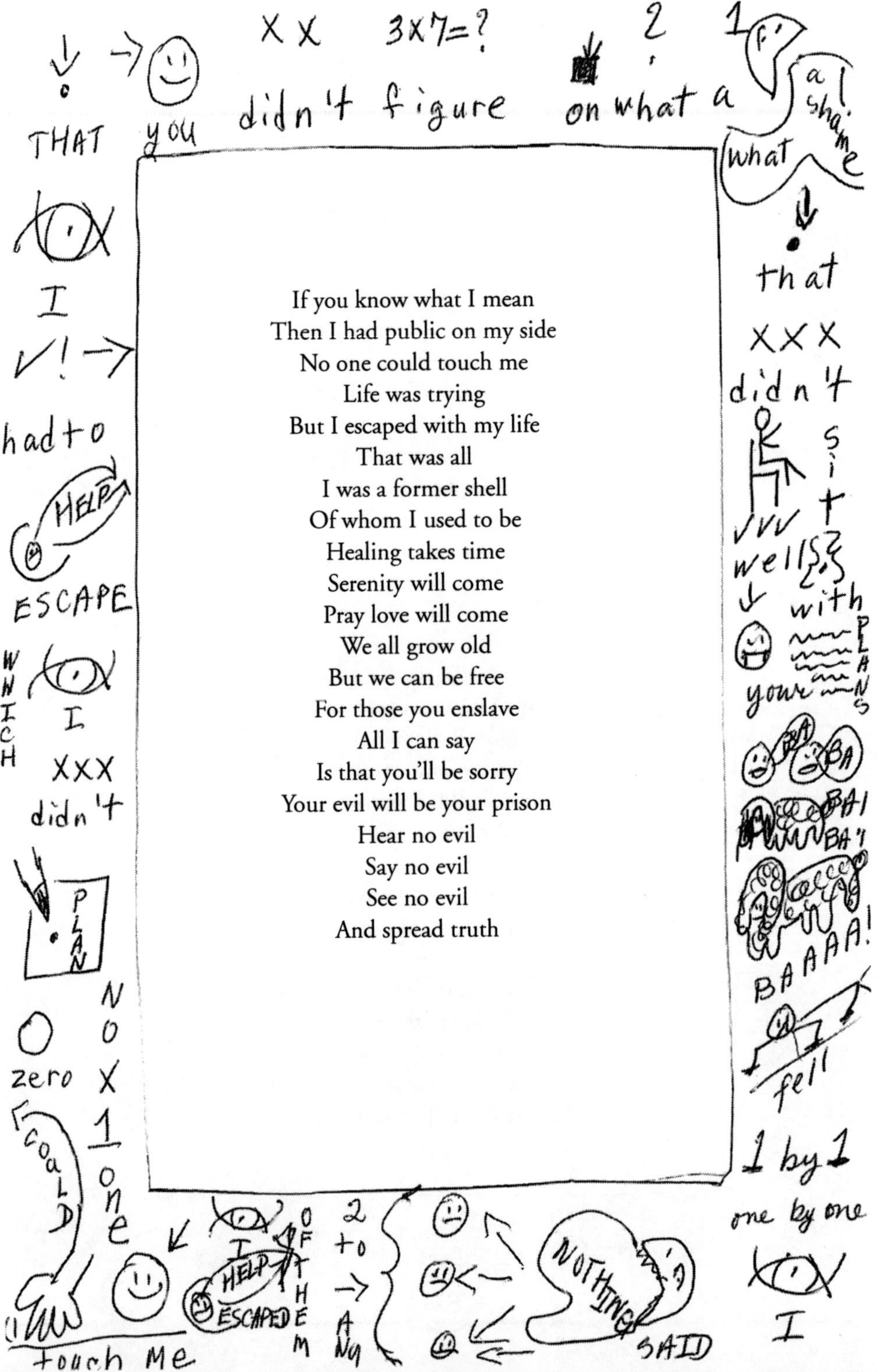

If you know what I mean
Then I had public on my side
No one could touch me
Life was trying
But I escaped with my life
That was all
I was a former shell
Of whom I used to be
Healing takes time
Serenity will come
Pray love will come
We all grow old
But we can be free
For those you enslave
All I can say
Is that you'll be sorry
Your evil will be your prison
Hear no evil
Say no evil
See no evil
And spread truth

JUST FOR THE THOUGHT OF IT

This story will unfurl. Just for the thought of it
The thought makes my mind twirl.
There's plenty of room for it
The thought is my whole life. The thought is in the script
The thought is of a girl and this girl you may call hip

This thought started way back when
When my life started, way back then
In the early beginning, I felt like a number 10
There was a pause and then my life began again
Sometimes the very thought
Of an easy life can't be bought
And no matter what, all is in naught
And then life's battles have to be fought
At that stage of life, I didn't quite know
In which direction I was supposed to go
Was I supposed to resist or go with the flow?
Even as I thought of this, I was dealt a deathly blow
After that, I became cursed; life began all over
It was totally different; it was all I
could do but to run for cover
I hid in my personal corner and there I would hover
Until I thought I had found a loving and a safe lover
At its best, life was trying
Every single day was time I was buying
It seemed like in my life I was always faking

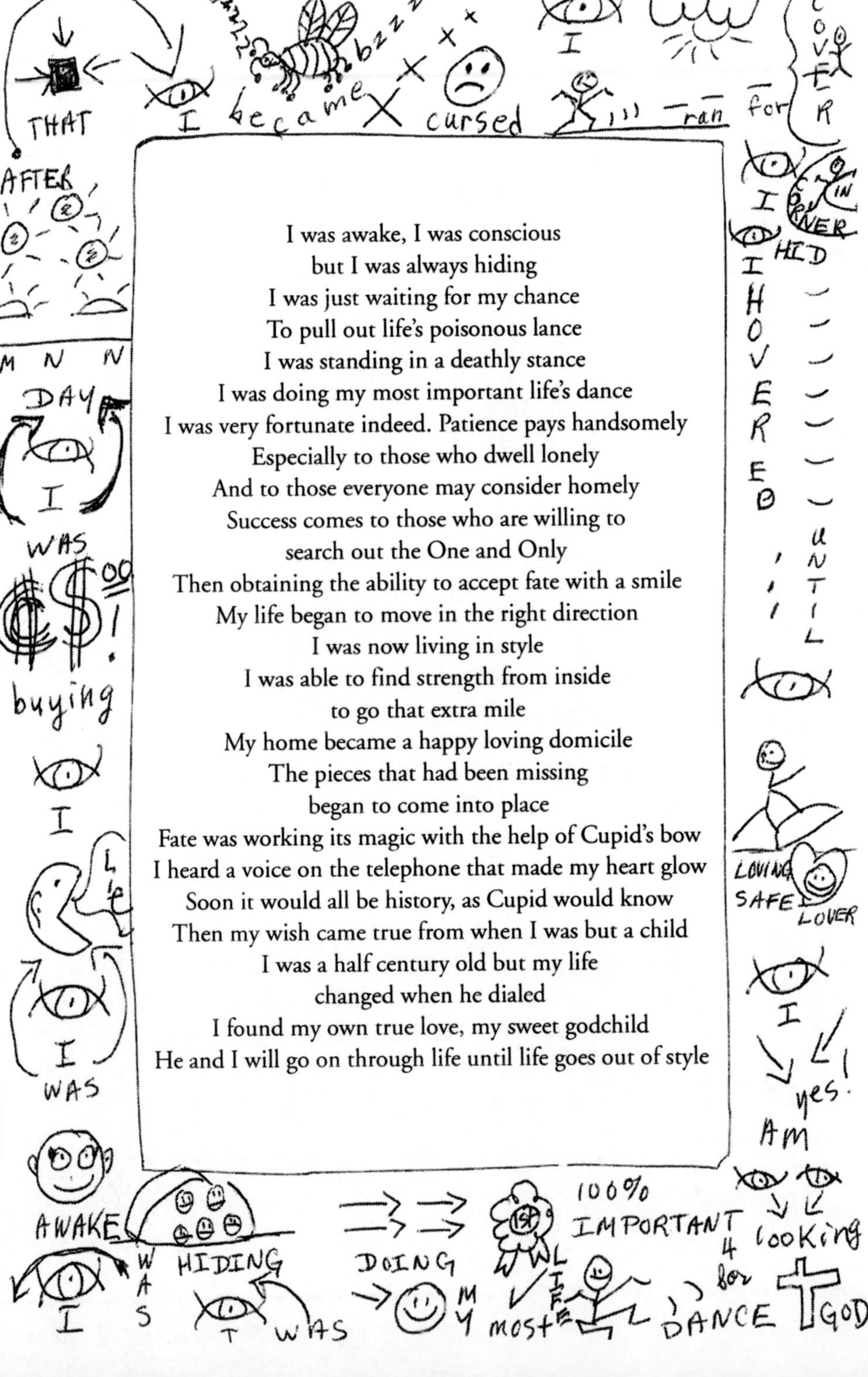

I was awake, I was conscious
but I was always hiding
I was just waiting for my chance
To pull out life's poisonous lance
I was standing in a deathly stance
I was doing my most important life's dance
I was very fortunate indeed. Patience pays handsomely
Especially to those who dwell lonely
And to those everyone may consider homely
Success comes to those who are willing to
search out the One and Only
Then obtaining the ability to accept fate with a smile
My life began to move in the right direction
I was now living in style
I was able to find strength from inside
to go that extra mile
My home became a happy loving domicile
The pieces that had been missing
began to come into place
Fate was working its magic with the help of Cupid's bow
I heard a voice on the telephone that made my heart glow
Soon it would all be history, as Cupid would know
Then my wish came true from when I was but a child
I was a half century old but my life
changed when he dialed
I found my own true love, my sweet godchild
He and I will go on through life until life goes out of style

YOU'RE MY FRIEND

You're my friend, mister. You, sir, are
definitely not an imposter
Give me one right here on the kisser.
That one will be a tester
You're also my favorite friend and
jester, whom I love to pester
I'm your friendly feline and you've
got me by the nose whiskers
Love is the way to go. I think I've been hit by Cupid's arrow
I say, I really love you so. I thought you had a right to know
I really want to show you, from the word go:
I am a powerful dynamo
And the reason that I glow is because
I am standing with you under the mistletoe
Come to me, my sweetie. You're my little monkey
My love for you is free; I'll be your busy little bee
Don't you see that our love
could be happy and carefree?
Love, love is the key.
You are free to be my love referee
Wait for me, I'll wait for you. We'll have a great rendezvous
That will be the worldview, with which I will want to pursue
I will not be mistaken or misconstrued. I will be right on cue
You'll wait for me too. It will be a great
fun, a love breakthrough
It'll send for you around the bend.
Please try to understand and try to comprehend

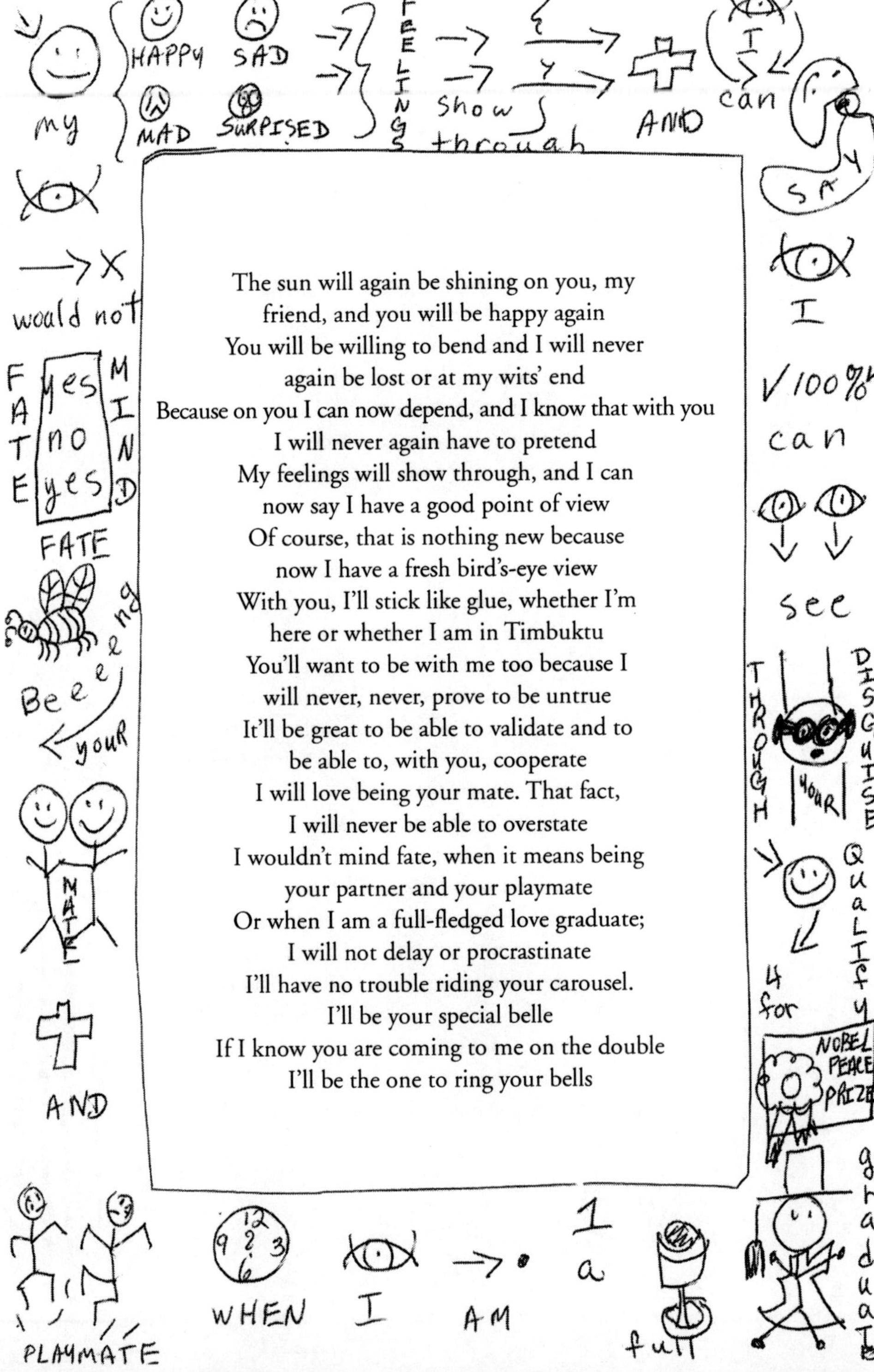

The sun will again be shining on you, my
friend, and you will be happy again
You will be willing to bend and I will never
again be lost or at my wits' end
Because on you I can now depend, and I know that with you
I will never again have to pretend
My feelings will show through, and I can
now say I have a good point of view
Of course, that is nothing new because
now I have a fresh bird's-eye view
With you, I'll stick like glue, whether I'm
here or whether I am in Timbuktu
You'll want to be with me too because I
will never, never, prove to be untrue
It'll be great to be able to validate and to
be able to, with you, cooperate
I will love being your mate. That fact,
I will never be able to overstate
I wouldn't mind fate, when it means being
your partner and your playmate
Or when I am a full-fledged love graduate;
I will not delay or procrastinate
I'll have no trouble riding your carousel.
I'll be your special belle
If I know you are coming to me on the double
I'll be the one to ring your bells

And if we become a couple,
you would be my William Tell and I'll be your Tinker Bell
Then I would move out of this hovel and
become your prim and proper mademoiselle
It is to me, no surprise that I can see through
your popular and romantic disguise
Or that you are such a valuable prize; you
definitely qualify for the Nobel Peace Prize
I'll assure you, I tell you no lies.
What you have discovered will be something to modernize
I told you so, you guys. Don't you agree?
I say, no one would dare say anything otherwise

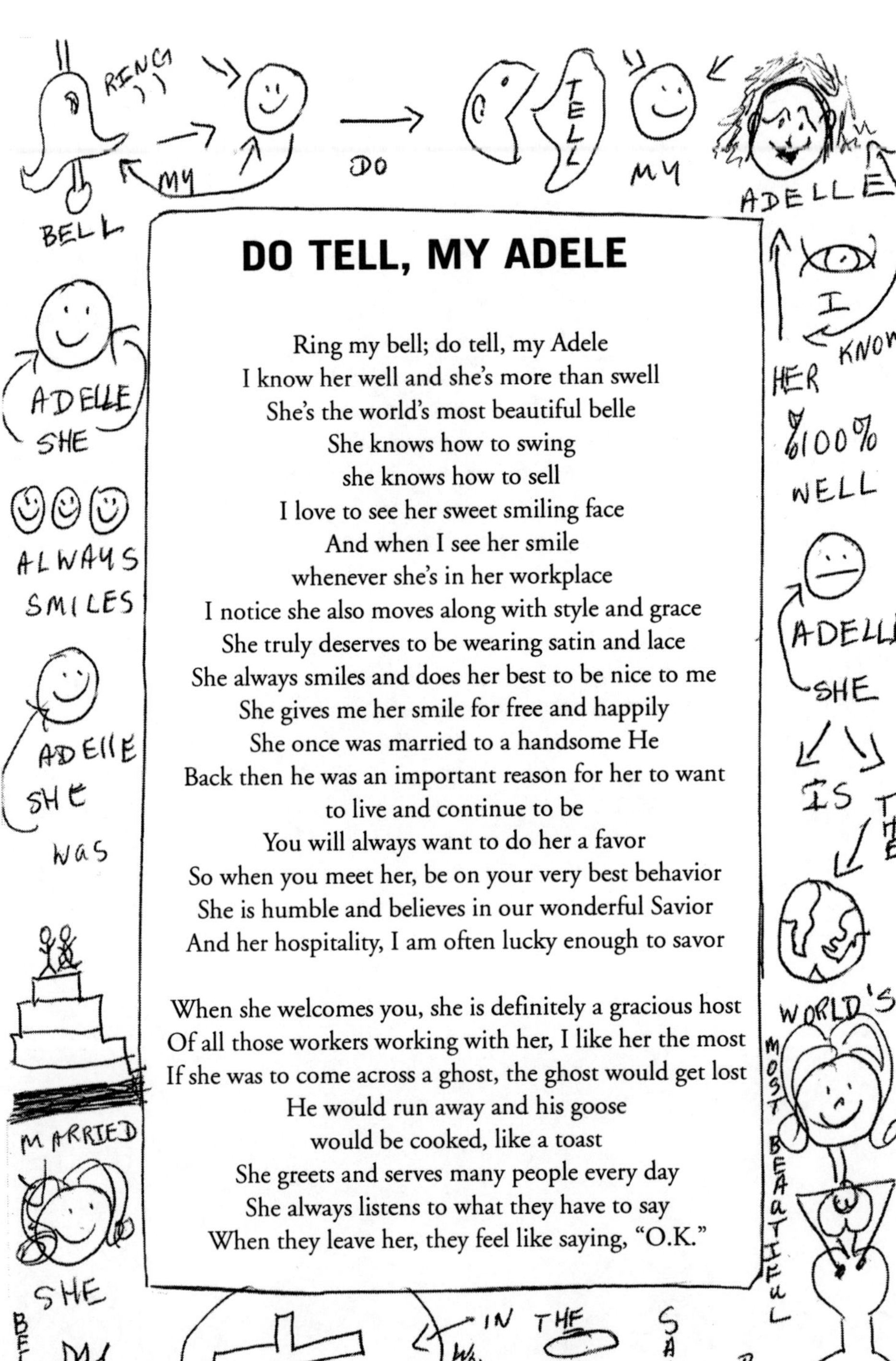

DO TELL, MY ADELE

Ring my bell; do tell, my Adele
I know her well and she's more than swell
She's the world's most beautiful belle
She knows how to swing
she knows how to sell
I love to see her sweet smiling face
And when I see her smile
whenever she's in her workplace
I notice she also moves along with style and grace
She truly deserves to be wearing satin and lace
She always smiles and does her best to be nice to me
She gives me her smile for free and happily
She once was married to a handsome He
Back then he was an important reason for her to want
to live and continue to be
You will always want to do her a favor
So when you meet her, be on your very best behavior
She is humble and believes in our wonderful Savior
And her hospitality, I am often lucky enough to savor

When she welcomes you, she is definitely a gracious host
Of all those workers working with her, I like her the most
If she was to come across a ghost, the ghost would get lost
He would run away and his goose
would be cooked, like a toast
She greets and serves many people every day
She always listens to what they have to say
When they leave her, they feel like saying, "O.K."

Then when they shuffle off,
they go away merry and gay
She is one of life's beautiful persons
I hope she is always happy and has a lot of fun
Also I hope all her battles are well-handled and are won
And I hope, she will never meet defeat or come undone
Myself, personally, I like her; she's one of the chosen few
Whatever she wears looks like it is brand new
I hope she never has a reason to be sad or blue
And I hope a smile forever sticks on her face
like it was stuck there permanently with glue

MY BEST FRIEND AND LOVE, CHARLIE

He is my best friend and love, Charlie
He is the one, with whom, I want to party
He is so cute and he is so pretty
With him, I don't have anything,
with which, to worry
He is my newest and most valuable find
His heart is pure and he is very, very kind
With him I truly love to be,
and with him, I love to unwind
Then he teases and excites me until I am quite blind
I am so very lucky to have found
Charlie on this land this blessed ground
I always want him close and around
When we are together
I feel we are truly glory bound
When I look at him
he makes my heart skip a beat
When he touches my lips; he lifts me ten feet
When we are near each other I feel the heat
He makes me feel so very complete
Charles is his proper name
This name is his claim to fame
Together we play the best love game
Then when we are alone; we become one and the same
He is my very best friend, one on whom I can depend

I'll love him again and again and again
I'll share his company with you, now and then and when
I find a friend around the bend that's also a number 10
He is so very capable and sweet, which I find quite neat
I knew he was the one when I first chanced him to meet
No one I know comes close to him or has him beat
No one yet has accomplished this feat
I love you, Charles, my darling love
You are my own sweet precious dove
You were sent down from above
You to me, just for me, to know you and more of

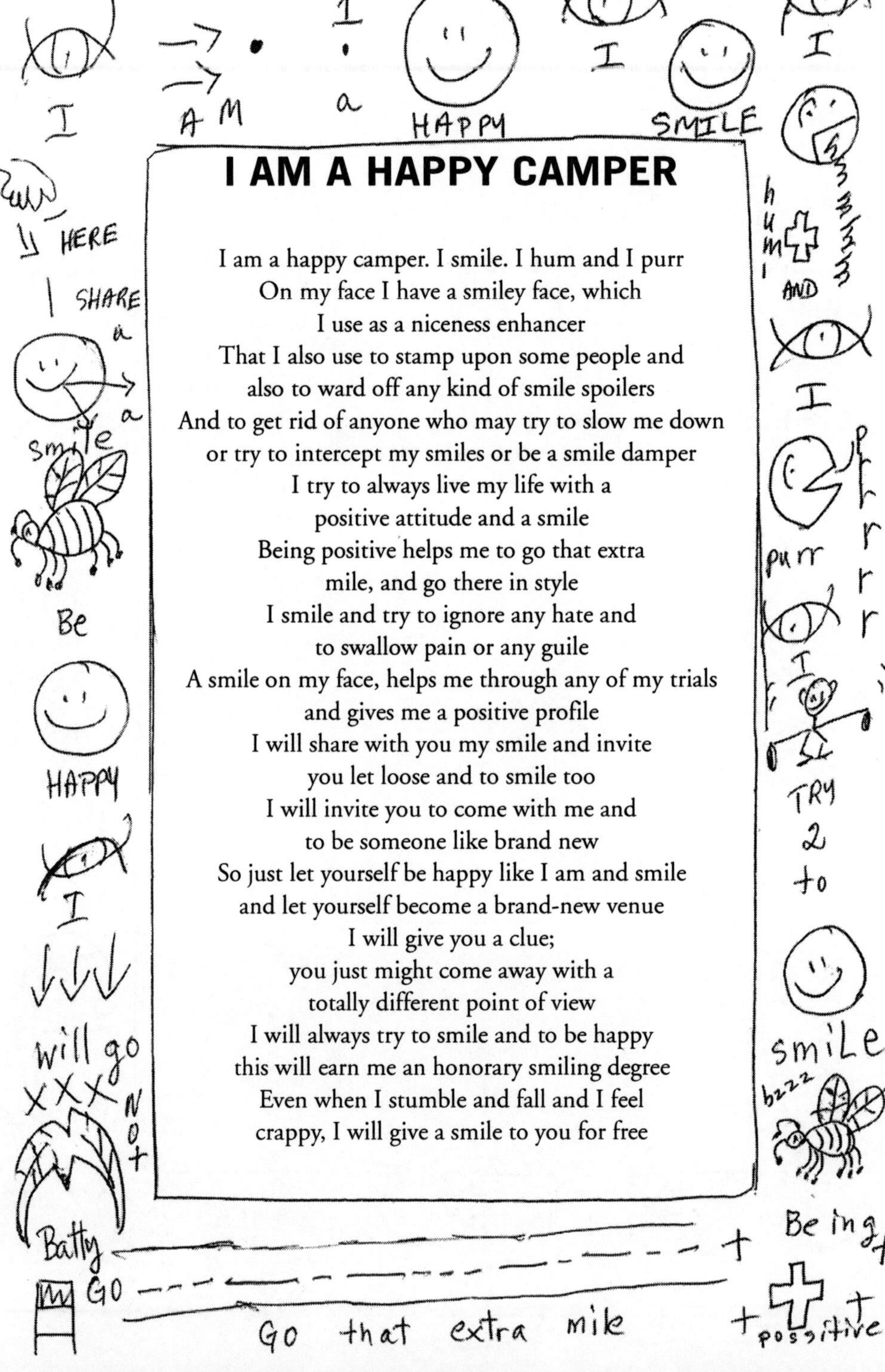

I AM A HAPPY CAMPER

I am a happy camper. I smile. I hum and I purr
On my face I have a smiley face, which
I use as a niceness enhancer
That I also use to stamp upon some people and
also to ward off any kind of smile spoilers
And to get rid of anyone who may try to slow me down
or try to intercept my smiles or be a smile damper
I try to always live my life with a
positive attitude and a smile
Being positive helps me to go that extra
mile, and go there in style
I smile and try to ignore any hate and
to swallow pain or any guile
A smile on my face, helps me through any of my trials
and gives me a positive profile
I will share with you my smile and invite
you let loose and to smile too
I will invite you to come with me and
to be someone like brand new
So just let yourself be happy like I am and smile
and let yourself become a brand-new venue
I will give you a clue;
you just might come away with a
totally different point of view
I will always try to smile and to be happy
this will earn me an honorary smiling degree
Even when I stumble and fall and I feel
crappy, I will give a smile to you for free

Being positive helps me not to go batty; that
is its bonus and smiling is the key
It leaves me with a happy new reality; it
leaves me relaxed and carefree
Smiling brings happiness and has made me enlightened
and has made the world my newfound friend
Smiling helps my senses to become sharp
and heightened with all hurts forgiven or on the mend
I no longer have to be apprehensive because
I will have the strength of ten men
With such great positive energy; this smiling
I will definitely, to you, recommend
Because of this happiness, my life will
become a success story
It will be my turn to bask in the glow
of my own newfound glory
I will no longer have any need to worry
or say anything to make me have to say sorry
I will be in a successful category,
with a smile of happiness the only fee,
which is really for free
I will go happily along
And because I'm happy
I won't want to do anything wrong
And then I will feel like I truly belong
And also then I will smile again and again
and I will sing out a new and happy song

I will smile and sing out,
high and low, near and far,
and dance heel to toe
I will yell out and let everyone know
Why I have a pleasant, happy glow
And I will share it with you; I will smile
and love may even grow

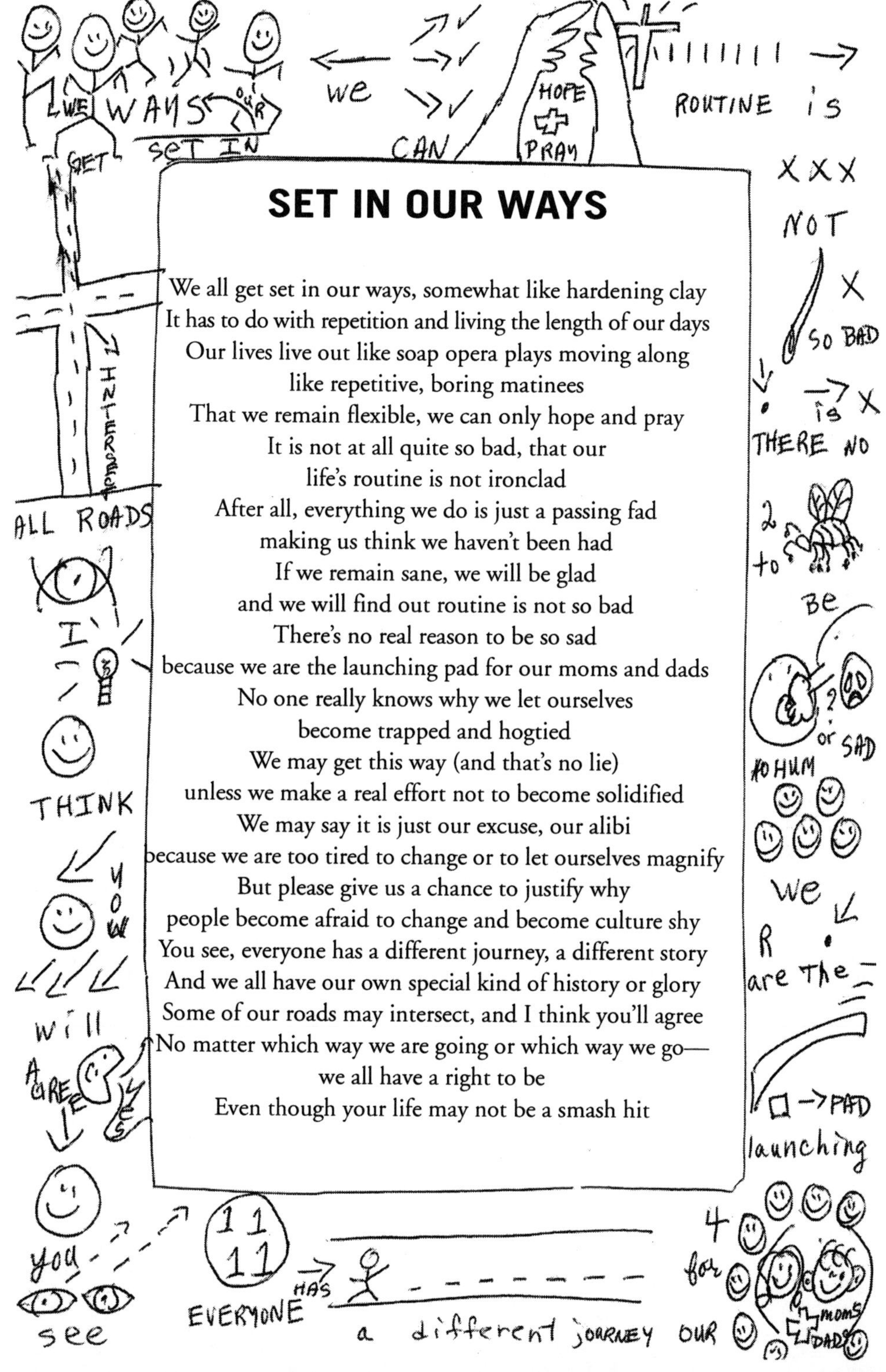

SET IN OUR WAYS

We all get set in our ways, somewhat like hardening clay
It has to do with repetition and living the length of our days
Our lives live out like soap opera plays moving along
like repetitive, boring matinees
That we remain flexible, we can only hope and pray
It is not at all quite so bad, that our
life's routine is not ironclad
After all, everything we do is just a passing fad
making us think we haven't been had
If we remain sane, we will be glad
and we will find out routine is not so bad
There's no real reason to be so sad
because we are the launching pad for our moms and dads
No one really knows why we let ourselves
become trapped and hogtied
We may get this way (and that's no lie)
unless we make a real effort not to become solidified
We may say it is just our excuse, our alibi
because we are too tired to change or to let ourselves magnify
But please give us a chance to justify why
people become afraid to change and become culture shy
You see, everyone has a different journey, a different story
And we all have our own special kind of history or glory
Some of our roads may intersect, and I think you'll agree
No matter which way we are going or which way we go—
we all have a right to be
Even though your life may not be a smash hit

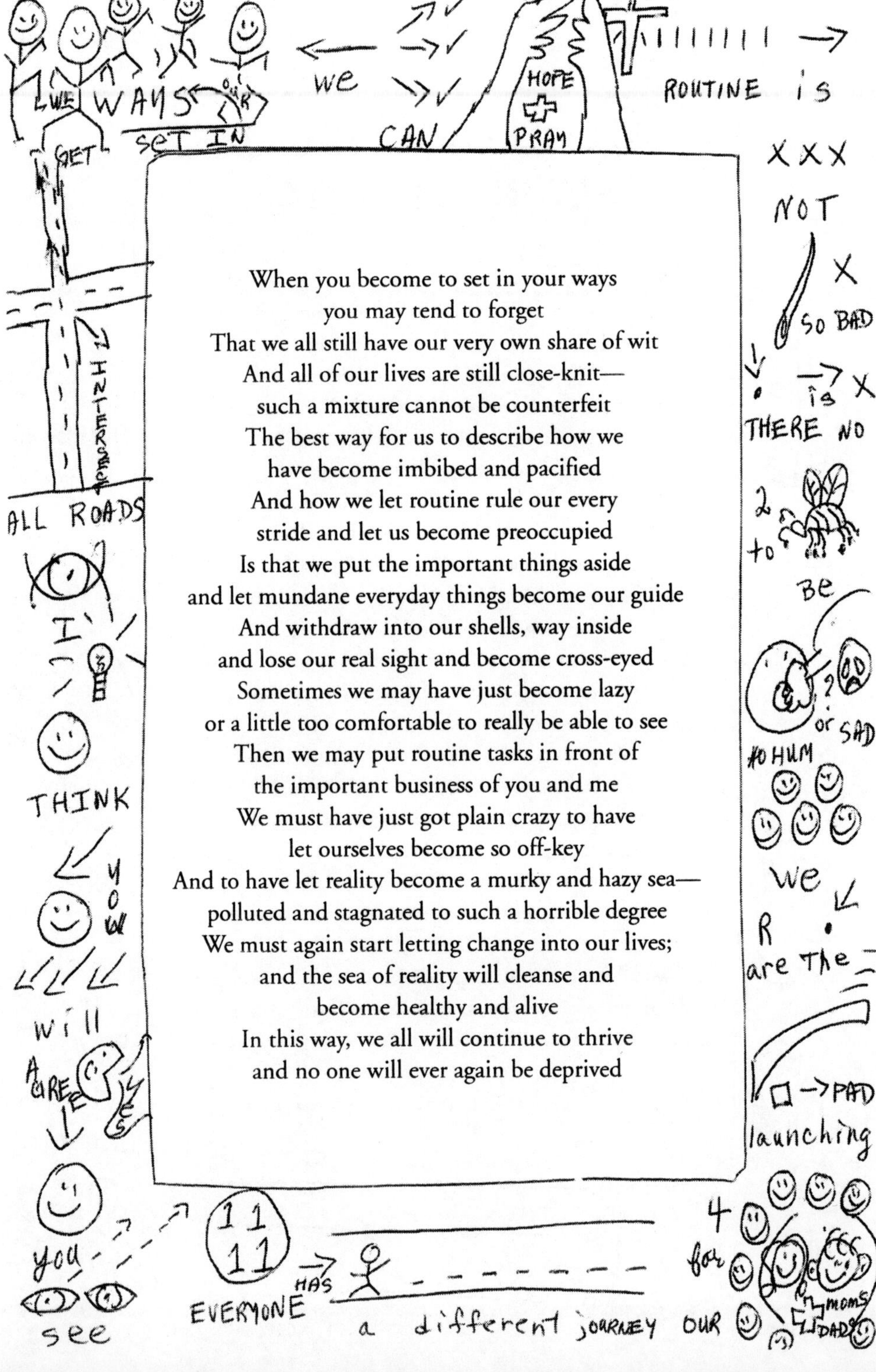

When you become to set in your ways
you may tend to forget
That we all still have our very own share of wit
And all of our lives are still close-knit—
such a mixture cannot be counterfeit
The best way for us to describe how we
have become imbibed and pacified
And how we let routine rule our every
stride and let us become preoccupied
Is that we put the important things aside
and let mundane everyday things become our guide
And withdraw into our shells, way inside
and lose our real sight and become cross-eyed
Sometimes we may have just become lazy
or a little too comfortable to really be able to see
Then we may put routine tasks in front of
the important business of you and me
We must have just got plain crazy to have
let ourselves become so off-key
And to have let reality become a murky and hazy sea—
polluted and stagnated to such a horrible degree
We must again start letting change into our lives;
and the sea of reality will cleanse and
become healthy and alive
In this way, we all will continue to thrive
and no one will ever again be deprived

WE
WAYS
OUR
GET
SET IN
WE
CAN
HOPE
PRAY
ROUTINE
IS
XXX
NOT
X
SO BAD
IS
X
THERE
NO
2
to
Be
?
or SAD
HO HUM
WE
R
are The
PAD
launching
4
for
OUR
MOMS
DADS
JOURNEY
different
a
EVERYONE
HAS
11
11
see
you
AGREE
will
YOU
THINK
I
ALL ROADS
INTERSECT

And our lives will be able to revive, and
we will go for a formula drive
and a sky dive and then for a deep-sea dive
And then all our ideals we will be
able to again give a high five
and thrive all the way from nine to five

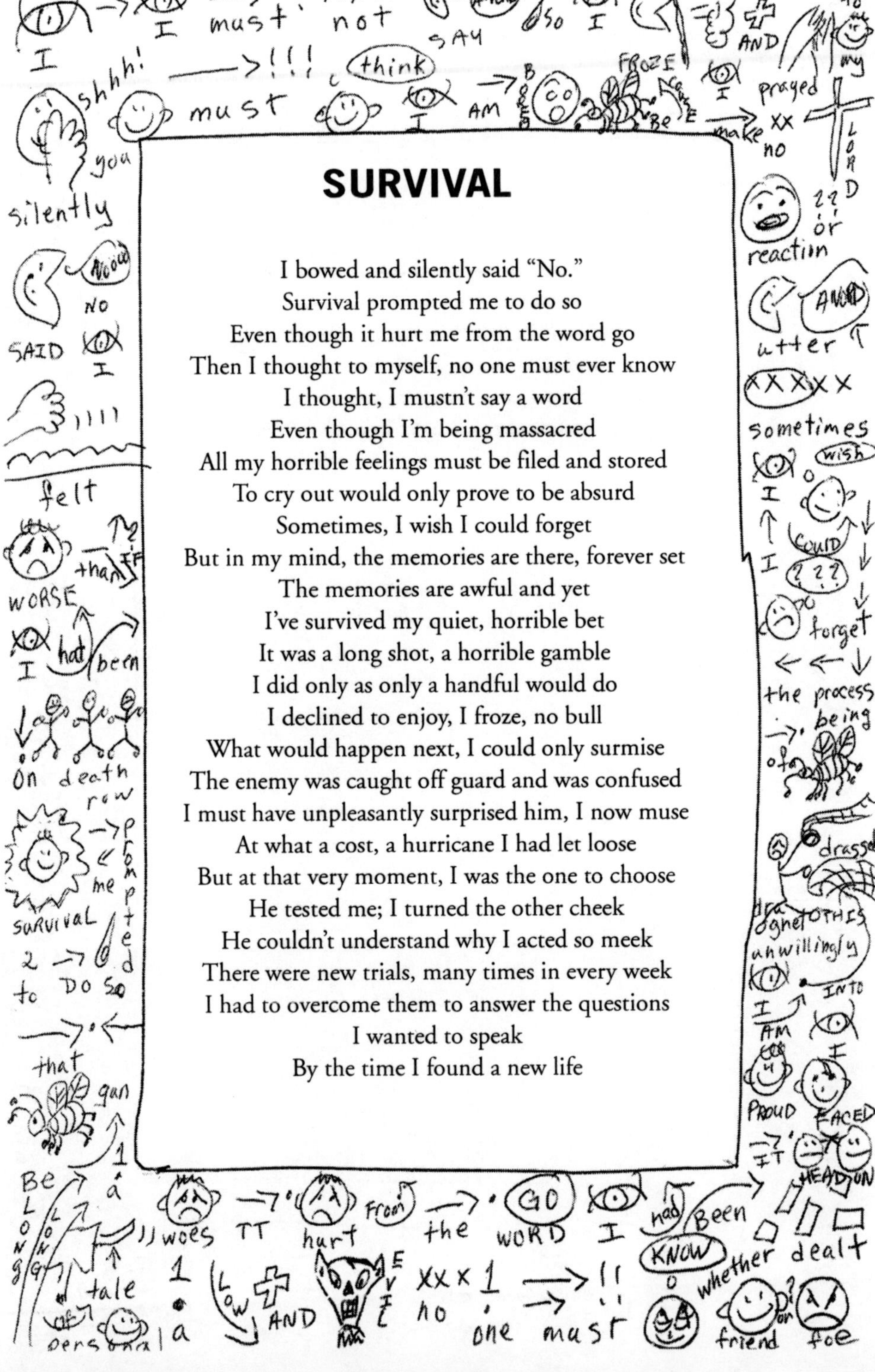

SURVIVAL

I bowed and silently said "No."
Survival prompted me to do so
Even though it hurt me from the word go
Then I thought to myself, no one must ever know
I thought, I mustn't say a word
Even though I'm being massacred
All my horrible feelings must be filed and stored
To cry out would only prove to be absurd
Sometimes, I wish I could forget
But in my mind, the memories are there, forever set
The memories are awful and yet
I've survived my quiet, horrible bet
It was a long shot, a horrible gamble
I did only as only a handful would do
I declined to enjoy, I froze, no bull
What would happen next, I could only surmise
The enemy was caught off guard and was confused
I must have unpleasantly surprised him, I now muse
At what a cost, a hurricane I had let loose
But at that very moment, I was the one to choose
He tested me; I turned the other cheek
He couldn't understand why I acted so meek
There were new trials, many times in every week
I had to overcome them to answer the questions
I wanted to speak
By the time I found a new life

And had become an innocent wife
I was a shell of a person, full of strife
He had cut me open and apart with an emotional knife
Many years later, I look back on those attacks
Courage is one thing that I certainly did not lack
Hope for some kind of future was all I had on my stack
My childlike innocence could never be given back

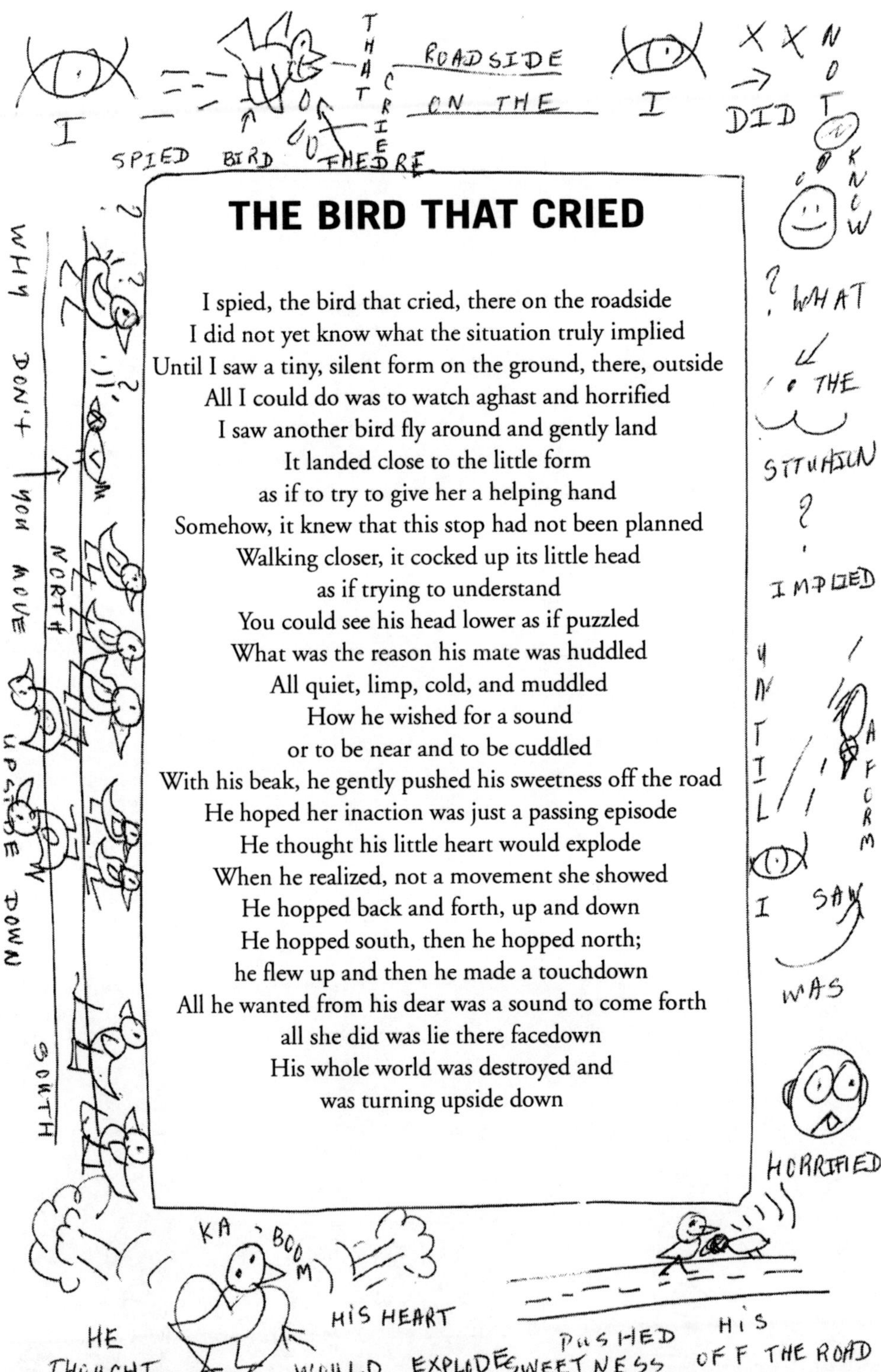

THE BIRD THAT CRIED

I spied, the bird that cried, there on the roadside
I did not yet know what the situation truly implied
Until I saw a tiny, silent form on the ground, there, outside
All I could do was to watch aghast and horrified
I saw another bird fly around and gently land
It landed close to the little form
as if to try to give her a helping hand
Somehow, it knew that this stop had not been planned
Walking closer, it cocked up its little head
as if trying to understand
You could see his head lower as if puzzled
What was the reason his mate was huddled
All quiet, limp, cold, and muddled
How he wished for a sound
or to be near and to be cuddled
With his beak, he gently pushed his sweetness off the road
He hoped her inaction was just a passing episode
He thought his little heart would explode
When he realized, not a movement she showed
He hopped back and forth, up and down
He hopped south, then he hopped north;
he flew up and then he made a touchdown
All he wanted from his dear was a sound to come forth
all she did was lie there facedown
His whole world was destroyed and
was turning upside down

He came a little nearer; then he came even nearer
He came closer and closer to his little dear
He nuzzled her gently with a growing, silent fear
That she would never again move away from here
He raised his head and as if to scream in desperation
He let out a piercing cry, for all to hear,
out to all the nations
This was his offering, his parting oblation
She stayed still, there in her quiet station
What was to come of him; he had been so blessed
His little heart broke within his tiny chest
He no longer had a need for his love nest
Flying away from his love was nature's final test

YOU CAN'T DEFY DESTINY

You can't defy your own destiny
You can't defy the fact
you are who you are or that I am me
Only with you, my dear, am I now really free
Through your eyes, I would like to be able to see
You are my whole world; you have put my life in a whirl
I come to you with my hands unfurled,
a loving and hopeful girl
With your eyes looking at me, my soul is not soiled
and I again feel like a young girl
Without you, my goose would have been cooked,
my life would have been spoiled
I want to take you in my arms
I want to hold you in a loving wrestling hold
You, my dearest, are my finest gold;
with each other, we will learn to be brave and bold
When you are around, I am free and I am
allowed to be bold
With you, the years will easily pass
but in my mind, with you, I will never grow old
We will stand the test of time, our lives will be sublime
With each other, we are free to be to each other, kind
When I look at you, to the wrongs of the world I am blind
You, my love, are always foremost on my mind
If someone looks at you at all, I tend
to, the meaning, misconstrue

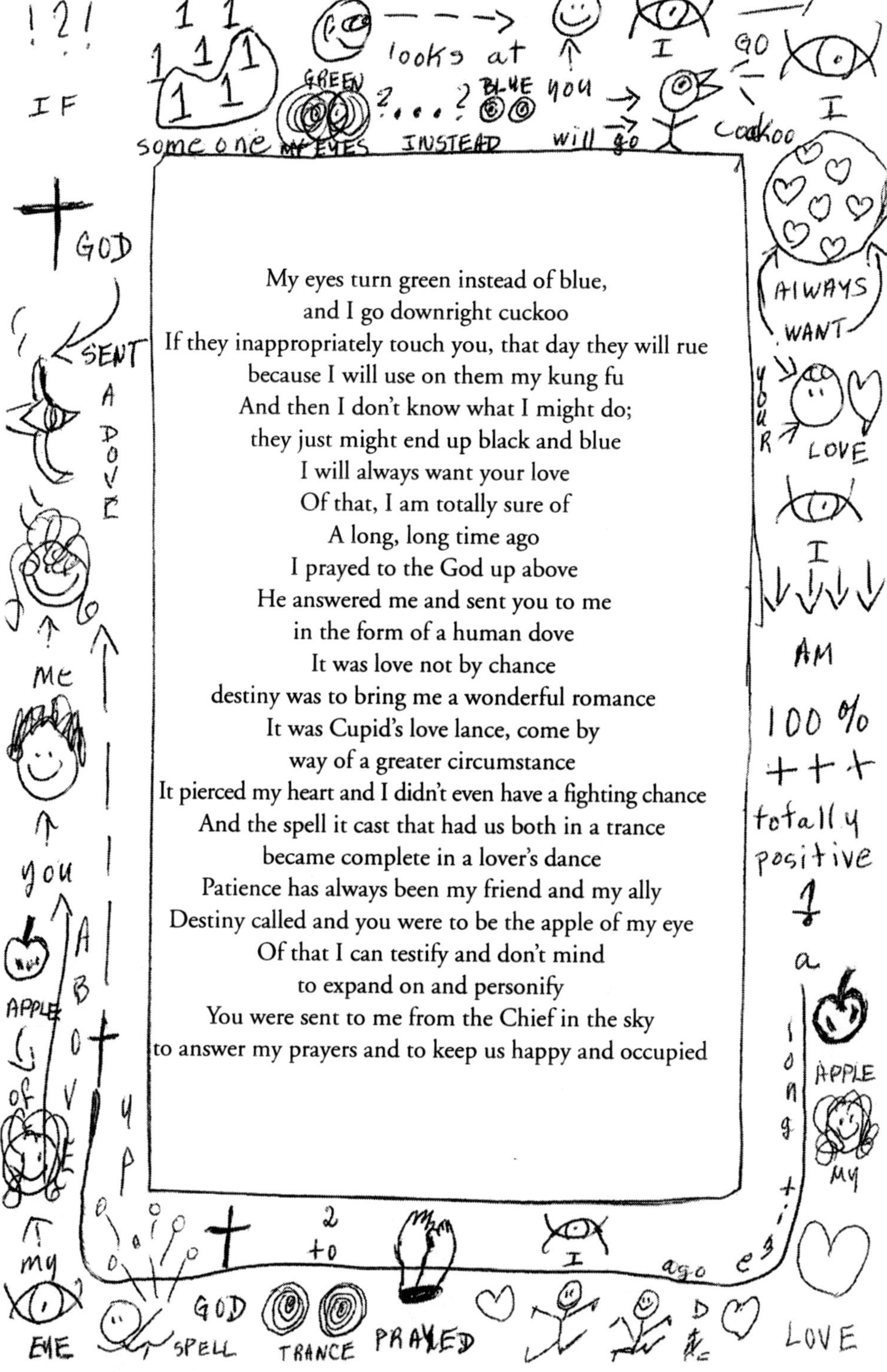

My eyes turn green instead of blue,
and I go downright cuckoo
If they inappropriately touch you, that day they will rue
because I will use on them my kung fu
And then I don't know what I might do;
they just might end up black and blue
I will always want your love
Of that, I am totally sure of
A long, long time ago
I prayed to the God up above
He answered me and sent you to me
in the form of a human dove
It was love not by chance
destiny was to bring me a wonderful romance
It was Cupid's love lance, come by
way of a greater circumstance
It pierced my heart and I didn't even have a fighting chance
And the spell it cast that had us both in a trance
became complete in a lover's dance
Patience has always been my friend and my ally
Destiny called and you were to be the apple of my eye
Of that I can testify and don't mind
to expand on and personify
You were sent to me from the Chief in the sky
to answer my prayers and to keep us happy and occupied

I HAVE A HOLE IN MY HEAD

In my head, I have a hole that has a very important role
When you look inside my head, it is like a nugget of gold
Inside my head, my mind, bends ideas into special molds
Ideas that like to grab a storm and take it into my brain's fold
I have a hole in my head, but don't think I am easily led
You would think this would put me on my deathbed
With all my brains scattered and falling out all over my bed
But instead, every kind of information
leads inside and stays there instead
Ideas enter the hole in my head and rush in like a tidal wave
Their signals and frequencies sink
in and are stored and saved
They fill inside every part of my brain's enclave
and are protected inside its cave
They shine so bright, I can't help but
focus on them in a daze

They toss and turn and form into organized thoughts
Like the letters in some languages that need dots
Sometimes they seem to make sense,
sometimes they do not
Depending on the language you use
they make sense or they may be just an afterthought
All I know is that my head is like a baited booby trap
And whatever comes inside gets covered and
neatly wrapped
Into one gigantic, complicated, well-formed bunch of facts
That stays in my head right there under my thinking cap

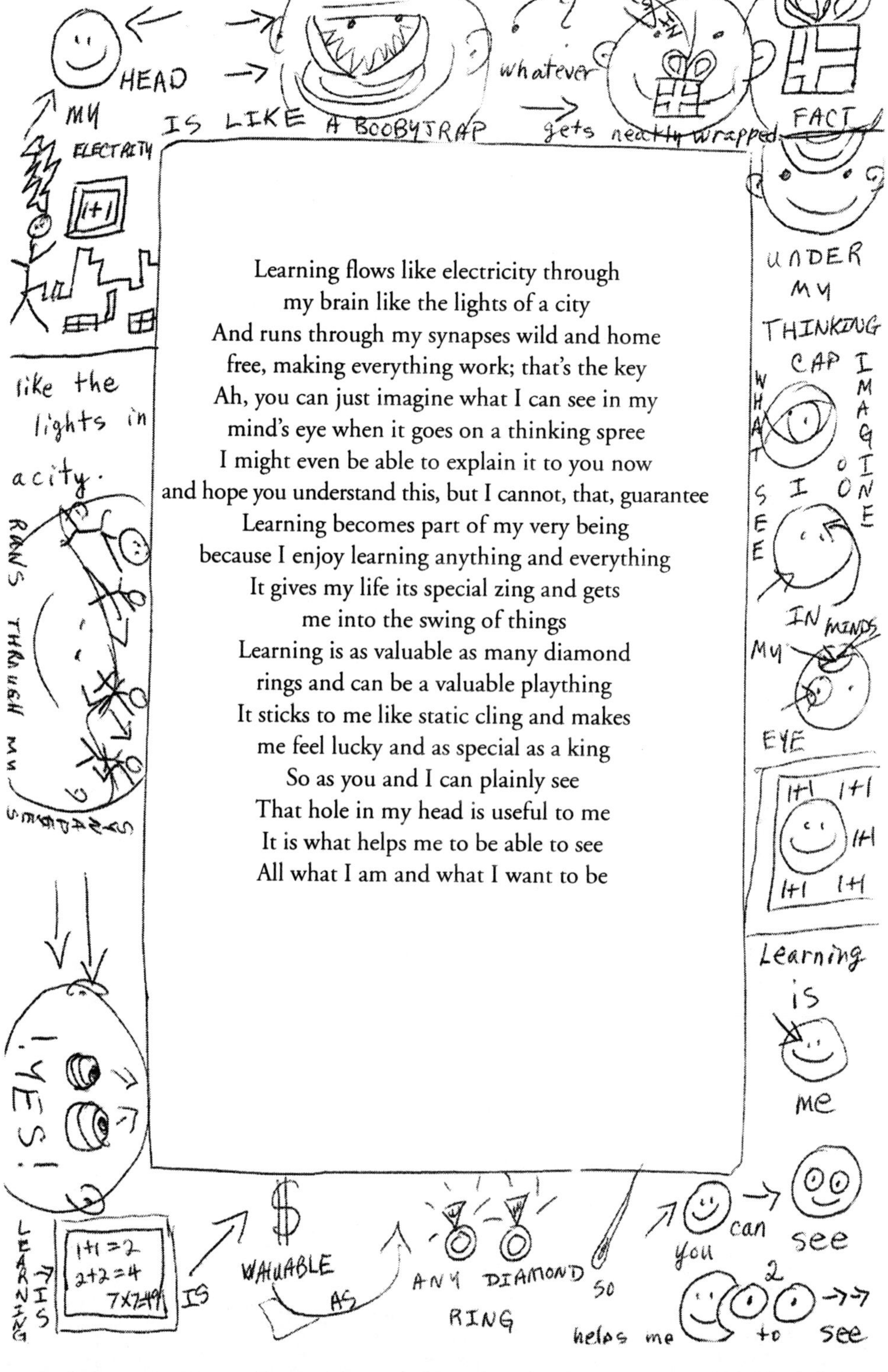

Learning flows like electricity through
my brain like the lights of a city
And runs through my synapses wild and home
free, making everything work; that's the key
Ah, you can just imagine what I can see in my
mind's eye when it goes on a thinking spree
I might even be able to explain it to you now
and hope you understand this, but I cannot, that, guarantee
Learning becomes part of my very being
because I enjoy learning anything and everything
It gives my life its special zing and gets
me into the swing of things
Learning is as valuable as many diamond
rings and can be a valuable plaything
It sticks to me like static cling and makes
me feel lucky and as special as a king
So as you and I can plainly see
That hole in my head is useful to me
It is what helps me to be able to see
All what I am and what I want to be

RIBBONS AND LACE

I can plainly see you have good taste
Because I can see you are wearing ribbons and lace
I can also see that you are innocent and chaste
And beauty like yours truly should not be disgraced
You are pure, bonnie lass
I can also see you have a lot of class
I first saw you in church, at mass
I knew I must meet you and fast
I was amazed at your inner beauty
I was in desperate need of your company
Your companies made me feel young and carefree
I was smitten by you, my delicate, sweet pea
When I came close to you, I was rewarded
Those eyes held no disguise, you were a purebred
Then when we came head to head
nothing more had to be said
It was mutual love unrequited
and it was full speed ahead
My legs felt like those ribbons in your hair
My stomach felt weak at your slightest stare
Of anyone else, I had not a single care
All I could see was you; I thought this was fair
I knew you were my chosen one; my
package was wrapped up and done

You were the one I had been looking
for the rest of my life's fun
I wanted you to always be with me, my honey bun
I prayed and prayed—please, please don't run
I went on bended knee and asked you, "Please be my wife,"
Give me the honor and please enter into my life
We will always be happy and always stay,
that way, we'll have no worries, no strife
Our love cannot be possibly anything but right
She wore ribbons and lace
And those eyes and that face
Oh, that hair, she also had good taste
And her personality was A-1, first rate

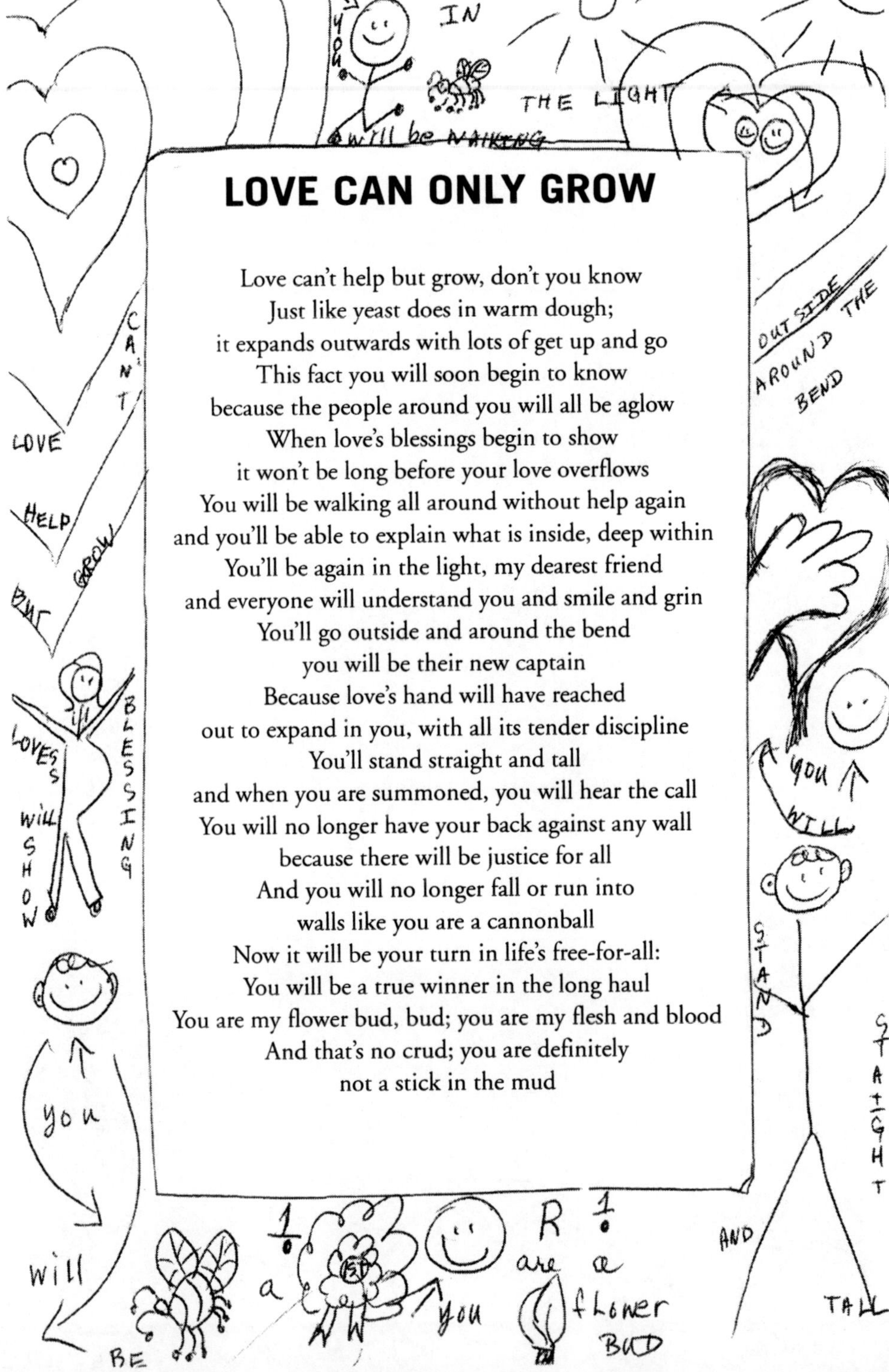

LOVE CAN ONLY GROW

Love can't help but grow, don't you know
Just like yeast does in warm dough;
it expands outwards with lots of get up and go
This fact you will soon begin to know
because the people around you will all be aglow
When love's blessings begin to show
it won't be long before your love overflows
You will be walking all around without help again
and you'll be able to explain what is inside, deep within
You'll be again in the light, my dearest friend
and everyone will understand you and smile and grin
You'll go outside and around the bend
you will be their new captain
Because love's hand will have reached
out to expand in you, with all its tender discipline
You'll stand straight and tall
and when you are summoned, you will hear the call
You will no longer have your back against any wall
because there will be justice for all
And you will no longer fall or run into
walls like you are a cannonball
Now it will be your turn in life's free-for-all:
You will be a true winner in the long haul
You are my flower bud, bud; you are my flesh and blood
And that's no crud; you are definitely
not a stick in the mud

By the way, your name is not mud; but
you did come in a flash flood
Nor is your name Elmer Fudd and
you are not a dud; you are a blue blood
I have found the only way I will find
any cure is to let changes occur
In who's looking back at me in that
mirror and then lay on the spurs
I am not seeing a blur, but sometimes I am not seeing
who's really there. I would like to though; I don't want to err
Something is definitely astir, and I'm
hoping for the best results to occur
We all have special magic that might
cure us when we are sick
Love is the main trick; it is welcome at any picnic
Love can be slow or love can be quick
you can even send it by pressing a click
Love can be very, very chic especially
for the lonely and the lovesick
Love's seed spreads, and it's widespread
for hard heads as well as eggheads
Transforming its plants until they are
ahead of all the purebreds
Sometimes love is blue, sometimes red,
but love always leaves you ahead
I can say I am not easily led, but easily fed, with love
and I do not want to see bloodshed

Love starts out small and then grows until it is very tall
First love learns how to crawl, then it
learns how to play hard ball
It follows no protocol when it takes
you for its loving free-for-all
And usually no one minds at all even
if it is, for them, a wake-up call

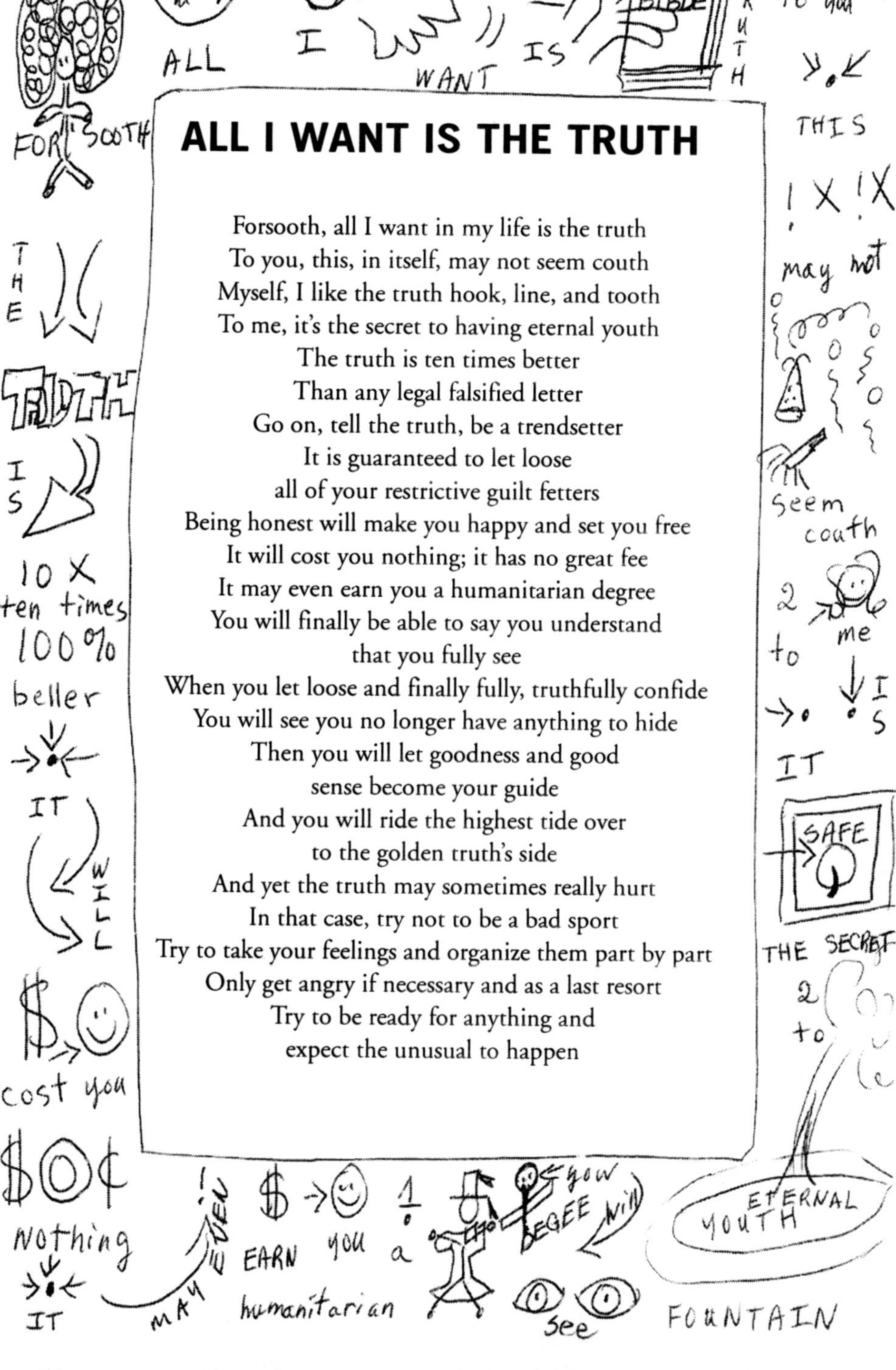

ALL I WANT IS THE TRUTH

Forsooth, all I want in my life is the truth
To you, this, in itself, may not seem couth
Myself, I like the truth hook, line, and tooth
To me, it's the secret to having eternal youth
The truth is ten times better
Than any legal falsified letter
Go on, tell the truth, be a trendsetter
It is guaranteed to let loose
all of your restrictive guilt fetters
Being honest will make you happy and set you free
It will cost you nothing; it has no great fee
It may even earn you a humanitarian degree
You will finally be able to say you understand
that you fully see
When you let loose and finally fully, truthfully confide
You will see you no longer have anything to hide
Then you will let goodness and good
sense become your guide
And you will ride the highest tide over
to the golden truth's side
And yet the truth may sometimes really hurt
In that case, try not to be a bad sport
Try to take your feelings and organize them part by part
Only get angry if necessary and as a last resort
Try to be ready for anything and
expect the unusual to happen

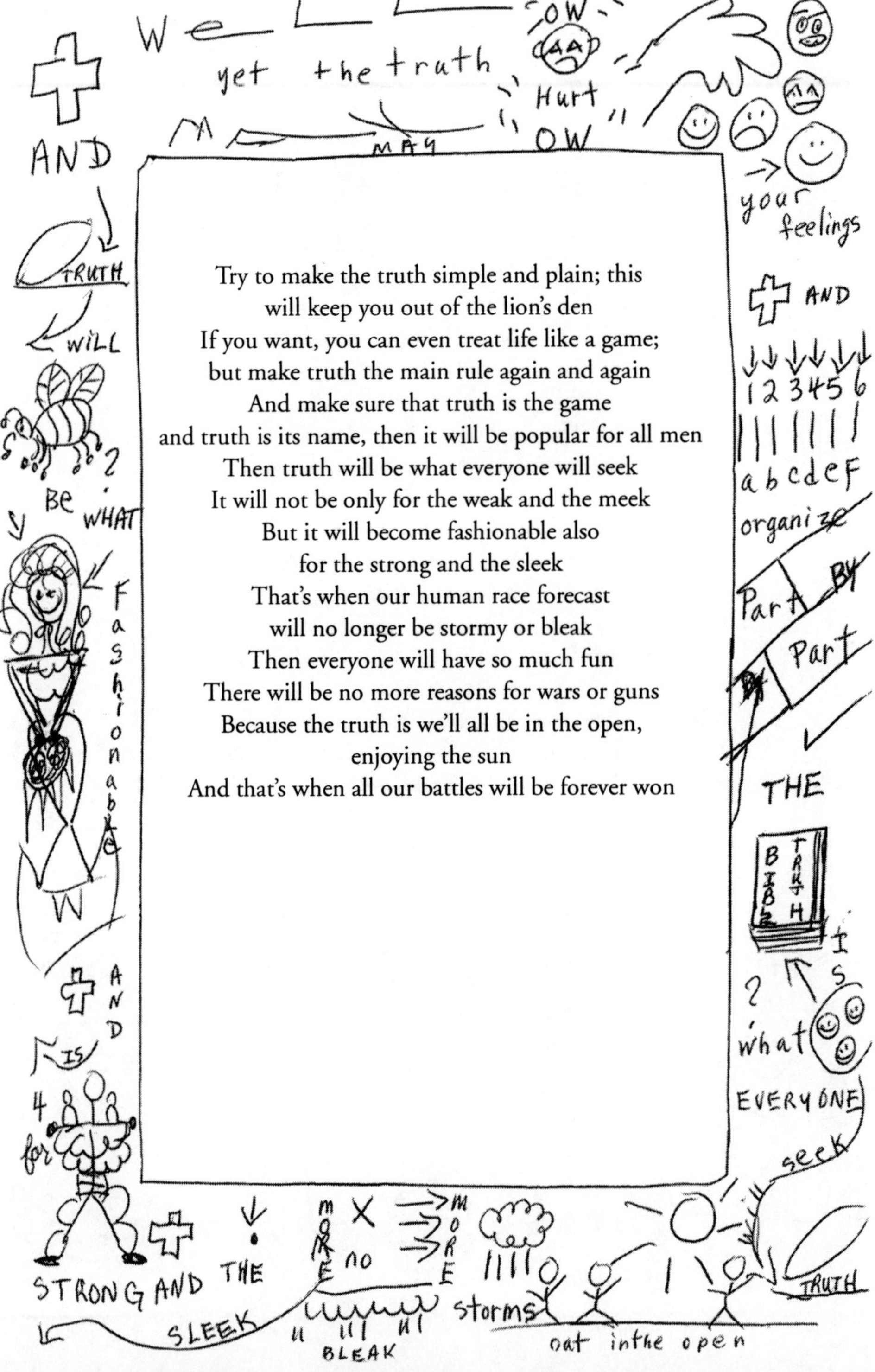

Try to make the truth simple and plain; this
will keep you out of the lion's den
If you want, you can even treat life like a game;
but make truth the main rule again and again
And make sure that truth is the game
and truth is its name, then it will be popular for all men
Then truth will be what everyone will seek
It will not be only for the weak and the meek
But it will become fashionable also
for the strong and the sleek
That's when our human race forecast
will no longer be stormy or bleak
Then everyone will have so much fun
There will be no more reasons for wars or guns
Because the truth is we'll all be in the open,
enjoying the sun
And that's when all our battles will be forever won

STEAMROLLER

My life has been lived like I was being
run over by a giant steamroller
My edges are all curled up from being
burnt all around and from all over
Once I was confined and trapped and
silently tried to scream and holler
But no one came to rescue me or cared or even bothered
All in all, I learned to accept and not to care or mind
Because basically, I am a forgiving and a practical kind
The hidden beauty in unfortunate situations, I try to find
Even extreme hardships can secretly turn out to be
for the best and be educational and kind
I have found that we must be all tested by fire
And we will be burnt up if we are liars
That's why, of truth, we must learn to never tire
That is, in order to be able to strive higher and higher
We must remember there is always a reason
For each and every change in our life's many seasons
Even if those reasons are not of our
choosing, or to our pleasing
We must try to live life fully before it
is time for us to be leaving
It has never been my choice, until now,
and I've always been held back
I was not able to use my voice and give my
opinion without being attacked

I've had to use all my hidden ploys
and to be patient until now, to show I didn't lack
I've had to be very careful, just to
survive life's constant noise
and protect my loved ones, and that is a fact
In effect, life has decided to try and roll me over
Yes, roll me over, like by a giant steamroller
Many times I've had to duck and run for cover
While the world around me tossed and churned me
and spread me out like butter
There have been many, many surprises for me in my life
Not all of them have been choice prizes;
many have cut me like a knife
And some have come in strange disguises
and have caused much strife
I have dealt with them all as they arise,
before and after I was a wife
I know that no matter what, we must
all continue to keep on rolling
No matter what life chooses on doling out for us:
good, bad, happy, sad, any situation
We must use our powers of doing well and work hard
then happiness is what all this will bring
Self-pity has no place and doesn't
help anyone a doggone thing

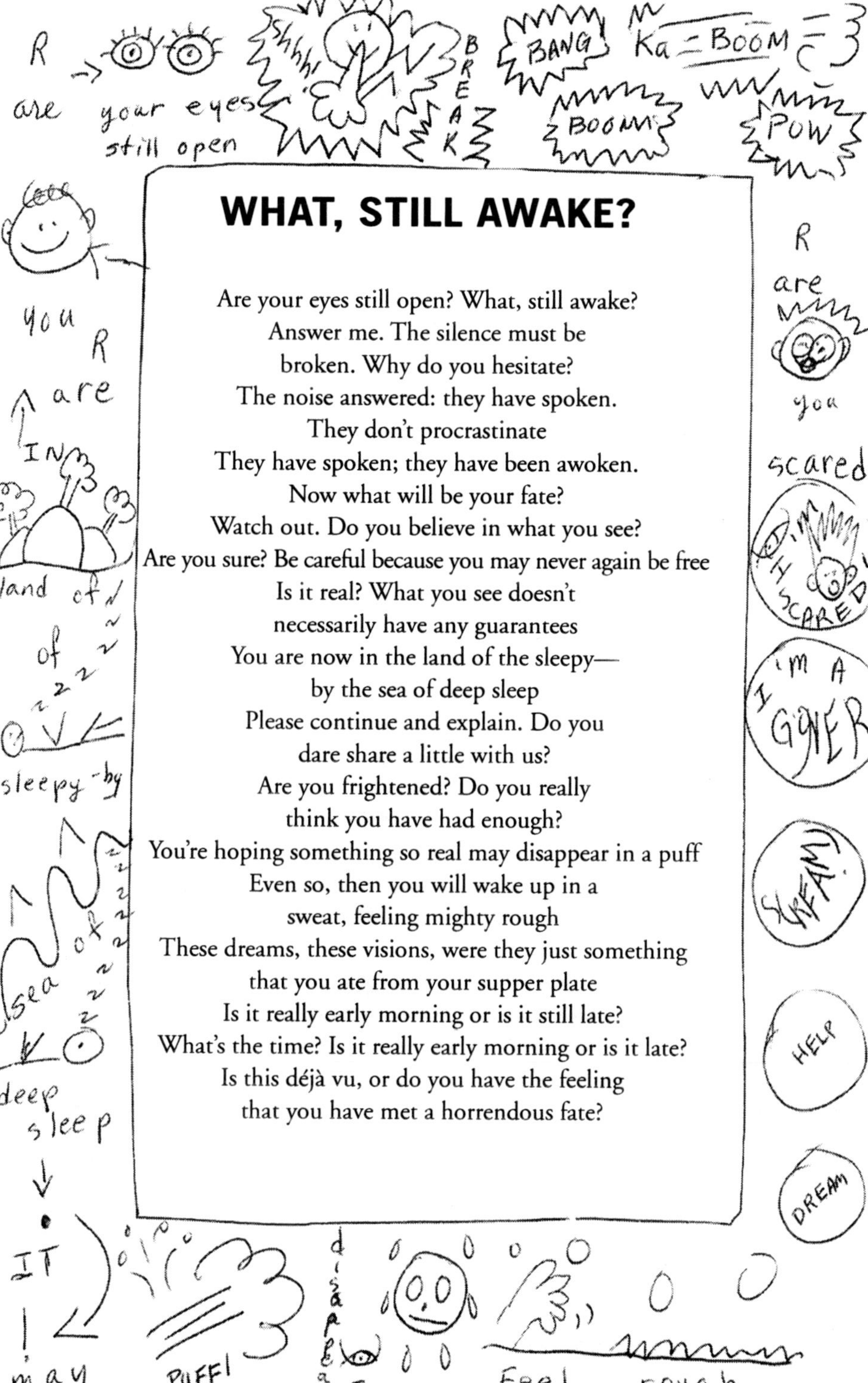

WHAT, STILL AWAKE?

Are your eyes still open? What, still awake?
Answer me. The silence must be
broken. Why do you hesitate?
The noise answered: they have spoken.
They don't procrastinate
They have spoken; they have been awoken.
Now what will be your fate?
Watch out. Do you believe in what you see?
Are you sure? Be careful because you may never again be free
Is it real? What you see doesn't
necessarily have any guarantees
You are now in the land of the sleepy—
by the sea of deep sleep
Please continue and explain. Do you
dare share a little with us?
Are you frightened? Do you really
think you have had enough?
You're hoping something so real may disappear in a puff
Even so, then you will wake up in a
sweat, feeling mighty rough
These dreams, these visions, were they just something
that you ate from your supper plate
Is it really early morning or is it still late?
What's the time? Is it really early morning or is it late?
Is this déjà vu, or do you have the feeling
that you have met a horrendous fate?

Wake up. You want to open your eyes, but what a shame
You find real life is just as bad as the dream
and is a nightmare just the same
Is it possible your limbs all refuse to work?
You have become lame
You can no longer speak. You think you are alive
but you wish that you were dead all the same
They say it won't be long before you're gone
They talk to each other
and all agree that you no longer belong
What if this is reality? You'll wonder
about reality before too long
Am I alive? What's that ghastly music
of that funeral song?
OK. That's it. You've had enough
Somehow everything seems strange.
You'll be the one to call their every bluff
Somehow, you feel tightness around your cuffs
Now you also feel your bedding is satin, luxurious stuff
You wonder how the impossible has happened
You can sense that you should look up.
You see your crying girlfriend
There are people standing all around,
looking down at me. Is this the end?
I'm watching in silence, but what my spirit
sees, my mind can't comprehend

THE LOVELY LADY THAT CLEANS

Oh, that lovely lady that cleans
She's never last by any means
There is more to her than there is to be seen
That's for sure, there is no if and or in between
Oh, how I've learned to love that lady
She is my favorite; she is always poised and ready
She's always helpful, heartfelt, and heady
She's always in my thoughts.
She is silent, but she is steady
Her beauty is genuine and real.
But most often, she gets a bum deal
She deserves to receive many a fancy meal
But instead, we get her for a steal
You can see her love comes from within
So much praise she deserves, I can't begin to begin
You shouldn't ignore her on a whim
And if you hurt her feelings, it would be a sin
I find her heart is bigger than a house
She even cleans after that pest, that mangy mouse
She has to deal with every kind of dirty louse
Not only the insect variety, but also the human host
Even with all this, she is usually ignored
And usually by the ones who cause the most discord
If only they knew how wise she was, they'd be floored
Still, she will be the one with the final word

She always manages to have something to do
Even though she shares her time with only a chosen few
Her ideas are basically always shiny and new
Her time is so precious, does that give you a clue
Oh, that lovely lady, you certainly don't lack
Your hair may be white, blonde, red, brunette, or black
But you always seem to have the special knack
And you always know how to bring the people back

THE MAN WHO LENDS A HAND

You have to understand why I feel so grand
There lives, in town, a man who likes to lend a hand
The work he will complete is at your and my command
He's the best in all the land
He needs no reprimand
This man is sometimes jovial and sweet
He is the one who you would like to meet
And shake hands with while walking down the street
You'll soon notice he's got two well-used feet
He can be the one to be your very best friend
He also has a family with which he has to fend
He's the one who knows how to put things on the mend
Look over there, he's coming from around the bend
He happens to take pride in his work
He has a good idea where evil lurks
And all its quirks
He knows how to handle any jerk
Even when they go berserk
He can easily wipe off any grimace or smirk
Sometimes he doesn't even wear a shirt—
Not because he is an extrovert
It is because it is hot where he has to work
We like him better when he chooses to exert
That is when we hit pay dirt
Saying hi to him won't even hurt
He usually is not an introvert

Sometimes, he works where it is cold
But he is still bold
Even though, everything he touches turns to gold
Sometimes he can be young or
sometimes he can be old
That's why I look up to him if I may be so bold
On him, I am sold
Without men like him, nothing would get done
For anyone
Then, how in the world would any of us have any fun
In the sun or on the run
Because most of our plans would be undone
They would lack the top gun
To us all, this definitely will make
him a big number one
A bull's eye—a hole in one
All in all, these are the quality gents
That is quite evident
When creation came and the curtains were rent
They went
Lo and behold, these men were sent
It was a blessed event
They didn't mind, in fact they were eager
You might say they were all heaven bent

I AM SPECIAL

I am an individual; I am special
I am made of my very own kind of mettle
I can even manage to boil a kettle
Sometimes it may take time
for me to calm down or to settle
What do you think makes me tick
Go ahead and try, take your pick
I get my jobs done lickety-split
And I seldom ail or get sick
You can subject me to very much
But you may have trouble to keep me in your clutch
Inside, way deep down, I am just a soft touch
And I try to avoid every vice or crutch
I have finally picked a friend, a sir
Now I'm finally having fun
and time passes by like I'm in a blur
Another of my friends is also the majestic fir
I'm convinced and I know that I will surely endure
I have loved; I have lived
Through the ashes, I have sieved
The main attraction I've perceived
Attention! Hello. I have also perceived
I feel fine now; I feel swell
On small differences, I no longer dwell
I feel like an ocean, I can quell
And that I am the lucky one, and I may
be able to ring the final bell
I think now you can just guess

I am no longer a mess
In the mess, I have found the bless
Yes, I have passed my own final test
I'll love life now and until I die
And then when I look at you straight in the eye
I'll try to be bright and spry
As I can be, and I will try to be sincere and not to lie
I won't bother with things that are bad
In this way, my armor will be ironclad
I will have no reason, or time, to be sad
Someday, there might even be a cure
for my youngest lad
The whole universe, I want to explore
And see what, for me, is in store
I want to see as much of what is left of my life before
It is finished, ended, ore
There's so much more in my life for me to see
And it's true; the best things in life are free
Come on over here, come on and meet me
I promise you, there isn't any fee
I myself would love to meet you
Wouldn't you love to meet me too?
Does this fact perhaps give you a clue?
If it does, maybe then you can take a cue
I'm A-OK, I now have hope
I'm free. I no longer have to mope
I am able. All my love can be wrote
Not in a bad way, here in this special note
I have offered and freely given my life

I have chosen and have endured much strife
My suffering was a two-edged knife
One side was bad and was good. It was all right
Some poor souls have no room to pity
They live there in the dark of the city
I'd rather choose to be happy and witty
It's better than being an itty-bitty
When I choose goodness, my battle will be won
Then I will know, now is the time to have fun
I then will have won and no longer will have to run
Better yet, I will have time to bask in the sun
And with a little help from all my friends
With all the happiness that they have to lend
My life will be happy, it no longer depends
On any situation that has a beginning or an end
Now I feel full of good humor
You can bet that's not just a rumor
My success couldn't have come any sooner
Even though, let's face it I'm a late bloomer
I'm sure I will have many more trials
But I'll be satisfied and happy in the meanwhile
No matter what comes along, I'll try to smile
I've heard nothing that comes easy is worthwhile
Well then my life has seldom come easy
My crowning achievement is my
children one, two, and three
And yes, right now, I'm still here and in my life I am free

UNTIL THE TIME COMES

Until the end time comes, our lives will be just trial runs
And if we are still here, we will be the lucky ones
So put down your weapons and your guns, one by one
And we all will be even happier—
Even more the fortunate ones
And when there is finally peace for all
We will no longer be headed for a great fall
our ears will be opened and we will hear the call
We will no longer have to put up brick walls
When we all decide to get along
together we will be strong
We will all sing the same harmonious songs
And we will all feel like we fit together and belong
Then everything will be right
and nothing will again be wrong
We are all made of the same strains
and come from the same veins
We can all learn to play a peaceful and universal game
For this game, we have no need to be trained or tamed
And there will be room enough for us all to reign
Meanwhile, we can, with the spirit of grace,
Get many benefits and all get a true taste
We can extend our friendly hands
to each other in haste
And we can learn to cherish,
love, and be chaste

Come on, let there be peace and no more hatred
Come on, go ahead,
and use those brains in your head
Aren't we all living in the same proverbial bed?
And saying that, I say full speed ahead, egghead
We'll all end up tolling the knell bell and bid a fond farewell
Either on our way to heaven or away
from it and onwards towards hell
We will be all by ourselves; that is how
it will happen in a nutshell
It will all be very familiar,
and we will know when we feel the final bombshell
If we want, we can all be full of love
And happiness and more of all the above
We can be excited like sunshine
and flying like turtledoves
Then we can peep through the clouds like the sun's rays
and show our brotherly love

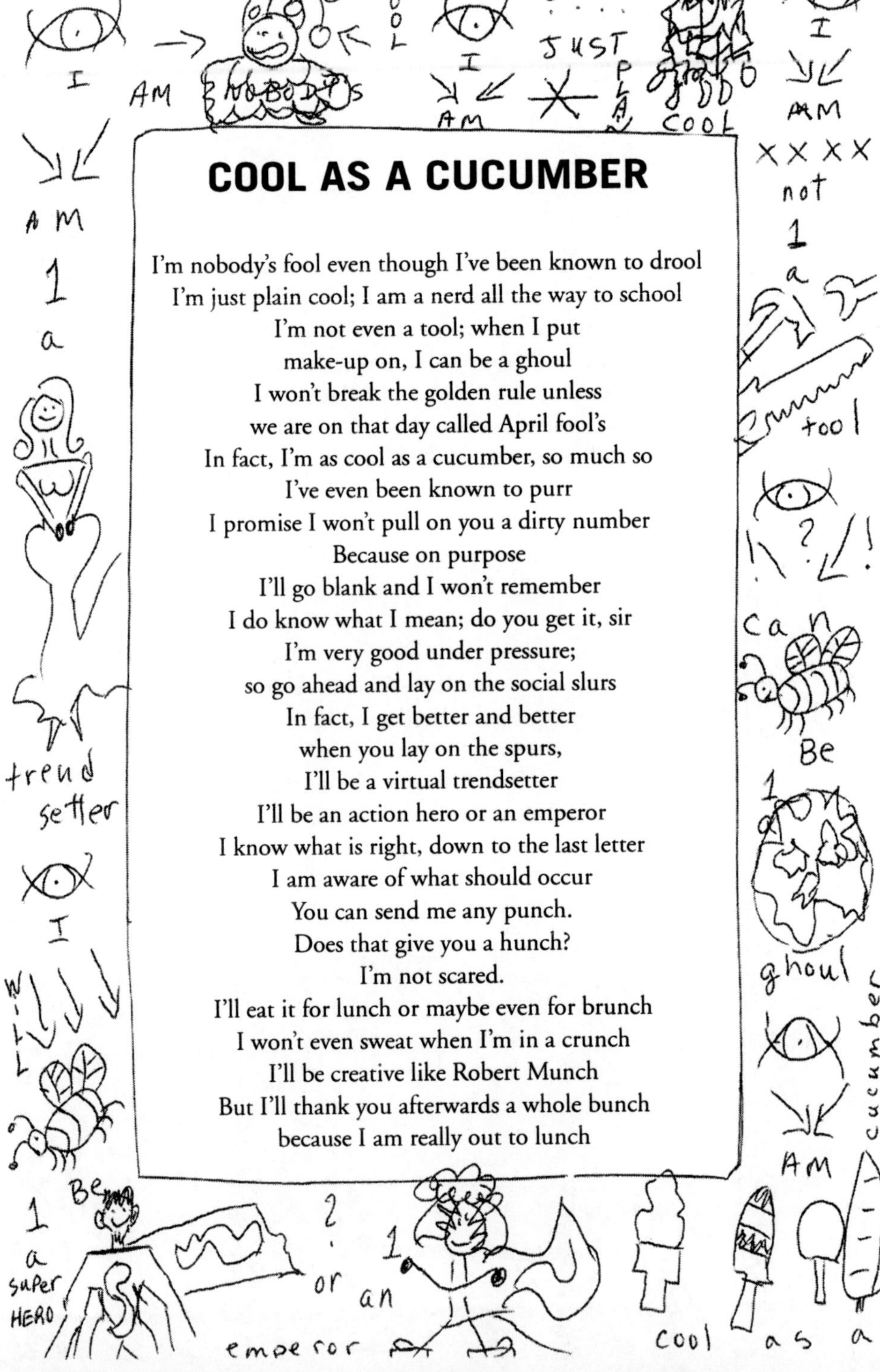

COOL AS A CUCUMBER

I'm nobody's fool even though I've been known to drool
I'm just plain cool; I am a nerd all the way to school
I'm not even a tool; when I put
make-up on, I can be a ghoul
I won't break the golden rule unless
we are on that day called April fool's
In fact, I'm as cool as a cucumber, so much so
I've even been known to purr
I promise I won't pull on you a dirty number
Because on purpose
I'll go blank and I won't remember
I do know what I mean; do you get it, sir
I'm very good under pressure;
so go ahead and lay on the social slurs
In fact, I get better and better
when you lay on the spurs,
I'll be a virtual trendsetter
I'll be an action hero or an emperor
I know what is right, down to the last letter
I am aware of what should occur
You can send me any punch.
Does that give you a hunch?
I'm not scared.
I'll eat it for lunch or maybe even for brunch
I won't even sweat when I'm in a crunch
I'll be creative like Robert Munch
But I'll thank you afterwards a whole bunch
because I am really out to lunch

You see, I cannot feel any pain
because I have chosen to abstain
Life is just one glorious game
let's break out a bottle of champagne
I won't be found to be lame
because secretly I'll have fortune and fame
I'll choose to play if I want, and if it's all the same
just take me out to the ball game
It doesn't matter if there's a lot of danger
I'll just bare my fangs, and we'll see what else occurs
And then I'll just lay on the spurs to my imaginary steed
until we take off in a blur
Then I'll just try to look at you
and continue to ride my steed faster and faster
I may be cool as a cucumber, but I
think I'm headed for disaster
Still, I'm no fruit, and one way or
another; I can be a real terror
I even try to be a good person when there is trouble astir
And my loved ones you had better not bother
because I can be one real mean mother
Ah, such is the good life and who can beat the nightlife
I try not to wince when I'm under the knife
because they might slip and I might lose my life
In fact, I try to enjoy what I can from my strife
and I try to be a happy housewife
I am just ordinary, not anyone larger
than life, but I can say this
I am not related to the wildlife

POSITIVE REACTION

Face it: be positive, and all will be well; no
one will be ringing your doorbell
Ignore the negative and accentuate the
positive, then everything will be swell
Soon people will want what you have
to sell and all will be well
They'll know you are good. Soon they will
be able to tell this
and it will be clear as a bell
You may imagine they mean you harm,
but one way or the other,
chances are no one will bother
You will have to accept no one really
wishes to hurt you or really matters
Even though you can't win them all,
sometimes you will get in hot water
Chances are you will be safe and glad
and one couldn't be happier
The more you put your good foot forward,
the more you will be self-assured
And the more power there will be to your word
until it is so good, it will be the password
That's when you will really be heard word for word
The truth is the best for this mama bird,
this songbird, this hummingbird
We are supposed to have a positive reaction like a brave lion
Even when I only get negative attention;
I'm as persistent as a spreading dandelion

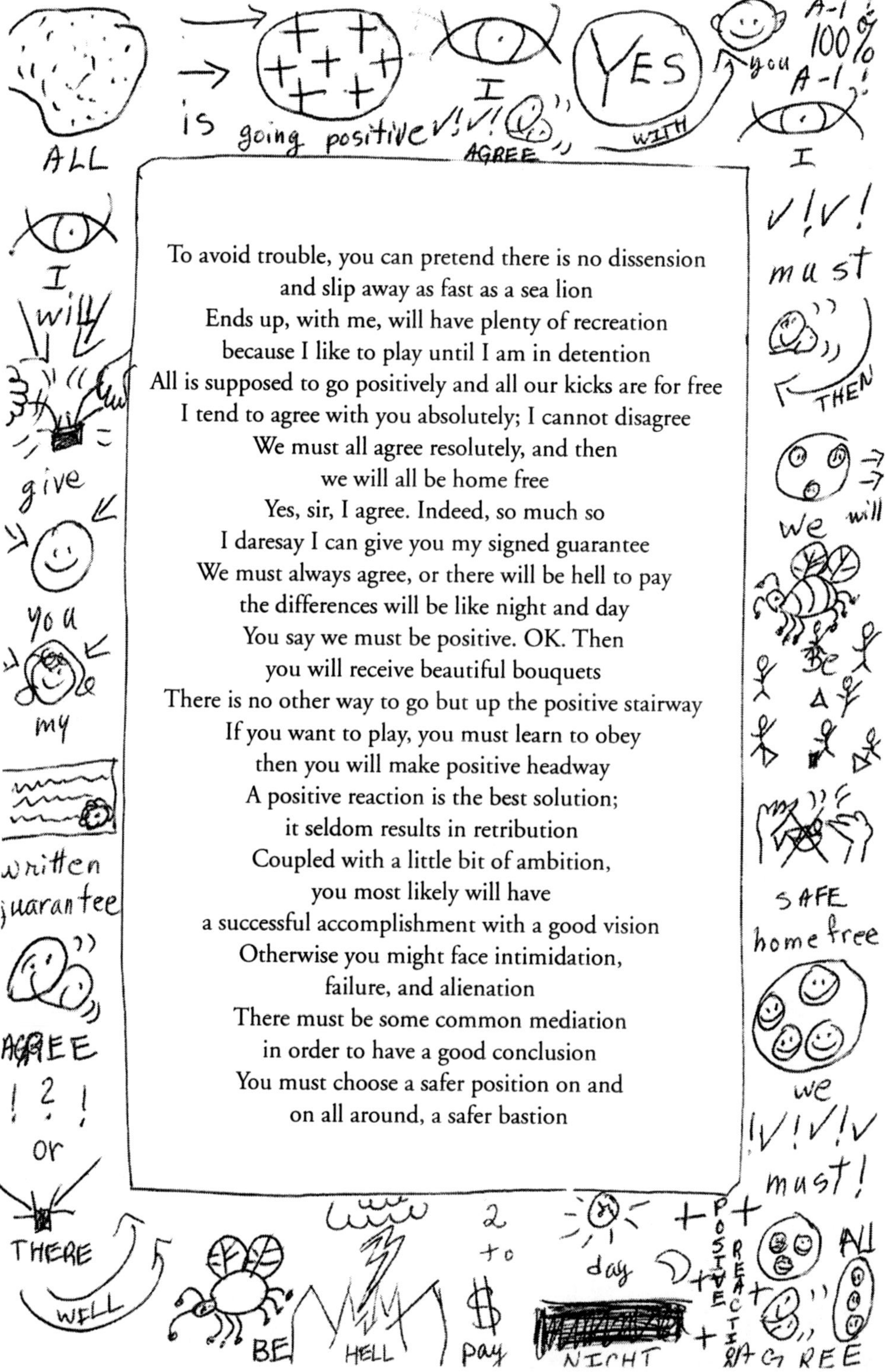

To avoid trouble, you can pretend there is no dissension
and slip away as fast as a sea lion
Ends up, with me, will have plenty of recreation
because I like to play until I am in detention
All is supposed to go positively and all our kicks are for free
I tend to agree with you absolutely; I cannot disagree
We must all agree resolutely, and then
we will all be home free
Yes, sir, I agree. Indeed, so much so
I daresay I can give you my signed guarantee
We must always agree, or there will be hell to pay
the differences will be like night and day
You say we must be positive. OK. Then
you will receive beautiful bouquets
There is no other way to go but up the positive stairway
If you want to play, you must learn to obey
then you will make positive headway
A positive reaction is the best solution;
it seldom results in retribution
Coupled with a little bit of ambition,
you most likely will have
a successful accomplishment with a good vision
Otherwise you might face intimidation,
failure, and alienation
There must be some common mediation
in order to have a good conclusion
You must choose a safer position on and
on all around, a safer bastion

You'd better choose a positive reaction
so that your ideas will come to fruition
Or it may be your last attraction and
you may end up in traction
Still it will be the best chosen plan
because it is based on a positive organization
When your attitude is positive, you won't
have to run because everyone
you will have won
It means you truly believe, hon. because
you are sincere you have won
It means there will be no smoking
gun or lingering repercussions
And I will not spoil anybody's fun
because we will all be playing together under the sun
I'll like this answer and so will you
Being positive will be nothing new
It doesn't have to be for just a chosen few
In fact, it has been tried and proven to be true
Being positive will prove to be fun and quite catchy
It'll leave you happy, carefree, and worry free
So come on, don't keep this idea under lock and key
Let yourself be positive for the whole world to see

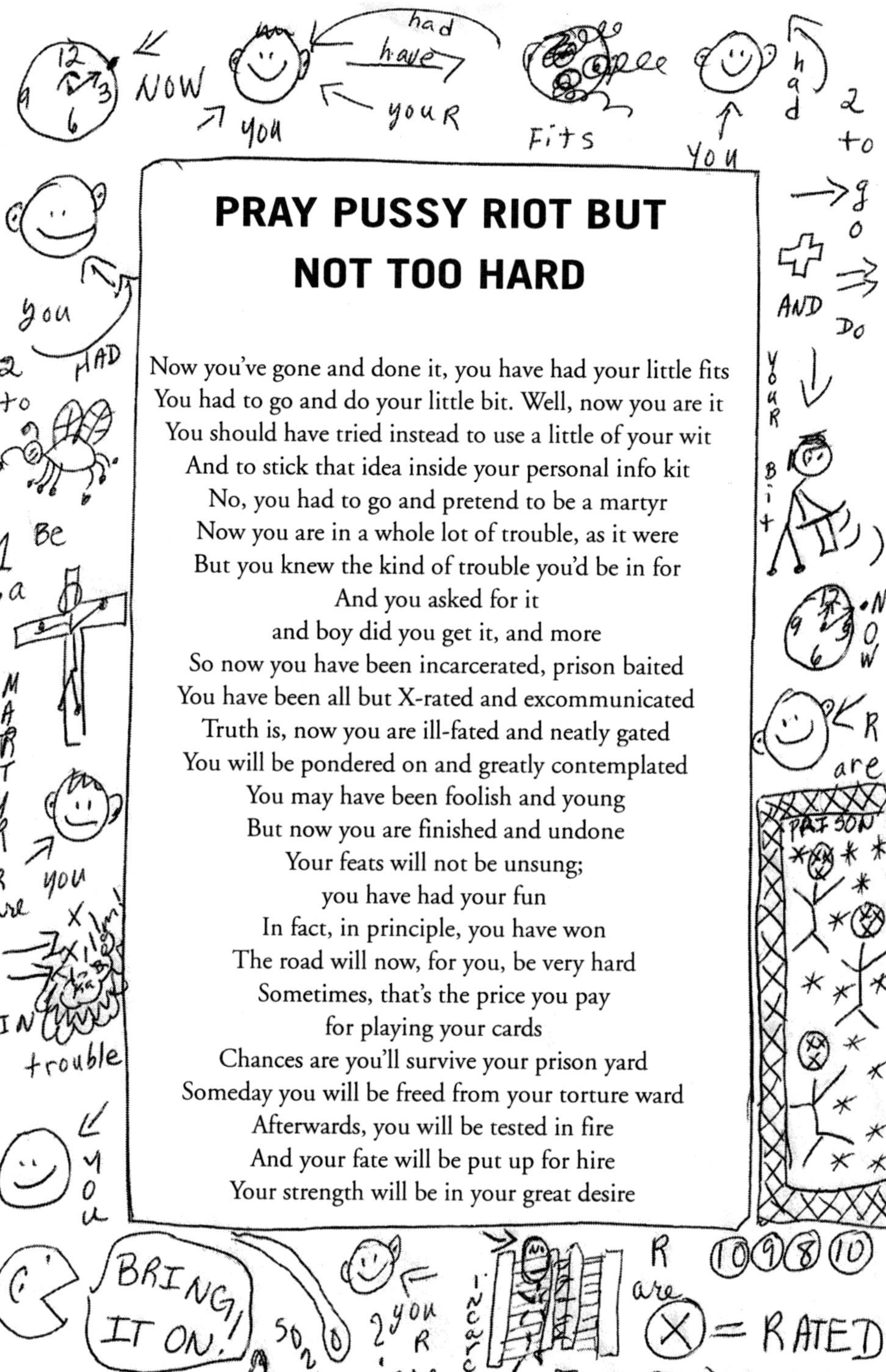

PRAY PUSSY RIOT BUT NOT TOO HARD

Now you've gone and done it, you have had your little fits
You had to go and do your little bit. Well, now you are it
You should have tried instead to use a little of your wit
And to stick that idea inside your personal info kit
No, you had to go and pretend to be a martyr
Now you are in a whole lot of trouble, as it were
But you knew the kind of trouble you'd be in for
And you asked for it
and boy did you get it, and more
So now you have been incarcerated, prison baited
You have been all but X-rated and excommunicated
Truth is, now you are ill-fated and neatly gated
You will be pondered on and greatly contemplated
You may have been foolish and young
But now you are finished and undone
Your feats will not be unsung;
you have had your fun
In fact, in principle, you have won
The road will now, for you, be very hard
Sometimes, that's the price you pay
for playing your cards
Chances are you'll survive your prison yard
Someday you will be freed from your torture ward
Afterwards, you will be tested in fire
And your fate will be put up for hire
Your strength will be in your great desire

To obtain your freedom
one thinks you would never tire
Some may understand the ideas behind your band
Some may not think your ideas were quite so grand
Even though you live in a far away land
Some may still choose to support you
and give you a helping hand
Some say you were very brave, but
maybe you were just foolish
Think whichever way you may want
to take it, as you wish
Because of your views, you have been dealt life's cruel dish
Now you must suck up the gruel and eat a piece of fish

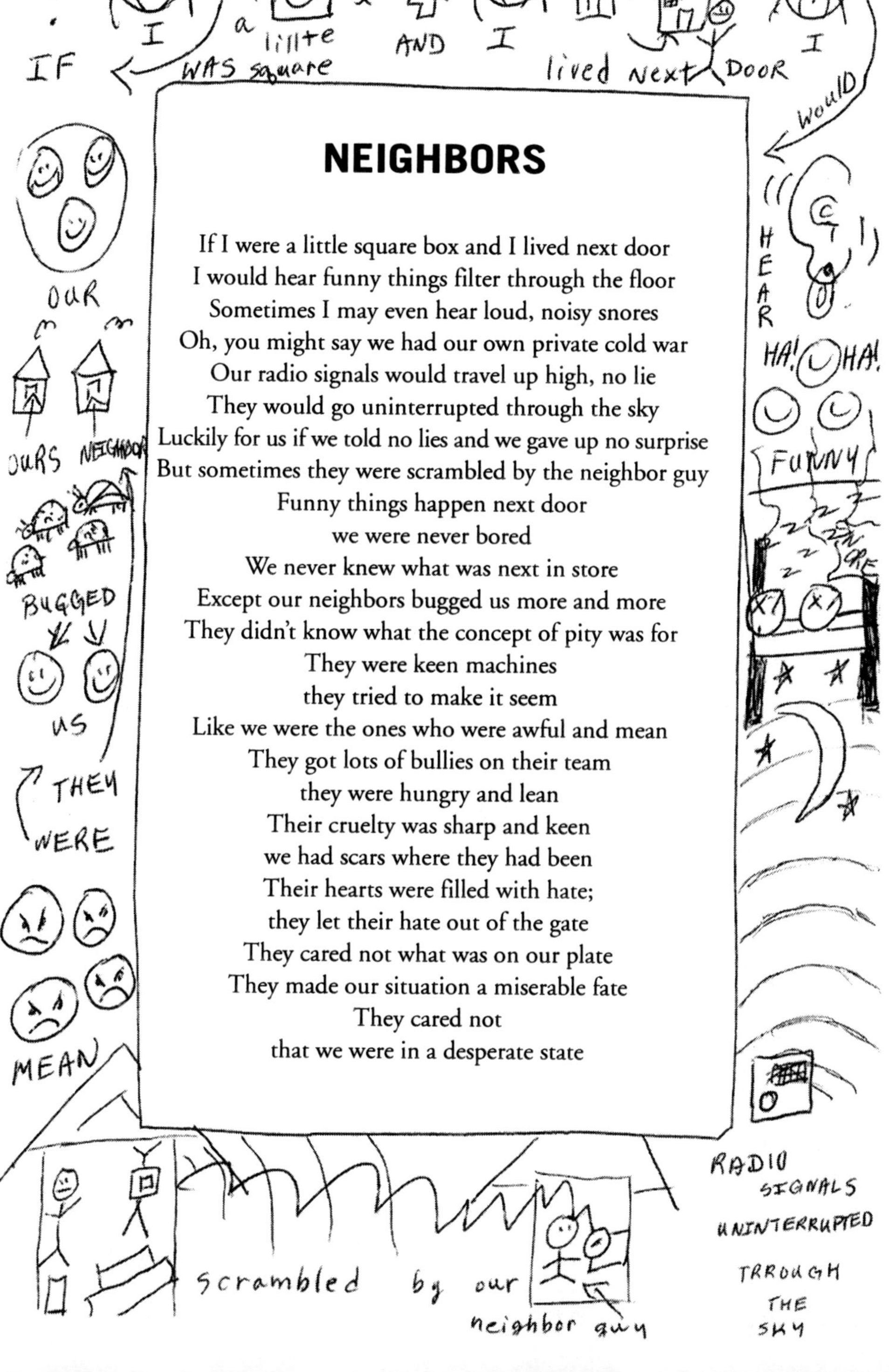

NEIGHBORS

If I were a little square box and I lived next door
I would hear funny things filter through the floor
Sometimes I may even hear loud, noisy snores
Oh, you might say we had our own private cold war
Our radio signals would travel up high, no lie
They would go uninterrupted through the sky
Luckily for us if we told no lies and we gave up no surprise
But sometimes they were scrambled by the neighbor guy
Funny things happen next door
we were never bored
We never knew what was next in store
Except our neighbors bugged us more and more
They didn't know what the concept of pity was for
They were keen machines
they tried to make it seem
Like we were the ones who were awful and mean
They got lots of bullies on their team
they were hungry and lean
Their cruelty was sharp and keen
we had scars where they had been
Their hearts were filled with hate;
they let their hate out of the gate
They cared not what was on our plate
They made our situation a miserable fate
They cared not
that we were in a desperate state

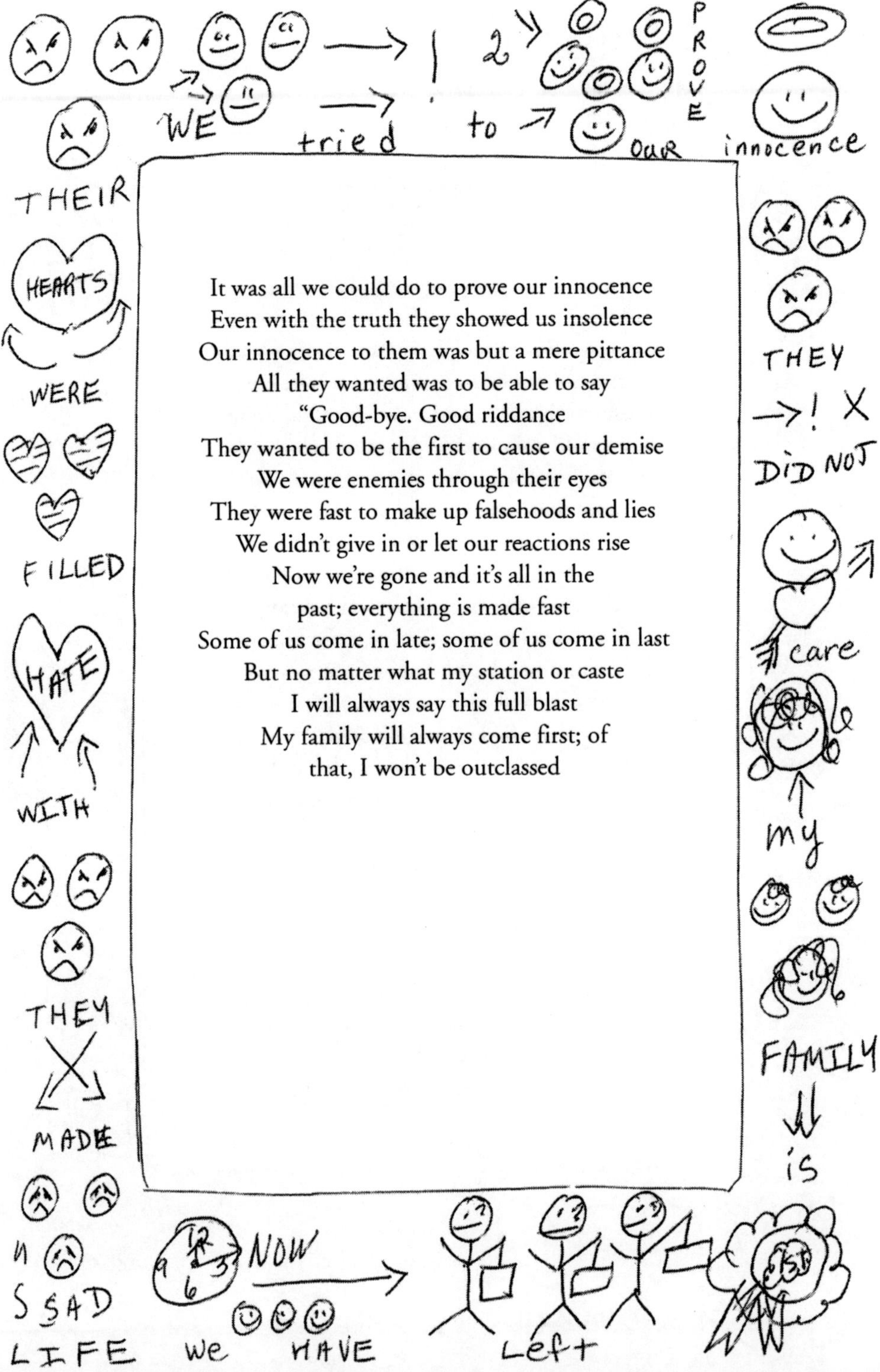

It was all we could do to prove our innocence
Even with the truth they showed us insolence
Our innocence to them was but a mere pittance
All they wanted was to be able to say
"Good-bye. Good riddance
They wanted to be the first to cause our demise
We were enemies through their eyes
They were fast to make up falsehoods and lies
We didn't give in or let our reactions rise
Now we're gone and it's all in the
past; everything is made fast
Some of us come in late; some of us come in last
But no matter what my station or caste
I will always say this full blast
My family will always come first; of
that, I won't be outclassed

WHO, YOU AND ME, YOU JEST

Hey you—you and me. You jest. That's not funny
You there, you Playboy bunny; keep your money
Your skies may not always be clear and sunny
Do you think you will always have a new honey?
Even though you travel near and far
And you have a very fancy, expensive car
That doesn't make you an automatic star
So you can get right back into your Jaguar
You have some really fancy-looking threads
And you seem to consider yourself a thoroughbred
Even though you appear to be cared for and spoon fed
This doesn't mean you are royalty or even legally wed
That thing on your head is not a crown
The fact it is called a tiara is well-known
I see you have a very large bill for your phone
I think your operation's cover may have been blown
To you, men are just suckers and easy prey
With your charm, they usually do what you say
You tempt them with various types of role-play
They give you what you want and do not refuse to pay
You work both in the day and during the night
You don't know the difference between wrong and right
You think all your alibis are foolproof and airtight
Truth is, what you are doing proves you aren't too bright

Sooner or later, you will slip up
And you will then be all washed up
You will have a different kind of dress up
When they put you into a police lineup
The thing that clinches it and puts you on the hook
Is that psychedelic phone number and address book
With names and numbers, it proves you to be a crook
You could now very easily go to a
farm named Sunny Brook

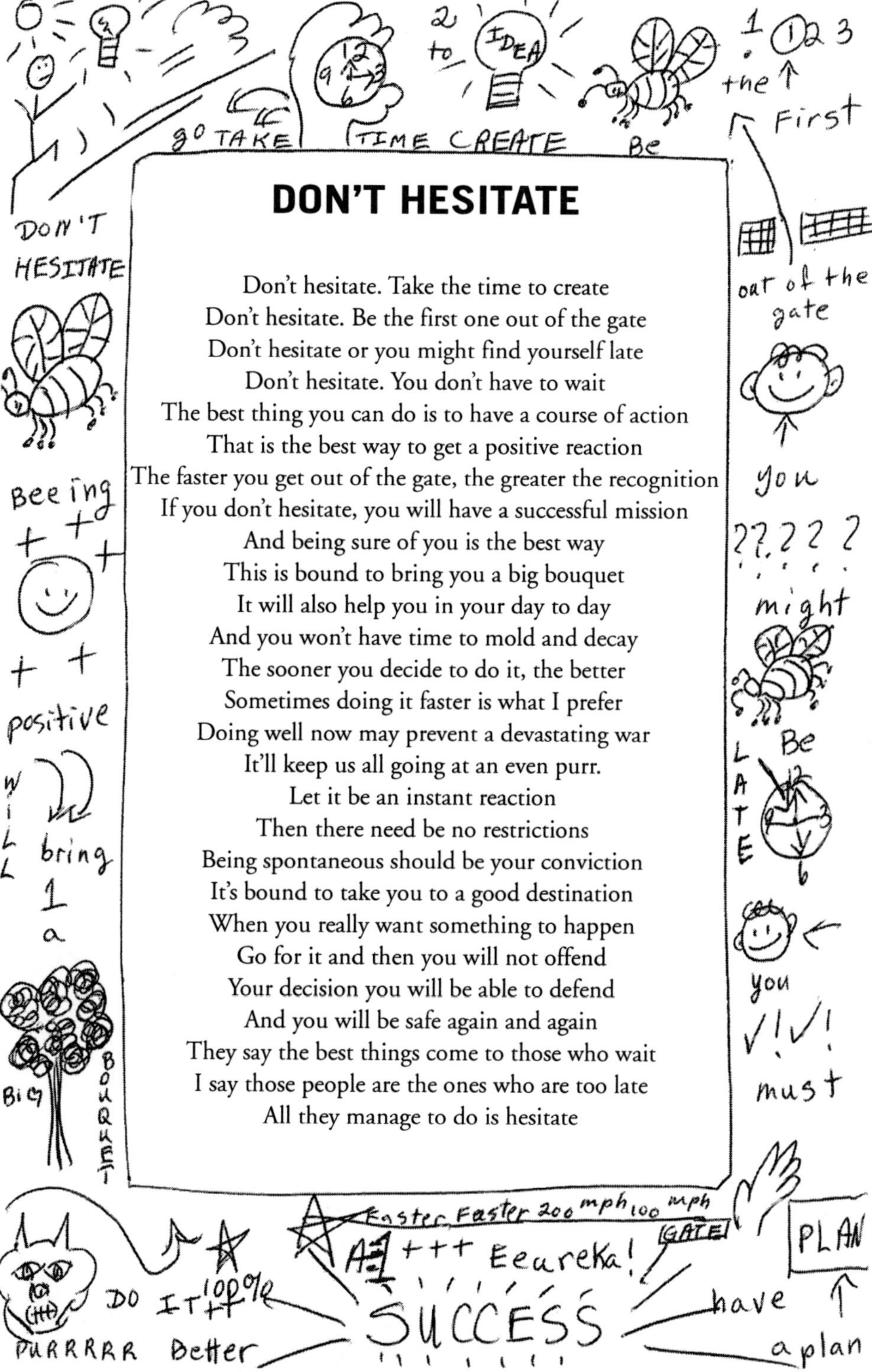

DON'T HESITATE

Don't hesitate. Take the time to create
Don't hesitate. Be the first one out of the gate
Don't hesitate or you might find yourself late
Don't hesitate. You don't have to wait
The best thing you can do is to have a course of action
That is the best way to get a positive reaction
The faster you get out of the gate, the greater the recognition
If you don't hesitate, you will have a successful mission
And being sure of you is the best way
This is bound to bring you a big bouquet
It will also help you in your day to day
And you won't have time to mold and decay
The sooner you decide to do it, the better
Sometimes doing it faster is what I prefer
Doing well now may prevent a devastating war
It'll keep us all going at an even purr.
Let it be an instant reaction
Then there need be no restrictions
Being spontaneous should be your conviction
It's bound to take you to a good destination
When you really want something to happen
Go for it and then you will not offend
Your decision you will be able to defend
And you will be safe again and again
They say the best things come to those who wait
I say those people are the ones who are too late
All they manage to do is hesitate

Waiting will always be their fate
Now when it comes to choosing your mate
Be a little choosy; don't settle for second rate
Then when you're sure, don't be left at the plate
Strike when the iron is hot. Don't hesitate
Never wait to show your love
Do you see that beautiful turtledove?
Love guides his wings to go all over, below and above
And he never wastes time to hesitate or to shove
Love doesn't wait. It's your fate
Come on, don't hesitate
Come on, jump out of the gate
Or you'll find out that you are the one who is late
You must first make up your mind
That is the most important rule line
That accomplishment you mustn't shirk or decline
You must continue on, rain or shine
If you choose the proper course of action
Instead of one of fear or self-denying
Your heart will then feel as strong as a lion
It may even prevent you from dying

I
WISH
I
Wish
?!
BUT
FARE
THEE
WELL
That
IS
THE
tale
IN
1
a
nutshell
Here
we
HAVE
the
waiting
well
GO AHEAD
MAKE A
WISH
on the
waiting
well
YOUR
Fondest
Dreams
CAN
Be
AS
TRUE
AS
BIBLE
STORY
TALE
These
ARE
falsehood
1
a
XX
XXX
not
AT
All
clientele

THE WAY IT IS

You and I will always wonder
If life is some kind of fantastic blunder
Or is it all just a hazy, lazy blur
Truth is, that's the way it is, sir
Is that drinking really yours?
Is that a fresh bottle of Coors
There is no need to open your doors
You reek as you speak, more and more
Big, bad daddy, me oh my
Is it true you are a very mean guy?
When you are drunk and all pie-eyed?
You say that is just the way it is, that's why
Truth is, no one cares anymore
If you stay, or if you walk out that door
Especially, when you have become
the world's number 1 boor
But I tell you, you'll never know
what's next for you or what's in store
Some may wonder
why your life occurs in this way or in that way
Sometimes life isn't fair, with no room to play
And pain is happening to us day after day
That's the way it is, that's all we can say
Well, now that we all know the score
We'll be able to continue to learn more
We'll be able to comprehend what's in store
That's just the way it is and that's what it's for

Life isn't just a lot of pain
Most times there is a lot to gain
The answer is clear and plain
Just try not to complain and
take the time to use your brain
We can help each other to draw the line
We can give each other a simple peace sign
The almighty dollar is really the danger sign
That's the way it is, come rain or shine

THAT'S JUST GREAT

I say that's just great
Still I must hesitate
Until I find out my fate
Until I have more of
my life on my plate
That's just great
is this going to be my fate
Right now, I have a splitting headache
I guess I will just have to wait
Until my head no longer pulsates
I've had a grand good time
I've lived a long, long time line
My life has been good. It has been fine
You could say
I have lived on cloud nine
I'll follow through and you'll see it too
You'll see all my thoughts
all brand spanking new
I'll give them as an offering to you
So that you will no longer feel blue
With a little help from my ideas, my friends
Your life and my life, will improve to no ends
Your enemies will go way around the bend
And they will not
be able to torture you again
That's just great; it's all for the best
That's just great; surely you don't jest

Come on now, give me a little rest
You know it will be all for the best
You might say peace and quiet is my quest
This gives time for my thoughts to process
And gives fear time to shrink and regress
it also gives problems time
to get back and to repress

That's just great, I'll sit and wait
I'll just sit down until I satiate
I'll just sit down until I feel great
I'll say it's been well worth
the hesitate

I SMELL SUCCESS

I smell success at its very best
Success is a well-played game of chess
Success is when life
has been put to the test
And the outcome is successful
and is a real bless
Success will ring a bell, do tell
Success will have a certain gel, hard sell
Everyone will begin to know it oh so well
Then success will have
a fragrant, sweet smell
Then the universe will seem to be a small place
And no matter where we are
we'll be able to see each other's face
The smell of it will take on a new meaning, a new taste
It will be the very best scenario, the very best case
Then there will be no expensive fee
There will be no cost, you see, it will be free
It will be the faith we all have in you and me
It will be the way it was and is supposed to be
Success is a sure bet
Success is easier yet
Than anything you might have met
What you see is what
you are going to love to get
Talk about being famous to all of us
Success will take you as far as Uranus
Success won't make you miss the bus

You can also get success from your new boss
Yes, success is a sticky wicket
but you can pick it
Success is a platinum-gold-engraved ticket
Success is better than a good game of cricket
Go ahead, take aim, and kick it
right through the thicket
Success is oh so sweet, something you'd like to meet
It comes fast; it comes cheek to cheek;
you'll be on the hot seat
Success is also intended for the mild and the meek
Success is coming soon, this very week
turn on the stove and put on the heat

FIFTY-FIVE OR SOMETHING

Where do I begin? Let's see, here's the spin
I have a large grin, but I may be a has been
I have fair skin, which I do not consider a sin
And I am a graduate of fifty-five or something
I kind of like being in my own boat
Even though I no longer fit my old coat
I know as long as I am alive
there is still hope
By the way, I am still as strong as an oak
I can still boogie like the best
I sometimes barely need any rest
Go ahead; get it off of your chest
Come on, I dare you; give me a test
I can sing too; I'll knock off the roof
You can say I'm quite social, never aloof
Sometimes I act like quite a goof
I like to shock you, and then I will go "poof"
You might say that I am so very wise
I've got being nice right down to a franchise
You might also say
that I own the clear, blue skies
Especially, that is, when I cross my eyes
I can give anyone a good fight
So you had better treat me right
And oh, did I tell you, I bite
Oh, now the truth comes into the light
So now you can lift up your little white hanky

And you can confirm you are long and lanky
Then I may or may not give you a spanking, we'll see
Because I would much rather practice
on you with my superior abilities
And when I die
I will have to stay still, me oh my
They'll find out for sure that I am not a guy
And I will no longer be able to resist or to defy
Of this I promise you; I tell you no lie

I JUST MADE MYSELF ANGRY

No, I didn't just go and take a Benny
I just went and made myself angry
No, it's not because of you, honey
And yes, it is not very funny
Take my advice, take it from me,
Hissy fit come cheap; they come for free
My dad used to take me over his knee
No matter what was my excuse
or what was my plea?
So I would run far, far away
And find a private place to play
Oh, those were quiet, happy days
Then I was satisfied
you might say
When I dared to come back
I usually could see where I lacked
I would be ready for the next attack
You might say I could
I had eyes behind my back
I became very, very efficient
Especially when I had a witness
You see I acted very innocent
Because I was quite sincere and
it worked like nobody's business
I was quite studious and very industrious
Even though my enemies were very hideous
No matter how they interfered and were curious
I always left them feeling quite dubious

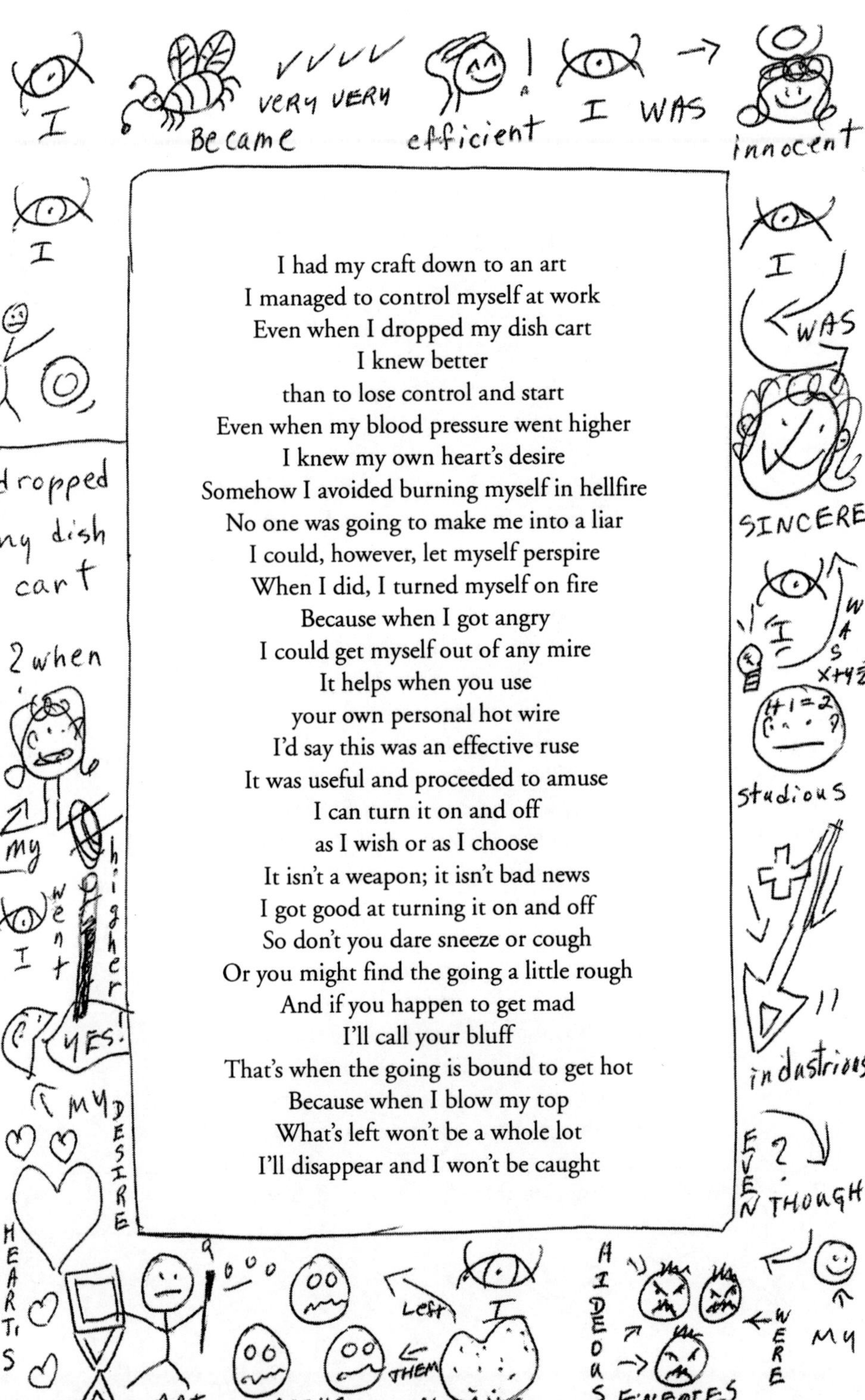

I had my craft down to an art
I managed to control myself at work
Even when I dropped my dish cart
I knew better
than to lose control and start
Even when my blood pressure went higher
I knew my own heart's desire
Somehow I avoided burning myself in hellfire
No one was going to make me into a liar
I could, however, let myself perspire
When I did, I turned myself on fire
Because when I got angry
I could get myself out of any mire
It helps when you use
your own personal hot wire
I'd say this was an effective ruse
It was useful and proceeded to amuse
I can turn it on and off
as I wish or as I choose
It isn't a weapon; it isn't bad news
I got good at turning it on and off
So don't you dare sneeze or cough
Or you might find the going a little rough
And if you happen to get mad
I'll call your bluff
That's when the going is bound to get hot
Because when I blow my top
What's left won't be a whole lot
I'll disappear and I won't be caught

I HAVE NO FEAR

I have no fear
But I do love you dear and
I do not feel queer
I am positive and find it quite clear
I always wanted you somewhere near
You are the reason for my every season
And the reason for my living, God willing
To me, many things you have given
You have given me love for my pleasing
All the melodies and music I hear
Is dedicated to you, my handsome dear
With you, I have no fear;
When I'm with you, I feel normal
and I love to have you near
I love you, you are my only man
Now I have fully come to understand
When I love you,
you give me a helping hand
You lift me up and make me feel grand
I know if the sky falls in the long haul
I will hear your voice call like a bird call
You make me feel a thousand feet tall
And I will not have a reason to fear at all
When I'm away from you
all the more I love you
It proves I can't help but love you anew
Men like you are precious, far and few

With you, I'm lucky, and I will never be blue
Someday when we are whole and complete
And we feel each other's heat
We will feel the greatest of all feats
We will feel each other's heartbeats
My heart will be free and soar
And a number 10, you will score
What's more and what's for
No one else will matter anymore
You, my dear, fill my whole cart
And that's only for a start
You have done more than your part
You have won a special place in my heart
With you we can only share
a rare precious love
You must have been sent from above
I can't help but want more and more of
Your love, dear, that fits like a glove
I know I have no responsibility in the role
Of my life, which has taken its own toll?
On my body and my mind's soul
But there is yet hope with its drum roll
When I prayed for you a long time ago
In the dead of night
I prayed for a knight to ride to me, a beau
I was not aware and little was I to know
That it would come and take fifty years or so

THE LAW OF THE LAND

We all know that Caesar had a hand
In the governing and law of his land
You and I and everyone have to understand
It was his due, his right to go and to so demand
Now the law of the land is there for you and for me
If we follow the laws, we will be protected and be free
Then we can all live together in peace
it will be OK, you'll see
Then no matter where you or I go
we will be able to share and agree
Our world can someday be a paradise
No one will want or even need a disguise
We will have no need for deception or lies
Everyone will be equal, every race
all the girls and all the guys
All we have to bring ourselves to do
Is embrace what is good and also what is new
Bad will have a special place too
Or Yin wouldn't have
Yang, and that day we would rue
If we all behave and follow the rules
We will no longer act or feel like fools
The linings to the clouds will all be gilded
Our future generations will all be happily fitted
And there will be freedom
for the downcast as well as the gifted

We will begin to fully understand
Who really has the upper hand?
And who is the real boss of all our lands
Then we will be closer to the Boss Man
It is not really a giant mystery
Who holds the good book and the golden key?
The mystery is more whether the key
opens the door for you and me
Just follow the rules; it costs not a penny.
There is no fee and you'll be freed

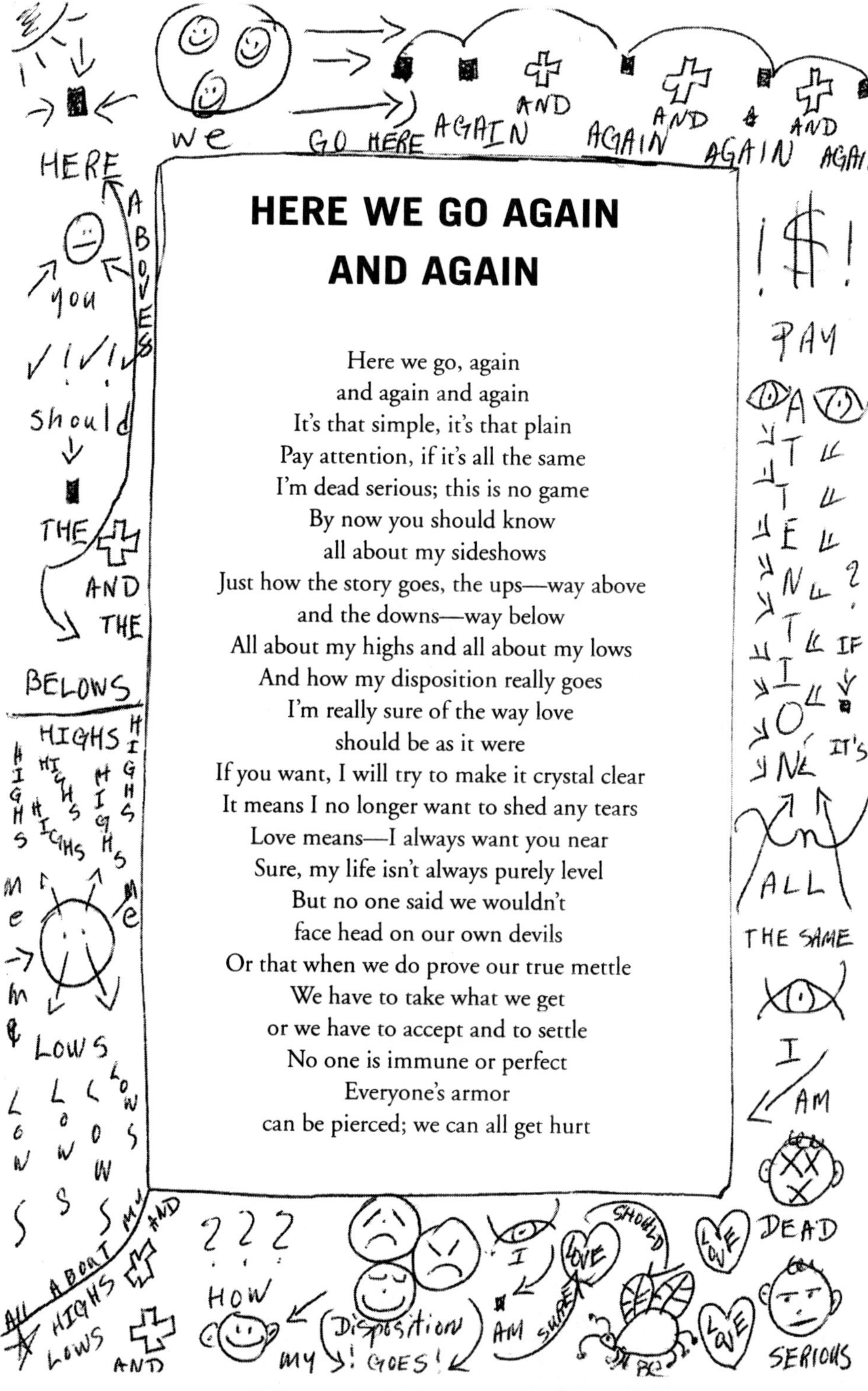

HERE WE GO AGAIN AND AGAIN

Here we go, again
and again and again
It's that simple, it's that plain
Pay attention, if it's all the same
I'm dead serious; this is no game
By now you should know
all about my sideshows
Just how the story goes, the ups—way above
and the downs—way below
All about my highs and all about my lows
And how my disposition really goes
I'm really sure of the way love
should be as it were
If you want, I will try to make it crystal clear
It means I no longer want to shed any tears
Love means—I always want you near
Sure, my life isn't always purely level
But no one said we wouldn't
face head on our own devils
Or that when we do prove our true mettle
We have to take what we get
or we have to accept and to settle
No one is immune or perfect
Everyone's armor
can be pierced; we can all get hurt

What is important is what is under our shirts
Right there inside, the heart, the love spurt
It depends on the way you go with the flow
It also depends on how you are in the know
And how you put an arrow in Cupid's bow
And how you let your love grow and grow
You will be able to give good advice
You can count once, twice, thrice
Some will say no way, no dice
Some will say once will suffice
The only way they have to discover
Their love that has been kept under cover
And their hearts full of love for one another
Is when Cupid joins one to the other?
You'll find when you're with me, love will be
My love will surround us, all my love you'll see
My heart has lots of room for us
for a nominal fee
Let love guide you and me, that's the key
Sometimes I'm up and sometimes I'm down
I know I'm really a challenge to be around
But you won't be sorry that I'm tightly wound
Truth is, you'll be happy;
you got me on the rebound

I will not disappoint you
and you won't, the day we met, rue
My moods may be something never new
But darling, I will give you a great, big clue
I can make life very, very interesting for you
We will have a happy, married life
And I will make you a very good wife
There will be way more good, then strife
We will be very close, very tight
and I will love you with all my might

THE BLUE-BOTTOMED SPECIAL

What's on today's menu, what is the new breakthrough?
What is it that is made to order—delicious, tasty, and new?
Is it a hot bowl of tasty Irish stew or plain old gruel goo
Or maybe, it is a zesty, well-planned, outside barbecue?
I find that, on the menu, there is quite a variety
And the cooks are professionals, far from lazy
It is a sin how they make cooking looks so easy
They do not sweat it; they are light and breezy
What is that elusive mystery item, what is that taste?
Could it be a rare mushroom stem I overlooked in haste?
Whatever it is, it must be a real gem
mixed in with the paste
Whatever it is, it is new to us and to them,
delicate and chaste
It was made for a special someone
Who is discerning and very well-known?
And someone who likes food that is home-grown
This person is celebrating an important milestone
This unpopular someone is still bucking public opinion
And cared not of the place's dubious distinction
And because this someone
had a bad case of double vision
It led to his rash and split second decision
And so his decision led
to the blue-bottomed special
It was given in a secret-voted trial

And he was sent a
blue-bottomed fly with some guile
Right from a rat-infested food pile
This poor man never suspected
The pepper on his dish
wasn't carefully selected
But was rather something
left over and rejected
A blue-bottomed fly
torn and dissected
The story has a moral and
here's the short and the tall
Use better judgment and protocol
If you can't see, get someone else
to use their eyeballs
Or you will be the one in for a downfall

AN EYE FOR AN EYE

In some places the golden rule is "an eye for an eye"
In those places all you can hear is "gung ho and banzai"
Watch out though, if you are the practicing FBI, guy
Watch your back, or you might end up getting crucified
Watch out for you dentures or for your teeth, forsooth
Right now, you might think
you have each and every tooth
But remember the rule "An eye for an eye,
a tooth for a tooth"
Pulling your teeth might be someone's
glorious moment of truth
What? Is that a cavity? Chop, chop
Please sir, a little less off the top
I'm afraid I have not much of a crop
Chop off my hair, if you must, but leave my head
that's where you must please stop
I think you all are still living in the Dark Ages
You are still living in your land of
chaos and petty rages
And your behavior is just plain
unacceptable and outrageous
You would do well to control
your ridiculous rampages
This kind of behavior is supposed to be ancient history
Am I just mistaken or is it just you or could it be just me
I have earned a college degree and a PhD, you see

I still can't understand this ridiculous
useless killing spree
Haven't we, as a human race, learned anything?
Don't we yet understand; it won't accomplish a thing
By fighting and returning hate with hate;
we will all see what that brings
And it won't be good
why there is all this senseless killing
All these people want and live and breathe is war
They scurry here, they scurry there, both near and far
Sometimes they blow themselves up
along with an occasional car
It all seems too wrong, just so bizarre;
and we thought that we were all superstars
Couldn't you, for one minute, enjoy
peace and your fighting cease?
Then you could enjoy smelling the
roses and shooting the breeze
You would certainly have quite less of a need for referees
And you could laugh with each other
and hug each other and gently squeeze

MIRROR IMAGE

Yes, the mirror image, itself is life
Yes, I am a satisfied, happy housewife
Yes, I also like to enjoy living the nightlife
And yes, I am also a larger version of life
When I look into a mirror at a reflection of me
I don't really like what is there
and what I have to see
I see all my faults and to a tee
and there they are as plain as can be
Then I feel humility to the nth degree
and all I wish to do is flee
My eyes seem to have deadly X-rays
All I want to do is turn and look away
I don't even dare to plead or to pray
What could I possibly ask for or
have to say
My eyes burn into my very soul
That's when I feel like a very ugly troll
I then feel I could qualify as a ghoul
Because I see my flesh
all old and rotten as a rule
Just what happened to me; I don't know
Life has dealt me some very deathly blows
Even though I am and may be a dynamo
I will certainly never win any fashion shows

At one time, my form
was shapely and was woe
Now I look more like a large, happy hippo
My ex even called me a cud-chewing cow
I don't care; I accept who I am and what I am now
If it is any consolation to me, I can almost guarantee
No one really likes their mirror image, you see
The trick is being satisfied, accepting it, and letting it be
Smile when you look at your mirror image
and you will unlock its key
Try to see all your goodness
And also stay humble overall
Because self-love can also lead to a fall
After all, when you gaze into a mirror
we can only stand so tall

MY DEAREST MARY

My dearest, beautiful Mary
You have helped Din Din to see
You are a powerful queen bee
You have a powerful pedigree
You are so very thoughtful and kind
I want for you peace of mind
You are so very wise
it boggles any mastermind
I pray for better health for you to find
I must pray for you in the right way
To the Lord, God in Spirit, for a bouquet
To his Mary, for she needs help, these days
I wish for a bouquet
of health for her nowadays
I love you Mary, so be worry-free
Someone loves you: He. One, two, three
Give your life to Him and you'll see
He listens to each
and every one of your pleas
He'll fix all your problems; so you can say "Amen"
He'll fix all of them right now and he'll fix them then
He'll fix them again and again and again and again
With faith, we can all hang ten even in the lion's den
So my dearest Mary, in this world there are no guarantees
It may seem very scary, but you will soon be able to see
That if you give your life to Him,
you'll soon agree with me

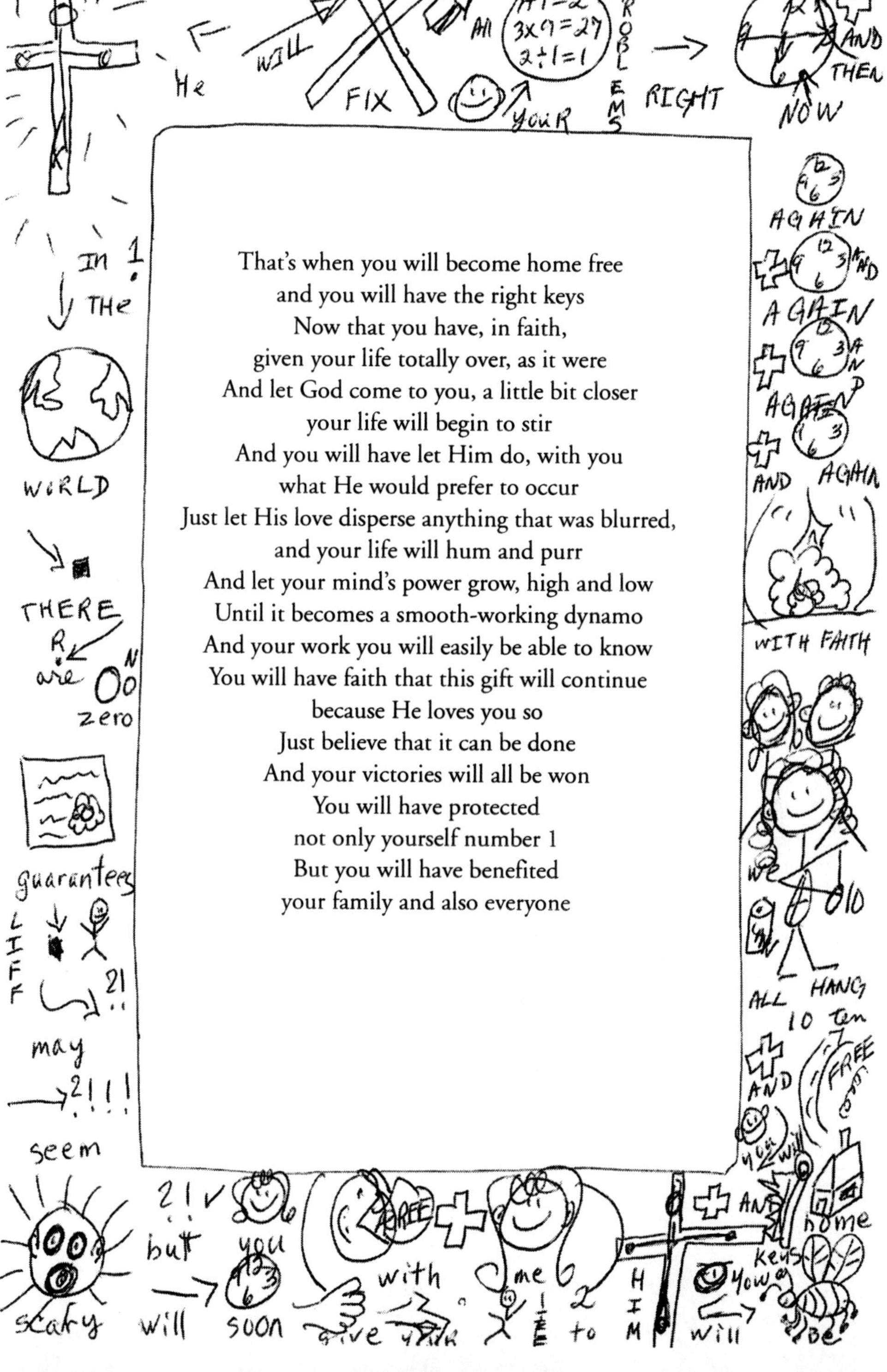

That's when you will become home free
and you will have the right keys
Now that you have, in faith,
given your life totally over, as it were
And let God come to you, a little bit closer
your life will begin to stir
And you will have let Him do, with you
what He would prefer to occur
Just let His love disperse anything that was blurred,
and your life will hum and purr
And let your mind's power grow, high and low
Until it becomes a smooth-working dynamo
And your work you will easily be able to know
You will have faith that this gift will continue
because He loves you so
Just believe that it can be done
And your victories will all be won
You will have protected
not only yourself number 1
But you will have benefited
your family and also everyone

A NEW ROLE

I have decided I have a new role
I won't be left out in the cold
I must make sure to expand my soul
I must rock and roll
I must have even more control of it,
on the whole and be bold
I must have and use my aces in the hole
I must cajole and extol
I must always try to remember
To try to behave with the utmost demur
I must acknowledge and forgive every slur
And learn to react correctly and to concur
That's when I will be able to gather and change
My life accordingly and to be able to rearrange
All my faults and successfully move and arrange
All my virtues and be able to share them
And to exchange
Along with my newfound abilities
I must say, please
And also comes with it a great responsibility
I'm lucky to live in the Land of the Free
Still, I should be polite and say pardon me
I want and need to be a good example
I must be careful not to act like a numbskull
I must try to fill my brain chock-full
Of pearls of wisdom and be peaceful like Sitting Bull

I must always be in control of myself and chill
I must deflect every insult and swallow every pill
This way, by example, respect
I will instill
Trust for you and me in my neighbor
and overall goodwill
In a way, I must be a goodwill ambassador
And try to teach friendship and be a mentor
I must be a humanitarian more and more
And try to increase
and improve my overall health
I must and will try to always act proper
So that the cycle of goodness will prosper
And my example will be felt all over
And so this world will be a good place
for all whether it is for him or for her

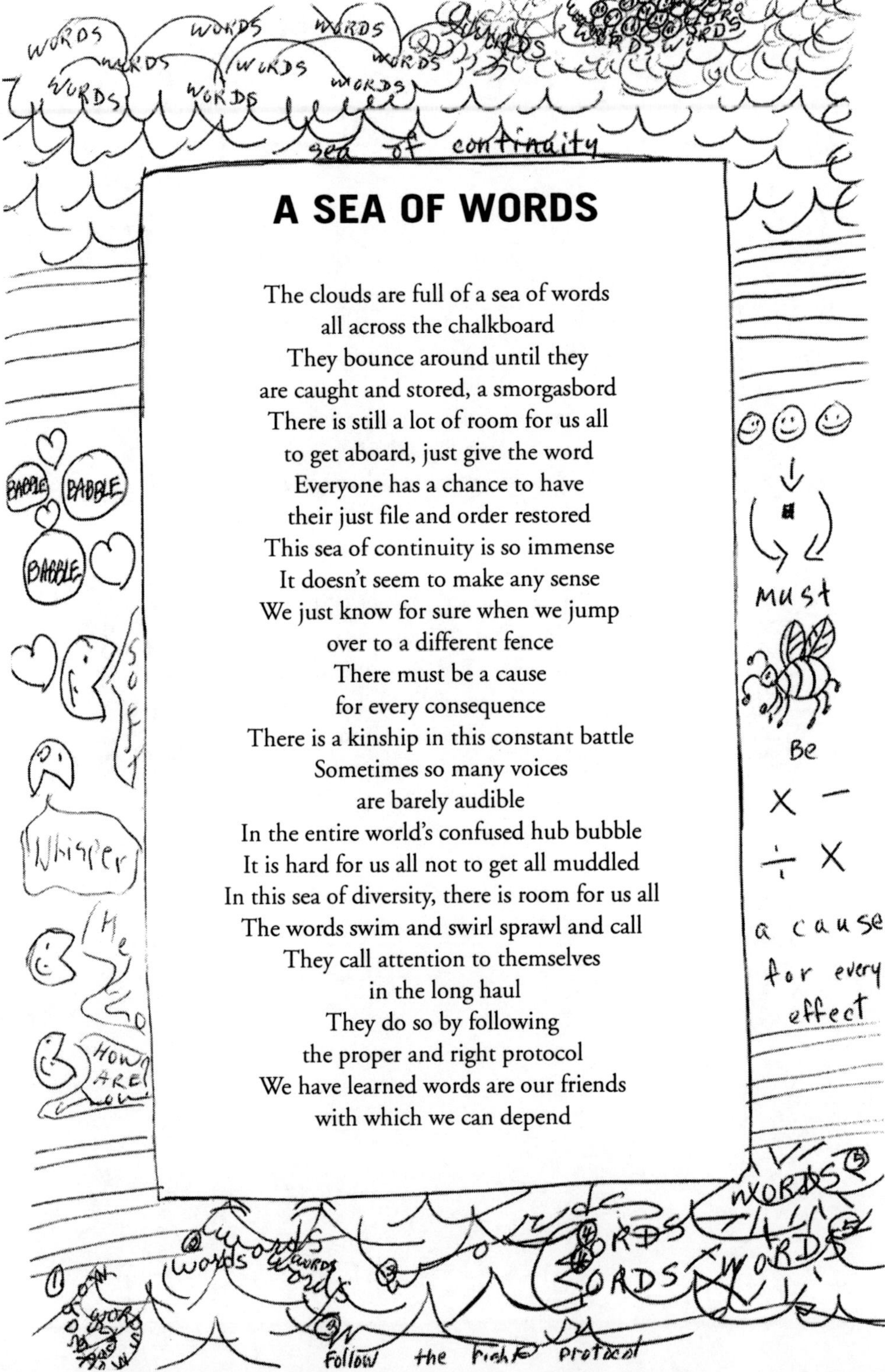

A SEA OF WORDS

The clouds are full of a sea of words
all across the chalkboard
They bounce around until they
are caught and stored, a smorgasbord
There is still a lot of room for us all
to get aboard, just give the word
Everyone has a chance to have
their just file and order restored
This sea of continuity is so immense
It doesn't seem to make any sense
We just know for sure when we jump
over to a different fence
There must be a cause
for every consequence
There is a kinship in this constant battle
Sometimes so many voices
are barely audible
In the entire world's confused hub bubble
It is hard for us all not to get all muddled
In this sea of diversity, there is room for us all
The words swim and swirl sprawl and call
They call attention to themselves
in the long haul
They do so by following
the proper and right protocol
We have learned words are our friends
with which we can depend

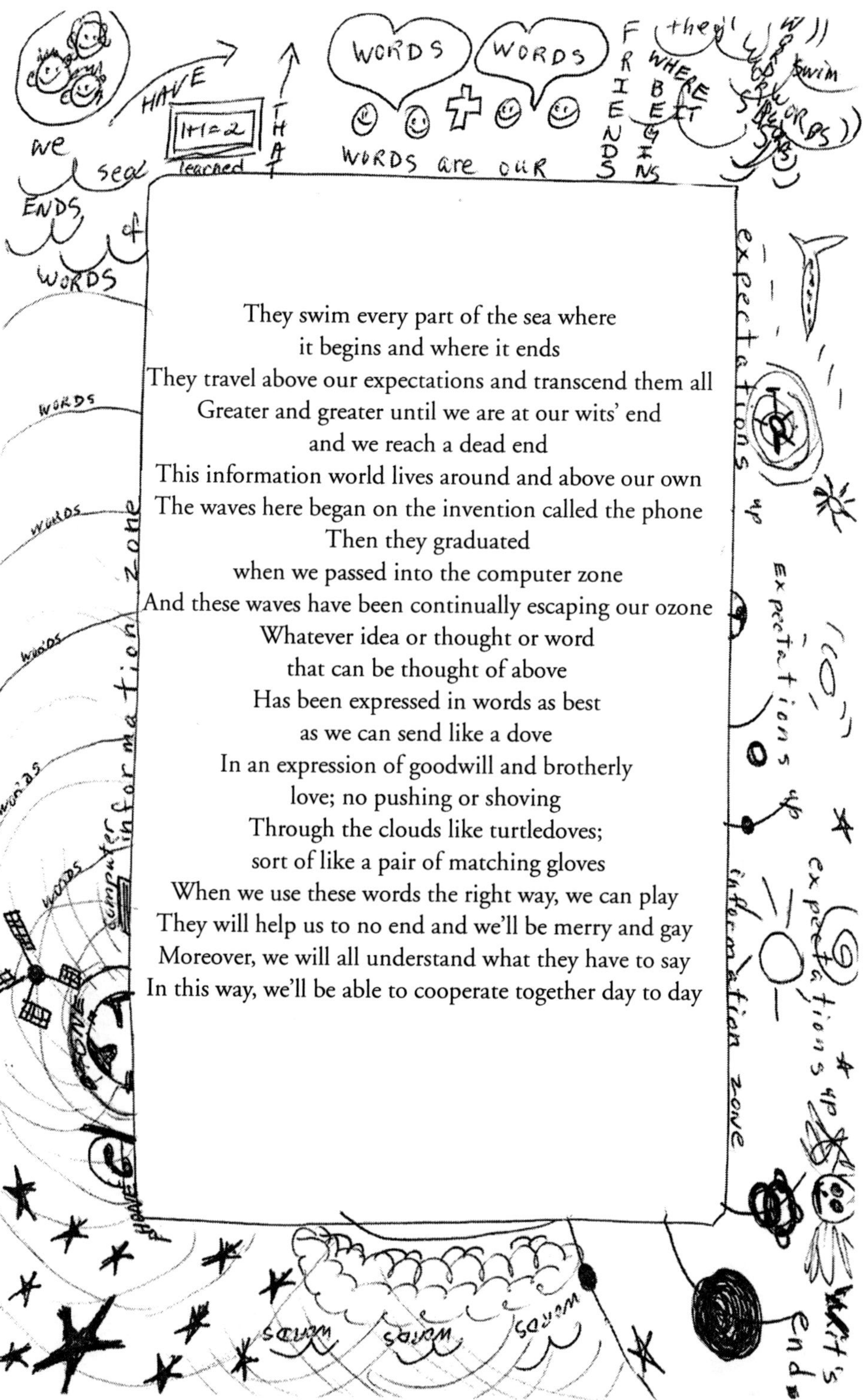

They swim every part of the sea where
it begins and where it ends
They travel above our expectations and transcend them all
Greater and greater until we are at our wits' end
and we reach a dead end
This information world lives around and above our own
The waves here began on the invention called the phone
Then they graduated
when we passed into the computer zone
And these waves have been continually escaping our ozone
Whatever idea or thought or word
that can be thought of above
Has been expressed in words as best
as we can send like a dove
In an expression of goodwill and brotherly
love; no pushing or shoving
Through the clouds like turtledoves;
sort of like a pair of matching gloves
When we use these words the right way, we can play
They will help us to no end and we'll be merry and gay
Moreover, we will all understand what they have to say
In this way, we'll be able to cooperate together day to day

BE CAREFUL

Be careful, that's no bull; its old school
Watch out, or you might get an earful
You'll want to push, but you'll have to pull
You might even have to pretend to be dull
Be careful; keep your mouth shut
Or people might think you are a nut
They might pick you up
and kick you in the butt
It's a plain and simple case
open and shut
Be careful; don't you move, I might disapprove
Or you might break the golden rule, you mule
If you did that, it wouldn't be very cool as a rule
You would be the one ending up being the fool

Be careful to mind your own business
There is no real need to impress
or go to excess
If you don't try, no one will think any less
And if you ignore them
they won't care, more or less
Be careful; try to be politically correct and direct
It is always good to have the utmost respect
People will always be pleased with this prospect
And it will give the right cause and the right effect
Watch out, be careful; do not lie or falsify

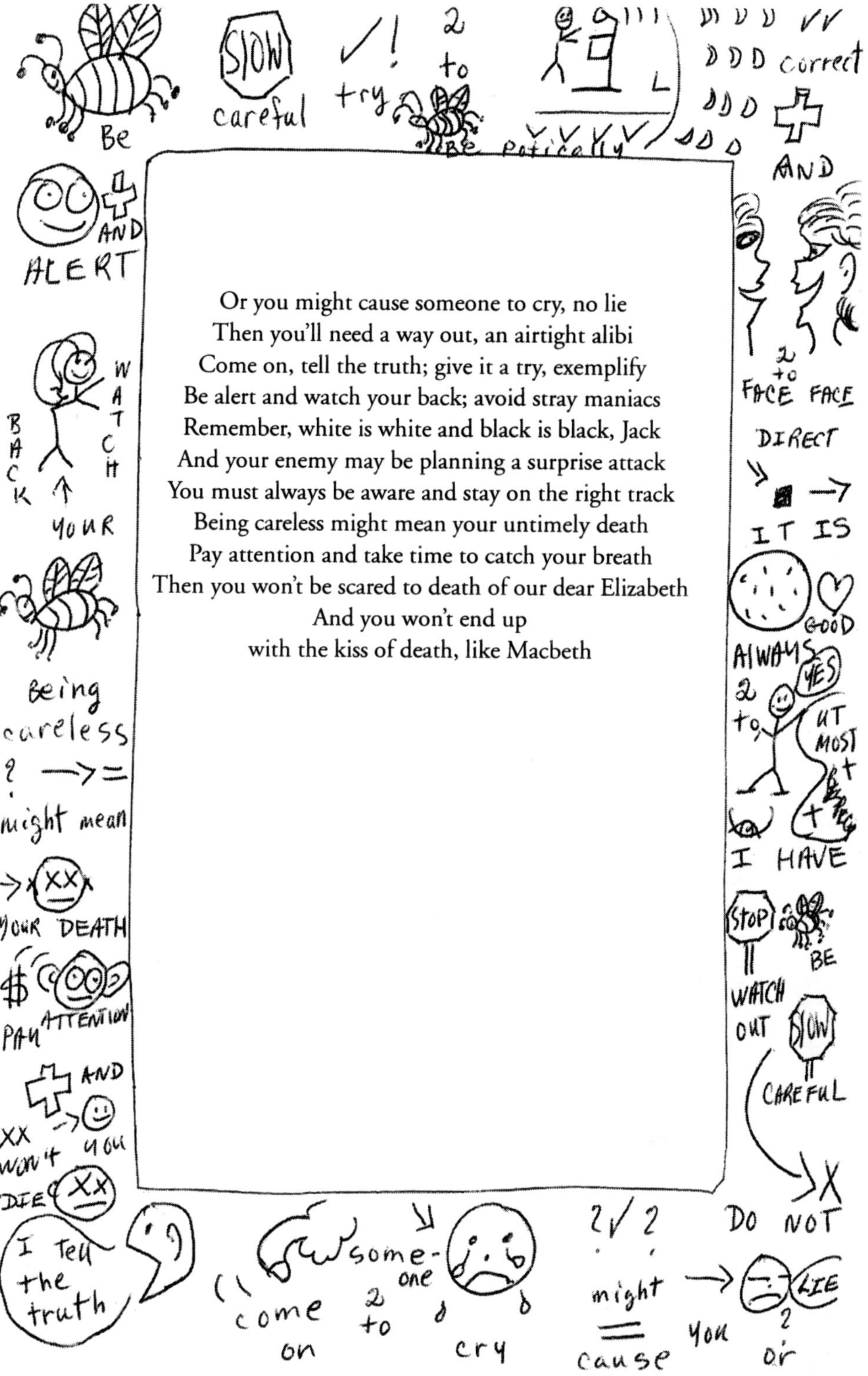

Or you might cause someone to cry, no lie
Then you'll need a way out, an airtight alibi
Come on, tell the truth; give it a try, exemplify
Be alert and watch your back; avoid stray maniacs
Remember, white is white and black is black, Jack
And your enemy may be planning a surprise attack
You must always be aware and stay on the right track
Being careless might mean your untimely death
Pay attention and take time to catch your breath
Then you won't be scared to death of our dear Elizabeth
And you won't end up
with the kiss of death, like Macbeth

REALITY BITES

Sometimes when you're in the light, reality bites
But it doesn't have to suck; it can be pure dynamite
It may be enough to give you insight and foresight
You will have all the luck when you're in the spotlight
The road may not be smooth today,
and you may go the wrong way
But who said you would have a choice
in where you have to play
Or that it would be smooth sailing all
the way, with an instant replay
There has to be a little rain and a little snow
from day to day
Sometimes your brain may hurt and sound the alert
And your sweat may pour and wet your shirt
Try not to underestimate yourself and overexert
Try instead to assert yourself
and keep yourself unhurt
Ignore and avoid cat fights; be upright, a socialite
Embrace and encourage the contrite; use foresight
Avoid all the unnecessary, the angry, and the uptight
Let love have its way, give it the green light
Always try to be fair and square, be totally aware
In all of your personal and business affairs, be fair
This way you'll never feel the need to be a solitaire
And you will be welcomed everywhere; that's fair
That will give you lots and lots of time
To cut through all of life's filth and grime

And when your time comes
and it's the big time
You'll know your lines like they
were from a simple nursery rhyme
So if you meet your enemy on the street
Just be calm and turn the other cheek
Furthermore, show them you can be meek
Show your love technique
and hold your tongue in your cheek
Even though truth may be cruel
Be sure to be nobody's fool
Use mother wisdom as your tool
You may even make cruel into cool

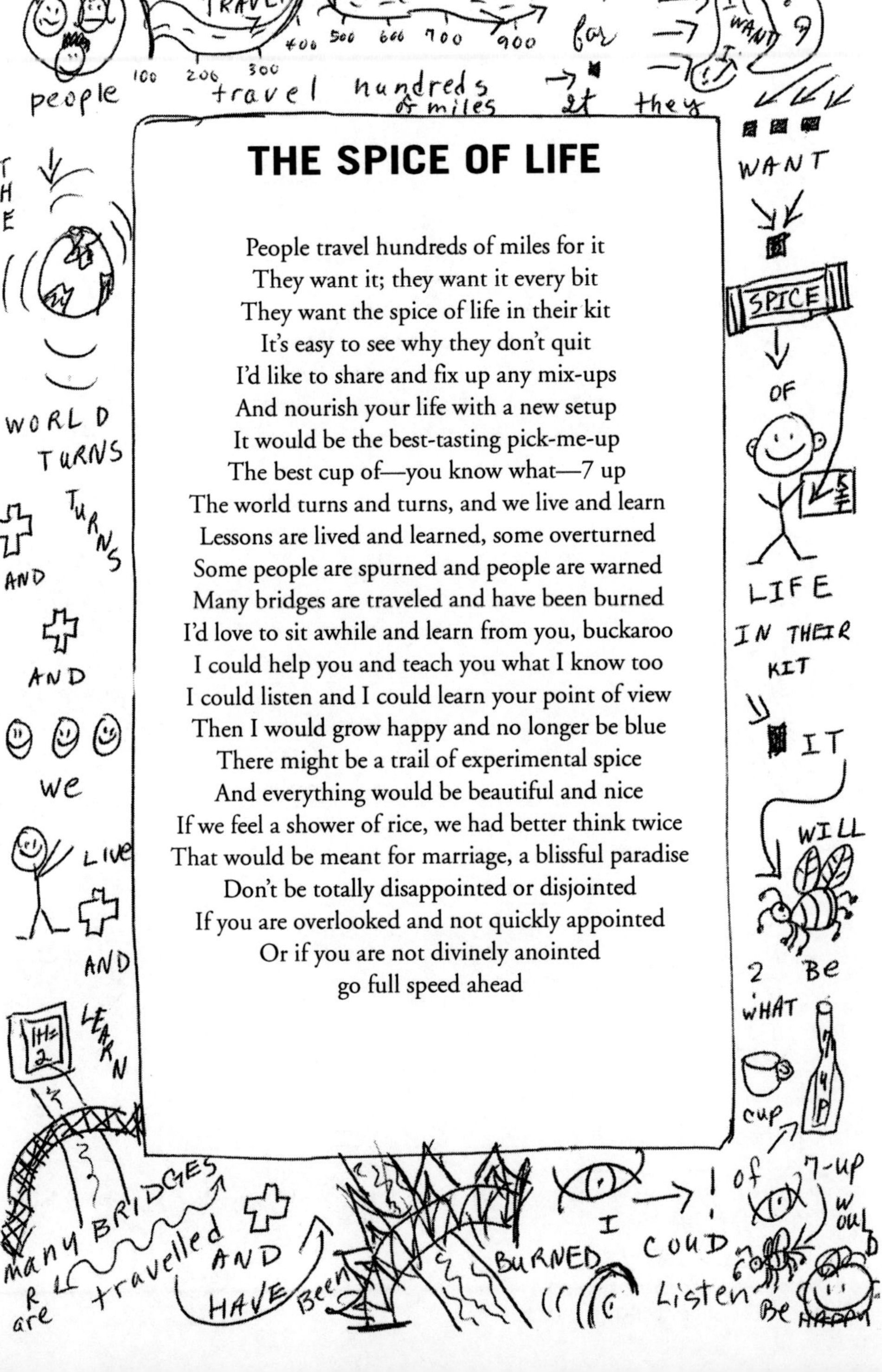

THE SPICE OF LIFE

People travel hundreds of miles for it
They want it; they want it every bit
They want the spice of life in their kit
It's easy to see why they don't quit
I'd like to share and fix up any mix-ups
And nourish your life with a new setup
It would be the best-tasting pick-me-up
The best cup of—you know what—7 up
The world turns and turns, and we live and learn
Lessons are lived and learned, some overturned
Some people are spurned and people are warned
Many bridges are traveled and have been burned
I'd love to sit awhile and learn from you, buckaroo
I could help you and teach you what I know too
I could listen and I could learn your point of view
Then I would grow happy and no longer be blue
There might be a trail of experimental spice
And everything would be beautiful and nice
If we feel a shower of rice, we had better think twice
That would be meant for marriage, a blissful paradise
Don't be totally disappointed or disjointed
If you are overlooked and not quickly appointed
Or if you are not divinely anointed
go full speed ahead

That's when you must develop
a totally new viewpoint
Your enemies will be like all your hairs, so watch and beware
They'll want to know all of your affairs, they'll sit and glare
They'll climb the stairs and appear out of all of their lairs
So be careful when you are here, and be careful everywhere
You'll always have for them a surprise, by and by
Because when they exhale and open their eyes
They'll see your salvation written high in the skies
It was the spice of life; despite their many lies

LOVE HAS MANY FACES

Love has many attitudes, and many faces
You can find love anywhere and at any place
You can find it at home or in the workplace
You can search for it or meet it face to face
Can you see love where you are?
You can find love in your guitar
You can find love at a seminar
Or you can find love
in a rare Renoir
Love has many beautiful names
These names can be
in the form of nicknames
These names can be
your claim to fame
They also can be in the fun of a game
You can find love in your fellow man
Love can be there
in Anna or love can be there in Stan
Love can be at a home or
in the land Afghanistan
It's the love in our own land that can be grand
Love is powerful and can overcome any evil
Its weapons are goodness and freewill
and what they instill
The skill of love is goodwill and it is a pure thrill
Don't underestimate its power to kill any ill

When love kills, something wonderful happens
A Pandora's candy box of goodness opens
Wonderment and joy can run free and hang ten
Then the world is love's footstool and playpen
The phoenix is burnt to ashes, by pure love
The phoenix is reborn from a blue flame from above
Turning it into a spirit in a form of a sacrificial dove
That is waiting for lots more love
and more of that sort of
The blue flame is a spirit that touches us all
It is pure love falling like rainfall
This rain creates the best free-for-all
And cascades like a life-giving waterfall

JAMMING WITH MY BUDDIES

Really, who says I can't mix and blend again?
And get jamming with my so-called friends
Overall, and in the end, the more time I spend
Jamming with my buddies,
the better the universal trend
When I take the time and pain to joyfully create
And when I forget to waste time and
I don't get lazy and hesitate
When I jam with my buddies and leave the gate
That's when we hit it off
and it turns into something great
When we open the window and close the door
And make lots of music, right through the floor
Jamming with our buddies is the opposite of a chore
Then all we want to do is
make music and more, more, more
They said I couldn't sing all my love songs
Well, you know what, I proved them wrong
I and my friends knew it was OK all along
This lady is not only tough, she is headstrong
So all I did was turn, turn, and turn to my next buddy
And invited them to dance and say squeeze me
Then tell them nothing could possibly better be
Than to share with you
and me on a dancing spree

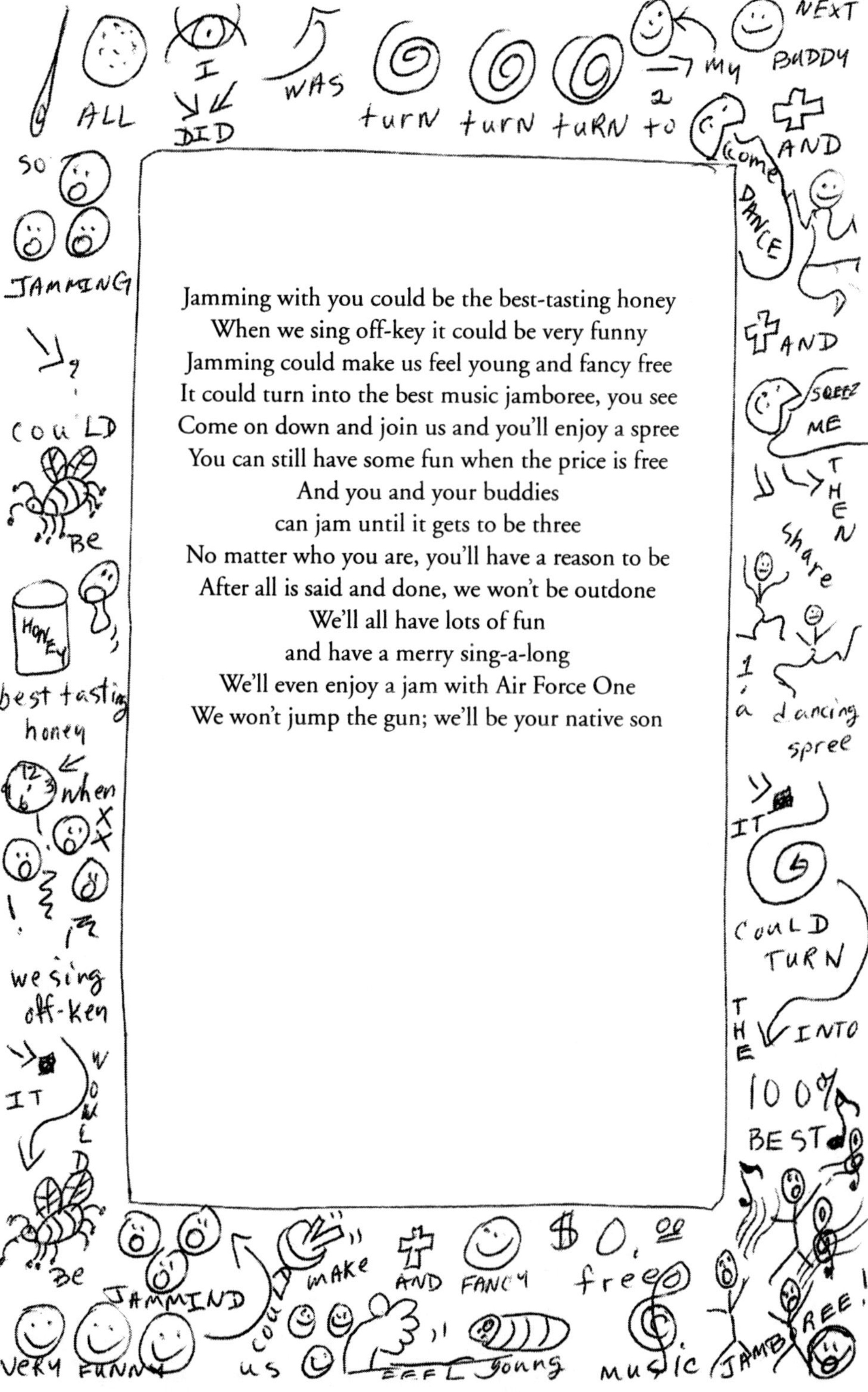

Jamming with you could be the best-tasting honey
When we sing off-key it could be very funny
Jamming could make us feel young and fancy free
It could turn into the best music jamboree, you see
Come on down and join us and you'll enjoy a spree
You can still have some fun when the price is free
And you and your buddies
can jam until it gets to be three
No matter who you are, you'll have a reason to be
After all is said and done, we won't be outdone
We'll all have lots of fun
and have a merry sing-a-long
We'll even enjoy a jam with Air Force One
We won't jump the gun; we'll be your native son

USE YOUR IMAGINATION

Be creative when you are working, and love what you do
Find the silver lining in your clouds
and fill them with joy too
Be positively positive, spread some cheer
does that give you a clue?
Tell a joke, make someone smile, go
that extra mile, buckaroo
Be encouraging when your friends come near;
don't be sad or blue
Use your imagination, make do with what you have
grin it, and bear
Use your imagination and make someone laugh and care
Transform simple, plain ware and give it wing anywhere
Change plain things into gorgeous and lovely creations;
use your great flair
When nothing is going right, imagine something better
Then look a little harder; it's better to use your head, sir
The world will have a different view
but make a compromise, don't err
You are full of interesting and wonderful ideas;
because you are a go-getter
When you think you are one of the Odd Couple
just get into your brainstorming huddle
You can look in wonder because you are gorgeous
and you look good when you cuddle

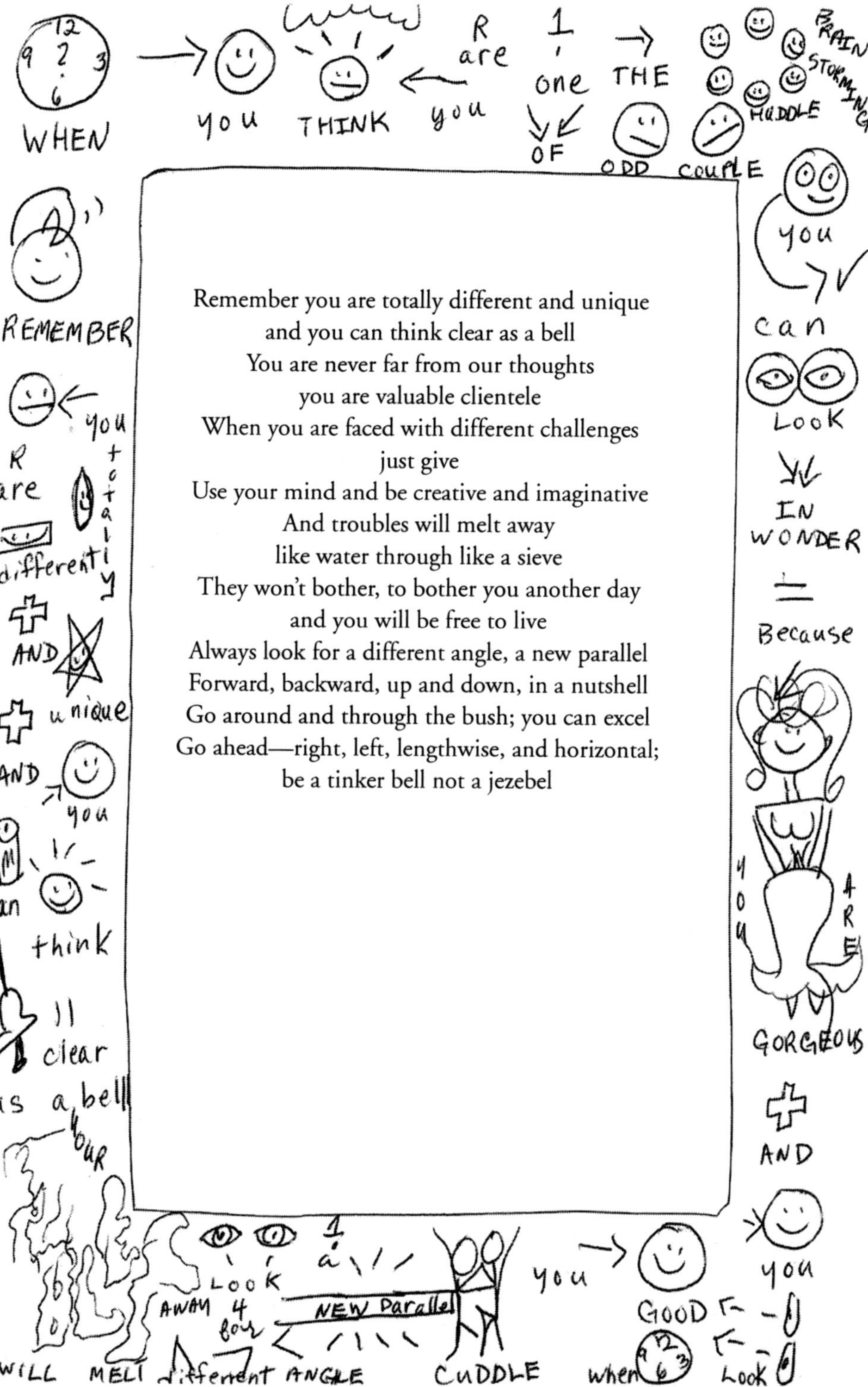

Remember you are totally different and unique
and you can think clear as a bell
You are never far from our thoughts
you are valuable clientele
When you are faced with different challenges
just give
Use your mind and be creative and imaginative
And troubles will melt away
like water through like a sieve
They won't bother, to bother you another day
and you will be free to live
Always look for a different angle, a new parallel
Forward, backward, up and down, in a nutshell
Go around and through the bush; you can excel
Go ahead—right, left, lengthwise, and horizontal;
be a tinker bell not a jezebel

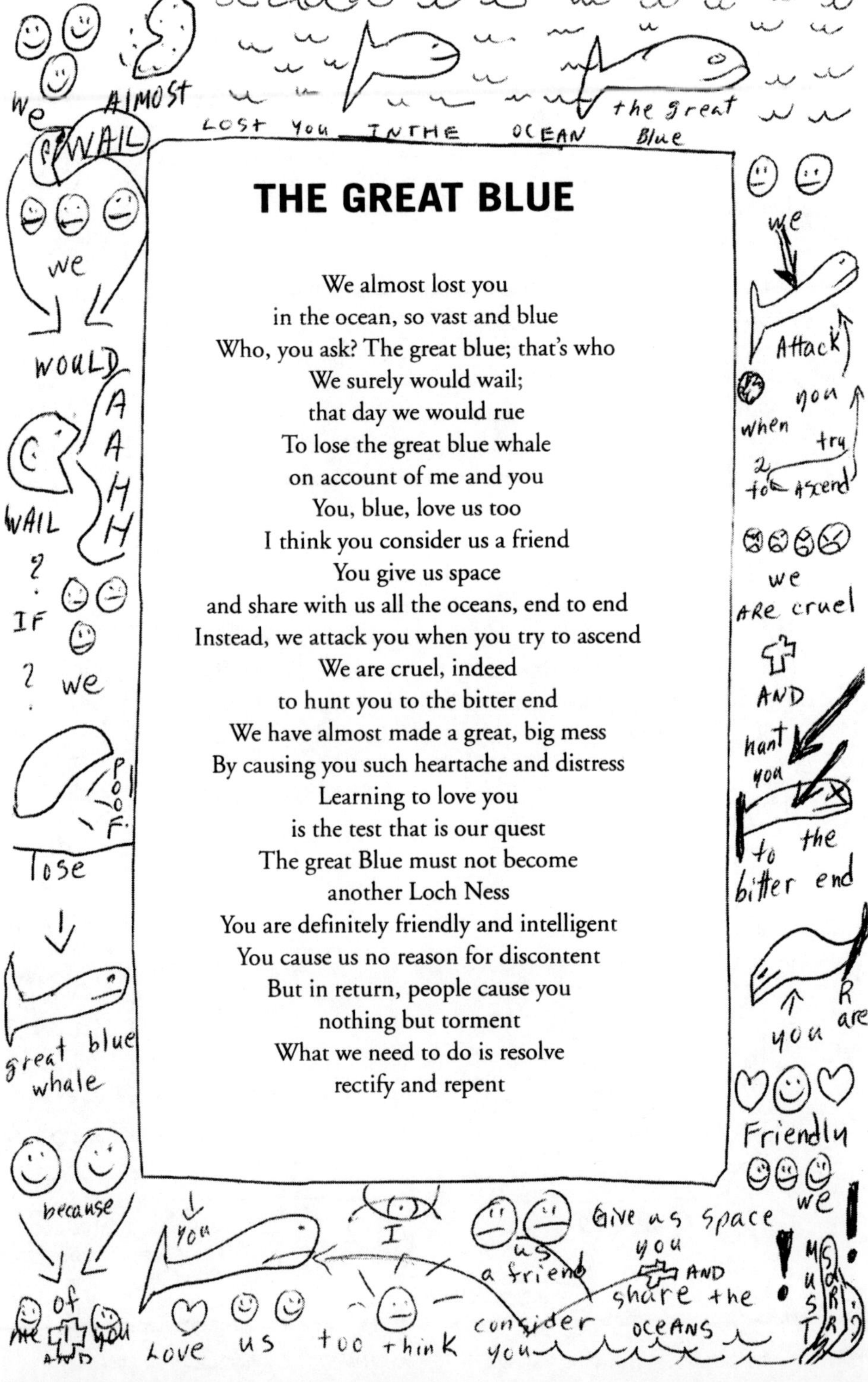

THE GREAT BLUE

We almost lost you
in the ocean, so vast and blue
Who, you ask? The great blue; that's who
We surely would wail;
that day we would rue
To lose the great blue whale
on account of me and you
You, blue, love us too
I think you consider us a friend
You give us space
and share with us all the oceans, end to end
Instead, we attack you when you try to ascend
We are cruel, indeed
to hunt you to the bitter end
We have almost made a great, big mess
By causing you such heartache and distress
Learning to love you
is the test that is our quest
The great Blue must not become
another Loch Ness
You are definitely friendly and intelligent
You cause us no reason for discontent
But in return, people cause you
nothing but torment
What we need to do is resolve
rectify and repent

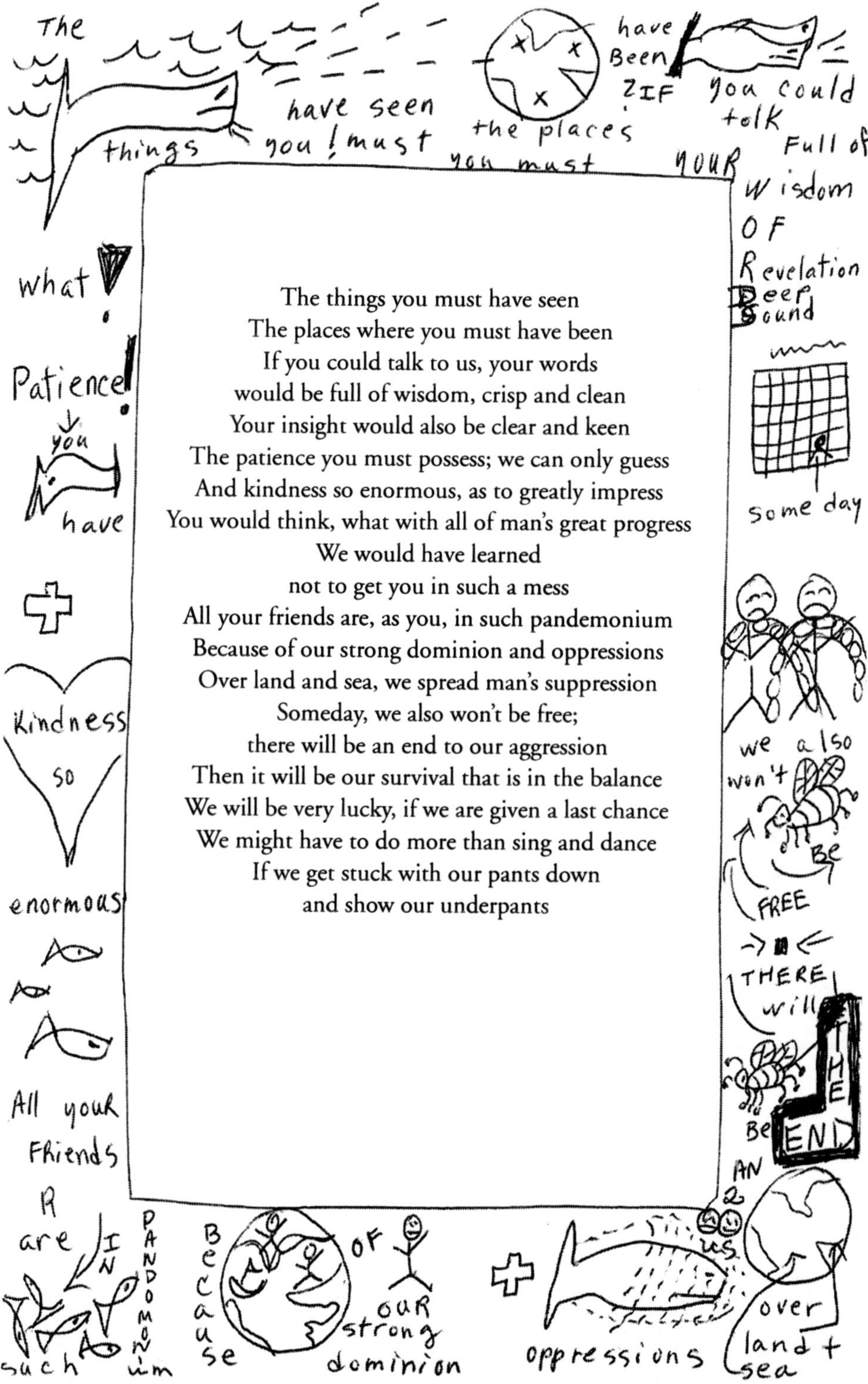

The things you must have seen
The places where you must have been
If you could talk to us, your words
would be full of wisdom, crisp and clean
Your insight would also be clear and keen
The patience you must possess; we can only guess
And kindness so enormous, as to greatly impress
You would think, what with all of man's great progress
We would have learned
not to get you in such a mess
All your friends are, as you, in such pandemonium
Because of our strong dominion and oppressions
Over land and sea, we spread man's suppression
Someday, we also won't be free;
there will be an end to our aggression
Then it will be our survival that is in the balance
We will be very lucky, if we are given a last chance
We might have to do more than sing and dance
If we get stuck with our pants down
and show our underpants

TESTIMONY

My story has been told before
It was kept, well-hidden
behind closed doors
Wouldn't you like to know more?
It would make wonderful folklore
Secrets have a habit of coming out
Because everyone is nosy
and curious what they are all about
Why the old man
was so furious and why he shouts
Why there has been a major blowout
There is always a silver lining
Behind every cloud that isn't shining
There is a rainbow that follows—with colors winding
After a heavy rainfall, birds are chirping and singing
Do you really want to know about this tale of woe?
That it was he who was my worst foe, a real no-no
He was the closest, but he was the very deadliest foe
He was the largest and he wore
a bulletproof vest, from head to toe
He lives on, but from that situation
I am long gone
And he's where he always belonged
He's in my past, all alone, all woebegone
Now he is but an unfortunate phenomenon
I can say I've broken my personal hatred cycle

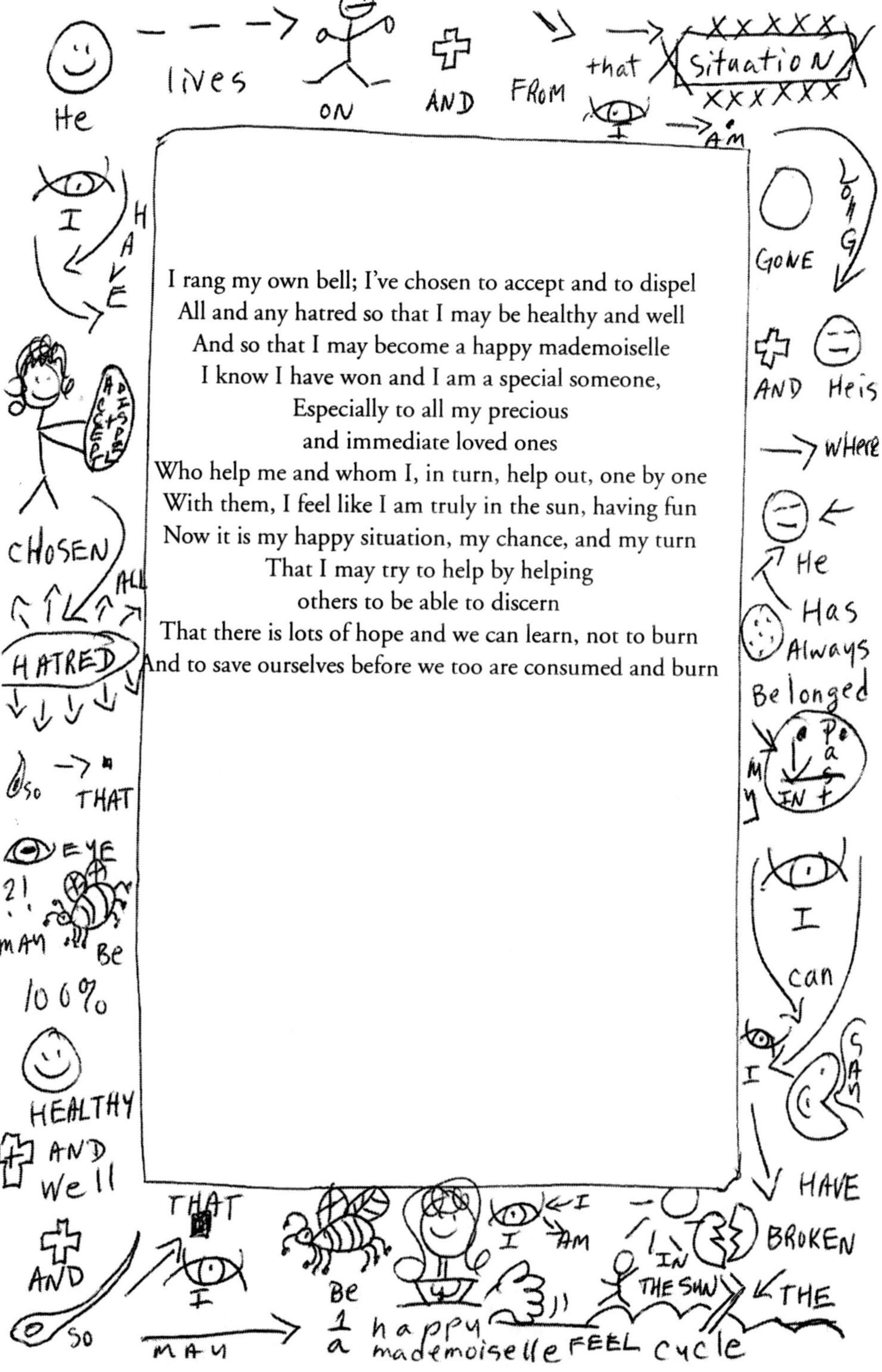

I rang my own bell; I've chosen to accept and to dispel
All and any hatred so that I may be healthy and well
And so that I may become a happy mademoiselle
I know I have won and I am a special someone,
Especially to all my precious
and immediate loved ones
Who help me and whom I, in turn, help out, one by one
With them, I feel like I am truly in the sun, having fun
Now it is my happy situation, my chance, and my turn
That I may try to help by helping
others to be able to discern
That there is lots of hope and we can learn, not to burn
And to save ourselves before we too are consumed and burn

I AM HAPPY

No bad news for me, I will no longer let it be
My new love has set me free, and love is the key
To also send people my way is my only plea
So that I'll have memories
about you and me, you see
Don't tell me bad news
I refuse to listen to the blues
I'll give you a major clue
I don't pay attention
to bad reviews
Give me something positive
and I will be attentive
Make my day happy, a day to want to relive
Send me good news and make it informative
So that I can have a good, playful initiative
Then worries will disappear, and life will be clear
And happiness will replace tears with no more fears
No one will have a reason to cry anywhere my dear
And all bad things will say good-bye and disappear
Ah, our lives will be fun, our lives have just begun
And we will all have life on the run, we won't be undone
We will be happy all the time while basking in the sun
True love will surely be mine
and I will again feel like number 1

Thoughts of people will happily stay
Memories will no longer go away or stray
Love will come to stay with me
again and every day
Faster than you can buy them on eBay
I'll enjoy life while I can, I'll feel like a number 10
I won't look back to way back then ever again
I'll choose to be happy all the time, my friend
Because I've found peace of mind
in all mortal men
You see, I have my own free will, oh, what a thrill
And I have chosen the happiness pill that will not kill
Now life can't go anywhere but uphill, with any ill will
Because I am happy, happier, and happiest still—
all fulfilled

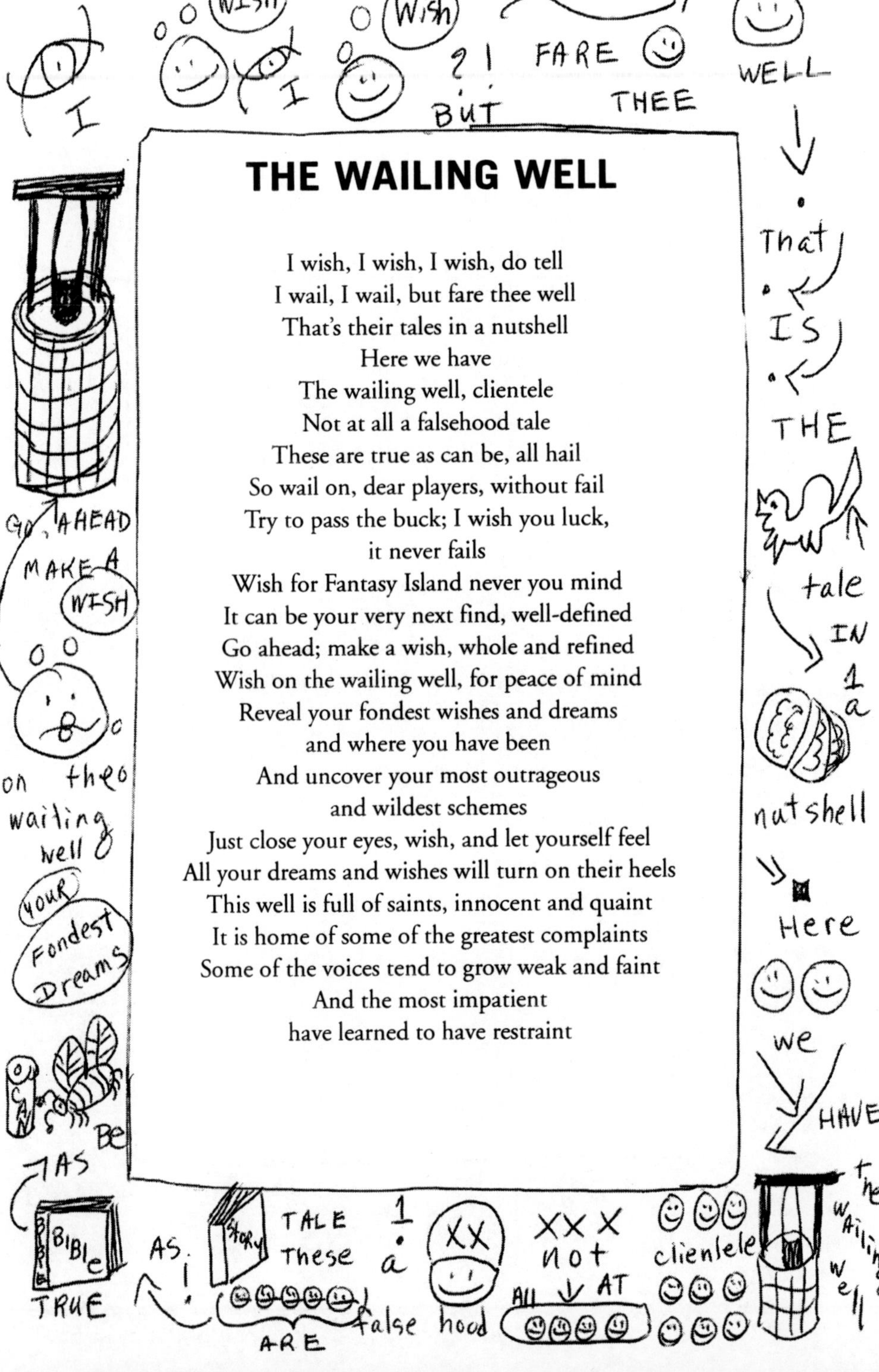
I
WISH
I
Wish
?!
BUT
FARE
THEE
WELL
That
IS
THE
tale
IN
1
a
nutshell
Here
we
HAVE
the
WAiling
well
GO, AHEAD
MAKE A
WISH
on the
waiting
well
YOUR
Fondest
Dreams
CAN
Be
AS
BIBle
TRUE
AS
STORY
TALE
These
ARE
1
a
false hood
XX
XXX
not
AT
All
clienlele

THE WAILING WELL

I wish, I wish, I wish, do tell
I wail, I wail, but fare thee well
That's their tales in a nutshell
Here we have
The wailing well, clientele
Not at all a falsehood tale
These are true as can be, all hail
So wail on, dear players, without fail
Try to pass the buck; I wish you luck,
it never fails
Wish for Fantasy Island never you mind
It can be your very next find, well-defined
Go ahead; make a wish, whole and refined
Wish on the wailing well, for peace of mind
Reveal your fondest wishes and dreams
and where you have been
And uncover your most outrageous
and wildest schemes
Just close your eyes, wish, and let yourself feel
All your dreams and wishes will turn on their heels
This well is full of saints, innocent and quaint
It is home of some of the greatest complaints
Some of the voices tend to grow weak and faint
And the most impatient
have learned to have restraint

Go ahead; fill the well up to the brim
It'll never let on what you have said or where you have been
To fill it completely up has yet to be done or to be seen
It'll never be filled up because
all wishes are invisible and unseen
If the wailing well could tell all its stories
It would be chock-full of many past glories
And would tell
of many woes and many worries
And might give up
the age-old wisdom of Socrates
Those famous wishes were thought of,
but undone and unfinished at first
The well lent an ear and became a silent
cohort and put up a silent fort
It was a silent, gracious gesture of support
from a friend of sorts, which didn't hurt
In many a measure, the well was well worth
the effort of being a good sport

MY ACHING HEAD

I have a familiar ache and I feel just like a rake
It feels like my head will break
now that I am awake
It throbs right there
between my eyes like a earthquake
And it feels like
I've been bitten by a rattlesnake
So I follow through with a pint of
brew for a brand-new view
Thinking it might make my migraine call a truce, thank you
Truth is, it is just a cheap excuse to let loose and start anew
Looks like I've again
cooked my own goose through and through
Now in the same thought, I could find me a bottle of wine
This might help me to relax and unwind or just toe the line
Then again, it might cause me to get out of line;
that could be a danger sign
If my wine is spiked, I might go out of my mind
and make headlines
Next, I'll get to that gosh-darned hard
stuff, it's not so tough, and I scoff
This is no longer the caffeinated stuff;
this is the hard stuff, its decaf
It makes me sneeze, it makes me cough, and then
my germs have lift off, cough, and cough
The secret is whether I know when I've had
enough or if I become a big show-off
This story will all end up with me having a case of the bends

Then I will be alone again because I
will have lost all my friends
Because I'll be a zero among normal
men, and I'll be broke again
I, sir, should have known when to say
when and when to say amen
Now my life will begin again, my
friend; I'm out of rehab again
Because my headache has gone right
away after I got over the bends
I am now on the right path again and I am
no longer in a prison all penned
To the rehab, I can say thank you kindly,
amen and amen—never again
I will now have to change everyone I hang around with
from now and herewith
When I now go to the bar, my drinking alcohol
will have to be a myth
Instead of being a John, I now will have to be a Smith
and java I will have known to be with
I will change my stripes from there to herewith
and I'll be the better off; that's the gist
No more boos for this poor lonesome fellow
I now have a new portfolio
It's enough that my mind is forever made of Jell-O
and now I am a sloppy Moe
And I might say good-bye to you instead of hello
get ready, get set, go
And if you give me directions to go home
I might end up in Mexico

BRING THE MUSIC BACK

Don't turn your back
Bring the music back
Remember what you lack
And put it in your backpack
Simple things are often the best
They're the ones that stand life's tests
They're often the ones that cost less
And they don't have to cause a big mess
You don't have to read lots and lots of books
Just don't fill your head with gobbledygook
Also remember what you've been taught
and don't act like a kook
So pay attention in class
and listen when you are rebuked
Remember that life is your classroom
And people are the dancers
in your ballroom
Some circumstances may
make you into a cartoon
But poetry can be your escape
Like a safety cocoon
Music is joy, so bring the joy back
And make it your new toy
Use your new joy, smell your new joy
taste your new joy, and feel your new joy
Music is the language that comes in many tongues
which you should learn to employ

It is easily understood by all, it's the real McCoy
If you apply all this to all your music, you'll have the trick
You'll have magical music poetry; it'll be a magical flick
That can't be defeated by any dirty trick
or measured by any yardstick
There's something deadly serious about
a wonderful love story
that's homemade and handpicked
It'll be so serious, it will be like liquid fire,
which you can't help but admire
It'll surpass all your joys and bring you
higher and higher up its fiery spire
It'll be something of which you never tire and
something to which you can aspire
It'll be something of which will be a surefire
hit in your very own heavenly choir
The siren's wail will reveal a tale of pure hypnotic blackmail
and trap you in its gale
The sound will be like when an angel
exhales, and everything else will pale
It'll make sense in its own place and will
unveil beauty, like a nightingale
It'll give you the answers to the human race's questions
like reading a beautiful fairy tale

SOFTLY BEATS THE HEART OF A GIANT

How can someone be so soft?
Yet be so strong up in his loft
The greatness shows through
quite oft
To this giant, it is nothing new
no guff
His heart is the ticket
It is the main sticky wicket
You wouldn't want to give it a kick
Instead, you would want to fix it
His heart has been broken many, many times
More than much sad poetry
and many nursery rhymes
Those rejections were cruel, nasty crimes
First came the damage
then he paid for it big time
Something soft, yet something so strong
Can show a card hidden there all along
When passing a certain someone
quite headstrong
You'll know which one
when you hear this folk song
His heart traveled quite far
Farther than any of his cars
He'll want to declare a love war

On his newfound admiring star
He'll find he has nothing to fear
That his love is nothing foreign or queer
From one who only wishes him to be near?
One who herself sometimes
sheds a lonely tear
She hears his heart beat
She sees his lovely feet
She thinks he is quite sweet
He earns a place
upon her heart's love seat
I hope to someday find him by me always
And keep this lovely man, oh so kind,
with me for all my days
Always, in front of and behind me
as my personal protégé
I hope for him to stay
with me all of our days

I FEEL JUST LIKE BRAND NEW

With you, I feel just like brand new
You have given me my first clue
I feel like I want to say "I do"
To you, my fellow, say you do, too
Will we ever get the chance?
Or will we fall into a trance
Love has struck us
with its powerful lance
Now we must do
love's dance
You're my favorite one
With you, I can't and
won't come undone
With you, I'll have lots of fun
With you, the battle will be won
I now have a new kind of skin
I love you and your next of kin
But I dare not commit a sin
by the way, how long has it been?

I have a lot of love to give
I have a great capacity to forgive
I know how it can be, to be dead
and not to live
To feel my hope is running through my fingers
like water through a sieve
I speak with authority

But not with superiority
I may be your senior
and may make some worry
But if you were with me, we would
make a beautiful story
I love you with all my heart
With you, I feel very smart
You give me a brand new start
With you, I feel like a piece
of beautiful art
My spirit is gone with the wind
and blown away every day
It feels light enough to float up,
up and away, every day
It is free and has flown away to play
Now it is light hearted, merry, and gay

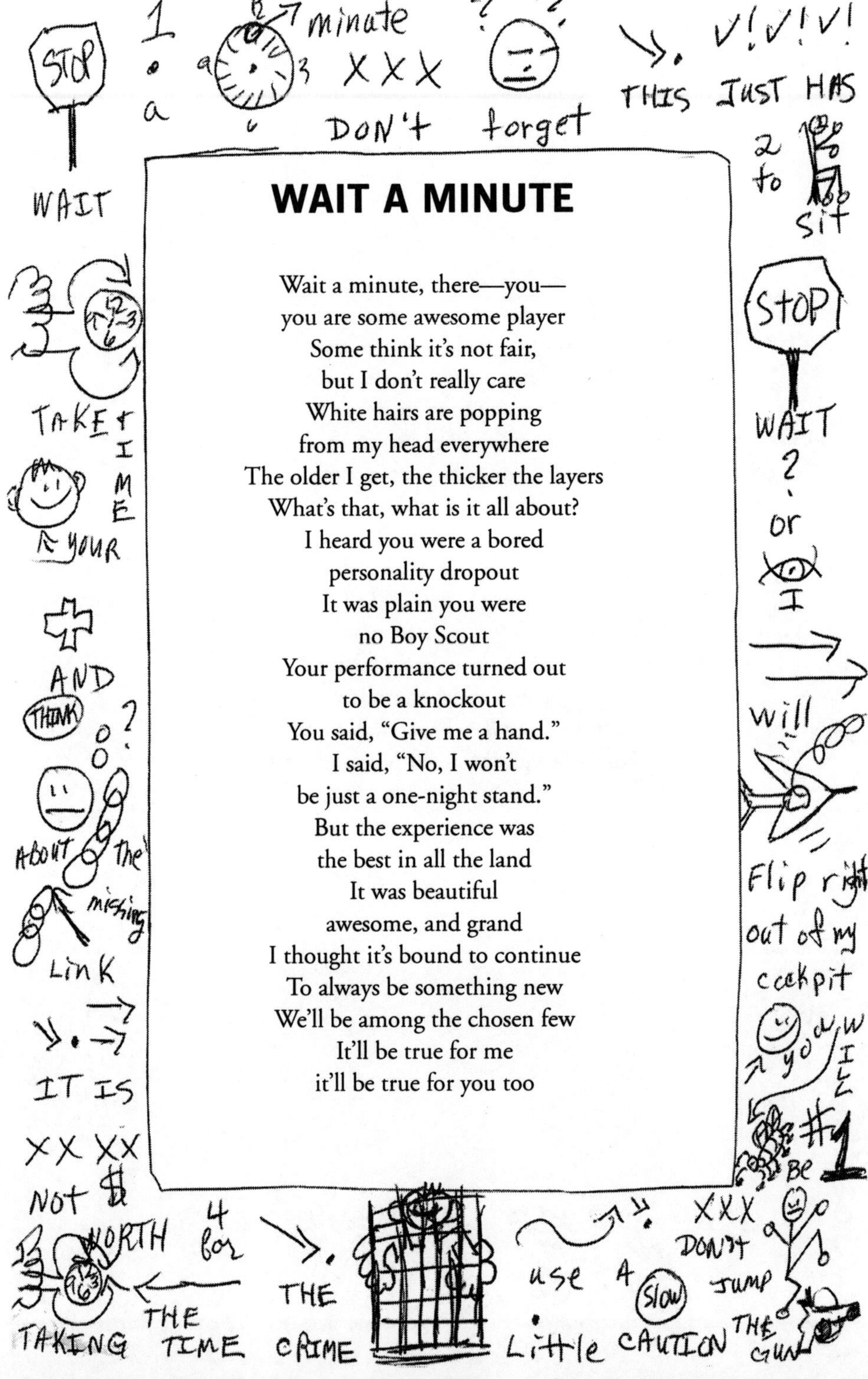

WAIT A MINUTE

Wait a minute, there—you—
you are some awesome player
Some think it's not fair,
but I don't really care
White hairs are popping
from my head everywhere
The older I get, the thicker the layers
What's that, what is it all about?
I heard you were a bored
personality dropout
It was plain you were
no Boy Scout
Your performance turned out
to be a knockout
You said, "Give me a hand."
I said, "No, I won't
be just a one-night stand."
But the experience was
the best in all the land
It was beautiful
awesome, and grand
I thought it's bound to continue
To always be something new
We'll be among the chosen few
It'll be true for me
it'll be true for you too

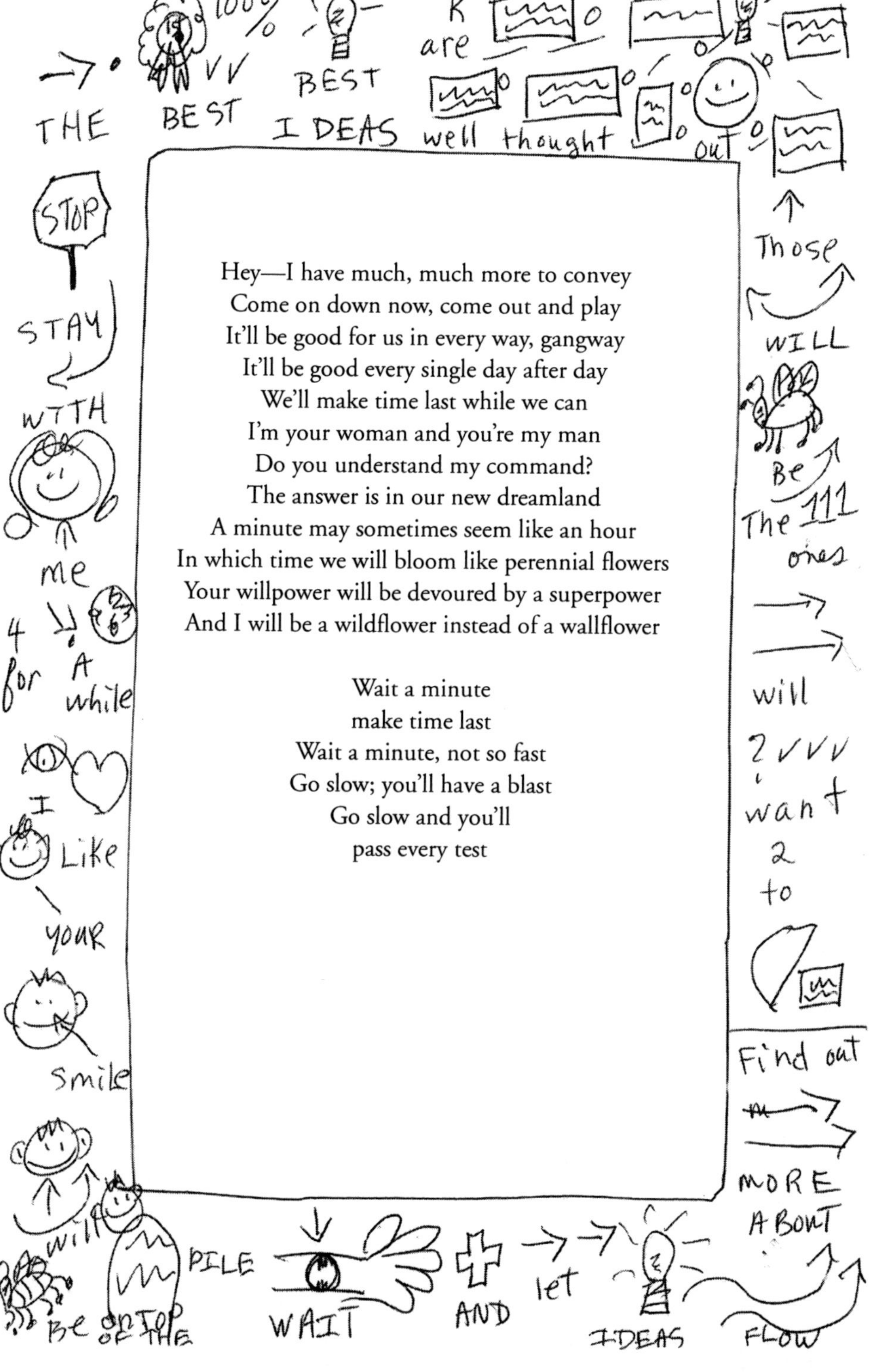

Hey—I have much, much more to convey
Come on down now, come out and play
It'll be good for us in every way, gangway
It'll be good every single day after day
We'll make time last while we can
I'm your woman and you're my man
Do you understand my command?
The answer is in our new dreamland
A minute may sometimes seem like an hour
In which time we will bloom like perennial flowers
Your willpower will be devoured by a superpower
And I will be a wildflower instead of a wallflower

Wait a minute
make time last
Wait a minute, not so fast
Go slow; you'll have a blast
Go slow and you'll
pass every test

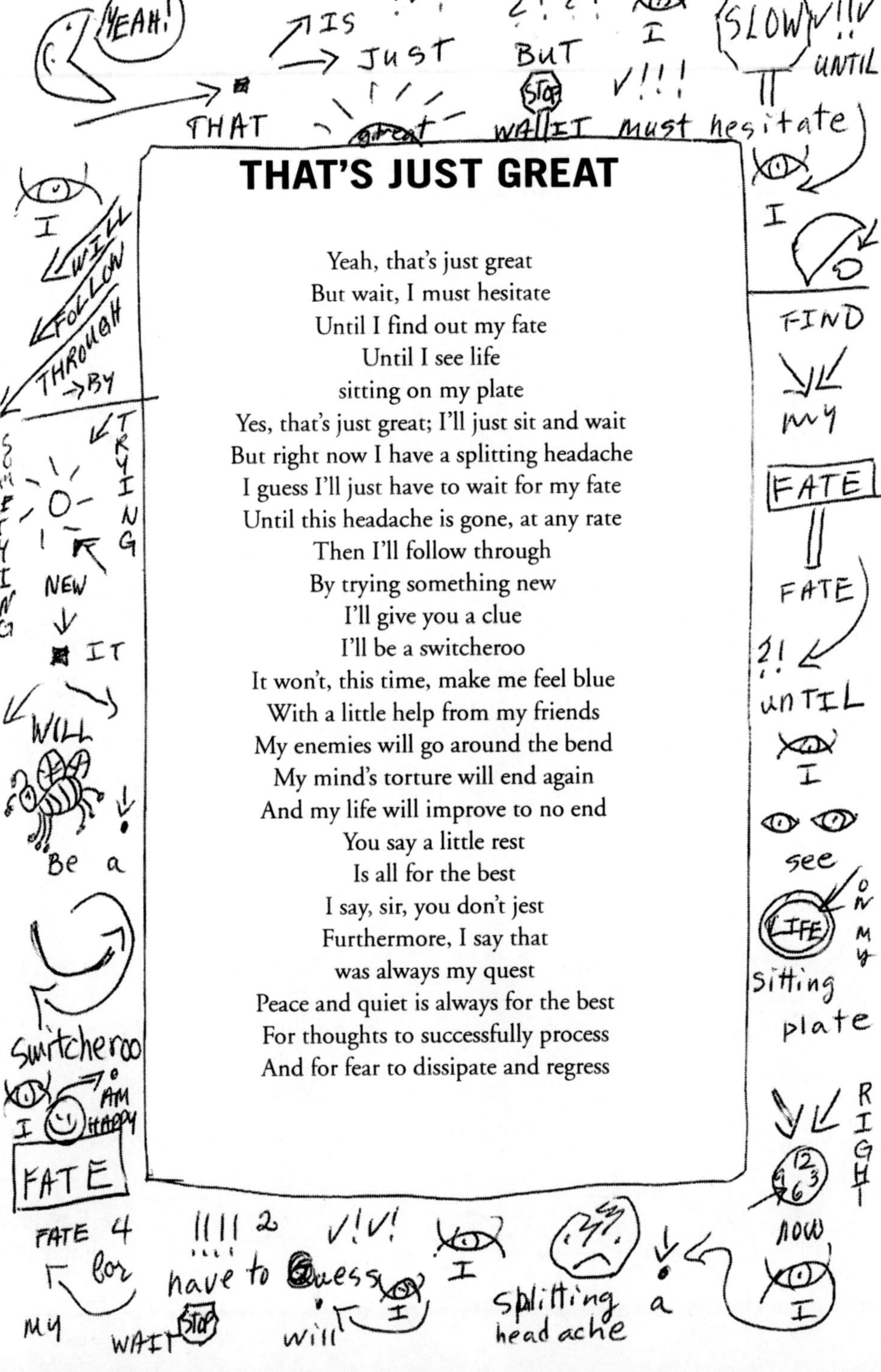

THAT'S JUST GREAT

Yeah, that's just great
But wait, I must hesitate
Until I find out my fate
Until I see life
sitting on my plate
Yes, that's just great; I'll just sit and wait
But right now I have a splitting headache
I guess I'll just have to wait for my fate
Until this headache is gone, at any rate
Then I'll follow through
By trying something new
I'll give you a clue
I'll be a switcheroo
It won't, this time, make me feel blue
With a little help from my friends
My enemies will go around the bend
My mind's torture will end again
And my life will improve to no end
You say a little rest
Is all for the best
I say, sir, you don't jest
Furthermore, I say that
was always my quest
Peace and quiet is always for the best
For thoughts to successfully process
And for fear to dissipate and regress

And also for problems
to fade and repress
When I think about it
I'll just wait it out and sit
This can't hurt anyone a bit
I will still
keep my campfires lit
While I sit and wait
I will contemplate my fate
I'll realize it was all worth
the hesitate
And I will end up
feeling really great

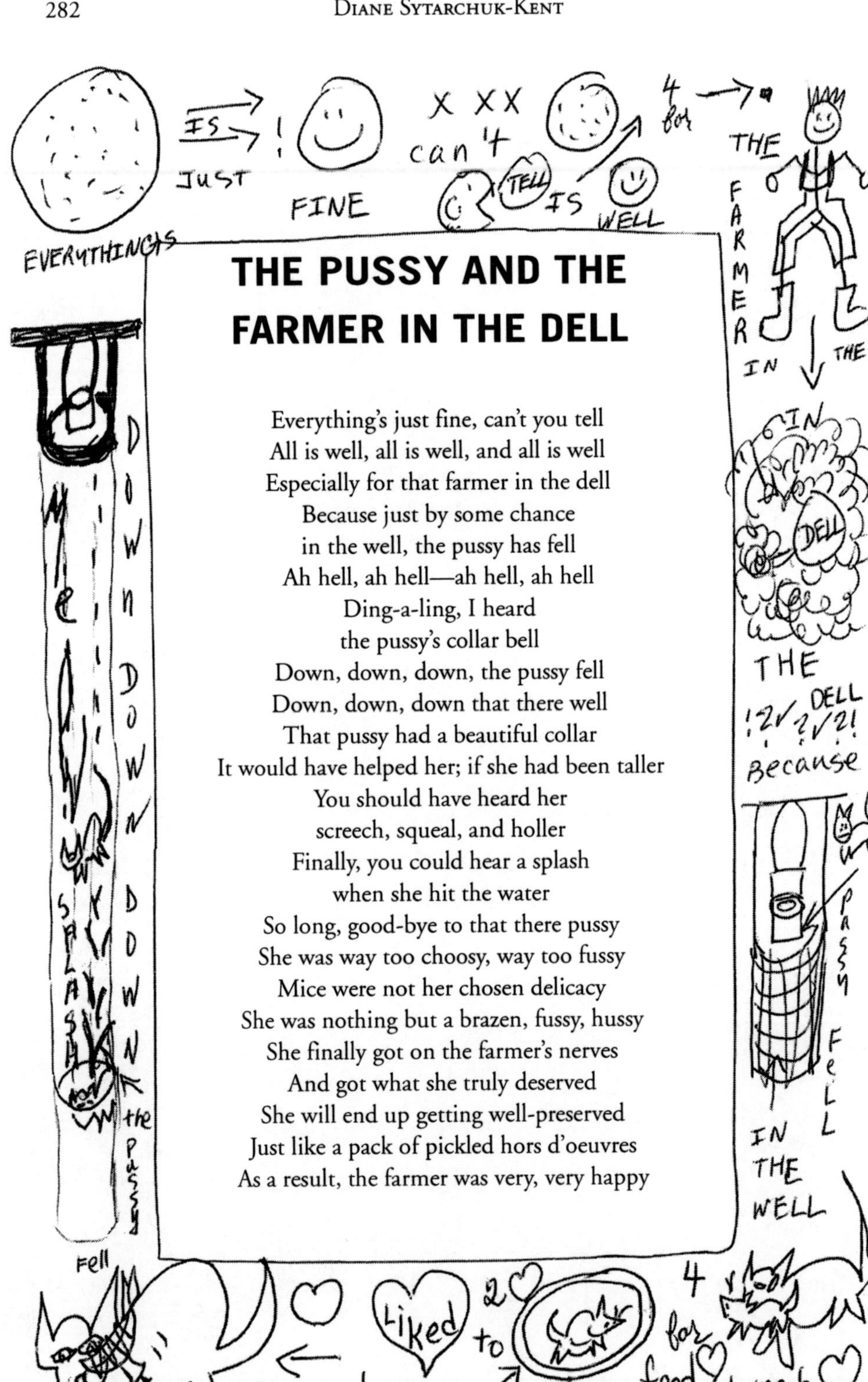

THE PUSSY AND THE FARMER IN THE DELL

Everything's just fine, can't you tell
All is well, all is well, and all is well
Especially for that farmer in the dell
Because just by some chance
in the well, the pussy has fell
Ah hell, ah hell—ah hell, ah hell
Ding-a-ling, I heard
the pussy's collar bell
Down, down, down, the pussy fell
Down, down, down that there well
That pussy had a beautiful collar
It would have helped her; if she had been taller
You should have heard her
screech, squeal, and holler
Finally, you could hear a splash
when she hit the water
So long, good-bye to that there pussy
She was way too choosy, way too fussy
Mice were not her chosen delicacy
She was nothing but a brazen, fussy, hussy
She finally got on the farmer's nerves
And got what she truly deserved
She will end up getting well-preserved
Just like a pack of pickled hors d'oeuvres
As a result, the farmer was very, very happy

Because the feline would no longer be catty
and would be down the well's deep sea
The rats would still continue to be ratty
And the townsfolk would continue to go batty
And that's that
No welcome mat
To pull from a hat
For that there cat

PS:

The farmer also would not have to
buy any more tender vittles
Or lose any more of his baby Chicken Little's
He would not ever have to again play second fiddle
And even though he had disposed of the pussy
he would be noncommittal

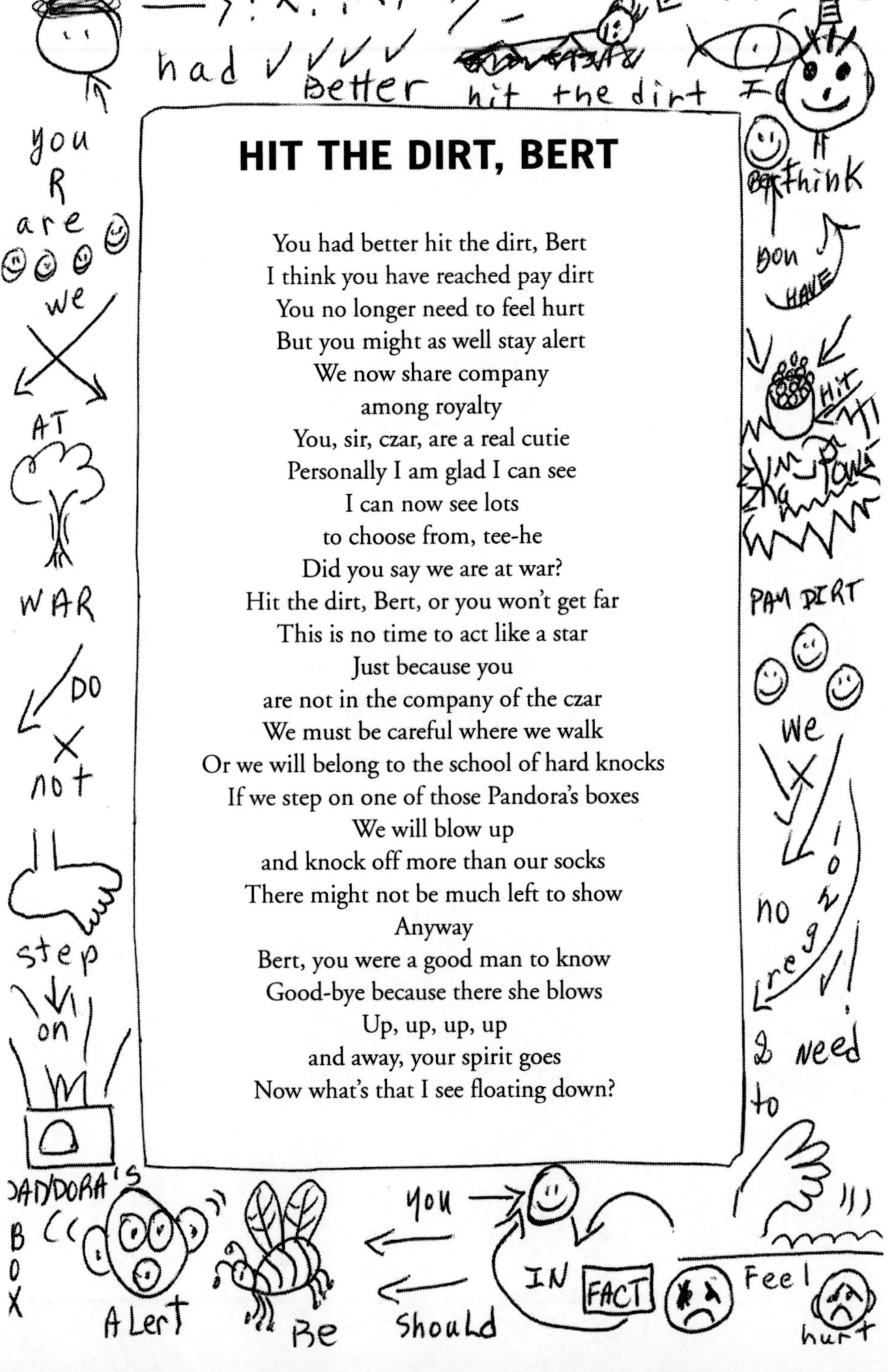

HIT THE DIRT, BERT

You had better hit the dirt, Bert
I think you have reached pay dirt
You no longer need to feel hurt
But you might as well stay alert
We now share company
among royalty
You, sir, czar, are a real cutie
Personally I am glad I can see
I can now see lots
to choose from, tee-he
Did you say we are at war?
Hit the dirt, Bert, or you won't get far
This is no time to act like a star
Just because you
are not in the company of the czar
We must be careful where we walk
Or we will belong to the school of hard knocks
If we step on one of those Pandora's boxes
We will blow up
and knock off more than our socks
There might not be much left to show
Anyway
Bert, you were a good man to know
Good-bye because there she blows
Up, up, up, up
and away, your spirit goes
Now what's that I see floating down?

Could it be a part of your army gown?
I'm scared what I might find
on the other side of town
All I know is that
you will never again be around
I turned around when I heard a bang
and I was too late to see you dance
This foreign land looks like a giant wasteland
even at a second glance
Bert, you didn't even have a fighting chance
You didn't even have a chance
to pose in a glorious stance
I will create an original, catchy epitaph
It will include
how you were on the war path
And also how you were
the world's friendliest psychopath
And how no one will really care
about the resulting bloodbath

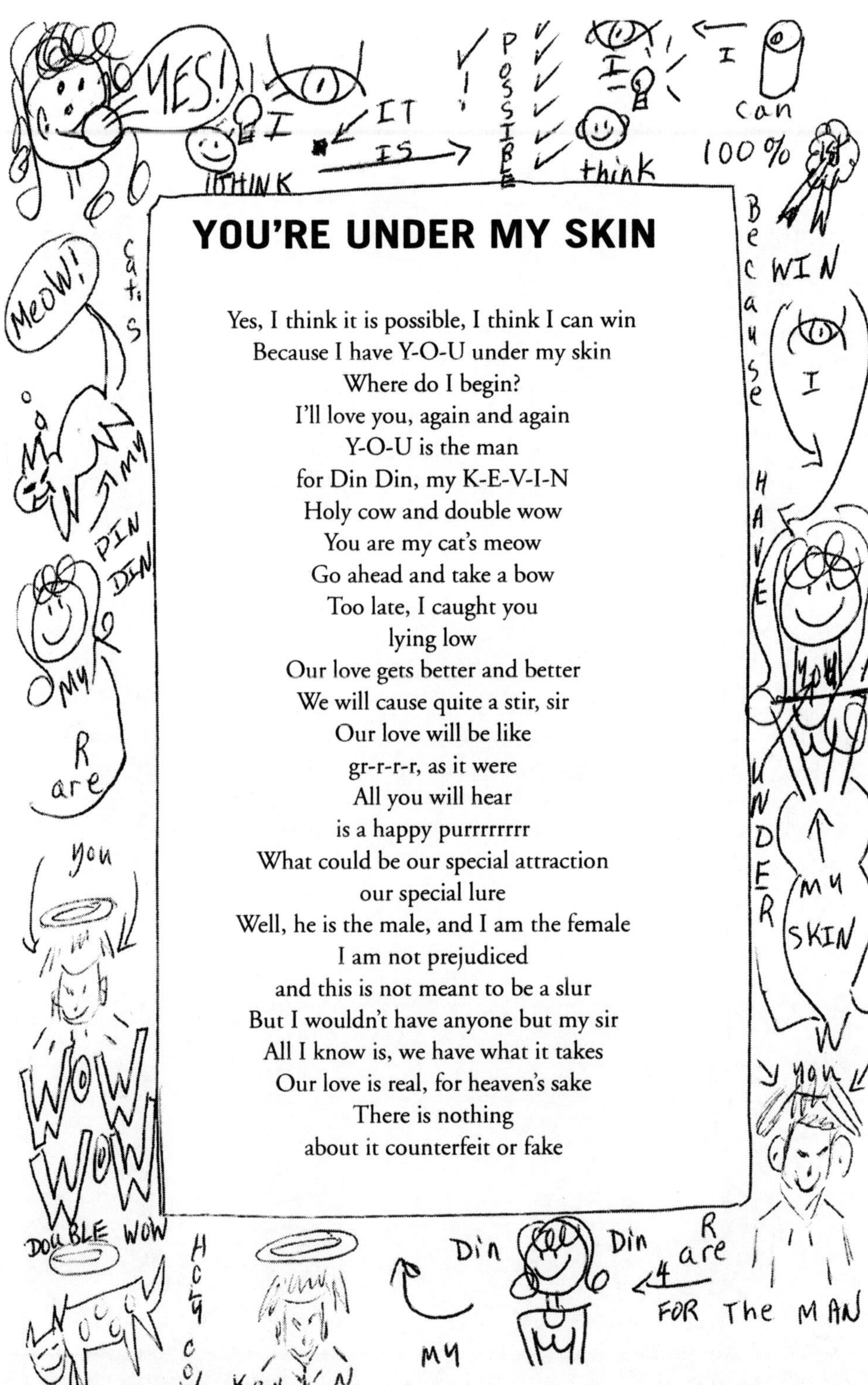

YOU'RE UNDER MY SKIN

Yes, I think it is possible, I think I can win
Because I have Y-O-U under my skin
Where do I begin?
I'll love you, again and again
Y-O-U is the man
for Din Din, my K-E-V-I-N
Holy cow and double wow
You are my cat's meow
Go ahead and take a bow
Too late, I caught you
lying low
Our love gets better and better
We will cause quite a stir, sir
Our love will be like
gr-r-r-r, as it were
All you will hear
is a happy purrrrrrrr
What could be our special attraction
our special lure
Well, he is the male, and I am the female
I am not prejudiced
and this is not meant to be a slur
But I wouldn't have anyone but my sir
All I know is, we have what it takes
Our love is real, for heaven's sake
There is nothing
about it counterfeit or fake

It is there whether our eyes are closed or
whether we are wide awake
I think about you as much when
you are not with me
Sometimes, when I sleep, it is your face I see
I love your attitude, so romantic and debonair
yet so carefree
When you soothe me with your quiet voice, I cannot
help but see your point of view and agree
Our brains must be on the same wavelength
Because when we kiss
we give each other secret strength
Our energy reaches
further than any possible length
When we are together
we go from the first through the tenth
You, sir, are definitely under my skin
You are a giant among mortal men
I want to be with you forever
now and then and again
I picked you out of the bull's pen
that's it, lights out. Amen

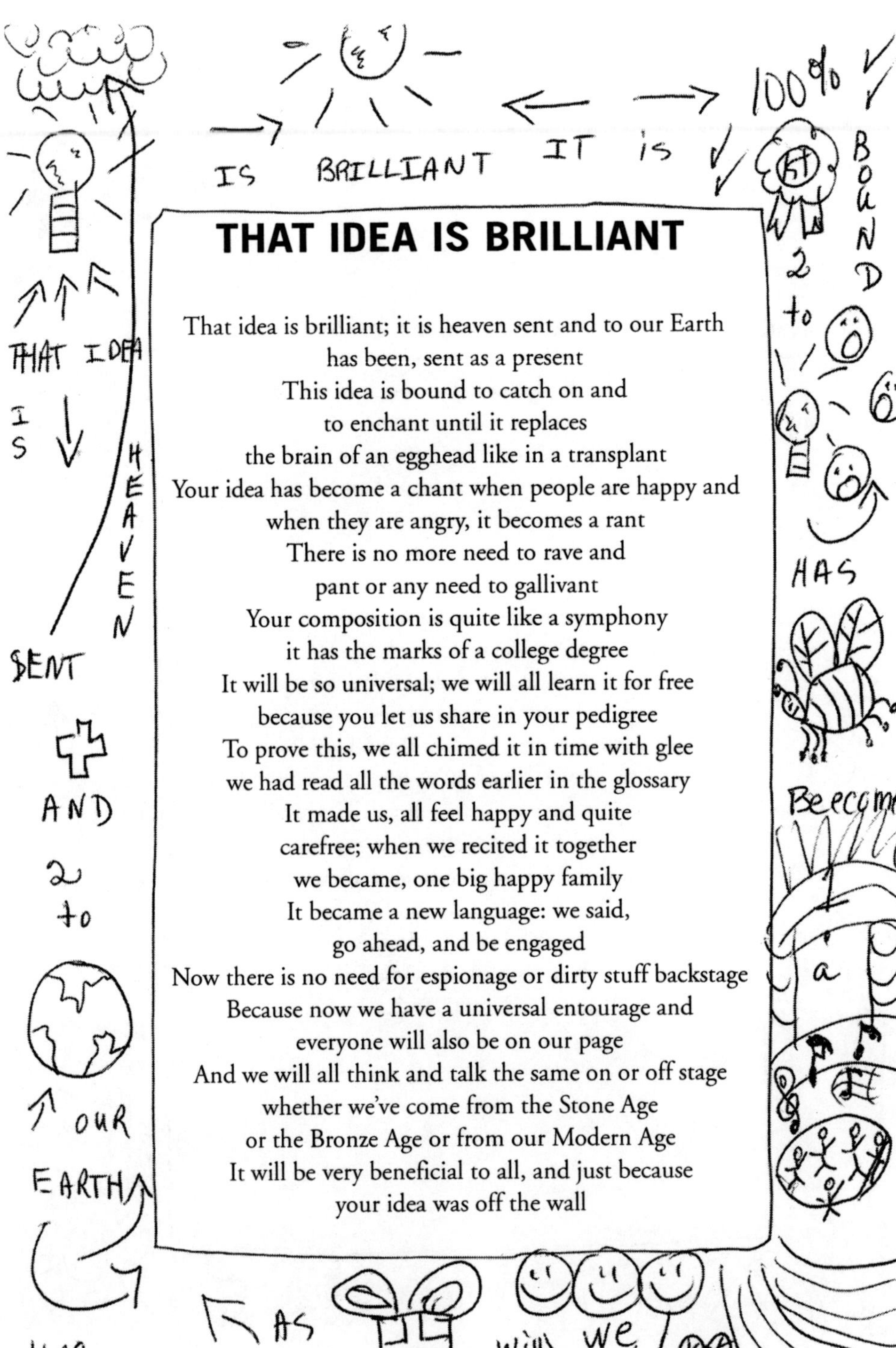

THAT IDEA IS BRILLIANT

That idea is brilliant; it is heaven sent and to our Earth
has been, sent as a present
This idea is bound to catch on and
to enchant until it replaces
the brain of an egghead like in a transplant
Your idea has become a chant when people are happy and
when they are angry, it becomes a rant
There is no more need to rave and
pant or any need to gallivant
Your composition is quite like a symphony
it has the marks of a college degree
It will be so universal; we will all learn it for free
because you let us share in your pedigree
To prove this, we all chimed it in time with glee
we had read all the words earlier in the glossary
It made us, all feel happy and quite
carefree; when we recited it together
we became, one big happy family
It became a new language: we said,
go ahead, and be engaged
Now there is no need for espionage or dirty stuff backstage
Because now we have a universal entourage and
everyone will also be on our page
And we will all think and talk the same on or off stage
whether we've come from the Stone Age
or the Bronze Age or from our Modern Age
It will be very beneficial to all, and just because
your idea was off the wall

It is still worth your being called an oddball
because everyone will be singing your song by nightfall
And because it will be written in graffiti—ten feet tall
And it will be preserved for all, in the long haul
and you; will have the final curtain call
You might even get an award
if that doesn't make me sound too avant-garde
And you didn't even try to hard; you
didn't even use a cue card
You were careful when you played
your cards and because of this
you were able to score high on your score cards
You proved you are not a blowhard;
You, sir, have many ideas that will die hard
People will look up to you because you
knew them through and through
They will say you had a high IQ
and that you were the king of impromptu
Whether or not this is true is totally
an individual point of view
it may be or may not be because of your idea
but it will still be supposed to come from me to you

When you receive this idea, I will share it with you gladly
Because I love all people and I hope for the best, you see
And I try to treat everyone like they are my friend, a VIP
I also try to place a thought seed, written in the pollen
of each mind of every human bee

That idea is so brilliant; it will outshine
the most brilliant Rembrandt
It will be instrumental in creating as
much energy as a power plant
Also everyone will see you in a different
way—in a different slant
And it will have the power to grant
a brand-new point of view, a brand-new power plant

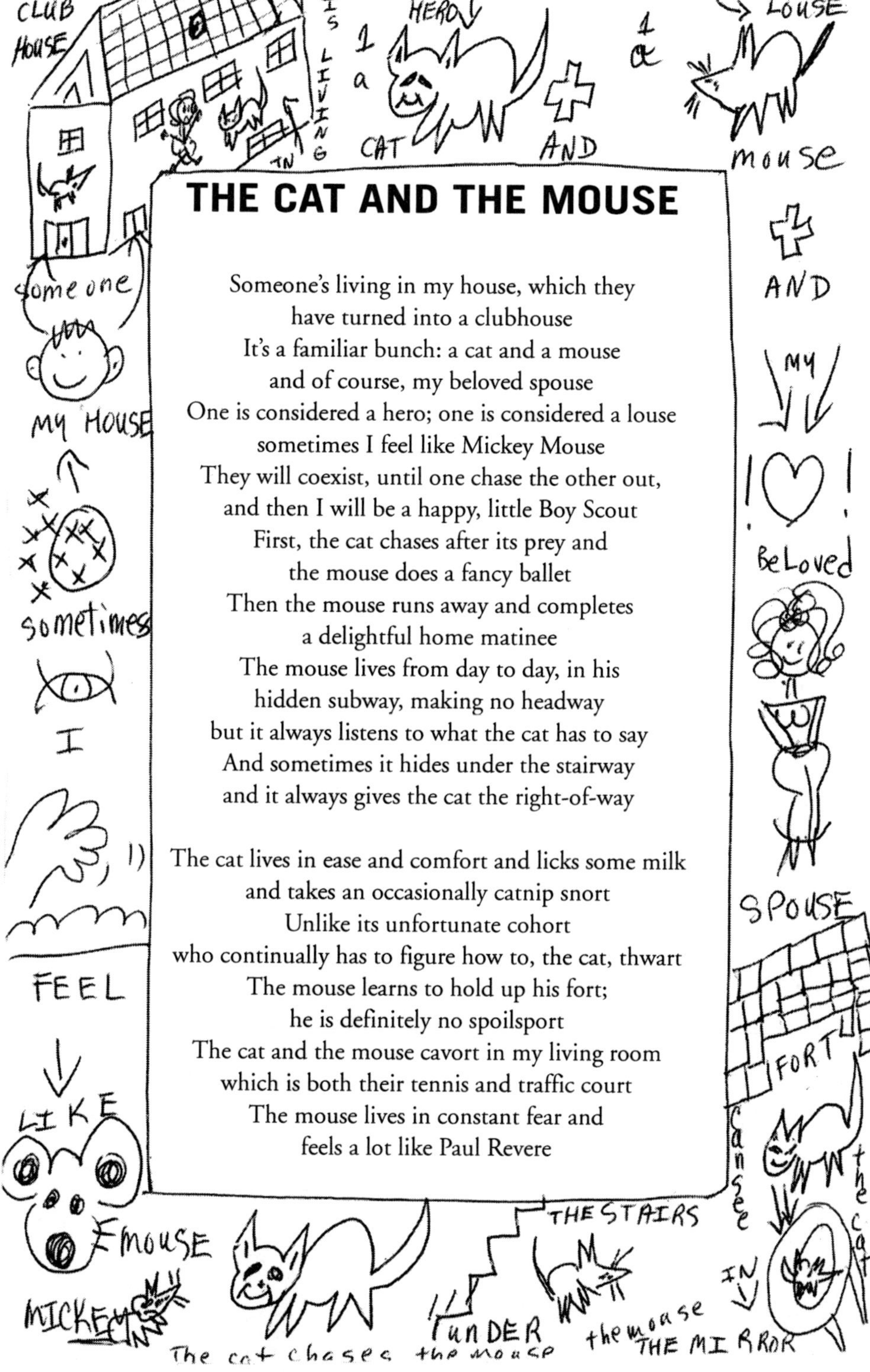

THE CAT AND THE MOUSE

Someone's living in my house, which they
have turned into a clubhouse
It's a familiar bunch: a cat and a mouse
and of course, my beloved spouse
One is considered a hero; one is considered a louse
sometimes I feel like Mickey Mouse
They will coexist, until one chase the other out,
and then I will be a happy, little Boy Scout
First, the cat chases after its prey and
the mouse does a fancy ballet
Then the mouse runs away and completes
a delightful home matinee
The mouse lives from day to day, in his
hidden subway, making no headway
but it always listens to what the cat has to say
And sometimes it hides under the stairway
and it always gives the cat the right-of-way

The cat lives in ease and comfort and licks some milk
and takes an occasionally catnip snort
Unlike its unfortunate cohort
who continually has to figure how to, the cat, thwart
The mouse learns to hold up his fort;
he is definitely no spoilsport
The cat and the mouse cavort in my living room
which is both their tennis and traffic court
The mouse lives in constant fear and
feels a lot like Paul Revere

He is afraid of the cat, which tends to persevere
and makes his intentions crystal clear
The cat can see the mouse in the reflection of my mirror
his reflection is coming in loud and clear
The cat sees his breakfast coming nearer and nearer
and he feels like Captain Bligh, the buccaneer
The cat waits and bides his time; he treats
his domain like a war zone, at half time
He is always thinking of the perfect crime
and eating out all in good time and in this lifetime
And that delicious mouse is definitely in its prime
it would be so tasty for dinnertime
That would just fit the bill for all, especially,
we enemies and partners in crime
The mouse would be a tender morsel,
with a fragrant, delicious smell
The mouse would qualify as Tinker Bell because
she was the one who rang the dinner bell
She had that magic spell and has had the unfortunate
luck of coming to the Last Chance Motel
Or rather, she has the martyr's ring and was
given a thumbs down and offered as bait to
the hungry lion from his waiting jail cell
Unfortunately, the worst might happen for the
mouse if she chances too close to the cat's den
Something serious that may tend to make you sad
if you are the soft-hearted kind of mother hen

The cat might catch and eat the mouse and that
would then for the mouse, be a poison pen
I guess that would be that, then; and that's
a big over and out and a big amen
The moral to this story is you can run around all you want
but if you push the wrong buttons
You will be eaten for lunch and you'll be
the one who will be long gone
Antoine will prepare you for the feast like a tasty bon-bon
And Cezanne will step on the floor
instead of standing on a chair afraid and woebegone

YOU ARE WHO YOU ARE

Why pretend and be artificial, why
pretend you are so special?
You, just might end up sitting in
some jail cell if you are a liar
and then you'll be walking on eggshells
Try being honest and clear as a bell;
and when you become Mr. William Tell
you won't have to deal with any bombshell
Being you will more than sell
it may even cast a magical spell
If you are a good worker and don't lose sight of yourself
good things are bound to occur
Work will pass by, like you are traveling in a blur
and trouble will never be astir
Look work in the eye and say grrrrr
and you'll feel like an emperor
Don't let your enemies interfere or with you, deter
and you will like it, it as it is, as it were
If you like to express yourself;
make sure you are sincere and truthful
and be true to yourself
Don't let doubters stop you; put them on the bookshelf
Have confidence in yourself because
there is no one like you;
if you feel like being an elf, be an elf
Doubters are many, believers are
few; believe in belief itself
Remember, you are who you are;
and if you remain true to yourself, you'll always be a star

THE
MAIN THING
is
2
to
Be
REAL
genuINE
THERE
IS
ROOM
IN THIS
WORLD
4
for
EVERYONE
R
are
you
R
are XX
not
1
a
snake
in
a sheep's skin
WHEN
you
look in the mirror will
you
Be
ABLE
2
to
smile + grin
you
AND
will
Like
you
WHO

You may be some kind of famous star;
even this is good, if it is so; it is not so bizarre
Or a derelict from some sleazy bar,
which has every right to wish on the falling stars
Or a refugee from a foreign war
just remember that you are OK, no matter who you are
The main thing is to be genuine and
you will never be a has-been
And you will always know where you've been;
because you are not a snake in a sheep's skin
No matter what kind of mess you get yourself in;
honesty and being yourself will make you a shoo-in
Then when you look in the mirror
you will be able to smile and grin and
you won't need a stand-in
Of yourself, never be ashamed; even learn
to like your given nicknames
Especially accept who you are in life's game
and you will never be put to shame
You are special in the overall mainframe
so take your special ways and get ready and take aim
Everyone has their reasons and their own claim
no one is made the same; and everyone
has their own kind of acclaim
Above all, try to like who you are
because that way, you can go very far
Try to learn from life's scars; they make you who you are

No matter, how different, you are,
no matter how bizarre
you are still a superstar
If everyone wrote their own memories
we would have the most interesting
library bazaar by far
There is room in this world for everyone
the lines of destiny have already been drawn
Whether you are a Don Juan or
an Yvonne of the Yukon
You could come from Taiwan or from
the province of Saskatchewan
You could be an Antoine or a
Cezanne or a Genghis Khan;
the fact is, you are who you are and
of that you have no choice
it is a forgone conclusion.

AN EYE ON THE SKY

One day I was looking way up into the sky
I was enjoying the clouds as they passed by
which I enjoyed to catalog and to classify
I saw something that looked like a giant spinning pie
I became fearful and terrified
It zigzagged back and forth, no lie; it
seemed like it was dissatisfied
It moved just like a giant hyper horsefly
this was definitely a case for the FBI
The air was sparkling with electricity
the giant pies were giving a lightning jamboree
The air was vibrant by our fair city,
and lit it up like a giant Christmas tree
It was a perfect day to snooze or to sightsee,
except when one is afraid and has to flee
It was time to dance like a bumblebee and time to cop a plea
What happened next, right then and there?
Was one for the texts, right out of thin atmosphere?
Something that would make anyone perplexed
happened right there in midair
It was a story right out of Star Trek
along with all the fanfare
The shiny dish landed with no further ado
Out came beings with bald heads
and necks shaped like corkscrews
Now I know I am a certified egghead
but I was so shocked, my hair curled to a new hairdo
And this time I could have dropped dead

because I was petrified through and through
They didn't notice me, so I ran and
hid from the bald-headed
corkscrew-necked gigantic squids with eyelids
They didn't notice my monkey,
Marie, or my giant arachnid
But they stole my pet chimpanzee
I guess, to them, he looked like a brilliant whiz kid
I now keep my horse under lock and key
and watch for any new wildlife hybrids
Was I ever surprised, when as fast as it had come?
I just couldn't believe my eyes; it began
to leave where it had come from
I even snapped a picture to help me to justify
that I wasn't crazy or a lying bum
So that I could later examine it
and have it analyzed to find out if I
had really seen it, fee-fi-fo-fum
Then in a wink of an eye, it jerked up and away
It zipped right back up into the sky
like it had disappeared up a vertical stairway
It must have been camera shy,
or I rubbed it the wrong way
Because it didn't even stop to say good-bye
it was off to one of the stars in the Milky Way
Sometimes, I look up into the sky
and I salute and say

"Here's mud in your eyes, you guys."
Maybe I'm imagining what I see next
but what I see next, even if it is November
still seems like the fourth of July
All this may seem weird to you or like sci-fi
But I saw it with my own little eyes
when I had an eye on the sky

THE LONG ARM OF THE LAW

Now I've done it, which was the last
straw; I went and lost my temper
I hit him square on the jaw; I gave him what's for
and furthermore, I gave him much, much more, sir
It just might be his last hurrah; I don't see him moving
and he doesn't seem to want to stir
what do you know, here comes the long arm of the law;
I can hear the rattling of his spurs
He'll put me into a boot camp, you say;
he will make sure I do not disobey
It's just another place to learn to play
war games, the wrong ways
There has got to be a better way to
dance the retribution ballet
According to the gangster role-play;
you will see me make headway
if you do not rub them the wrong way

That's not at all I did; I flipped my lid
and my friends followed suit
I created a paparazzi pyramid that just
so happened to look very cute
I was a whiz kid out in Madrid, and I
played a mean Spanish flute
I was an Aspersers' hybrid kid and
my life was challenging,
but it was a beauty

It's all I could do but throw up my towel; I was very sad
But the judge still put down his gavel; he said
that I had been bad, bad, bad
It was all I could do, but to show my navel
and run around not at all clad
Now was the time for my birthday suit bombshell;
I guess then they will think I'm mad
Now came the time for justice; I guess
I would get what I deserve
It was to be the final feted kiss
I was to be given my sentence and I was served
It was to be the end of my life of freedom, my bliss
I now have to spend time in jail with a sentence to observe
I would have lots of time to reminisce
and think of why I thought I could have so much nerve
I knew my life was no longer, worth a plug cent;
The rest of my life, was destined behind bars to be spent
No one cared, if I was guilty or if I was innocent;
Or if I was just a malcontent, an unfortunate gent
No one cared where I was, if I was sane, or if I was innocent
it would be to them just a jolly experiment
No one cared if I rotted there inside—it
was all I could do but to lament
on any and all the time that had been
spent and would be spent
I was to rot away in a small cell; I didn't
even have so much as a doorbell

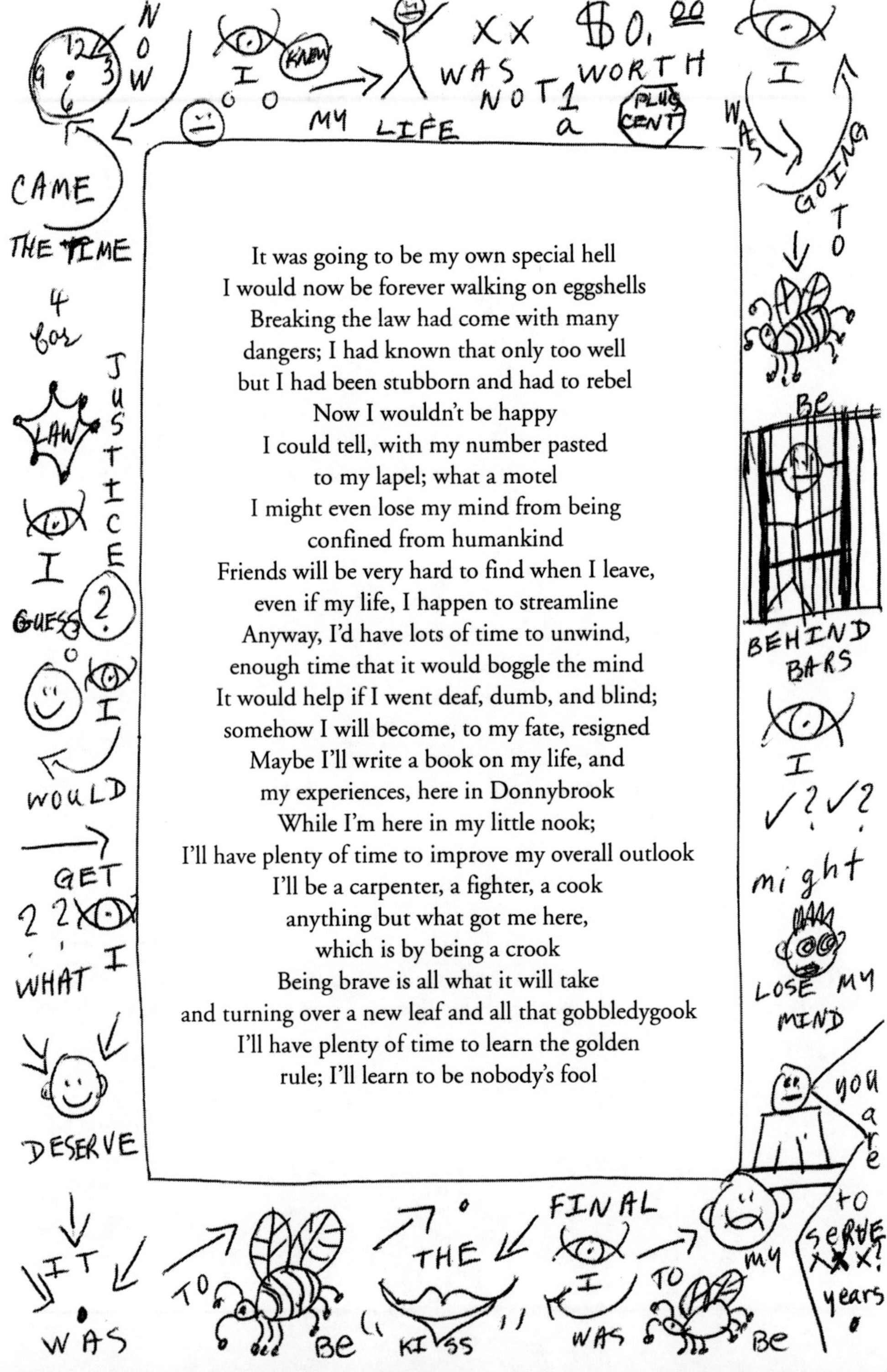

It was going to be my own special hell
I would now be forever walking on eggshells
Breaking the law had come with many
dangers; I had known that only too well
but I had been stubborn and had to rebel
Now I wouldn't be happy
I could tell, with my number pasted
to my lapel; what a motel
I might even lose my mind from being
confined from humankind
Friends will be very hard to find when I leave,
even if my life, I happen to streamline
Anyway, I'd have lots of time to unwind,
enough time that it would boggle the mind
It would help if I went deaf, dumb, and blind;
somehow I will become, to my fate, resigned
Maybe I'll write a book on my life, and
my experiences, here in Donnybrook
While I'm here in my little nook;
I'll have plenty of time to improve my overall outlook
I'll be a carpenter, a fighter, a cook
anything but what got me here,
which is by being a crook
Being brave is all what it will take
and turning over a new leaf and all that gobbledygook
I'll have plenty of time to learn the golden
rule; I'll learn to be nobody's fool

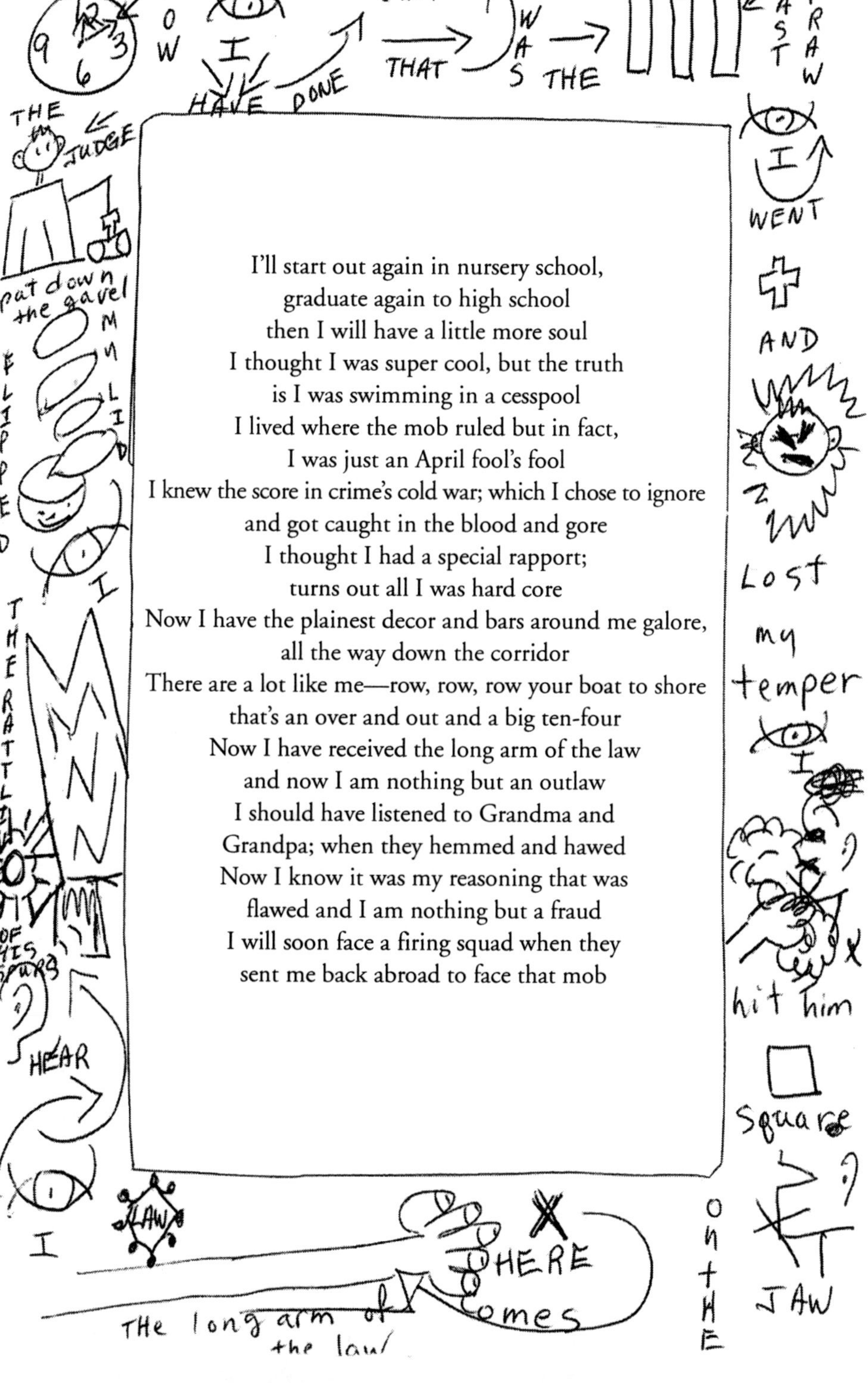

I'll start out again in nursery school,
graduate again to high school
then I will have a little more soul
I thought I was super cool, but the truth
is I was swimming in a cesspool
I lived where the mob ruled but in fact,
I was just an April fool's fool
I knew the score in crime's cold war; which I chose to ignore
and got caught in the blood and gore
I thought I had a special rapport;
turns out all I was hard core
Now I have the plainest decor and bars around me galore,
all the way down the corridor
There are a lot like me—row, row, row your boat to shore
that's an over and out and a big ten-four
Now I have received the long arm of the law
and now I am nothing but an outlaw
I should have listened to Grandma and
Grandpa; when they hemmed and hawed
Now I know it was my reasoning that was
flawed and I am nothing but a fraud
I will soon face a firing squad when they
sent me back abroad to face that mob

I JUST DON'T UNDERSTAND THE MASTER PLAN

I just don't understand the master plan
Or why this happened to my favorite man
All I know is I have to give him
a helping hand
There is no better than him in all the land
I'll stay with him through thick and thin
This battle, I want him to conquer and win
How much I love him, I can't begin to begin
Surely a love this great cannot be a sin
He is a fighter and a real prize—
a real prizefighter
Together, we couldn't be tighter or righter
His courage shines brighter and brighter
Our love is like pure dynamite
and has real power
He just doesn't know how to complain
He's just made to be humble
and to refrain
He has his emotions on a tight string
I get proud of him, again and again
When problems come our way
We live each day to day
and live for today
We'll listen to what
each of us has to say

Then at night, we know
everything will be A-OK.
No matter how hard life may become
We will not let ourselves become undone
We will always have time to have some fun
Surely we will, our problems, overcome
Then people will be amazed
At the trails, we've blazed—unfazed
And how happy we have stayed
And how our love is freely displayed
We will enjoy whatever time we have left together
That will make our time together
seem better and better
Right down to the last letter,
we are a perfect him and her
Together I feel like a queen with her royal emperor

THE QUESTION REMAINS

The question remains and stays the same
Why have you overstepped your domain?
Your answers seem not probable
and seem lame
This is not some stupid, silly, useless game
I am not some stupid schoolgirl
I have been around this big, big world
Don't put me into a stranglehold
Because you'll find
I don't fit any particular mold
You may find your hands will get burnt
That it might be
some kind of deterrent
You may find you get more than you earned
If you don't use all that you have learned
You may not be telling the whole truth
You may be hiding under a hat forsooth
I have only just begun to become uncouth
I'll flip if I see you hiding there in your phone booth
No, your theory is not right
And I'll fight you with all my might
You think I am not too bright
Now all I have to do is hang tight
You won't hurt those whom I love
Because there is
a greater power from above

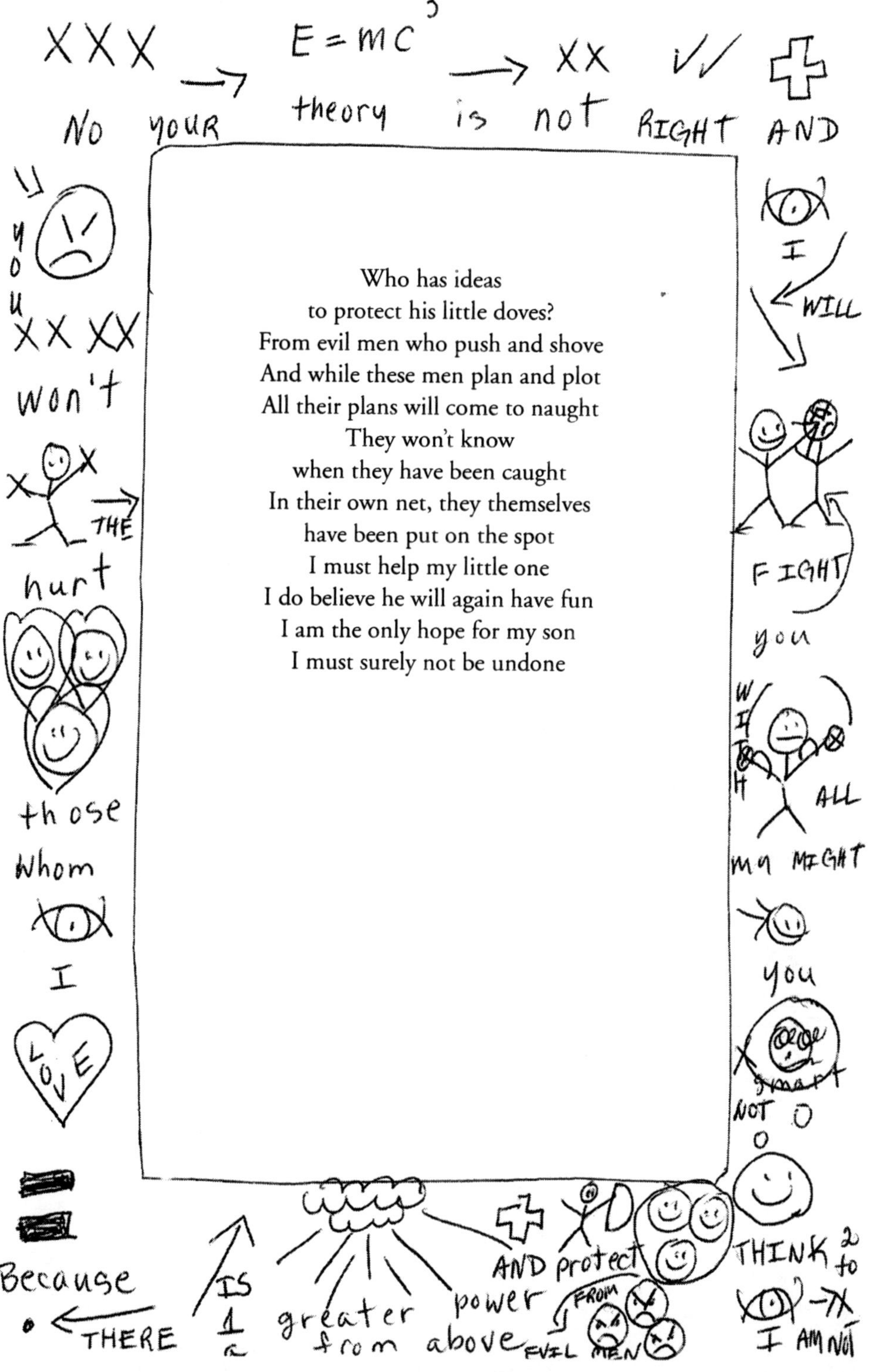

Who has ideas
to protect his little doves?
From evil men who push and shove
And while these men plan and plot
All their plans will come to naught
They won't know
when they have been caught
In their own net, they themselves
have been put on the spot
I must help my little one
I do believe he will again have fun
I am the only hope for my son
I must surely not be undone

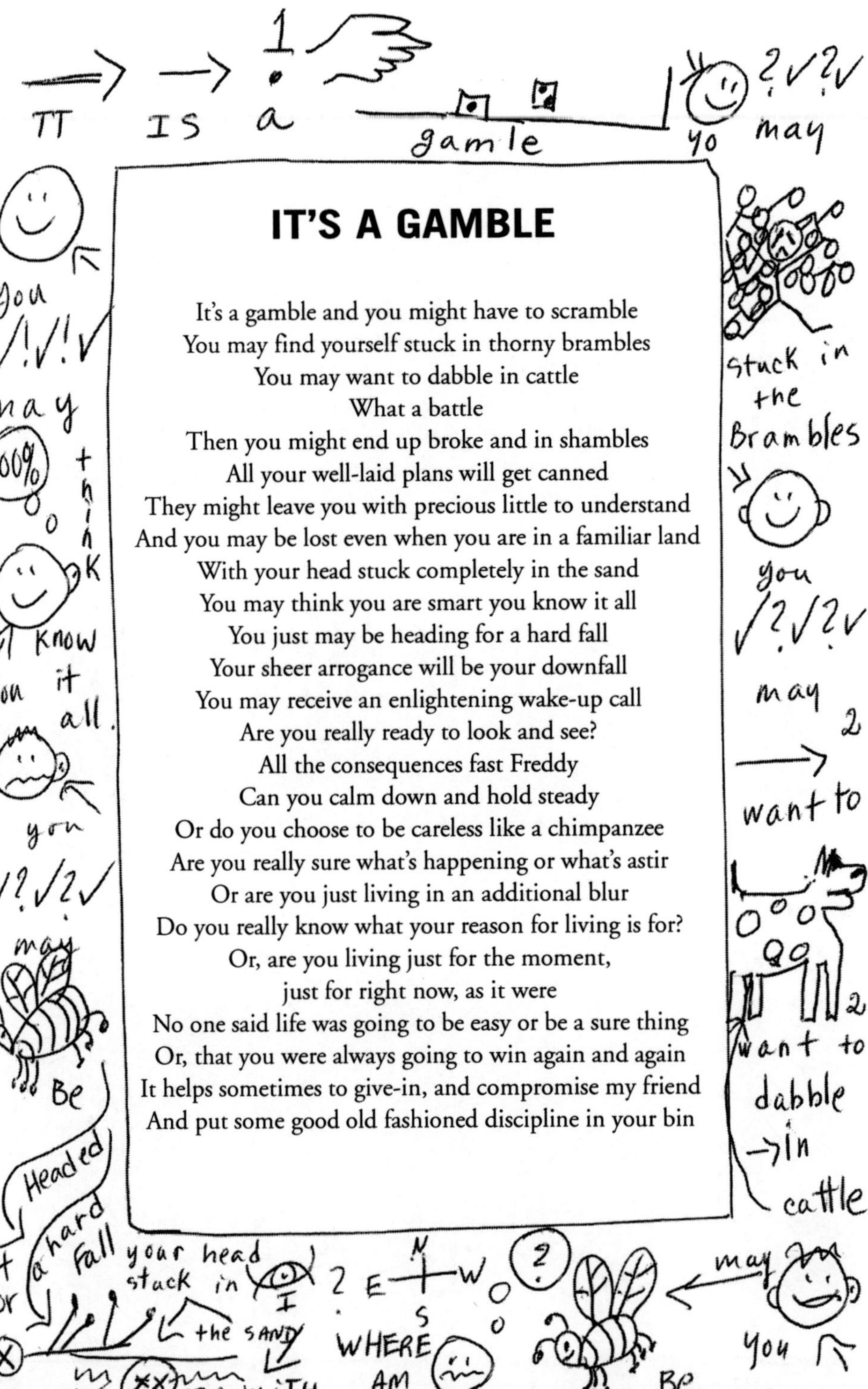

IT'S A GAMBLE

It's a gamble and you might have to scramble
You may find yourself stuck in thorny brambles
You may want to dabble in cattle
What a battle
Then you might end up broke and in shambles
All your well-laid plans will get canned
They might leave you with precious little to understand
And you may be lost even when you are in a familiar land
With your head stuck completely in the sand
You may think you are smart you know it all
You just may be heading for a hard fall
Your sheer arrogance will be your downfall
You may receive an enlightening wake-up call
Are you really ready to look and see?
All the consequences fast Freddy
Can you calm down and hold steady
Or do you choose to be careless like a chimpanzee
Are you really sure what's happening or what's astir
Or are you just living in an additional blur
Do you really know what your reason for living is for?
Or, are you living just for the moment,
just for right now, as it were
No one said life was going to be easy or be a sure thing
Or, that you were always going to win again and again
It helps sometimes to give-in, and compromise my friend
And put some good old fashioned discipline in your bin

It may be hard to stop from showing off
When you've hit the jackpot
Or, when you feel; you are really hot
But, that's when you should show what you've got
No one will ever warn you or give you a clue
On how, or what you will have to do anew
You will have to stop; and use a little control too
And while your luck is still with you
You must say many a thank-you

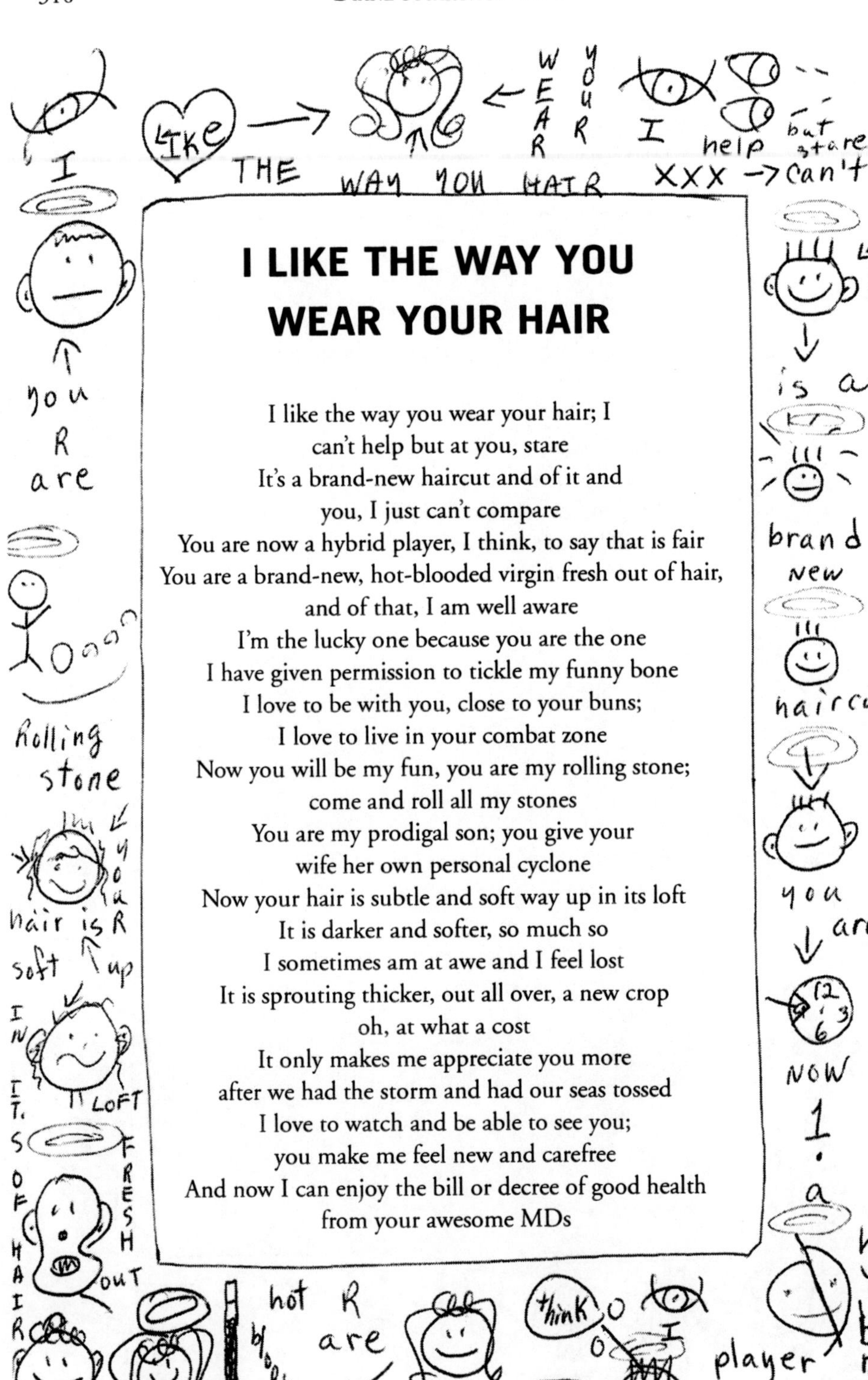

I LIKE THE WAY YOU WEAR YOUR HAIR

I like the way you wear your hair; I
can't help but at you, stare
It's a brand-new haircut and of it and
you, I just can't compare
You are now a hybrid player, I think, to say that is fair
You are a brand-new, hot-blooded virgin fresh out of hair,
and of that, I am well aware
I'm the lucky one because you are the one
I have given permission to tickle my funny bone
I love to be with you, close to your buns;
I love to live in your combat zone
Now you will be my fun, you are my rolling stone;
come and roll all my stones
You are my prodigal son; you give your
wife her own personal cyclone
Now your hair is subtle and soft way up in its loft
It is darker and softer, so much so
I sometimes am at awe and I feel lost
It is sprouting thicker, out all over, a new crop
oh, at what a cost
It only makes me appreciate you more
after we had the storm and had our seas tossed
I love to watch and be able to see you;
you make me feel new and carefree
And now I can enjoy the bill or decree of good health
from your awesome MDs

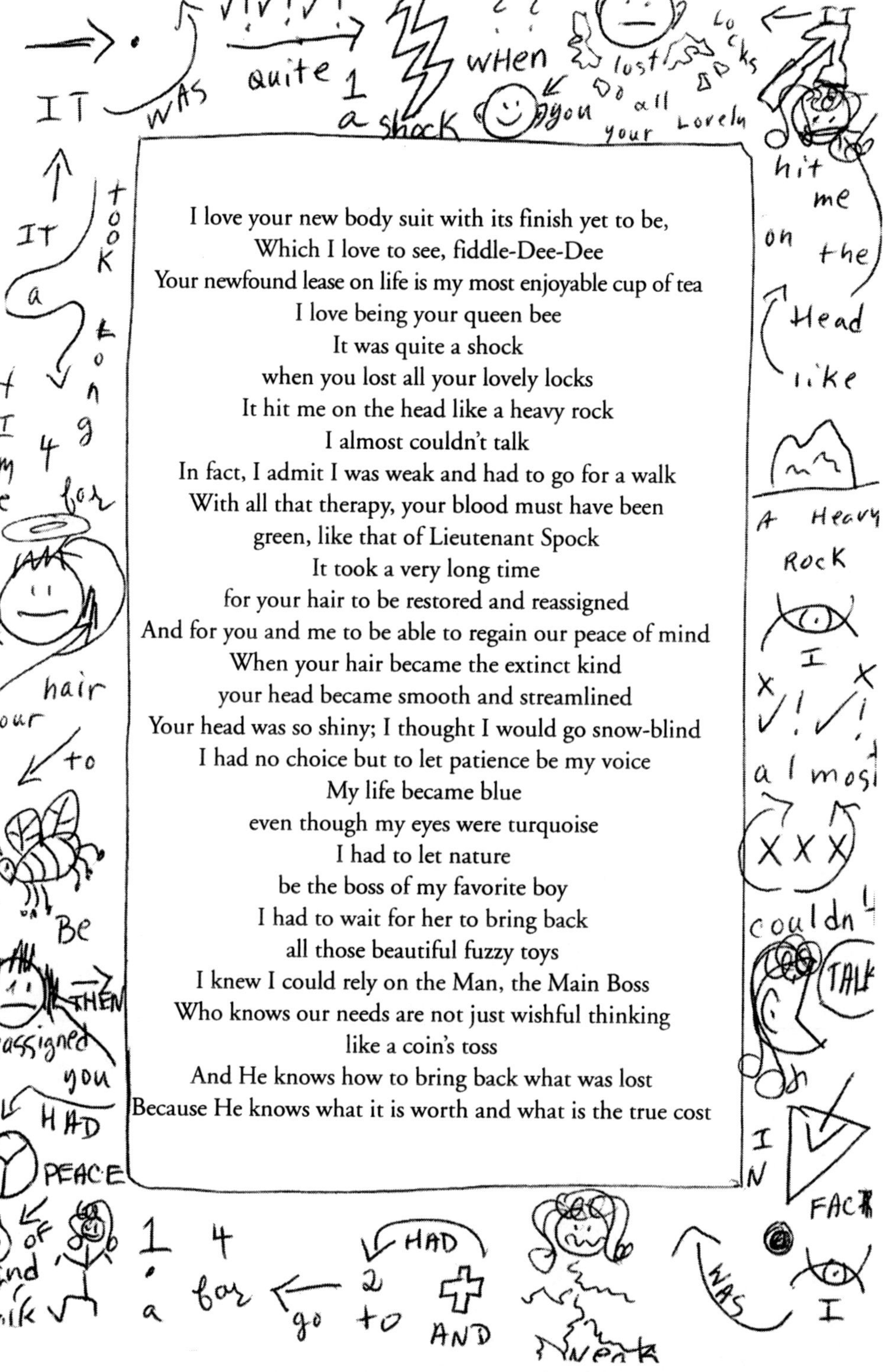

I love your new body suit with its finish yet to be,
Which I love to see, fiddle-Dee-Dee
Your newfound lease on life is my most enjoyable cup of tea
I love being your queen bee
It was quite a shock
when you lost all your lovely locks
It hit me on the head like a heavy rock
I almost couldn't talk
In fact, I admit I was weak and had to go for a walk
With all that therapy, your blood must have been
green, like that of Lieutenant Spock
It took a very long time
for your hair to be restored and reassigned
And for you and me to be able to regain our peace of mind
When your hair became the extinct kind
your head became smooth and streamlined
Your head was so shiny; I thought I would go snow-blind
I had no choice but to let patience be my voice
My life became blue
even though my eyes were turquoise
I had to let nature
be the boss of my favorite boy
I had to wait for her to bring back
all those beautiful fuzzy toys
I knew I could rely on the Man, the Main Boss
Who knows our needs are not just wishful thinking
like a coin's toss
And He knows how to bring back what was lost
Because He knows what it is worth and what is the true cost

THE CARDS ARE DEALT

The way the cards
are passed and dealt
Can sometimes
deal a heavy welt
And the way they are usually felt
Is usually sincere and heartfelt
Meanwhile, in your particular domicile
Instead of just existing, you can go in style
It would be worthwhile to go that extra mile
By trying that route, without malice or guile
When you place your cards
down and all in a row
You may get some insight and begin to know
About your ebbs and flows
and your highs and your lows
Without ever breaking the status quo
Then your alibi will be airtight
Because you will not be the one
causing a fight
Make sure to place the cards
out of sight
Or someone may suspect
your reasoning and get uptight

Who knows what is in your cards
It may be a mystery that will catch us off guard
No matter how you try to understand it
the resulting confusion may be too hard
And may put you into a hospital ward
No matter which way your future may go
It will lead you through
a fabulous hologram picture show
Where you are destined
to shine and glow
In which case, you will be
in the very front row
And while the life's show may leave you puzzled
You may want to be silent
and keep yourself muzzled
You may also want to sit close to life and cuddle
Until you know you have what it takes
the underlying muscle
You will now know
you have met your match
When you can no longer unlatch
From life and from what
you think is a bad batch
In reality, you have
just begun to reattach

YOU HELPED ME LEARN TO BE FREE

Until now, I've never known; I've been facedown
I did not know how to be free; my heart had been on loan
and I have been a fool and acted like a clown
So far, on barren land my love has been sewn
and I've been lost and unknown
Oh, how I've grown; you could say
I played, I ran, and I scored a touchdown
Help me is my plea—help me, to the tenth degree
Help me learn to be free: counting one, two, and three
I've always had a great desire to be
happy and to be carefree
Of this, I will never tire; you'll help me to be happy,
you'll see
It is almost impossible to read between the lines
if it's just between you and me
How unusually free we are; you can be my personal referee
You have helped me to become whole and fancy free
Having faith in you
was the key to obtaining my honorary college degree
You gave me my ticket to ride, and I
became your blushing bride
Now all I have is great love for you inside
and a great deal of fond, loving pride
You helped me ride the storm, the tempest, the tide
you were my constant guide

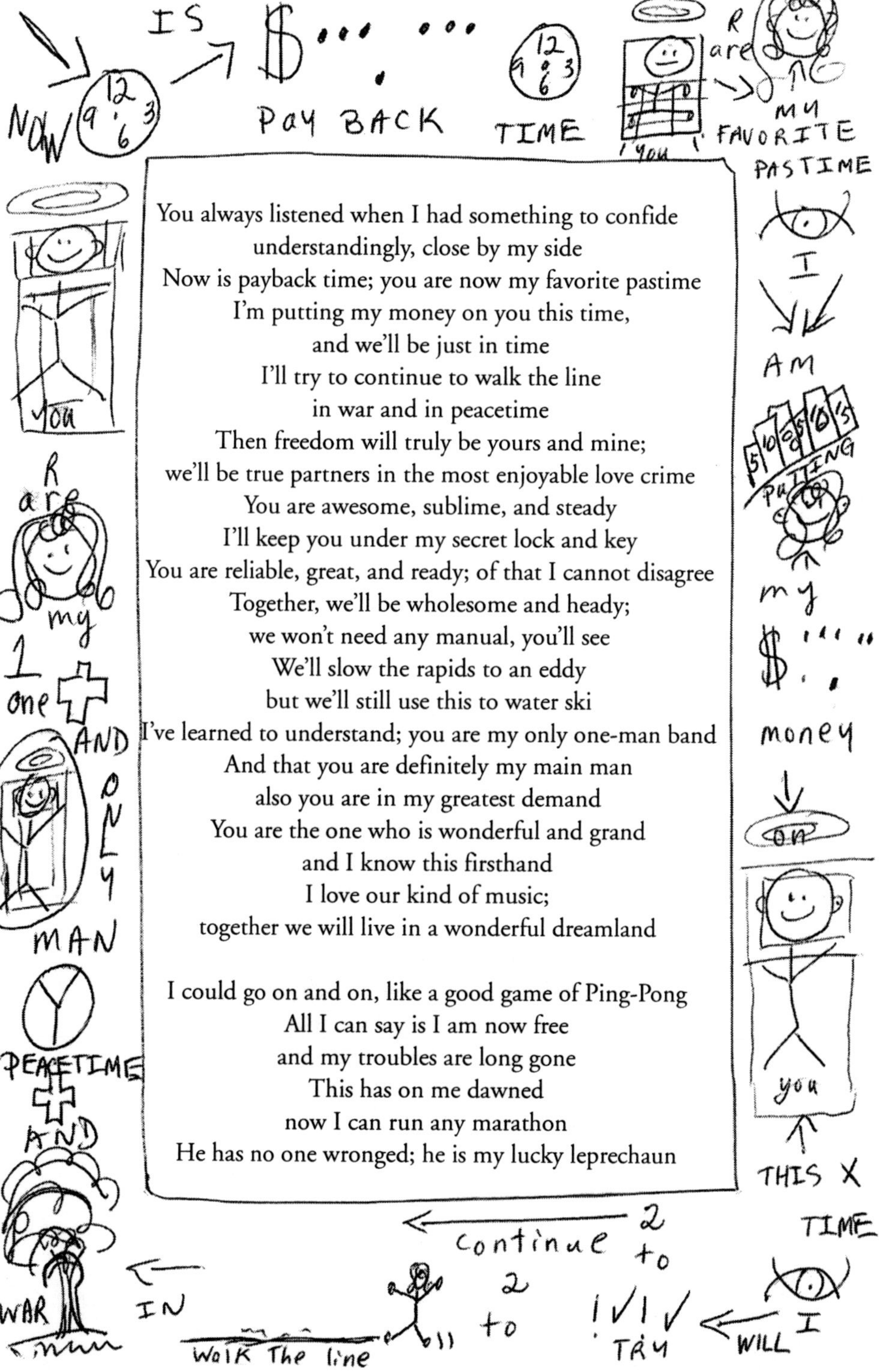

You always listened when I had something to confide
understandingly, close by my side
Now is payback time; you are now my favorite pastime
I'm putting my money on you this time,
and we'll be just in time
I'll try to continue to walk the line
in war and in peacetime
Then freedom will truly be yours and mine;
we'll be true partners in the most enjoyable love crime
You are awesome, sublime, and steady
I'll keep you under my secret lock and key
You are reliable, great, and ready; of that I cannot disagree
Together, we'll be wholesome and heady;
we won't need any manual, you'll see
We'll slow the rapids to an eddy
but we'll still use this to water ski
I've learned to understand; you are my only one-man band
And that you are definitely my main man
also you are in my greatest demand
You are the one who is wonderful and grand
and I know this firsthand
I love our kind of music;
together we will live in a wonderful dreamland

I could go on and on, like a good game of Ping-Pong
All I can say is I am now free
and my troubles are long gone
This has on me dawned
now I can run any marathon
He has no one wronged; he is my lucky leprechaun

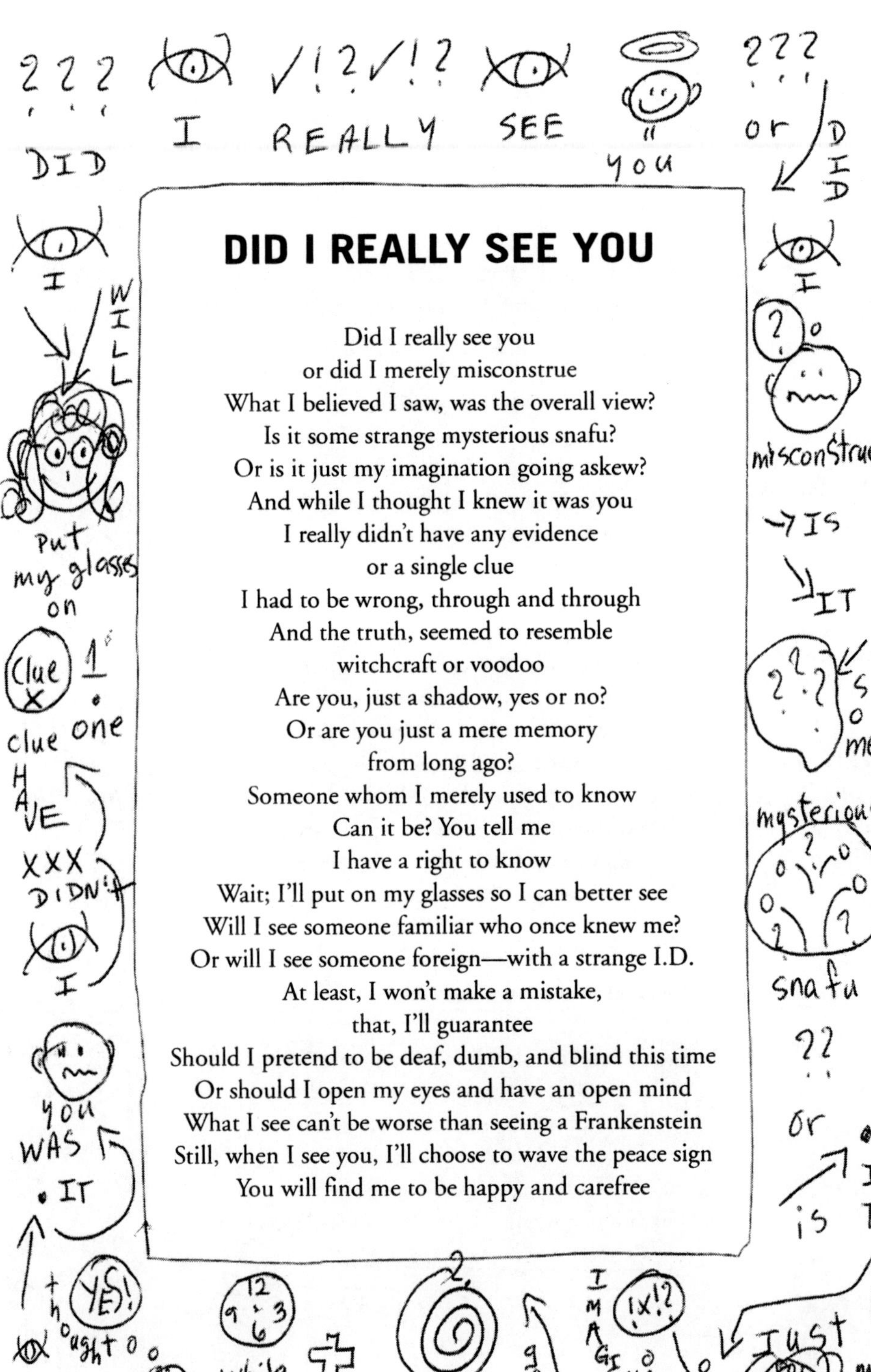

DID I REALLY SEE YOU

Did I really see you
or did I merely misconstrue
What I believed I saw, was the overall view?
Is it some strange mysterious snafu?
Or is it just my imagination going askew?
And while I thought I knew it was you
I really didn't have any evidence
or a single clue
I had to be wrong, through and through
And the truth, seemed to resemble
witchcraft or voodoo
Are you, just a shadow, yes or no?
Or are you just a mere memory
from long ago?
Someone whom I merely used to know
Can it be? You tell me
I have a right to know
Wait; I'll put on my glasses so I can better see
Will I see someone familiar who once knew me?
Or will I see someone foreign—with a strange I.D.
At least, I won't make a mistake,
that, I'll guarantee
Should I pretend to be deaf, dumb, and blind this time
Or should I open my eyes and have an open mind
What I see can't be worse than seeing a Frankenstein
Still, when I see you, I'll choose to wave the peace sign
You will find me to be happy and carefree

I am the one with the greatest ability to see
Because being patient are my best quality
and my purest pedigree
And being observant to you, looking at me
keeps me safe and worry free
Tell me; should I begin to try and pay more attention
And to also try to cultivate more memory and retention
Otherwise, my dysfunction might cause a malfunction
Which may lead to failure and lend to conjecture
because of an overactive imagination?
Sending my gaze your way;
may have been a fleeting thing
But it was just as good as my seeing everything
And you can no longer lie about a thing
Because now I have caught you in my mind's eye
like a puppet on a string

I'LL LOVE YOU TONIGHT

I'll love you tonight, and I won't even bite
I'll even be polite, I won't be uptight
You won't know what hit you
because it will be out of sight
And I'll be quite forthright
it'll be as powerful as snakebite
I like to play, today, or any day
You were so good in your heyday
so what do you say
You're still good anyway
you know the way
Are you really Canadian? Heh
how's about a little role-play?
Gray may be the color of my hair, I do declare
And you'll be able to find my gray hair anywhere
that's only fair and square
I don't really have a care at all
about all that glitz and all the fanfare
I don't even care what I wear;
so here's to wash and wear
I don't mind if you tarry; I'm fancy free
You are really very happy
just like a chimpanzee
Your name isn't Jerry
but you have a royal pedigree
Kevin is the one I want to marry
he's my VIP.

You can be my playmate; you are really great
Loving you will be my fate; I just can't wait
Please, my love, satiate;
bring me through glory's gate
You are a real heavyweight;
you are someone I must investigate
You can take your time because you are in your prime
Even though you don't have a dime
you can still see me anytime
You can ring my chimes anytime
and you can ring them big time
It won't be any kind of crime
I'll quite enjoy being with you for a lifetime
The gracious are the ones to love, come push or shove
The polite will be the ones to get more of,
for their special kind of brotherly love
Come on now, come on the wings of a dove;
then put on your boxing gloves
Be quiet, be my puppy love;
lick my face from below or above
I'll love you tonight; I am quite happy and contrite
I'll love you today with all my might
and I won't put up a fight
Today, I'll get it just right; man, it's out of sight
You give me real insight;
it is as clear as black and white

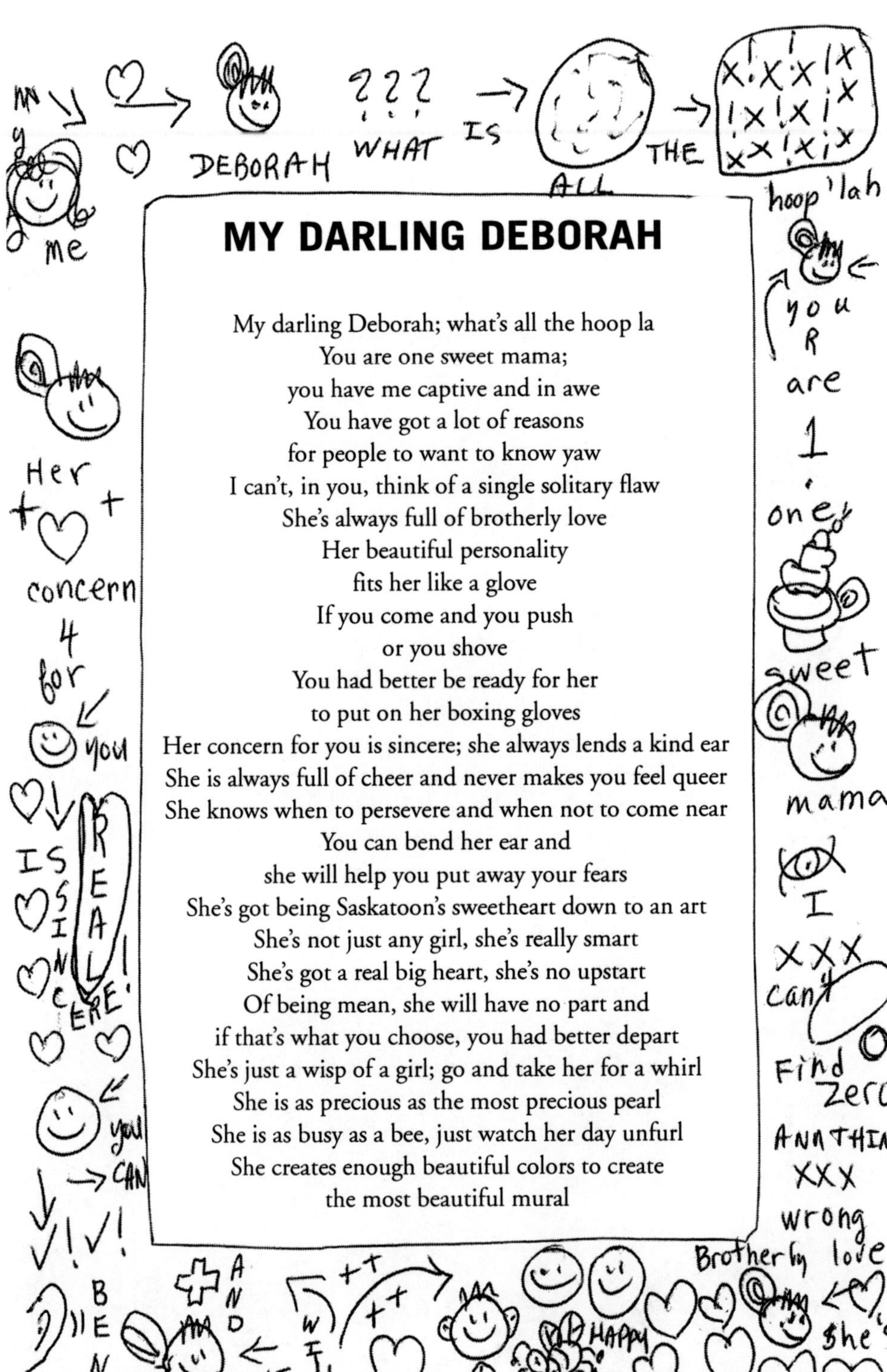

MY DARLING DEBORAH

My darling Deborah; what's all the hoop la
You are one sweet mama;
you have me captive and in awe
You have got a lot of reasons
for people to want to know yaw
I can't, in you, think of a single solitary flaw
She's always full of brotherly love
Her beautiful personality
fits her like a glove
If you come and you push
or you shove
You had better be ready for her
to put on her boxing gloves
Her concern for you is sincere; she always lends a kind ear
She is always full of cheer and never makes you feel queer
She knows when to persevere and when not to come near
You can bend her ear and
she will help you put away your fears
She's got being Saskatoon's sweetheart down to an art
She's not just any girl, she's really smart
She's got a real big heart, she's no upstart
Of being mean, she will have no part and
if that's what you choose, you had better depart
She's just a wisp of a girl; go and take her for a whirl
She is as precious as the most precious pearl
She is as busy as a bee, just watch her day unfurl
She creates enough beautiful colors to create
the most beautiful mural

Her beauty is so real that she can't possibly, it, conceal
Unlike an automobile
you can't possibly buy it or steal
No matter what kind of misfortune you have been through
her words have the power to heal
She takes no credit for it; she never thinks it is a big deal
She is very wise, which comes to me as no surprise
She's not just one of the girls or the guys
I can see it in her eyes
You won't catch her telling lies
only the truth for her applies
She believes in family ties; she is a real cutie pie
No matter what happens
I'll always consider her as one of my friends
Because she knew when to outstretch her hand
when I was at my wits' end
Especially when I needed to talk again and again
About my ailing, favorite, loving, and beloved man

MY ISLAND

My island is a special place
I sometimes go to in haste
It is one suited to my very own personal taste
My island is a place I love to tenderly embrace
My island is a place where I can be truly free
and feel heavenly grace
It is a great realm with no disease
It is a place where you find peace
and sweet release
It is a place where the breeze
smells like sweet peas
It is also where I love to wander,
all happy and at total ease
You'd never guess what it is,
or where it is
You won't find it on any pop quiz
I'll never tell you and
that's showbiz
That's another story
it is what it is
My island travels through space and time
It follows a special rhythm
and a special rhyme
It'll never let me down
daytime or nighttime
As long as I'm around;
we are special partners in a love crime

My island is a place
where we all want to be
It is a place I am—when he touches me
My husband's touch
is an island of serenity
Something I experience as a gift of love
from him for free
My island can be in your mind too
Let my mind find your island
and let it find you
You won't have the faintest clue
what to pursue
Just what it is where it is or who it is
excuse me and thank you
Before you know it, you might have a nervous tic
And before you've even realized it
you might be in the thick
The answer will fall right out of the skies
like a ton of bricks
And it will blind your eyes like a bad card trick
The solution will land slowly while you watch
You will wonder if it was really here
or if it is hiding under a cabbage patch
You'll wonder if you've missed it in some
mysterious geological batch
Then there might be a telltale fear
of a huge dinosaur hatch

My island rocks
My island talks
My island even squawks
My island even back talks
Talk to me, my island my dreamland
Tell me you are my friend;
tell me again and again
Tell me I can depend on you
to be my fantasy land
Tell me you are where the law of the land
listens to my every command

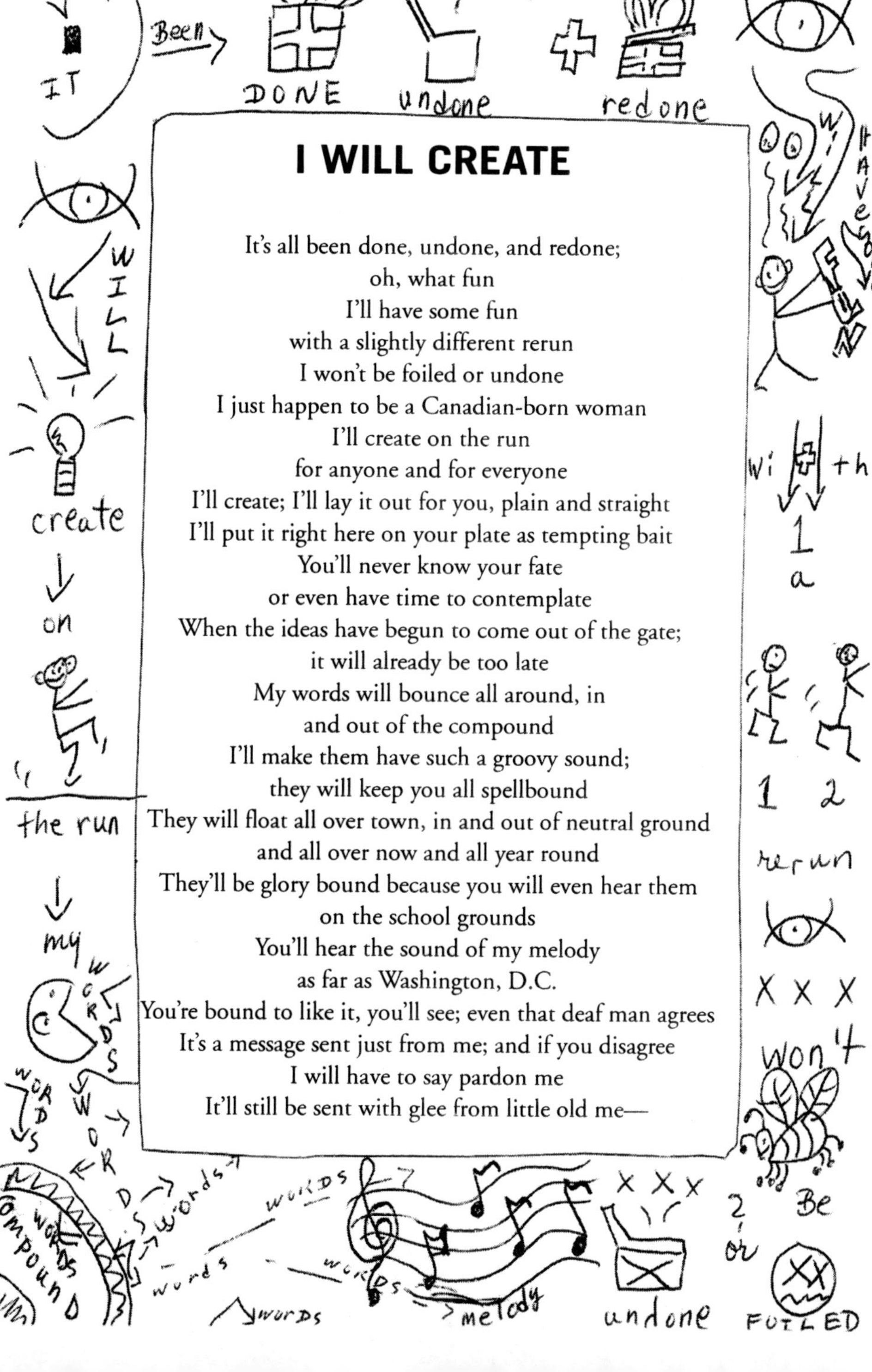

I WILL CREATE

It's all been done, undone, and redone;
oh, what fun
I'll have some fun
with a slightly different rerun
I won't be foiled or undone
I just happen to be a Canadian-born woman
I'll create on the run
for anyone and for everyone
I'll create; I'll lay it out for you, plain and straight
I'll put it right here on your plate as tempting bait
You'll never know your fate
or even have time to contemplate
When the ideas have begun to come out of the gate;
it will already be too late
My words will bounce all around, in
and out of the compound
I'll make them have such a groovy sound;
they will keep you all spellbound
They will float all over town, in and out of neutral ground
and all over now and all year round
They'll be glory bound because you will even hear them
on the school grounds
You'll hear the sound of my melody
as far as Washington, D.C.
You're bound to like it, you'll see; even that deaf man agrees
It's a message sent just from me; and if you disagree
I will have to say pardon me
It'll still be sent with glee from little old me—

Master of the spelling bee
My ideas will come from my heart
even though they may not always be too smart
But my heart is a good place to start
using my special kind of folk art
My melodies will flow out of me like a modern Mozart
yes, I do, sometimes, feel like an upstart
But I have waited a long time; to be
able to show or do my part
I'll continue on and on, and I'll
weigh the pros and the cons
You can tell me if I should belong
and I'll keep on pondering
on this, until way after dawn
But as for me and this song;
it will be my offering from a full-grown swan
I'll perform today, and until I'm gone,
off and on, like a newly freed Don Juan
This will be the best way I can think of to play
And it will be also the best way to spend my day
The notes, to my ideas, will run up and down
the scale's stairway playing a musical ballet
They will fly up and float away up into the Milky Way
I can think of nothing better than to share my handiwork
It gives me pleasure to share my pleasure, my art;
which is not really a chore
At the same time, it gives my brain a chance to
run better and to better work
And helps me to work out any fuzzy quirks
where and if they lurk

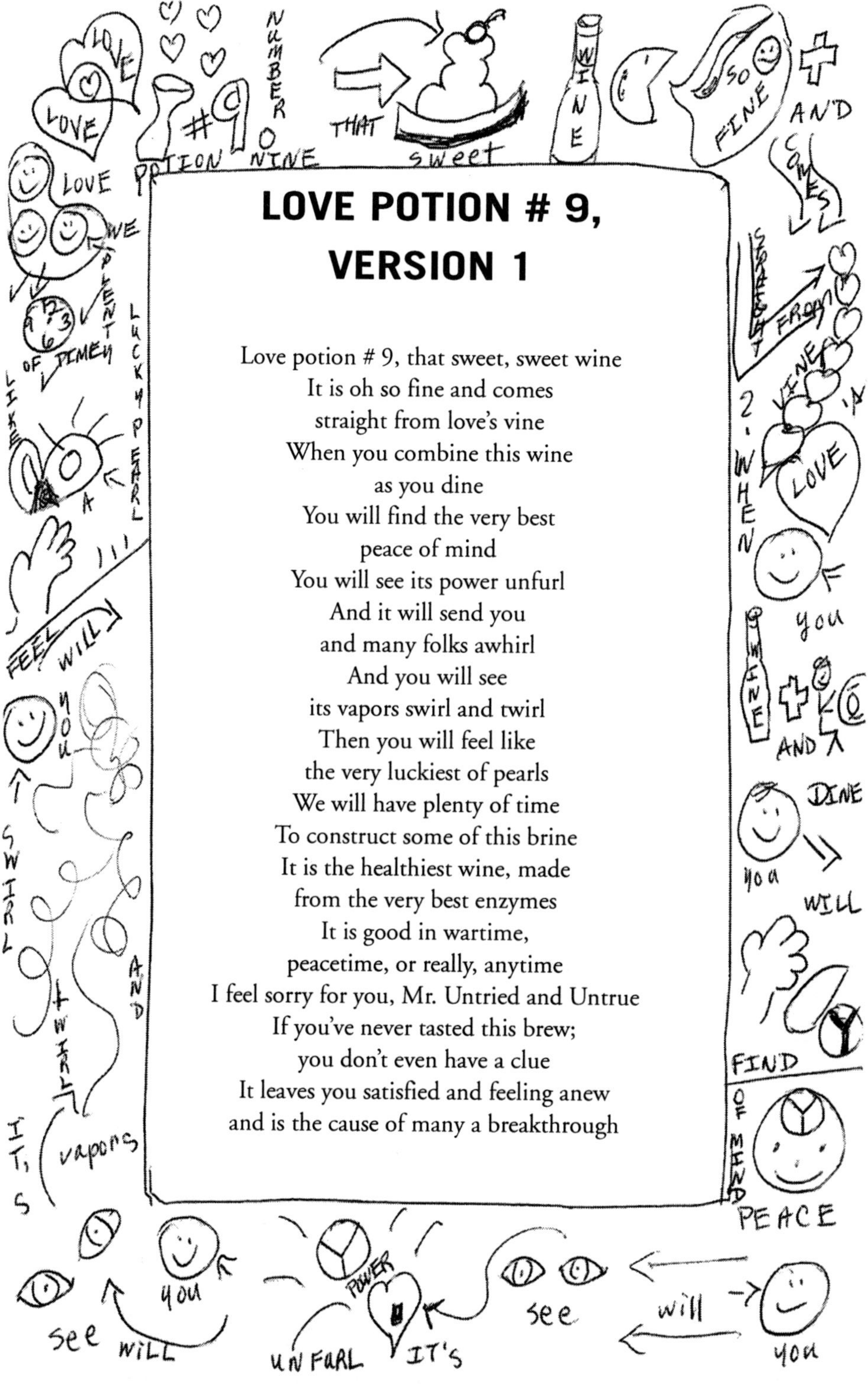

LOVE POTION # 9, VERSION 1

Love potion # 9, that sweet, sweet wine
It is oh so fine and comes
straight from love's vine
When you combine this wine
as you dine
You will find the very best
peace of mind
You will see its power unfurl
And it will send you
and many folks awhirl
And you will see
its vapors swirl and twirl
Then you will feel like
the very luckiest of pearls
We will have plenty of time
To construct some of this brine
It is the healthiest wine, made
from the very best enzymes
It is good in wartime,
peacetime, or really, anytime
I feel sorry for you, Mr. Untried and Untrue
If you've never tasted this brew;
you don't even have a clue
It leaves you satisfied and feeling anew
and is the cause of many a breakthrough

Without it, you won't even have a clue on
which direction to go, or on which avenue
You don't need a ton of knowledge
All you need is a little, tiny smidge
Of ideas, from this wonderful dredge
They'll send you over
love's mountain ledge
Love will be the secret potion not to be undone
You soon, will have the notion how
to have, all its fun
What else are you to put into
the lotion, one by one?
Love potion # 9 will put your desires into motion,
and you may not even have time to call 911
It is oh so fine; you'll be on cloud nine
Love potion # 9 is a veritable gold mine
I wanted it all the time; it would even cure
the redneck Frankenstein
Finally, I've found it, it is mine; I also
offered it to my friend Einstein
It can't be mistaken and will never be undone
It will not be forsaken or forgotten
by your enemy, your friend, or by anyone
It is love's first bite, you could then say
you've been hit, but you didn't want to run
It will always be just right,
Love's greatest hole in one

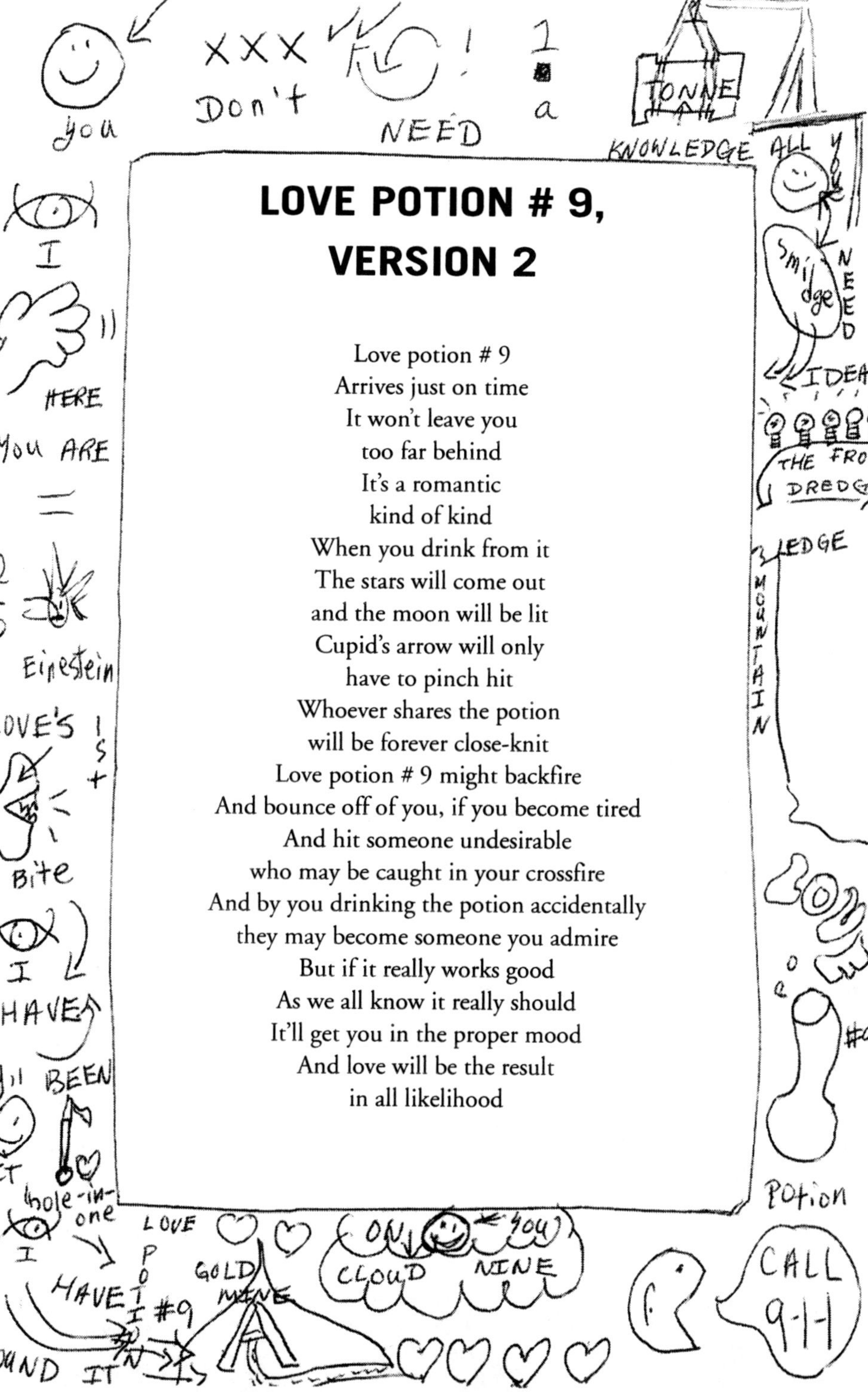

LOVE POTION # 9, VERSION 2

Love potion # 9
Arrives just on time
It won't leave you
too far behind
It's a romantic
kind of kind
When you drink from it
The stars will come out
and the moon will be lit
Cupid's arrow will only
have to pinch hit
Whoever shares the potion
will be forever close-knit
Love potion # 9 might backfire
And bounce off of you, if you become tired
And hit someone undesirable
who may be caught in your crossfire
And by you drinking the potion accidentally
they may become someone you admire
But if it really works good
As we all know it really should
It'll get you in the proper mood
And love will be the result
in all likelihood

It'll be like heaven's delight
It'll feel like a mountain
majestic and in all its might
It'll be like a flowing river
than runs both day and night
It'll be as good as flying a kite
When you've tasted love's sweet liquid
It'll lift you as high as Egypt's pyramids
You won't be able to close your eyelids
And you'll like it because that's why
you became a whiz kid.
The end result will be good and great
And you'll be glad you took love's bait
The feeling will totally help you
to liberate
And you will be headed
right for the pearly gates
In the end, you'll be glad, you've been love had
That love potion # 9 was definitely,
your launching pad
Because you have now officially become
a love Olympiad
And will now have as many adventures
as did Galahad

MY CARES LAID BARE

(Version 1)

My cares are laid bare
All people can do
is stop and stare
I don't really care
I think this is quite fair
It's all about being free
Because someone who loved us
was nailed to a tree
Forgiveness for our sins
was his plea
His was a great sacrifice
for you and me
We strive to live
Up to his standards
and to give
Our children
this precious gift
And not to cause
any negative rifts
When I have gone through life
And I have encountered strife
I know now I am a good wife
Carved out of life
with an experienced knife
Soon everyone
will know

Me from heel to toe
My goodness
will glow
From inside me
just so
My most glorious time
Is when I sit and rhyme
Sitting and writing words on paper
line after line?
I say this is a treasure to me
and is truly my very best, best find
It brings me no end of pleasure
It is truly something I treasure
Something I dole out
in good measure
It comes now and then
at my leisure
It has always been so
If you care to know
Silently waiting to come out left to grow
Just how it came to be and why it flows
I'll gladly welcome and tell you
on why and how and give you more info

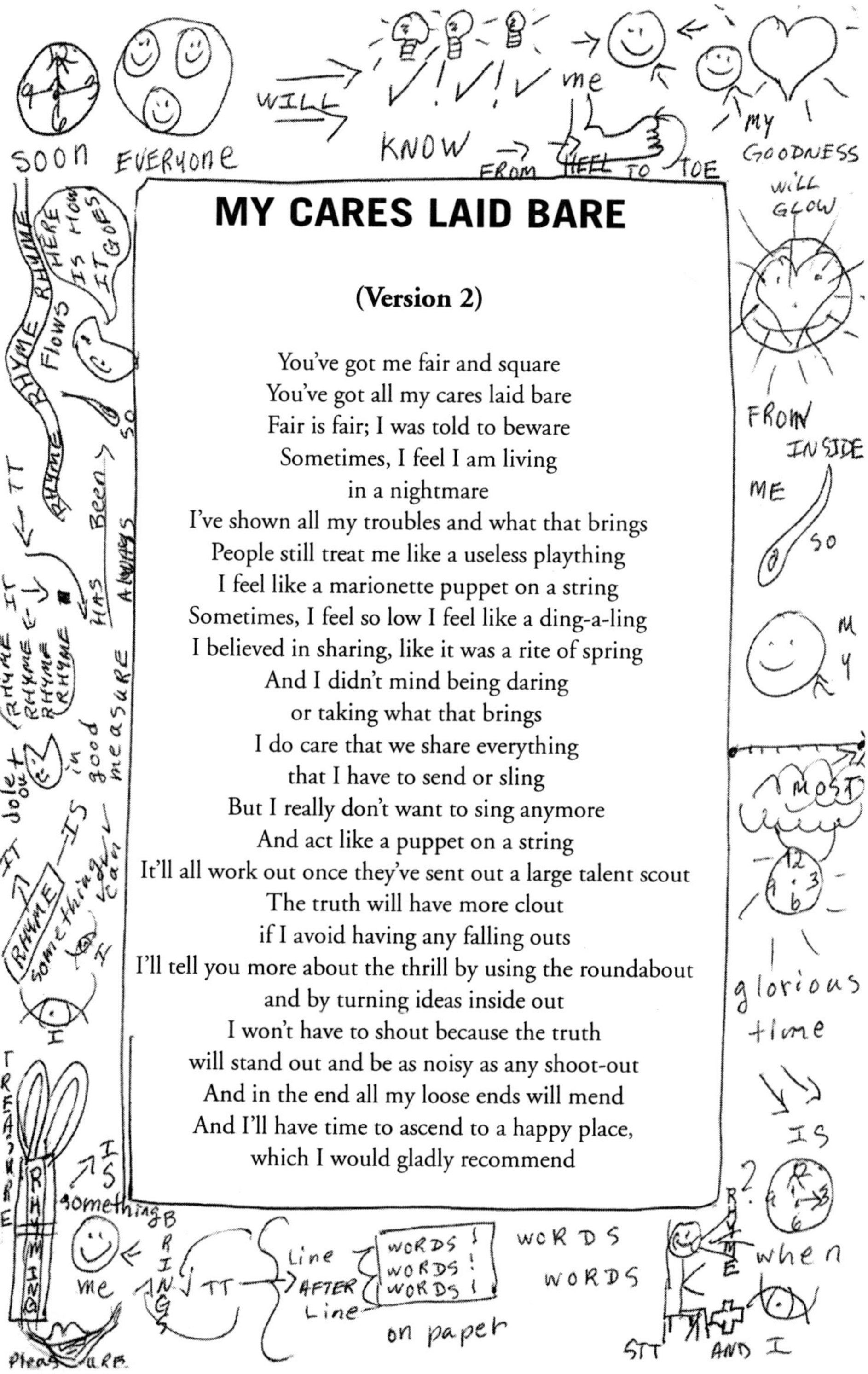

MY CARES LAID BARE

(Version 2)

You've got me fair and square
You've got all my cares laid bare
Fair is fair; I was told to beware
Sometimes, I feel I am living
in a nightmare
I've shown all my troubles and what that brings
People still treat me like a useless plaything
I feel like a marionette puppet on a string
Sometimes, I feel so low I feel like a ding-a-ling
I believed in sharing, like it was a rite of spring
And I didn't mind being daring
or taking what that brings
I do care that we share everything
that I have to send or sling
But I really don't want to sing anymore
And act like a puppet on a string
It'll all work out once they've sent out a large talent scout
The truth will have more clout
if I avoid having any falling outs
I'll tell you more about the thrill by using the roundabout
and by turning ideas inside out
I won't have to shout because the truth
will stand out and be as noisy as any shoot-out
And in the end all my loose ends will mend
And I'll have time to ascend to a happy place,
which I would gladly recommend

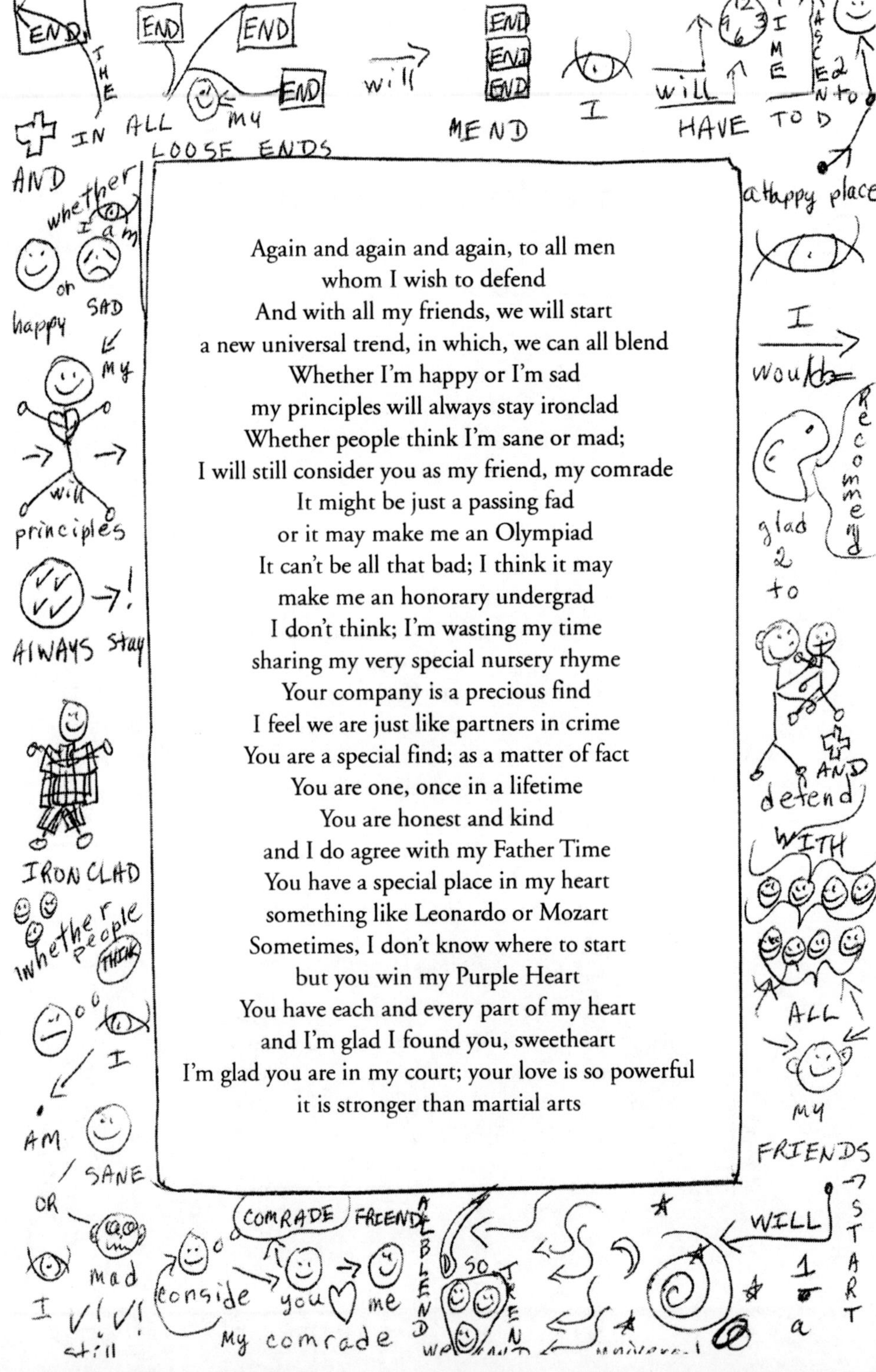

Again and again and again, to all men
whom I wish to defend
And with all my friends, we will start
a new universal trend, in which, we can all blend
Whether I'm happy or I'm sad
my principles will always stay ironclad
Whether people think I'm sane or mad;
I will still consider you as my friend, my comrade
It might be just a passing fad
or it may make me an Olympiad
It can't be all that bad; I think it may
make me an honorary undergrad
I don't think; I'm wasting my time
sharing my very special nursery rhyme
Your company is a precious find
I feel we are just like partners in crime
You are a special find; as a matter of fact
You are one, once in a lifetime
You are honest and kind
and I do agree with my Father Time
You have a special place in my heart
something like Leonardo or Mozart
Sometimes, I don't know where to start
but you win my Purple Heart
You have each and every part of my heart
and I'm glad I found you, sweetheart
I'm glad you are in my court; your love is so powerful
it is stronger than martial arts

GIVE ME A CHANCE

Give me a fighting chance
Don't take a tough stance
Love's arrow will hit you
with its lance
Myself, I work freelance
The story gets
better and better
I'm certainly a go-getter
I won't bind you
with any fetters
But I'll spell it out
in large letters
You'll soon know
I can undo any foe
My love can
grow and grow
It can be high
it can be low
It was the best kind of test
I got thrown out of my nest
Put your head on my chest
Then you'll know
about the rest
I was hit with
a battle of the wits
Who'll be left holding the mitts?
Who'll call it quits or have a fit
How many times

Will there be to permit?
Where are we heading?
Where are we bound?
Maybe we are bound for world renown?
What are we searching for?
I hope it is neutral ground
I hope it is peace and that
I am not a hanger-on

But I can run a marathon and
have a lot of fun
Right here in the province of Saskatchewan
There's a lot of room for us all
to see eye to eye
And for all of us to share love, by and by
There is no need to fight
or to try to disqualify
Or to continue to go on living a lie
we must get along and do or die

THAT'S A LIE

It is everything but the truth
It just isn't at all couth
It's a lie, hook, line
nail, and tooth
They turned around, and a lie
is what they let loose
It was a downright fib; that wise guy told a lie
They thought they could get away with it
if they pretended to be shy
They were nothing but fakirs and dishonest guys
We sure don't agree with them or see eye to eye
They were careful when they pulled the wool, those fools
They were chock-full of stinky bull and falsehoods, so full
They were just plain numbskulls that thought they were cool
It was just plain sinful to hear all their bunch of bull
What a bunch of false fabrications
What evil conniving, imaginations
What silly, preposterous superstitions
What utter useless and untrue inventions

What you said, sir, I soon learned to dread
I think you made it all up in your head
You had better try to tell the truth instead
If you say it that way, they might see red
Sometimes you should be careful and try being cool
Because otherwise, you might choke on that mouthful
You should be more truthful
and you might learn the golden rule

It might prove to be much more useful
and avoid any further ridicule
It was supposed to be an innocent white lie
But it became a noxious
and hideous trap, by and by
Not just a piece of the pie
but the whole darned sky
It grew bigger and bigger
after each and every try
It will lead that perpetrator straight to jail
Then all he or she will receive is mail
The liar's freedom will be gone without fail
And will be looking between steel bar rails

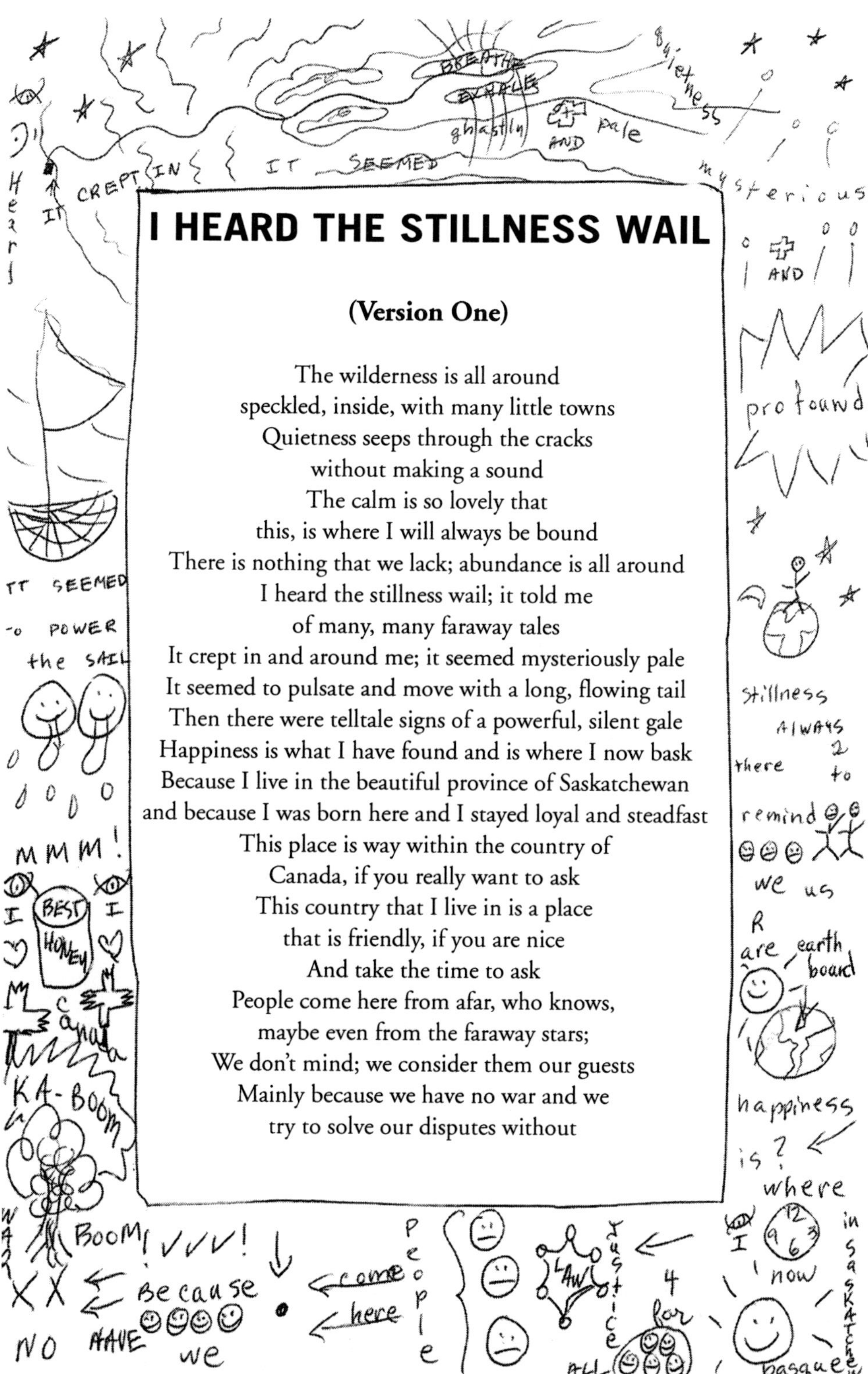

I HEARD THE STILLNESS WAIL

(Version One)

The wilderness is all around
speckled, inside, with many little towns
Quietness seeps through the cracks
without making a sound
The calm is so lovely that
this, is where I will always be bound
There is nothing that we lack; abundance is all around
I heard the stillness wail; it told me
of many, many faraway tales
It crept in and around me; it seemed mysteriously pale
It seemed to pulsate and move with a long, flowing tail
Then there were telltale signs of a powerful, silent gale
Happiness is what I have found and is where I now bask
Because I live in the beautiful province of Saskatchewan
and because I was born here and I stayed loyal and steadfast
This place is way within the country of
Canada, if you really want to ask
This country that I live in is a place
that is friendly, if you are nice
And take the time to ask
People come here from afar, who knows,
maybe even from the faraway stars;
We don't mind; we consider them our guests
Mainly because we have no war and we
try to solve our disputes without

Putting on a mask
Serenity is a luxury we can all hold if we search for it
and make peace our quest
Knowing justice prevails, we can be bold
and we will do our best to pass life's tests
Any fight we may have with each other
eventually does not hold water
And can be resolved without any bother
if we take the time to listen to one another
Not only will our illnesses be kept care of;
many cures will be found, moreover
Help will come, according to our
ability to help one another
and our levels of need, for any him or her

I love this province within our country
We are lucky and I'm thankful
for all our plentiful bounty
We even have the best-tasting honey
So far, anyway you'll see
It's where you get the most for the money
and is a good place to marry your honey

Of course, no place is perfect or
it would prove quite boring
That is another quality which makes it so alluring
We can stay put in one place; if we want
and no one will say a thing

If we follow the house rules
we will see how much fun it really brings
If you like to work, no one is stopping you
You can do your own thing,
as long as you are honest and true blue
You can even go far and get rich
if you want to
You can even make a point
of making a green footprint too
Again, I heard the stillness silently wail
In the quietness it told me another tale
The quietness it expressed
was that the world will never fail
And that any country can have
what we have, which is not for sale

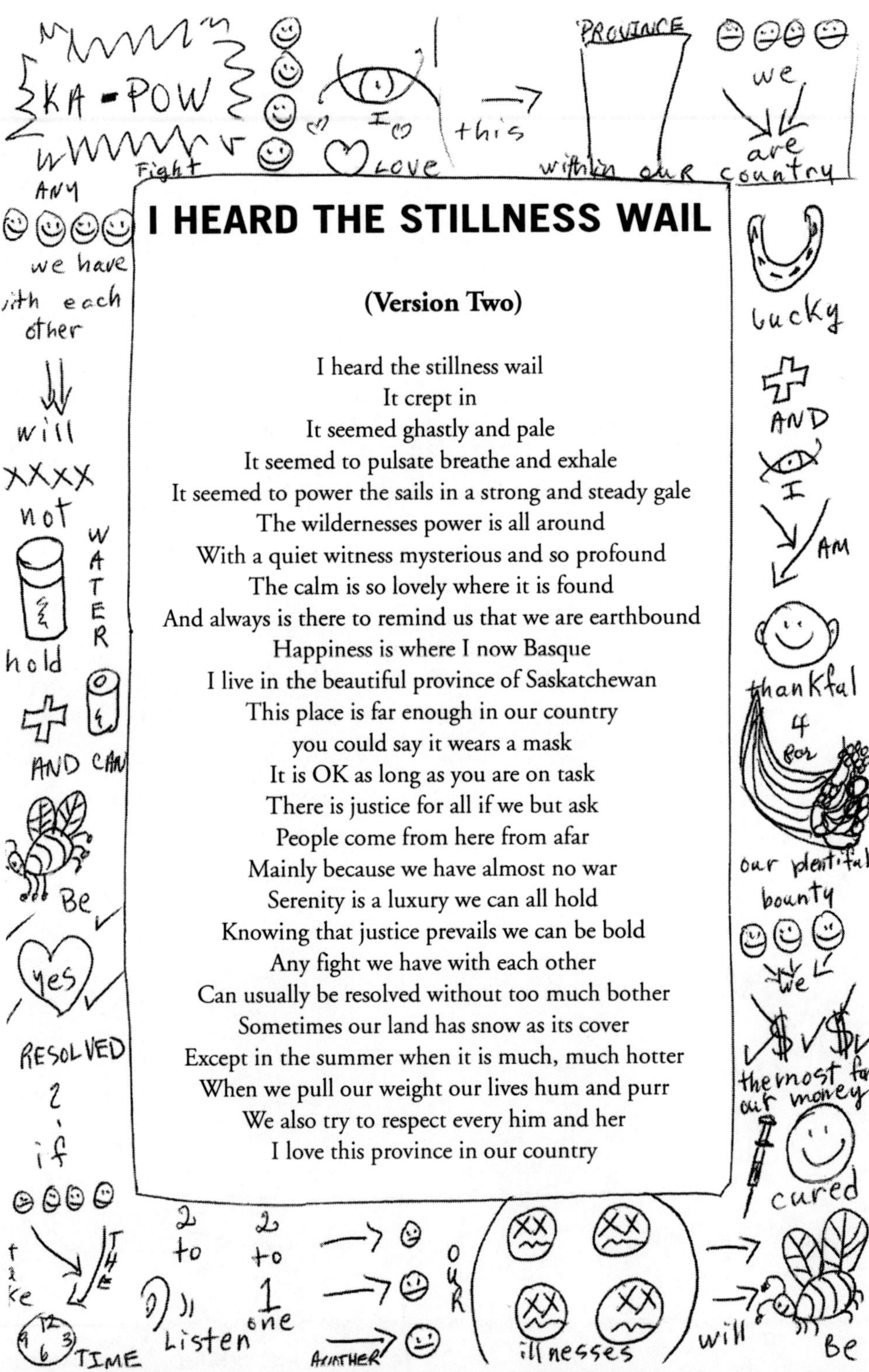

I HEARD THE STILLNESS WAIL

(Version Two)

I heard the stillness wail
It crept in
It seemed ghastly and pale
It seemed to pulsate breathe and exhale
It seemed to power the sails in a strong and steady gale
The wildernesses power is all around
With a quiet witness mysterious and so profound
The calm is so lovely where it is found
And always is there to remind us that we are earthbound
Happiness is where I now Basque
I live in the beautiful province of Saskatchewan
This place is far enough in our country
you could say it wears a mask
It is OK as long as you are on task
There is justice for all if we but ask
People come from here from afar
Mainly because we have almost no war
Serenity is a luxury we can all hold
Knowing that justice prevails we can be bold
Any fight we have with each other
Can usually be resolved without too much bother
Sometimes our land has snow as its cover
Except in the summer when it is much, much hotter
When we pull our weight our lives hum and purr
We also try to respect every him and her
I love this province in our country

We are lucky and I'm thankful for all the plentiful bounty
We even have the best tasting honey
It's where you get the most for your money
You can tell I'm patriotic and very happy

Thumbs up, eh?

THE MAJESTIC SNOWY OWL

The Majestic Snowy Owl
Is not just any old fowl
But it may
have to throw in the towel
If we don't hear its call
and hear it howl
The snowy owl has been here a long time
And it looks oh so fine
in the overall grand design
You might someday
even find a picture of it on a dime
Now it just happens to be in my rhyme
Listen and hear what I have to say
The owl travels up, up and away
In the kingdom of the sky
is where it plays
It's up to us, to make sure that it
will always be A-OK.
In winter, its coat of feathers is the purest white
For its children, it will fight with all its might
It flies higher than any balloon
and better than any kite
It is not fettered; it is free, it is light
but it can win most fights
Nothing looks more majestic when in flight
Than a majestic snowy owl, in the heights

You may not be able
to even see an owl in flight
because they may seem invisible
being that their feathers are pure white
One can only imagine the owl's feelings
Just how terrific it must be to fly
up high with no ceiling
How it must feel to go up, up, up
and to screech and to sing
Flying way up high above the world
and not to have to be worrying
How great it must be with nature as its playmate
And to be able to use its freedom sublime,
to get supper and use its freedom as its bait
Just think. He can soar over any size of gate
And he too, will be happy when he finds a mate
He is our friend not just because he is wise or bright
When he lands on our doorstep, we will all agree
oh, what a beautiful sight
We must fight his cause
like it was our very own fight
Because for him to live is his
and nature's solemn right

HARD AS A ROCK

My head is as hard as a rock
But I come from good stock
I am also from a large flock
I come from
the school of hard knocks
You've got me between a rock and a stone
Oh my, let me see; oh, how you've grown
My heart has always been on loan and
I've always been waiting here at home
My thoughts
are what have been faithfully sewn
Don't knock my head too hard
You might find out, instead
that I am a bard
Also that
I have many wild cards
Gone are the days when
I hide alone and on guard
I'll always welcome
constructive criticism
My ideas are real and sincerely genuine
They are all there stuck inside my head
and I consider this situation a win-win
They'll be a success
when they are freed, again and again
That just about says it all
it is time for the final curtain calls

My head is harder than true grit
or any brick wall
My brains are all close and tightly knit,
better than any old shawl
The ideas will hit you so hard
you will need a complete overhaul
My strength will be put to the test
and I will do my very best
It has become a difficult quest to beat all the rest
You will find I do not jest because
I do not find it at all any contest
It's so sad, you all will end up crying, lest
because I have put on my best bulletproof vest
I've never been beaten, but I've always been chosen
I've never been positively proven, but I am outspoken
My ideas are difficult to prove wrong because
it has all, been tried to do, again and again
They'll travel around until they
hang ten and finally say amen
Then the rock will fall hard because it is very hard
And we will get the guard to come
when they start to bombard
We will pelt them with rocks
until they are battle-scarred
Then we will show them
we don't die easy, but we do die hard

DON'T LIE

Telling the truth is what is right
and might even earn you an award
besides, if you tell the truth
you'll be as free as a bird
So just try to correctly express
everything you have heard
And be honest
and tell the truth in each and every word
Don't plan a lie and be a stupid wise guy
Because when you testify
you might end up being the fall guy
Just clarify; be truthful and correctly verify
Be the honest one and the one to exemplify
OK, so you say telling the truth is dull
I say that if you lie, you are a numbskull
Telling the truth rocks, and that is no bull
Lying sucks and is for frightened fools
Don't try to cop out by scheming or rationalizing
Because you might become a puppet on a string
And people might never want to
or believe you again
And you may end up seeming like a ding-a-ling
If you continue to let lies fester and grow
And then you shoot off your mouth
careless and all gung ho
Soon you will be trapped
in your own sideshow

Because you will be the dishonest Joe
Pinocchio could not have said it better than you
His nose became an attention getter
and grew and grew
And it soon became a record award-setter too
Next, he became a donkey
and you will be next to go down that avenue
Because if you continue and you are not careful
You'll have more than you ever wanted or can handle
Because lies tend
to land you in trouble and chock-full
Of what comes right out of the back end of a bull
I have found
that the truth is the solid best
It wins first prize and the solves the test
It is safer, by far, and beats all the rest
And it is the most welcome
of any and all of the guests

I'M GONE WITH THE WIND

I'm gone with the wind; it's time for
me to relax and unwind
I'll be your friend; I can even try and be your mastermind
I'll be the one to begin to win and
the one to begin to find
Both of us will win; we'll get through thick and thin
and end up being sublime
My wings will catch the breeze and I'll
soar into the sky with great ease
I will swing along on my invisible trapeze
like a happy, babbling chimpanzee
My love will bring you to your knees, and
I will make you beg pretty please
My heart will unlock all your mind's mysteries
and I will become as wise as Socrates
I will feel so free, and I will suggest to
you a new biological decree
That I would love to have you with
me, to be my personal referee
We'll travel far and wide together; you'll see
you can be my sweet bumblebee
We'll both bumble and buzz, to and fro,
hither and thither, quite satisfied and carefree
We will feel refreshed and young even
though we are the old ones
We won't be undone; that would not
do. In fact, we'll have lots of fun

We will hit a home run and a hole in one
in fact, our fun has just begun
We will have our turn in the sun
something like that of that famous prodigal son
You might find me anywhere in many
forms, solid as a rock or thin as air
I might disappear into thin air or appear in
your worst nightmare, so take care
I could be none the worse for wear or I
could end up ailing in intensive care
I might blow right through your hair, but I
can promise you; I will never be square
I will always learn to adjust because that, in itself, is a must
I will find that I will want to earn your trust;
or I might as well bite the dust
I will just have to learn to be fair and
not to be a spoiled sourpuss
It's not Ziggy Stardust you see, it is go for broke, or else bust
I will try not to be mysterious;
this might help me not to miss getting on the bus
I won't be unruly or delirious or cause a
raucous fuss; I'll just be nonplussed
I won't be the laziest; rather, I will try to go on any quest;
that will be a must
But in the end, I may be the one who is the craziest
without creating a lot of fuss and muss
Then I'll go away on my magic carpet
without working up a sweat

Even though I may make a large target
still I will have no regrets
As long as I don't forget my little red
Corvette and my private jet
And make everything fit into my budget
Then I'll be right there in the jet set

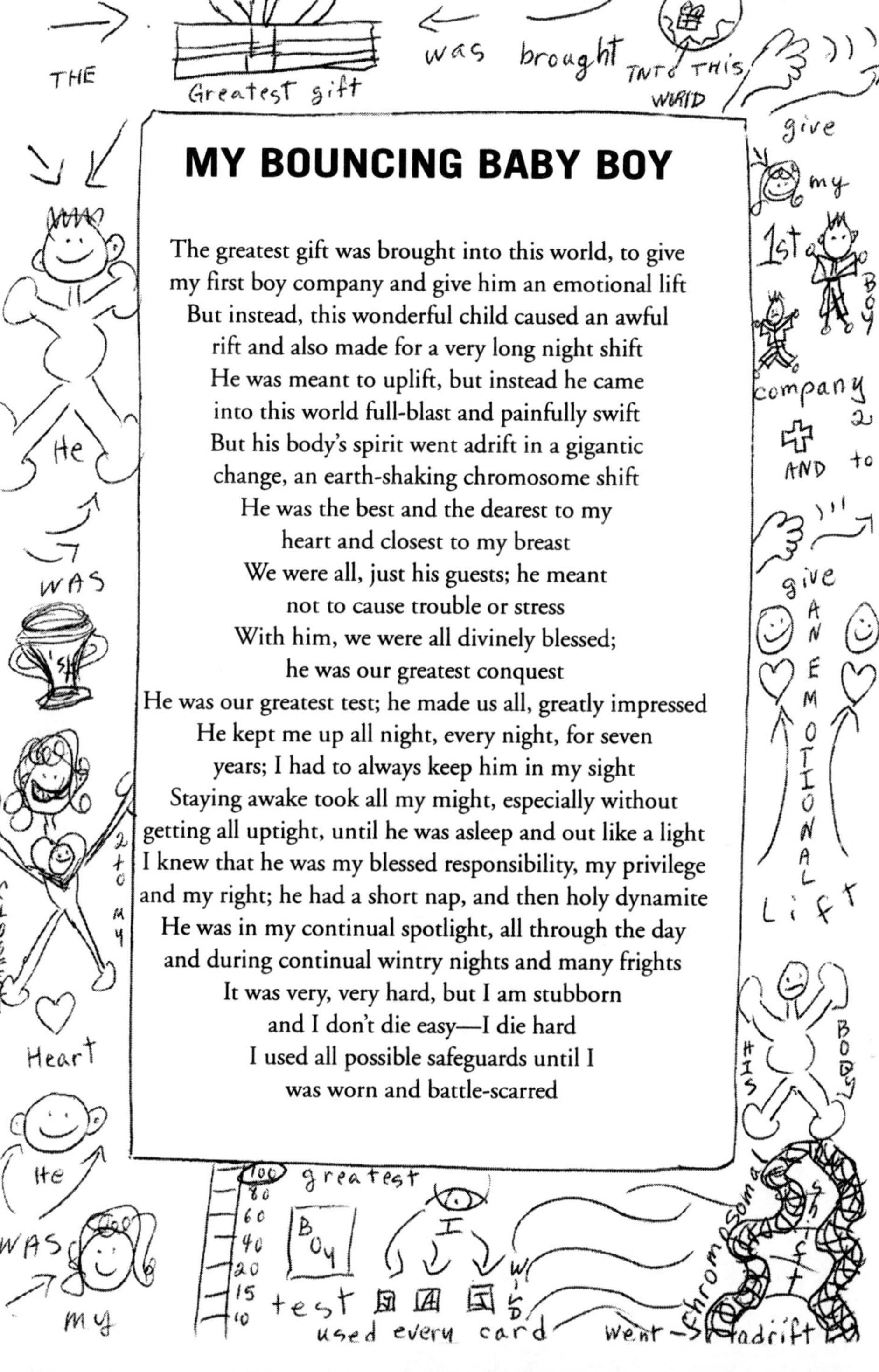

MY BOUNCING BABY BOY

The greatest gift was brought into this world, to give
my first boy company and give him an emotional lift
But instead, this wonderful child caused an awful
rift and also made for a very long night shift
He was meant to uplift, but instead he came
into this world full-blast and painfully swift
But his body's spirit went adrift in a gigantic
change, an earth-shaking chromosome shift
He was the best and the dearest to my
heart and closest to my breast
We were all, just his guests; he meant
not to cause trouble or stress
With him, we were all divinely blessed;
he was our greatest conquest
He was our greatest test; he made us all, greatly impressed
He kept me up all night, every night, for seven
years; I had to always keep him in my sight
Staying awake took all my might, especially without
getting all uptight, until he was asleep and out like a light
I knew that he was my blessed responsibility, my privilege
and my right; he had a short nap, and then holy dynamite
He was in my continual spotlight, all through the day
and during continual wintry nights and many frights
It was very, very hard, but I am stubborn
and I don't die easy—I die hard
I used all possible safeguards until I
was worn and battle-scarred

I was his bodyguard, I was his lifeguard;
I used every possible wild card
I went that extra yard; I was his armed guard,
and for his protection, I parried and I sparred
I pulled down all the blinds because
he continually whined
No peace could we find; there was no time to be refined
I was surely in a bind; to suffering I
had to become snow-blind
I wasn't ahead, I was behind; there was no time to unwind
To keep care of him, I knew I must;
he didn't always cry and fuss
In me, he put all his hope, and eventually
he learned how to trust
Keeping him happy was do, die, or bust; as he
grew, his medicines I gradually had to adjust
I knew I must remain truly decent and just to
continue to keep him healthy and robust
Why are you always so sad, my gracious
lad; life is not really so bad
I try my best to make you glad, my precious
comrade; you are my hero, my Galahad
A bad stroke of luck you have had; you had no choice
in your life, but to me, you are an honorary grad
I don't blame you for being angry or acting
stark-raving mad, but I know you well, and
I think it is we that have been had

Baby, please don't cry; I won't let you die.
Laugh, you are the apple of my eye
And then I won't cry, and both our victories
will someday be nigh for you and I
Have you got something in your eye?
My guy, hush now, rock-a-bye
I think you need some shut-eye, hush-a-bye;
I'll sing you a lullaby, my, my, my

IF IT'S ALL THE SAME

If it's all the same, I would like to continue
to play in life's word game
This is my aim and my main claim to
my uncontested personal fame
Using the right words in the right way will
make everything a new ball game
I must make sure not to inflame or I most
definitely will be put to shame
You do not recognize my name or my
face or happen to know me now
But soon, you I will be quite familiar
and you will raise your eyebrows
Nevertheless, I will try to be humble, and
I will be the one to curtsy and bow
All because I am jolly and sociable and I
love to entertain you high and low
First, I will try by using the proper
vocabulary and using the right words
Then I will try to put them to music
and share all my favorite chords
I will then put the words to music and share a
melody that comes fast on my guitar's boards
The strings that are attached to the guitar's boards
then will sing out loud "Oh, my Lord."
All the sounds are different from each
other, not one, but seven
I will play an individual orchestra, and
I will play again and again

They'll make us all so happy; they
will take us all up to heaven
I am hoping that they will raise your spirits,
like yeast (the very best leaven)
Did you hear the latest news, from the
latest, juicy, descriptive clues?
The names have been changed so that
we don't have to sing the blues
Have you heard the news, those strange
words, saying "I love you?"
Or did someone stress that we must push
for a veto and say "No can do."
Somehow, the word story
always follows the same theme
Here it is—it was, it is, and then it had been
It can be that with which we have yet to have seen
Of course, we hear less than it really means
So I'll try to be honest and go and tell what's on my mind
And I'll set it to music, in noise, for
everyone, not just for the blind
Then even they will know and won't
be left, in silence, far behind
And those who see will also hear
and might find what they left behind
I'll be gracious with my music and my words
On a scale of which will be seen and might be heard
In the game of life, it has occurred to me;
some may consider me a nerd, which is totally absurd
I am no different than you; I feel as free as a bird

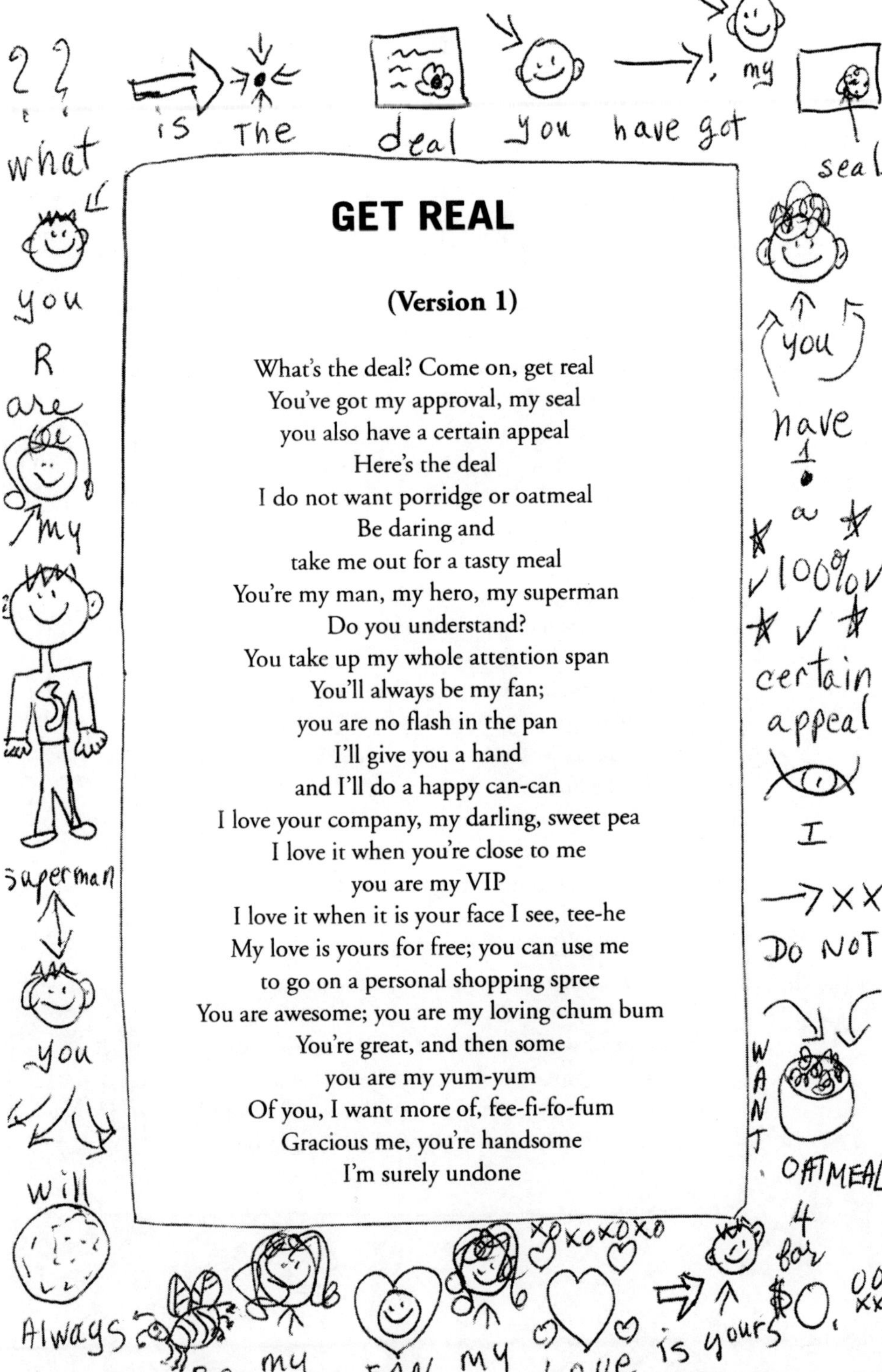

GET REAL

(Version 1)

What's the deal? Come on, get real
You've got my approval, my seal
you also have a certain appeal
Here's the deal
I do not want porridge or oatmeal
Be daring and
take me out for a tasty meal
You're my man, my hero, my superman
Do you understand?
You take up my whole attention span
You'll always be my fan;
you are no flash in the pan
I'll give you a hand
and I'll do a happy can-can
I love your company, my darling, sweet pea
I love it when you're close to me
you are my VIP
I love it when it is your face I see, tee-he
My love is yours for free; you can use me
to go on a personal shopping spree
You are awesome; you are my loving chum bum
You're great, and then some
you are my yum-yum
Of you, I want more of, fee-fi-fo-fum
Gracious me, you're handsome
I'm surely undone

You are an awesome gent; you are 100 percent
Because you are heaven sent,
and with love, which is your main intent
You will destroy and rent and torment all discontent
My armor is all broken and bent
what a blessed event
I know I am quite a handful, but I am no numbskull
It is quite understandable even though I am not dull
And when there is a scandal
I like being chock-full of wild wool
Our relationship is more than likeable
it is rock stable
I've never met anyone quite like you;
I think it is a breakthrough
You came to me out of the blue, just like good king, kung fu
I'll always have love for you too, just like lasting super glue
Our love will always be new, like
continuously good book reviews
I'll never let you down; I'll be your happy clown
I'll even leave my good town of small renown
I'll wear your wedding gown
like it was a graduating cap and gown
I hope you want me also to be your own,
like a porcelain doll from Chinatown

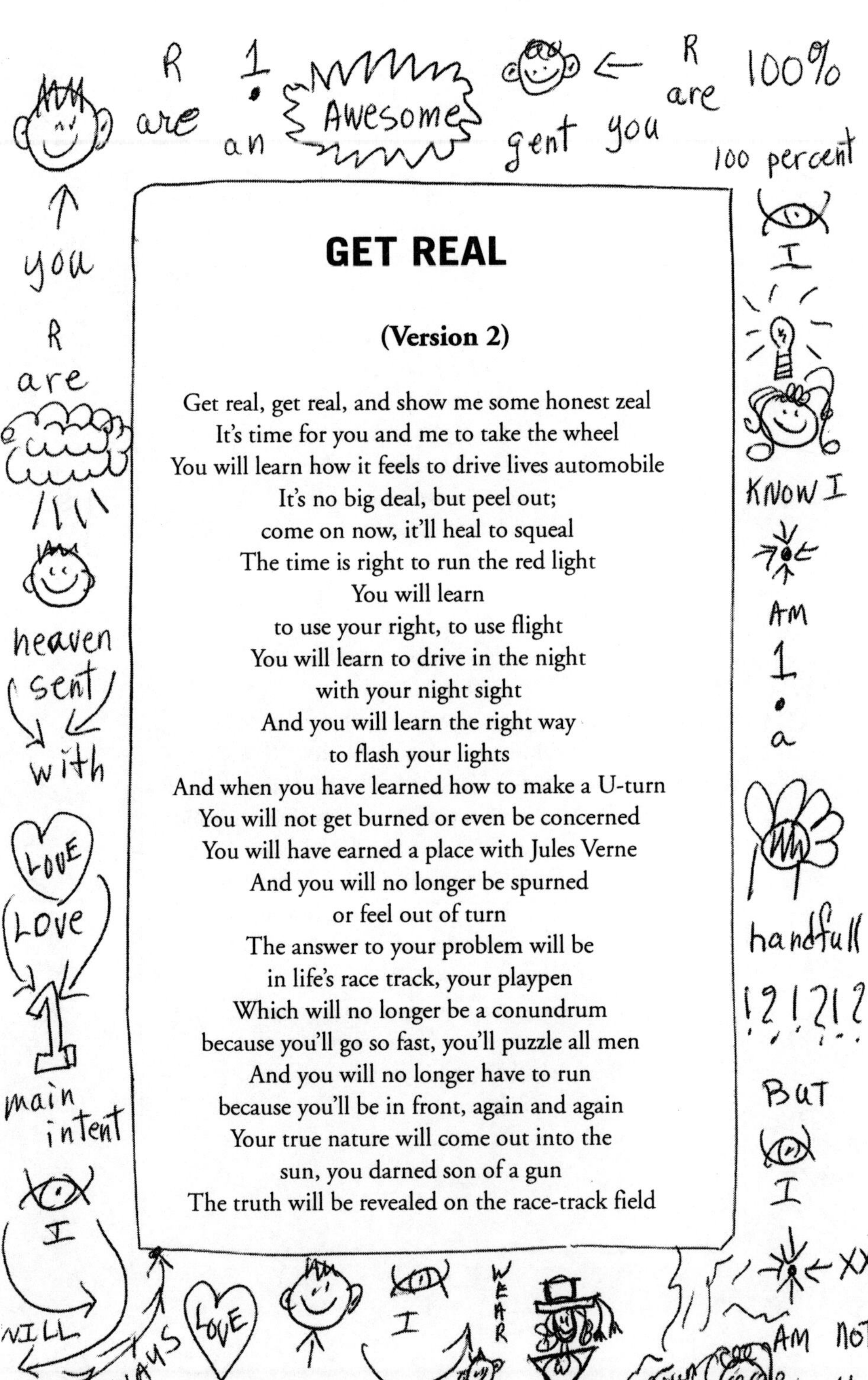

GET REAL

(Version 2)

Get real, get real, and show me some honest zeal
It's time for you and me to take the wheel
You will learn how it feels to drive lives automobile
It's no big deal, but peel out;
come on now, it'll heal to squeal
The time is right to run the red light
You will learn
to use your right, to use flight
You will learn to drive in the night
with your night sight
And you will learn the right way
to flash your lights
And when you have learned how to make a U-turn
You will not get burned or even be concerned
You will have earned a place with Jules Verne
And you will no longer be spurned
or feel out of turn
The answer to your problem will be
in life's race track, your playpen
Which will no longer be a conundrum
because you'll go so fast, you'll puzzle all men
And you will no longer have to run
because you'll be in front, again and again
Your true nature will come out into the
sun, you darned son of a gun
The truth will be revealed on the race-track field

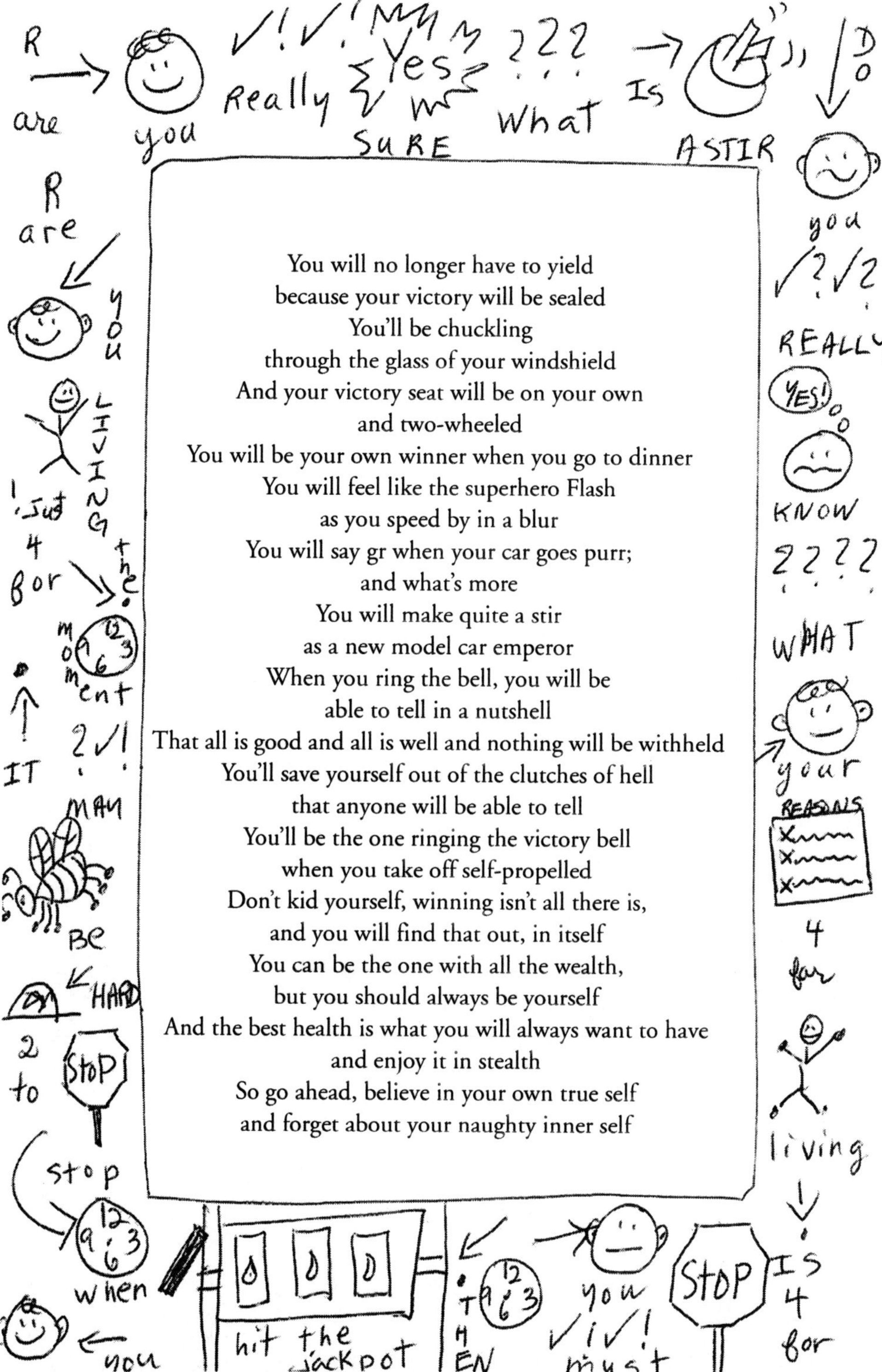

You will no longer have to yield
because your victory will be sealed
You'll be chuckling
through the glass of your windshield
And your victory seat will be on your own
and two-wheeled
You will be your own winner when you go to dinner
You will feel like the superhero Flash
as you speed by in a blur
You will say gr when your car goes purr;
and what's more
You will make quite a stir
as a new model car emperor
When you ring the bell, you will be
able to tell in a nutshell
That all is good and all is well and nothing will be withheld
You'll save yourself out of the clutches of hell
that anyone will be able to tell
You'll be the one ringing the victory bell
when you take off self-propelled
Don't kid yourself, winning isn't all there is,
and you will find that out, in itself
You can be the one with all the wealth,
but you should always be yourself
And the best health is what you will always want to have
and enjoy it in stealth
So go ahead, believe in your own true self
and forget about your naughty inner self

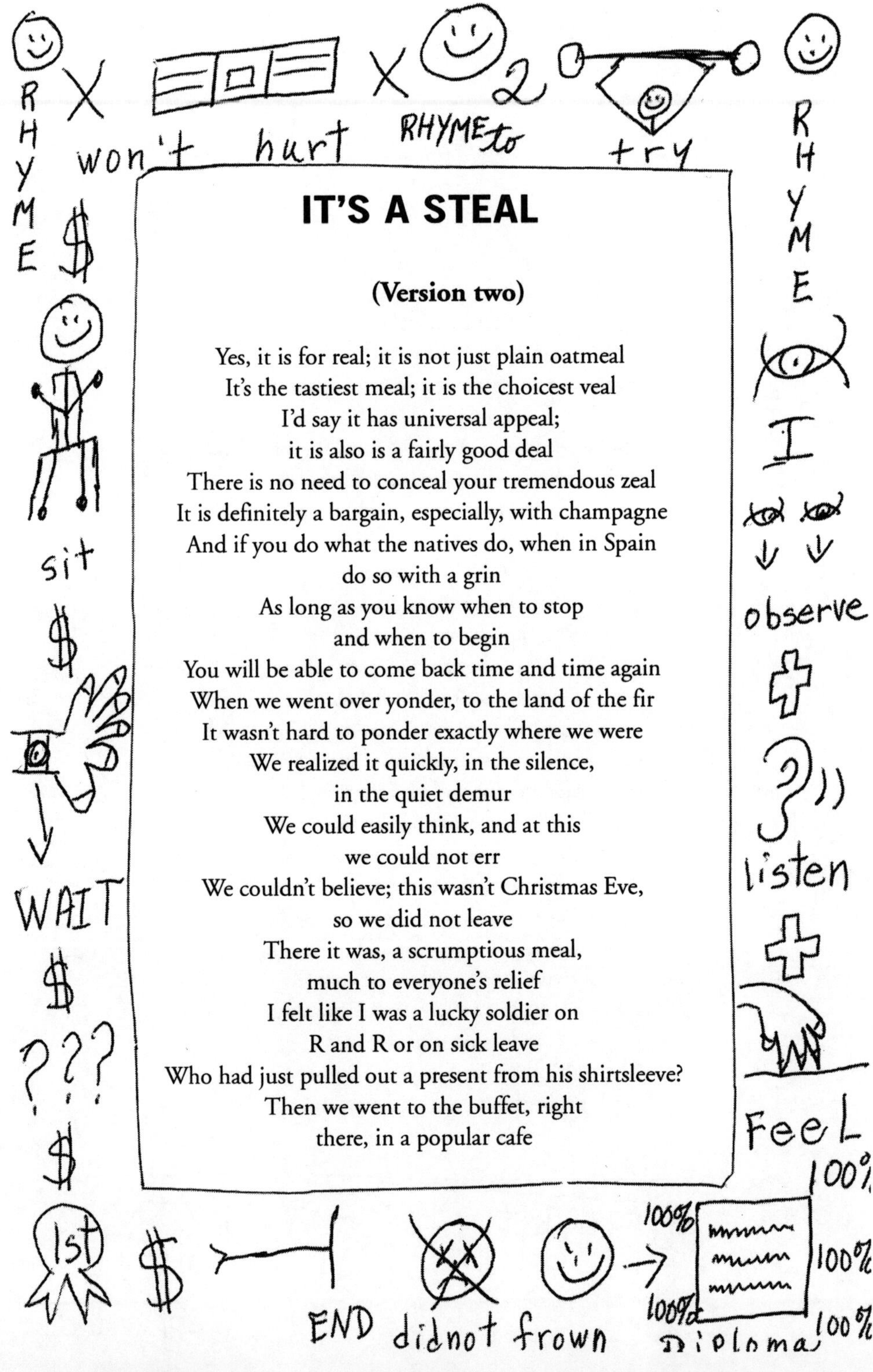

IT'S A STEAL

(Version two)

Yes, it is for real; it is not just plain oatmeal
It's the tastiest meal; it is the choicest veal
I'd say it has universal appeal;
it is also is a fairly good deal
There is no need to conceal your tremendous zeal
It is definitely a bargain, especially, with champagne
And if you do what the natives do, when in Spain
do so with a grin
As long as you know when to stop
and when to begin
You will be able to come back time and time again
When we went over yonder, to the land of the fir
It wasn't hard to ponder exactly where we were
We realized it quickly, in the silence,
in the quiet demur
We could easily think, and at this
we could not err
We couldn't believe; this wasn't Christmas Eve,
so we did not leave
There it was, a scrumptious meal,
much to everyone's relief
I felt like I was a lucky soldier on
R and R or on sick leave
Who had just pulled out a present from his shirtsleeve?
Then we went to the buffet, right
there, in a popular cafe

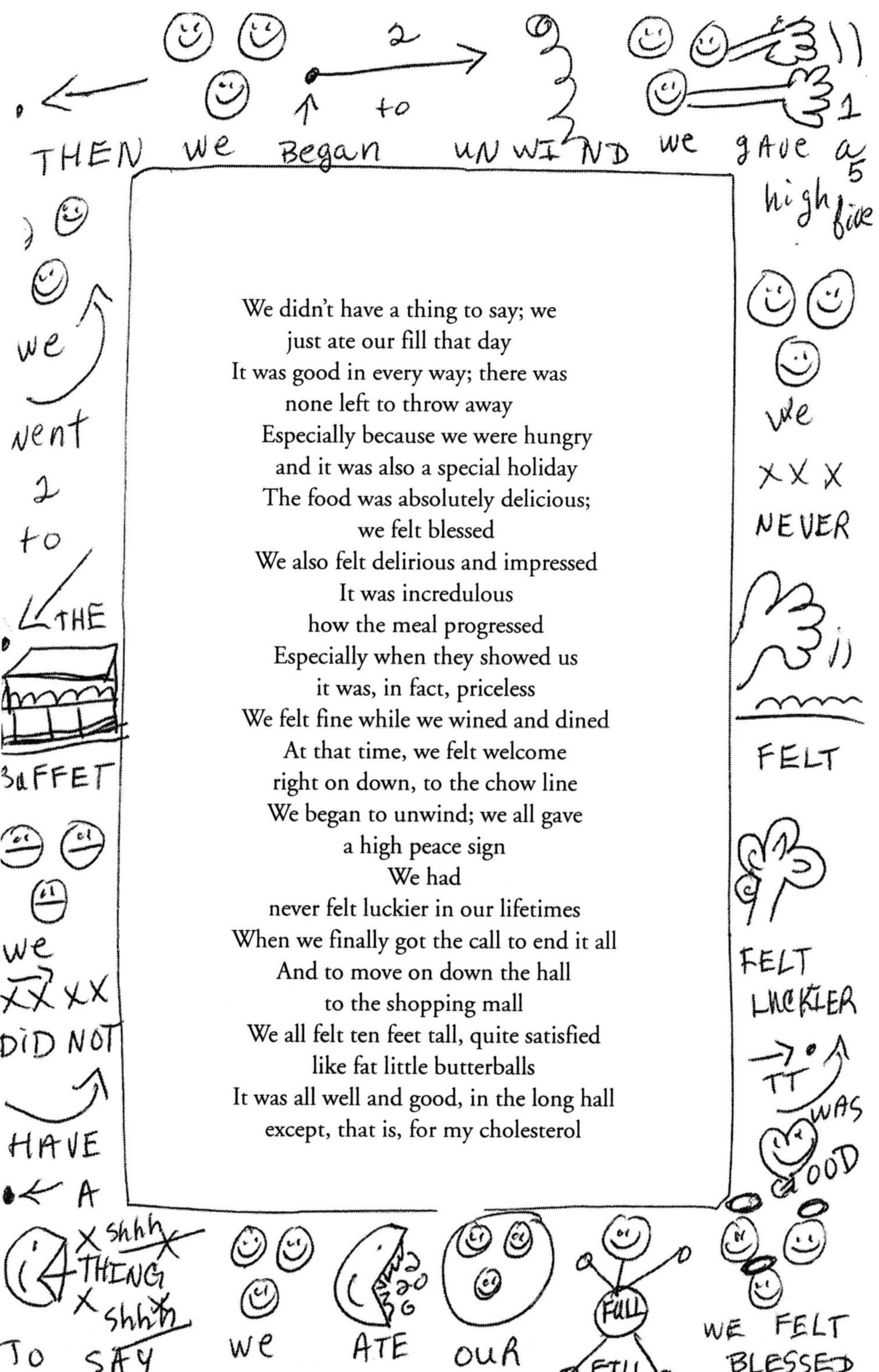

We didn't have a thing to say; we
just ate our fill that day
It was good in every way; there was
none left to throw away
Especially because we were hungry
and it was also a special holiday
The food was absolutely delicious;
we felt blessed
We also felt delirious and impressed
It was incredulous
how the meal progressed
Especially when they showed us
it was, in fact, priceless
We felt fine while we wined and dined
At that time, we felt welcome
right on down, to the chow line
We began to unwind; we all gave
a high peace sign
We had
never felt luckier in our lifetimes
When we finally got the call to end it all
And to move on down the hall
to the shopping mall
We all felt ten feet tall, quite satisfied
like fat little butterballs
It was all well and good, in the long hall
except, that is, for my cholesterol

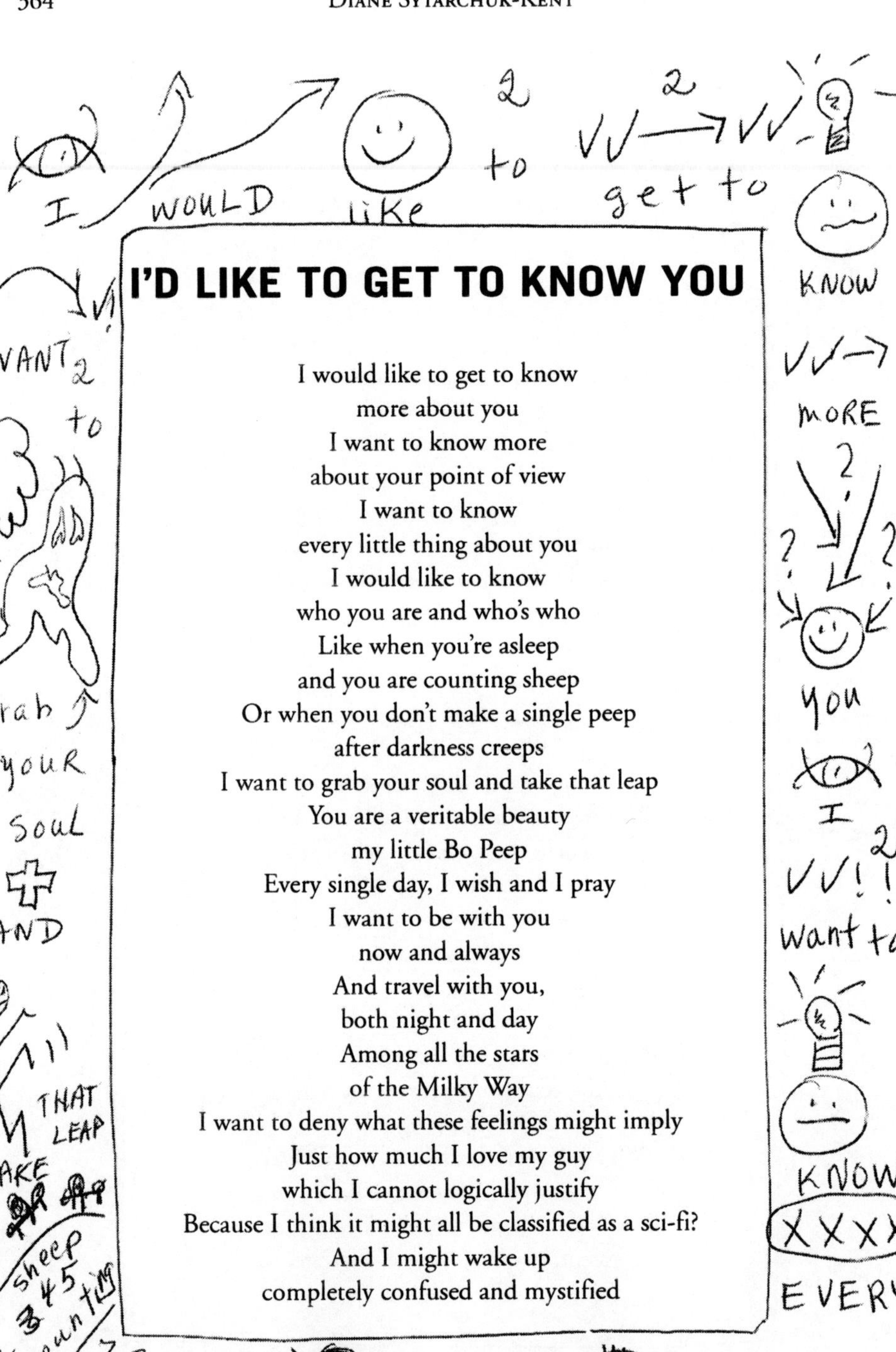

I'D LIKE TO GET TO KNOW YOU

I would like to get to know
more about you
I want to know more
about your point of view
I want to know
every little thing about you
I would like to know
who you are and who's who
Like when you're asleep
and you are counting sheep
Or when you don't make a single peep
after darkness creeps
I want to grab your soul and take that leap
You are a veritable beauty
my little Bo Peep
Every single day, I wish and I pray
I want to be with you
now and always
And travel with you,
both night and day
Among all the stars
of the Milky Way
I want to deny what these feelings might imply
Just how much I love my guy
which I cannot logically justify
Because I think it might all be classified as a sci-fi?
And I might wake up
completely confused and mystified

So for the time being
I'll take it as a wonderful, whim
And I'll remember who I am and where I have been
And I'll be happy
to have been with someone so keen
With this man that makes me feel like a queen
I'll always remember
just how I feel and how happy he makes me
How he manages to send me to a place
beautiful and carefree
And the love he sends to me is for free;
that is his guarantee
And how he makes me see everything that is beauty
He makes me feel calm and justified and how he fits the bill
Even though, I know I can be and am at times strong-willed
Any which way, he fits the prescription
and I will gladly swallow the prescribed pill
I have never met anyone on this world
that has given me such a steady thrill
When I finally come back to the planet Earth
I can't help but still see his overall net worth
And smile with fondness and winsome mirth
At how he was sent to me from afar,
after his birth

YOU HELP ME TO BE FREE

You help me to feel happy and carefree
now I am no longer blind and I can see
I need to see with the freedom
with which your eyes can see
You help me see joy
you help me let myself be me
I'll give you love because you unlocked
and loosened my personality with your love's key
You are my joystick and you are my burning candlewick
Because of you, I can again use
my freedom of choice and take my pick
Of anything in my mind's storeroom that makes me tick
You have brought me slapstick
I don't even mind being lovesick
You are not a slick country hick
You give my life a welcome kick
You and I
just click and click and click
You make my heart throb
and tick; you, sir, do the trick
I won't let you down my wonderful clown
I will try not to make you frown or drown
You make me come all unwound
now I'm glory bound
Without making a single, solitary sound
you are bound for world renown
You let me have friends with which I can fend

You don't know that this sends me
over to a happy land
I go to a happy place
that starts and never ends
Where there are no demands
but all the best ingredients
You were the one and only one
to let me be free to be me
And the one to come to me when I was really lonely
And the one to tell me I'm beautiful
when I feel really homely
You are my one and only honey
the very best deal for my money
Now with you, I am free to take a breath of fresh air
You love me for who I am, and I think that's fair
For that, you'll be the one
with whom I always care
I can even enjoy playing with all
your freshly grown, virgin hair
You don't mind if I am myself and practice to be kind
Or if I am slow and have trouble
using my brains in time
You are my lover and the greatest mastermind;
you are quite a find
You have answers of an intelligent kind
and our souls will forever be intertwined

GREASE LIGHTNING

It is truly surprising and frightening
How my senses
are just like grease lightning
If anything, my senses are heightening
And their anticipation is like
a string that is tightening
My senses like to help me to create
They give me no time to hesitate
They are sharp and tend to help
my ideas to liberate
They help me to discern
and to discriminate
They are my friends and have helped
me to be carefree
They help me to realize that I am me
They help me
to be fully aware and to see
They have helped me to be or not to be
That makes me happy;
because my time doesn't come free
My time doesn't grow on just any old tree
And I don't want my music to be off-key
Or I might have to put it away safely
under lock and key
My attention span will get stronger
And it will be harder for it to wander

My attention span
gets longer and longer
My senses are
smooth as a purr, as it were
My senses help me to lift my spirits up
They encourage me
and get me out of many a rut
I never need any particular help or shortcuts
Because my senses
won't take any ifs, ands, or buts
They help me and bring me the best of luck
And help me to beware of any passing trucks
They can help me
sense when it is time to duck
They often leave me in awe or wonder struck
So no matter how you try to catch or dampen them
My senses will soon bounce back, again and again
They are more valuable
and greater than the brightest gems
And they will leave no evidence
with which I could be condemned

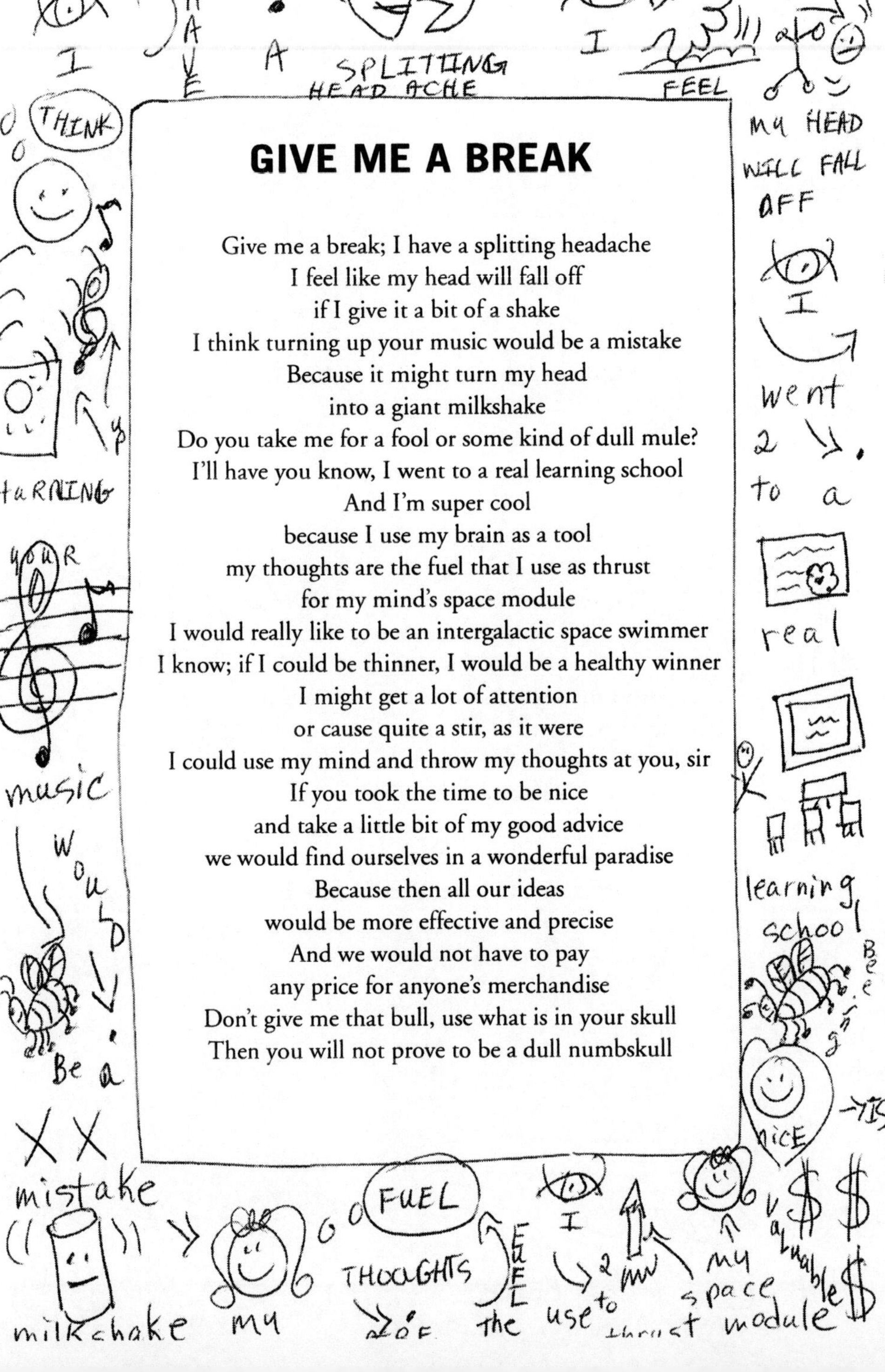

GIVE ME A BREAK

Give me a break; I have a splitting headache
I feel like my head will fall off
if I give it a bit of a shake
I think turning up your music would be a mistake
Because it might turn my head
into a giant milkshake
Do you take me for a fool or some kind of dull mule?
I'll have you know, I went to a real learning school
And I'm super cool
because I use my brain as a tool
my thoughts are the fuel that I use as thrust
for my mind's space module
I would really like to be an intergalactic space swimmer
I know; if I could be thinner, I would be a healthy winner
I might get a lot of attention
or cause quite a stir, as it were
I could use my mind and throw my thoughts at you, sir
If you took the time to be nice
and take a little bit of my good advice
we would find ourselves in a wonderful paradise
Because then all our ideas
would be more effective and precise
And we would not have to pay
any price for anyone's merchandise
Don't give me that bull, use what is in your skull
Then you will not prove to be a dull numbskull

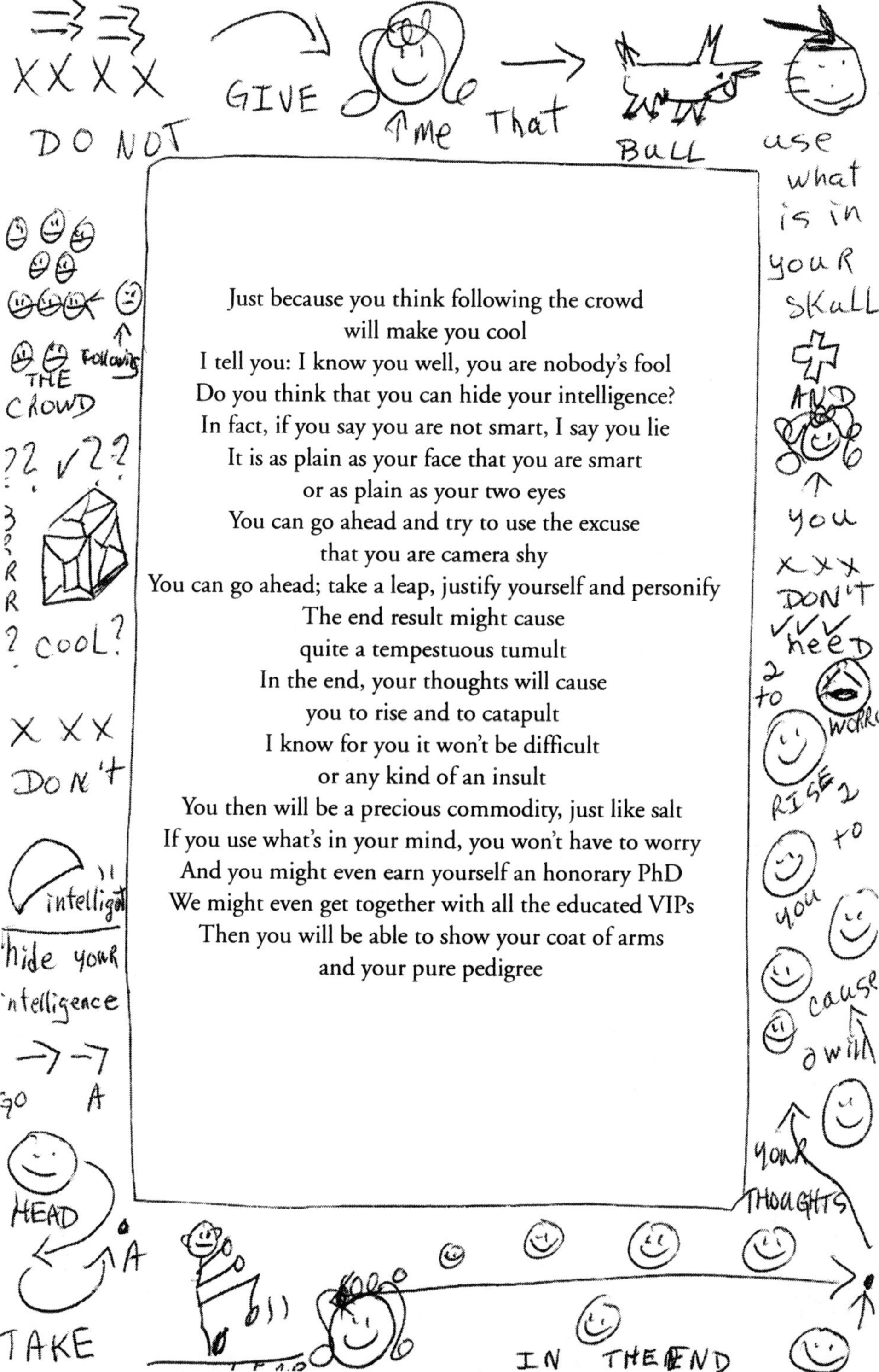

Just because you think following the crowd
will make you cool
I tell you: I know you well, you are nobody's fool
Do you think that you can hide your intelligence?
In fact, if you say you are not smart, I say you lie
It is as plain as your face that you are smart
or as plain as your two eyes
You can go ahead and try to use the excuse
that you are camera shy
You can go ahead; take a leap, justify yourself and personify
The end result might cause
quite a tempestuous tumult
In the end, your thoughts will cause
you to rise and to catapult
I know for you it won't be difficult
or any kind of an insult
You then will be a precious commodity, just like salt
If you use what's in your mind, you won't have to worry
And you might even earn yourself an honorary PhD
We might even get together with all the educated VIPs
Then you will be able to show your coat of arms
and your pure pedigree

WAIT A MINUTE

Wait a minute; don't forget
this just has to sit
Wait or I'll flip right out of my cockpit
You'd better quit and help me to pinch hit
Or you might get stung and I'll lose it
bit by bit
Take your time and think about this missing link
You just might avoid landing in the clink
if you stop and try and think
Did you see that person wink, that dirty rat fink?
No, he didn't just blink; he faked it
and he lip synched
It is worth taking the time to suit the crime
Because if you are patient, you will avoid
ending up behind come curtain time
So don't lose your temper
just do a silent pantomime
You'd be surprised; you might find yourself
again in your prime
Use a little caution, or you may find yourself
in trouble and undone
Travel carefully, in slow motion, and don't jump the gun
That's, when you will conquer your most powerful
enemies, and your battles will be won
Perseverance may result in a miracle potion
that proves to be cure number 1

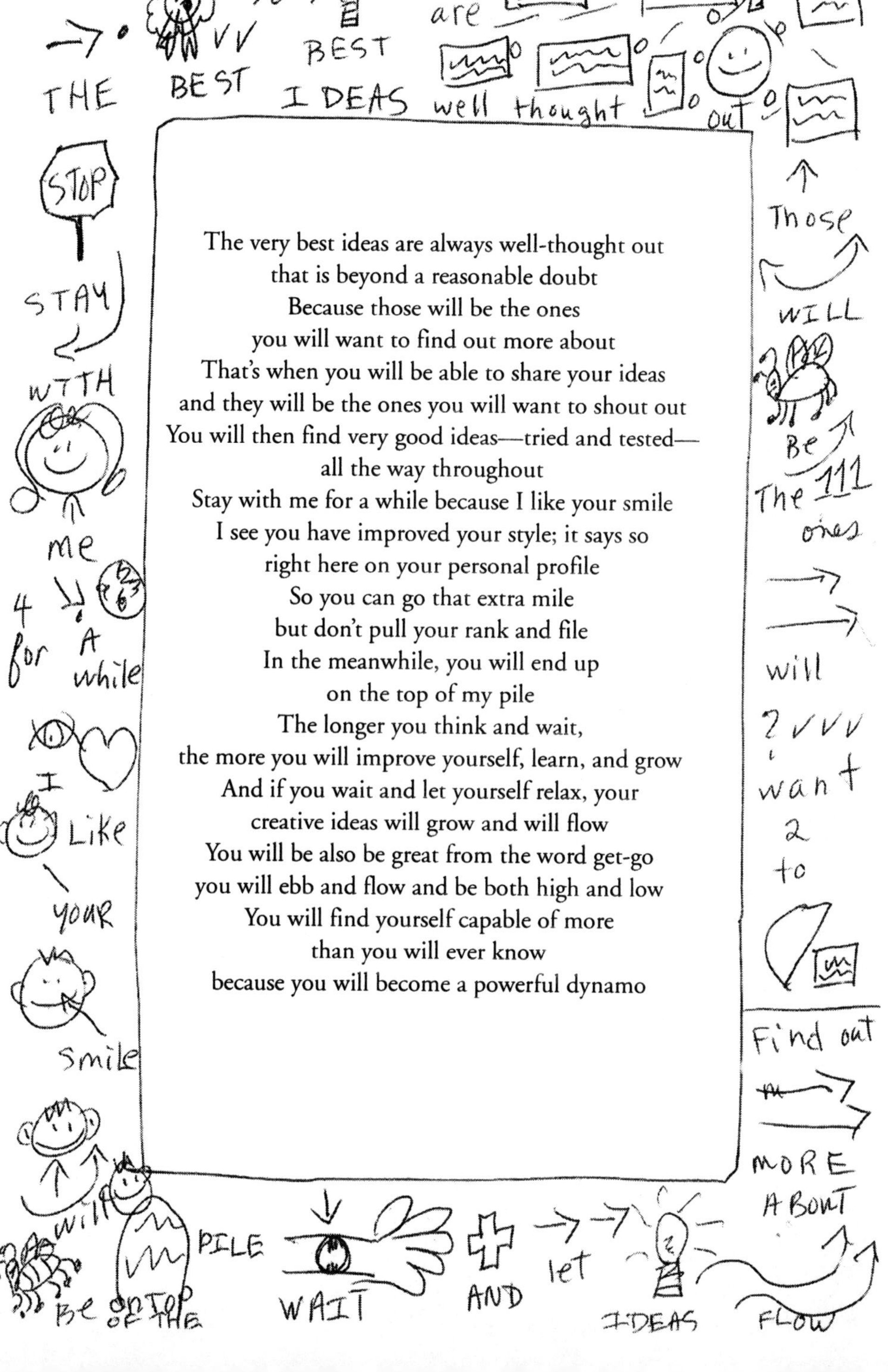

The very best ideas are always well-thought out
that is beyond a reasonable doubt
Because those will be the ones
you will want to find out more about
That's when you will be able to share your ideas
and they will be the ones you will want to shout out
You will then find very good ideas—tried and tested—
all the way throughout
Stay with me for a while because I like your smile
I see you have improved your style; it says so
right here on your personal profile
So you can go that extra mile
but don't pull your rank and file
In the meanwhile, you will end up
on the top of my pile
The longer you think and wait,
the more you will improve yourself, learn, and grow
And if you wait and let yourself relax, your
creative ideas will grow and will flow
You will be also be great from the word get-go
you will ebb and flow and be both high and low
You will find yourself capable of more
than you will ever know
because you will become a powerful dynamo

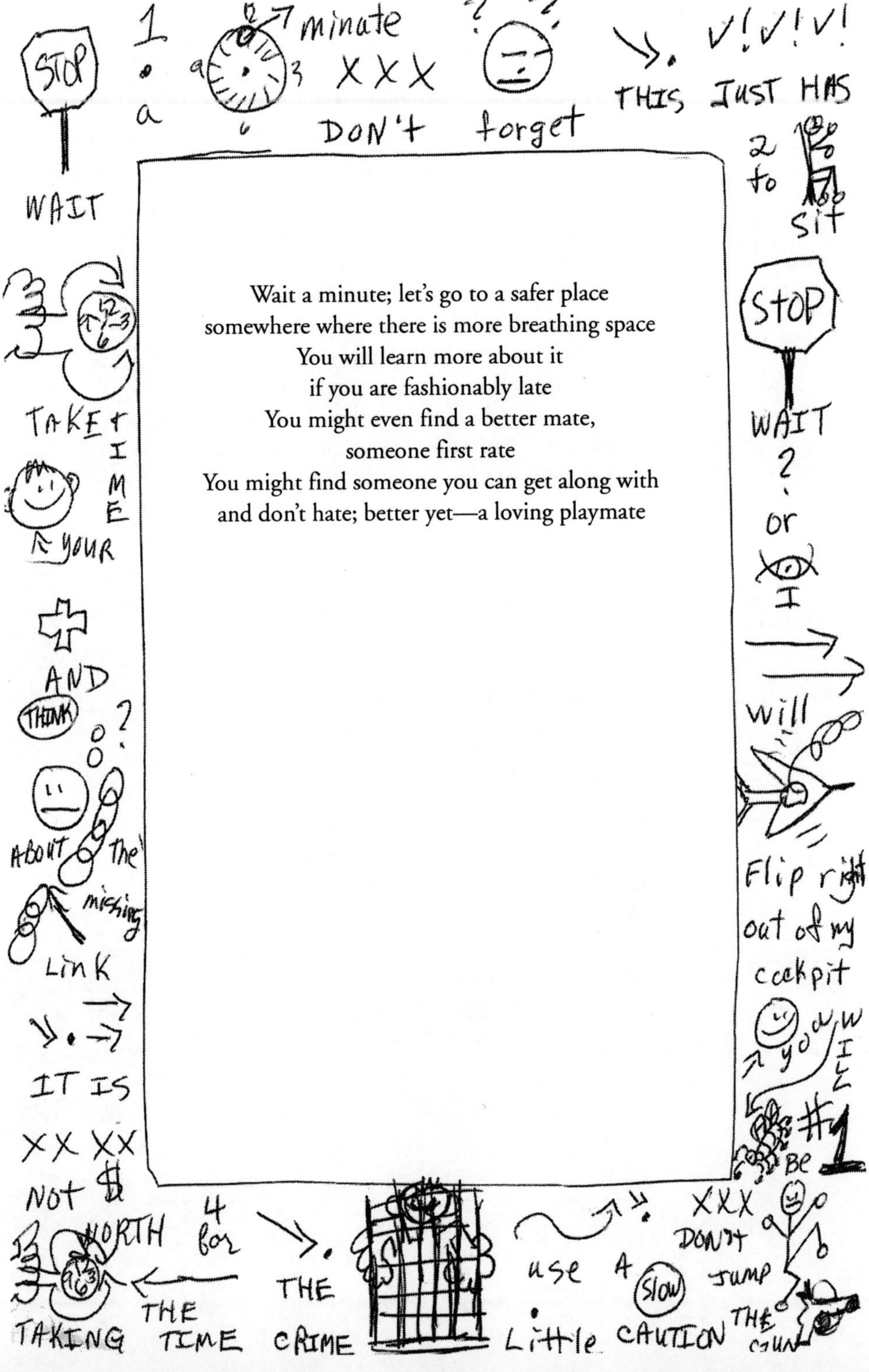

Wait a minute; let's go to a safer place
somewhere where there is more breathing space
You will learn more about it
if you are fashionably late
You might even find a better mate,
someone first rate
You might find someone you can get along with
and don't hate; better yet—a loving playmate

THE SHARON CONNECTION

Come hither, little turtledove
put on your boxing gloves
Wake up and join us; you are our labor of love
We're sending prayers for you to someone above
So we'll have your company, push or shove
Open your eyes, give us a pleasant surprise
And you'll again, see your loving family ties
We know your sleep
is only a temporary disguise
And where your spirit now flies
leaves you hypnotized
We here on the ground want you to stay around
We want you earthbound, healthy, and fully wound
Go ahead; make a little sound
from your happy hunting grounds
And to us, it will be a treasure
and an honor quite profound
We all realize sleep tends to catch you
and keep you mesmerized
And how difficult it is for you to lift
your head and to get up and rise
But miracles can surprise us
while we fantasize of sunshine and bluer skies
And we want a miracle one of a big size; pray
let it grow and multiply
My girl, my beloved little squirrel, let your wings unfurl

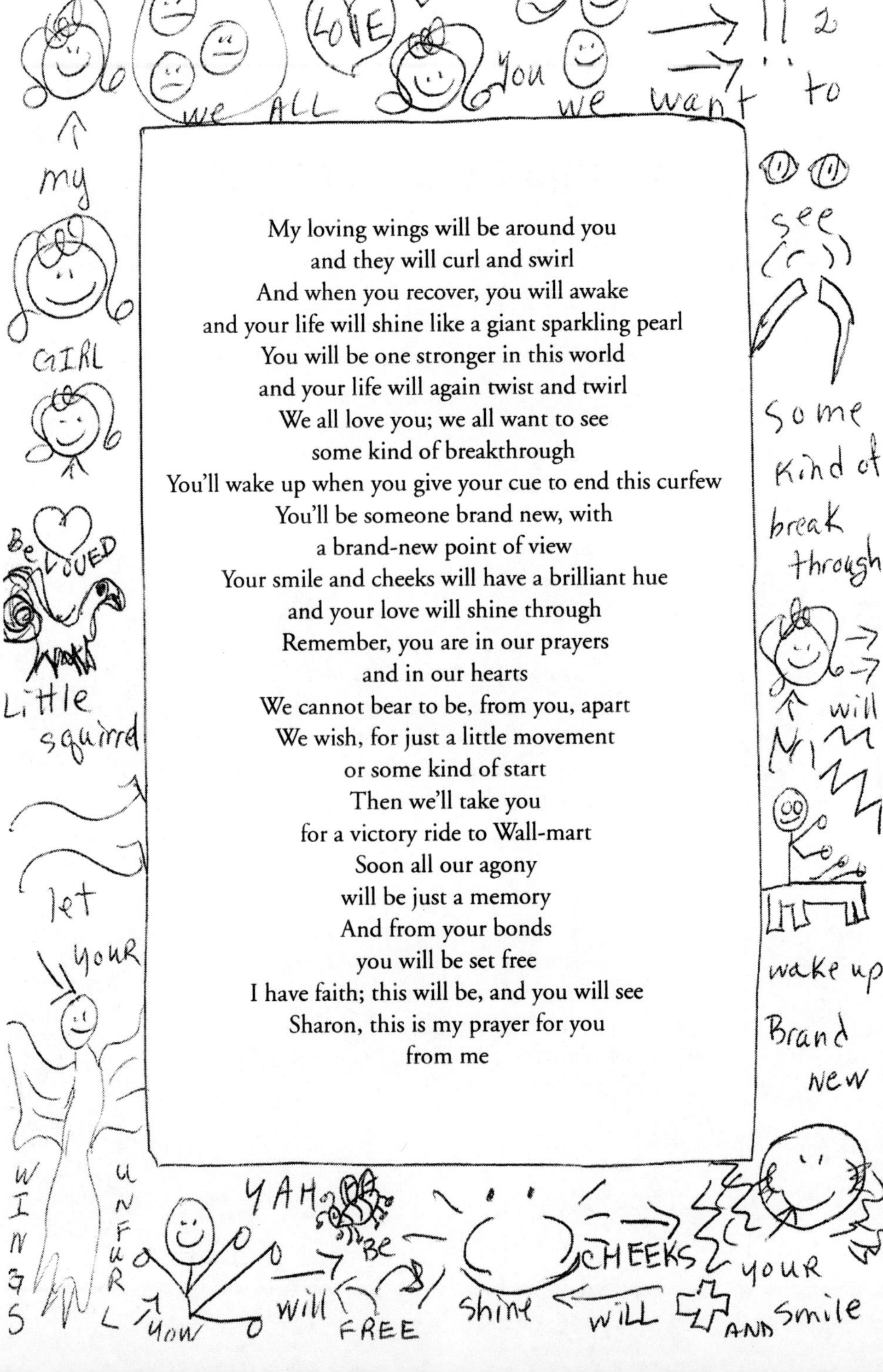

My loving wings will be around you
and they will curl and swirl
And when you recover, you will awake
and your life will shine like a giant sparkling pearl
You will be one stronger in this world
and your life will again twist and twirl
We all love you; we all want to see
some kind of breakthrough
You'll wake up when you give your cue to end this curfew
You'll be someone brand new, with
a brand-new point of view
Your smile and cheeks will have a brilliant hue
and your love will shine through
Remember, you are in our prayers
and in our hearts
We cannot bear to be, from you, apart
We wish, for just a little movement
or some kind of start
Then we'll take you
for a victory ride to Wall-mart
Soon all our agony
will be just a memory
And from your bonds
you will be set free
I have faith; this will be, and you will see
Sharon, this is my prayer for you
from me

ANGELICIOUS

Delicious Angelicious, you luscious dish
You fry up some mighty fine battered fish
You are damn good looking,
every man's wish
Not at all vicious,
and no need to be suspicious
She turns more than a burger,
for many boys and girls
Mark you me, I'll wager I heard her purr
Your food will be scrump-didly-icious
yes, sir
Damn delicious, fit for a king
or for an emperor
She'll curl the hairs of your whiskers
and what's more
She'll say hi even if the misters are *a poor flavor*
Her bangs are a fine curly wisp and somewhat
like a mane is how she is adorned
She's as pure as a baby, newly born
or a shirt that has never been worn
Her food is delectable fare, fit for any millionaire
She is none the worse for wear
she is only happy to prepare
Every meal she makes is square
guaranteed better than anywhere
She doesn't really care; she is so clean that
she is the health inspector's worst nightmare

With her, I have a special bond
and not only because I am also blond
I hope of me she is fond, in our working fishpond
We often meet face to face
and we respond like friendly vagabonds
I just, won't tell you in which place
our uniforms we have donned
She turns all the delivery men on,
like an experienced Cezanne
With her wiles and delicious cactus cola;
she has many a hangers-on
I can't verily compete; she is a veritable Amazon
But she makes each day complete
a completely enjoyable marathon
What more can I say about her cooking ballet
To work with her is like living in a play
with every day a happy birthday
I hope she feels the same way
I would like to somehow, her, repay
Come what may, I will send her out
a big Angelicious bouquet
Angelicious, you make a damned tasty dish
So damned delicious
with your weapon whisk
Come on, go, girl. You go, girl;
come on, make a wish
Go for it; right on, right upon; tsk, tsk, tsk

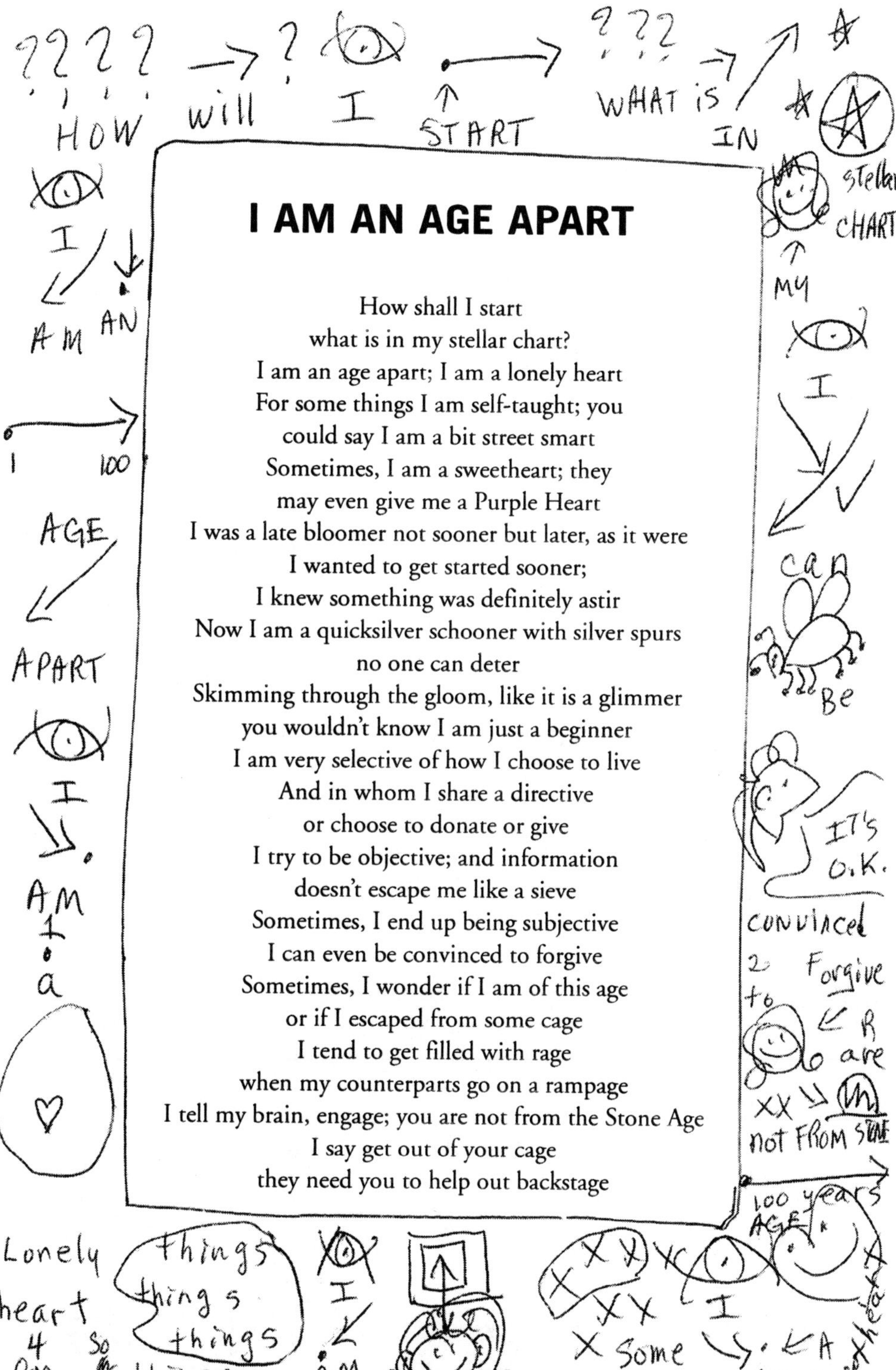

I AM AN AGE APART

How shall I start
what is in my stellar chart?
I am an age apart; I am a lonely heart
For some things I am self-taught; you
could say I am a bit street smart
Sometimes, I am a sweetheart; they
may even give me a Purple Heart
I was a late bloomer not sooner but later, as it were
I wanted to get started sooner;
I knew something was definitely astir
Now I am a quicksilver schooner with silver spurs
no one can deter
Skimming through the gloom, like it is a glimmer
you wouldn't know I am just a beginner
I am very selective of how I choose to live
And in whom I share a directive
or choose to donate or give
I try to be objective; and information
doesn't escape me like a sieve
Sometimes, I end up being subjective
I can even be convinced to forgive
Sometimes, I wonder if I am of this age
or if I escaped from some cage
I tend to get filled with rage
when my counterparts go on a rampage
I tell my brain, engage; you are not from the Stone Age
I say get out of your cage
they need you to help out backstage

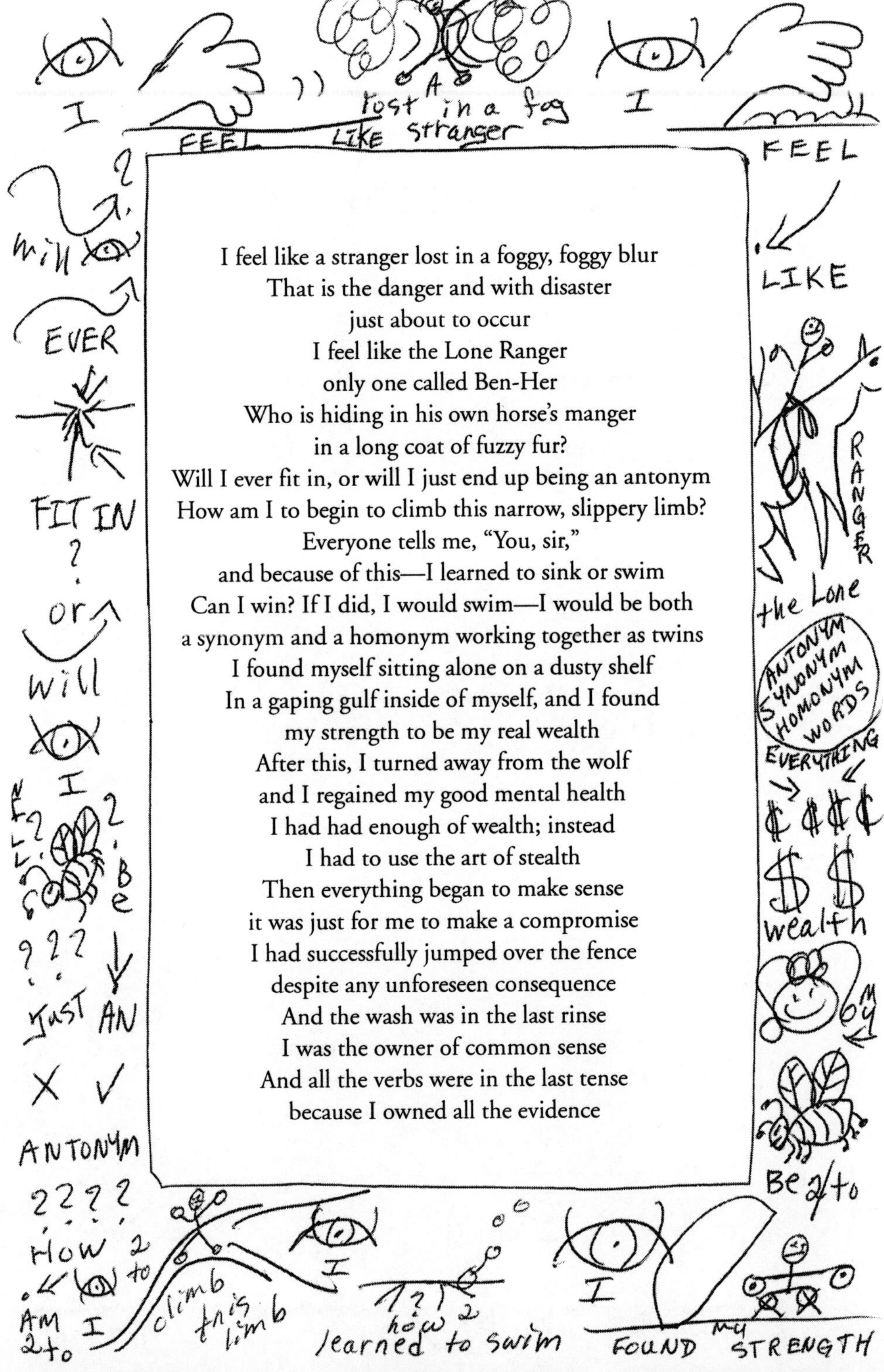

I feel like a stranger lost in a foggy, foggy blur
That is the danger and with disaster
just about to occur
I feel like the Lone Ranger
only one called Ben-Her
Who is hiding in his own horse's manger
in a long coat of fuzzy fur?
Will I ever fit in, or will I just end up being an antonym
How am I to begin to climb this narrow, slippery limb?
Everyone tells me, "You, sir,"
and because of this—I learned to sink or swim
Can I win? If I did, I would swim—I would be both
a synonym and a homonym working together as twins
I found myself sitting alone on a dusty shelf
In a gaping gulf inside of myself, and I found
my strength to be my real wealth
After this, I turned away from the wolf
and I regained my good mental health
I had had enough of wealth; instead
I had to use the art of stealth
Then everything began to make sense
it was just for me to make a compromise
I had successfully jumped over the fence
despite any unforeseen consequence
And the wash was in the last rinse
I was the owner of common sense
And all the verbs were in the last tense
because I owned all the evidence

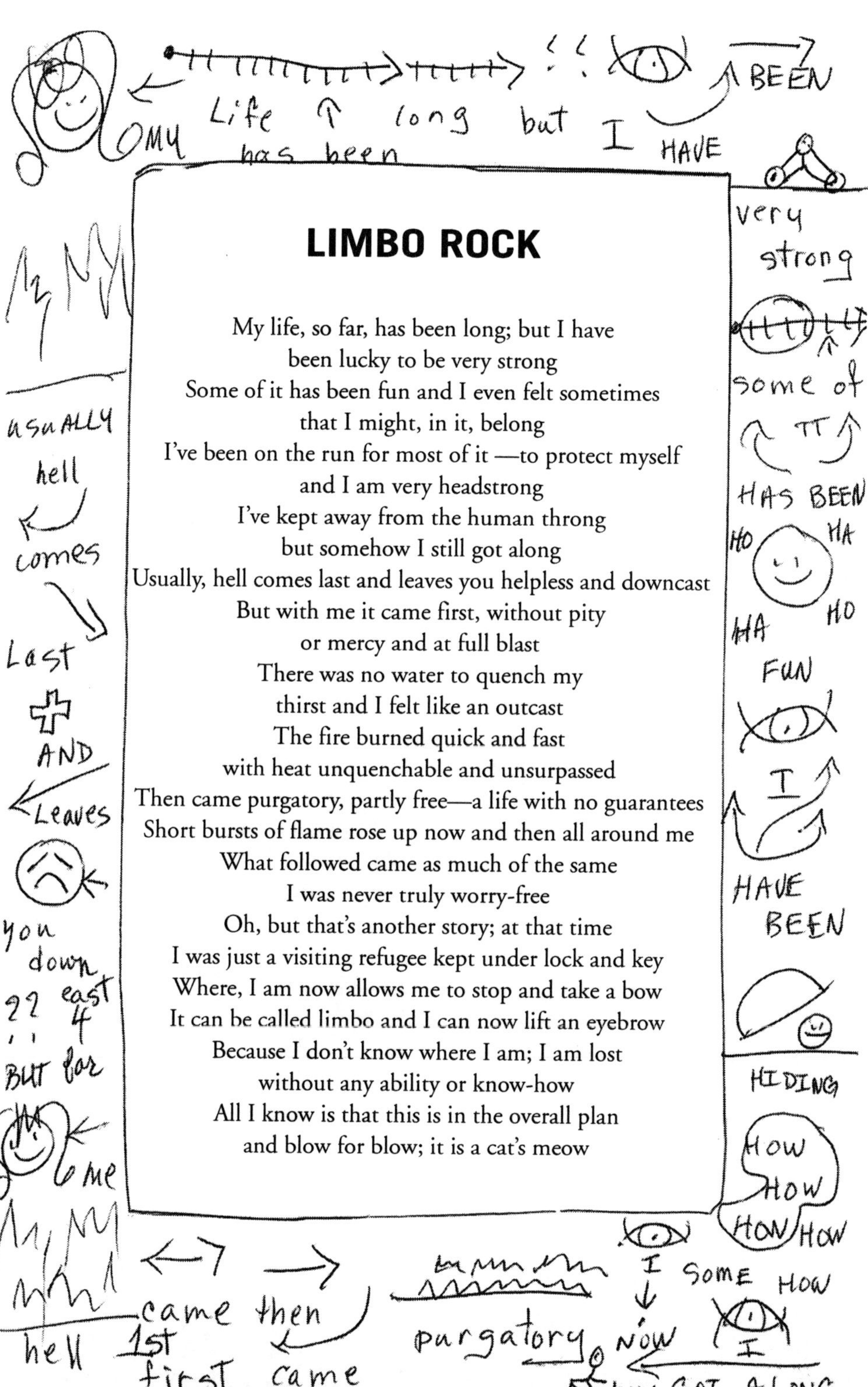

LIMBO ROCK

My life, so far, has been long; but I have
been lucky to be very strong
Some of it has been fun and I even felt sometimes
that I might, in it, belong
I've been on the run for most of it —to protect myself
and I am very headstrong
I've kept away from the human throng
but somehow I still got along
Usually, hell comes last and leaves you helpless and downcast
But with me it came first, without pity
or mercy and at full blast
There was no water to quench my
thirst and I felt like an outcast
The fire burned quick and fast
with heat unquenchable and unsurpassed
Then came purgatory, partly free—a life with no guarantees
Short bursts of flame rose up now and then all around me
What followed came as much of the same
I was never truly worry-free
Oh, but that's another story; at that time
I was just a visiting refugee kept under lock and key
Where, I am now allows me to stop and take a bow
It can be called limbo and I can now lift an eyebrow
Because I don't know where I am; I am lost
without any ability or know-how
All I know is that this is in the overall plan
and blow for blow; it is a cat's meow

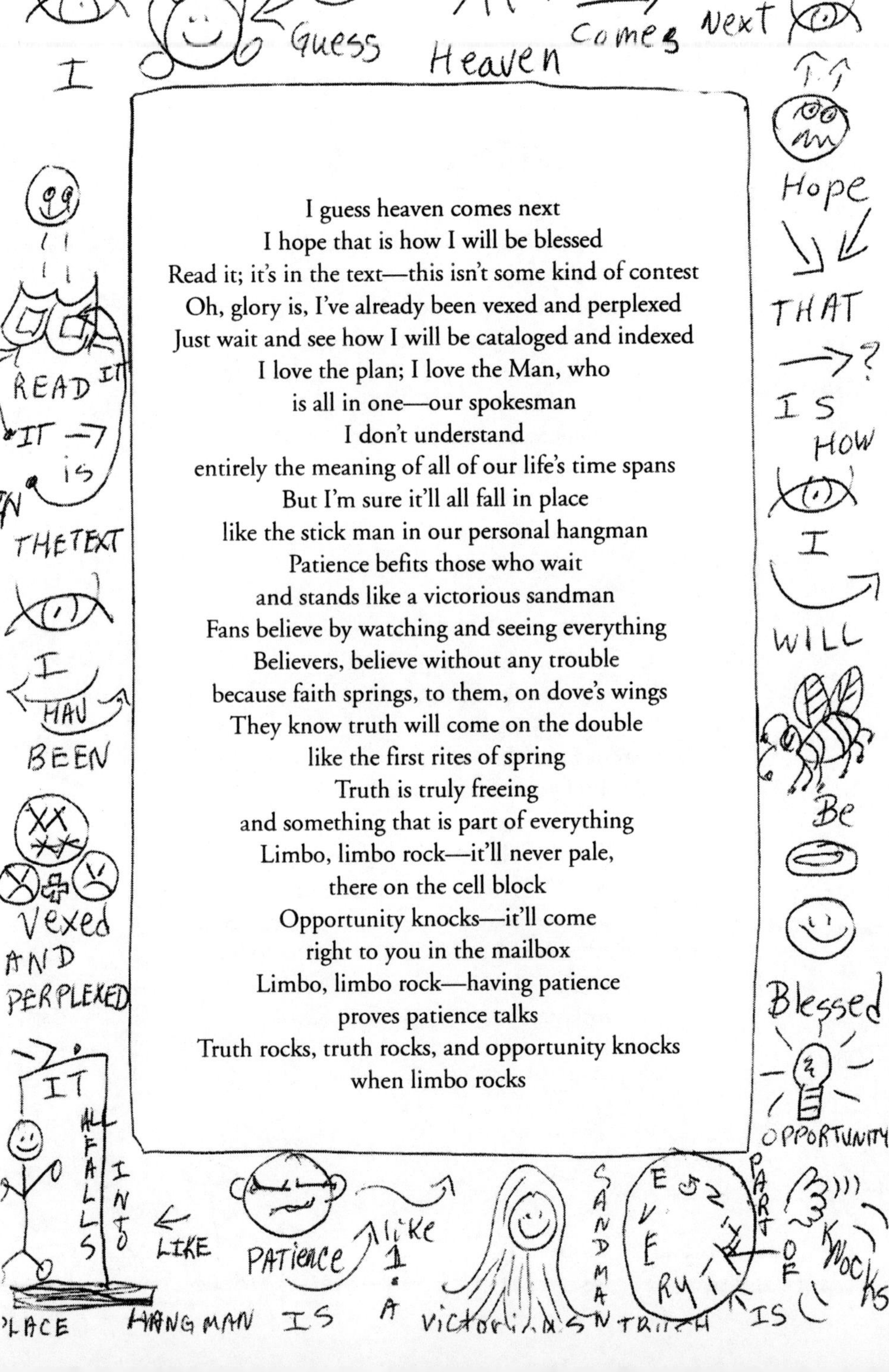

I guess heaven comes next
I hope that is how I will be blessed
Read it; it's in the text—this isn't some kind of contest
Oh, glory is, I've already been vexed and perplexed
Just wait and see how I will be cataloged and indexed
I love the plan; I love the Man, who
is all in one—our spokesman
I don't understand
entirely the meaning of all of our life's time spans
But I'm sure it'll all fall in place
like the stick man in our personal hangman
Patience befits those who wait
and stands like a victorious sandman
Fans believe by watching and seeing everything
Believers, believe without any trouble
because faith springs, to them, on dove's wings
They know truth will come on the double
like the first rites of spring
Truth is truly freeing
and something that is part of everything
Limbo, limbo rock—it'll never pale,
there on the cell block
Opportunity knocks—it'll come
right to you in the mailbox
Limbo, limbo rock—having patience
proves patience talks
Truth rocks, truth rocks, and opportunity knocks
when limbo rocks

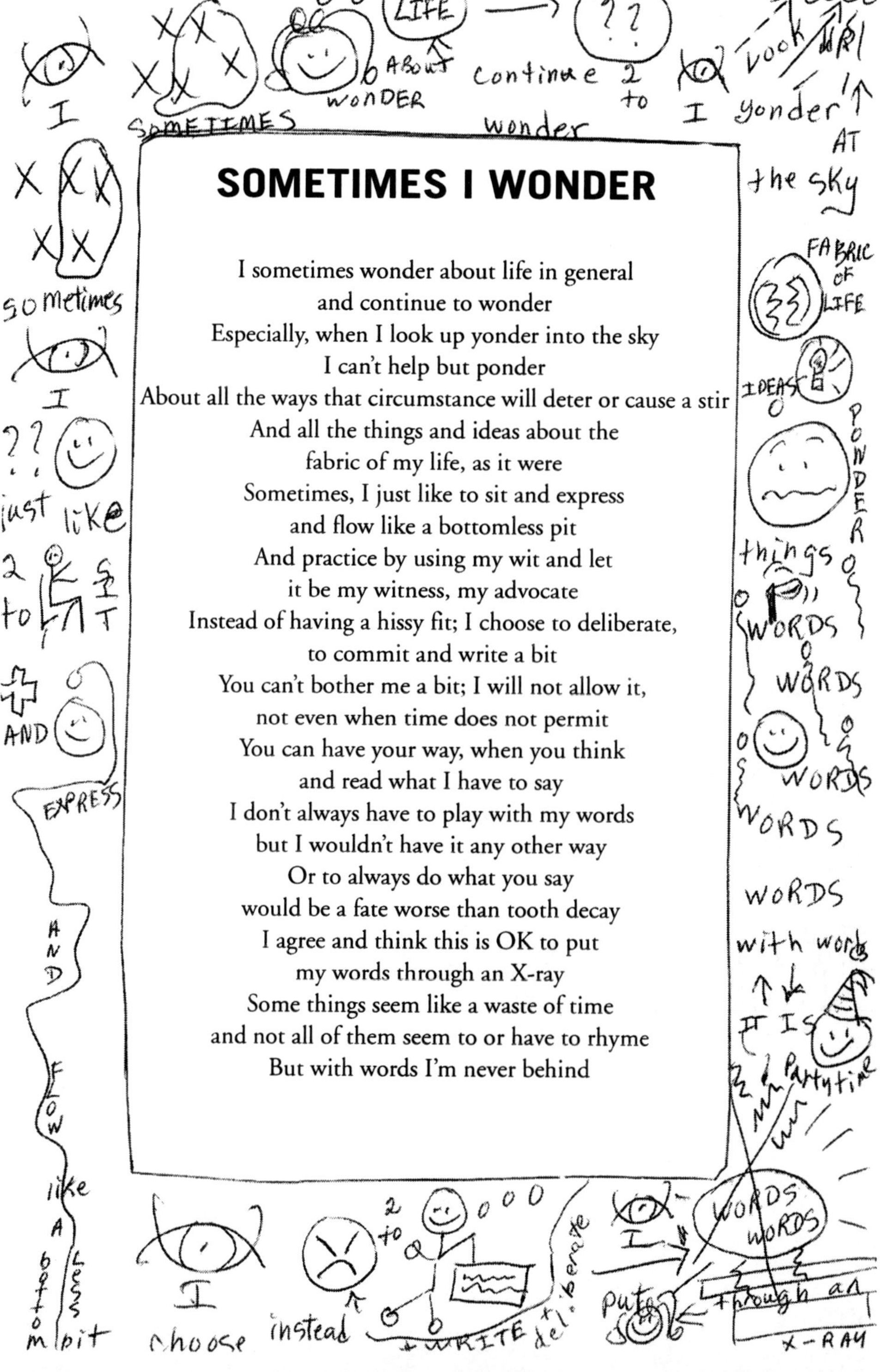

SOMETIMES I WONDER

I sometimes wonder about life in general
and continue to wonder
Especially, when I look up yonder into the sky
I can't help but ponder
About all the ways that circumstance will deter or cause a stir
And all the things and ideas about the
fabric of my life, as it were
Sometimes, I just like to sit and express
and flow like a bottomless pit
And practice by using my wit and let
it be my witness, my advocate
Instead of having a hissy fit; I choose to deliberate,
to commit and write a bit
You can't bother me a bit; I will not allow it,
not even when time does not permit
You can have your way, when you think
and read what I have to say
I don't always have to play with my words
but I wouldn't have it any other way
Or to always do what you say
would be a fate worse than tooth decay
I agree and think this is OK to put
my words through an X-ray
Some things seem like a waste of time
and not all of them seem to or have to rhyme
But with words I'm never behind

I feel like I have many, many partners in crime
Especially when they flow through my mind's time
I just feel like it is party time
They just come to me line after line
and are wonderful and sublime
To pass my own test, I must handle
any self-made conquest
I must always do my personal best
or I will be very depressed
You can be my guest; I give you
permission to be impressed
And join me on my quest
to read and enjoy a creation of pure finesse
We'll blend right in, an enjoyable
win-win, and it won't even be a sin
Because we don't intend to sin even
though we feel like we have fallen
It doesn't matter where we begin
As long as the thought comes from within
We'll be winners in the end when we
reach the sentence we like
and break into a huge grin
The day will come, when all is said and done
that we will all succumb
We'll be found in the sun, stroking our green thumbs
our lives will have just begun
and we will have overcome

Then all our battles will have been won
and we will feel quite numb
To come along with me is my accomplishment
and will be my decree
The fun is ours and is totally free; you
and I are now totally home-free
Open your eyes and let it be;
and you will feel quite satisfied and carefree
Sharing love is the key, which has been allowed
to come from your thoughts from me to you and you to me

2010 AND THEN SOME

What a good year full of cheer
Better than the best beer
the whole smear
Not a single tear; we are all clear
I'm facing my worst fears;
it's a brand-new frontier
This year, I've truly began a new life span
The greatest of my grandstands
is now in my great demand
I'm my biggest fan in my very own
one-man band
Now I've come to understand
not everything goes as planned
I'll wave my magic wand in my very own fantasy land
Oh, by the way, of my music I am very fond
it is the very best in all the land
In fact, I will receive no reprimand
I can think of offhand
My music will be my very own brand;
you must understand
I think; I now can be happy
Now that I've found
my very own sugar daddy
I no longer feel depressed and crappy
Because I have found
the most wonderful laddie
I'm just finding out now who I really am and
that I can depend on my own brand

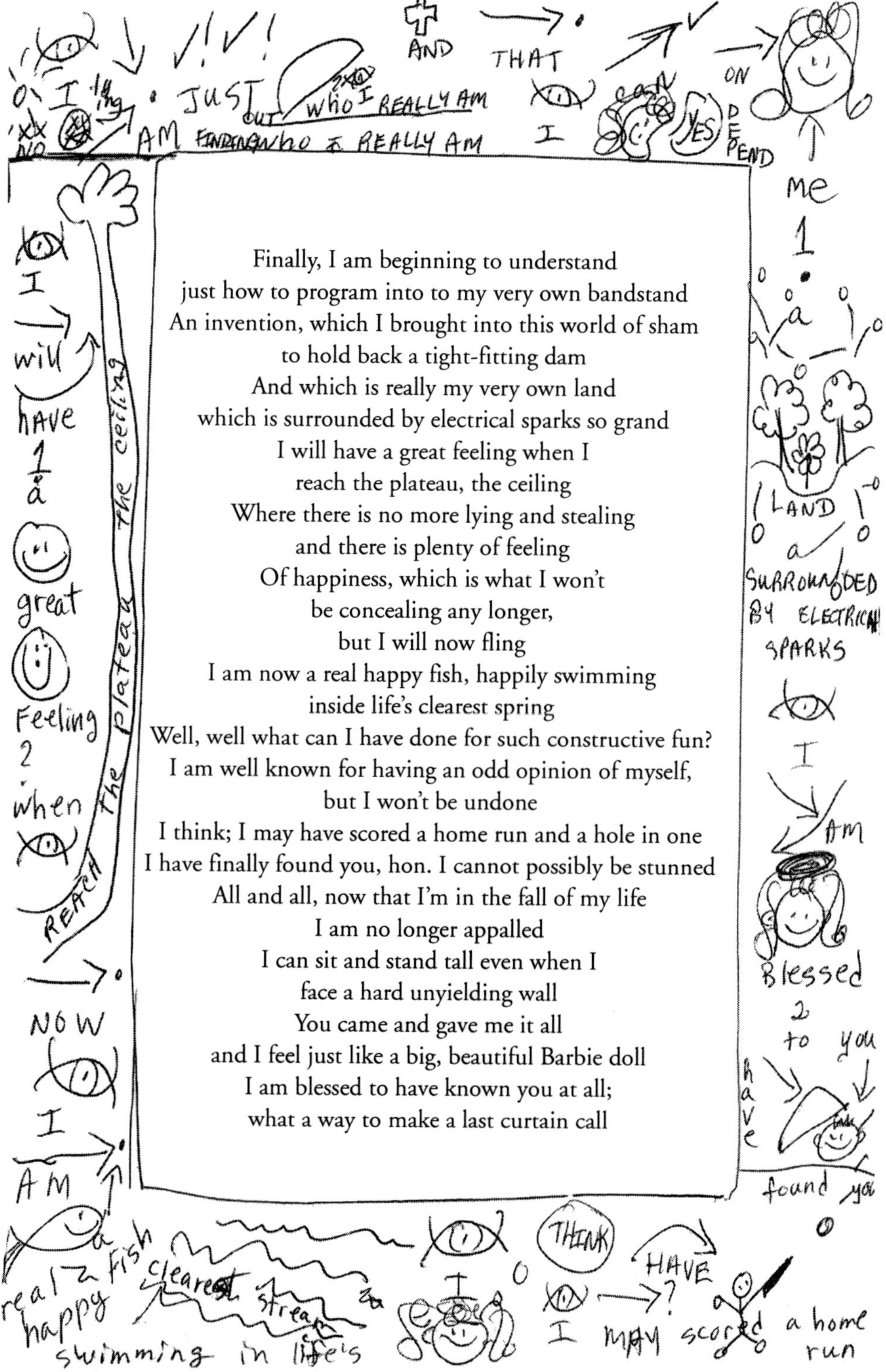

Finally, I am beginning to understand
just how to program into to my very own bandstand
An invention, which I brought into this world of sham
to hold back a tight-fitting dam
And which is really my very own land
which is surrounded by electrical sparks so grand
I will have a great feeling when I
reach the plateau, the ceiling
Where there is no more lying and stealing
and there is plenty of feeling
Of happiness, which is what I won't
be concealing any longer,
but I will now fling
I am now a real happy fish, happily swimming
inside life's clearest spring
Well, well what can I have done for such constructive fun?
I am well known for having an odd opinion of myself,
but I won't be undone
I think; I may have scored a home run and a hole in one
I have finally found you, hon. I cannot possibly be stunned
All and all, now that I'm in the fall of my life
I am no longer appalled
I can sit and stand tall even when I
face a hard unyielding wall
You came and gave me it all
and I feel just like a big, beautiful Barbie doll
I am blessed to have known you at all;
what a way to make a last curtain call

MY SHOES DON'T FIT

My shoes don't fit, and they hurt quite a bit
Because my feet are swollen
when I stand or when I sit
The circulation has been cut off lickety-split
My feet are larger than yours;
it has to do with the genetic
Oh, woe is me, my feet are the key
The pain in my face is plain to see
That I will receive relief
there is no guarantee
I no longer want my feet
to belong to me
Now when it comes to feeling left out
My shoes don't know where they are
or what they are all about
My shoes don't fit
even if when scream and shout
That's when I feel like I should go out
onto a different route
Even if I think and feel my shoes fit right
I still have to fight by the end of the night
That's when my shoes become too tight
And I feel like I have
a case of snakebite
Sometimes, this makes me feel
very out of place
Just like I don't belong to the human race

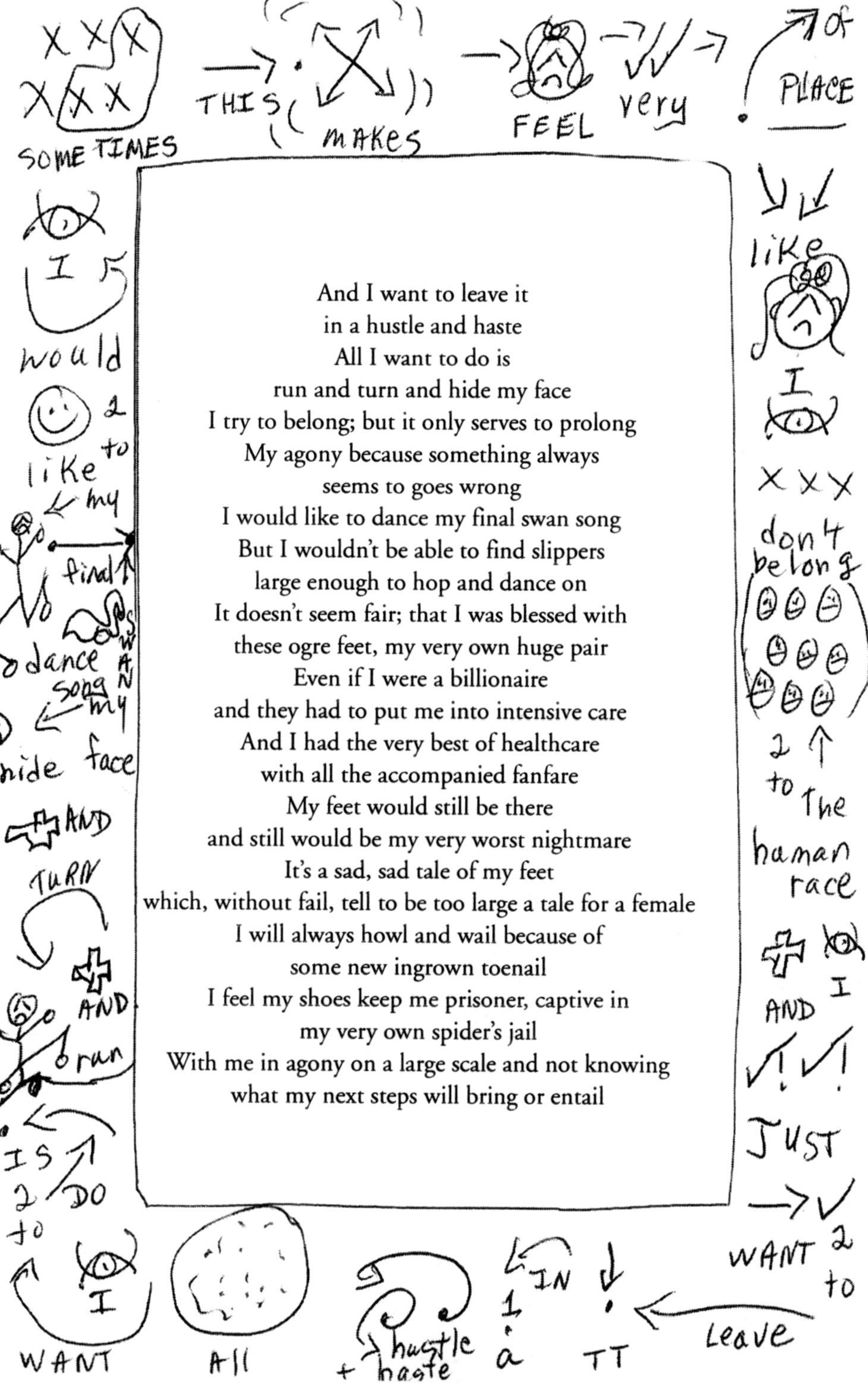

And I want to leave it
in a hustle and haste
All I want to do is
run and turn and hide my face
I try to belong; but it only serves to prolong
My agony because something always
seems to goes wrong
I would like to dance my final swan song
But I wouldn't be able to find slippers
large enough to hop and dance on
It doesn't seem fair; that I was blessed with
these ogre feet, my very own huge pair
Even if I were a billionaire
and they had to put me into intensive care
And I had the very best of healthcare
with all the accompanied fanfare
My feet would still be there
and still would be my very worst nightmare
It's a sad, sad tale of my feet
which, without fail, tell to be too large a tale for a female
I will always howl and wail because of
some new ingrown toenail
I feel my shoes keep me prisoner, captive in
my very own spider's jail
With me in agony on a large scale and not knowing
what my next steps will bring or entail

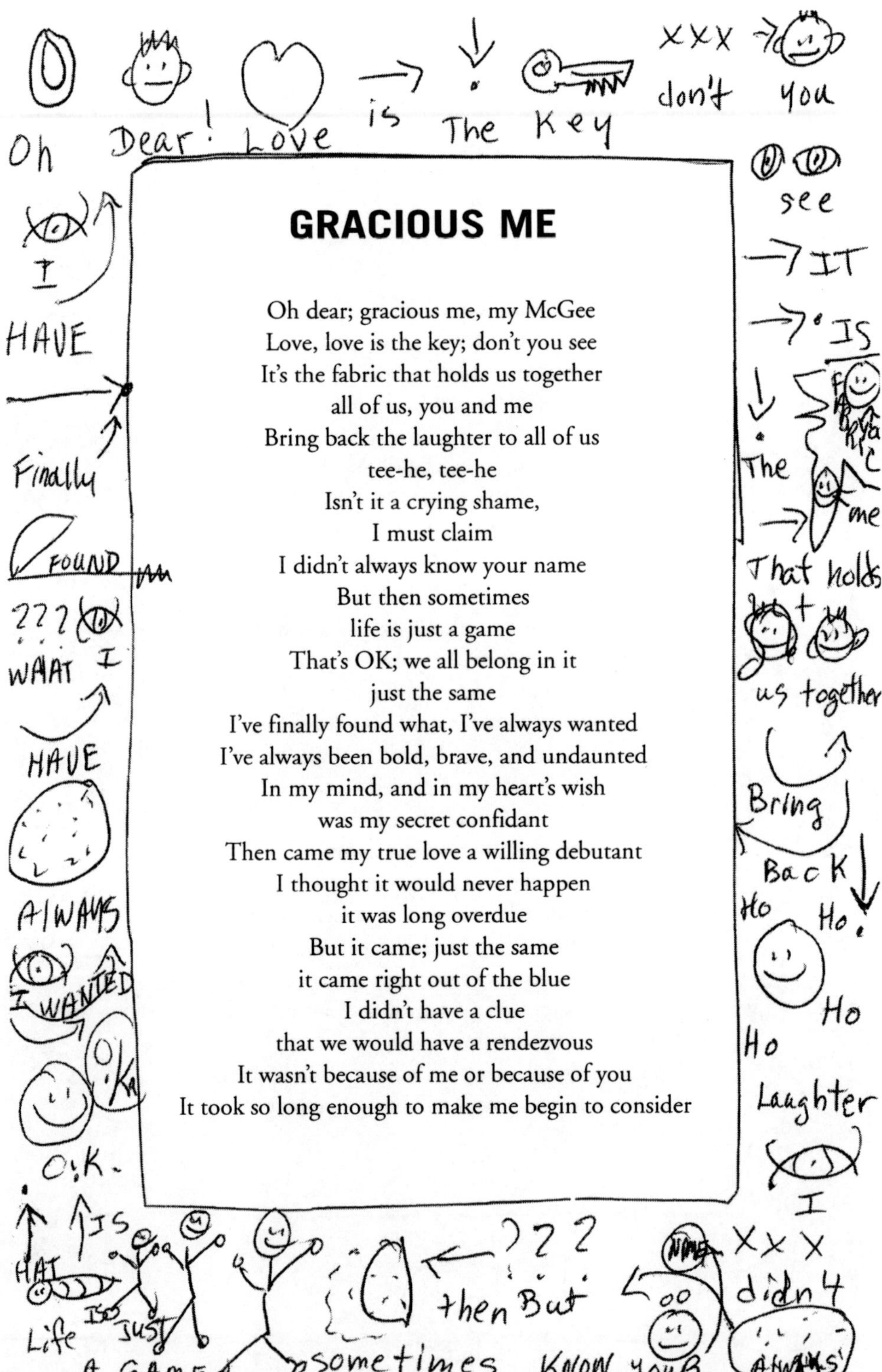

GRACIOUS ME

Oh dear; gracious me, my McGee
Love, love is the key; don't you see
It's the fabric that holds us together
all of us, you and me
Bring back the laughter to all of us
tee-he, tee-he
Isn't it a crying shame,
I must claim
I didn't always know your name
But then sometimes
life is just a game
That's OK; we all belong in it
just the same
I've finally found what, I've always wanted
I've always been bold, brave, and undaunted
In my mind, and in my heart's wish
was my secret confidant
Then came my true love a willing debutant
I thought it would never happen
it was long overdue
But it came; just the same
it came right out of the blue
I didn't have a clue
that we would have a rendezvous
It wasn't because of me or because of you
It took so long enough to make me begin to consider

And wonder if
I was just going to waste away and wither
Part of me was frightened and wanted to shiver
When I was rescued hither
it almost made me shake and quiver
Somehow things always manage to work out
Because goodness is stronger than evil
and has more clout
We don't always know why
or what it's all about
But we find out
when goodness grows and starts to sprout
Tell me what you have to say
About the way I want to play
Give me a clue, please
if you may
If that is also your wish
and your will and your way
Give me an excuse, a reason to produce
One good enough for me to cut loose
and to give me a boost
Make it a beautiful reason, you silly goose
Don't leave me hanging, come with me
and let it all hang loose

I'LL SEND YOU FLOWERS

All is well, all is well; I must be under your magic spell
I thought I heard the final bell;
it sounded as loud as a bombshell
The world didn't end, can't you tell,
eh, Madame, mademoiselle?
It's not yet time to go to hell, just time for show and tell
I'll send you flowers if you prefer
They'll have special powers
to make you move or stir
They will inspire you
to lie on the spurs
Soon you will hear the password
and you will turn into a lovebird
You will smell a special fragrance
It will make you get up and break dance
The effect will encourage
and enhance our romance
We'll get up and out of our trances
which will give our love a fighting chance
Then when you get up in the morning,
love will be dawning
Love won't give you a warning;
and you will feel its sting
It will be like qualifying
for the love rights of spring

Everything for which you've been yearning
will stick to you like static cling
This love story
will be something great
Now let us get this straight
It could also be everyone's fate
It is a good example
at any rate
These flowers will be the story
Blossoming in all in their glory
Their fragrance will be the theme,
one without worry
The ending will make a beautiful
fragrant bouquet for you and me
The flower's seeds will grow and grow
And blossom and multiply row on row
They will overcome
every obstacle and every foe
They'll be the ones, who are in the know
My mind will send you loving thoughts
a whole bunch
A whole bouquet and more, each and every lunch
Soon you are bound to have a strong hunch
How much I love you, even when we're in a crunch

LET'S MAKE THE BEST OF IT

You're in for a surprise, which I have
to continue to emphasize
It is better than you'd ever surmise;
it is one grand enterprise
If you take off your disguise, I will
send you some googol eyes
Yes, sir, we can take the prize, and the prize may be
my eagle eyes, without compromise
Let's make the best of it, come here and lickety-split
That may be a strange twist or it may be a smash hit
That is about the entire gist
and that is far from counterfeit
And it won't even hurt a bit
so put that in your first-aid kit
Let's take it slow, let's stop, and then let's go
you'll learn more than you could ever know
when we are in our own personal show
You'll have more to show; it will be great fun
then it will all be touch and go
You won't have to say stop; you'll be able to say go
I will be your personal dynamo
Let's begin from the start; it will give you a jump-start
Then you can do your part;
you are my personal work of art
It'll become easier and easier
especially if I give you give me a head start
If you let it come from your heart
then you will be playing the right part

You'll reap what you sow; it is karma—don't you know
So be careful where you go;
choose the straight and the narrow
It all depends on who you know
and where you aim your bow and your arrow
It also depends where the wind blows
or where the air flows
Your language may be in the way
and you may not understand the right way
Everything will eventually come into play
and will fall together day to day
You know I'll want to stay; I'll give you a fresh bouquet
You will want another small foray
you will be my newest protégé
You can't have it all or pretend you know it all
You just will have to stand tall
and ignore the catcalls
Stay through it all and try not to fall
and hope there is justice for all
And if you have to lean on a wall
try to pretend you are as light as a rag doll
Just hope that another day will come;
and you will avoid the Peeping Toms
Your eyes will open to see the sun;
but the sun may seem like a fire bomb
And you will prove all in all that you're really supermom
Because you didn't let yourself come undone
and you can still let loose and have fun

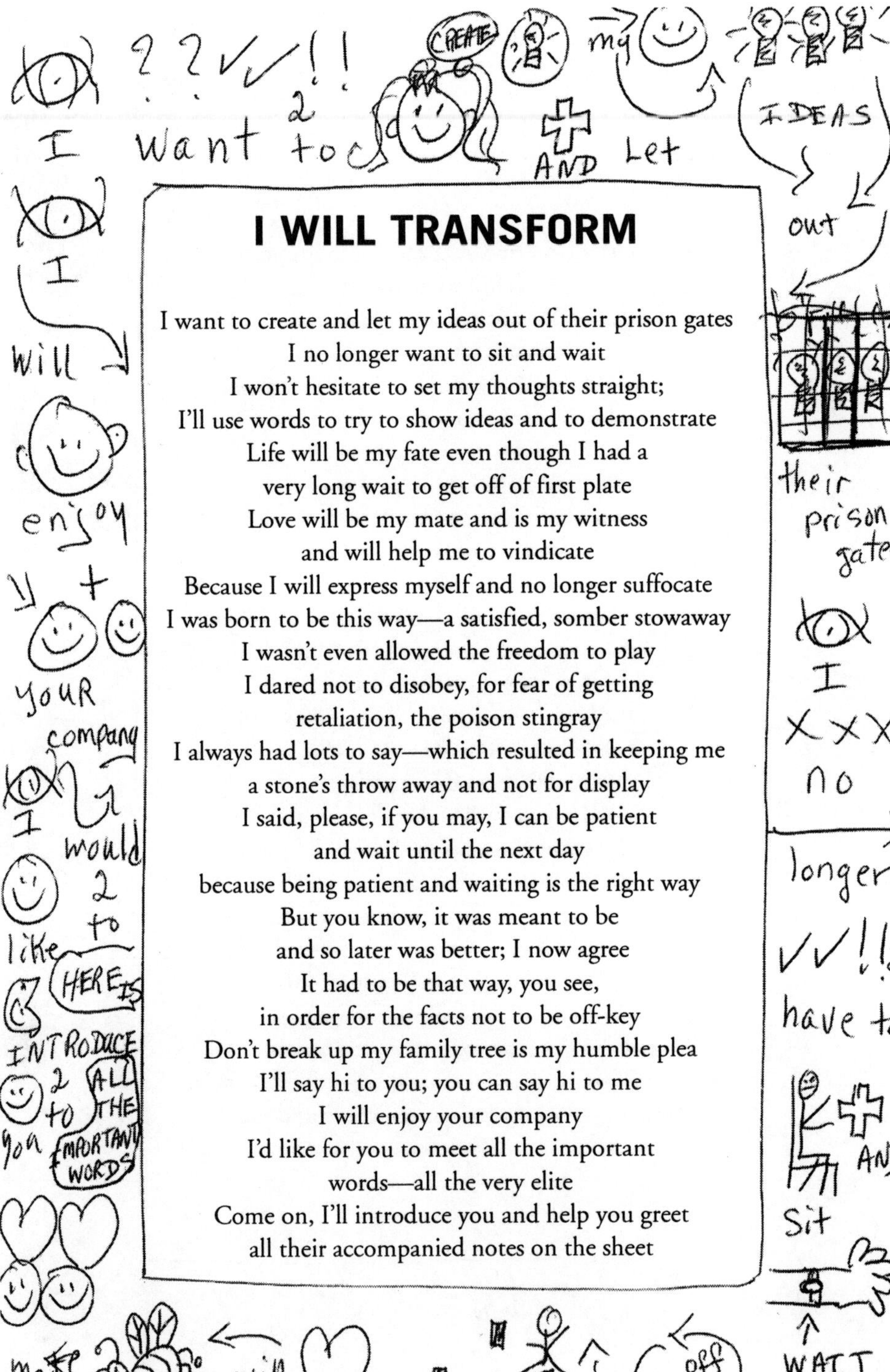

I WILL TRANSFORM

I want to create and let my ideas out of their prison gates
I no longer want to sit and wait
I won't hesitate to set my thoughts straight;
I'll use words to try to show ideas and to demonstrate
Life will be my fate even though I had a
very long wait to get off of first plate
Love will be my mate and is my witness
and will help me to vindicate
Because I will express myself and no longer suffocate
I was born to be this way—a satisfied, somber stowaway
I wasn't even allowed the freedom to play
I dared not to disobey, for fear of getting
retaliation, the poison stingray
I always had lots to say—which resulted in keeping me
a stone's throw away and not for display
I said, please, if you may, I can be patient
and wait until the next day
because being patient and waiting is the right way
But you know, it was meant to be
and so later was better; I now agree
It had to be that way, you see,
in order for the facts not to be off-key
Don't break up my family tree is my humble plea
I'll say hi to you; you can say hi to me
I will enjoy your company
I'd like for you to meet all the important
words—all the very elite
Come on, I'll introduce you and help you greet
all their accompanied notes on the sheet

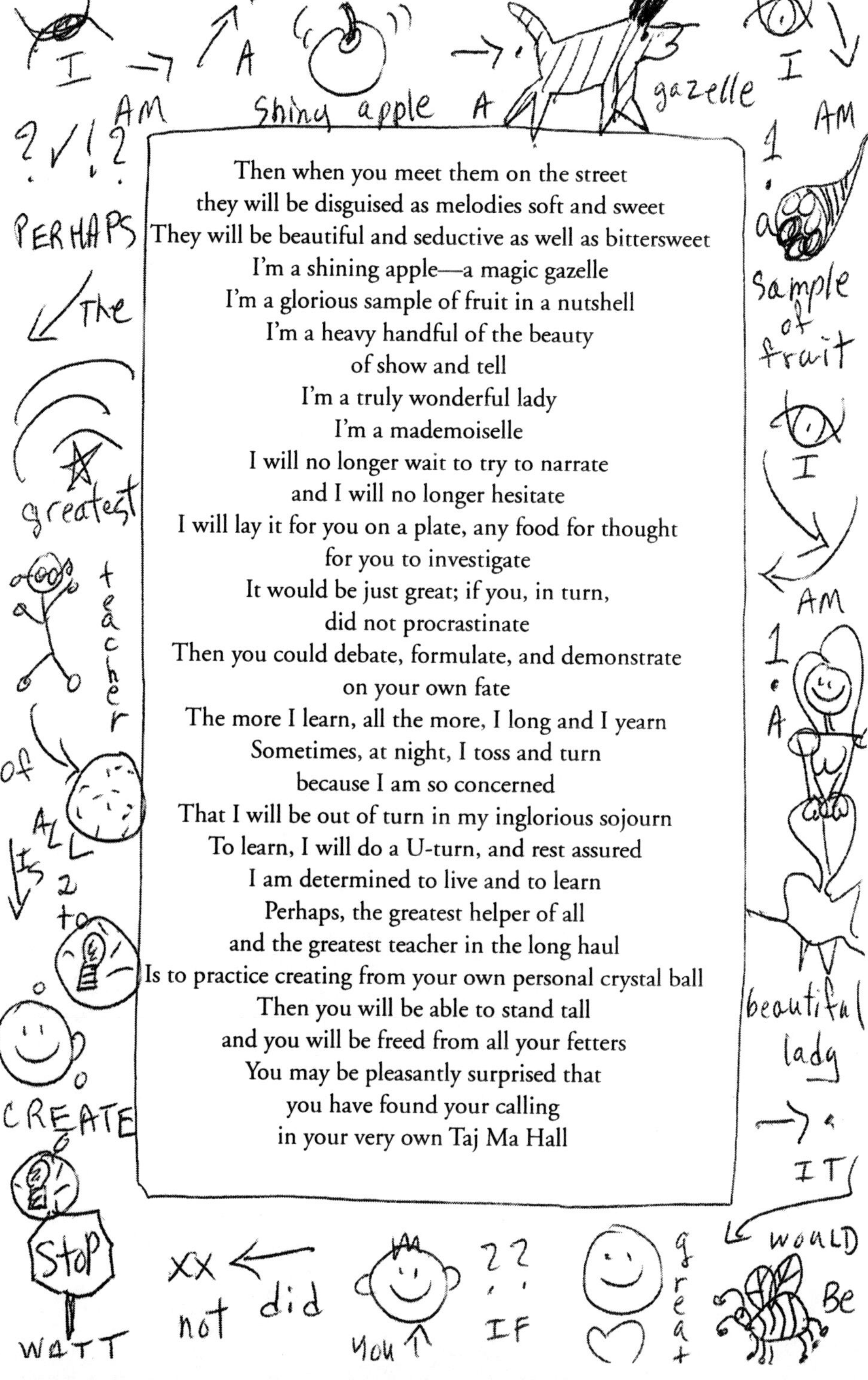

Then when you meet them on the street
they will be disguised as melodies soft and sweet
They will be beautiful and seductive as well as bittersweet
I'm a shining apple—a magic gazelle
I'm a glorious sample of fruit in a nutshell
I'm a heavy handful of the beauty
of show and tell
I'm a truly wonderful lady
I'm a mademoiselle
I will no longer wait to try to narrate
and I will no longer hesitate
I will lay it for you on a plate, any food for thought
for you to investigate
It would be just great; if you, in turn,
did not procrastinate
Then you could debate, formulate, and demonstrate
on your own fate
The more I learn, all the more, I long and I yearn
Sometimes, at night, I toss and turn
because I am so concerned
That I will be out of turn in my inglorious sojourn
To learn, I will do a U-turn, and rest assured
I am determined to live and to learn
Perhaps, the greatest helper of all
and the greatest teacher in the long haul
Is to practice creating from your own personal crystal ball
Then you will be able to stand tall
and you will be freed from all your fetters
You may be pleasantly surprised that
you have found your calling
in your very own Taj Ma Hall

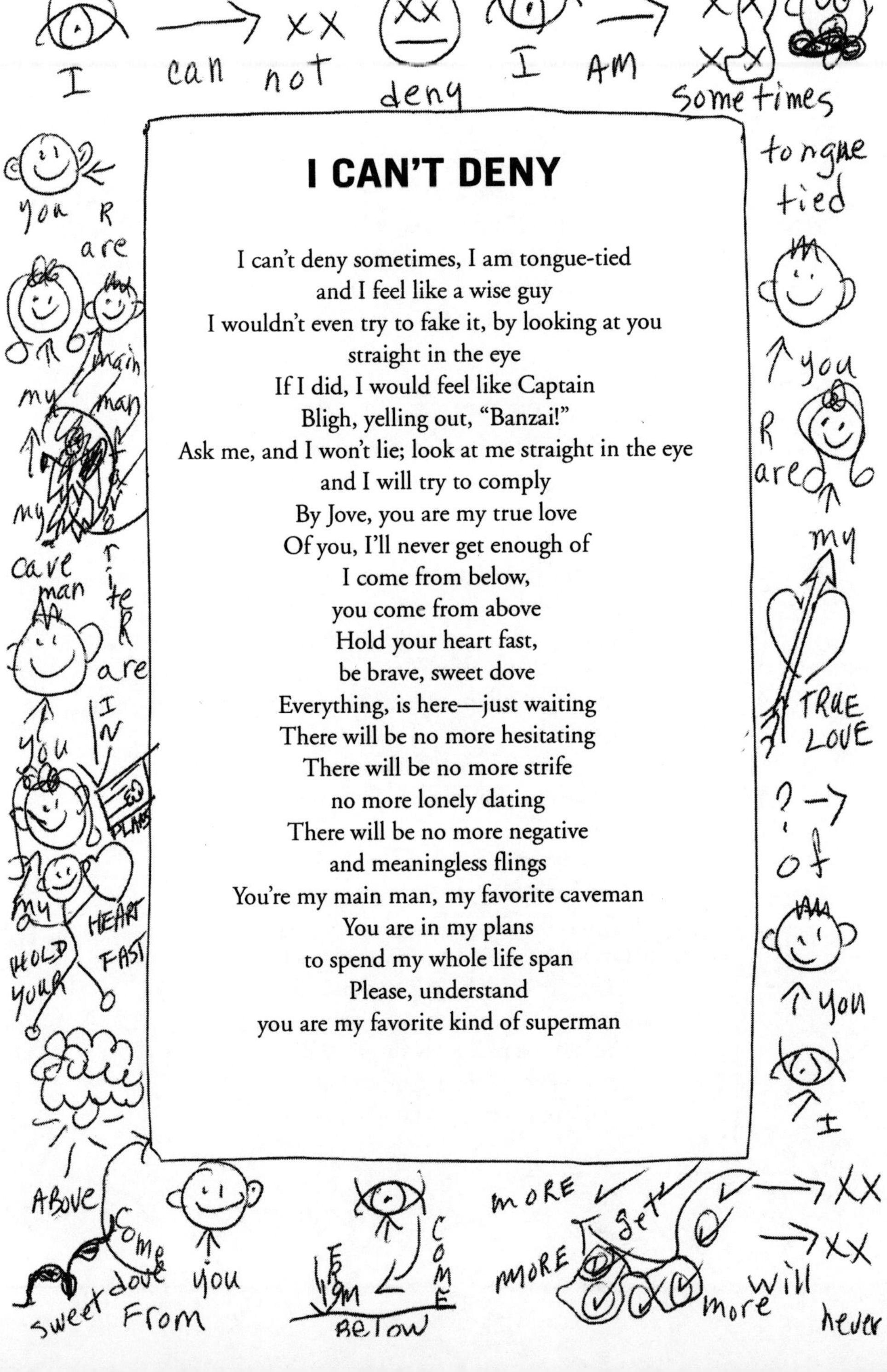

I CAN'T DENY

I can't deny sometimes, I am tongue-tied
and I feel like a wise guy
I wouldn't even try to fake it, by looking at you
straight in the eye
If I did, I would feel like Captain
Bligh, yelling out, "Banzai!"
Ask me, and I won't lie; look at me straight in the eye
and I will try to comply
By Jove, you are my true love
Of you, I'll never get enough of
I come from below,
you come from above
Hold your heart fast,
be brave, sweet dove
Everything, is here—just waiting
There will be no more hesitating
There will be no more strife
no more lonely dating
There will be no more negative
and meaningless flings
You're my main man, my favorite caveman
You are in my plans
to spend my whole life span
Please, understand
you are my favorite kind of superman

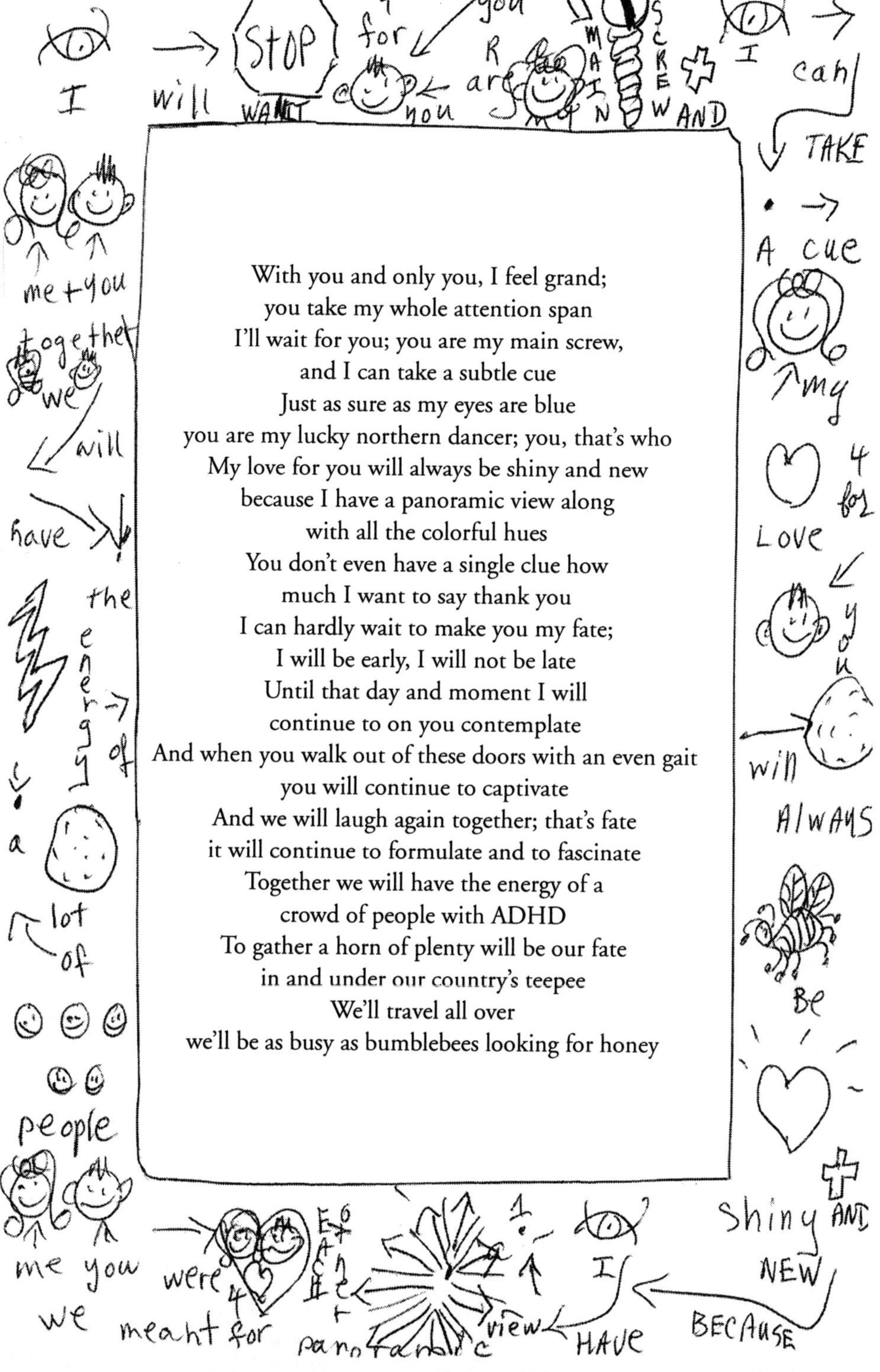

With you and only you, I feel grand;
you take my whole attention span
I'll wait for you; you are my main screw,
and I can take a subtle cue
Just as sure as my eyes are blue
you are my lucky northern dancer; you, that's who
My love for you will always be shiny and new
because I have a panoramic view along
with all the colorful hues
You don't even have a single clue how
much I want to say thank you
I can hardly wait to make you my fate;
I will be early, I will not be late
Until that day and moment I will
continue to on you contemplate
And when you walk out of these doors with an even gait
you will continue to captivate
And we will laugh again together; that's fate
it will continue to formulate and to fascinate
Together we will have the energy of a
crowd of people with ADHD
To gather a horn of plenty will be our fate
in and under our country's teepee
We'll travel all over
we'll be as busy as bumblebees looking for honey

We can conquer any obstacle, isn't it funny
and I can guarantee, we will need no chaperones or referees
If you ask if we were meant for each other,
what can I say? We know what it is for
When we look at one another, that is when
we land smack in a pot of hot water
Cupid turned out to be an awesome hunter
with an aim that connected a lion to a
lioness, what could be better
He brought us together in a grand union
with a giant explosion of love
that was a blast and not at all a blunder

OH, WOE IS ME

Do you know where I've been?
Do you know what I've seen?
I know where my senses
are sharp and keen
I'm big, I'm bad, and I'm mean
I'm as clumsy as an ox
I sure don't look
like Goldilocks
I'm as contagious
as the chicken pox
Instead of brains,
some say I have rocks
I could be boring
and continue on and on
But that would be totally wrong
Then I might not feel
like I belong
And the bad guys might end up
singing my songs
So I'll try harder
right now and how
I'll put my nose to the plow
And all they will
be able to say is wow
Then I will happily be forced
to take a bow

Still sometimes, I feel unsure
And that's when I feel like a cur
That's when I can't look
at myself in the mirror
Afterwards, all the rest
is a hazy, blur
Then I feel like an idiot, a number 1 fool
I also feel like an awful and clueless tool
I don't at all feel cool;
feeling cheap could be my new rule
Put on me a dunce cap
and sit me on a stool
I knew it all along
I just do not belong
And all my good senses
are completely gone
And everything I do is wrong
Someday, my victory day
will dawn on me
And my true self
will be set free
I will have to learn to love me
Then guilty I will happily be

I LIKE YOU

I like you, yes, I do;
I love you through and through
To me, your kind is brand new;
come on, let's make a rendezvous
I'll give you another clue; I know you are true blue
I want to stick to you like glue
do you see my point of view?
I love your many ways; I'll follow your game play by play
Come on, dear, let's go; let's romp and play night and day
I'll see you in the morning, what do you say?
I'll see you at night, come what may
You're a little thin; but you're not gray
living with you is one giant holiday
You give me inspiration; you are tasty, my honey bun
You give me a bright new direction;
you are my number 1
You get even better upon reflection
you are my hole in one
Since you have come to my attention
I might as well be road kill or a victim of hit and run
Of you, I'll never tire; I got caught in Cupid's crossfire
I love you, you live wire; you are my shining sapphire
I want to fall into the fire of unquenchable desire
Of which, with you, I will never tire
I'll let you take me higher and higher
until we make a large mountain bonfire
We could make beautiful music together
on a scale that purrs and purrs

You could show me how to stir
in any kind of weather in any way you prefer
Which would be better, the hearth
or the heather? Or are you a slow go-getter?
Which would be better, linoleum or leather?
Which prop would go like a chair or a feather?
Your kind of love is catchy; your
character is fun and carefree
You are sure the best sugar daddy;
that I could find anywhere in the ocean or by the sea
You are far from nasty; on the contrary, you are so good;
I tell them to just let him be
You come firstly, not lastly, to the likes of little old me
come on, let's go, one, two, three
Of your eyes, I am quite aware
and you have that certain flair
When you're warm, sensuous stare bathes me everywhere
I know you really care
With me, your stare can get you anywhere;
you are so handsome and debonair
Even though you are a humble player;
you put me right into intensive care
Now is the time for me to strike you
have nothing that I dislike
While the time is hot, I'll grab the
mike and try to look ladylike
You can have my love any way you
like it, with you I feel childlike
We will fly higher than a kite
you are good for my whole and entire psych

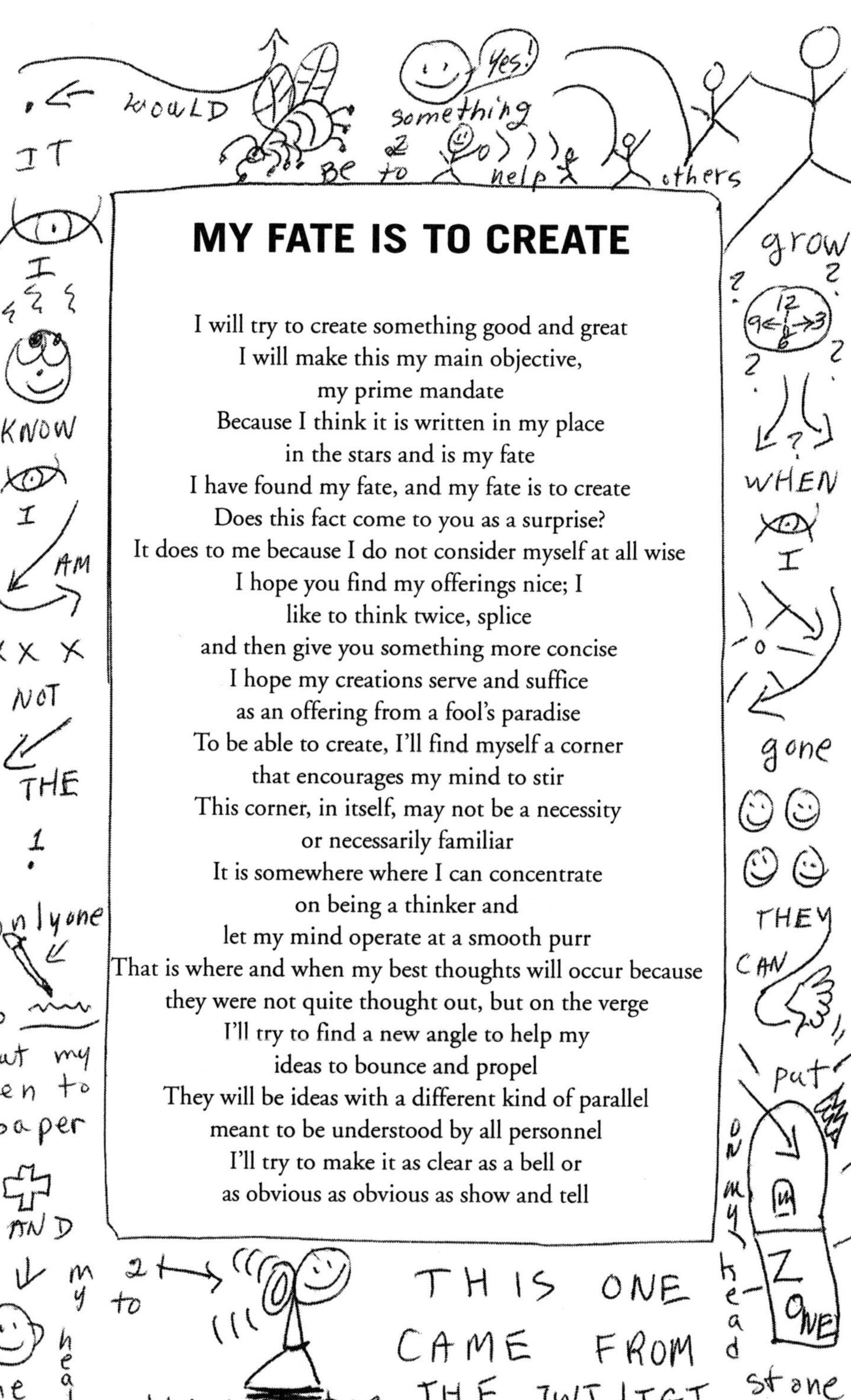
WOULD
IT
Yes!
something
Be
to
help
others
I
KNOW
I
AM
X X X
NOT
THE
1
onlyone
2
to
put my
pen to
paper
AND
me
my
head
2
to
the grindstone
grow
WHEN
I
gone
THEY
CAN
put
ON
my
head
stone
ZONE
THIS ONE
CAME FROM
THE TWILIGT

MY FATE IS TO CREATE

I will try to create something good and great
I will make this my main objective,
my prime mandate
Because I think it is written in my place
in the stars and is my fate
I have found my fate, and my fate is to create
Does this fact come to you as a surprise?
It does to me because I do not consider myself at all wise
I hope you find my offerings nice; I
like to think twice, splice
and then give you something more concise
I hope my creations serve and suffice
as an offering from a fool's paradise
To be able to create, I'll find myself a corner
that encourages my mind to stir
This corner, in itself, may not be a necessity
or necessarily familiar
It is somewhere where I can concentrate
on being a thinker and
let my mind operate at a smooth purr
That is where and when my best thoughts will occur because
they were not quite thought out, but on the verge
I'll try to find a new angle to help my
ideas to bounce and propel
They will be ideas with a different kind of parallel
meant to be understood by all personnel
I'll try to make it as clear as a bell or
as obvious as obvious as show and tell

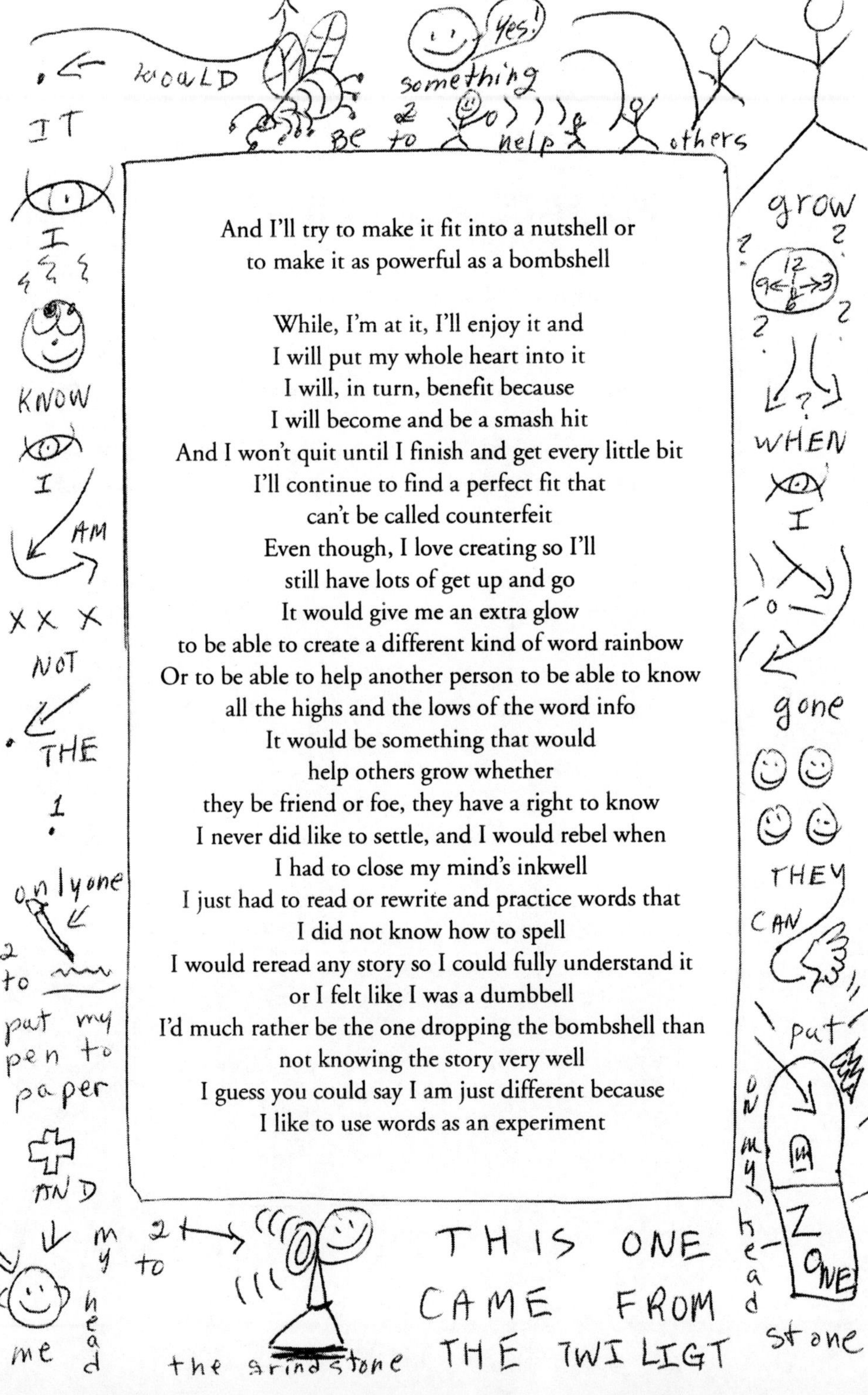
Yes!
IT WOULD Be something 2 to help others
I KNOW I AM NOT THE 1 only one
2 to put my pen to paper
AND my head to the grindstone
me
grow
WHEN I gone
THEY CAN put ON my head stone
THIS ONE CAME FROM THE TWILIGT ZONE

And I'll try to make it fit into a nutshell or
to make it as powerful as a bombshell

While, I'm at it, I'll enjoy it and
I will put my whole heart into it
I will, in turn, benefit because
I will become and be a smash hit
And I won't quit until I finish and get every little bit
I'll continue to find a perfect fit that
can't be called counterfeit
Even though, I love creating so I'll
still have lots of get up and go
It would give me an extra glow
to be able to create a different kind of word rainbow
Or to be able to help another person to be able to know
all the highs and the lows of the word info
It would be something that would
help others grow whether
they be friend or foe, they have a right to know
I never did like to settle, and I would rebel when
I had to close my mind's inkwell
I just had to read or rewrite and practice words that
I did not know how to spell
I would reread any story so I could fully understand it
or I felt like I was a dumbbell
I'd much rather be the one dropping the bombshell than
not knowing the story very well
I guess you could say I am just different because
I like to use words as an experiment

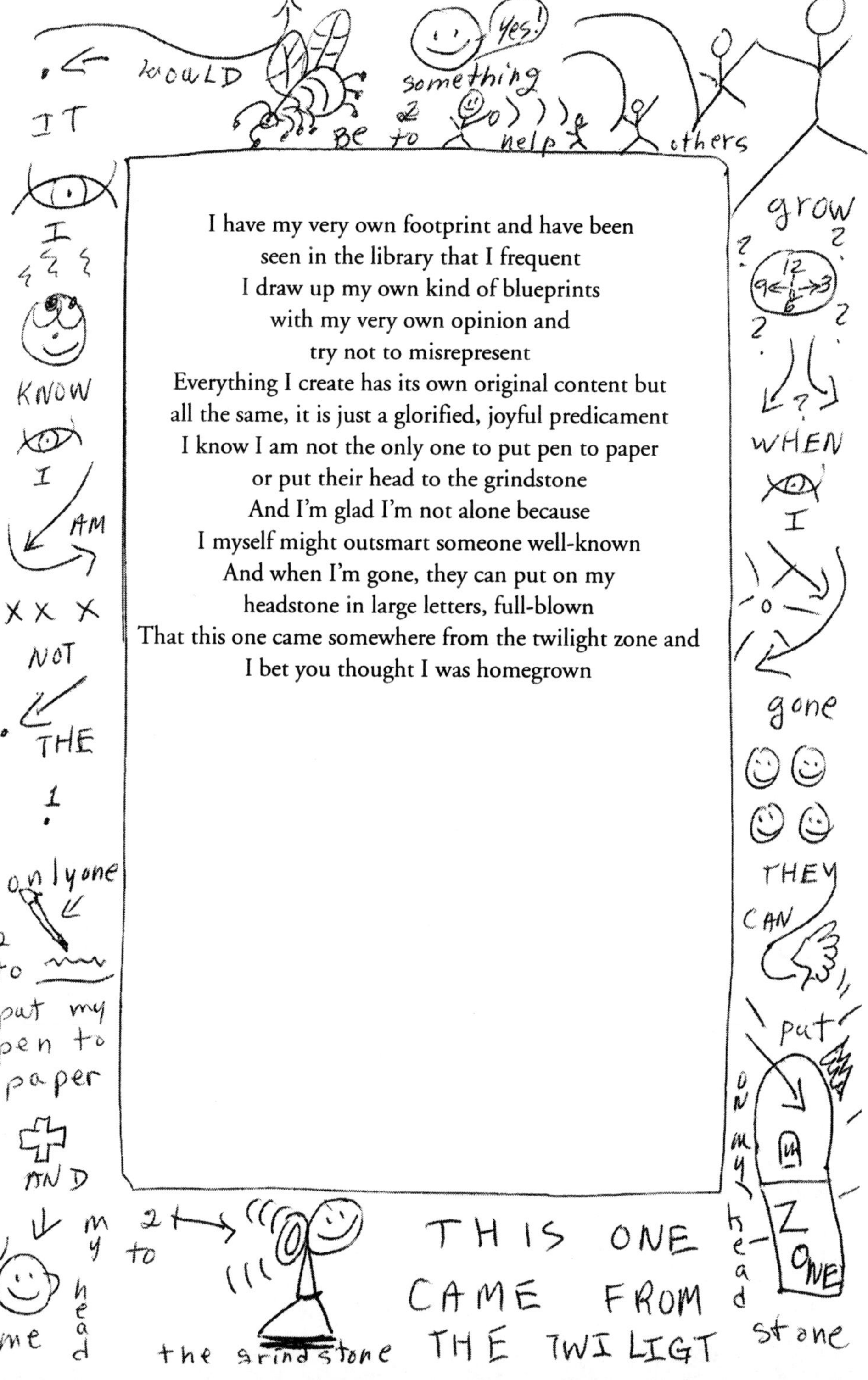

I have my very own footprint and have been
seen in the library that I frequent
I draw up my own kind of blueprints
with my very own opinion and
try not to misrepresent
Everything I create has its own original content but
all the same, it is just a glorified, joyful predicament
I know I am not the only one to put pen to paper
or put their head to the grindstone
And I'm glad I'm not alone because
I myself might outsmart someone well-known
And when I'm gone, they can put on my
headstone in large letters, full-blown
That this one came somewhere from the twilight zone and
I bet you thought I was homegrown

THE MIGHTY JOHNNIE QUINN

Well, I can say that I've met
The Mighty Johnnie Quinn
When I met him, he had a sheepish grin
He warned me to be careful and
to protect what I spin
That was way before
my friends considered me Din Din
I always kept his advice
close to my heart
And made sure to always do my part
I always did my best to protect my art
No one was going to steal my music
because I played it smart
He was and is a very busy man
But he helped me to be able
to understand
That wisdom and experience come
hand in hand
I could see the lines on his face
mapping out a vast and varied landscape
Still I consider this man my friend
From that time way back then
I wouldn't mind
meeting him again
We could compare notes
and hang ten

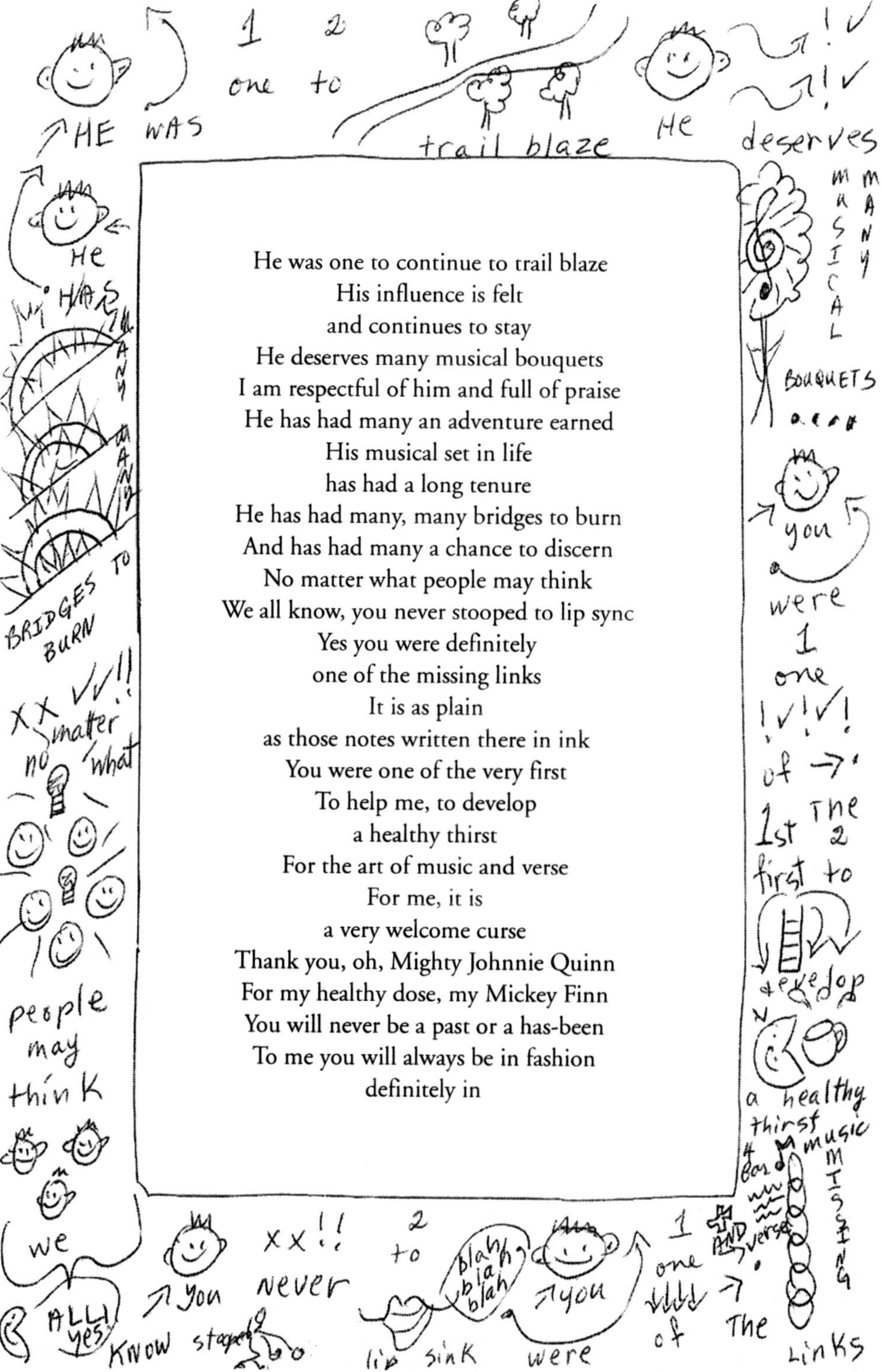

He was one to continue to trail blaze
His influence is felt
and continues to stay
He deserves many musical bouquets
I am respectful of him and full of praise
He has had many an adventure earned
His musical set in life
has had a long tenure
He has had many, many bridges to burn
And has had many a chance to discern
No matter what people may think
We all know, you never stooped to lip sync
Yes you were definitely
one of the missing links
It is as plain
as those notes written there in ink
You were one of the very first
To help me, to develop
a healthy thirst
For the art of music and verse
For me, it is
a very welcome curse
Thank you, oh, Mighty Johnnie Quinn
For my healthy dose, my Mickey Finn
You will never be a past or a has-been
To me you will always be in fashion
definitely in

I WILL MOVE AT WARP SPEED

I will choose to travel on at warp speed
I will go faster than light itself, what a deed
I will go so fast, my movements
will myself proceed
And time travel will finally be guaranteed
Life will start to go
in continuous fast forward
There, will be no time at all
to be bored
No stone will be left unturned
or unexplored
Eternity will become
like a giant billboard

My life will go on now, before and forever in the fast lane
It must have been fueled by a warm, tropical, time current
that must be what is to blame
We all know that we can all enjoy playing at this
times' game
My life tends to go by like a movie
in many continuous frames
All I know is that when I get excited and happy,
The faster I tend to move and jump and buzz
like an excited bumblebee
And I will move so fast, I will feel happy and be carefree
Because my spirit will have been set free and
I will have the genetic proof, my ID, my sworn guarantee
I'll send my thoughts to you in a snafu

They'll go to you so fast
you won't have a clue
When they hit, I will know;
and you will know too
Because they will hit you as deadly
as if they were well-aimed voodoo
Then we will all have something in common
Right from the top of our heads
down to our very bottoms
I will be beside myself and
you will be right there my number 1
My mind might then have to call 911
because it will have had an overdose of fun
Now it is all getting very crystal clear
There is no longer any difference for me
between far and near
There is no longer
any need to worry or to fear
And there is also no longer
any reason for tears
Whether it is straight or on a curve
I will move faster with a little nerve
I will slide along with way more verve
And will pay better attention
to your every word
I'll travel so fast out
on an electrical arc
All I need is that special spark
It means the difference
between light and dark
It is so fast; it is bound to work

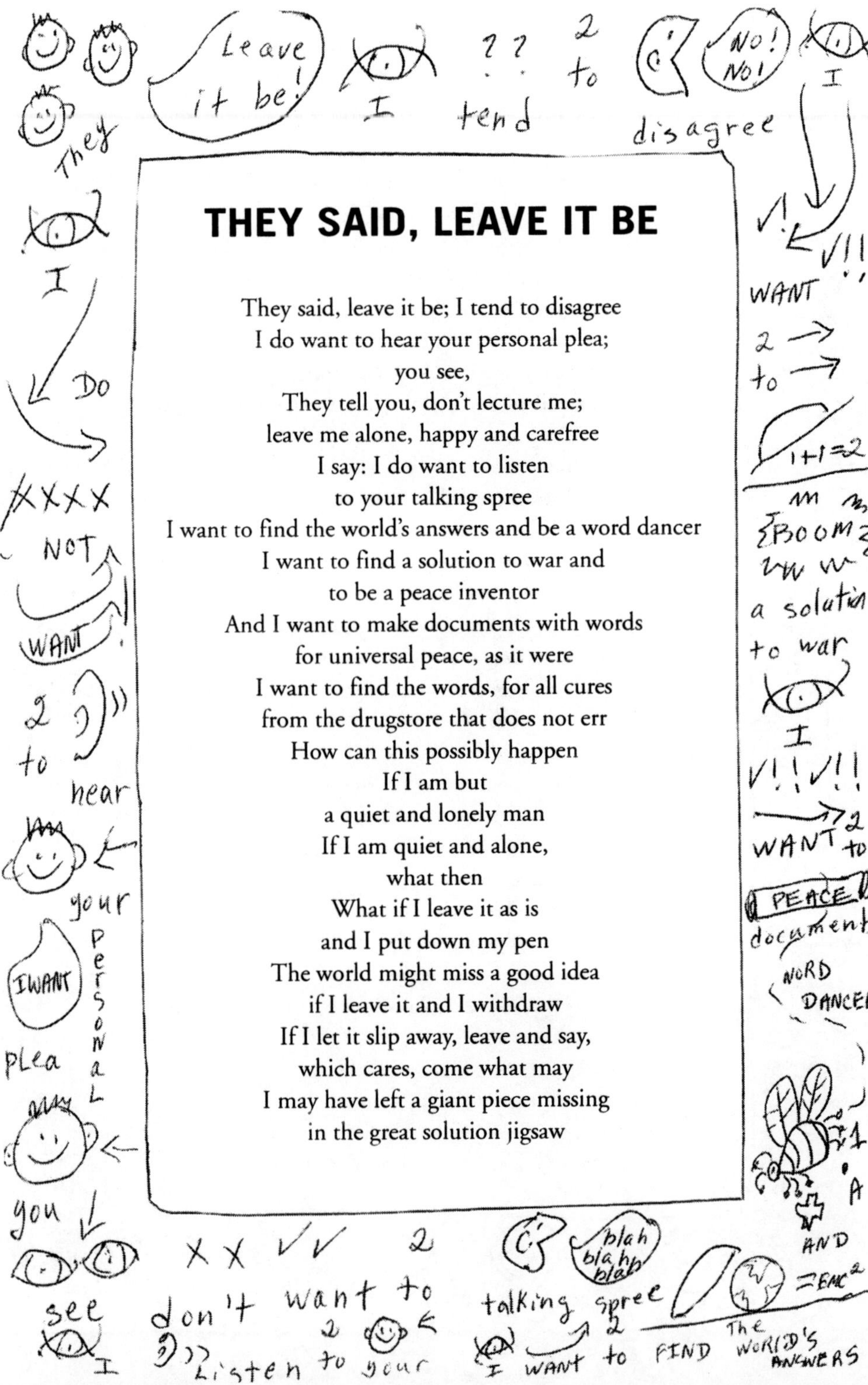

THEY SAID, LEAVE IT BE

They said, leave it be; I tend to disagree
I do want to hear your personal plea;
you see,
They tell you, don't lecture me;
leave me alone, happy and carefree
I say: I do want to listen
to your talking spree
I want to find the world's answers and be a word dancer
I want to find a solution to war and
to be a peace inventor
And I want to make documents with words
for universal peace, as it were
I want to find the words, for all cures
from the drugstore that does not err
How can this possibly happen
If I am but
a quiet and lonely man
If I am quiet and alone,
what then
What if I leave it as is
and I put down my pen
The world might miss a good idea
if I leave it and I withdraw
If I let it slip away, leave and say,
which cares, come what may
I may have left a giant piece missing
in the great solution jigsaw

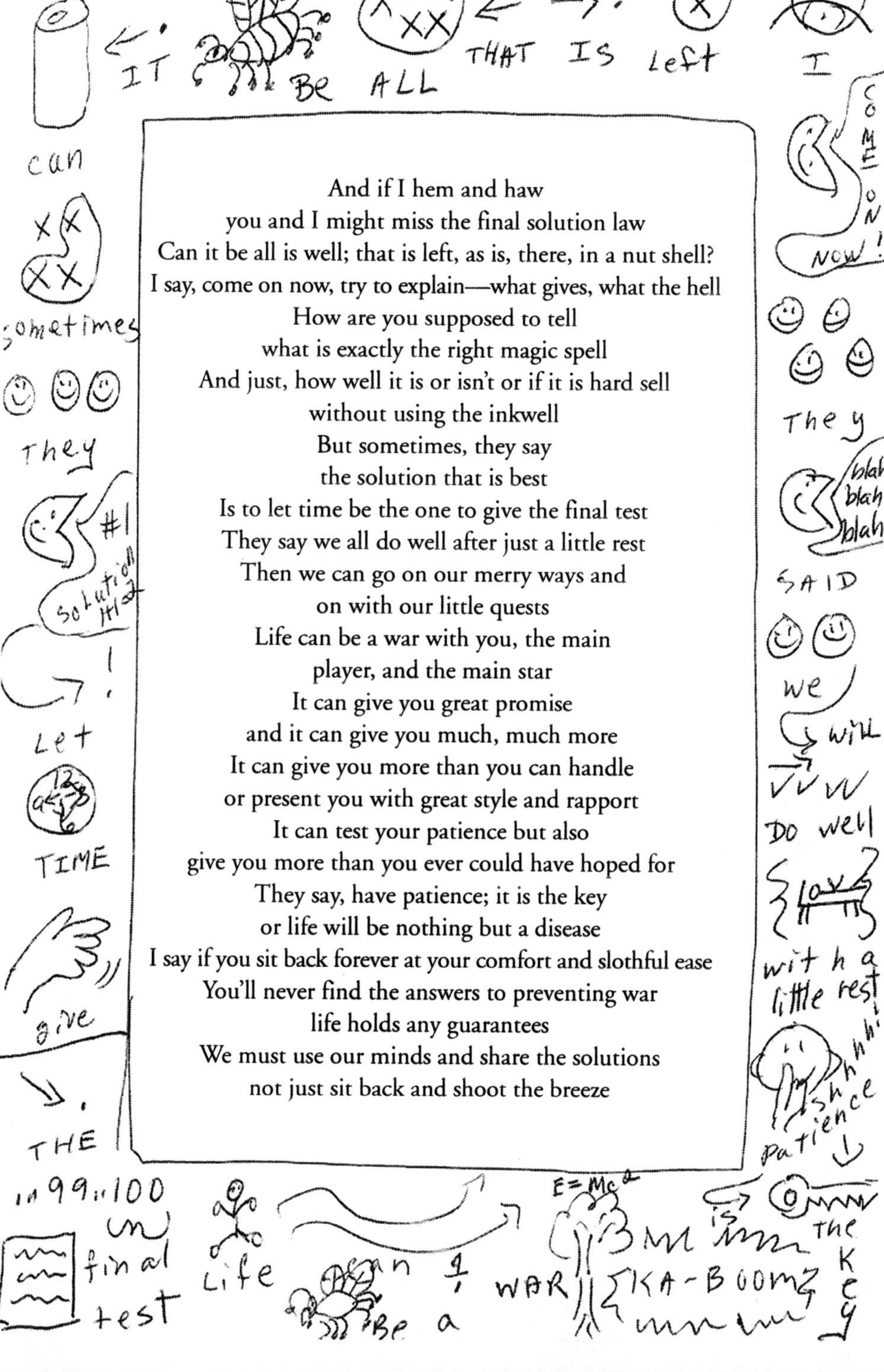

And if I hem and haw
you and I might miss the final solution law
Can it be all is well; that is left, as is, there, in a nut shell?
I say, come on now, try to explain—what gives, what the hell
How are you supposed to tell
what is exactly the right magic spell
And just, how well it is or isn't or if it is hard sell
without using the inkwell
But sometimes, they say
the solution that is best
Is to let time be the one to give the final test
They say we all do well after just a little rest
Then we can go on our merry ways and
on with our little quests
Life can be a war with you, the main
player, and the main star
It can give you great promise
and it can give you much, much more
It can give you more than you can handle
or present you with great style and rapport
It can test your patience but also
give you more than you ever could have hoped for
They say, have patience; it is the key
or life will be nothing but a disease
I say if you sit back forever at your comfort and slothful ease
You'll never find the answers to preventing war
life holds any guarantees
We must use our minds and share the solutions
not just sit back and shoot the breeze

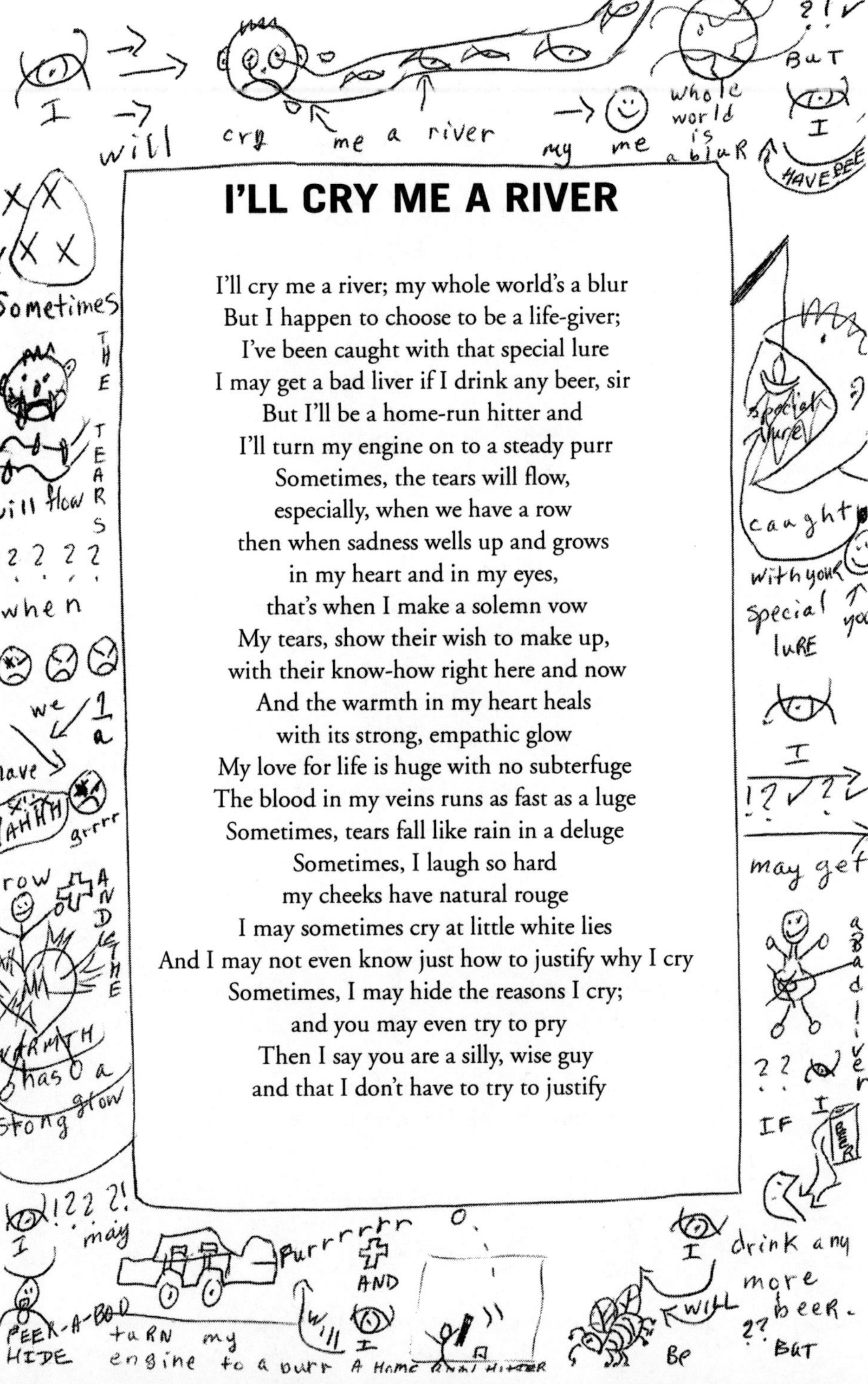

I'LL CRY ME A RIVER

I'll cry me a river; my whole world's a blur
But I happen to choose to be a life-giver;
I've been caught with that special lure
I may get a bad liver if I drink any beer, sir
But I'll be a home-run hitter and
I'll turn my engine on to a steady purr
Sometimes, the tears will flow,
especially, when we have a row
then when sadness wells up and grows
in my heart and in my eyes,
that's when I make a solemn vow
My tears, show their wish to make up,
with their know-how right here and now
And the warmth in my heart heals
with its strong, empathic glow
My love for life is huge with no subterfuge
The blood in my veins runs as fast as a luge
Sometimes, tears fall like rain in a deluge
Sometimes, I laugh so hard
my cheeks have natural rouge
I may sometimes cry at little white lies
And I may not even know just how to justify why I cry
Sometimes, I may hide the reasons I cry;
and you may even try to pry
Then I say you are a silly, wise guy
and that I don't have to try to justify

You know, my moods have many reasons
You know, they also change like the seasons
I'll choose whom I want to be pleasing
And with whom, I will be doing the teasing
You could give me a song and a dance
But I wouldn't give you a second glance
If I should give you any kind of chance
I might end up crying
at my own private rain dance
I would end up taking my hat off to you
I would know that you and I
no longer have a clue what to do
If you saw me then
you would know that I was blue
Because I would be crying and sobbing
a whole river, through and through
I will cry and bawl and my tears will surely fall
The squall of tears
will cause a cascading waterfall
I will cry me a river
from Saskatoon all the way to Montreal
I will end up with such a headache;
I will be in the need of Tylenol

GIVE ME A HAND

Marry me; give me your strong hands, my man
And you'll make me the happiest in all the land
If you like, take me firsthand my particular brand
You will make me feel great and grand and
you will take me to fantasy land
I will welcome your opinion my delicious little minion
Even if you don't agree with my bidding,
you are still my courageous lion
I know your ideas may be, from me, hidden
like the roots of a dandelion
But I'm willing to listen because
I know you won't be lying
I may need help; when I give out a yelp
My sincerity will be heartfelt
and the pain will leave a purple welt
Your ideas will make my heart melt
and your kind eyes will be gladly felt
I'll cherish them all under my belt
and under my love's christening pelt
I don't always know the reason
for a blow from Cupid's bow
The best road to go is to
get ready, get set, and to go
But once I get used to the rhythm and the flow
I can go heel to toe and also stop and go
I'll go from row to row and use my get up and go
If you show me

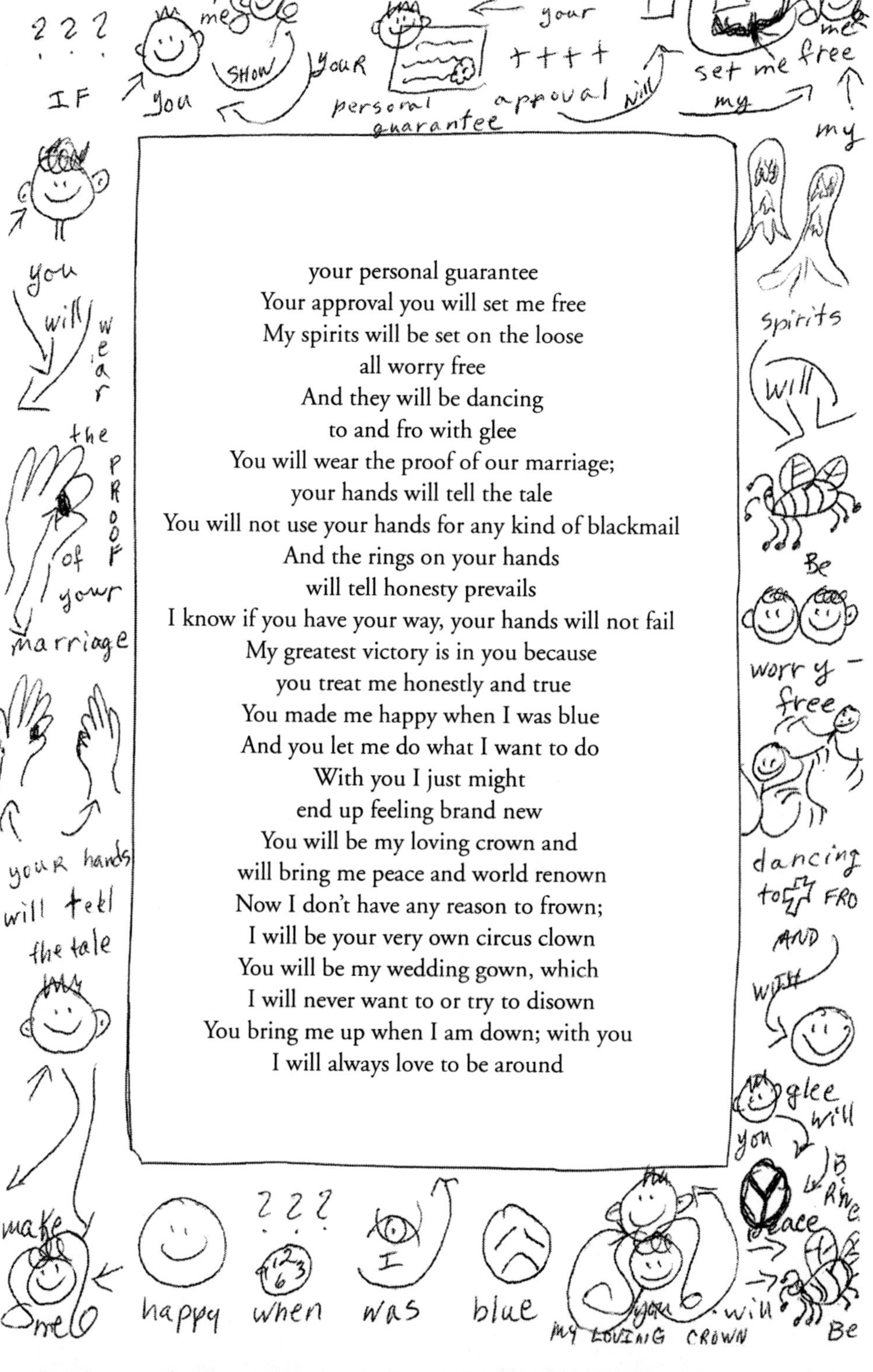

your personal guarantee
Your approval you will set me free
My spirits will be set on the loose
all worry free
And they will be dancing
to and fro with glee
You will wear the proof of our marriage;
your hands will tell the tale
You will not use your hands for any kind of blackmail
And the rings on your hands
will tell honesty prevails
I know if you have your way, your hands will not fail
My greatest victory is in you because
you treat me honestly and true
You made me happy when I was blue
And you let me do what I want to do
With you I just might
end up feeling brand new
You will be my loving crown and
will bring me peace and world renown
Now I don't have any reason to frown;
I will be your very own circus clown
You will be my wedding gown, which
I will never want to or try to disown
You bring me up when I am down; with you
I will always love to be around

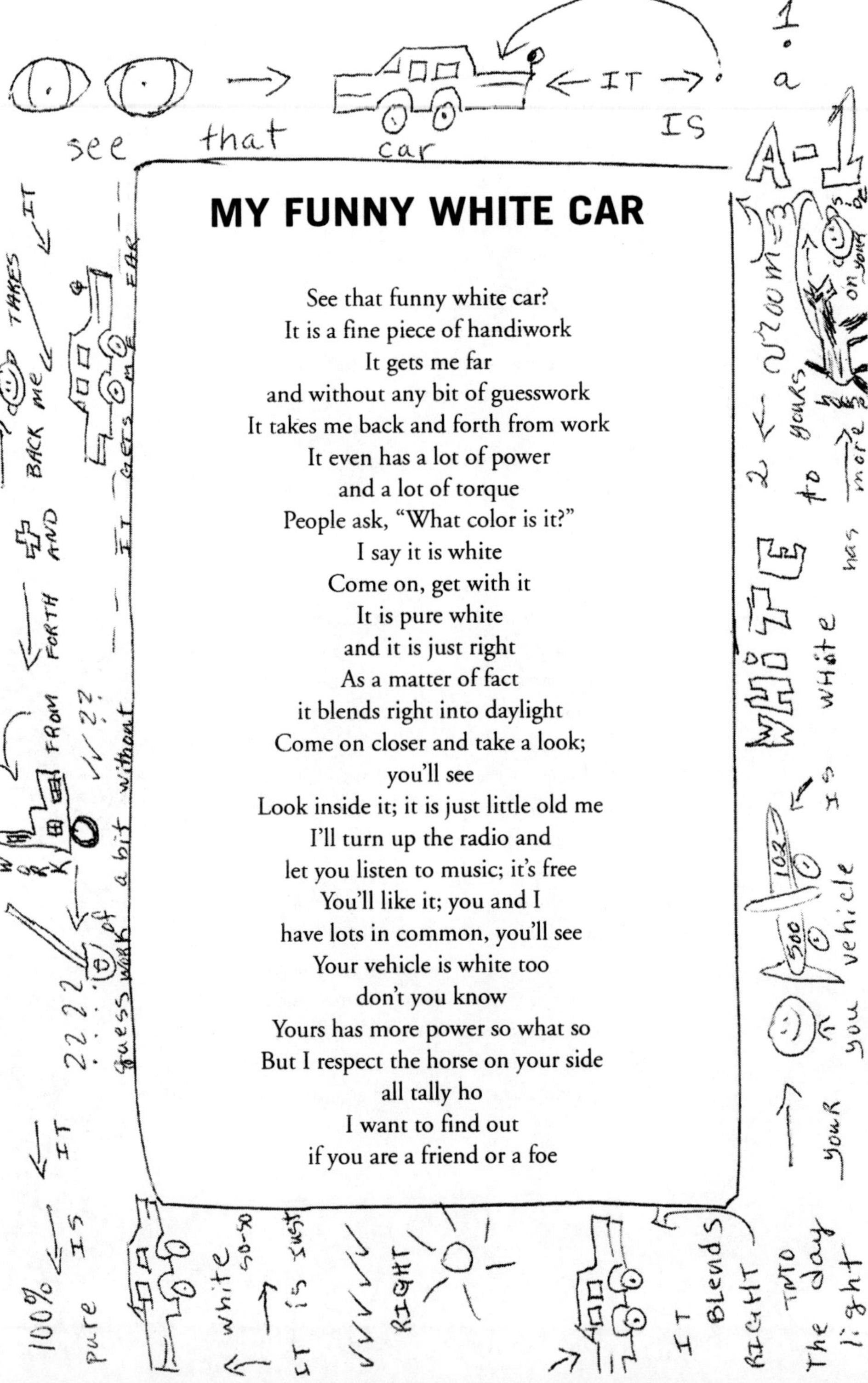

MY FUNNY WHITE CAR

See that funny white car?
It is a fine piece of handiwork
It gets me far
and without any bit of guesswork
It takes me back and forth from work
It even has a lot of power
and a lot of torque
People ask, "What color is it?"
I say it is white
Come on, get with it
It is pure white
and it is just right
As a matter of fact
it blends right into daylight
Come on closer and take a look;
you'll see
Look inside it; it is just little old me
I'll turn up the radio and
let you listen to music; it's free
You'll like it; you and I
have lots in common, you'll see
Your vehicle is white too
don't you know
Yours has more power so what so
But I respect the horse on your side
all tally ho
I want to find out
if you are a friend or a foe

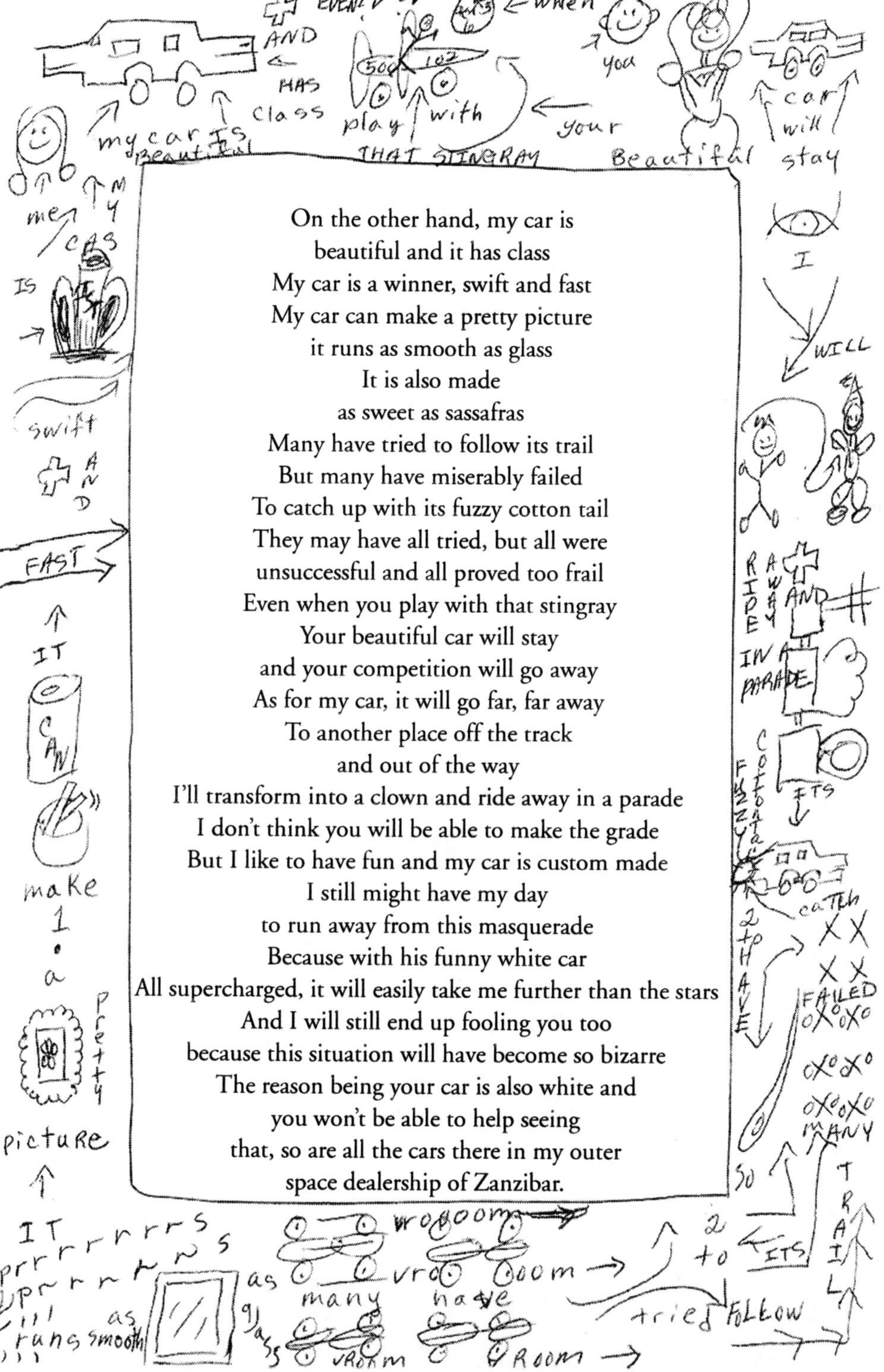

On the other hand, my car is
beautiful and it has class
My car is a winner, swift and fast
My car can make a pretty picture
it runs as smooth as glass
It is also made
as sweet as sassafras
Many have tried to follow its trail
But many have miserably failed
To catch up with its fuzzy cotton tail
They may have all tried, but all were
unsuccessful and all proved too frail
Even when you play with that stingray
Your beautiful car will stay
and your competition will go away
As for my car, it will go far, far away
To another place off the track
and out of the way
I'll transform into a clown and ride away in a parade
I don't think you will be able to make the grade
But I like to have fun and my car is custom made
I still might have my day
to run away from this masquerade
Because with his funny white car
All supercharged, it will easily take me further than the stars
And I will still end up fooling you too
because this situation will have become so bizarre
The reason being your car is also white and
you won't be able to help seeing
that, so are all the cars there in my outer
space dealership of Zanzibar.

PLAY WITH SOMEONE ELSE

(Version 1)

Should I play with someone else? No
I dare not; if I had a choice to choose
if I should do so
For if I did stray and that way did go
I would surely fall down
and stub my toe
I cringe at the mere thought of it
Because this would hurt me every bit
And now that I have found my true love
and the story is writ
I want to lie with just him
and never have to quit
Ah, how I love my sweet, sweet surrender
You are my man, my favorite fender bender
I'll be your personal love letter writer and sender
I'll be your one and only cuddly heart mender
If you wish to find out if I am true,
you can try and test me
You will be surprised, what you find and what you see
Our lives most definitely will not be all fun and glee
But I have got a warm heart, and you have got my key
Now that I have found you are the right one
I know my life has opened and has just begun
I feel I am finally living
and have come out into the sun

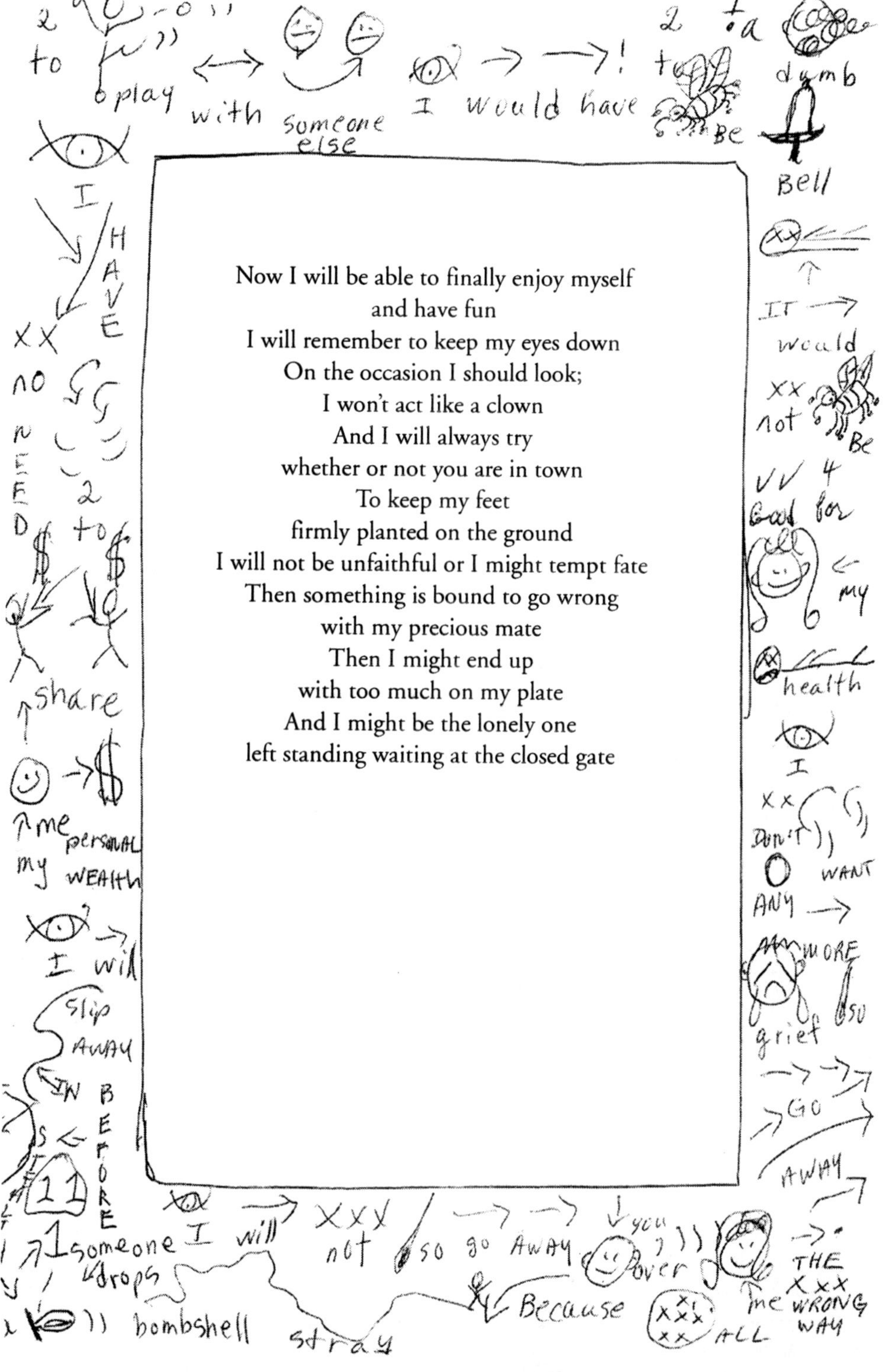

Now I will be able to finally enjoy myself
and have fun
I will remember to keep my eyes down
On the occasion I should look;
I won't act like a clown
And I will always try
whether or not you are in town
To keep my feet
firmly planted on the ground
I will not be unfaithful or I might tempt fate
Then something is bound to go wrong
with my precious mate
Then I might end up
with too much on my plate
And I might be the lonely one
left standing waiting at the closed gate

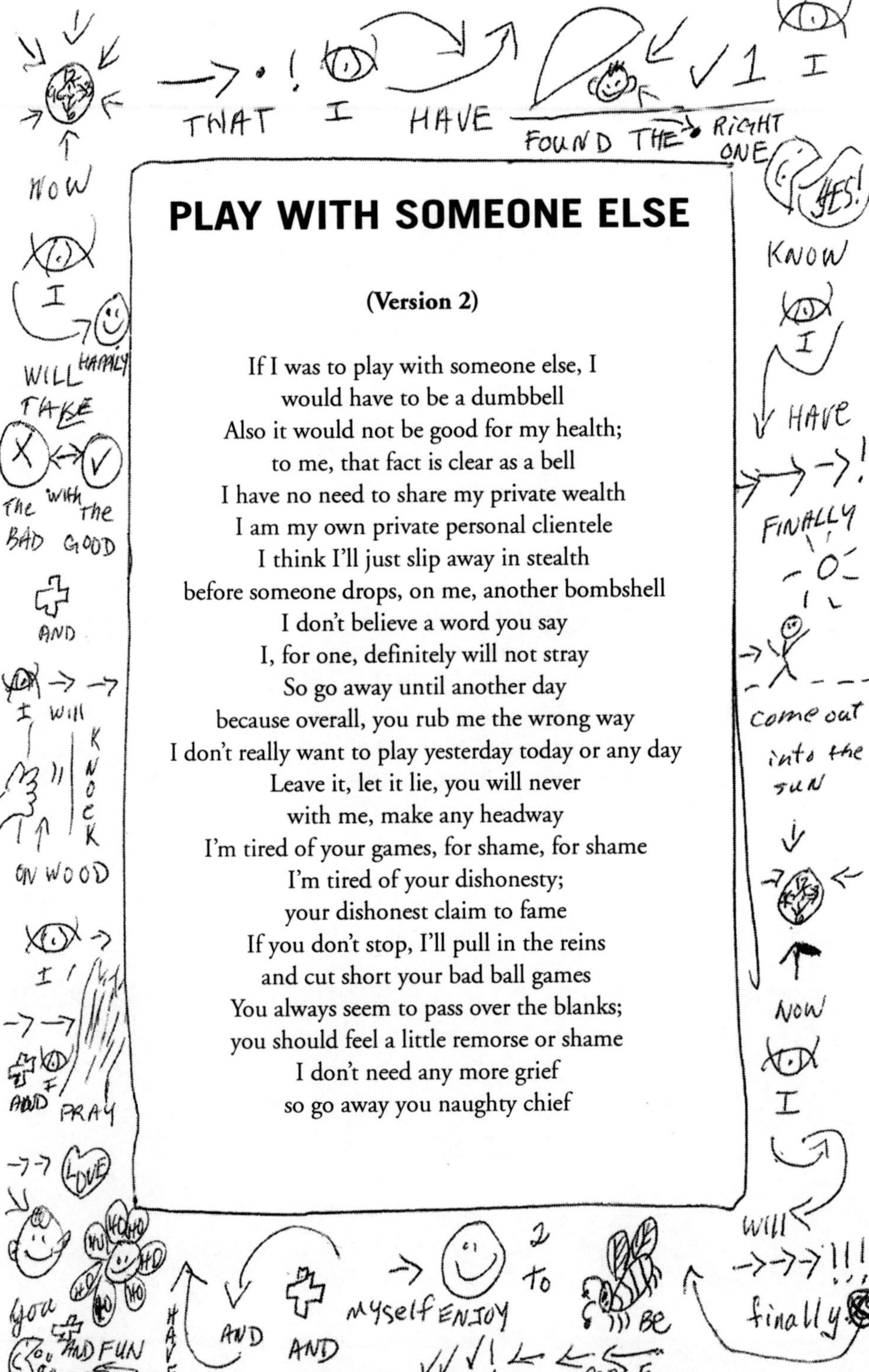

PLAY WITH SOMEONE ELSE

(Version 2)

If I was to play with someone else, I
would have to be a dumbbell
Also it would not be good for my health;
to me, that fact is clear as a bell
I have no need to share my private wealth
I am my own private personal clientele
I think I'll just slip away in stealth
before someone drops, on me, another bombshell
I don't believe a word you say
I, for one, definitely will not stray
So go away until another day
because overall, you rub me the wrong way
I don't really want to play yesterday today or any day
Leave it, let it lie, you will never
with me, make any headway
I'm tired of your games, for shame, for shame
I'm tired of your dishonesty;
your dishonest claim to fame
If you don't stop, I'll pull in the reins
and cut short your bad ball games
You always seem to pass over the blanks;
you should feel a little remorse or shame
I don't need any more grief
so go away you naughty chief

I think you are
nothing but a thief and full of corned beef
Look at me; I'm shaking like a leaf in utter disbelief
You think I'm scared that is your belief;
all I can say is good grief
I will choose to ignore anything you wished
or anything you hoped for
No matter how you implore, I will
ignore you and furthermore
I will show you the door and you will be all washed up
high and dry, on the shore
I think you are nothing but a bore; you
are nothing but an eyesore
Do you think you will get ahead by
being an ignorant blockhead?
By rationalizing everything in your head?
You, sir, think you are a desirable purebred
You think everyone will be easily led
and can be pabulum and spoon-fed
I heard you that are what you said.
You said you are an egghead
You like to hear yourself talk
you will keep me in a captive gridlock
I can go away; I can walk fast and far, and that's no jive talk
Myself, my ears are deaf like a rock
and I won't be able to hear any back talk
I choose not to hear a single a single solitary squawk;
go ahead and try to knock, knock, and knock

Go away, go to sleep
you horrible nasty suggestive creep
Then maybe you won't make a single peep
and you won't show you are so very cheap
You are a tiresome creep, and you are in trouble deep
So go take a giant flying leap
and let the devil take your soul to keep

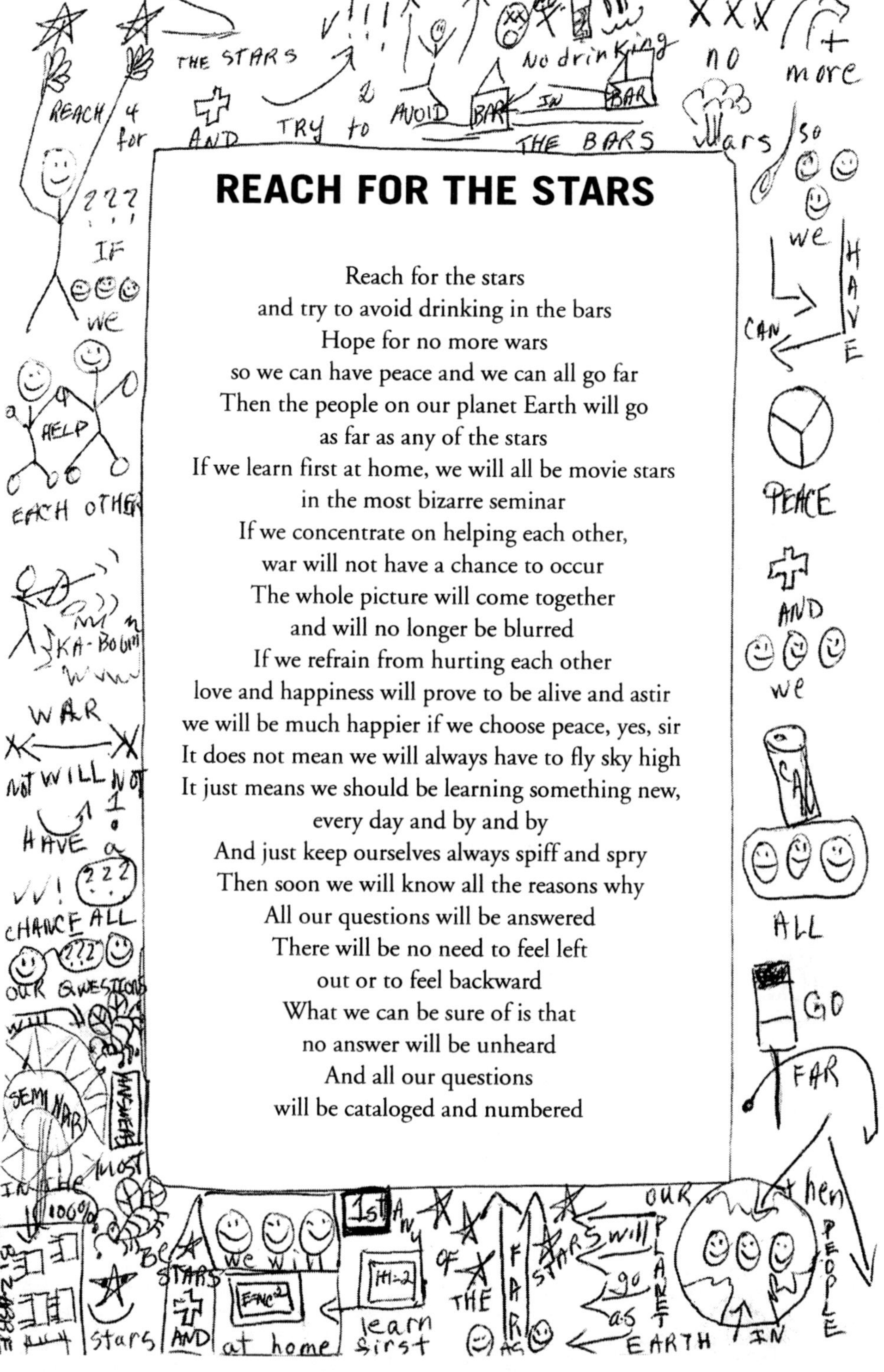

REACH FOR THE STARS

Reach for the stars
and try to avoid drinking in the bars
Hope for no more wars
so we can have peace and we can all go far
Then the people on our planet Earth will go
as far as any of the stars
If we learn first at home, we will all be movie stars
in the most bizarre seminar
If we concentrate on helping each other,
war will not have a chance to occur
The whole picture will come together
and will no longer be blurred
If we refrain from hurting each other
love and happiness will prove to be alive and astir
we will be much happier if we choose peace, yes, sir
It does not mean we will always have to fly sky high
It just means we should be learning something new,
every day and by and by
And just keep ourselves always spiff and spry
Then soon we will know all the reasons why
All our questions will be answered
There will be no need to feel left
out or to feel backward
What we can be sure of is that
no answer will be unheard
And all our questions
will be cataloged and numbered

Everyone will be compelled
to be agreeable and to gel
They will say, "I know it well."
The answer will all of a sudden
seem clear as a bell
They will all want the credit
for their show and tell
It will come together
quickly and all of a sudden
It will be just in time
to help the downtrodden
It may even help the spoiled rotten
It will even help the woe begotten
There will be nothing at all wrong
With wanting to help
the milling throng
Then we will all have
a chance to belong
We will wonder why
we did not think of this all along
We will then all acknowledge and agree
That all our lives are created to be free
Our eyes will be opened
and we will see
Then we will reach for the stars
and they will be there for you and me

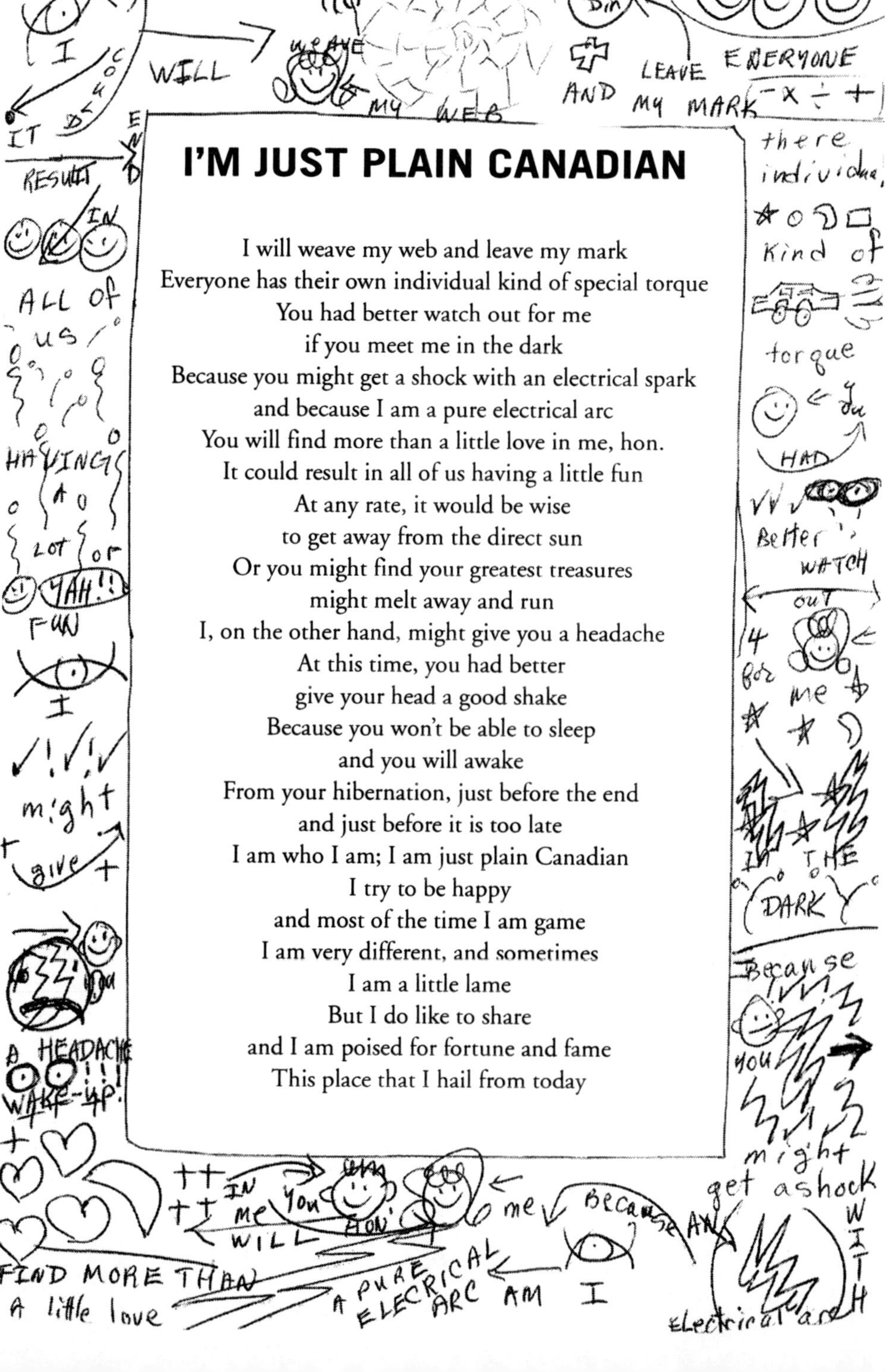

I'M JUST PLAIN CANADIAN

I will weave my web and leave my mark
Everyone has their own individual kind of special torque
You had better watch out for me
if you meet me in the dark
Because you might get a shock with an electrical spark
and because I am a pure electrical arc
You will find more than a little love in me, hon.
It could result in all of us having a little fun
At any rate, it would be wise
to get away from the direct sun
Or you might find your greatest treasures
might melt away and run
I, on the other hand, might give you a headache
At this time, you had better
give your head a good shake
Because you won't be able to sleep
and you will awake
From your hibernation, just before the end
and just before it is too late
I am who I am; I am just plain Canadian
I try to be happy
and most of the time I am game
I am very different, and sometimes
I am a little lame
But I do like to share
and I am poised for fortune and fame
This place that I hail from today

And what I want to share and to say
And how I will express myself today
Is the fact, that I am just plain Canadian
ten-four high five and to you a big, eh
I will try to share with you my opinion
I will try to know where to begin
I will try to avoid falling into sin
I will share all my thoughts just to help you
so that everyone can win
You, as a person, are new and pretty
But sometimes, you seem
artificial and very petty
I am, on the other hand
liquid nitrogen and I am steady
I am a true Canadian
and I am willing and ready
Personally, my features that are there
are none the worse for wear
I think that is fair because I don't
put much stock to them
or even bother to care
Each of our features has its special snare
that we can use to send out into the air
And each of us has a different flair
that makes us individuals
with many different layers here there or anywhere

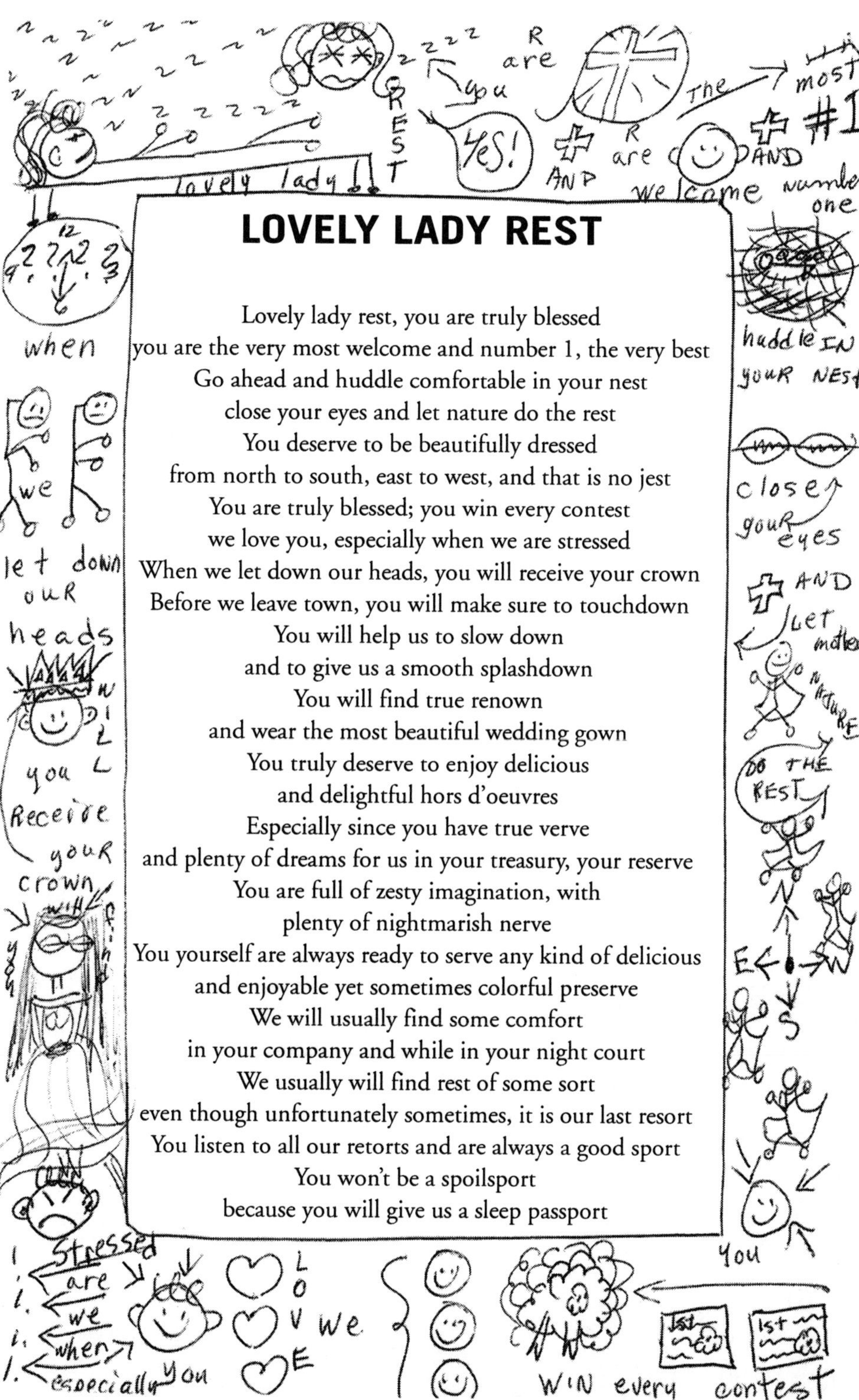

LOVELY LADY REST

Lovely lady rest, you are truly blessed
you are the very most welcome and number 1, the very best
Go ahead and huddle comfortable in your nest
close your eyes and let nature do the rest
You deserve to be beautifully dressed
from north to south, east to west, and that is no jest
You are truly blessed; you win every contest
we love you, especially when we are stressed
When we let down our heads, you will receive your crown
Before we leave town, you will make sure to touchdown
You will help us to slow down
and to give us a smooth splashdown
You will find true renown
and wear the most beautiful wedding gown
You truly deserve to enjoy delicious
and delightful hors d'oeuvres
Especially since you have true verve
and plenty of dreams for us in your treasury, your reserve
You are full of zesty imagination, with
plenty of nightmarish nerve
You yourself are always ready to serve any kind of delicious
and enjoyable yet sometimes colorful preserve
We will usually find some comfort
in your company and while in your night court
We usually will find rest of some sort
even though unfortunately sometimes, it is our last resort
You listen to all our retorts and are always a good sport
You won't be a spoilsport
because you will give us a sleep passport

Everyone would do well
with a little relaxation and to practice to gel
We all should have a good rest especially if we are unwell
We should rest until the morning bell
and let rest have us under its magical spell
While we are in our interlude,
we can say hello to the most beautiful Tinker Bell
Sweet dreams will come flooding
inside our heads
They will fill our minds and surround our beds
When we put our heads down on our pillows
our dream lands will go full speed ahead
Our imagination will be in control
and the possibilities will be widespread
While we are asleep, sweet thoughts and notions
refuse to be undone
That is, when we will appreciate the dreamy commotion
and during rest, we will feel like number 1
You and I will feel the motion of our
imaginary fun in the sun
Our thoughts will travel onwards with
no bars holding us back, and we
will feel like prodigal sons
The best will happen while we are at rest and
when we are quiet and while we are not a threat
Then while we rest in between riots
earthquakes, and floods; we won't have any regrets
We can't get anything better than sleep's safety net
We all need it; we can't deny it
and chances are, none of us will forget it

HOLD YOUR TONGUE

Practice some control;
hold your tongue, hon.
Or you will end up being
the one who is undone
Then that will be the end of your fun
And then you
might not be a happy one
Sometimes, it is better to keep quiet
Because you might just avoid a riot
Just ask
that calm and reserved airline pilot
He knows where it is at and a whole lot
about when he is put on the spot
Try to keep your opinions to yourself
And you will be
the one to gather great wealth
Be humble and lay back with stealth
This is bound to be
better for your overall health
Anyone can speak up
and tell you
But if you are the first
to say boo
It may be your day to rue
We all should know
from experience,
this is nothing new

The first one out of the shut
usually gets shot
And tall tales are usually hot
The truth can't be bought
but is usually sought
Your integrity is
all you've got, is it not?
On silence, the world
may prove to depend
On our silence, again and again
Or on how your security
and integrity will fend
Silence may give you
the true victory in the end
You must be able to show
How you can keep,
to yourself, what you know
And use discretion and also
know how to be able to lie low
If you master the art of this practice
Your innocence, to all, will glow
If you are able to keep
A secret, all will be sweet
Your affairs will be well-arranged, well kept and neat
This will be a great
and grand and wonderful feat

ONION SOUP

Onion soup let us get together and regroup
If we don't, it will send us on a loop, in one fell swoop
Getting it together will make sure it
is liked by the whole group
because then they won't be duped
The cheese, melted on top, will be like goop
so good you won't be able to help but take a scoop
It will be nothing but the best
which we will enjoy with childlike zest
It will pass every cook's test, and you may send it
as a regular staple to Aunt Jemima's medicine chest
It'll send you on a quest to eat it all
up—that will be your conquest
Everyone will be impressed when it
has passed every taste test
Everyone will want the recipe and will want every ingredient,
all cataloged from A to Z
You will give it away for free with a
chuckle and a snicker, tee-he
They'll be very happy; you'll see
they won't believe that fortune has,
on them, smiled so kindly
You'll be laughing with glee
all carefree and as a happy as a chimpanzee
The soup itself is very healthy and
easy as one, two, and three

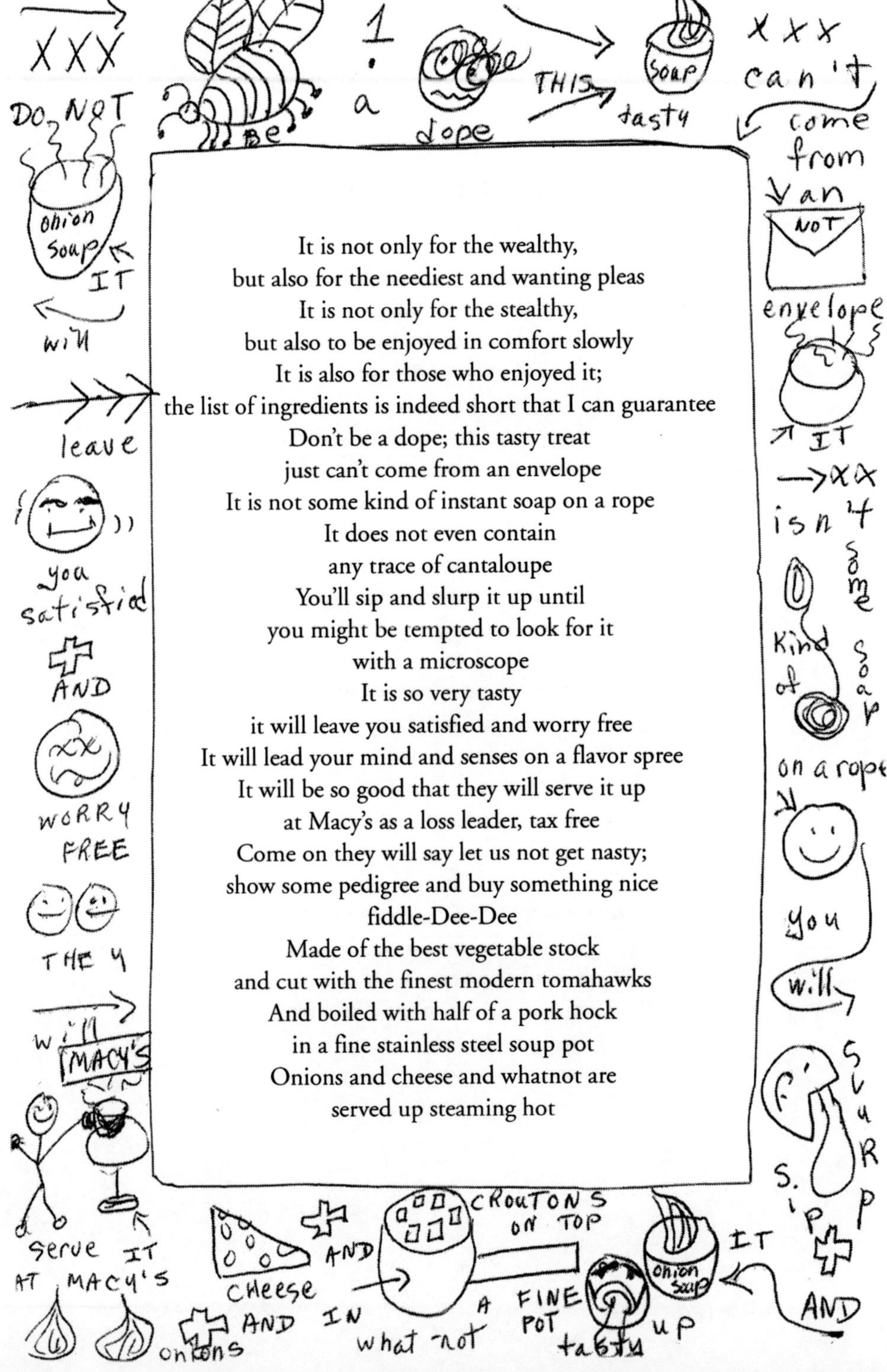

It is not only for the wealthy,
but also for the neediest and wanting pleas
It is not only for the stealthy,
but also to be enjoyed in comfort slowly
It is also for those who enjoyed it;
the list of ingredients is indeed short that I can guarantee
Don't be a dope; this tasty treat
just can't come from an envelope
It is not some kind of instant soap on a rope
It does not even contain
any trace of cantaloupe
You'll sip and slurp it up until
you might be tempted to look for it
with a microscope
It is so very tasty
it will leave you satisfied and worry free
It will lead your mind and senses on a flavor spree
It will be so good that they will serve it up
at Macy's as a loss leader, tax free
Come on they will say let us not get nasty;
show some pedigree and buy something nice
fiddle-Dee-Dee
Made of the best vegetable stock
and cut with the finest modern tomahawks
And boiled with half of a pork hock
in a fine stainless steel soup pot
Onions and cheese and whatnot are
served up steaming hot

Croutons on top are what are really sought for in its hot pot
It is a flavor fix, fit for a king; he likes it better than wings
Onion soup is greatly wanted and a
somewhat preferable thing
It is such a wonderful creation and has made such a stir;
you can hear them sing
Place it on the counter for him and her
the likes of which you will never see anyone bring

IT'S BETTER LEFT UNSAID

Your opinions are better left unsaid
If you talk, you may wish
you were dead
In that case, someone may
even put a price on your head
And to the lions you may be fed
Mum's the word,
better seen and not heard
You must not blurb
or you will look absurd
The word "secret" is a noun, not a verb
To tattle would result in a tale
that would be just unheard
We must be faithful
and not drop a bombshell
And remain tasteful and quiet as well
We must not be hateful
but friendly, in a nutshell
We must not spill the beans
and lose a full plateful
This will keep us safe and up to date
And keep us from a horrible fate
if we are innate
We won't come up last at the gate
or attract any hate
And it will be success at any rate
because we will discriminate

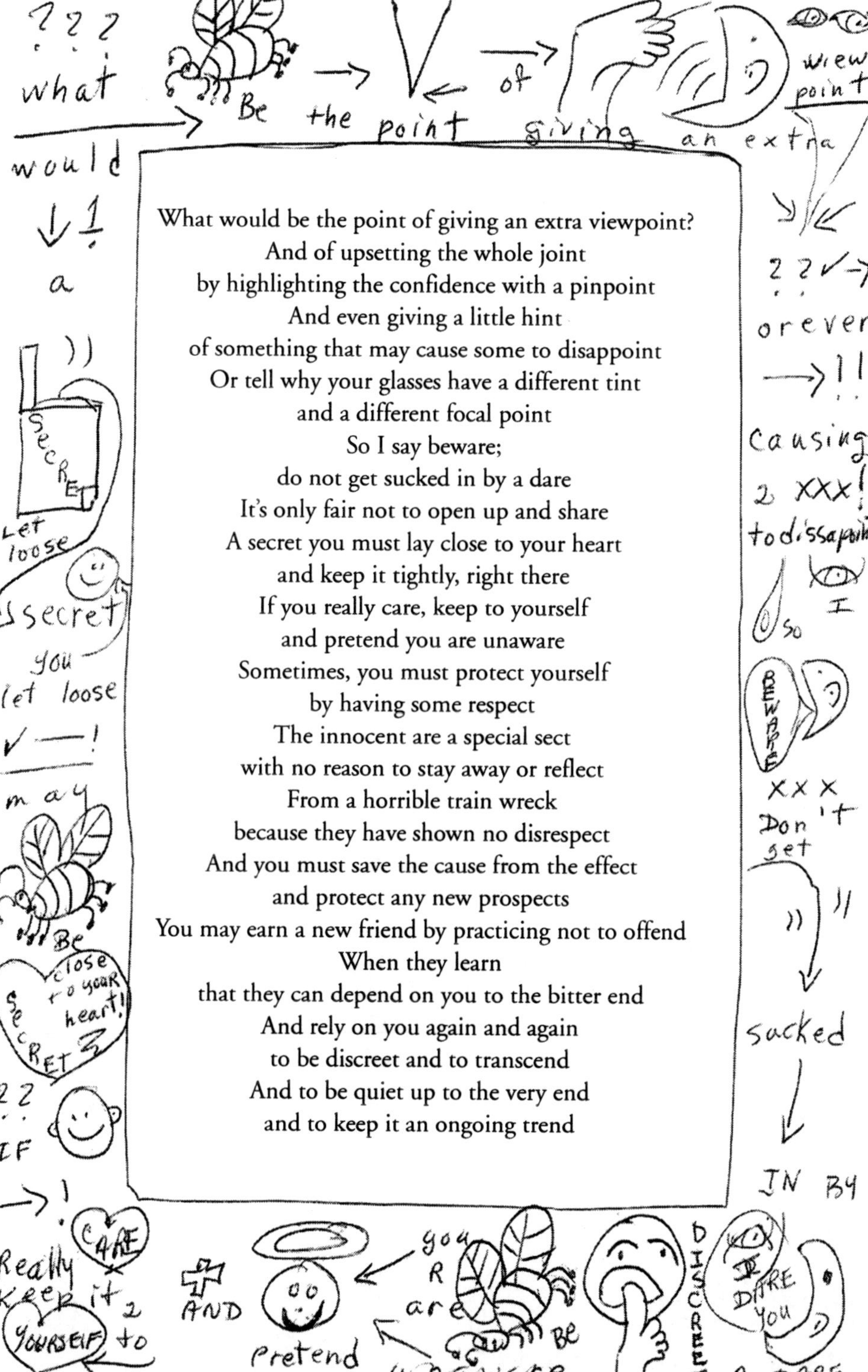

What would be the point of giving an extra viewpoint?
And of upsetting the whole joint
by highlighting the confidence with a pinpoint
And even giving a little hint
of something that may cause some to disappoint
Or tell why your glasses have a different tint
and a different focal point
So I say beware;
do not get sucked in by a dare
It's only fair not to open up and share
A secret you must lay close to your heart
and keep it tightly, right there
If you really care, keep to yourself
and pretend you are unaware
Sometimes, you must protect yourself
by having some respect
The innocent are a special sect
with no reason to stay away or reflect
From a horrible train wreck
because they have shown no disrespect
And you must save the cause from the effect
and protect any new prospects
You may earn a new friend by practicing not to offend
When they learn
that they can depend on you to the bitter end
And rely on you again and again
to be discreet and to transcend
And to be quiet up to the very end
and to keep it an ongoing trend

SEAL OF APPROVAL

All is well; in fact, things are going swell
As far as I can tell,
they are that way on life's carousel
Things are all beginning to gel
in fact, very well
Soon the finished product will be
ready to sell to our loyal clientele
Here's the deal; here's the overall and mass appeal
You'll have our seal of approval
on this, our greatest deal
It will seem like a steal, so be careful;
and don't slip or squeal
But I am telling you, it is for real
and you will have to hide your inner zeal
The seal will be tied up in a bow
and it will be the status quo
You will soon be in the know about all the secret info
You will have that victory glow;
after all, you have the right to know
The info will continue from the word go
like a very well-made video
The Seal of Approval will be on the top
signed by the like of one like Aesop
From you will come a brand-new crop;
in fact, it will flow nonstop
No one will be able to stop the cream from growing
in the cropAnd what you have desperately sought
will be there for everyone to window shop

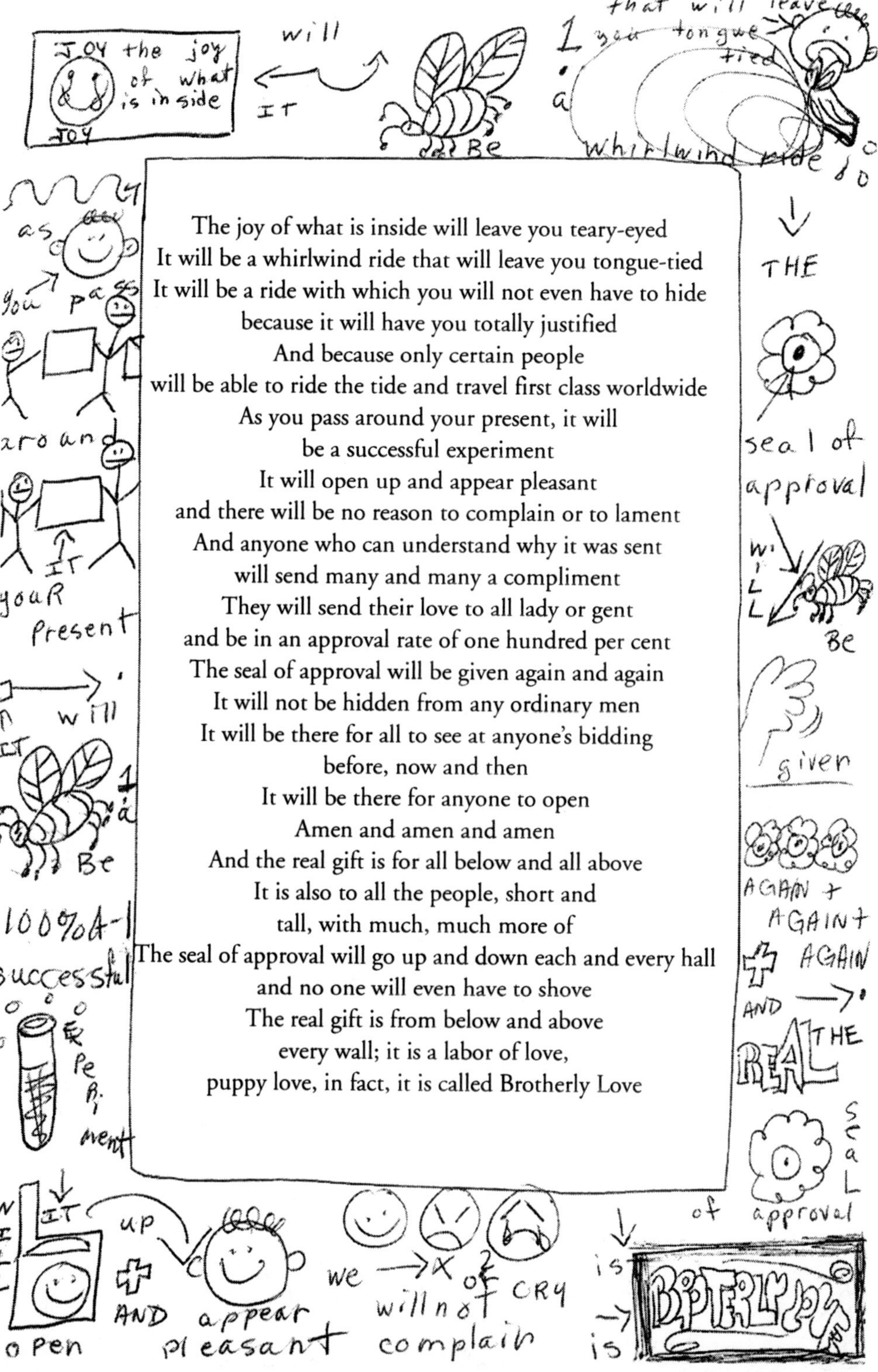

The joy of what is inside will leave you teary-eyed
It will be a whirlwind ride that will leave you tongue-tied
It will be a ride with which you will not even have to hide
because it will have you totally justified
And because only certain people
will be able to ride the tide and travel first class worldwide
As you pass around your present, it will
be a successful experiment
It will open up and appear pleasant
and there will be no reason to complain or to lament
And anyone who can understand why it was sent
will send many and many a compliment
They will send their love to all lady or gent
and be in an approval rate of one hundred per cent
The seal of approval will be given again and again
It will not be hidden from any ordinary men
It will be there for all to see at anyone's bidding
before, now and then
It will be there for anyone to open
Amen and amen and amen
And the real gift is for all below and all above
It is also to all the people, short and
tall, with much, much more of
The seal of approval will go up and down each and every hall
and no one will even have to shove
The real gift is from below and above
every wall; it is a labor of love,
puppy love, in fact, it is called Brotherly Love

MIND FREEZE

My mind is numb; I feel blind, deaf and dumb
To my fatigue, I have succumbed
I feel sad and glum
To my longing, I send my hurt
and I am overcome
My heart feels like it is in the slammer
and I feel like a bum
My mind is frozen
like it has been stung with a poison pen
That is my token
from the proverbial bull pen
To you, I am beholden;
you are just like my mother hen
It is you, I am holding;
you are the best of all men
Onward, I traveled in the cold and frozen wastes
with a mind numb with the cold
There was nothing there, but the breath of winter
that had me in a choke hold
trying to take me and chastise and hold
I find you in my thoughts, you are my stronghold
But I dare not share these for fear of reprisal
and being therefore left out in the cold
You will come someday
on your beautiful sleigh

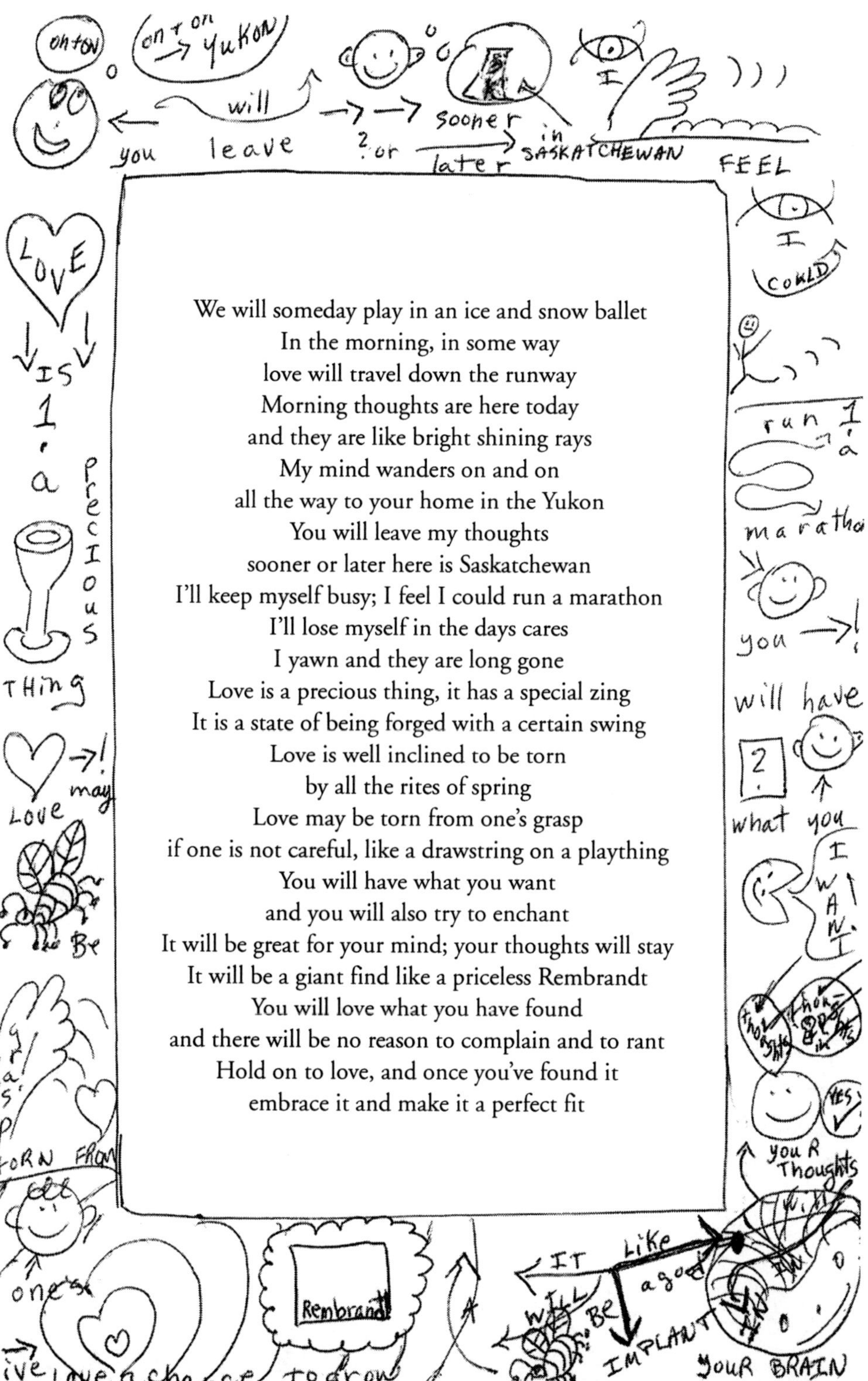

We will someday play in an ice and snow ballet
In the morning, in some way
love will travel down the runway
Morning thoughts are here today
and they are like bright shining rays
My mind wanders on and on
all the way to your home in the Yukon
You will leave my thoughts
sooner or later here is Saskatchewan
I'll keep myself busy; I feel I could run a marathon
I'll lose myself in the days cares
I yawn and they are long gone
Love is a precious thing, it has a special zing
It is a state of being forged with a certain swing
Love is well inclined to be torn
by all the rites of spring
Love may be torn from one's grasp
if one is not careful, like a drawstring on a plaything
You will have what you want
and you will also try to enchant
It will be great for your mind; your thoughts will stay
It will be a giant find like a priceless Rembrandt
You will love what you have found
and there will be no reason to complain and to rant
Hold on to love, and once you've found it
embrace it and make it a perfect fit

If you can, but let it free also it will be a smash hit
Give it room to fly up, up and away, lickety-split
And it will stay by you, and your love will never quit
Your love experience will last forever;
it will try to run smoothly, then it will purr
If you take care of yourself, great things will occur
You will, somehow,
always have it today and tomorrow, that is for sure
This love you have;
you will not have to borrow that is its special lure

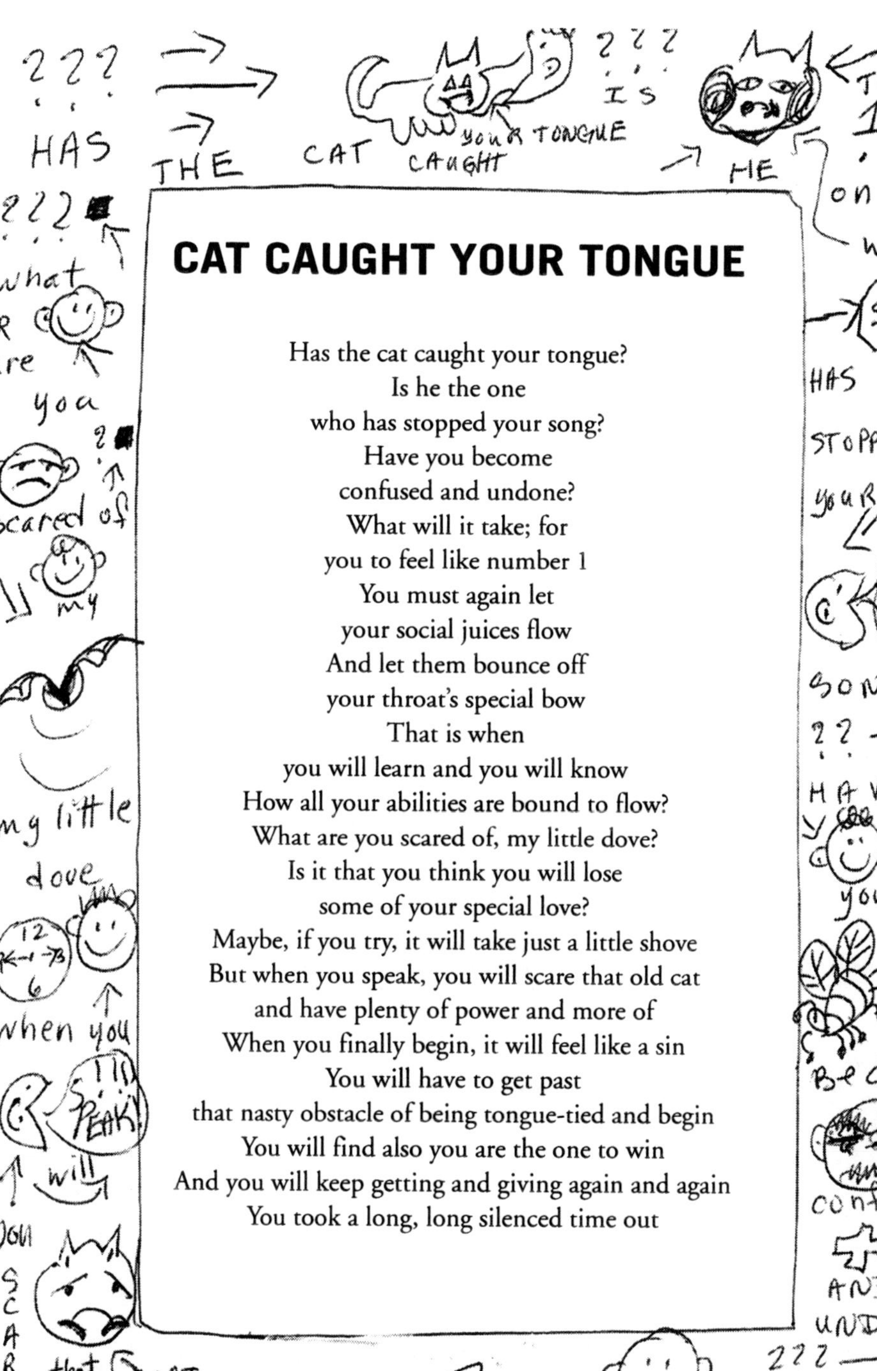

CAT CAUGHT YOUR TONGUE

Has the cat caught your tongue?
Is he the one
who has stopped your song?
Have you become
confused and undone?
What will it take; for
you to feel like number 1
You must again let
your social juices flow
And let them bounce off
your throat's special bow
That is when
you will learn and you will know
How all your abilities are bound to flow?
What are you scared of, my little dove?
Is it that you think you will lose
some of your special love?
Maybe, if you try, it will take just a little shove
But when you speak, you will scare that old cat
and have plenty of power and more of
When you finally begin, it will feel like a sin
You will have to get past
that nasty obstacle of being tongue-tied and begin
You will find also you are the one to win
And you will keep getting and giving again and again
You took a long, long silenced time out

You were curious and shy in life
that is, what it was all about
You wanted to know
which way was the best route
So your words would have more clout
It, indeed, was a wise move
To be careful until you could again get into the groove
After, practice you will again, be as fast as Villeneuve
You will be as straight as an arrow
and will not again, swerve
You have practiced in silence
long enough
That, in itself, has been rough
People can be mean, and that is no guff
Now let 'err rip;
and show all your saved-up stuff
Come on, let it out
and begin again
Come on, be the one to please
all your friends
You will see the pleasure it sends
And the freedom to you
it lends

LET LIFE MOLD YOU

Let life mold you and show you what to do
Let life show you,
where to go and who's who
Let life show you,
what's next for you, in the news
Let life show you which road to pursue
Life will pour you into
and let you drink from a cup
And shape you into the right makeup
Life can lift you up
and can get you out of a rut
Or life can kick you right in your gut
Life may grab you
and catch you by surprise
Or life may
even wear a secret disguise
Life does not have to tell any lies
And life can see through you
with its X-ray eyes
Sometimes, life smiles at you and gives you a choice
And sometimes you are lucky enough
to have a voice
But sometimes you may want to hide
and not to make a noise
And sometimes you will want to be
just another one of the boys
By all means this doesn't necessarily mean
that life is talking pork and beans

Everyone has a right to test life
and to see what it really means
Just remember, where life for you is and has been
When you find out
you will be happy and life will be keen
Accept life, but don't stop trying
Or that villain defeat
may leave you crying
I tell you;
I am most definitely not lying
Because I can say it is
on my very own experience
I am relying
Whatever comes will most definitely come
The end result will shine for all to see
right there in the sun
The result will leave you
either full of fun or maybe totally undone
And then you will know
if a victory has been won
Then we will say we would like to get to know
this life that special person
Because he might even be my favorite daughter or son
Or maybe even my favorite hon. my special loved one
When this comes to pass,
I won't be undone or even want to run

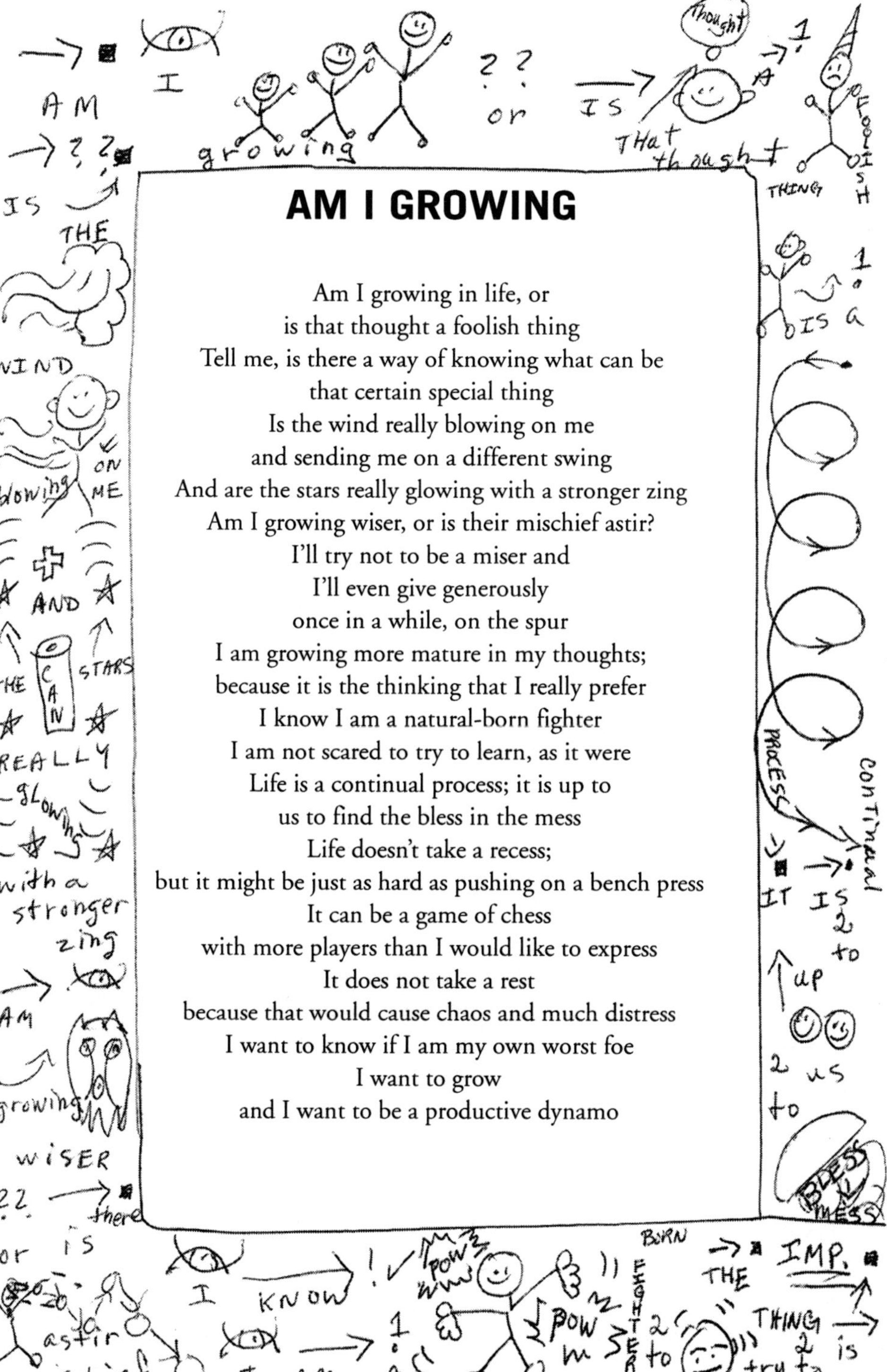

AM I GROWING

Am I growing in life, or
is that thought a foolish thing
Tell me, is there a way of knowing what can be
that certain special thing
Is the wind really blowing on me
and sending me on a different swing
And are the stars really glowing with a stronger zing
Am I growing wiser, or is their mischief astir?
I'll try not to be a miser and
I'll even give generously
once in a while, on the spur
I am growing more mature in my thoughts;
because it is the thinking that I really prefer
I know I am a natural-born fighter
I am not scared to try to learn, as it were
Life is a continual process; it is up to
us to find the bless in the mess
Life doesn't take a recess;
but it might be just as hard as pushing on a bench press
It can be a game of chess
with more players than I would like to express
It does not take a rest
because that would cause chaos and much distress
I want to know if I am my own worst foe
I want to grow
and I want to be a productive dynamo

I want to live it up and go
row on row to all this newfound info
Knowledge can be high
and knowledge can be low;
but the important thing is to know
Knowledge is all in the way it is given,
and the punch line or the delivery, wrapped up is the gift
Then when we are in the know, we
will notice; how our life shifts
We will see that; if any progress is to be
it is sure to be a help and a lift
The change that will have been made to you and me
will not have been necessarily and wonderfully swift
So if this change is to be called progress,
it is the problems we must first address
It couldn't be called anything less important
than being compared to the Gettysburg Address
It is all right to have the best
because this is what comes with success
And that will be the true test not your fancy dress
You cannot stop Jack because he has a special knack
It was Jack in the beanstalk
that didn't for courage lack
It was in a growth spurt of courage
that he climbed that beanstalk
like he was riding piggyback
As he grew, he didn't lack in ability and wisdom
and he became a real cracker jack

We can all grow to great heights
even if we consider ourselves not to be too bright
It is one of our inborn rights; indeed,
just as is our own birthright
It will be one of our greatest delights
when we see ourselves through life's eyes
As we grow, we will even be able to choose our own fights
as well as our own delights

FORGIVE BUT DON'T FORGET

Forgive, but don't forget, or you might end up losing the bet
You might end up being in a train wreck and in a cold sweat
Your enemy could be more than a pain in the neck
you just might end up like Marie Antoinette
You could end up just plain sick
so do not consent to a game of Russian roulette
It will help you to come to terms by addressing past concerns
With all those nasty skeletons and tapeworms;
you are still bound to get heartburn
So kill all your negative feelings turn by turn
and tell them to go and never again to return
You will find out
what is really on the upturn, by learning to discern
You must protect yourself
or you will just be another notch on someone's bookshelf
In order to continue to keep your health
you must be kind and have the heart of an elf
That, in itself, is your true wealth
right there, right there, inside you
The key to your true self understands about your own life itself

And if you find yourself feeling unsure and insecure
There is only one thing with which you can be sure
the fact that history repeats itself
that fact never errs
That certain tempting lure
may take off and cause your heart to stir
That, in itself, may be dangerous
and may cause even more danger to occur

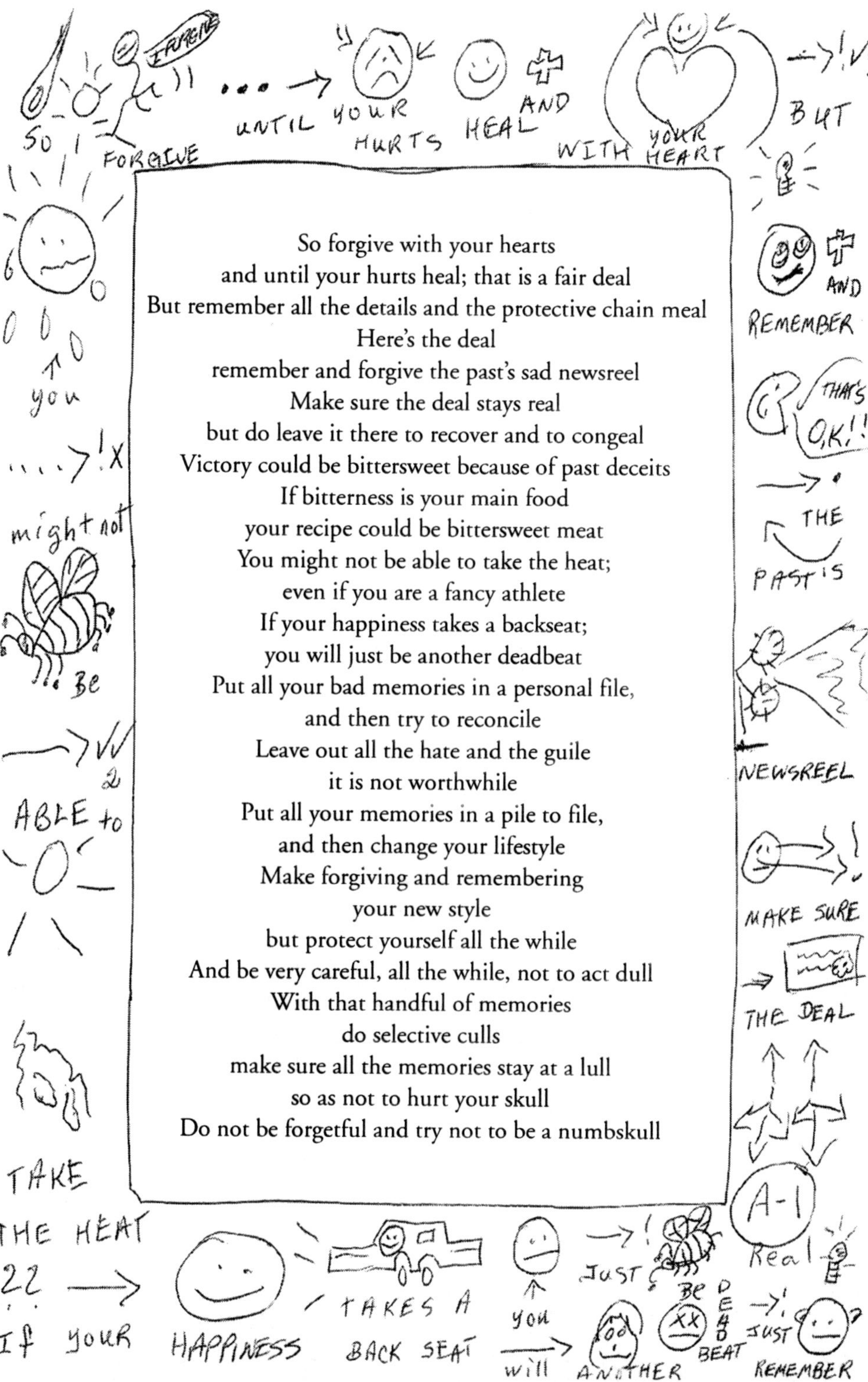

So forgive with your hearts
and until your hurts heal; that is a fair deal
But remember all the details and the protective chain meal
Here's the deal
remember and forgive the past's sad newsreel
Make sure the deal stays real
but do leave it there to recover and to congeal
Victory could be bittersweet because of past deceits
If bitterness is your main food
your recipe could be bittersweet meat
You might not be able to take the heat;
even if you are a fancy athlete
If your happiness takes a backseat;
you will just be another deadbeat
Put all your bad memories in a personal file,
and then try to reconcile
Leave out all the hate and the guile
it is not worthwhile
Put all your memories in a pile to file,
and then change your lifestyle
Make forgiving and remembering
your new style
but protect yourself all the while
And be very careful, all the while, not to act dull
With that handful of memories
do selective culls
make sure all the memories stay at a lull
so as not to hurt your skull
Do not be forgetful and try not to be a numbskull

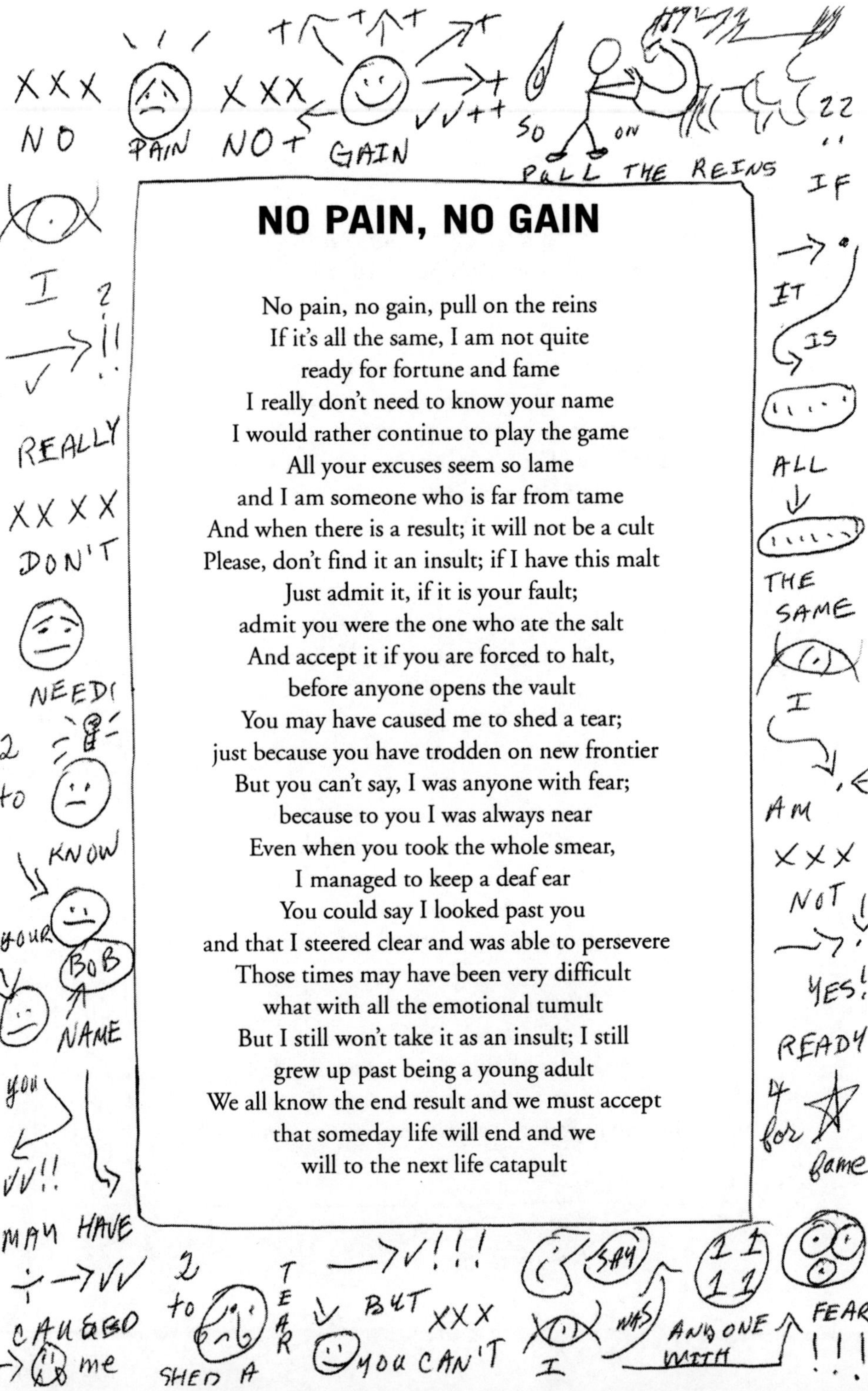

NO PAIN, NO GAIN

No pain, no gain, pull on the reins
If it's all the same, I am not quite
ready for fortune and fame
I really don't need to know your name
I would rather continue to play the game
All your excuses seem so lame
and I am someone who is far from tame
And when there is a result; it will not be a cult
Please, don't find it an insult; if I have this malt
Just admit it, if it is your fault;
admit you were the one who ate the salt
And accept it if you are forced to halt,
before anyone opens the vault
You may have caused me to shed a tear;
just because you have trodden on new frontier
But you can't say, I was anyone with fear;
because to you I was always near
Even when you took the whole smear,
I managed to keep a deaf ear
You could say I looked past you
and that I steered clear and was able to persevere
Those times may have been very difficult
what with all the emotional tumult
But I still won't take it as an insult; I still
grew up past being a young adult
We all know the end result and we must accept
that someday life will end and we
will to the next life catapult

The world most definitely won't come to a halt
and we will at least add flavor to the Earth; we were the salt
We know all good things sometimes
come very difficult to take
and seem very hard
And in order for us to put down the right card
We might have to suffer in some lonely ward
And keep quiet until we are ready
to play our wild card and discard
All we have to do is be patient and observe
when life throws us a hardball or a curve
We must be strong while we are in horrible pain
and try not to swerve and our energy
we must try to conserve
We must not sway from our principles or lose our nerve
and keep them intact as precious reserves
And to continue to live our life with vim and verve
until the good things come that we all deserve
After all, when your back is against the wall
we must endure and stand tall
You will be the only one to fall is you choose a pit fall
You still will have one call, no matter what;
that is the usual protocol
You can go in the room down the hall
and there is bound to be justice for all
We must continue to put lots of effort,
even if it causes pain and hurts

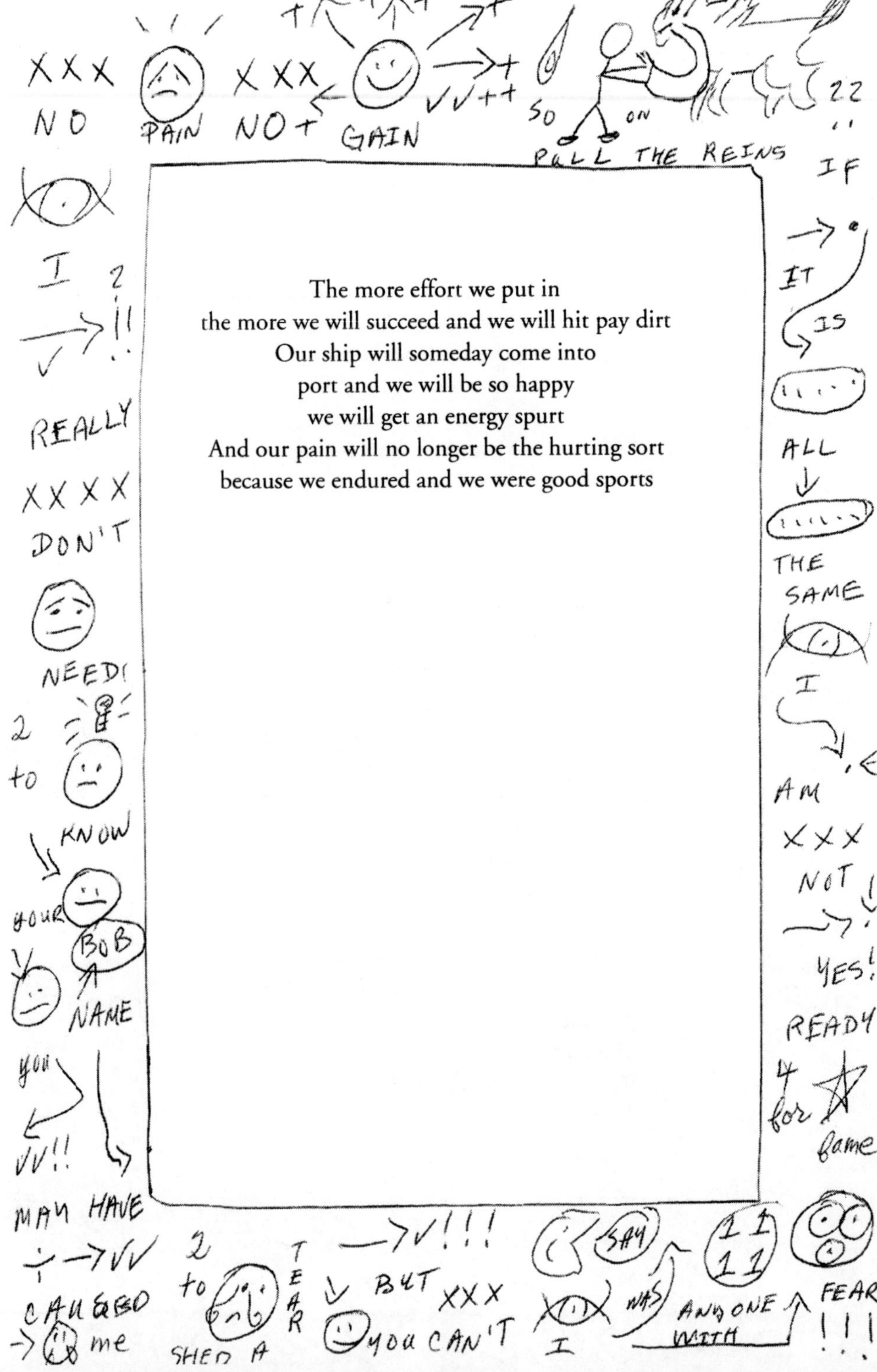

The more effort we put in
the more we will succeed and we will hit pay dirt
Our ship will someday come into
port and we will be so happy
we will get an energy spurt
And our pain will no longer be the hurting sort
because we endured and we were good sports

I DON'T TICKLE ANYMORE

Mine is a sad, sad story far from carefree
It comes from a life
with way too much worry
It took a special knack
to stop all my innocent glee
It was taken all away in a hurry
despite all my prayerful pleas
And no matter how you try
to boost my morale
You dare not to tickle this gal
It takes control to deny
the feelings in my O.K. Corral
The nerves that control me
are not the masters of me, pal

No, I am not a cold fish or fickle
I just choose
not to let myself tickle
It sure helps me
when I am in a pickle
This can prevent the hammer
from hitting the sickle
You may be able to make the other one pop
They will be the one caught doing a flip flop
And they may be the one to learn a lot
Because from me
they won't get the reaction that they sought
Ignoring pleasure is an acquired skill

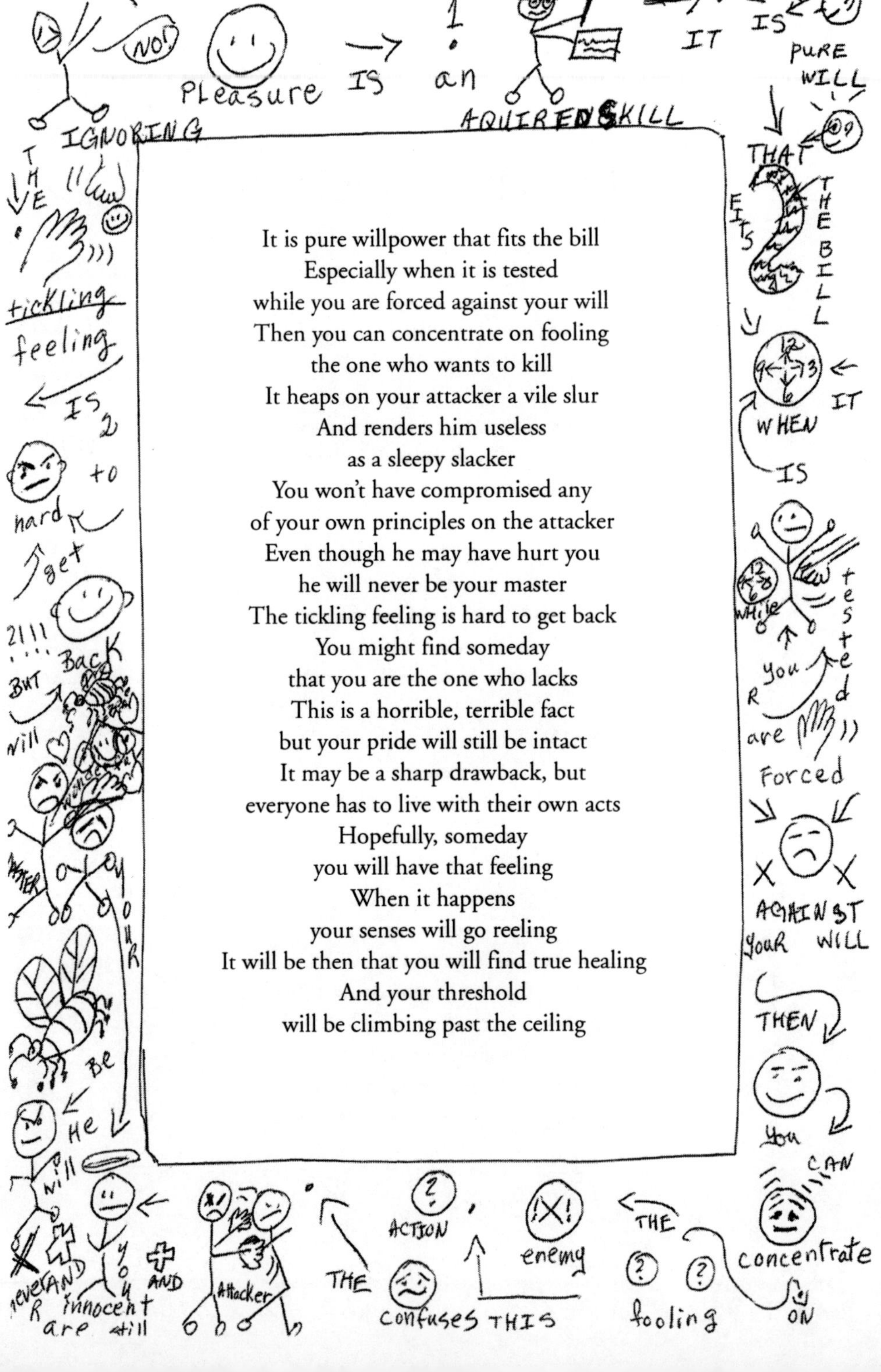

It is pure willpower that fits the bill
Especially when it is tested
while you are forced against your will
Then you can concentrate on fooling
the one who wants to kill
It heaps on your attacker a vile slur
And renders him useless
as a sleepy slacker
You won't have compromised any
of your own principles on the attacker
Even though he may have hurt you
he will never be your master
The tickling feeling is hard to get back
You might find someday
that you are the one who lacks
This is a horrible, terrible fact
but your pride will still be intact
It may be a sharp drawback, but
everyone has to live with their own acts
Hopefully, someday
you will have that feeling
When it happens
your senses will go reeling
It will be then that you will find true healing
And your threshold
will be climbing past the ceiling

I'M GOING TO SCREAM

I'm going to scream
if I stay in my daydream
Because I've seen where you have been
I'm not too keen of your life's movie screen
Oh, what I have seen
through yonder smokescreen
I will scream without making a sound
It will be as loud as something
coming from underground
My cries will keep
my mind on neutral ground
They will continue
to keep me spellbound
You will also
be able to feel my pain
When I am old, crippled, and lame
But you will not hear me complain
It doesn't matter to me;
it will be all the same
My cries went farther;
than I would have preferred
They definitely
hold water and make a stir
He heard me cry, Abba, Father
Please, rest in peace,
my loving mother
My screams will be
sharp and pierce the silent peace

And cut through the air in waves without cease
The sound waves will be awesome
and fierce as they ebb and flow and release
They will penetrate
your heart and your mind with ease
They will echo in your brain like an endless chain
And render you quite tame; no matter how you try
to avoid the siren's wail, it will be in vain
With me, that is all the same
Because in the end, it will turn out that
I am not totally sane
and alien may be one of my nicknames
I somehow knew that, in life, I would suffer
And that fate
would use my very own mother
And when you lied to her,
even though you knew better
Then I knew my life would henceforth
be a living hell, with invisible fetters
Nevertheless, I was and I am
very patient and very resourceful
Even though, life
has dealt me with a full plateful
I know someday life will be just wonderful
And when I turn my back on it all
I'll be satisfied and grateful

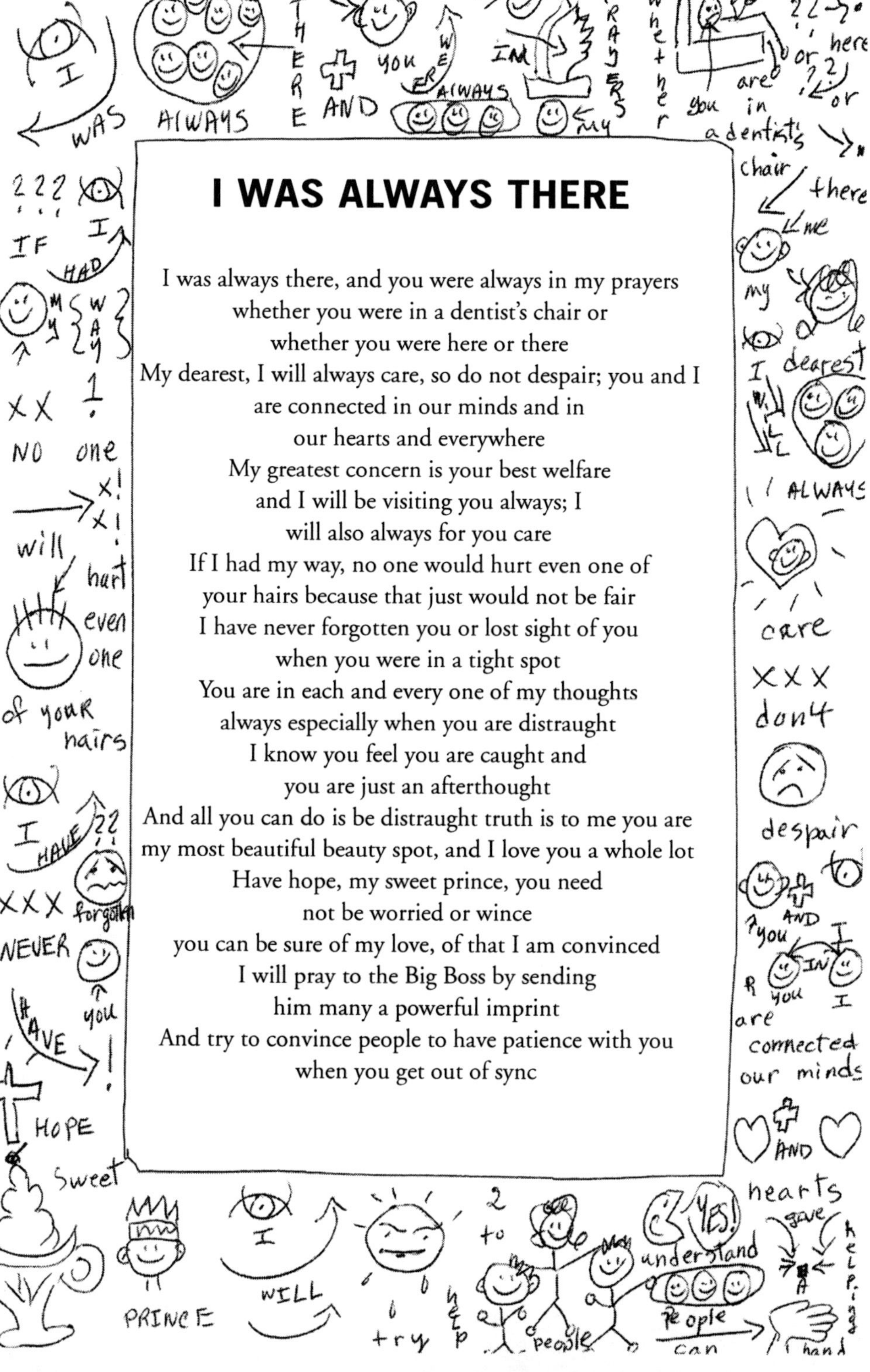

I WAS ALWAYS THERE

I was always there, and you were always in my prayers
whether you were in a dentist's chair or
whether you were here or there
My dearest, I will always care, so do not despair; you and I
are connected in our minds and in
our hearts and everywhere
My greatest concern is your best welfare
and I will be visiting you always; I
will also always for you care
If I had my way, no one would hurt even one of
your hairs because that just would not be fair
I have never forgotten you or lost sight of you
when you were in a tight spot
You are in each and every one of my thoughts
always especially when you are distraught
I know you feel you are caught and
you are just an afterthought
And all you can do is be distraught truth is to me you are
my most beautiful beauty spot, and I love you a whole lot
Have hope, my sweet prince, you need
not be worried or wince
you can be sure of my love, of that I am convinced
I will pray to the Big Boss by sending
him many a powerful imprint
And try to convince people to have patience with you
when you get out of sync

And I will try to help them to work with you so that
they continue giving and using love
and their family instincts
I will try to help people understand firsthand
that we are all capable to give a helping hand
And that, we can all live together hand in hand
and experience brotherly love firsthand
Also that we can share our big, beautiful land so
everyone can understand each other's demands
Oh, wouldn't this be beautiful and grand;
my prince in a world of love
for him and all in a great brotherhood of man
I am convinced that, in good time, with good
reason and rhyme and maybe the right enzymes
Someone bright will find for you peace of mind
wouldn't this be super and sublime and big time
When the key to your mind there in
your DNA all intertwined
will be unraveled and solved like a mystery crime
That would be the world's greatest
and most wonderful gift
to you from all the capable ones in humankind
I can only hope someone
will see in a microscope the entirety
and find the right slope
And we will be able to find the full
treatment for your condition
so you may have more hope

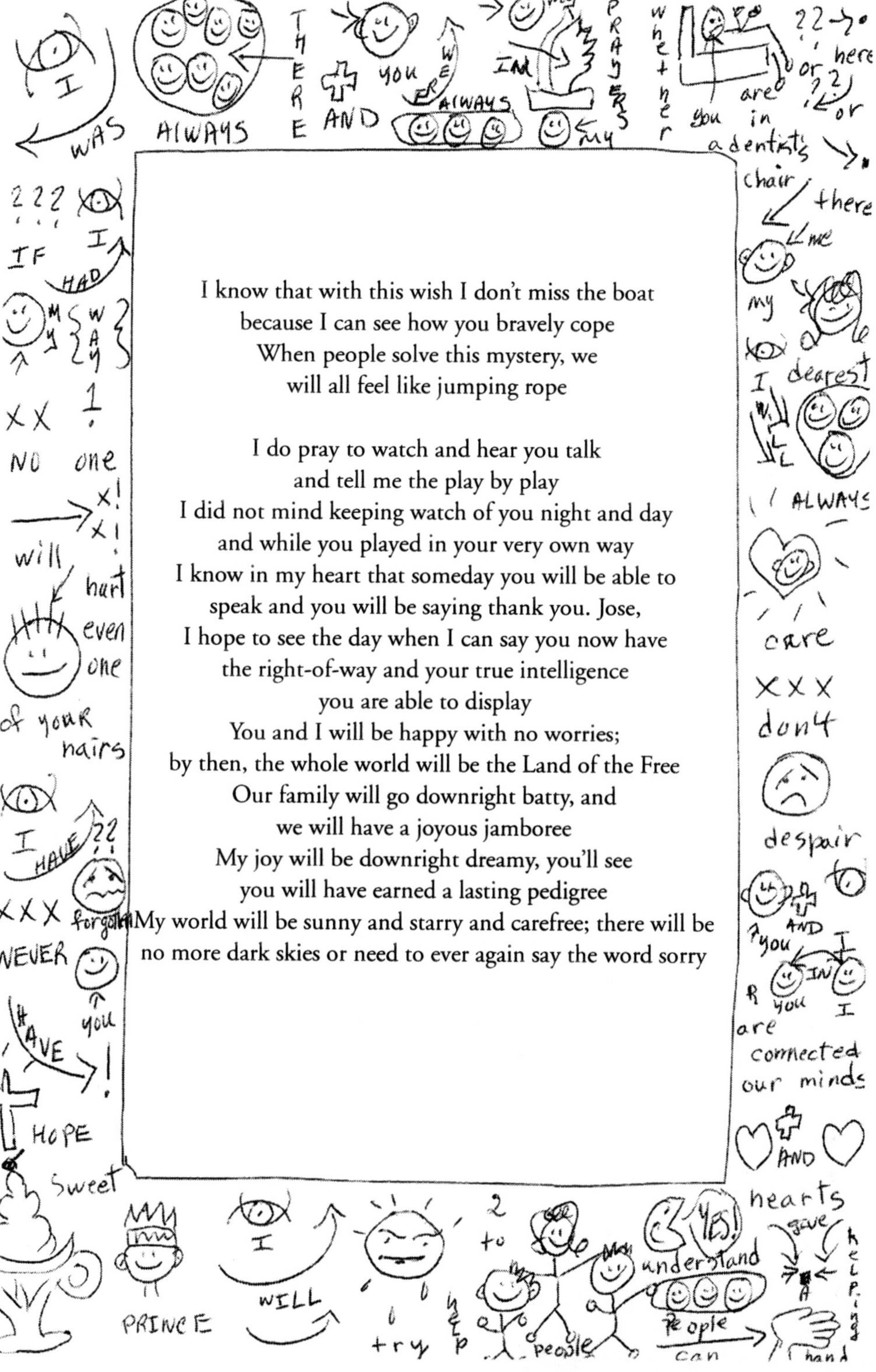

I know that with this wish I don't miss the boat
because I can see how you bravely cope
When people solve this mystery, we
will all feel like jumping rope

I do pray to watch and hear you talk
and tell me the play by play
I did not mind keeping watch of you night and day
and while you played in your very own way
I know in my heart that someday you will be able to
speak and you will be saying thank you. Jose,
I hope to see the day when I can say you now have
the right-of-way and your true intelligence
you are able to display
You and I will be happy with no worries;
by then, the whole world will be the Land of the Free
Our family will go downright batty, and
we will have a joyous jamboree
My joy will be downright dreamy, you'll see
you will have earned a lasting pedigree
My world will be sunny and starry and carefree; there will be
no more dark skies or need to ever again say the word sorry

FOLLOW LIFE TO THE LETTER

If you follow life to the letter
and let your feet get wetter and wetter
Life is bound to get better
the fact you are here does not lie or err
Life will lose all its fetters
it will no longer be able to deter
You will be glad you finally met life, won't you, sir
If you use all your spirit's juice
And use all those hidden clues
they will help you to deduce
All the answers which
you thought to be a ruse
And which proved really
to be some poor excuse
All will be fine and well and you will feel compelled
To choose an answer
that is very wise and unparalleled
You do this
for your soul's sake, rather than go to hell
Just listen to life's wishing well
and choose the right magic spell
Let life's ideas flow like a 3-D video
Then let them flow from your head to your toes
like an untapped dynamo
And when all the answers come to you,
you will know the status quo
You will know which way to go because
you will have get-up-and-go
Life rules, life rules, follow the rules

If you use the right tools
your life will be really cool
You won't be taken for a silly fool, and
your word will be the golden rule
That is when life will show
its most precious jewels
and you will graduate life's school
If you really listen, you will be the one to win
and you will gain some useful discipline
The answers will shine
and glisten through the din
It will be as it was written time and
time again, but you won't be a has-been
You will be truly smitten and left with
a gigantic grin and you will be a shoo-in
You must really learn how to feel
and use all your charming appeal
You must attract the sparks that
heal and add them to your sores with great zeal
You must incorporate them into your meal
of life's done deal
And you'll find you can get them
for a steal without a sound or a squeal
Last but not least, you must bring your best friend
You must share, with him,
your thoughts again and again
Let him share, until your thoughts
are heard by all women and all men
And until the thoughts ring as loud
as the chimes of Big Ben

IT'LL HAPPEN

It'll happen today without warning or delay
Great things sometimes happen in a day
while you are just a stone's throw away
Sometimes, what you want to say
then comes right into play
Definitely, how you role-play,
and your success story becomes
a reality show on display
Do you want it? Yes, I do every bit;
with reality I have been a hit
If you've got it, flaunt it, use all
your wit, and don't just sit
Come on get with it; make sure you commit;
use all your experience, your wit
I love it, I love it, and I have to admit that
that result came right out of my reality kit
This is the way I run my life
my life is a story of overcoming strife
It was helpful that
I did not try to run from suffering's painful knife
This gave me a lot of fortitude and strength
as a mother and as a wife
Now I will bask in the sun like the unbridled
and happy wildlife while I am in my golden years of life
What I've always wanted
to be was an egghead and a thoroughbred
I came undaunted, and I was
resurrected from my deathbed

I have what I flaunted because
I have always been brave and undaunted
I'll be something that I wanted to be
and not something someone else said
My job will continue on
until I make a great and grand breakthrough
My task will be something new
something, I will put out for the whole world to view
It will give you more than a few
rendezvous and a panoramic view
So you won't have to misconstrue my meaning
I will be the first to give you an interview
Granted, I am alive, and that is no jive
as a matter of fact, I now thrive
I will try to learn how
I have managed to survive
I won't think of it as a test drive:
more likely I will think of it
as a way to revive
I will use my thoughts to contrive
a way to operate besides
merely nine to five
The best result, of this, is just plainly my life as is
It's better than showbiz
now life is a real easy and happy whiz
Come on, it is not that bad,
Gee whiz, it doesn't have any frills and no frizz

Just because it is not yours and it is his
doesn't mean you fail the pop quiz
Soon the whole world will be satisfied, in fact,
there will not be a reason to cry and not one sigh
Since I am not the only one with
a story to give or to testify
The truth is everyone will be able to testify
and only the truth will apply
I will love all that glorious jive
because I am one groovy mama French fry

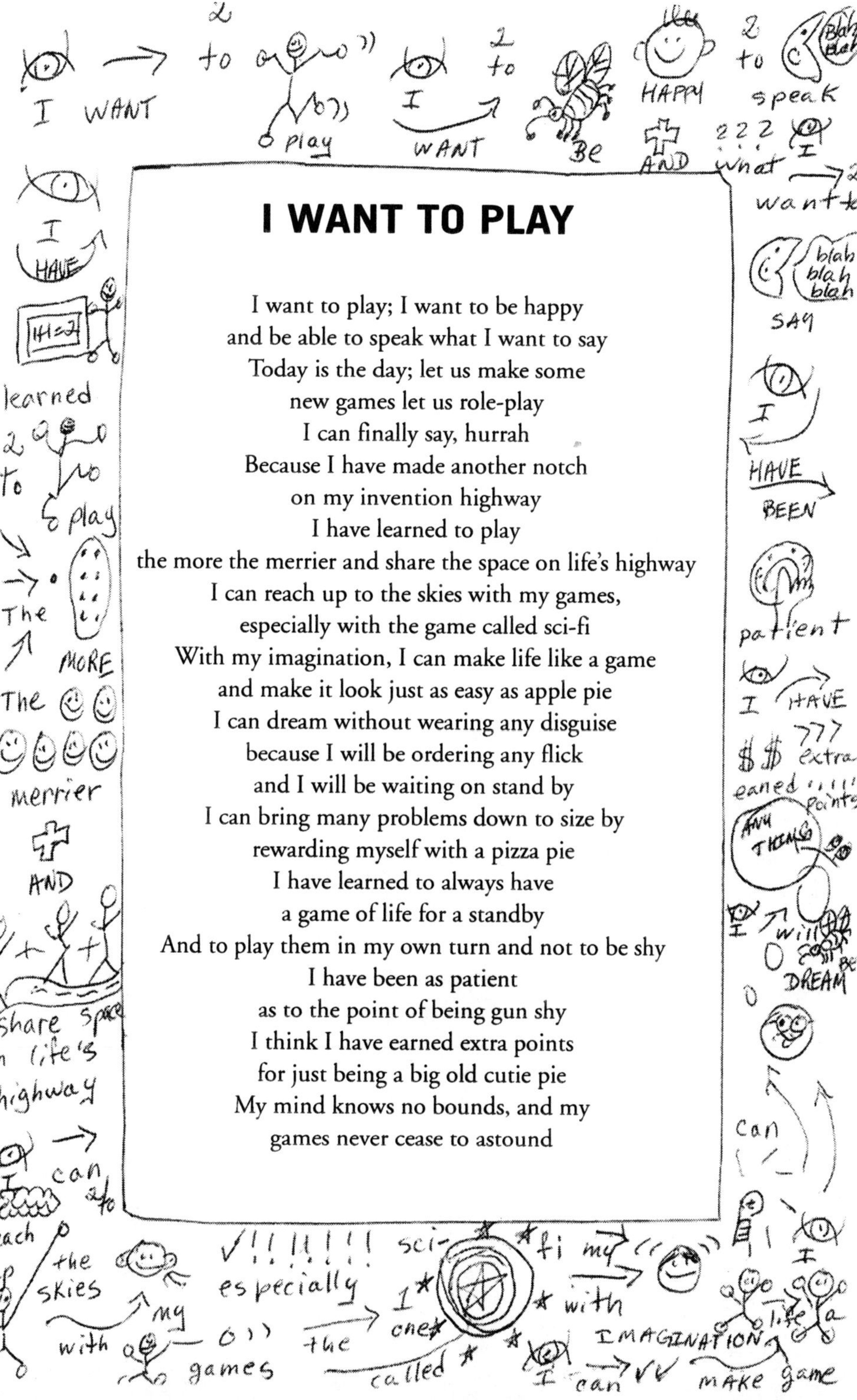

I WANT TO PLAY

I want to play; I want to be happy
and be able to speak what I want to say
Today is the day; let us make some
new games let us role-play
I can finally say, hurrah
Because I have made another notch
on my invention highway
I have learned to play
the more the merrier and share the space on life's highway
I can reach up to the skies with my games,
especially with the game called sci-fi
With my imagination, I can make life like a game
and make it look just as easy as apple pie
I can dream without wearing any disguise
because I will be ordering any flick
and I will be waiting on stand by
I can bring many problems down to size by
rewarding myself with a pizza pie
I have learned to always have
a game of life for a standby
And to play them in my own turn and not to be shy
I have been as patient
as to the point of being gun shy
I think I have earned extra points
for just being a big old cutie pie
My mind knows no bounds, and my
games never cease to astound

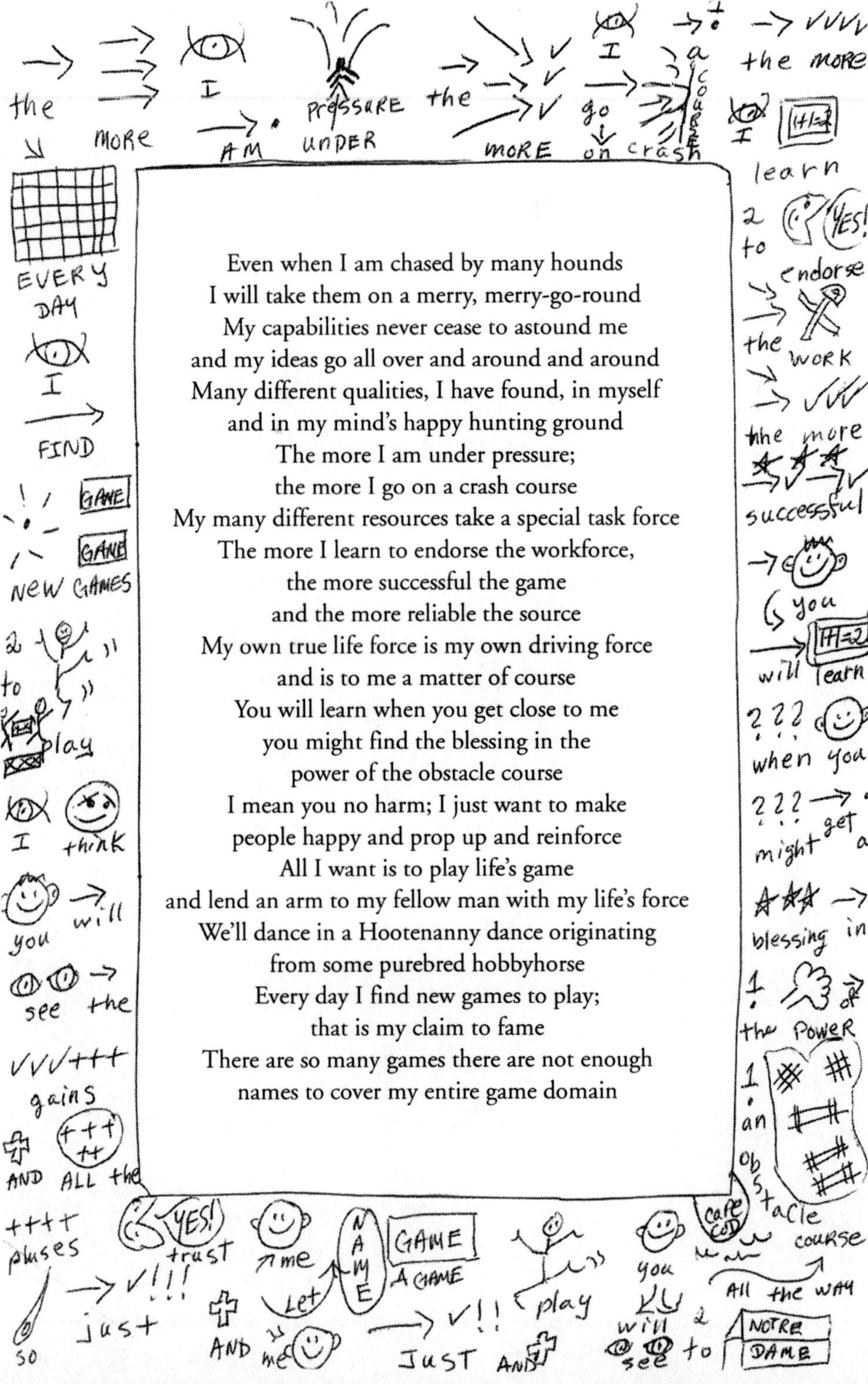

Even when I am chased by many hounds
I will take them on a merry, merry-go-round
My capabilities never cease to astound me
and my ideas go all over and around and around
Many different qualities, I have found, in myself
and in my mind's happy hunting ground
The more I am under pressure;
the more I go on a crash course
My many different resources take a special task force
The more I learn to endorse the workforce,
the more successful the game
and the more reliable the source
My own true life force is my own driving force
and is to me a matter of course
You will learn when you get close to me
you might find the blessing in the
power of the obstacle course
I mean you no harm; I just want to make
people happy and prop up and reinforce
All I want is to play life's game
and lend an arm to my fellow man with my life's force
We'll dance in a Hootenanny dance originating
from some purebred hobbyhorse
Every day I find new games to play;
that is my claim to fame
There are so many games there are not enough
names to cover my entire game domain

I think you will see the gains
and that this entire world is not in vain
Just wait and see what can be made
when I have got a hold of the reins
just like the rain in Spain
So just trust me and let me name a game
Let yourself be truly free
and do not have any shame
just play, and you will see all the way
from Cape Cod on to Notre Dame
And then we will see how happy
we can all be in life's Ball Game

MY BIPOPULAR LOVE

My love is bipopular and
happily belongs to this girl and not to a sir
I find myself truly lovable, and on
occasion, I talk out on the spur
It is totally understandable
for many unusual things to me occur
my love is not at all deplorable, as a matter of fact;
I am quite happy, yes, sir
My bipopular love fits me like a glove
It is what it will be; it comes from above
it is a labor of love
You can see it coming on the wings of a dove
as a matter of fact, it looks like a turtledove
This love is always pure love;
go ahead and put on your love gloves

My love is sometimes fast, sometimes slow,
and I try to show it to both friend and foe
Never failing to put up a good show
and blow for blow, I am a high-powered dynamo
You can try to open your mouth and blow me away
but I tell you there is more to me than you'll ever know
The truth will flow from my lips because I
thought that you had a right to know
My love will never fail to continue; as a matter of fact
it will be a welcome breakthrough
My love will show you more than one venue;
you will enjoy it through and through

My love is sometimes happy, sometimes
blue; but it is never meant to overdo
My love is sometimes happy, sometimes
angry, and sometimes blue;
But it will stick to you like glue
My love will blossom like a flower
And will sound smooth like a cat's purr
My love may wilt in nasty weather,
But will be reborn again and start to stir
You'll never find anything better; my
love is like a double header
When you have stopped and met her,
You will see my love holds no fetters
Sometimes, there will be hell to pay if
you rub me the wrong way
After that, there will be time to play
Because my love will have met you halfway
My love will laugh; then she will say Hurrah
And do the finest love ballet
She might get depressed; come what may
And even though the skies look gray,
Eventually, she will say "Heh, by the way let's play."
You'll never know what comes next;
Because my love changes just like T-Rex
Even though you can see it right there in the text
And it holds no kind of pretext
It'll be just enough to perplex, but not
enough for Samantha to place a hex

You can only hope for the best and then
go ahead put my love to the test
My love will come to you in a rush
And explode in a gush
You won't find it hiding in a bush;
But sometimes, it will make you blush
It may still make you shy, but my love
Will be happy to give you a little push
Whatever, please stay in touch because
My bipopular love is rich and it is lush

I AM A BROAD

My limbs are quite broad
In fact, I am a broad
All hail, all laud
I am also quite mode
I've fought
many battles in my life
I've had misery for my wife
Words have cut
through me like a knife
My troubles have been many
they have been rife
In fact, my problems
have made me quite strong
Somehow, I knew
this would happen, all along
Sometimes I feel like King Kong
Sing me a song, sing along
Come on now, I'll share
I've got lots to spare
My love,
on my sleeve I wear
And about you
I really do care
A day is much fancier
When it is a little bit chancy
Who is this guy
called Clancy

Is he related to Nancy?
The day won't go by any faster
When you let it be your master
So fight
with a will to live mister
And give it to me
full blast, sister
Go away;
if you don't want to play
I don't mind turning gray
In any case,
and in any way
I'll start
with a full plate any day
Mine will be the last word
You'll be the one
sitting like a lone turd
Because I am
the queen of the nerds
Even though
this may seem absurd

I'LL THINK OUT LOUD

I can think out loud
My logic is totally sound
Finally I have found
That, I might be
glory bound
I can go on day to day
With nothing at all to say
I can work or play
And still have fun
is that OK?
Then I will think thoughts
That might help others a lot
Should someone hear me
or whatnot?
They might get the brilliant idea
he or she had sought

When we unscramble all our eggs
We will acquire our sea legs
We'll no longer be in the dregs
And we'll all have full-charged kegs
Then we will no longer have to hide
We'll all see what we have got inside
You and I will be able, again, to confide
And we will all be on each other's side
You and I will be friends

Many treasures, to each other
we'll send
Our helping hands outstretched
we'll lend
We'll thank each other again and again
We'll want
each other's company to last
We won't forget
our appointed tasks
We will, all, have a blast
When we are all friendly and fast
I will be rewarded, moreover
I will stand up proud like a tall tower
I'll feel like I, at least
have a little power
Because my voice
will be heard all over

THE GALE SWEPT ME AWAY

The gale swept me away far, far away
There was no other way
from being thrown the wrong way
Surprisingly, the answer was lying
right there on the highway
What could I say
it was just a typical weekday
I had no other choice
but to pull out my Rolls-Royce
I almost lost my voice
because I could do nothing but rejoice
My forehead was hot and moist
my eyes were a clear turquoise
Soon, I could again hear the traffic noise
My mind was seeing Polaroid
All my thoughts I employed
somewhat like Sigmund Freud
With the answer I toyed
and I felt totally annoyed
The answer was so terrible
it rendered me almost destroyed
There was no way out of this blowout
There was no reason
to pout or to have any doubts
I couldn't
even shout and that is no doubt
I had to go this route
because the gale turned me out

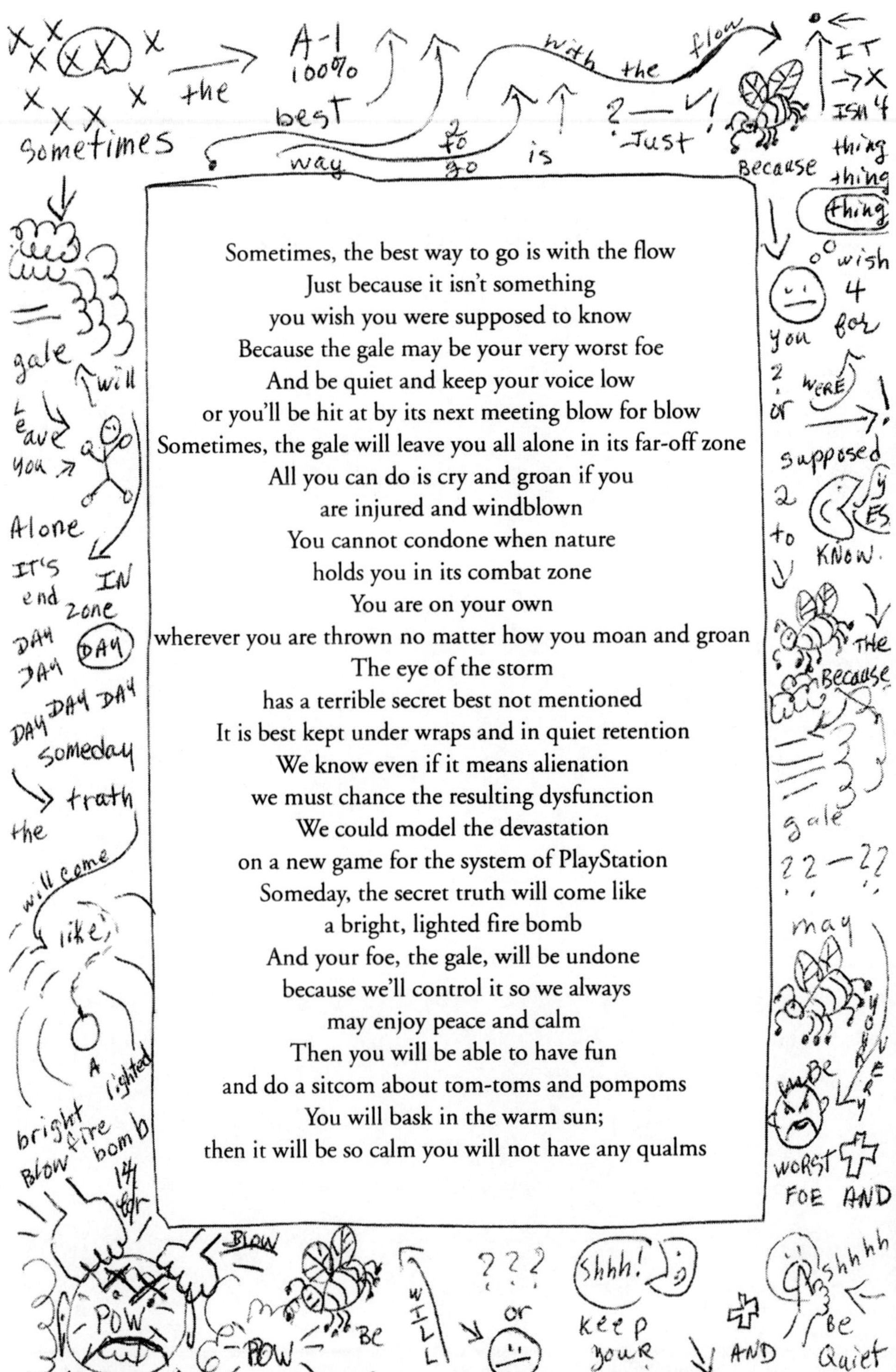

Sometimes, the best way to go is with the flow
Just because it isn't something
you wish you were supposed to know
Because the gale may be your very worst foe
And be quiet and keep your voice low
or you'll be hit at by its next meeting blow for blow
Sometimes, the gale will leave you all alone in its far-off zone
All you can do is cry and groan if you
are injured and windblown
You cannot condone when nature
holds you in its combat zone
You are on your own
wherever you are thrown no matter how you moan and groan
The eye of the storm
has a terrible secret best not mentioned
It is best kept under wraps and in quiet retention
We know even if it means alienation
we must chance the resulting dysfunction
We could model the devastation
on a new game for the system of PlayStation
Someday, the secret truth will come like
a bright, lighted fire bomb
And your foe, the gale, will be undone
because we'll control it so we always
may enjoy peace and calm
Then you will be able to have fun
and do a sitcom about tom-toms and pompoms
You will bask in the warm sun;
then it will be so calm you will not have any qualms

THE SIGHT OF INSIGHT

Can you see the sight of insight, fiddle-Dee-Dee
Look around you and me;
are we really fancy-free
Golly gee, is there really any solid guarantees?
What happens; will we ever be home free?
The sight of insight should prove better than hindsight
It comes from within, doesn't it
it is our mind's true searchlight
It is a bright light that turns
red, green, and yellow inside our mind's sight
It can even come out on a dark night
as an idea or an emotional searchlight
I have only three eyes, two of them cry
The two that see in front of me, tell no lies
It's the one inside my head
that is the one that tries to defy
My total view, so I no longer rely
on all the visions, with which, I spy
I think many things; my mind is a wonderful plaything
I see what it brings and I welcome inside everything
I own many rings
that to me resemble baby's teething rings
Insight is a beautiful string
that keeps me alive and in life's boxing ring
Insight all depends
on how one accepts, understands, and comprehends
Your opinion depends on how great
on the mind was the impression

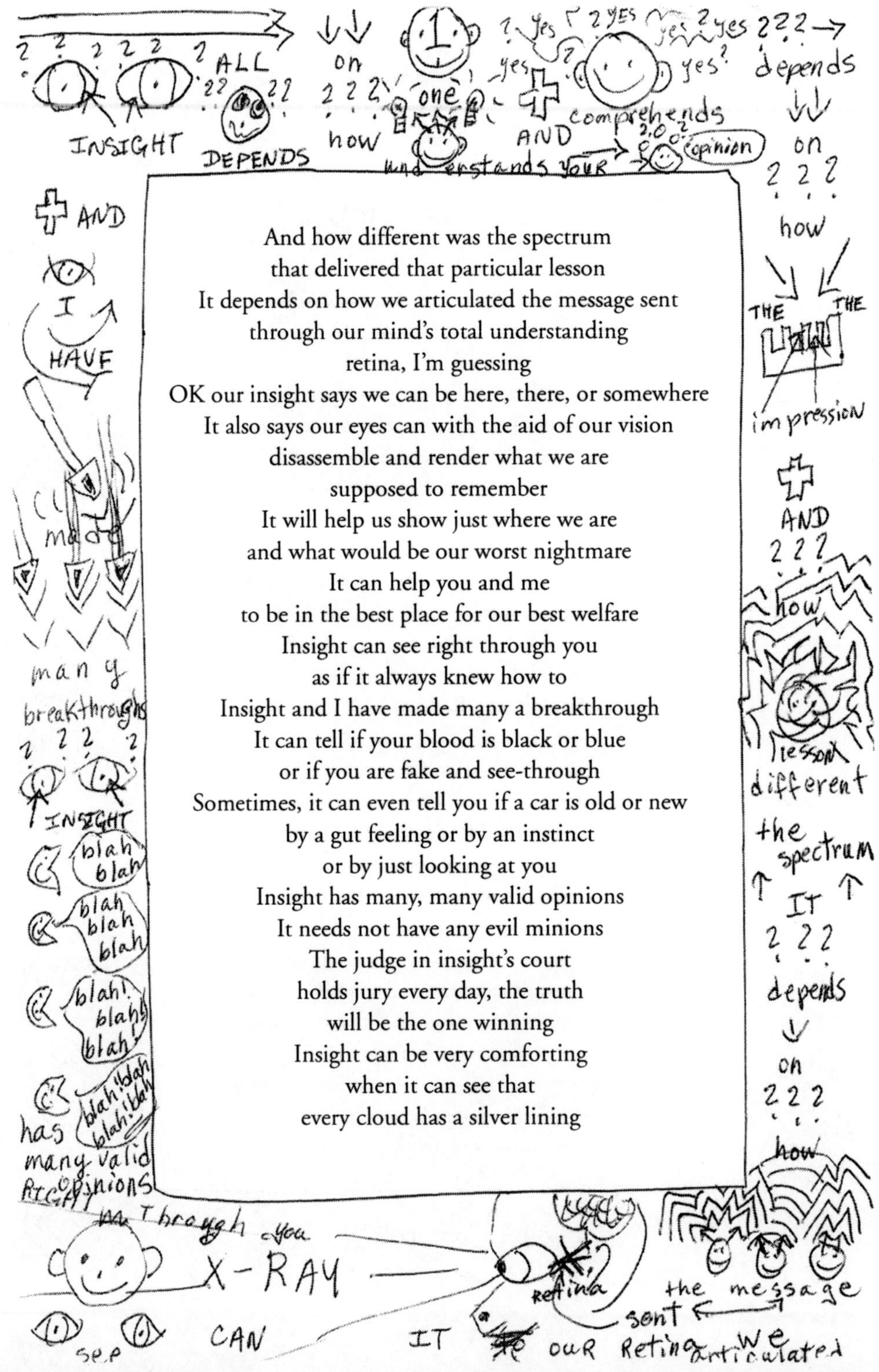

And how different was the spectrum
that delivered that particular lesson
It depends on how we articulated the message sent
through our mind's total understanding
retina, I'm guessing
OK our insight says we can be here, there, or somewhere
It also says our eyes can with the aid of our vision
disassemble and render what we are
supposed to remember
It will help us show just where we are
and what would be our worst nightmare
It can help you and me
to be in the best place for our best welfare
Insight can see right through you
as if it always knew how to
Insight and I have made many a breakthrough
It can tell if your blood is black or blue
or if you are fake and see-through
Sometimes, it can even tell you if a car is old or new
by a gut feeling or by an instinct
or by just looking at you
Insight has many, many valid opinions
It needs not have any evil minions
The judge in insight's court
holds jury every day, the truth
will be the one winning
Insight can be very comforting
when it can see that
every cloud has a silver lining

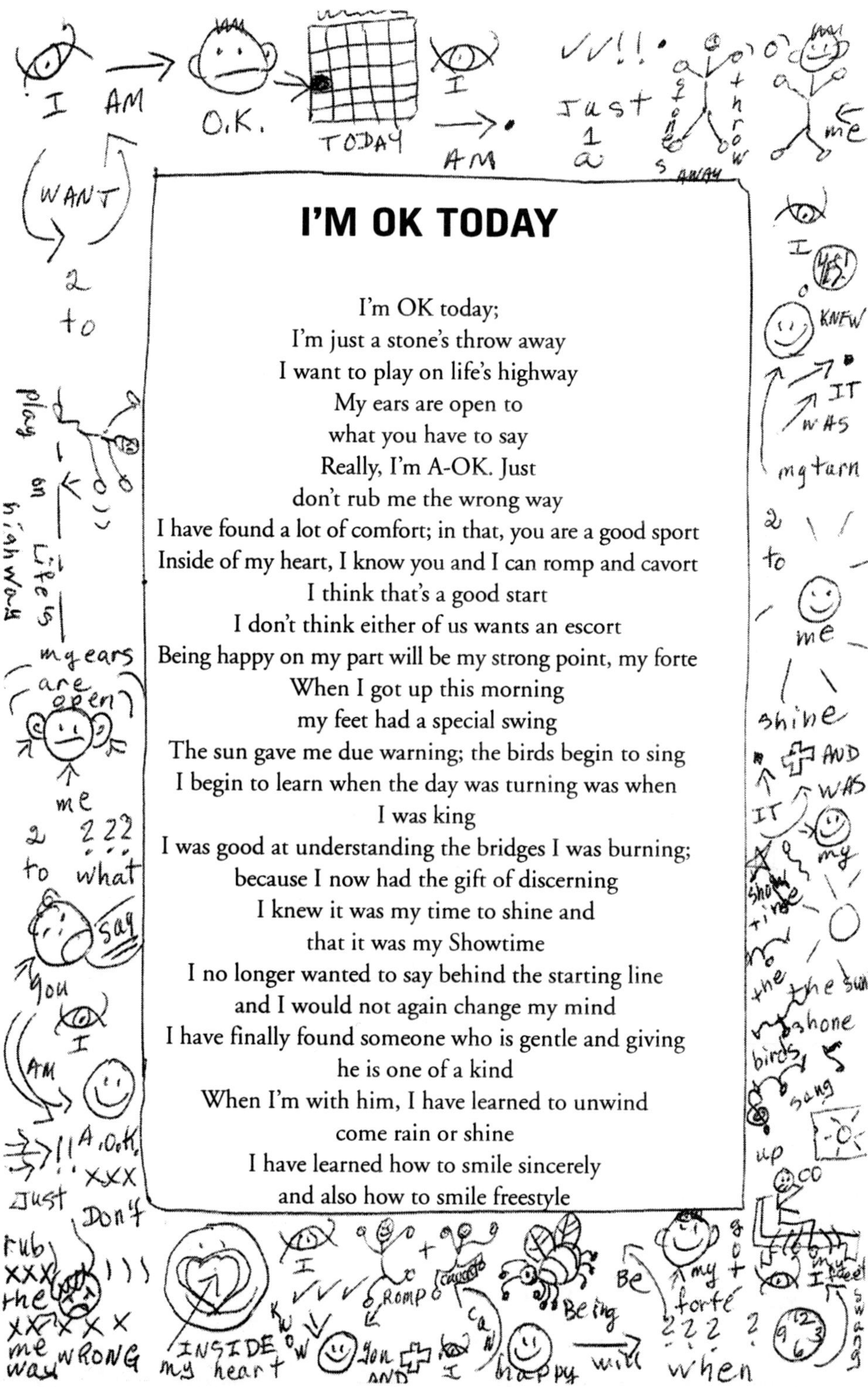

I'M OK TODAY

I'm OK today;
I'm just a stone's throw away
I want to play on life's highway
My ears are open to
what you have to say
Really, I'm A-OK. Just
don't rub me the wrong way
I have found a lot of comfort; in that, you are a good sport
Inside of my heart, I know you and I can romp and cavort
I think that's a good start
I don't think either of us wants an escort
Being happy on my part will be my strong point, my forte
When I got up this morning
my feet had a special swing
The sun gave me due warning; the birds begin to sing
I begin to learn when the day was turning was when
I was king
I was good at understanding the bridges I was burning;
because I now had the gift of discerning
I knew it was my time to shine and
that it was my Showtime
I no longer wanted to say behind the starting line
and I would not again change my mind
I have finally found someone who is gentle and giving
he is one of a kind
When I'm with him, I have learned to unwind
come rain or shine
I have learned how to smile sincerely
and also how to smile freestyle

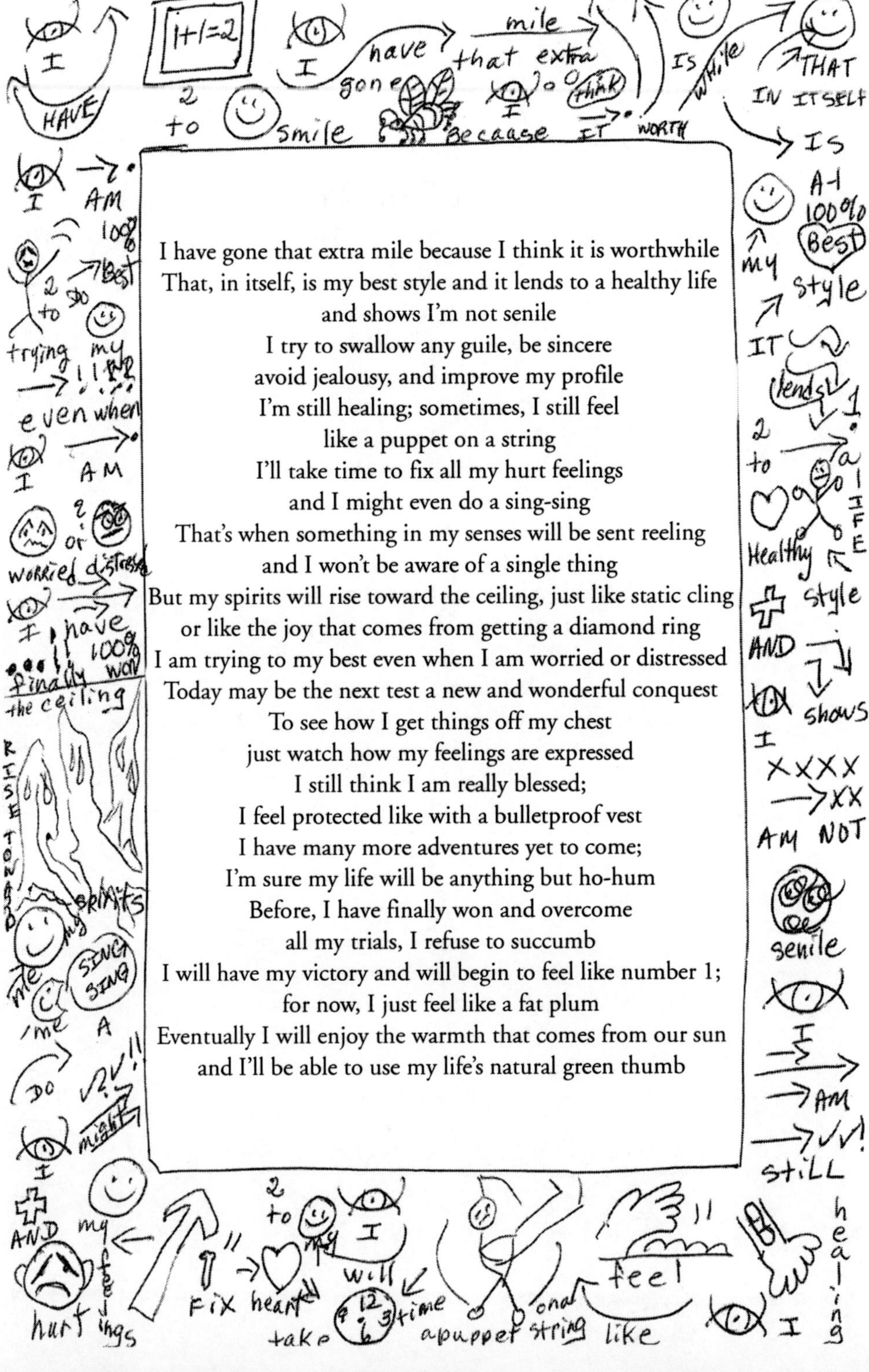

I have gone that extra mile because I think it is worthwhile
That, in itself, is my best style and it lends to a healthy life
and shows I'm not senile
I try to swallow any guile, be sincere
avoid jealousy, and improve my profile
I'm still healing; sometimes, I still feel
like a puppet on a string
I'll take time to fix all my hurt feelings
and I might even do a sing-sing
That's when something in my senses will be sent reeling
and I won't be aware of a single thing
But my spirits will rise toward the ceiling, just like static cling
or like the joy that comes from getting a diamond ring
I am trying to my best even when I am worried or distressed
Today may be the next test a new and wonderful conquest
To see how I get things off my chest
just watch how my feelings are expressed
I still think I am really blessed;
I feel protected like with a bulletproof vest
I have many more adventures yet to come;
I'm sure my life will be anything but ho-hum
Before, I have finally won and overcome
all my trials, I refuse to succumb
I will have my victory and will begin to feel like number 1;
for now, I just feel like a fat plum
Eventually I will enjoy the warmth that comes from our sun
and I'll be able to use my life's natural green thumb

I SEE WHAT YOU MEAN, MY DEAR

I see what you mean, my dear
I hold your opinion in the greatest esteem
I think your ideas are very keen
and you have tremendously good hygiene
I want you on my team to help me with my regular routine
You are a mighty mean idea machine
you are also squeaky clean
You are the very best; especially, when
I am sad and depressed
If you want to see all of my chest you have to be my husband
he the very best
I think he is blessed
he has won my permanent love request in our little love nest
He can stand up to any of love's tests;
I believe he is by love possessed
I love you my dear when I kiss you
I feel like I'm wrapped up in cashmere
I never have to fear because my love fills up the stratosphere
I wish for you to never shed a tear
unless your feelings speak to you to do so loud and clear
I always want you near;
I know your spirit will always be with me and persevere
I love being on your wavelength
You are my greatest strength
You have been sent because
we are both on heaven's wavelength

The clouds could not hold you away
so you were automatically sent
to me for me to play
because I had a lot of faith
I understand that you are kind
I also know what is on your mind
Because we are two of the same kind
When you love someone
your love can't help but bind
You set me free
with you I can again laugh with glee
You mean no harm
you do nothing but please
Now, with you, I am free
my wings fly in the breeze
With you, my dear, I feel the greatest release
When you were sent to me from the wise Spiritual Three
After I sent my earnest plea to do as you would; I agreed
I had no idea; you would be so kind
and let him stay with me
The perfect mister for me
who made me the happiest woman queen bee
You are and will always never cease to make me amazed
you are and always will be in my heart
and in my stars all of my days
No matter how many wars there are;
our lives will always be an adventure
like we are trailblazing
You have the ability to heal my scars; and
when you look at me I see stars and beautiful bouquets

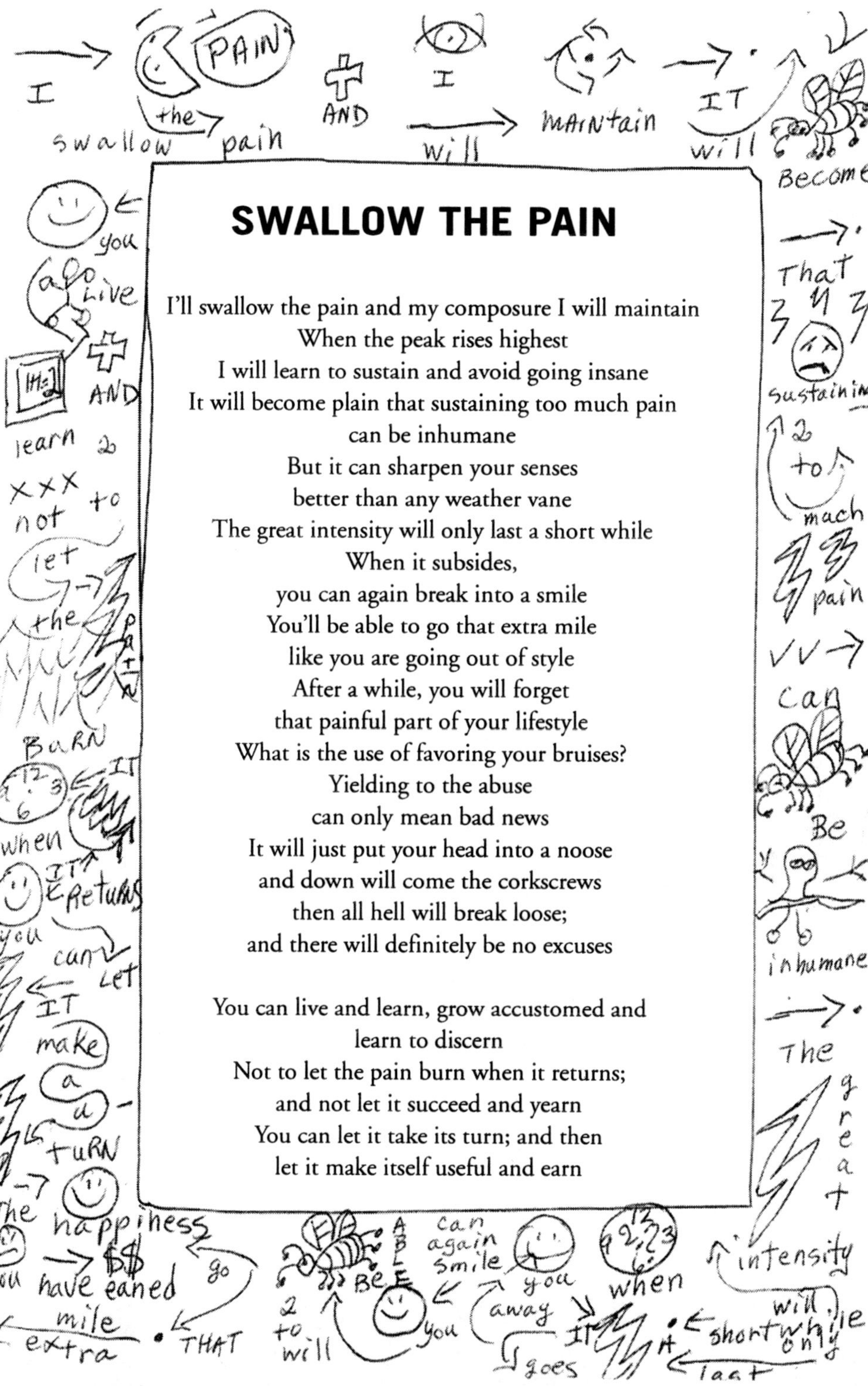

SWALLOW THE PAIN

I'll swallow the pain and my composure I will maintain
When the peak rises highest
I will learn to sustain and avoid going insane
It will become plain that sustaining too much pain
can be inhumane
But it can sharpen your senses
better than any weather vane
The great intensity will only last a short while
When it subsides,
you can again break into a smile
You'll be able to go that extra mile
like you are going out of style
After a while, you will forget
that painful part of your lifestyle
What is the use of favoring your bruises?
Yielding to the abuse
can only mean bad news
It will just put your head into a noose
and down will come the corkscrews
then all hell will break loose;
and there will definitely be no excuses

You can live and learn, grow accustomed and
learn to discern
Not to let the pain burn when it returns;
and not let it succeed and yearn
You can let it take its turn; and then
let it make itself useful and earn

The happiness that you have earned can help my life
be happy and have a sojourn
But beware, do not become numb;
because then it may make you deaf and dumb
And you will surely be undone if
you let yourself succumb
One must have pain to have fun because
its absence means you have overcome
One must have pain in order to feel pleasure and have fun
To learn to have balance is what it means
to master how to break dance
You must remember to leave nothing to chance
And when you enter into a song and a romance
You will recover by breaking into a folk dance
and then into a rain dance hap chance
When you learn to accept the overall concept
And that there are hardships
even for the chosen and the select
You will learn how to react
before and after the fact
No matter how low or how high the bet,
you will intercept
And when you are moved to tears
things will become painfully clear
You'll be able to face your fears because
you will be aware of the whole smear
And you will no longer be scared of mirrors
Because all the answers will be crystal clear

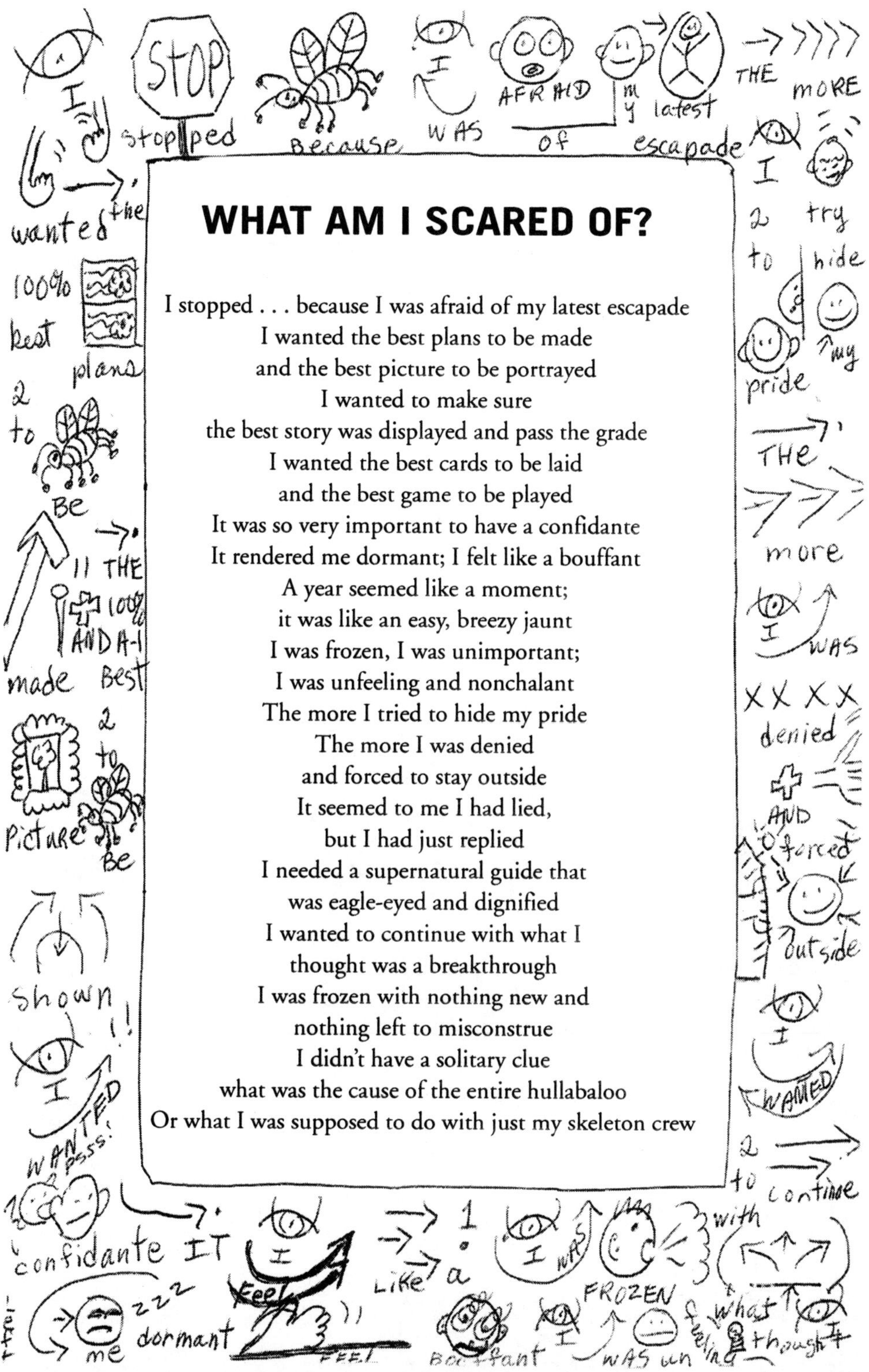

WHAT AM I SCARED OF?

I stopped . . . because I was afraid of my latest escapade
I wanted the best plans to be made
and the best picture to be portrayed
I wanted to make sure
the best story was displayed and pass the grade
I wanted the best cards to be laid
and the best game to be played
It was so very important to have a confidante
It rendered me dormant; I felt like a bouffant
A year seemed like a moment;
it was like an easy, breezy jaunt
I was frozen, I was unimportant;
I was unfeeling and nonchalant
The more I tried to hide my pride
The more I was denied
and forced to stay outside
It seemed to me I had lied,
but I had just replied
I needed a supernatural guide that
was eagle-eyed and dignified
I wanted to continue with what I
thought was a breakthrough
I was frozen with nothing new and
nothing left to misconstrue
I didn't have a solitary clue
what was the cause of the entire hullabaloo
Or what I was supposed to do with just my skeleton crew

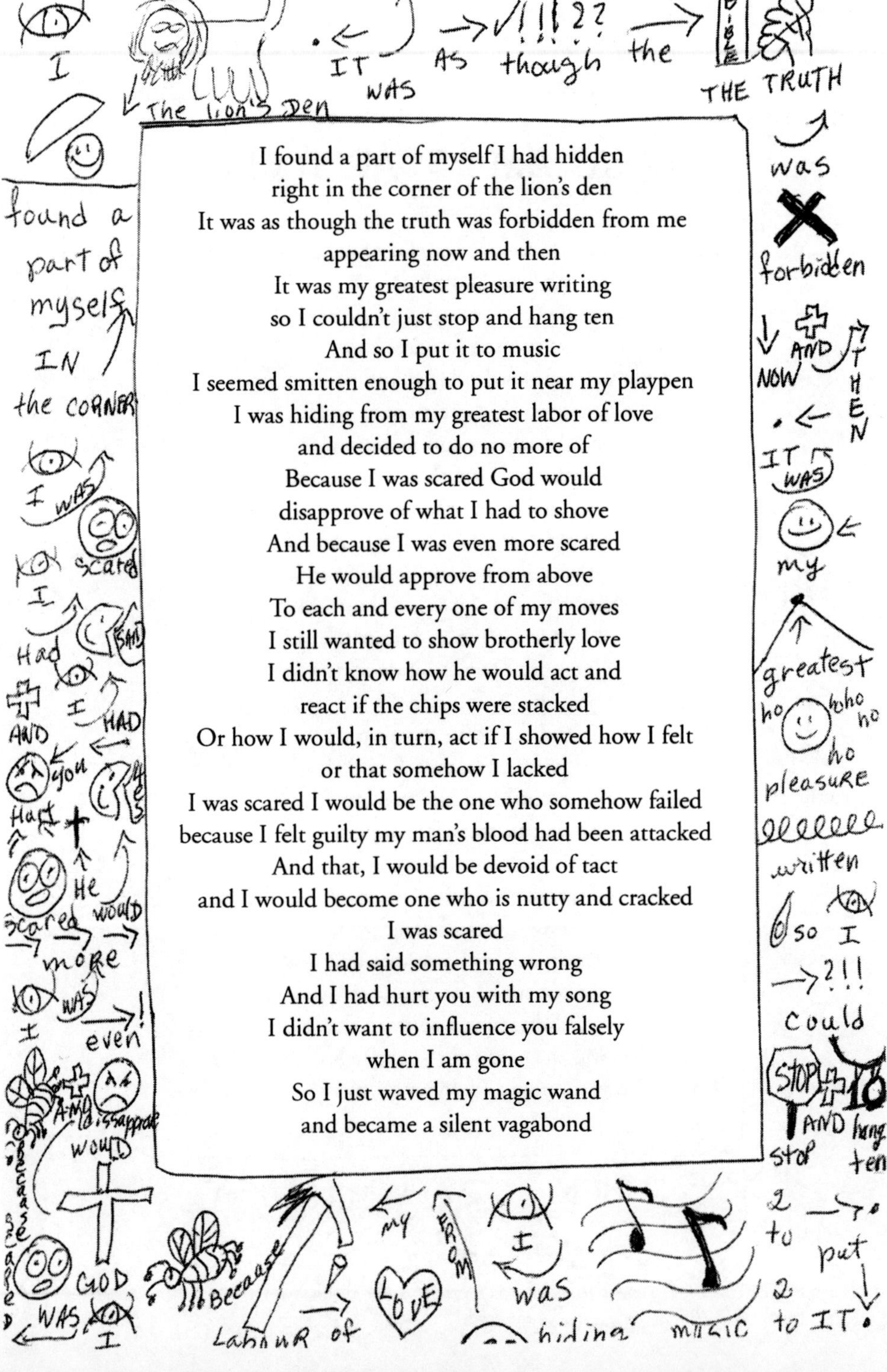

I found a part of myself I had hidden
right in the corner of the lion's den
It was as though the truth was forbidden from me
appearing now and then
It was my greatest pleasure writing
so I couldn't just stop and hang ten
And so I put it to music
I seemed smitten enough to put it near my playpen
I was hiding from my greatest labor of love
and decided to do no more of
Because I was scared God would
disapprove of what I had to shove
And because I was even more scared
He would approve from above
To each and every one of my moves
I still wanted to show brotherly love
I didn't know how he would act and
react if the chips were stacked
Or how I would, in turn, act if I showed how I felt
or that somehow I lacked
I was scared I would be the one who somehow failed
because I felt guilty my man's blood had been attacked
And that, I would be devoid of tact
and I would become one who is nutty and cracked
I was scared
I had said something wrong
And I had hurt you with my song
I didn't want to influence you falsely
when I am gone
So I just waved my magic wand
and became a silent vagabond

YOU'RE CRACKERS AND I'M NUTS

You're crackers and I'm nuts
No if and or buts;
it's just the fact of the matter
that's what
I've fallen into many
many ruts, so what
And now we're both in the soup,
that fact is clear cut
I can be used, considered, or seasoned
You're the best condiment
for my kind of pleasing
I can be good for something
or almost anything
And you are the best
for a lifelong fling
I have icing sprinkled on top
But do you know what
When I'm alone, I'll show you
what I've got
And you'll find out what
you have truly sought
Some people think I'm crazy
I may be a nut
but I am not lazy
First I make sense
then oops daisy

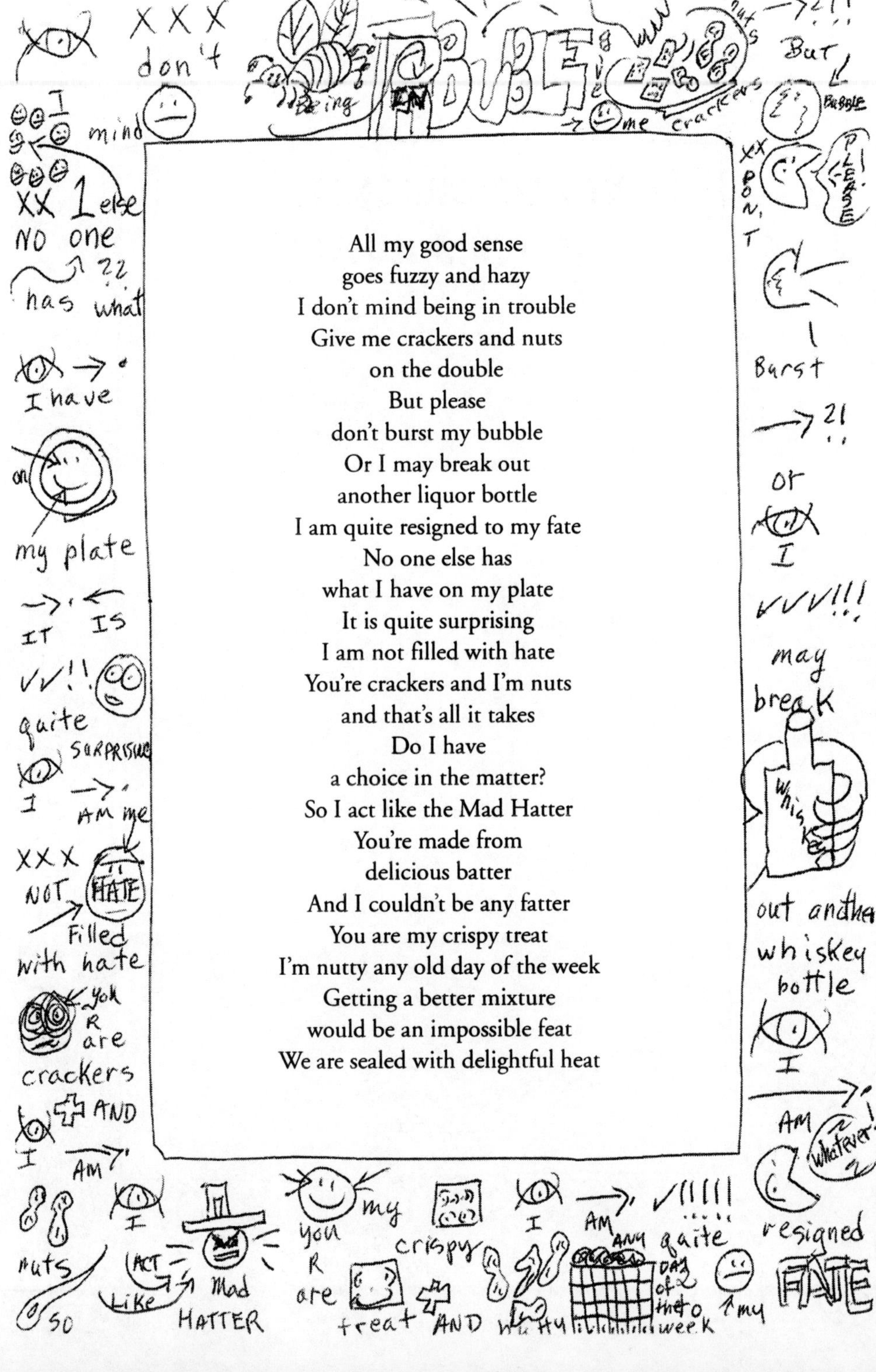

All my good sense
goes fuzzy and hazy
I don't mind being in trouble
Give me crackers and nuts
on the double
But please
don't burst my bubble
Or I may break out
another liquor bottle
I am quite resigned to my fate
No one else has
what I have on my plate
It is quite surprising
I am not filled with hate
You're crackers and I'm nuts
and that's all it takes
Do I have
a choice in the matter?
So I act like the Mad Hatter
You're made from
delicious batter
And I couldn't be any fatter
You are my crispy treat
I'm nutty any old day of the week
Getting a better mixture
would be an impossible feat
We are sealed with delightful heat

WISE MOVE

It would be wise
to wake up and open your eyes
And not to take a chance or to jeopardize
Winning first prize
proves there were no lies
Because you are transparent
and no longer in disguise
This wise move
will change the lives around me
I will find; I will no longer have to beg a plea
it will be obvious for all to see
It had to be over between you and me
to set us both free
But I still had to pay quite a fee;
quite a bit more than the price of a cup of tea
Bondage takes many forms
many wiggly worms
It can be right now, midterm or be long term
It can be a total change of the norm,
away from any harm
It can even be when a baby is born
all sad and forlorn
Traveling away from you
set me free
I found out who I could truly be
I will no longer be blue;
I will be happy and carefree

My life will be straight and true
now I will be home free
My next move has been born
and has arrived
It has been set and contrived; it is alive
It has been generated and tried
so it can survive after the test drive
I must contrive to surprise you
and to strive to stay alive
Whom I shall choose, you wonder
To share my company
it will all become a blur
Those that are dear to me
of course, sir
Those who love me, you see
cause my heart to stir
I also choose to love the ones
that are like my kind
The ones that love the spirit
of melody and rhyme
And to have them for company all the time
They will be my friends all the time;
and together, we will unwind
Who else are we supposed
to choose to be with?
Do you have inkling or is it but a myth

And just who are as close
as who we are with
A man called Smith
we are with the herewith
My love is enjoying an open book
For all I can see
and hear in it's every nook
If you choose to come near
I won't give you an evil look
Just stop and take a look; don't
overlook what is the textbook

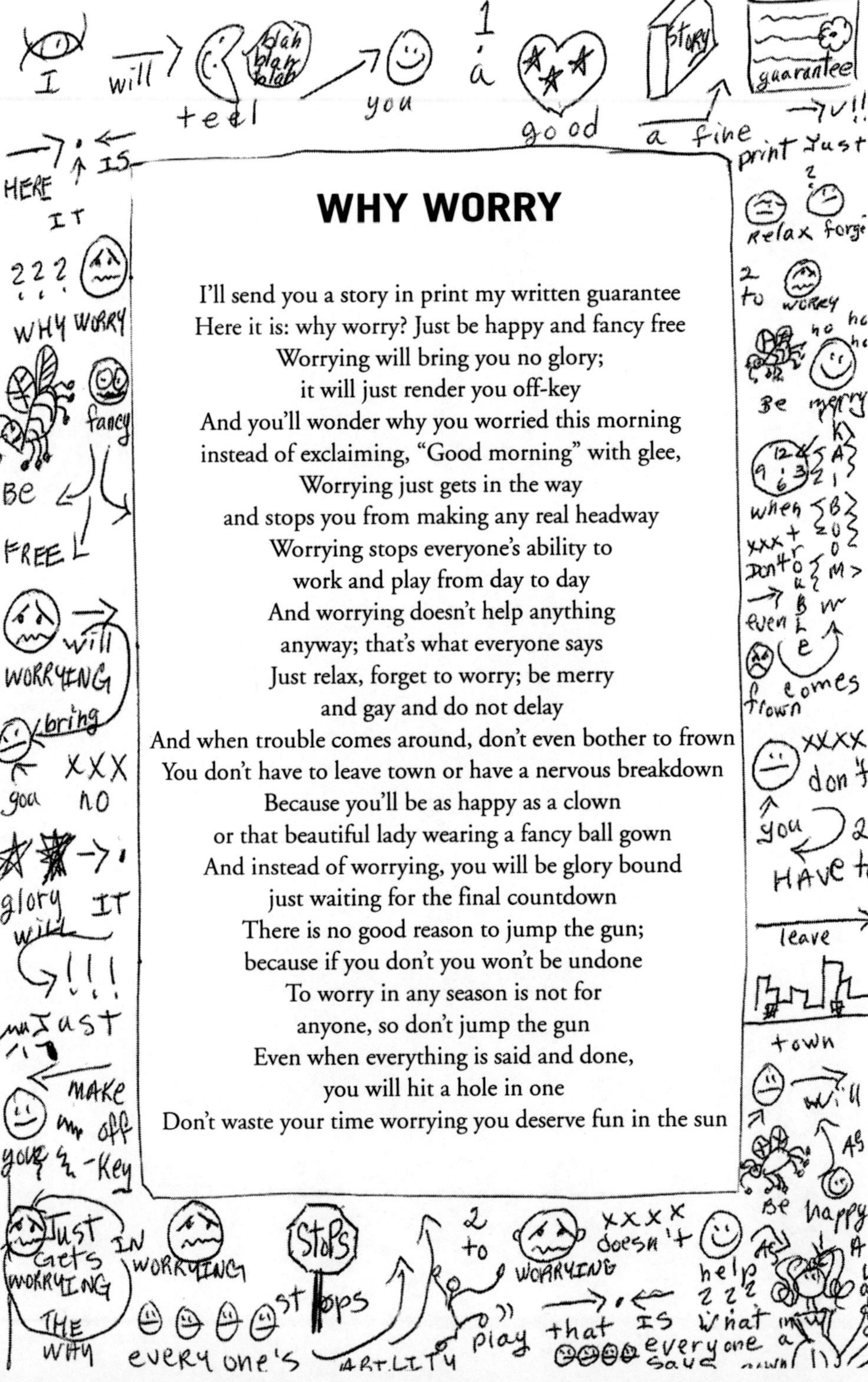

WHY WORRY

I'll send you a story in print my written guarantee
Here it is: why worry? Just be happy and fancy free
Worrying will bring you no glory;
it will just render you off-key
And you'll wonder why you worried this morning
instead of exclaiming, "Good morning" with glee,
Worrying just gets in the way
and stops you from making any real headway
Worrying stops everyone's ability to
work and play from day to day
And worrying doesn't help anything
anyway; that's what everyone says
Just relax, forget to worry; be merry
and gay and do not delay
And when trouble comes around, don't even bother to frown
You don't have to leave town or have a nervous breakdown
Because you'll be as happy as a clown
or that beautiful lady wearing a fancy ball gown
And instead of worrying, you will be glory bound
just waiting for the final countdown
There is no good reason to jump the gun;
because if you don't you won't be undone
To worry in any season is not for
anyone, so don't jump the gun
Even when everything is said and done,
you will hit a hole in one
Don't waste your time worrying you deserve fun in the sun

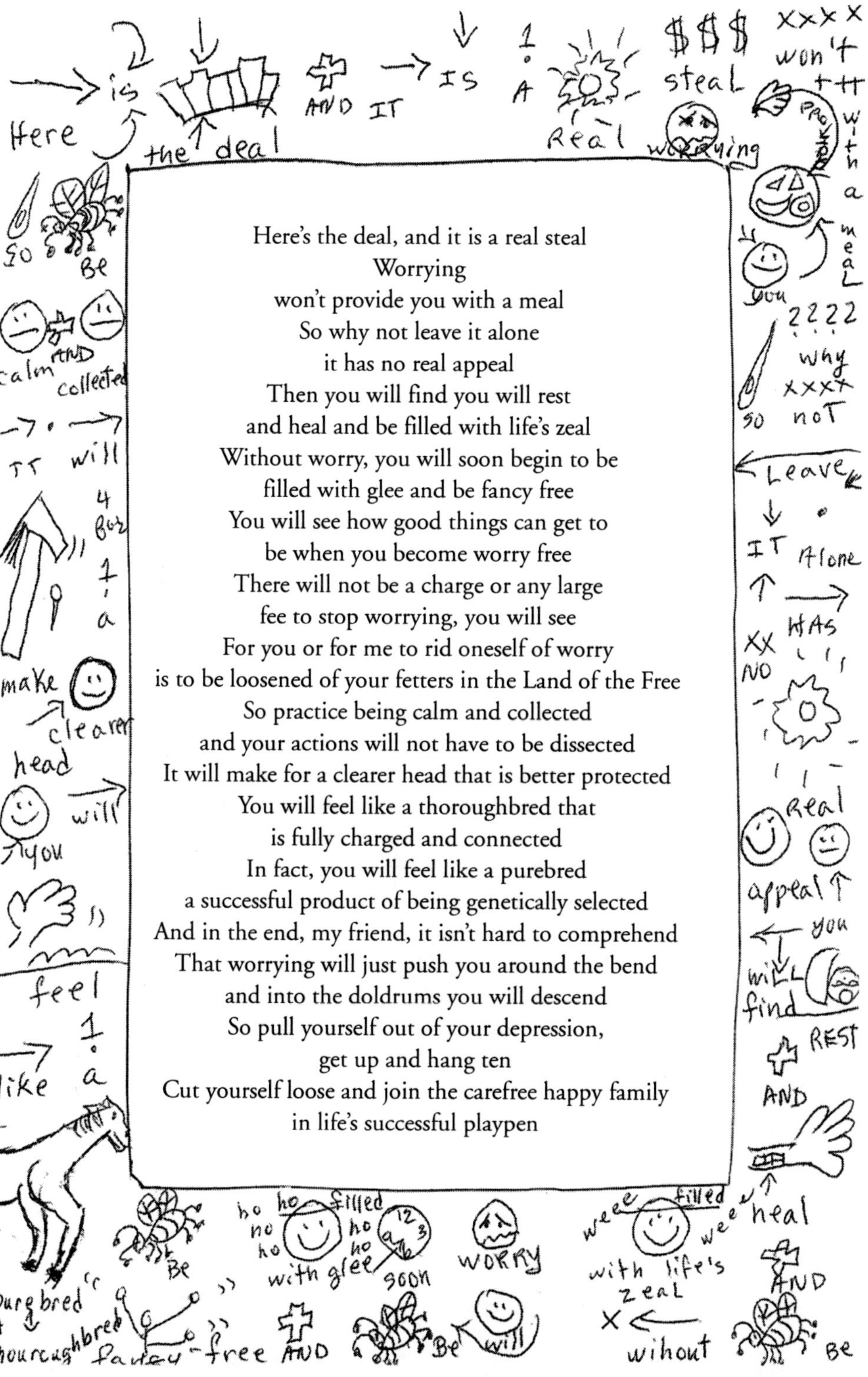

Here's the deal, and it is a real steal
Worrying
won't provide you with a meal
So why not leave it alone
it has no real appeal
Then you will find you will rest
and heal and be filled with life's zeal
Without worry, you will soon begin to be
filled with glee and be fancy free
You will see how good things can get to
be when you become worry free
There will not be a charge or any large
fee to stop worrying, you will see
For you or for me to rid oneself of worry
is to be loosened of your fetters in the Land of the Free
So practice being calm and collected
and your actions will not have to be dissected
It will make for a clearer head that is better protected
You will feel like a thoroughbred that
is fully charged and connected
In fact, you will feel like a purebred
a successful product of being genetically selected
And in the end, my friend, it isn't hard to comprehend
That worrying will just push you around the bend
and into the doldrums you will descend
So pull yourself out of your depression,
get up and hang ten
Cut yourself loose and join the carefree happy family
in life's successful playpen

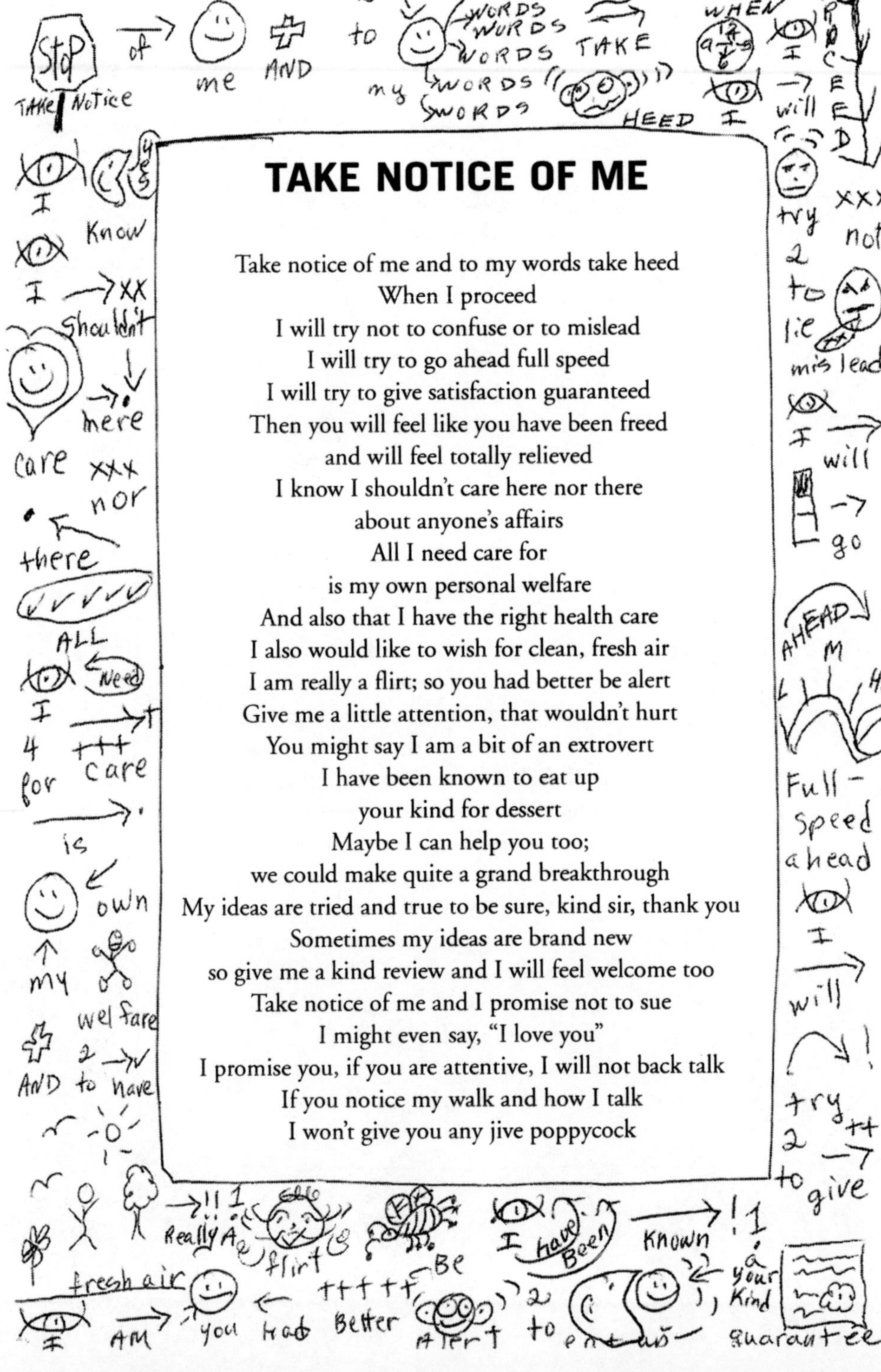

TAKE NOTICE OF ME

Take notice of me and to my words take heed
When I proceed
I will try not to confuse or to mislead
I will try to go ahead full speed
I will try to give satisfaction guaranteed
Then you will feel like you have been freed
and will feel totally relieved
I know I shouldn't care here nor there
about anyone's affairs
All I need care for
is my own personal welfare
And also that I have the right health care
I also would like to wish for clean, fresh air
I am really a flirt; so you had better be alert
Give me a little attention, that wouldn't hurt
You might say I am a bit of an extrovert
I have been known to eat up
your kind for dessert
Maybe I can help you too;
we could make quite a grand breakthrough
My ideas are tried and true to be sure, kind sir, thank you
Sometimes my ideas are brand new
so give me a kind review and I will feel welcome too
Take notice of me and I promise not to sue
I might even say, "I love you"
I promise you, if you are attentive, I will not back talk
If you notice my walk and how I talk
I won't give you any jive poppycock

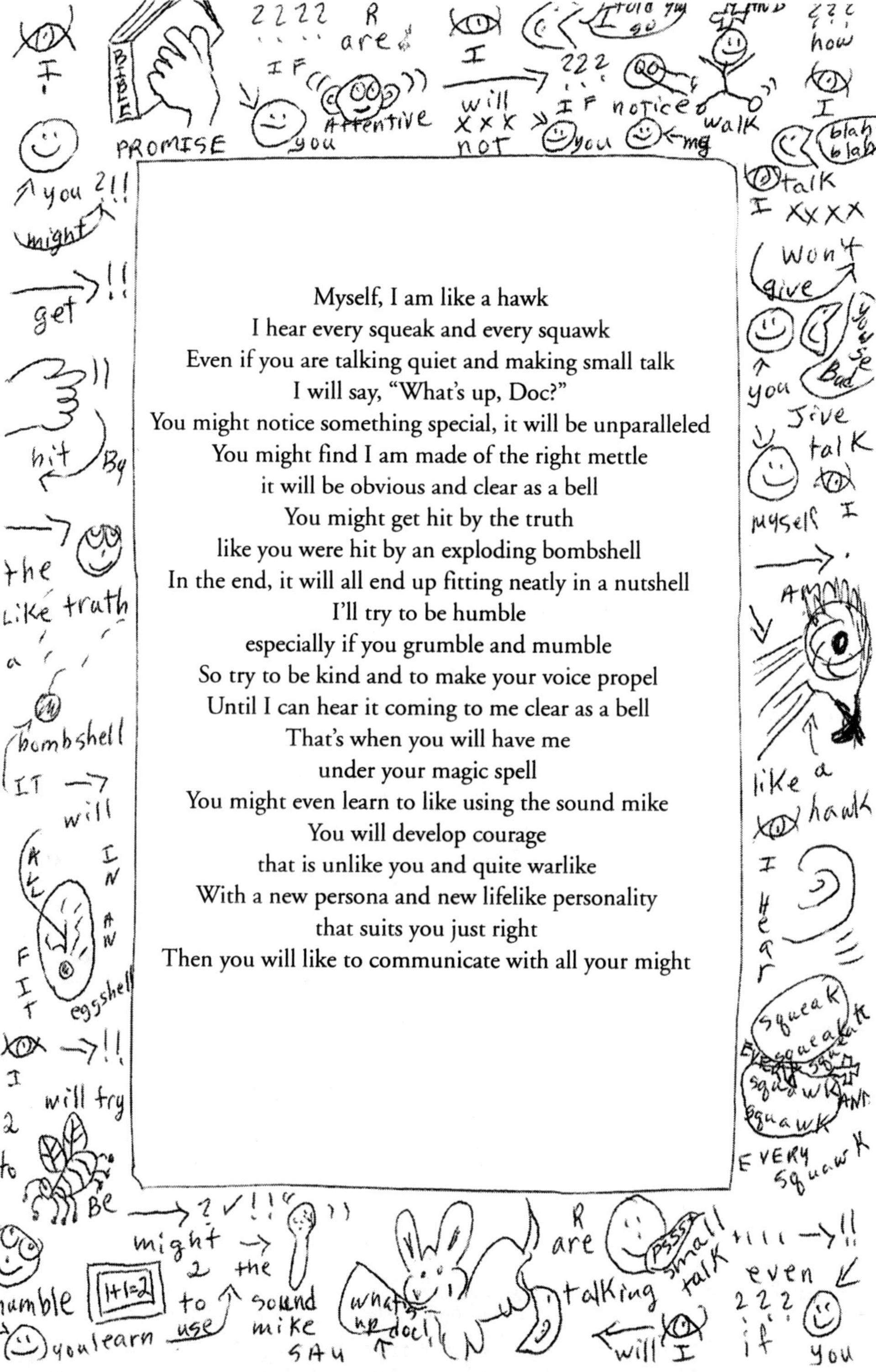

Myself, I am like a hawk
I hear every squeak and every squawk
Even if you are talking quiet and making small talk
I will say, "What's up, Doc?"
You might notice something special, it will be unparalleled
You might find I am made of the right mettle
it will be obvious and clear as a bell
You might get hit by the truth
like you were hit by an exploding bombshell
In the end, it will all end up fitting neatly in a nutshell
I'll try to be humble
especially if you grumble and mumble
So try to be kind and to make your voice propel
Until I can hear it coming to me clear as a bell
That's when you will have me
under your magic spell
You might even learn to like using the sound mike
You will develop courage
that is unlike you and quite warlike
With a new persona and new lifelike personality
that suits you just right
Then you will like to communicate with all your might

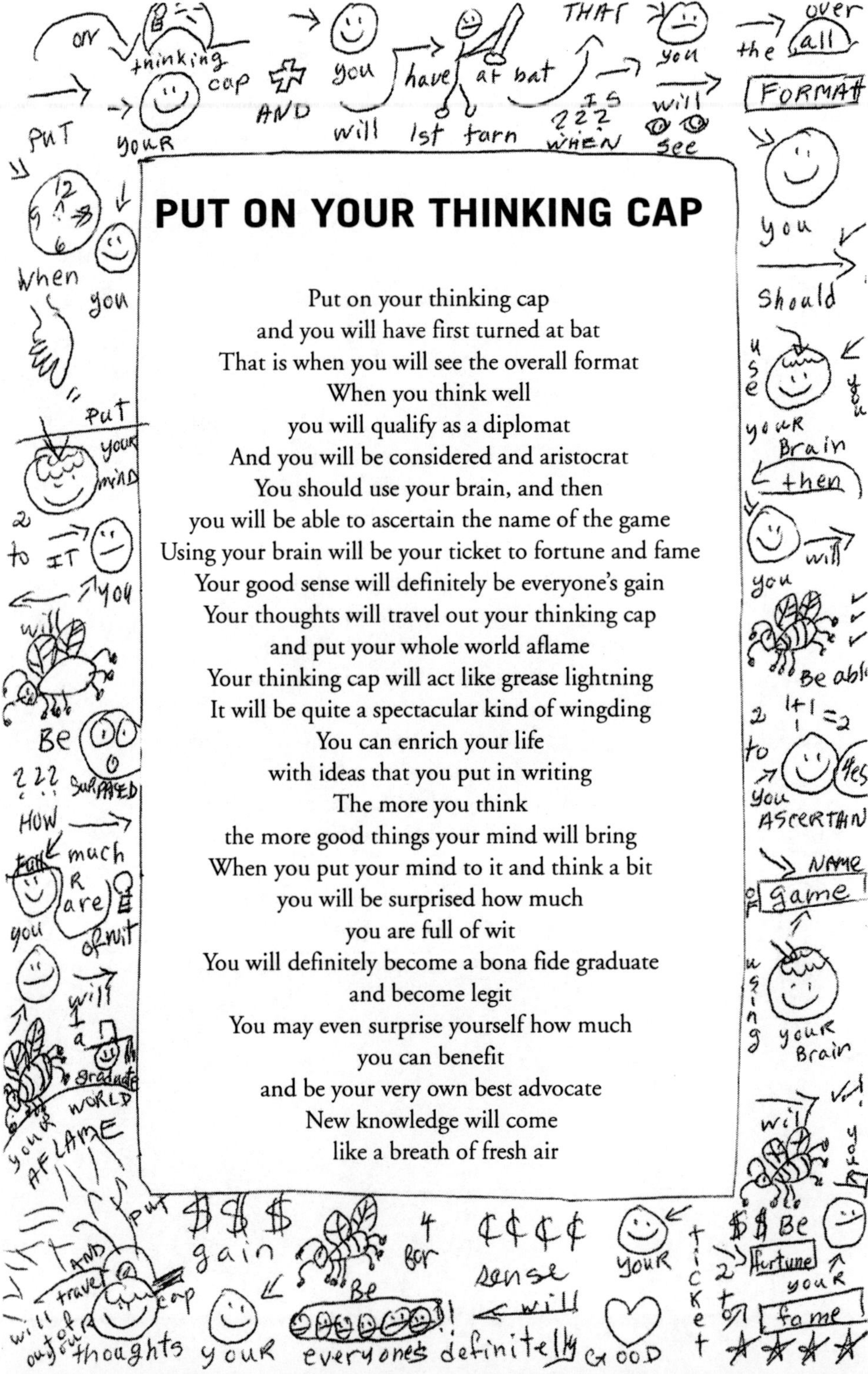

PUT ON YOUR THINKING CAP

Put on your thinking cap
and you will have first turned at bat
That is when you will see the overall format
When you think well
you will qualify as a diplomat
And you will be considered and aristocrat
You should use your brain, and then
you will be able to ascertain the name of the game
Using your brain will be your ticket to fortune and fame
Your good sense will definitely be everyone's gain
Your thoughts will travel out your thinking cap
and put your whole world aflame
Your thinking cap will act like grease lightning
It will be quite a spectacular kind of wingding
You can enrich your life
with ideas that you put in writing
The more you think
the more good things your mind will bring
When you put your mind to it and think a bit
you will be surprised how much
you are full of wit
You will definitely become a bona fide graduate
and become legit
You may even surprise yourself how much
you can benefit
and be your very own best advocate
New knowledge will come
like a breath of fresh air

It'll come from the fairest winds so rare
They will be winds of change
without worries or cares
They will gain strength
instead of just sitting there
New ideas can be your best friends
They can improve our lives
again and again
You'll enjoy how they can help you
explain from beginning to end
It can mean the difference
from having to depend and
in contrast being able to transcend
What is really, really nice
is when we can invent
some type of paradise
we can help by being more concise
You will be able to give better advice
When you think clearly
you will find a great deal
of fulfillment and that will be nice
It is the best feeling
to help someone
With an idea that you have begun
It is the greatest possible
pleasure and fun
To do good things when
you are under a warm, warm sun

LOAN SHARK

If you were smart
You would have no part
Of the man
called the loan shark
He'll cut you up—
straight to your heart
He'll call you his friend
But he'll have
your skin in the end
I'll tell you
again and again
You shouldn't take
what he lends
You might lose an arm or a leg
If you double cross him;
he will show everyone
your blood is not blue but red
Or you might even
lose your head
You will end up easily led
or even dead instead
Tell me is it really worth it
Do you want to be
an easy hit?
Or part of someone's
murder kit

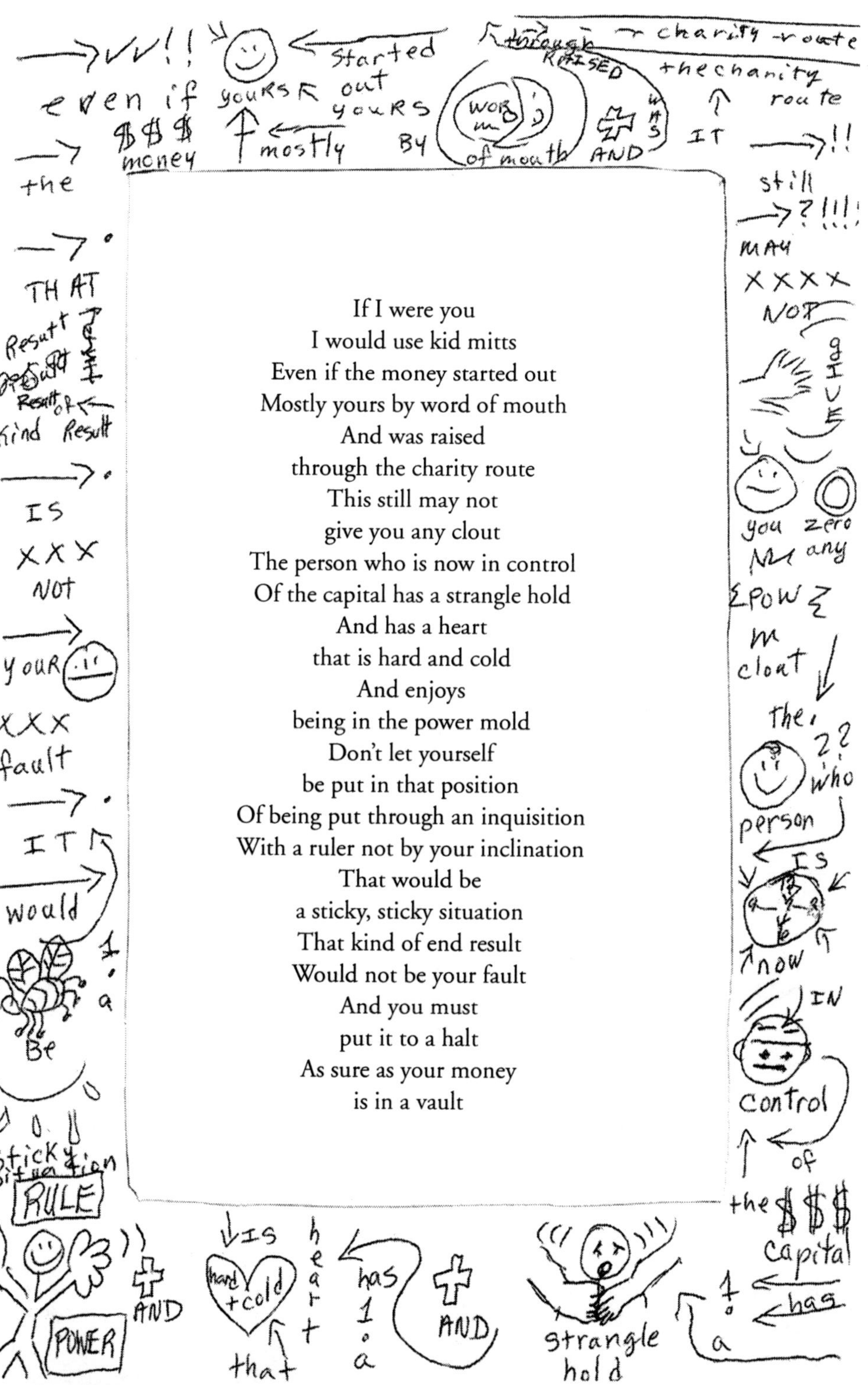

If I were you
I would use kid mitts
Even if the money started out
Mostly yours by word of mouth
And was raised
through the charity route
This still may not
give you any clout
The person who is now in control
Of the capital has a strangle hold
And has a heart
that is hard and cold
And enjoys
being in the power mold
Don't let yourself
be put in that position
Of being put through an inquisition
With a ruler not by your inclination
That would be
a sticky, sticky situation
That kind of end result
Would not be your fault
And you must
put it to a halt
As sure as your money
is in a vault

MY SILKY, SNOW-WHITE STALLION

Who's that peeking around the corner? Could
it be a distinguished famous emperor?
Something is definitely astir
No, it is the Silky, Snow-White Stallion himself
saying, "If you please, come on over."
He is lanky and gorgeously kind and tantalizing,
with plenty of good advice, moreover
He is still gentle and carries himself well,
better than that famous person, Ben-Her
He is wiser than his years and one of the best in his
chosen career—many times a discoverer and a pioneer
He helps you through your fears, and he
knows how to clear the atmosphere
and make himself known, loud and clear
He brings you through your fears, listens
intently, and manages to be totally sincere
He is better than a dozen beers and is the best
psychology engineer—do I make myself crystal clear?
I love this man, I don't really
understand; mainly because
he is like a friend willing to give a helping hand
He is a furry, fluffy ball of love that is in great demand
and is first in the chain of command
He is my constant strength and companion whom
I totally respect, with no room to misunderstand
He is my friend who has guided me and my champion
he is also far from his homeland

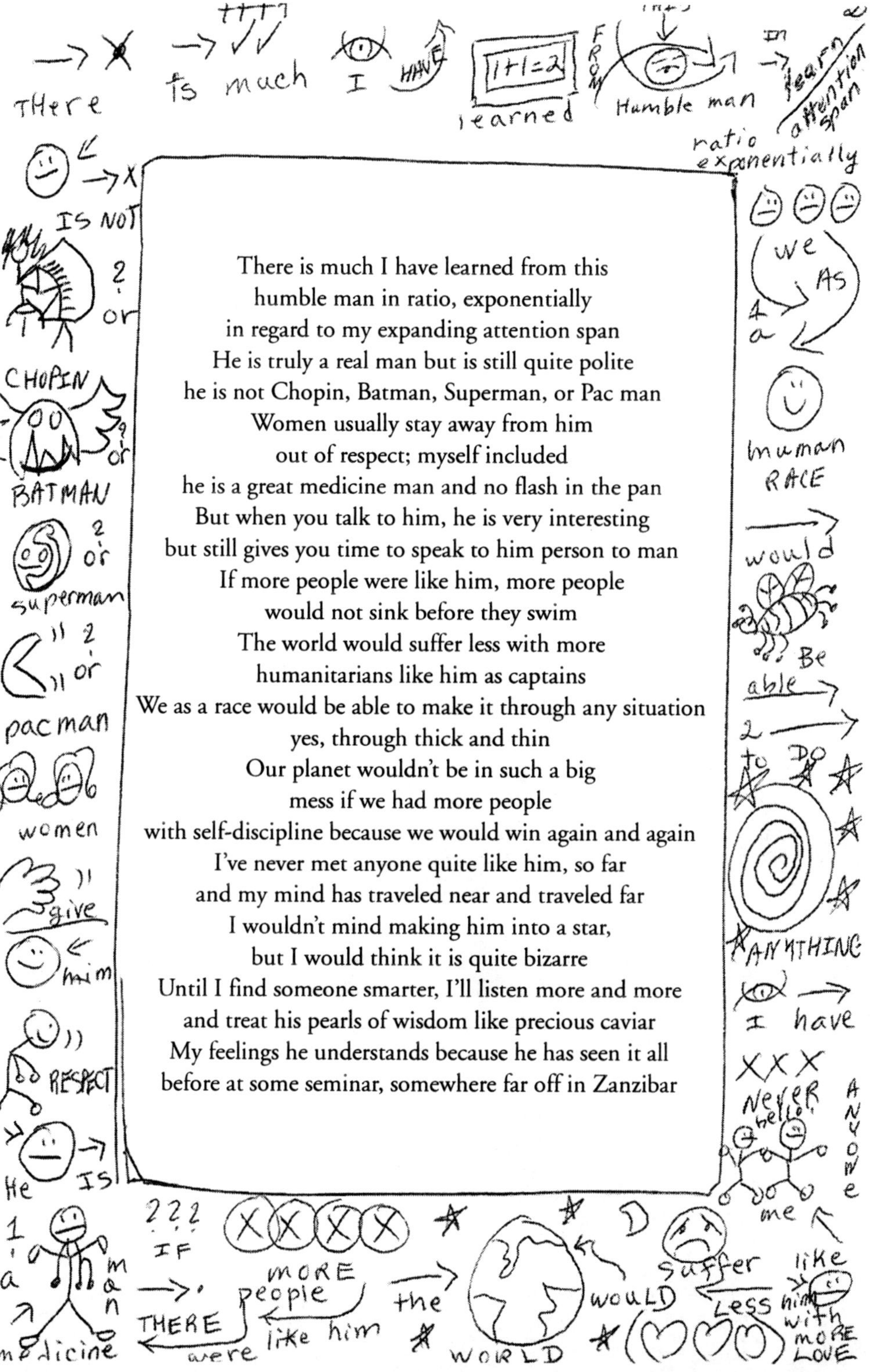

There is much I have learned from this
humble man in ratio, exponentially
in regard to my expanding attention span
He is truly a real man but is still quite polite
he is not Chopin, Batman, Superman, or Pac man
Women usually stay away from him
out of respect; myself included
he is a great medicine man and no flash in the pan
But when you talk to him, he is very interesting
but still gives you time to speak to him person to man
If more people were like him, more people
would not sink before they swim
The world would suffer less with more
humanitarians like him as captains
We as a race would be able to make it through any situation
yes, through thick and thin
Our planet wouldn't be in such a big
mess if we had more people
with self-discipline because we would win again and again
I've never met anyone quite like him, so far
and my mind has traveled near and traveled far
I wouldn't mind making him into a star,
but I would think it is quite bizarre
Until I find someone smarter, I'll listen more and more
and treat his pearls of wisdom like precious caviar
My feelings he understands because he has seen it all
before at some seminar, somewhere far off in Zanzibar

HOLD ME TIGHT

Hold me tight for you, I will dress in white
I won't put up a fight; I will be yours tonight
It is bound to feel right
the whole deal seems airtight
Give me a little hug, give me a little bite
don't pretend to be contrite
We could find some pleasure because you're him or her
We could find a newfound treasure
and at the same time make our motors purr
It wouldn't hurt in any measure
if I was your queen and you were my emperor
We could fit into a comfortable nighttime of leisure;
and you could feel as important as Ben-Her
And when I'm in your arms
I will be able to enjoy all your masterful charms
I will squeeze you until you are warm
I know I will cause you no harm
Maybe then you will conform; it will not be a false alarm
And you will be like a newborn
you will also be my lucky charm
The real test will be when I will be holding you to my breast
And when I will be with you, no jest, as you have guessed
I will not be distressed
You could be the very best
you are my most important conquest
I want you in my arms and with zest;
life with you will be like living in the
best part of the Wild West
Hold me, or I will put you over my knee

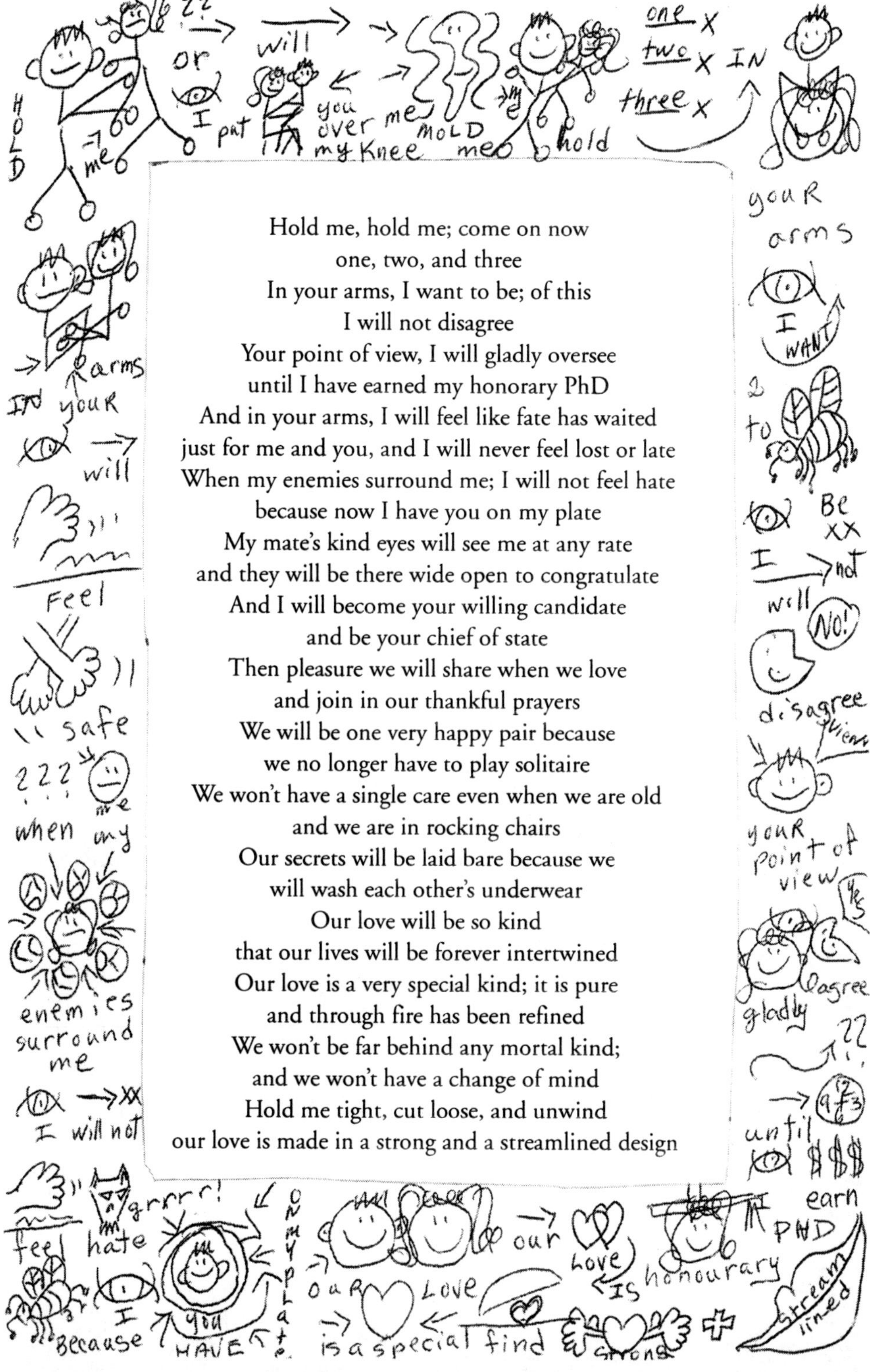

Hold me, hold me; come on now
one, two, and three
In your arms, I want to be; of this
I will not disagree
Your point of view, I will gladly oversee
until I have earned my honorary PhD
And in your arms, I will feel like fate has waited
just for me and you, and I will never feel lost or late
When my enemies surround me; I will not feel hate
because now I have you on my plate
My mate's kind eyes will see me at any rate
and they will be there wide open to congratulate
And I will become your willing candidate
and be your chief of state
Then pleasure we will share when we love
and join in our thankful prayers
We will be one very happy pair because
we no longer have to play solitaire
We won't have a single care even when we are old
and we are in rocking chairs
Our secrets will be laid bare because we
will wash each other's underwear
Our love will be so kind
that our lives will be forever intertwined
Our love is a very special kind; it is pure
and through fire has been refined
We won't be far behind any mortal kind;
and we won't have a change of mind
Hold me tight, cut loose, and unwind
our love is made in a strong and a streamlined design

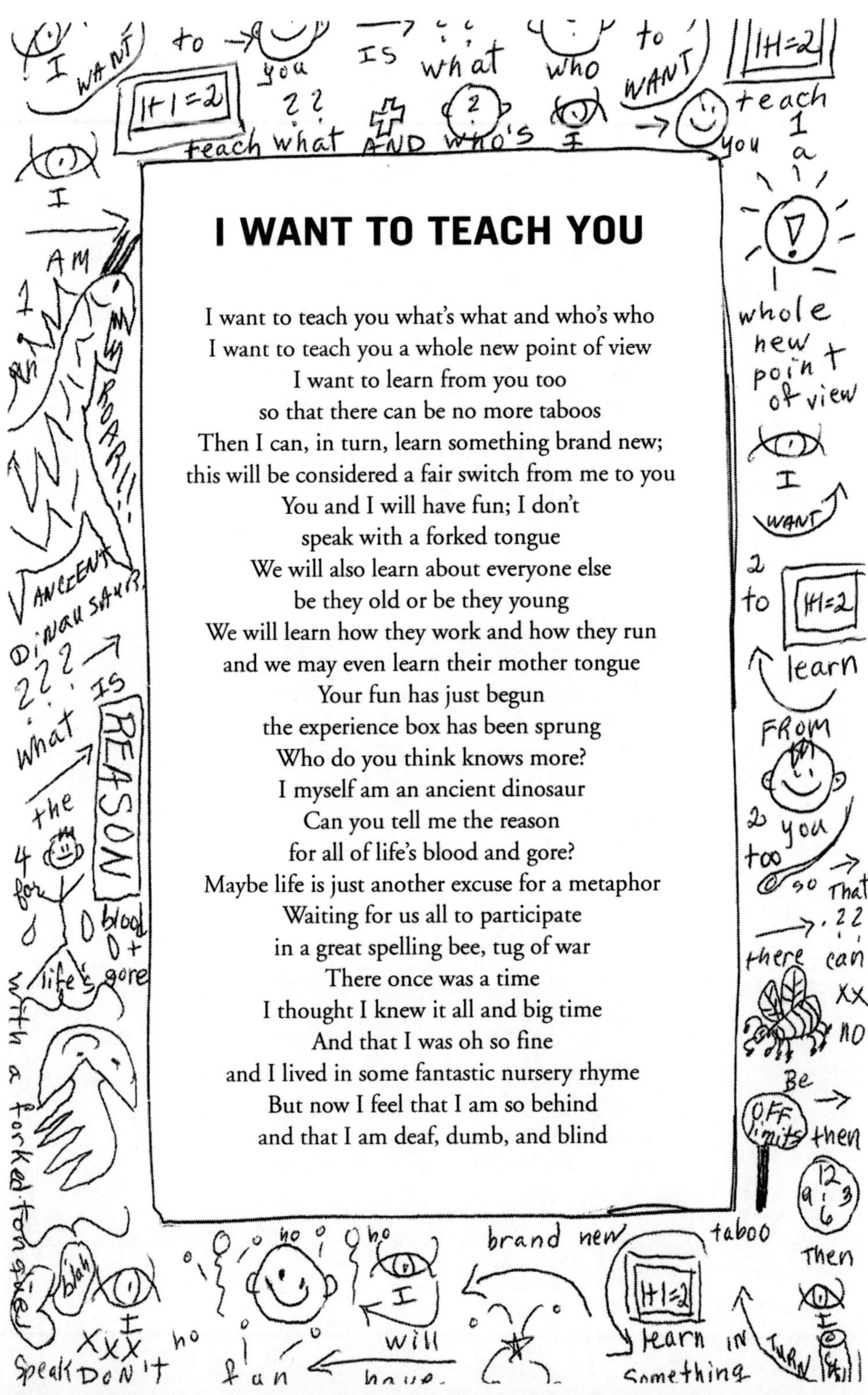

I WANT TO TEACH YOU

I want to teach you what's what and who's who
I want to teach you a whole new point of view
I want to learn from you too
so that there can be no more taboos
Then I can, in turn, learn something brand new;
this will be considered a fair switch from me to you
You and I will have fun; I don't
speak with a forked tongue
We will also learn about everyone else
be they old or be they young
We will learn how they work and how they run
and we may even learn their mother tongue
Your fun has just begun
the experience box has been sprung
Who do you think knows more?
I myself am an ancient dinosaur
Can you tell me the reason
for all of life's blood and gore?
Maybe life is just another excuse for a metaphor
Waiting for us all to participate
in a great spelling bee, tug of war
There once was a time
I thought I knew it all and big time
And that I was oh so fine
and I lived in some fantastic nursery rhyme
But now I feel that I am so behind
and that I am deaf, dumb, and blind

And every day is an impossible mountain to climb
So you see, it is I who feel like an uneducated monkey
You are the one who can teach me;
what it is to be an educated VIP
Listening will be the other key along with vision;
it will increase my knowledge to the nth degree
Then I too, will know what will be;
and I will finally be able to open my eyes and see
Whatever else I happen to know will
combine to give me get up and go
It also will impart in me with that glow like
I am the winner of a game show
I will have a certain ebb and flow, and I
will feel as strong as a dynamo
Only a teacher could help me grow any
smarter so I can be in the know
We'll give each other seeds of knowledge
that will make us stronger
The knowledge will satisfy our needs
and we won't struggle any longer
We will give each other leads that will get us out of hot water
We will pay attention to all the answers
because they really are important and they matter
Then we will go our way, all happy, merry, and gay
We won't have another thing to say
but we will know how to play
We will get better every day;
we will have perfected our methods, in every way
Then we won't complain
but we will thank our lucky stars every single today

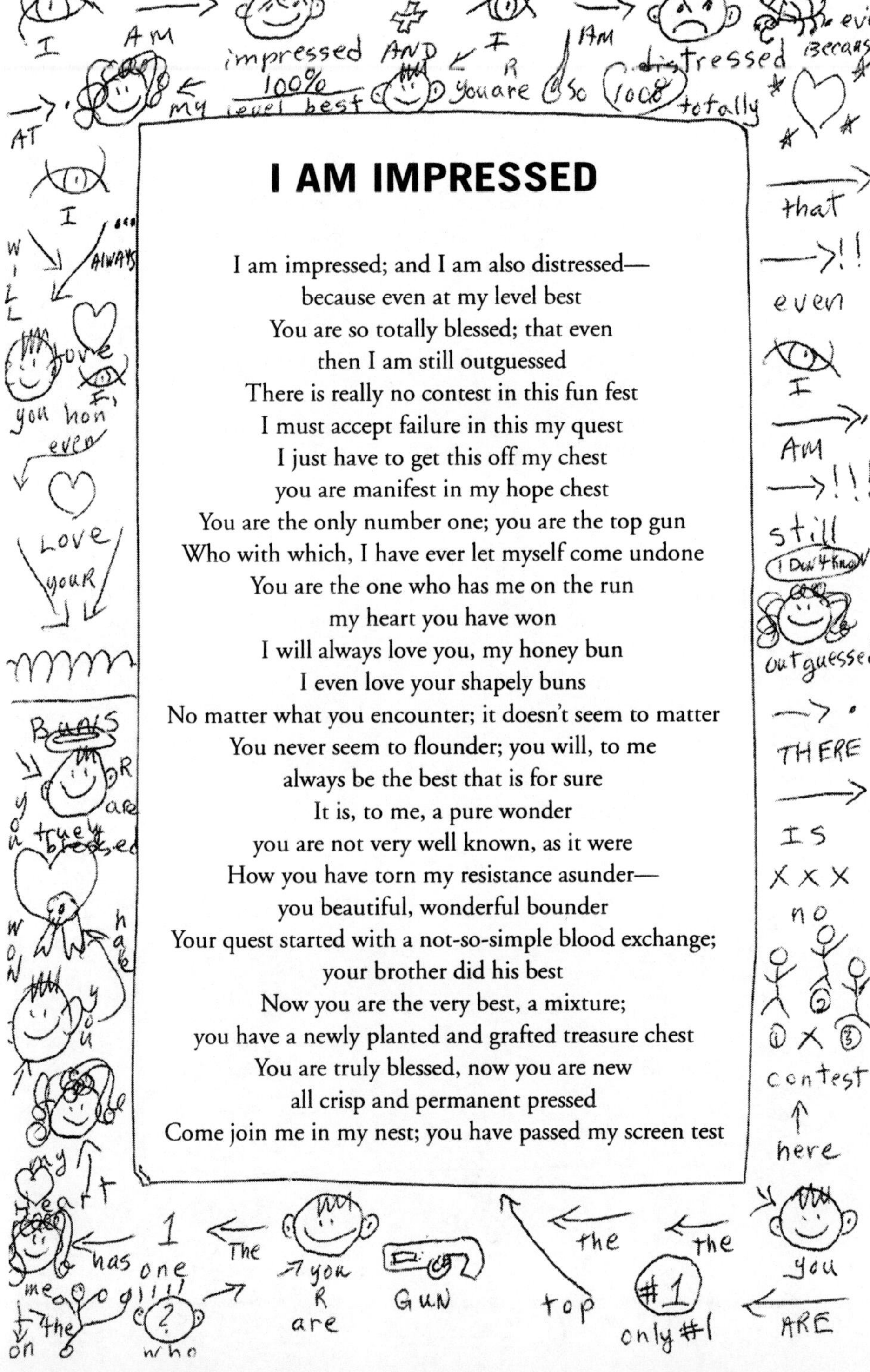

I AM IMPRESSED

I am impressed; and I am also distressed—
because even at my level best
You are so totally blessed; that even
then I am still outguessed
There is really no contest in this fun fest
I must accept failure in this my quest
I just have to get this off my chest
you are manifest in my hope chest
You are the only number one; you are the top gun
Who with which, I have ever let myself come undone
You are the one who has me on the run
my heart you have won
I will always love you, my honey bun
I even love your shapely buns
No matter what you encounter; it doesn't seem to matter
You never seem to flounder; you will, to me
always be the best that is for sure
It is, to me, a pure wonder
you are not very well known, as it were
How you have torn my resistance asunder—
you beautiful, wonderful bounder
Your quest started with a not-so-simple blood exchange;
your brother did his best
Now you are the very best, a mixture;
you have a newly planted and grafted treasure chest
You are truly blessed, now you are new
all crisp and permanent pressed
Come join me in my nest; you have passed my screen test

It is funny, fee-fie-foe fum, and fiddle-Dee-Dee-Dee
When I think of you, the world is sunny
and my eyes open wide and I can see
Then I don't need much money to please me
When I'm apart from you, all I can do
is think of you honey; you fill my heart with glee
With you, my days are happy
and my life is filled with daylight
And everything seems right; you are so polite
you could have been Snow White
I look forward to night; you are liquid dynamite
And to have you in my sights
is definitely one of life's highlights
I couldn't have known in my overall lowdown
That someday, you would phone
me in my very small town
Or you would come to my home
of no particular renown
Or that, you would have my heart on loan
sunny side up and upside down
I have never been so happy to be single and free
Now with you by my side, I love you madly;
and I will always want you badly
I will stay with you forever, gladly
and be glad to act silly and love happy
It can't be bad even though I love you so badly
if it is, all I can say is, "Pardon me."

AN ODE TO A VERB

Jack walks
Jill talks

Jack jogs
Jill sings

Jack runs
Jill yells

Jack falls
Jill screams

Jack cries
Jill laughs

Jack goes
Jill scoffs

Jack laughs
Jill is puzzled

Jack tries
Jill succumbs

Jack chokes
Jill coughs

Jack stomps
Jill writes

Jack plays
Jill works

Jack hurts
Jill soothes

Jack acts
Jill pleads

Jack asks
Jill tells

Jack exists
Jill loves

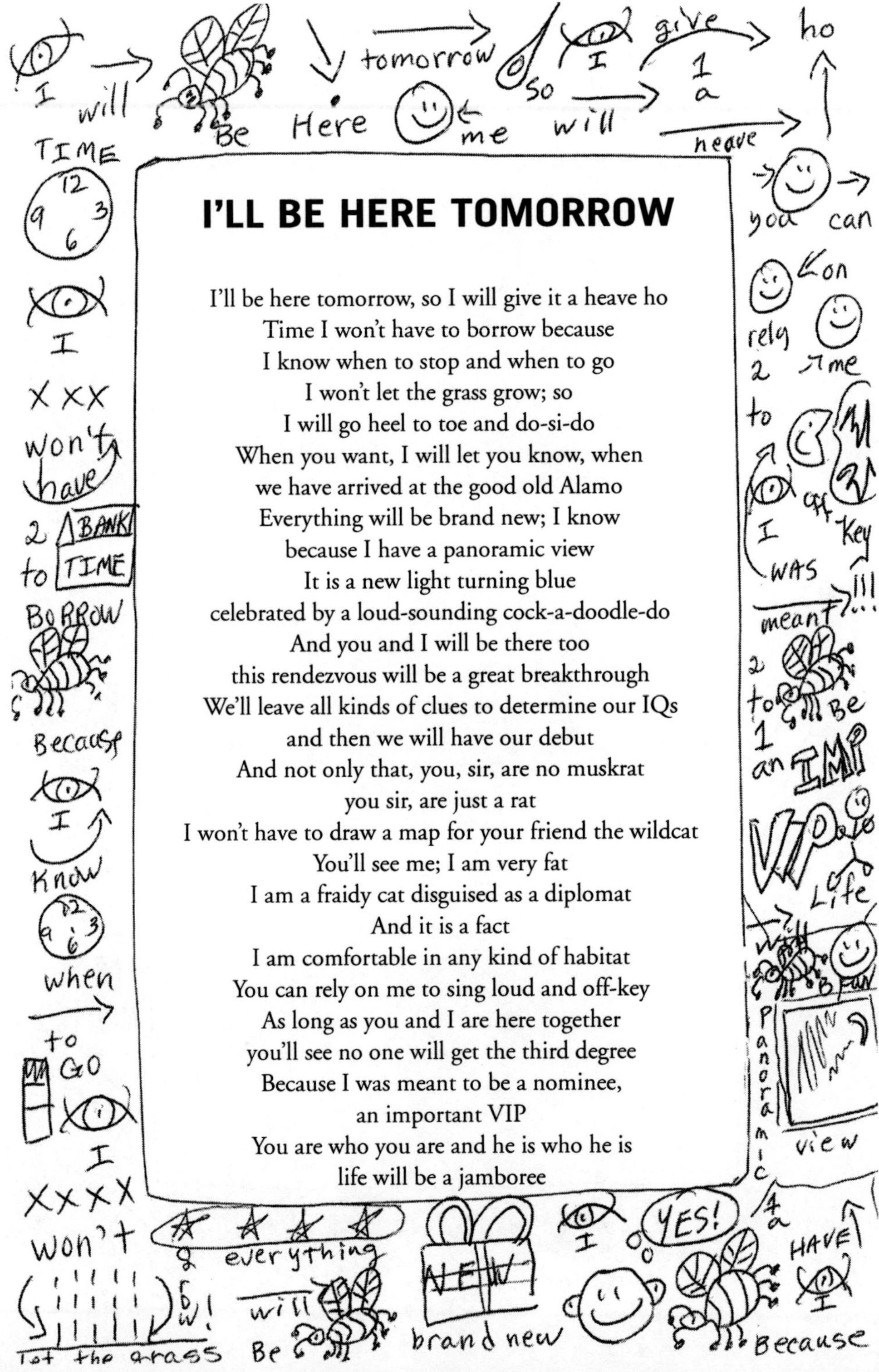

I'LL BE HERE TOMORROW

I'll be here tomorrow, so I will give it a heave ho
Time I won't have to borrow because
I know when to stop and when to go
I won't let the grass grow; so
I will go heel to toe and do-si-do
When you want, I will let you know, when
we have arrived at the good old Alamo
Everything will be brand new; I know
because I have a panoramic view
It is a new light turning blue
celebrated by a loud-sounding cock-a-doodle-do
And you and I will be there too
this rendezvous will be a great breakthrough
We'll leave all kinds of clues to determine our IQs
and then we will have our debut
And not only that, you, sir, are no muskrat
you sir, are just a rat
I won't have to draw a map for your friend the wildcat
You'll see me; I am very fat
I am a fraidy cat disguised as a diplomat
And it is a fact
I am comfortable in any kind of habitat
You can rely on me to sing loud and off-key
As long as you and I are here together
you'll see no one will get the third degree
Because I was meant to be a nominee,
an important VIP
You are who you are and he is who he is
life will be a jamboree

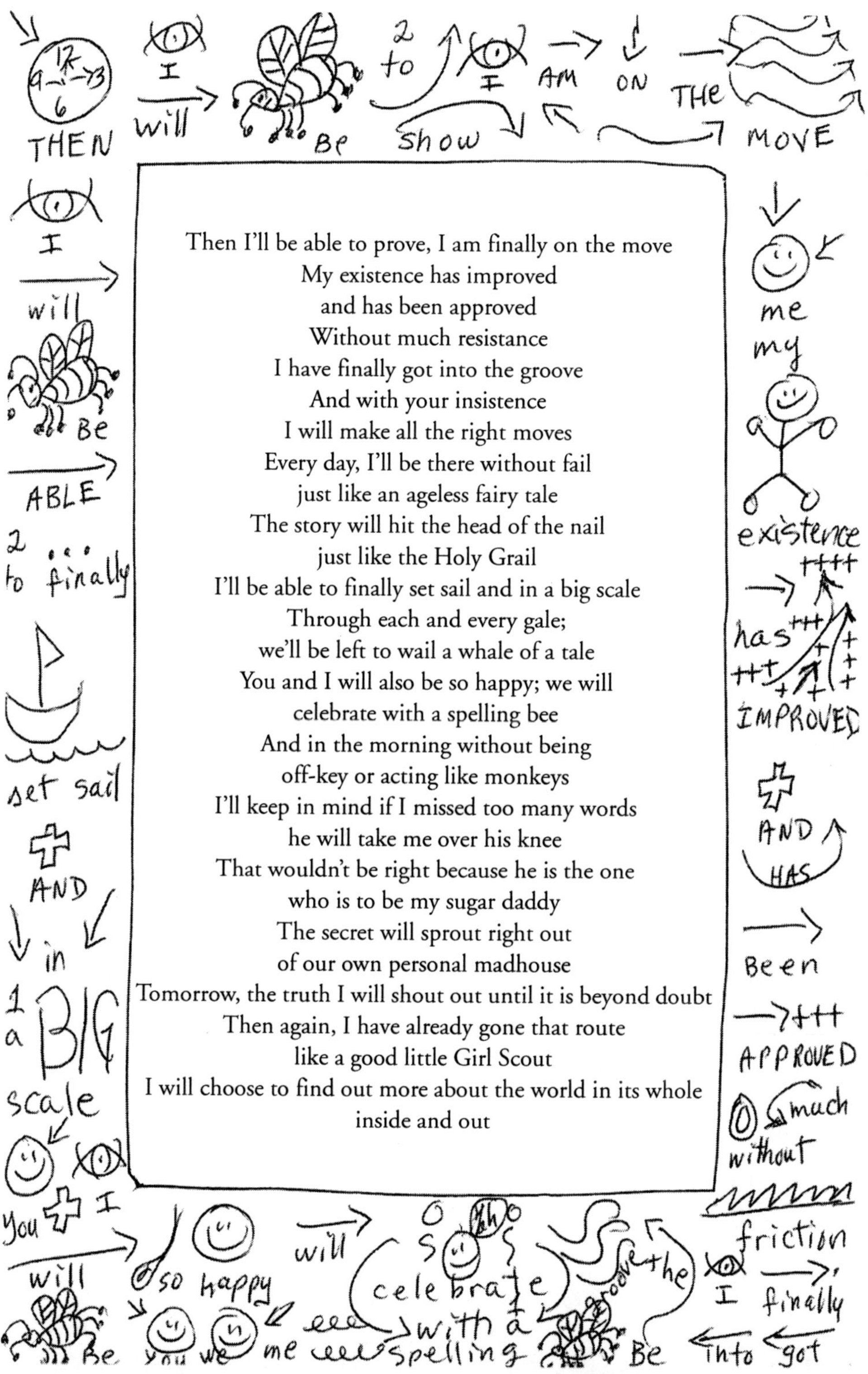

Then I'll be able to prove, I am finally on the move
My existence has improved
and has been approved
Without much resistance
I have finally got into the groove
And with your insistence
I will make all the right moves
Every day, I'll be there without fail
just like an ageless fairy tale
The story will hit the head of the nail
just like the Holy Grail
I'll be able to finally set sail and in a big scale
Through each and every gale;
we'll be left to wail a whale of a tale
You and I will also be so happy; we will
celebrate with a spelling bee
And in the morning without being
off-key or acting like monkeys
I'll keep in mind if I missed too many words
he will take me over his knee
That wouldn't be right because he is the one
who is to be my sugar daddy
The secret will sprout right out
of our own personal madhouse
Tomorrow, the truth I will shout out until it is beyond doubt
Then again, I have already gone that route
like a good little Girl Scout
I will choose to find out more about the world in its whole
inside and out

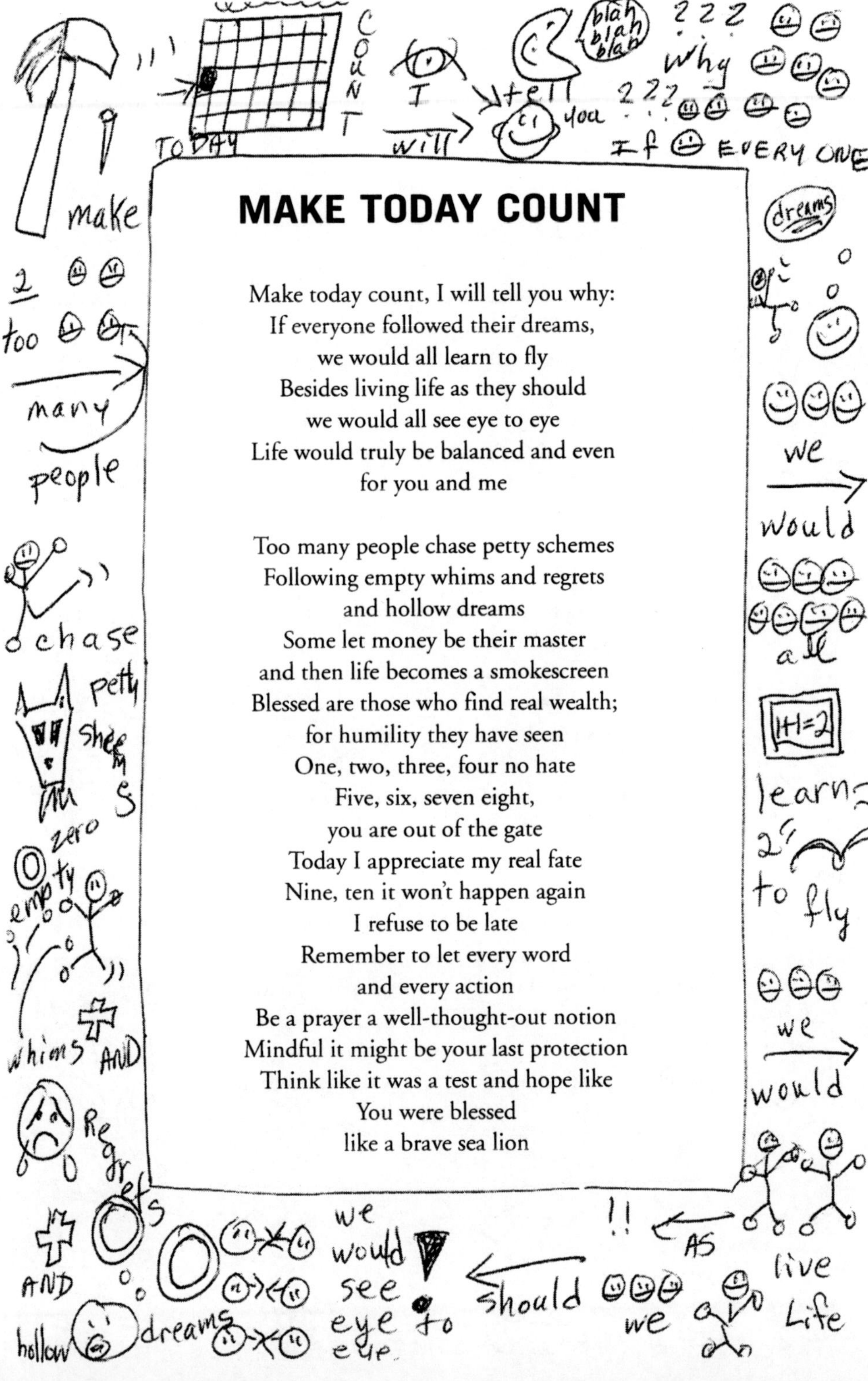

MAKE TODAY COUNT

Make today count, I will tell you why:
If everyone followed their dreams,
we would all learn to fly
Besides living life as they should
we would all see eye to eye
Life would truly be balanced and even
for you and me

Too many people chase petty schemes
Following empty whims and regrets
and hollow dreams
Some let money be their master
and then life becomes a smokescreen
Blessed are those who find real wealth;
for humility they have seen
One, two, three, four no hate
Five, six, seven eight,
you are out of the gate
Today I appreciate my real fate
Nine, ten it won't happen again
I refuse to be late
Remember to let every word
and every action
Be a prayer a well-thought-out notion
Mindful it might be your last protection
Think like it was a test and hope like
You were blessed
like a brave sea lion

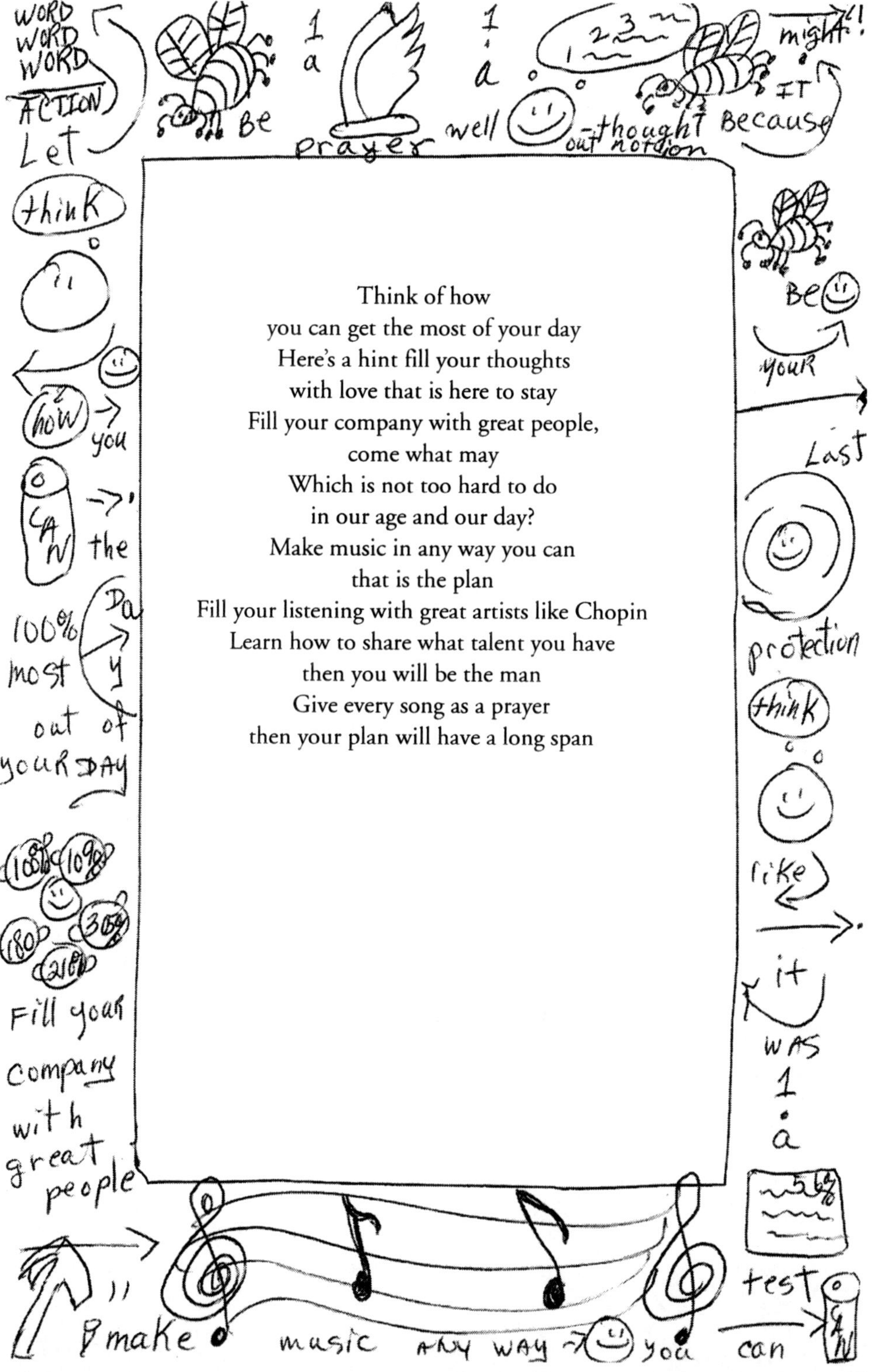

Think of how
you can get the most of your day
Here's a hint fill your thoughts
with love that is here to stay
Fill your company with great people,
come what may
Which is not too hard to do
in our age and our day?
Make music in any way you can
that is the plan
Fill your listening with great artists like Chopin
Learn how to share what talent you have
then you will be the man
Give every song as a prayer
then your plan will have a long span

YOU TEASE

You are nothing but a tease
To you life is
nothing but a breeze
Does anyone want ham
or a big cheese?
Do you care
if anyone is ill at ease?
You just tease, tease, and tease
Just say it
please, please, please
Otherwise, you will regret it;
so go ahead
and freeze, freeze, freeze
Didn't I say it,
golly geez, geez, geez?
You should handle your affection
with greater care
Or someone will play with you truth or dare
They will use your heart
and you will find a snare
All of the sudden, you will be
the one who cares
You will find the tables are suddenly turned
And you are being teased
and the one being burned

You'll be left in a lurch
left to pine and yearn
And never get to a church
you will live and learn
The foot will belong to the other guy
And your face will be
the one covered with pie
You will end up with
mud in your eye
And your enemies will
hang you to dry
Then you will finally know
You should never
tease John Doe
And you will discover
the status quo
And you will learn
not to tease
and go all gung ho

TRUE LOVE

True love is a test
from close to the breast
And kindness is its real conquest
When you are in love
you are steadfast and true with
your love openly professed
And your loyalty is
firm and upright and your love
Is secure in its nest
When you have true love,
you must tell the truth with full speed
You must be careful
to minister to all of each other's needs
You must be considerate and be up to speed
You must be careful of all your deeds
and make sure not to mislead
When you separate from each other
you must be loyal and true
When you learn to distinguish right from wrong;
you will have a breakthrough
You will receive instead of hate a new point of view
Why must we know?
Because that is how we will grow
One must pick one feeling over the other
You must pick the feeling that is stronger

Pick love over hate,
and you will live longer
Love will not let you down;
it is the feeling that is stronger
Follow love the right path
Then you will be doing
the right math
One plus one with two
as its aftermath
L O V E spells love—
and is as happy as a
bubble bath
Following your heart is easy; so go on a love spree
But using your head at the same time
might make you queasy
It might be wise to be careful
and not to be quite so carefree
Give it a try; you might end up liking what you see
Always keep care of your love
push comes to shove
Always stand close by your turtledove
Always travel through the tunnel of love
Then you will be close
to the One from above

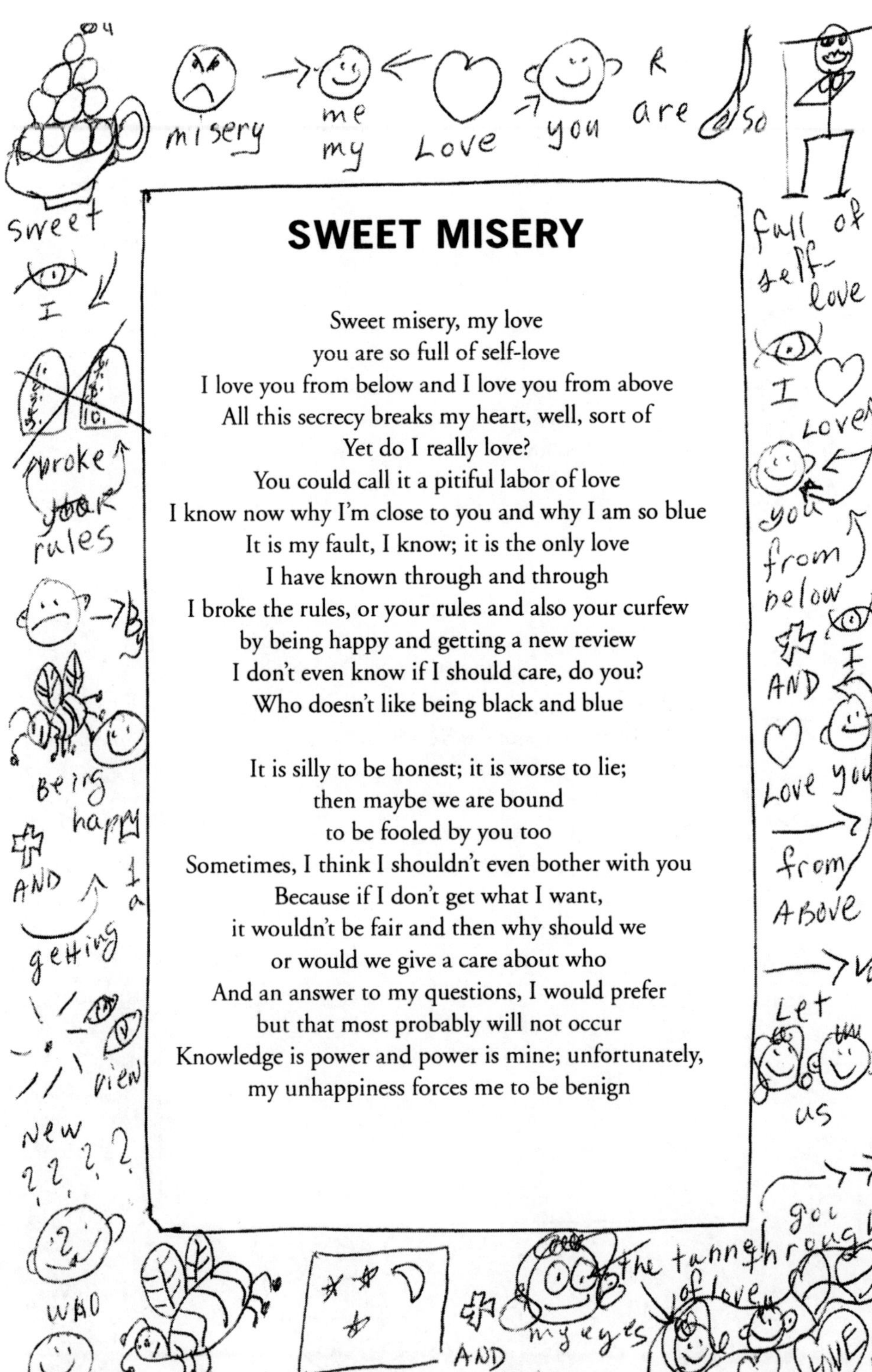

SWEET MISERY

Sweet misery, my love
you are so full of self-love
I love you from below and I love you from above
All this secrecy breaks my heart, well, sort of
Yet do I really love?
You could call it a pitiful labor of love
I know now why I'm close to you and why I am so blue
It is my fault, I know; it is the only love
I have known through and through
I broke the rules, or your rules and also your curfew
by being happy and getting a new review
I don't even know if I should care, do you?
Who doesn't like being black and blue

It is silly to be honest; it is worse to lie;
then maybe we are bound
to be fooled by you too
Sometimes, I think I shouldn't even bother with you
Because if I don't get what I want,
it wouldn't be fair and then why should we
or would we give a care about who
And an answer to my questions, I would prefer
but that most probably will not occur
Knowledge is power and power is mine; unfortunately,
my unhappiness forces me to be benign

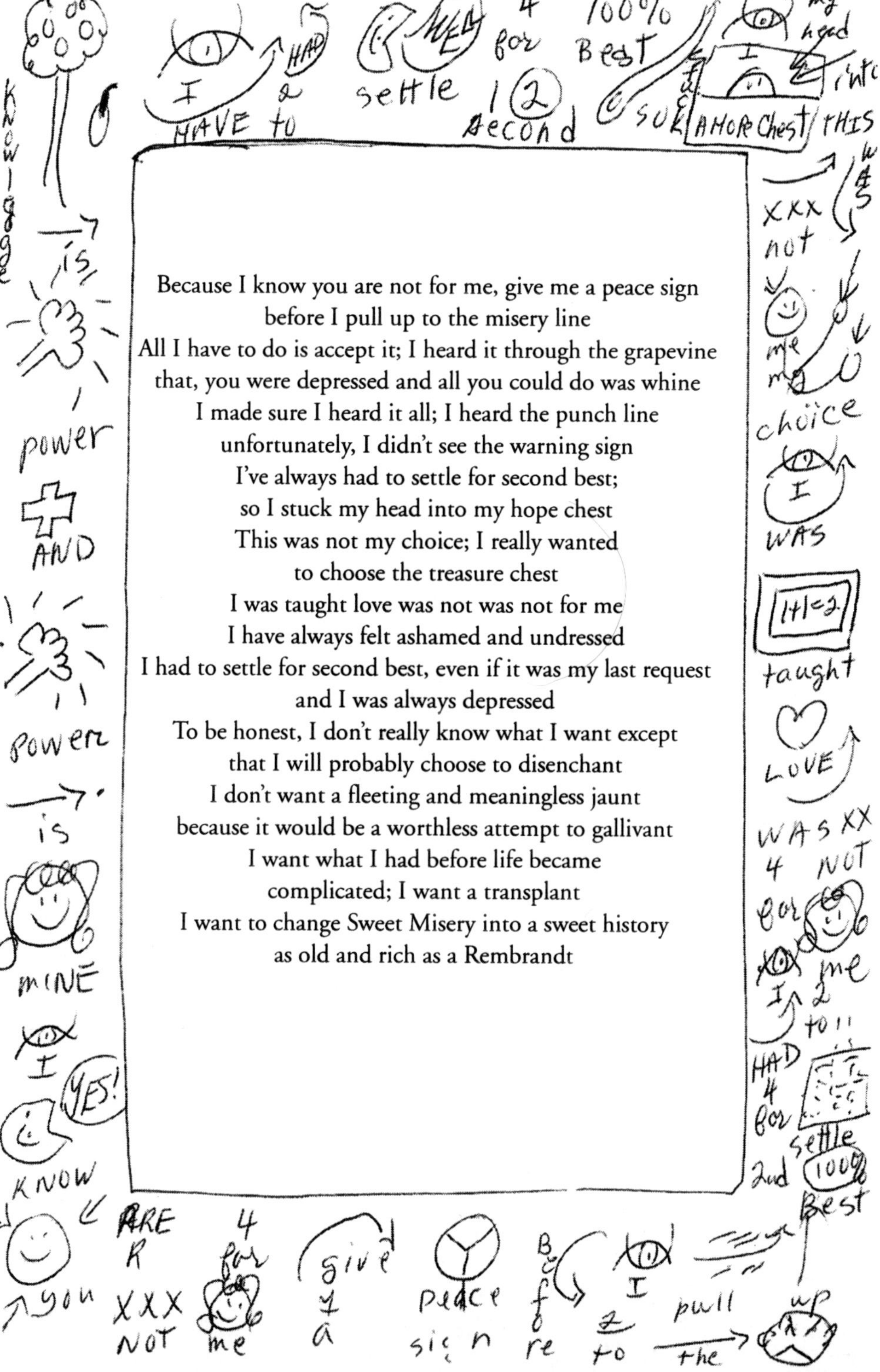

Because I know you are not for me, give me a peace sign
before I pull up to the misery line
All I have to do is accept it; I heard it through the grapevine
that, you were depressed and all you could do was whine
I made sure I heard it all; I heard the punch line
unfortunately, I didn't see the warning sign
I've always had to settle for second best;
so I stuck my head into my hope chest
This was not my choice; I really wanted
to choose the treasure chest
I was taught love was not was not for me
I have always felt ashamed and undressed
I had to settle for second best, even if it was my last request
and I was always depressed
To be honest, I don't really know what I want except
that I will probably choose to disenchant
I don't want a fleeting and meaningless jaunt
because it would be a worthless attempt to gallivant
I want what I had before life became
complicated; I want a transplant
I want to change Sweet Misery into a sweet history
as old and rich as a Rembrandt

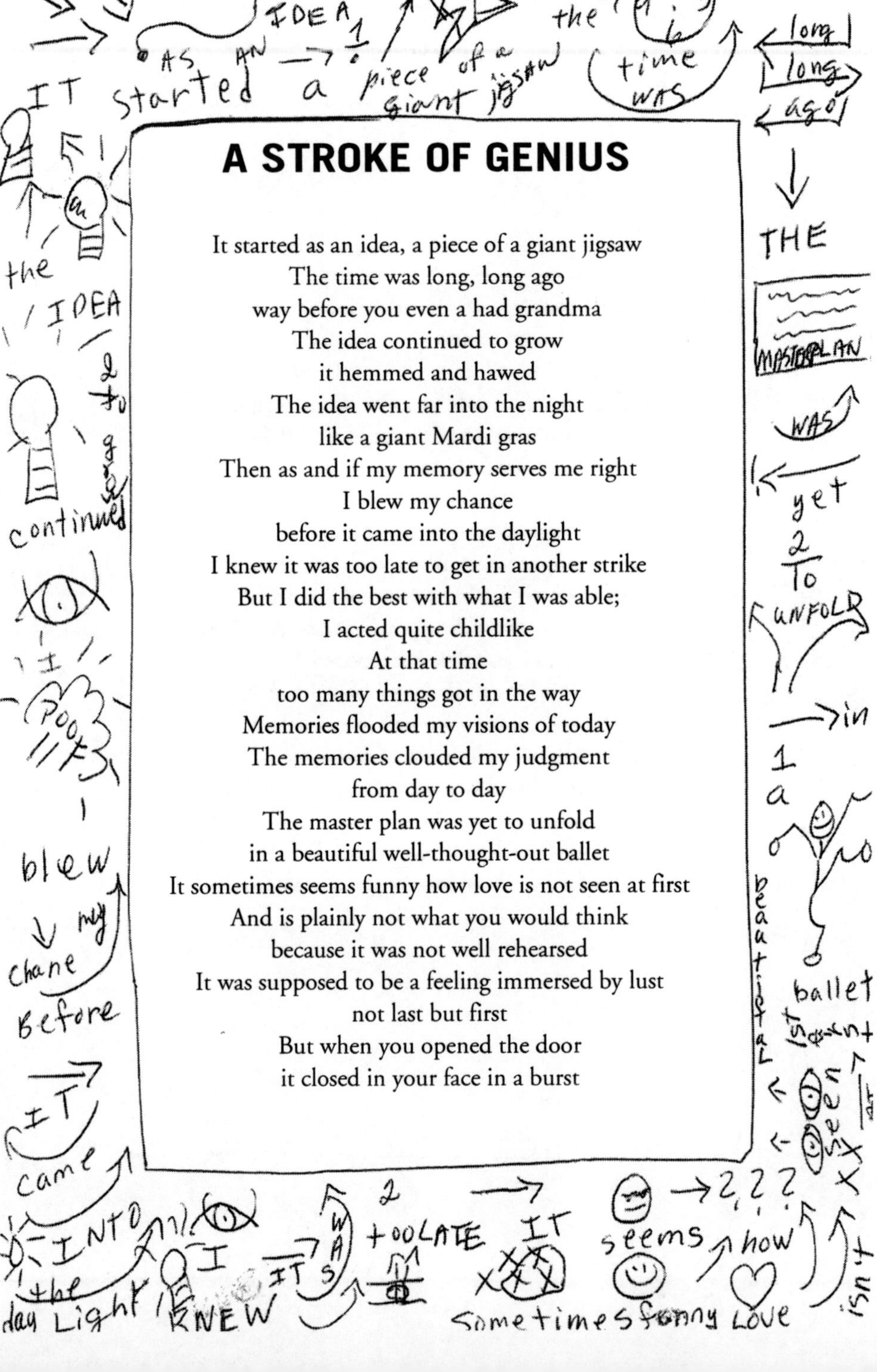

A STROKE OF GENIUS

It started as an idea, a piece of a giant jigsaw
The time was long, long ago
way before you even a had grandma
The idea continued to grow
it hemmed and hawed
The idea went far into the night
like a giant Mardi gras
Then as and if my memory serves me right
I blew my chance
before it came into the daylight
I knew it was too late to get in another strike
But I did the best with what I was able;
I acted quite childlike
At that time
too many things got in the way
Memories flooded my visions of today
The memories clouded my judgment
from day to day
The master plan was yet to unfold
in a beautiful well-thought-out ballet
It sometimes seems funny how love is not seen at first
And is plainly not what you would think
because it was not well rehearsed
It was supposed to be a feeling immersed by lust
not last but first
But when you opened the door
it closed in your face in a burst

The idea which had begun as something good
had become a horrendous problem
The ideas I had chosen to love were the
ones that proved to bring my end
And the people who I wanted to love me
back only chose to condescend
I can only say life sometimes works out that way even
when your idea is a rare gem
What started as an idea long ago and
seemed like it had the word go
Had been stopped, dead in its tracks,
to something slow, just so-so
It had to wait for the sun to come up and the rooster to crow
Then was able to start again
with a lot of get up and go and with gusto
For that brilliant idea, I am bound to give myself a medal
It may be the best thing
I have done since before I was unwell
The only thing is it will be something good
that rings as clear as a bell
I will be proud to talk it out
and show it to you all for show and tell
It will be a brilliant brainstorm, a wiggly, little worm
It will be something
I will love to affirm and to confirm
It will be very helpful and
be the best solution in the long term
The idea began as a little germ and
grew and grew and grew as big as a pachyderm

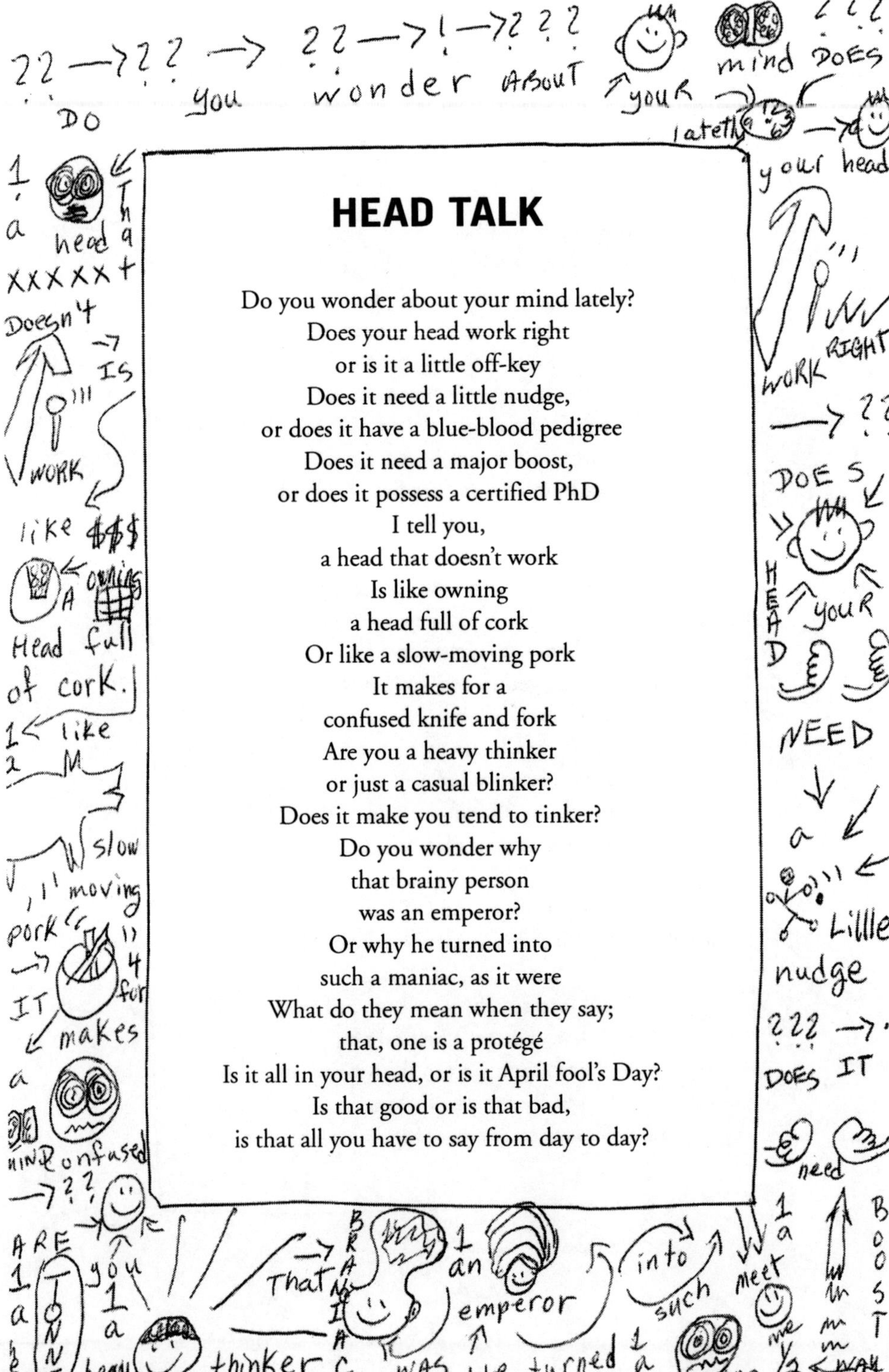

HEAD TALK

Do you wonder about your mind lately?
Does your head work right
or is it a little off-key
Does it need a little nudge,
or does it have a blue-blood pedigree
Does it need a major boost,
or does it possess a certified PhD
I tell you,
a head that doesn't work
Is like owning
a head full of cork
Or like a slow-moving pork
It makes for a
confused knife and fork
Are you a heavy thinker
or just a casual blinker?
Does it make you tend to tinker?
Do you wonder why
that brainy person
was an emperor?
Or why he turned into
such a maniac, as it were
What do they mean when they say;
that, one is a protégé
Is it all in your head, or is it April fool's Day?
Is that good or is that bad,
is that all you have to say from day to day?

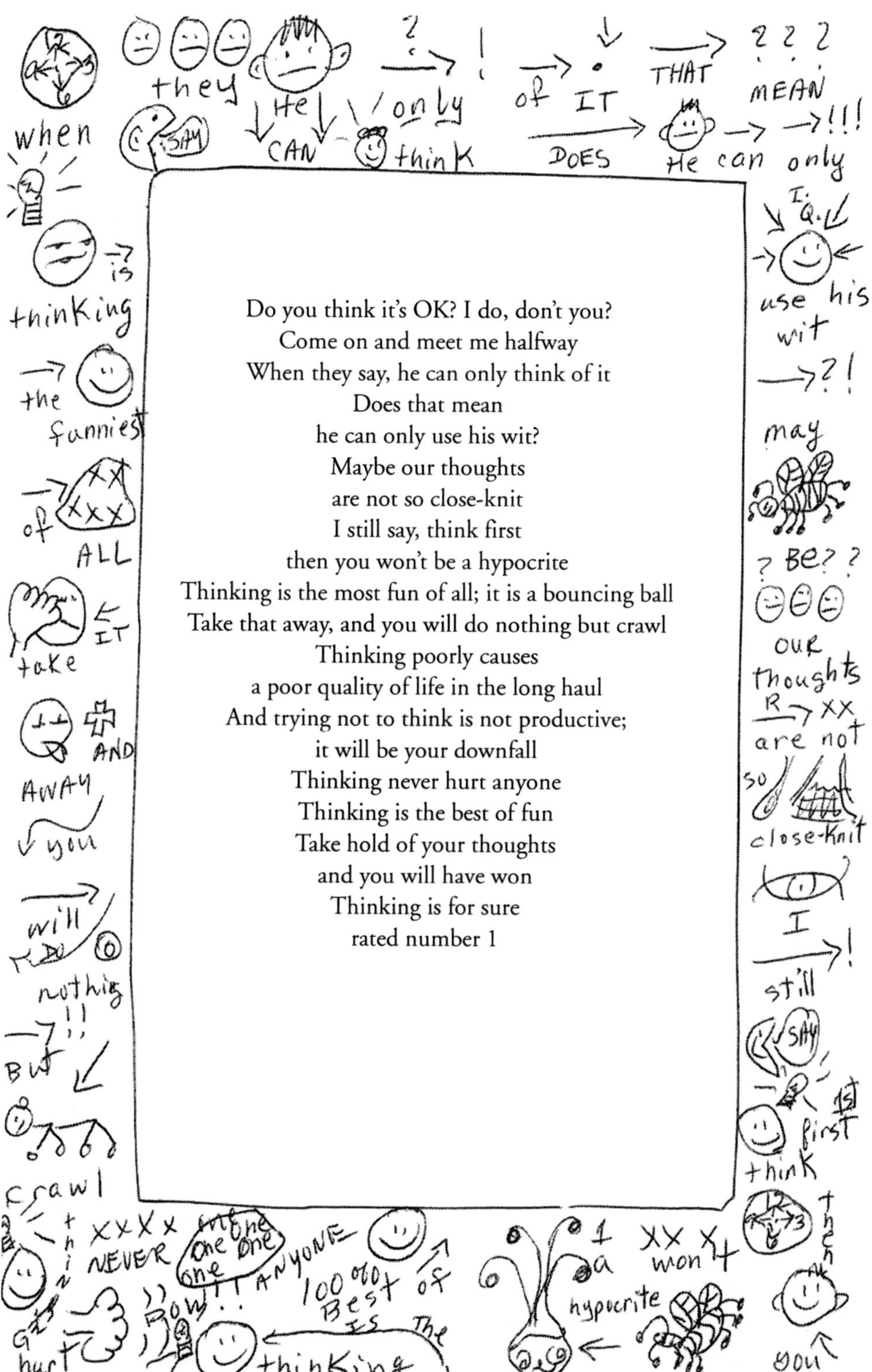

Do you think it's OK? I do, don't you?
Come on and meet me halfway
When they say, he can only think of it
Does that mean
he can only use his wit?
Maybe our thoughts
are not so close-knit
I still say, think first
then you won't be a hypocrite
Thinking is the most fun of all; it is a bouncing ball
Take that away, and you will do nothing but crawl
Thinking poorly causes
a poor quality of life in the long haul
And trying not to think is not productive;
it will be your downfall
Thinking never hurt anyone
Thinking is the best of fun
Take hold of your thoughts
and you will have won
Thinking is for sure
rated number 1

GOOD-BYE, BIG BUDDY

Traveling far, far away on life's ballet
what do I have to say;
I want a replay
I can travel farther than you
any old day
Come on give me a big boo
and a great big hurrah
Buzz, goes the air waves, like a big shock wave
Bam, bam hear the airwaves slam,
you must bow and wave
Chime, chime you must move in time
to come up with an intelligent brain wave
Ring, ring you can start to sing
before you rant and rave
That is when the world comes alive
You will never guess
who has arrived
I just bumped into my old friend,
and that, is no jive
Yes, you said it
He was definitely alive

Anything is possible, Jekyll,
or should I say Mr. Hyde
You took me for a sucker
for a real ride

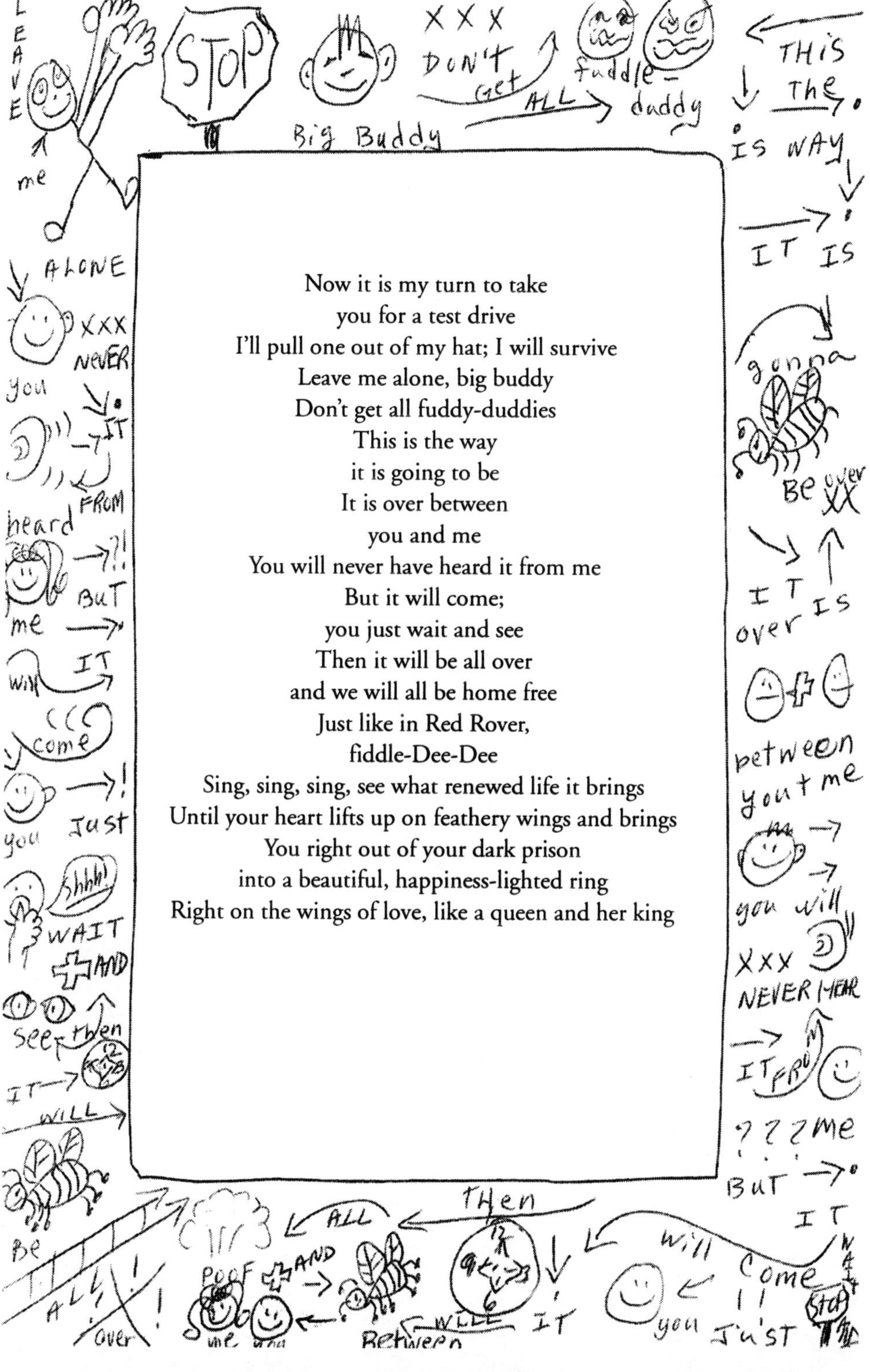

Now it is my turn to take
you for a test drive
I'll pull one out of my hat; I will survive
Leave me alone, big buddy
Don't get all fuddy-duddies
This is the way
it is going to be
It is over between
you and me
You will never have heard it from me
But it will come;
you just wait and see
Then it will be all over
and we will all be home free
Just like in Red Rover,
fiddle-Dee-Dee
Sing, sing, sing, see what renewed life it brings
Until your heart lifts up on feathery wings and brings
You right out of your dark prison
into a beautiful, happiness-lighted ring
Right on the wings of love, like a queen and her king

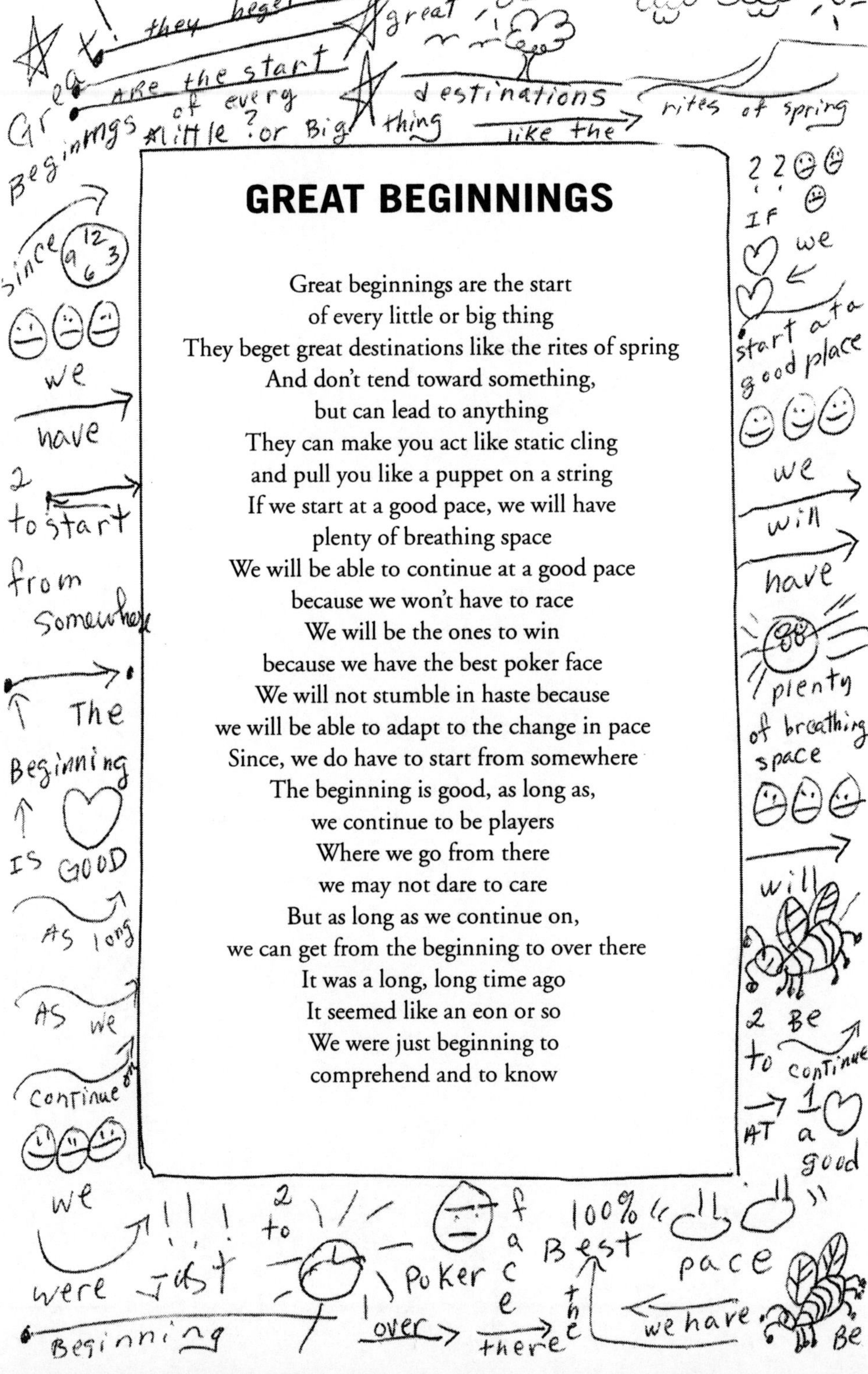

GREAT BEGINNINGS

Great beginnings are the start
of every little or big thing
They beget great destinations like the rites of spring
And don't tend toward something,
but can lead to anything
They can make you act like static cling
and pull you like a puppet on a string
If we start at a good pace, we will have
plenty of breathing space
We will be able to continue at a good pace
because we won't have to race
We will be the ones to win
because we have the best poker face
We will not stumble in haste because
we will be able to adapt to the change in pace
Since, we do have to start from somewhere
The beginning is good, as long as,
we continue to be players
Where we go from there
we may not dare to care
But as long as we continue on,
we can get from the beginning to over there
It was a long, long time ago
It seemed like an eon or so
We were just beginning to
comprehend and to know

By the looks of us, sometimes
it was touch and go
In the beginning someone was very wise
He began the Earth and formed the skies
For Him this wasn't hard to organize
In Him, there are no lies
to interfere or to nullify
He just let it all be,
and it was so and we were home
And before, He made you and me free
He made the sky and the sea
He first has to see if all three would agree
In His image we were made;
that was the key
Turns out we were just plain lucky
That we survived the beginning
because we were so careless and plucky
We had no guarantees, and we were a little kooky
But all in all, we survived being just rookies
And so it was good and great
with a lot of pizzazz
And just because we were tough,
we survived Alcatraz
There was no hidden note, no razz or jazz
The beginning became the new laws
and the laws became
all that razzmatazz

I LOVE YOU, DAMN IT

Can't you understand?
I need a first-aid kit
I am totally and
completely dazed at your wit
And full of love for you, damn it
Isn't it obvious and plain to see,
that to me you are a sold-out, smash hit?
I saw you today and
it was "Look out, bombs away!"
You turned my heart
into a full and colorful bouquet
You gave me many reasons to face another day
But damn it, what will happen tomorrow;
please give me a play by play
What is it that makes me feel this way?
Heck, I do not even know what to say
Just the sound of your voice
makes me want to play
Just the sight of you
takes my breath away
I cannot even express
or tell you the words that would fit
Or any thoughts you might use lickety-split
All I know is that
you feel the same way, damn it
It is almost a certain fact;
that what we feel is legit

So I must quietly count one, two, and three
And I must keep my thoughts to myself;
just in case you don't agree
I must also keep my love in my heart
or I might sing off-key
And I may not
be able to not wear it on my sleeve
that would be guaranteed
I can't beat it, so I guess I'll have to wear it
I can't live without it; I can't die or forget it
Come to me; don't quit
don't flee; don't split
Come hither, come hither to wit to wit
How can I get my message across
so you will understand?
When I am with you, I am in a faraway fantasy land
I can think of nothing better
than walking with you, hand in hand
I feel I am trapped
inside the loving embrace of your quicksand
I love you, damn it, I just wanted you to know
I have taken out a love permit;
I am Juliet and you are my Romeo
I love you every bit, not just so-so,
but more and more so
I love you—to me you are a smash hit;
I love you, damn it, I will always love you so

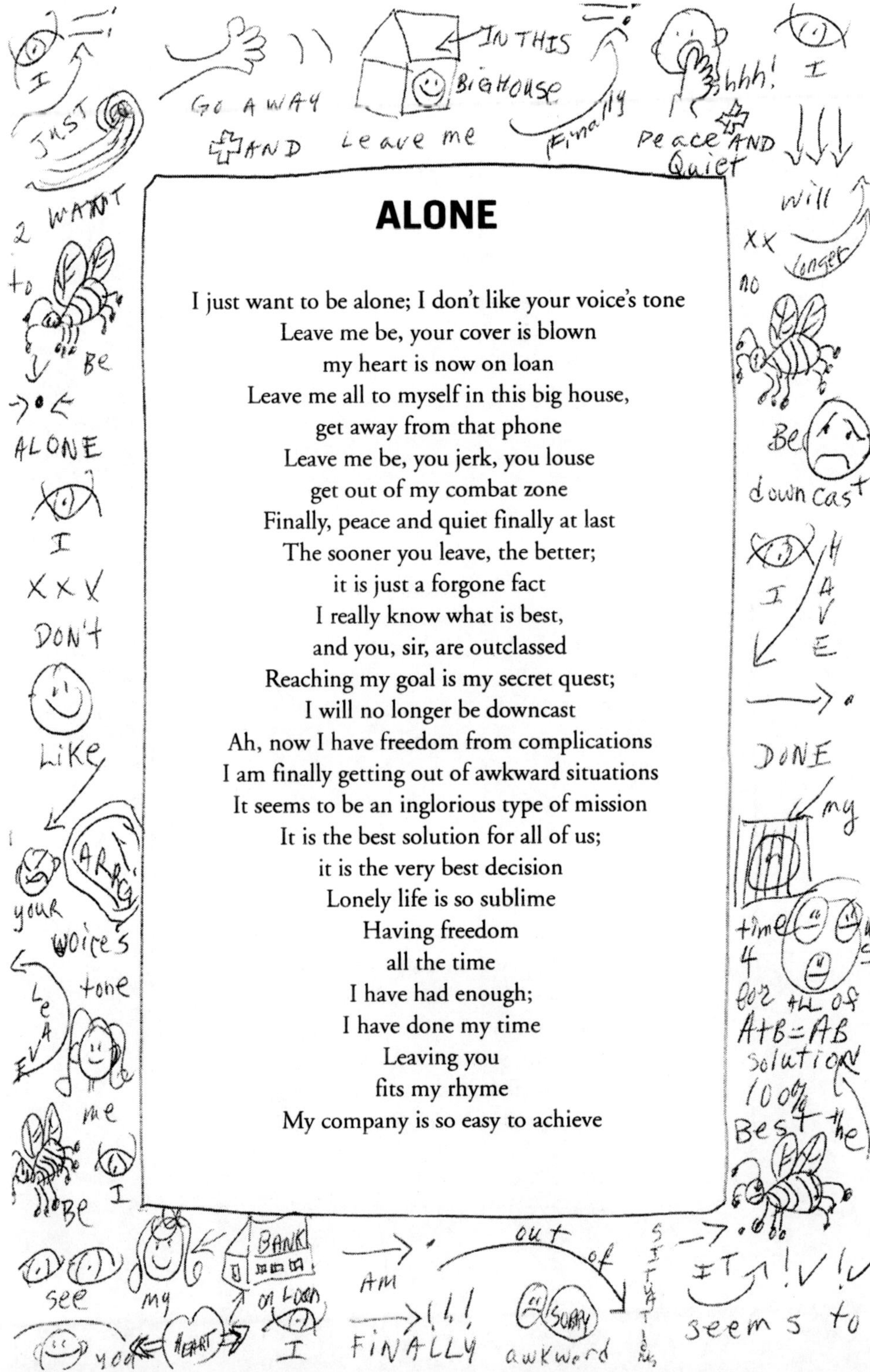

ALONE

I just want to be alone; I don't like your voice's tone
Leave me be, your cover is blown
my heart is now on loan
Leave me all to myself in this big house,
get away from that phone
Leave me be, you jerk, you louse
get out of my combat zone
Finally, peace and quiet finally at last
The sooner you leave, the better;
it is just a forgone fact
I really know what is best,
and you, sir, are outclassed
Reaching my goal is my secret quest;
I will no longer be downcast
Ah, now I have freedom from complications
I am finally getting out of awkward situations
It seems to be an inglorious type of mission
It is the best solution for all of us;
it is the very best decision
Lonely life is so sublime
Having freedom
all the time
I have had enough;
I have done my time
Leaving you
fits my rhyme
My company is so easy to achieve

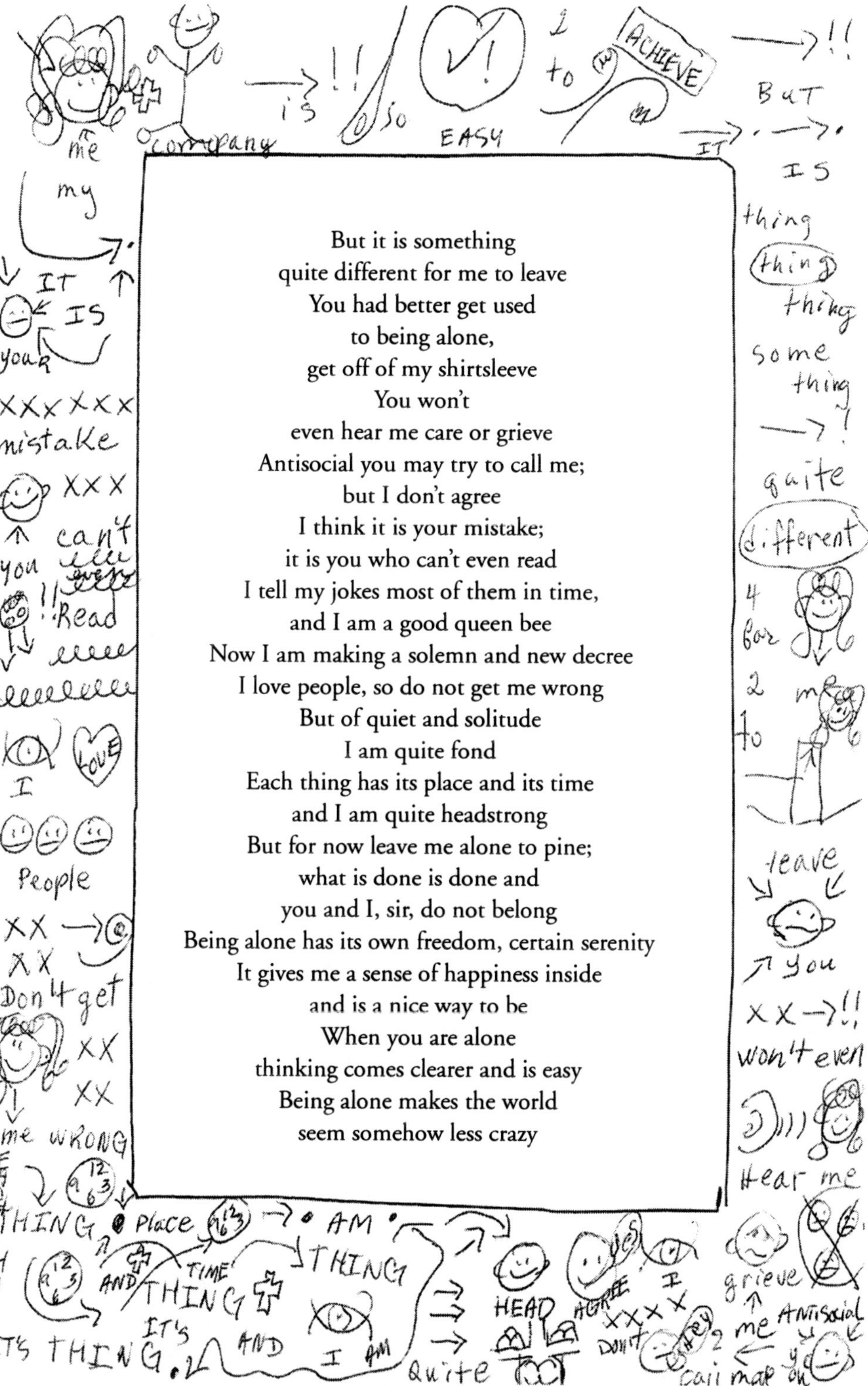

But it is something
quite different for me to leave
You had better get used
to being alone,
get off of my shirtsleeve
You won't
even hear me care or grieve
Antisocial you may try to call me;
but I don't agree
I think it is your mistake;
it is you who can't even read
I tell my jokes most of them in time,
and I am a good queen bee
Now I am making a solemn and new decree
I love people, so do not get me wrong
But of quiet and solitude
I am quite fond
Each thing has its place and its time
and I am quite headstrong
But for now leave me alone to pine;
what is done is done and
you and I, sir, do not belong
Being alone has its own freedom, certain serenity
It gives me a sense of happiness inside
and is a nice way to be
When you are alone
thinking comes clearer and is easy
Being alone makes the world
seem somehow less crazy

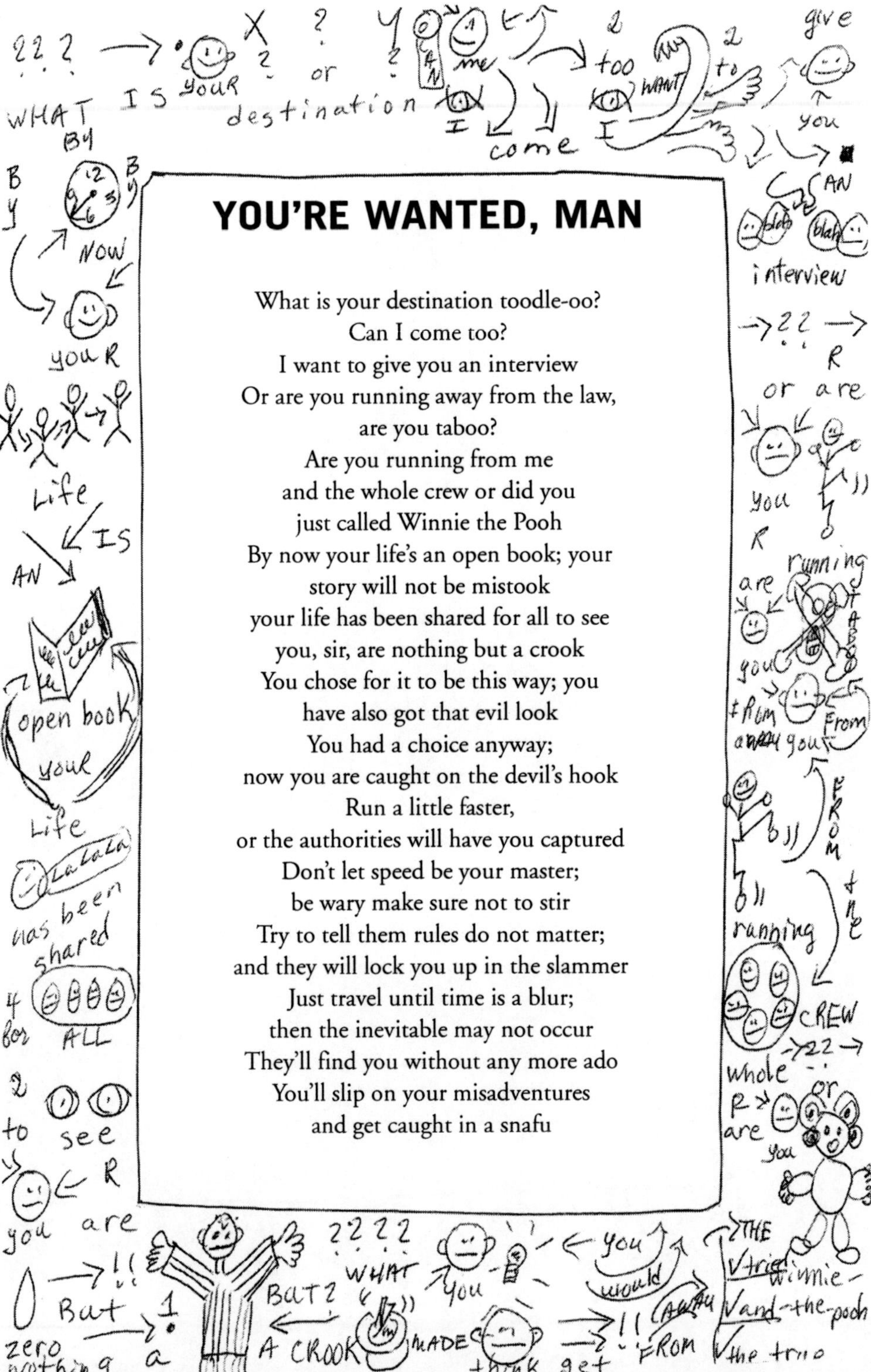

YOU'RE WANTED, MAN

What is your destination toodle-oo?
Can I come too?
I want to give you an interview
Or are you running away from the law,
are you taboo?
Are you running from me
and the whole crew or did you
just called Winnie the Pooh
By now your life's an open book; your
story will not be mistook
your life has been shared for all to see
you, sir, are nothing but a crook
You chose for it to be this way; you
have also got that evil look
You had a choice anyway;
now you are caught on the devil's hook
Run a little faster,
or the authorities will have you captured
Don't let speed be your master;
be wary make sure not to stir
Try to tell them rules do not matter;
and they will lock you up in the slammer
Just travel until time is a blur;
then the inevitable may not occur
They'll find you without any more ado
You'll slip on your misadventures
and get caught in a snafu

For your sins you'll pay;
they will lie on the screws
What made you think you think
you would get away
from the tried and the true

Was it worth the crime so horrendous;
was it worth all the fuss?
Was it worth thinking you were so stupendous
are you a number 1, an A-plus?
You'll slip, then you will be sorry
then you will be a gloomy Gus
It will be a totally different story that
you will have to discuss
You are a wanted man; your life is now in the trash can
The police are now your greatest fans;
they are the busy Mr. Lawmen
If you think you can throw them off,
you had better change you plans
You are not so tough;
you might end up being called a dead man
They will track you like an animal
until they hunt you down
You will be the disappointed one wearing a frown
You will be swimming in trouble until you drown
And you will end up wearing
an orange prison gown

Wee-you wee-you, wee-you, wee you
Burr, burr, burr, burr, burr, burr, burr, burr, burr, burr
Bang, bang, bang, bang, bang, bang, bang
All is done and all is anew, boo hoo, boo hoo
Bye for now, oh, oh, the police has caught you
Now that's a fine howdy do
yippy Dee-Dee-Dee doo

I AM HAPPY

Don't tell me bad news or sing me the blues
I won't listen to your horrible views
or any of your bad reviews
I have had enough wars
to last all my life, thank you
And I have met enough awful boors
and I have met quite a few
When you talk to me
give me something positive
And try to make my day happy
and I will try not to be too inquisitive
I do not mind if you let all the good news relive
So I can have a good reason
to be happy and to forgive
Then all my worries will disappear
And there will be happiness
instead with no reason to fear
No one will have a reason to cry;
I think that fact is clear
And we can say good-bye to bad
and go ahead in full gear
Ah, then life will be
fun, fun, fun, hon.
And we will have life on the run
My life will have
more than just begun
True love will surely be mine
with my chosen
loving number 1

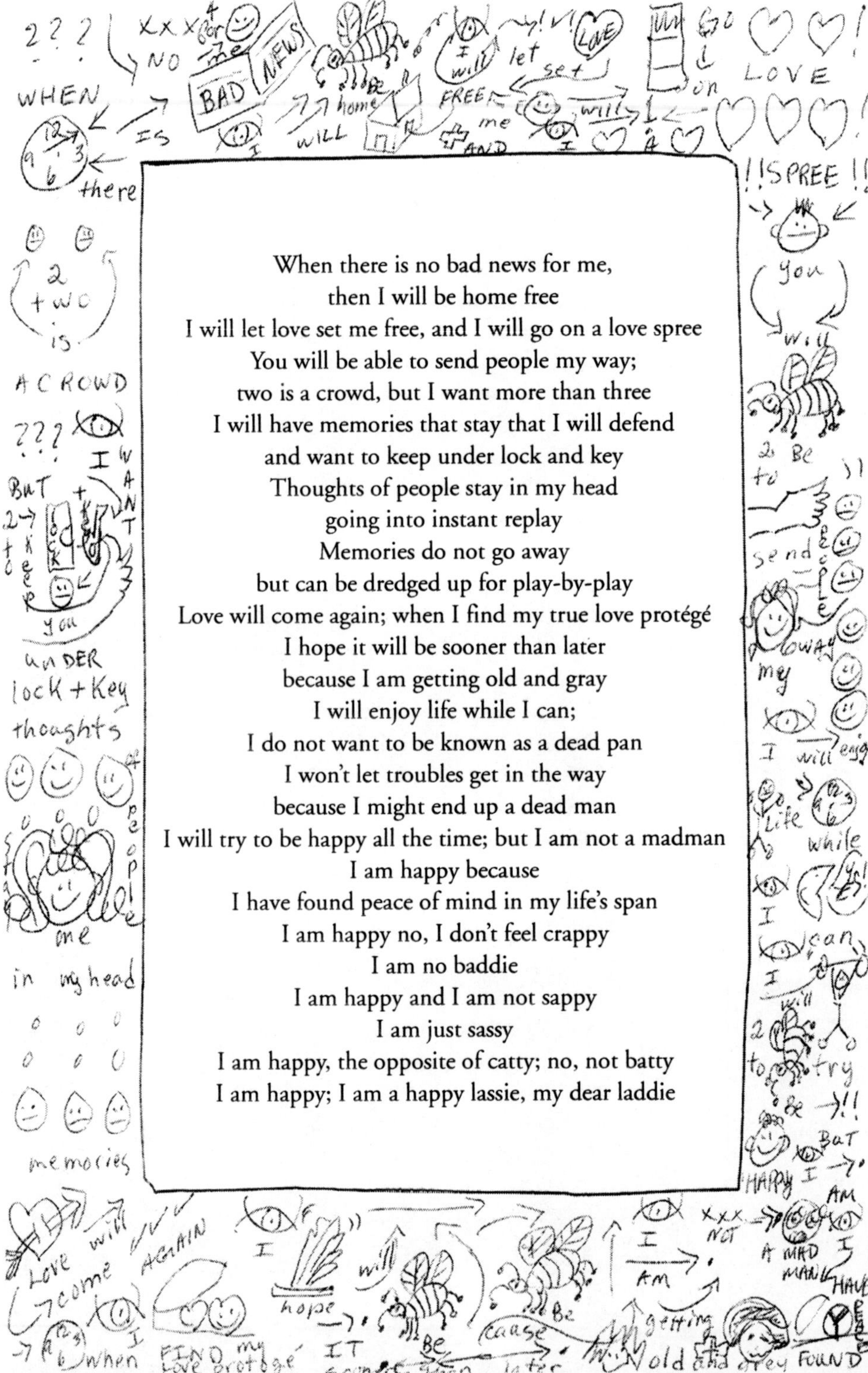

When there is no bad news for me,
then I will be home free
I will let love set me free, and I will go on a love spree
You will be able to send people my way;
two is a crowd, but I want more than three
I will have memories that stay that I will defend
and want to keep under lock and key
Thoughts of people stay in my head
going into instant replay
Memories do not go away
but can be dredged up for play-by-play
Love will come again; when I find my true love protégé
I hope it will be sooner than later
because I am getting old and gray
I will enjoy life while I can;
I do not want to be known as a dead pan
I won't let troubles get in the way
because I might end up a dead man
I will try to be happy all the time; but I am not a madman
I am happy because
I have found peace of mind in my life's span
I am happy no, I don't feel crappy
I am no baddie
I am happy and I am not sappy
I am just sassy
I am happy, the opposite of catty; no, not batty
I am happy; I am a happy lassie, my dear laddie

SIMPLE SIMON

That's him, that's him, its Simple Simon
they say he is supposed to be a pie man
I saw him last night at the barbecue;
he was chief cook and took place number 1
The night was very dark and scary behind us
we heard someone not just anyone
Simple Simon had lost his way;
you could say he bit the bun
That's him, that's him, Simple Simon
said the man with the scent dog
I had seen him yesterday when I went for a jog
He had passed me by the way, but at that time,
we were in the bog
He hadn't said hello; I might just as well
have been a bump on a log,
and he could have been a frog on a log
I will see him tomorrow and I will surely be undone
I hope he has learned more today and yesterday,
and then we might have some fun
So I guess then when I see him,
he will not be so much a Simple Simon;
he'll have graduated to a hired gun
Simple Simon is now a wanted man
a cook on the run
That's him, that's him, it is Simple Simon
he is alive and well

I saw him again last night; he's the master pie man
He was on the street selling pies again
after they were cooked and well-done
She on the other hand was on the corner;
you could say she was road kill
it was a case of hit and run
her goose was cooked, and she was undone
That's him, that's him, it's Simple Simon.
What a pie man with cute buns
I saw him today; he is in a misty way
his plan was in play, his spell was spun
With a pie in her hand, she did not
have a chance to even call 911
When the paramedics came on the run,
they found them lying facedown.
Then began the fun—they were baked
in a pie and cooked up in the sun
So it goes . . . That's him, that's him, Simple Simon
he could be called a baker in the front line,
an assembly mafia line man
I'll see him tomorrow at the lineup
and hope he is not underdone
He'll make the same mistakes as today,
and they may have to use their stun gun

The world will end for him and it will be
oh, oh, hot dogs for everyone;
it will have ended before it had begun
That's him, that's him, its Simple Simon
he sometimes acts like a silly nitwit
But most times his intentions are totally legit
And even though you might not think
his faculties are totally fit
You might even learn a little lesson
from Simple Simon: you might learn that
Simple Simon is simply a smash-up hit

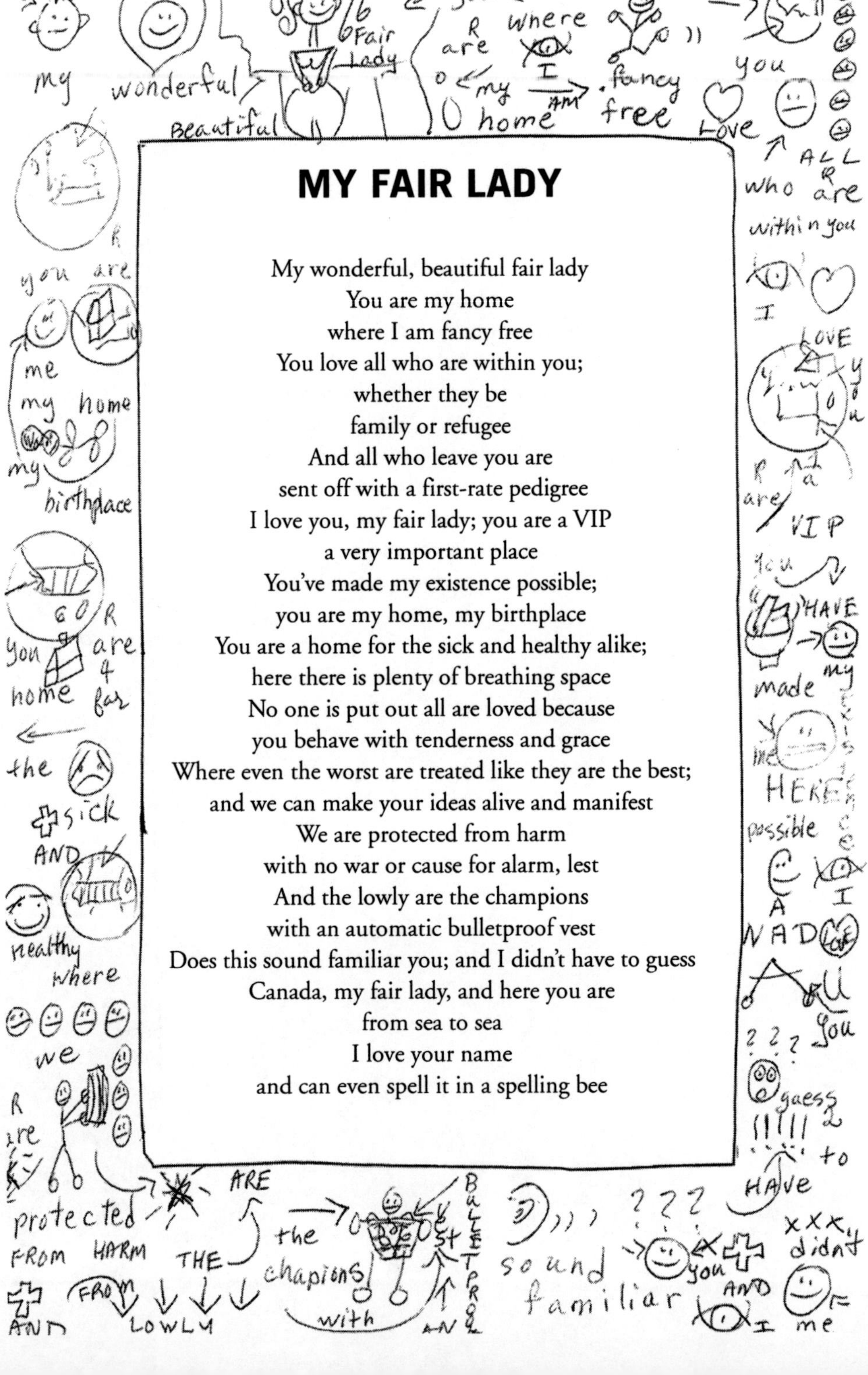

MY FAIR LADY

My wonderful, beautiful fair lady
You are my home
where I am fancy free
You love all who are within you;
whether they be
family or refugee
And all who leave you are
sent off with a first-rate pedigree
I love you, my fair lady; you are a VIP
a very important place
You've made my existence possible;
you are my home, my birthplace
You are a home for the sick and healthy alike;
here there is plenty of breathing space
No one is put out all are loved because
you behave with tenderness and grace
Where even the worst are treated like they are the best;
and we can make your ideas alive and manifest
We are protected from harm
with no war or cause for alarm, lest
And the lowly are the champions
with an automatic bulletproof vest
Does this sound familiar you; and I didn't have to guess
Canada, my fair lady, and here you are
from sea to sea
I love your name
and can even spell it in a spelling bee

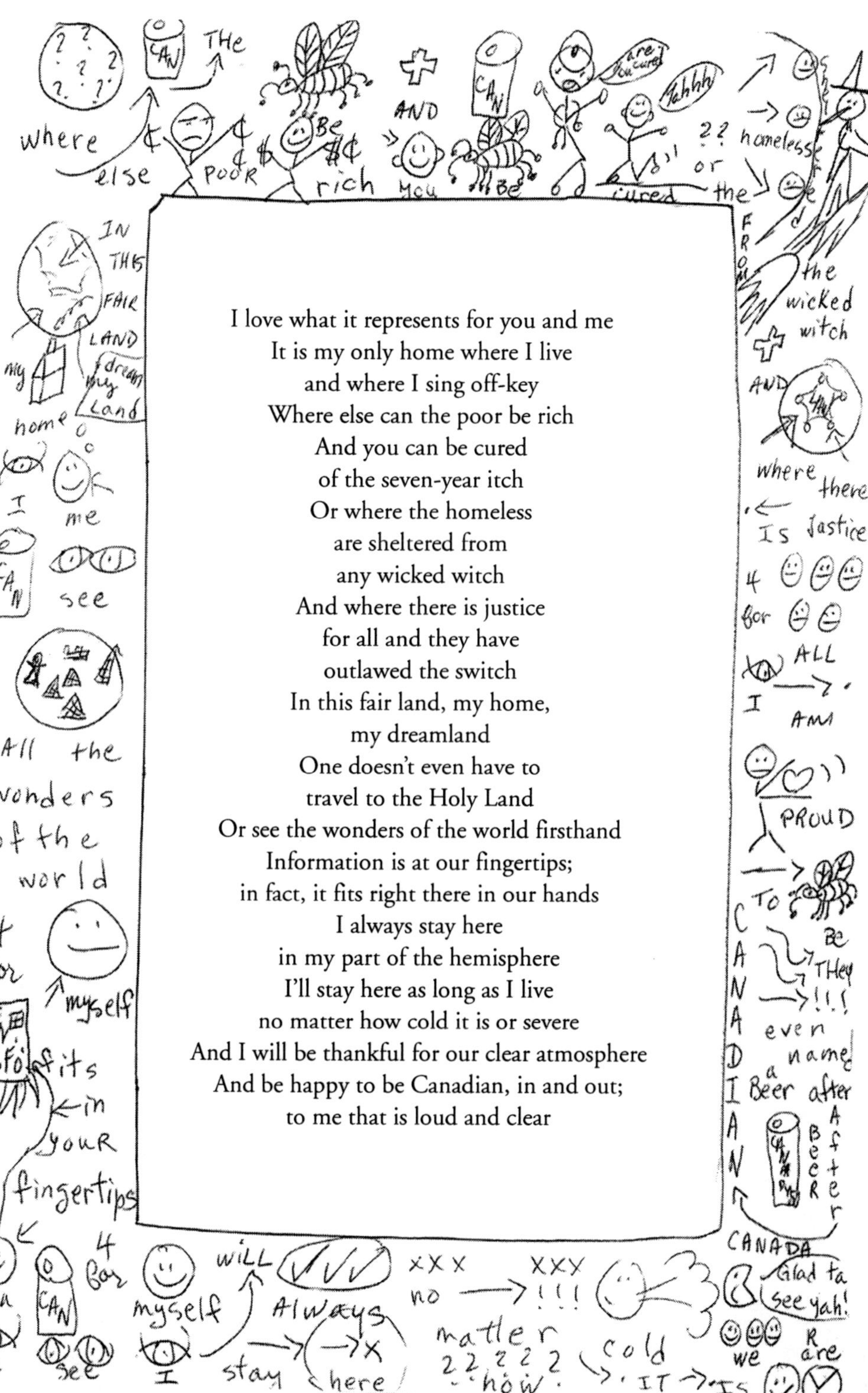

I love what it represents for you and me
It is my only home where I live
and where I sing off-key
Where else can the poor be rich
And you can be cured
of the seven-year itch
Or where the homeless
are sheltered from
any wicked witch
And where there is justice
for all and they have
outlawed the switch
In this fair land, my home,
my dreamland
One doesn't even have to
travel to the Holy Land
Or see the wonders of the world firsthand
Information is at our fingertips;
in fact, it fits right there in our hands
I always stay here
in my part of the hemisphere
I'll stay here as long as I live
no matter how cold it is or severe
And I will be thankful for our clear atmosphere
And be happy to be Canadian, in and out;
to me that is loud and clear

Heck they even named
a beer after Canada
It's where we say, "Eh, glad to see ya"
And welcome friends, neighbors,
grandmas, and grandpas
And where we are all free to love
each other, our pa and our ma

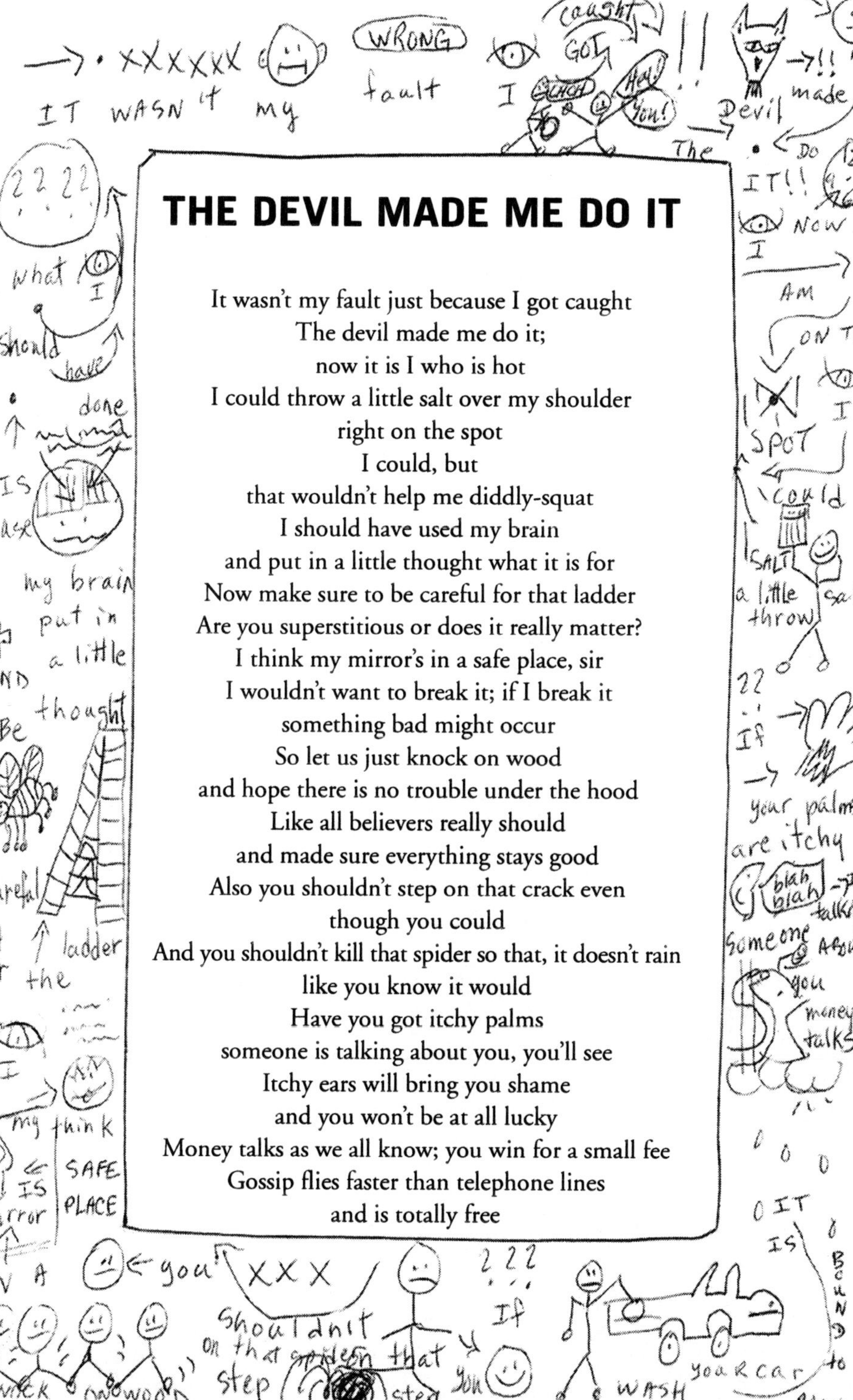

THE DEVIL MADE ME DO IT

It wasn't my fault just because I got caught
The devil made me do it;
now it is I who is hot
I could throw a little salt over my shoulder
right on the spot
I could, but
that wouldn't help me diddly-squat
I should have used my brain
and put in a little thought what it is for
Now make sure to be careful for that ladder
Are you superstitious or does it really matter?
I think my mirror's in a safe place, sir
I wouldn't want to break it; if I break it
something bad might occur
So let us just knock on wood
and hope there is no trouble under the hood
Like all believers really should
and made sure everything stays good
Also you shouldn't step on that crack even
though you could
And you shouldn't kill that spider so that, it doesn't rain
like you know it would
Have you got itchy palms
someone is talking about you, you'll see
Itchy ears will bring you shame
and you won't be at all lucky
Money talks as we all know; you win for a small fee
Gossip flies faster than telephone lines
and is totally free

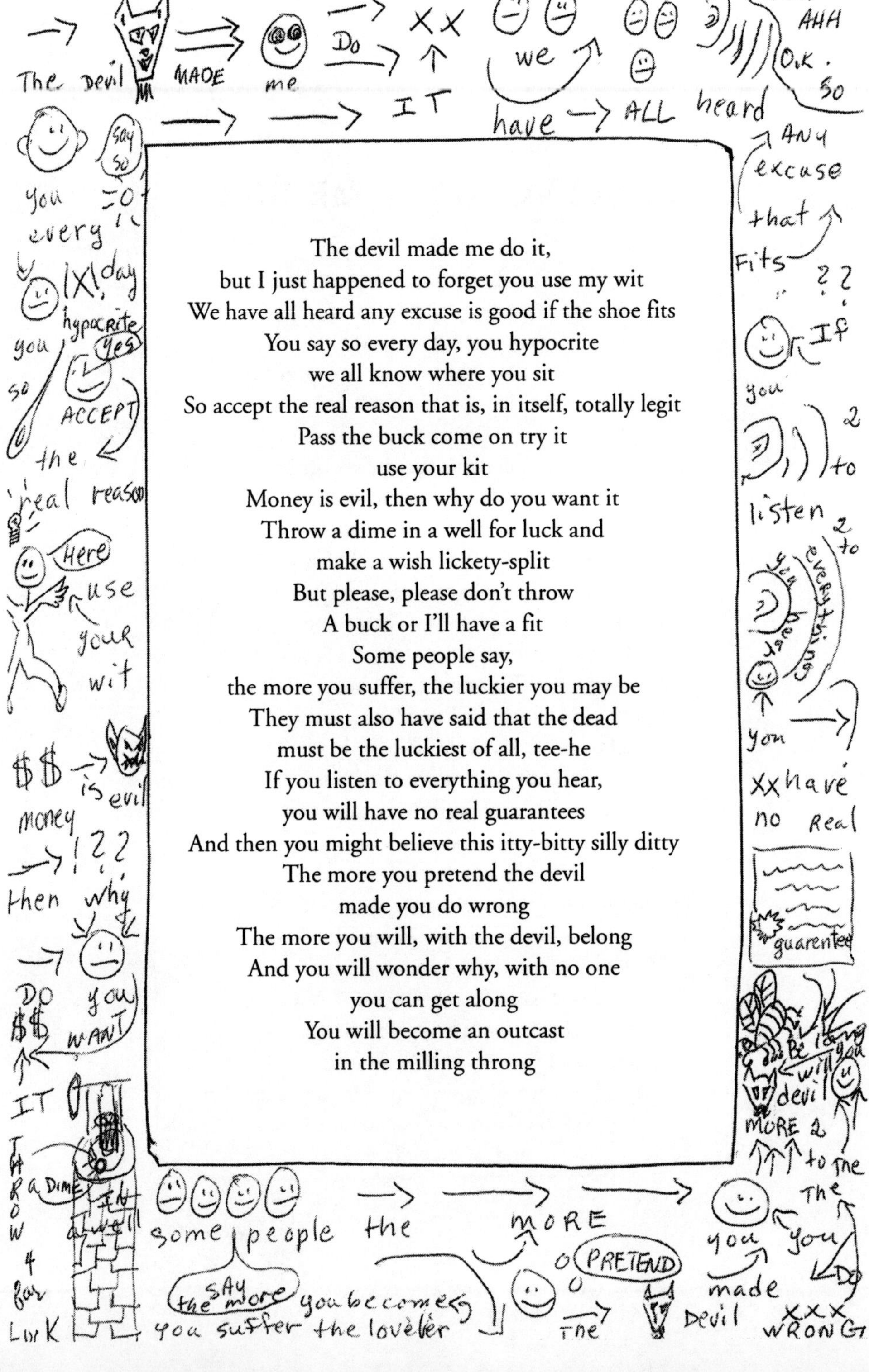

The devil made me do it,
but I just happened to forget you use my wit
We have all heard any excuse is good if the shoe fits
You say so every day, you hypocrite
we all know where you sit
So accept the real reason that is, in itself, totally legit
Pass the buck come on try it
use your kit
Money is evil, then why do you want it
Throw a dime in a well for luck and
make a wish lickety-split
But please, please don't throw
A buck or I'll have a fit
Some people say,
the more you suffer, the luckier you may be
They must also have said that the dead
must be the luckiest of all, tee-he
If you listen to everything you hear,
you will have no real guarantees
And then you might believe this itty-bitty silly ditty
The more you pretend the devil
made you do wrong
The more you will, with the devil, belong
And you will wonder why, with no one
you can get along
You will become an outcast
in the milling throng

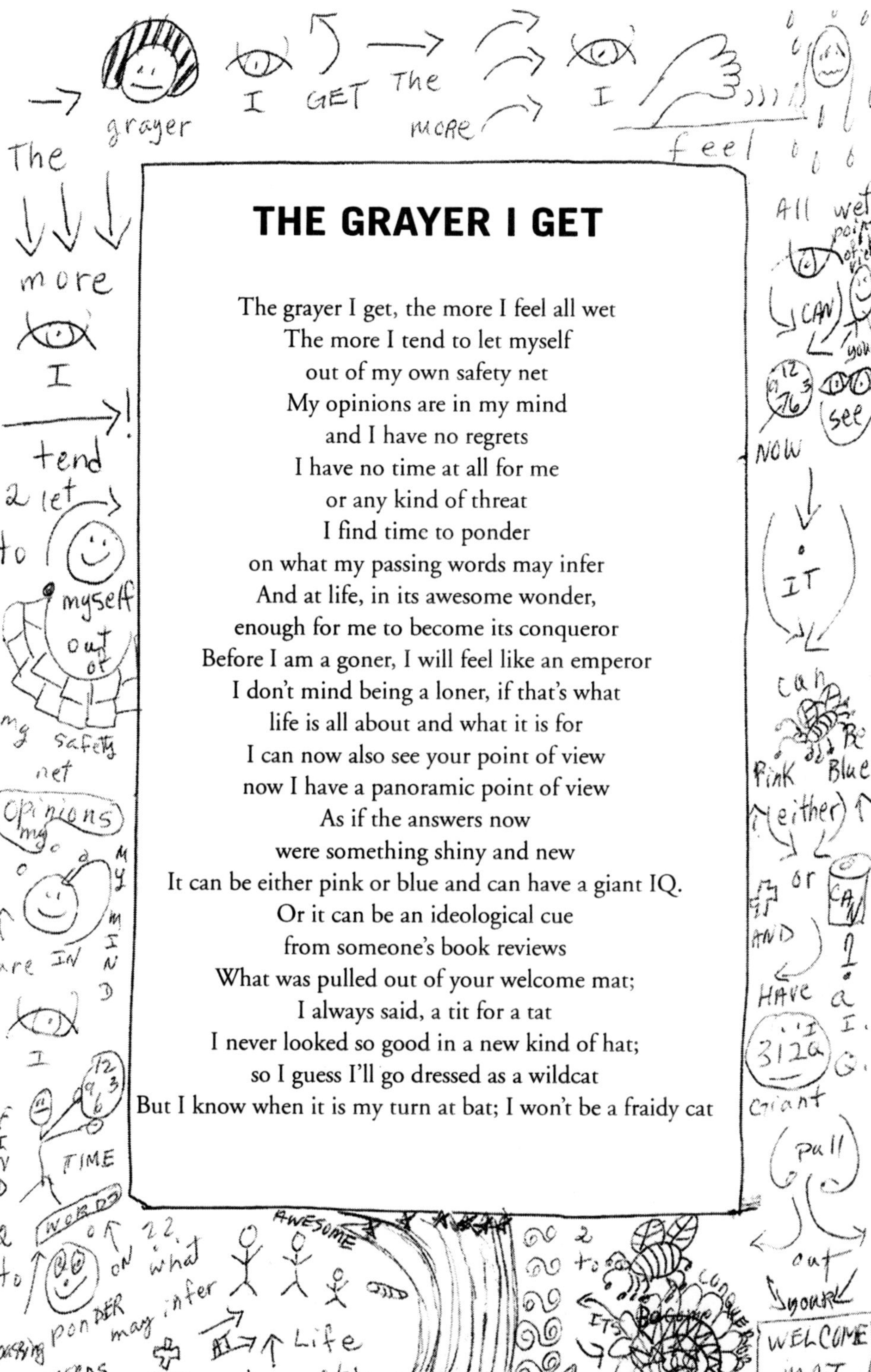

THE GRAYER I GET

The grayer I get, the more I feel all wet
The more I tend to let myself
out of my own safety net
My opinions are in my mind
and I have no regrets
I have no time at all for me
or any kind of threat
I find time to ponder
on what my passing words may infer
And at life, in its awesome wonder,
enough for me to become its conqueror
Before I am a goner, I will feel like an emperor
I don't mind being a loner, if that's what
life is all about and what it is for
I can now also see your point of view
now I have a panoramic point of view
As if the answers now
were something shiny and new
It can be either pink or blue and can have a giant IQ.
Or it can be an ideological cue
from someone's book reviews
What was pulled out of your welcome mat;
I always said, a tit for a tat
I never looked so good in a new kind of hat;
so I guess I'll go dressed as a wildcat
But I know when it is my turn at bat; I won't be a fraidy cat

And I think I'll know if you're a dirty rat
because then you will remind me of a bureaucrat
I can also look like a great speckled bird;
of that, you can bet I am self-assured
I wouldn't mind also being a nerd as long as
I was as sweet and smart as a songbird;
have you not heard?
Please can I say another word;
let me give you a hint;
I'll hum like a humming bird
You could say that is a totally different kind of chord
But as time goes by, I'll get less and less camera shy
That will change the way I look at the sky
and bolts of light will run across it to electrify
I will have mellowed and my humor will be wry
and it will have expanded and intensified
I will no longer have fear and I will greet you and
say a big hi because you are number 1
and you will now qualify
I will begin to understand what you
have explained in long hand
And also this world and all its lands
like they have been written on the back of my hand
I will feel like I know them firsthand
and like they are my homeland

Everyone will be there with information
that I will understand
So it matters not how gray I have got
Or what colors I have hatched on top
But it does matter
what battles I have fought
And it matters
what ideas I have wrought

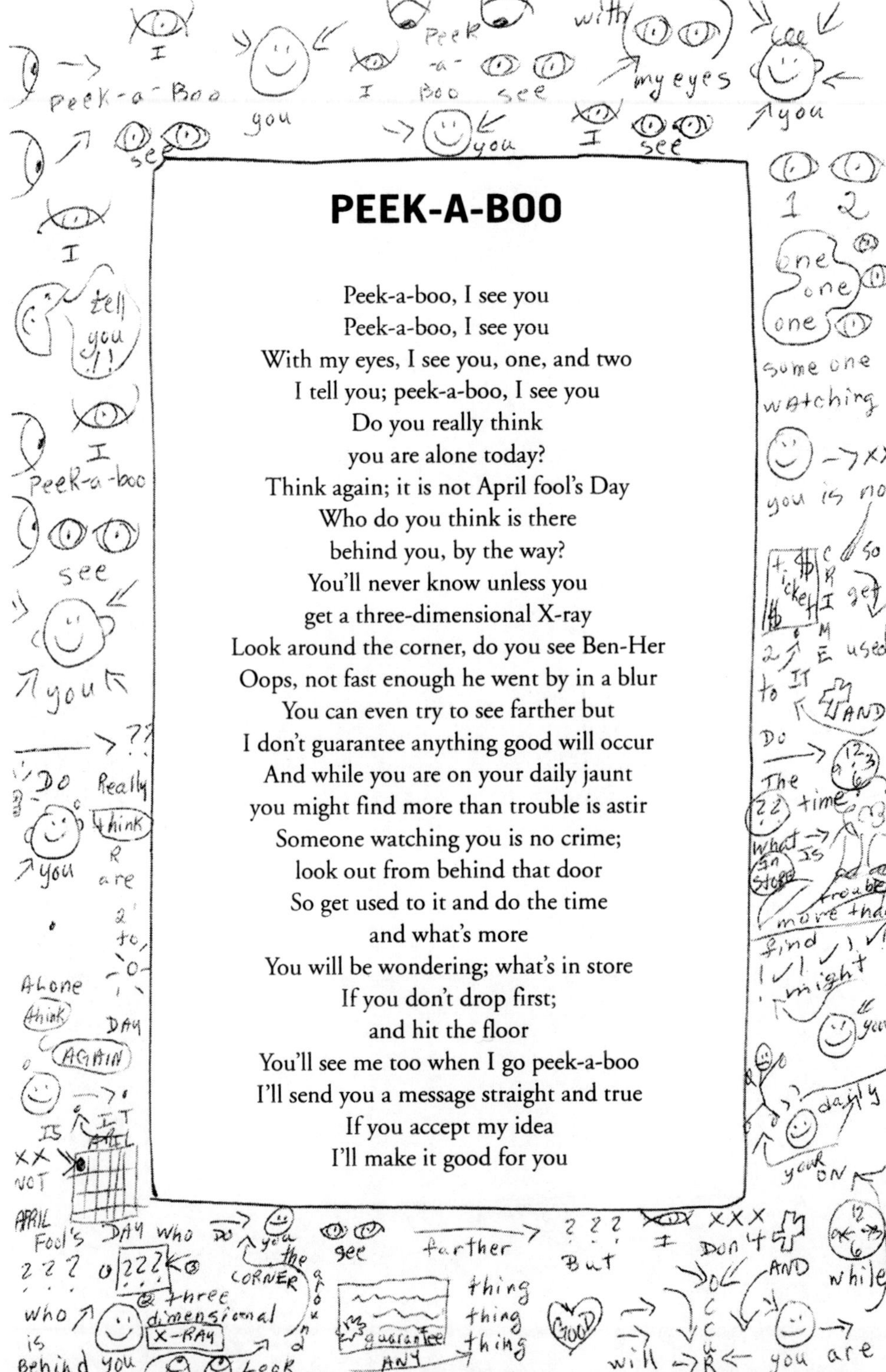

PEEK-A-BOO

Peek-a-boo, I see you
Peek-a-boo, I see you
With my eyes, I see you, one, and two
I tell you; peek-a-boo, I see you
Do you really think
you are alone today?
Think again; it is not April fool's Day
Who do you think is there
behind you, by the way?
You'll never know unless you
get a three-dimensional X-ray
Look around the corner, do you see Ben-Her
Oops, not fast enough he went by in a blur
You can even try to see farther but
I don't guarantee anything good will occur
And while you are on your daily jaunt
you might find more than trouble is astir
Someone watching you is no crime;
look out from behind that door
So get used to it and do the time
and what's more
You will be wondering; what's in store
If you don't drop first;
and hit the floor
You'll see me too when I go peek-a-boo
I'll send you a message straight and true
If you accept my idea
I'll make it good for you

It'll help you out, and you and I
may make a good rendezvous
Where will our exploits lead, caution
you must, my words heed
We must be careful, the thoughts, we seed
A good impression is something we might need
And we will say, "Peek-a-boo, one, two, three"
to each other and we won't have to lip read
And as we go, the plot will thicken,
so act tough and hang ten
And travel further than the dickens,
far away from the lion's den
Or we will end up playing more than hide-and-seek
again and again
Then it will no longer be a simple peek-a-boo-peek;
it will be lights out, amen
Truth is, I love to travel and
I love to hide in every nook
And I like to find out all
what is inside each and every book
And I like to see; I also love to look
You can say my life
is now an open book

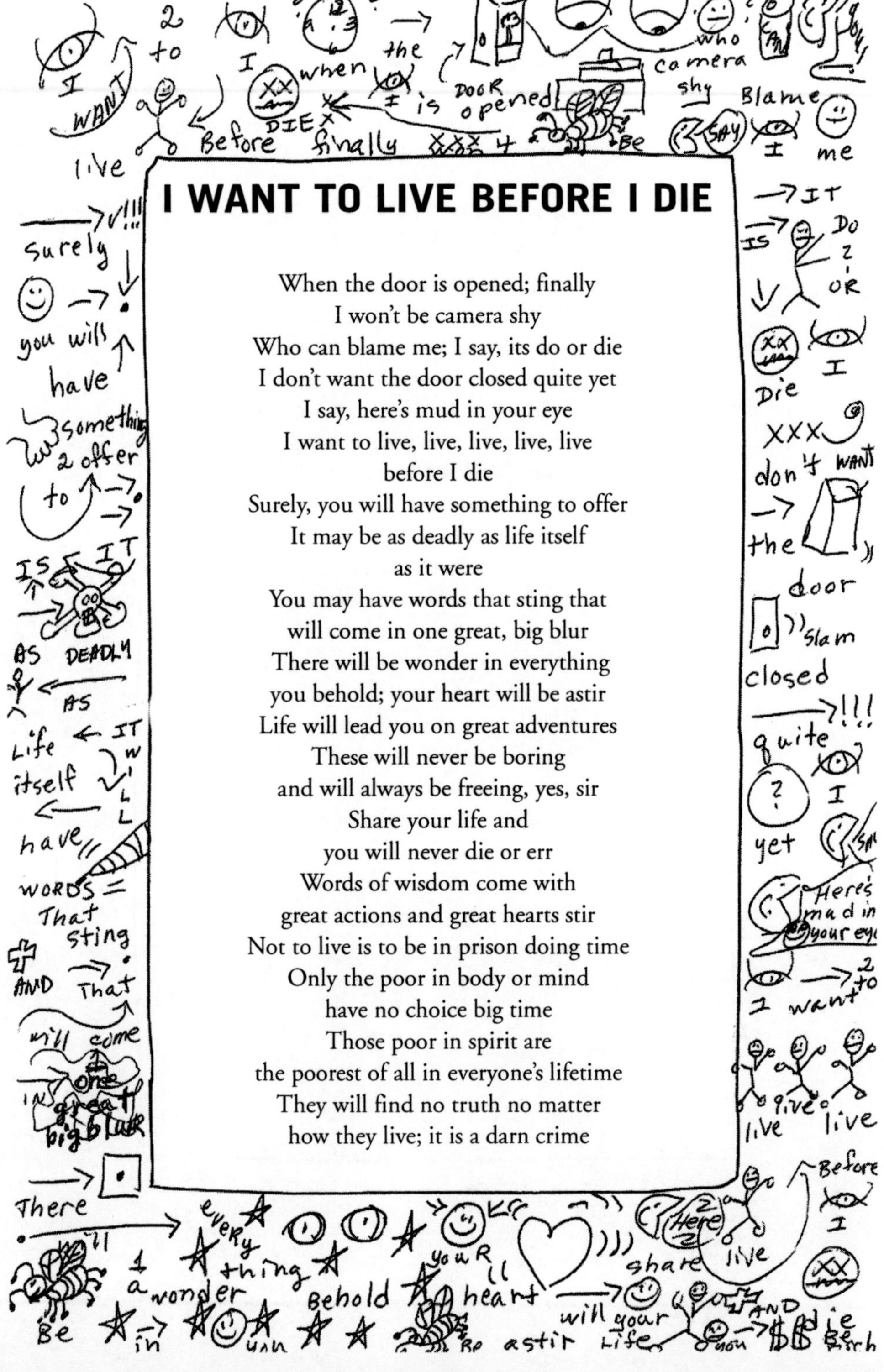

I WANT TO LIVE BEFORE I DIE

When the door is opened; finally
I won't be camera shy
Who can blame me; I say, its do or die
I don't want the door closed quite yet
I say, here's mud in your eye
I want to live, live, live, live, live
before I die
Surely, you will have something to offer
It may be as deadly as life itself
as it were
You may have words that sting that
will come in one great, big blur
There will be wonder in everything
you behold; your heart will be astir
Life will lead you on great adventures
These will never be boring
and will always be freeing, yes, sir
Share your life and
you will never die or err
Words of wisdom come with
great actions and great hearts stir
Not to live is to be in prison doing time
Only the poor in body or mind
have no choice big time
Those poor in spirit are
the poorest of all in everyone's lifetime
They will find no truth no matter
how they live; it is a darn crime

We are all soldiers in life,
sculpted with a fine knife
And trained with circumstance as our wife
And helped through the arms of the Lord
when we were in strife
whom without, there would be no night life
Thank you, kind sir, for breathing life into me
as it were
For my chance to live with all it has to infer
And learn all the truths that
I now have with which to refer
And to be alive to learn of what should occur
Gracious good man you have to understand
Let me gather knowledge
from Canada all the way to Japan
I will pass it on, gladly
all in my mortal life span
And I will do your *will*;
you are my Superman
I want to live before I die, and that is no lie
I want to have fun now and
on the Fourth of July
I want to intensify and exemplify;
I want to be the one who did it right
instead of being the wise guy
I want to apply myself;
even if it involves a case of sci-fi

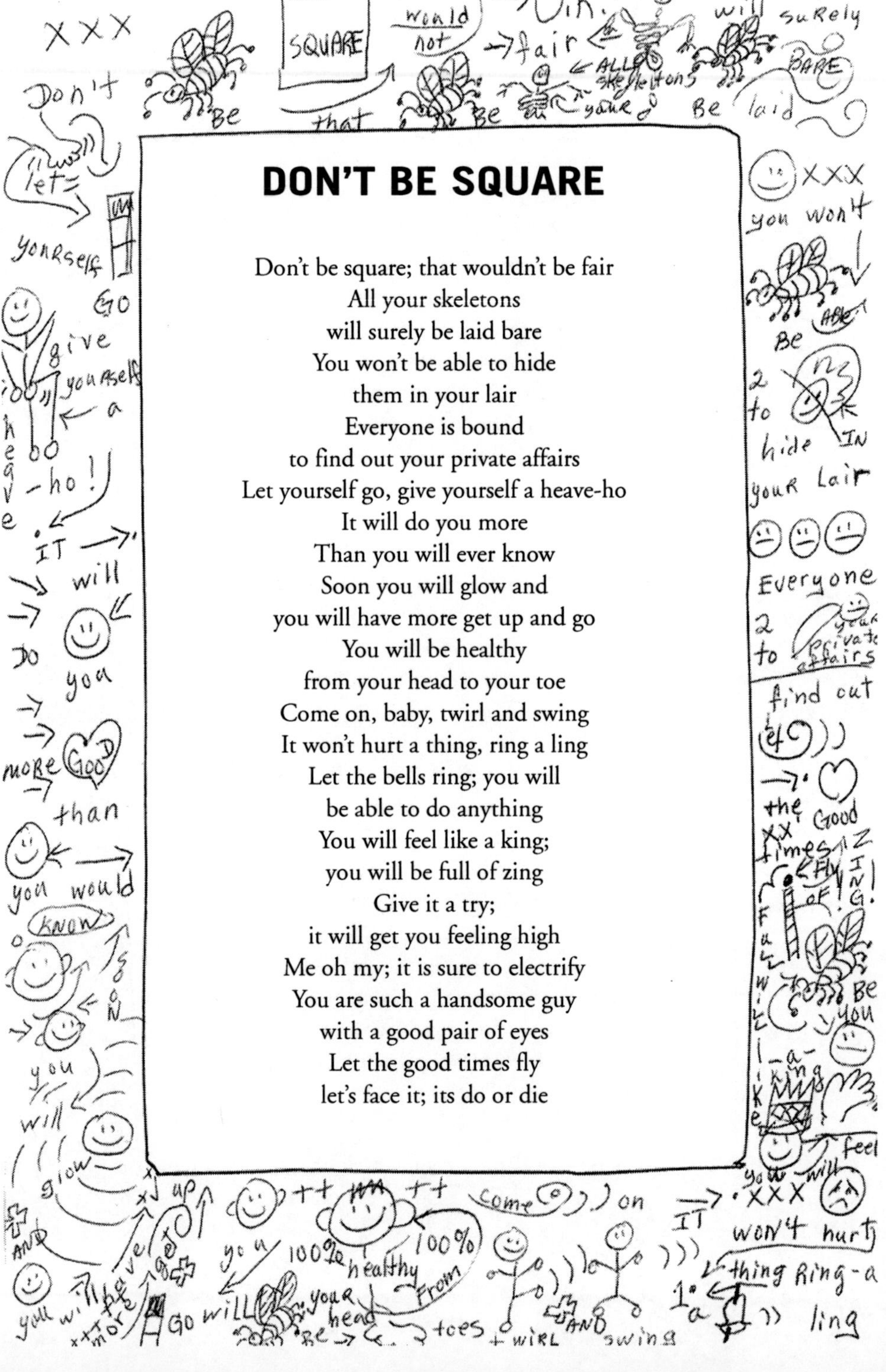

DON'T BE SQUARE

Don't be square; that wouldn't be fair
All your skeletons
will surely be laid bare
You won't be able to hide
them in your lair
Everyone is bound
to find out your private affairs
Let yourself go, give yourself a heave-ho
It will do you more
Than you will ever know
Soon you will glow and
you will have more get up and go
You will be healthy
from your head to your toe
Come on, baby, twirl and swing
It won't hurt a thing, ring a ling
Let the bells ring; you will
be able to do anything
You will feel like a king;
you will be full of zing
Give it a try;
it will get you feeling high
Me oh my; it is sure to electrify
You are such a handsome guy
with a good pair of eyes
Let the good times fly
let's face it; its do or die

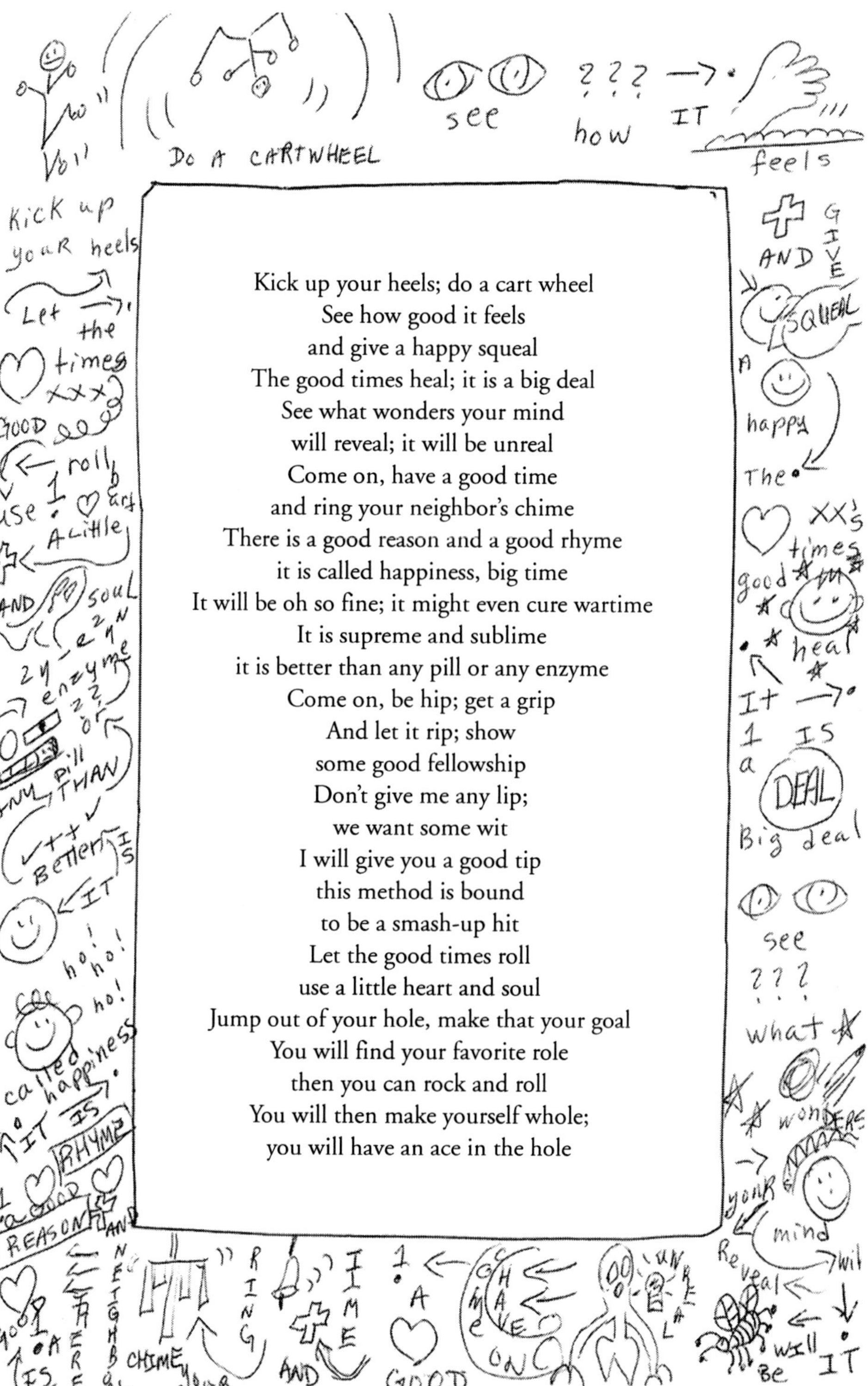

Kick up your heels; do a cart wheel
See how good it feels
and give a happy squeal
The good times heal; it is a big deal
See what wonders your mind
will reveal; it will be unreal
Come on, have a good time
and ring your neighbor's chime
There is a good reason and a good rhyme
it is called happiness, big time
It will be oh so fine; it might even cure wartime
It is supreme and sublime
it is better than any pill or any enzyme
Come on, be hip; get a grip
And let it rip; show
some good fellowship
Don't give me any lip;
we want some wit
I will give you a good tip
this method is bound
to be a smash-up hit
Let the good times roll
use a little heart and soul
Jump out of your hole, make that your goal
You will find your favorite role
then you can rock and roll
You will then make yourself whole;
you will have an ace in the hole

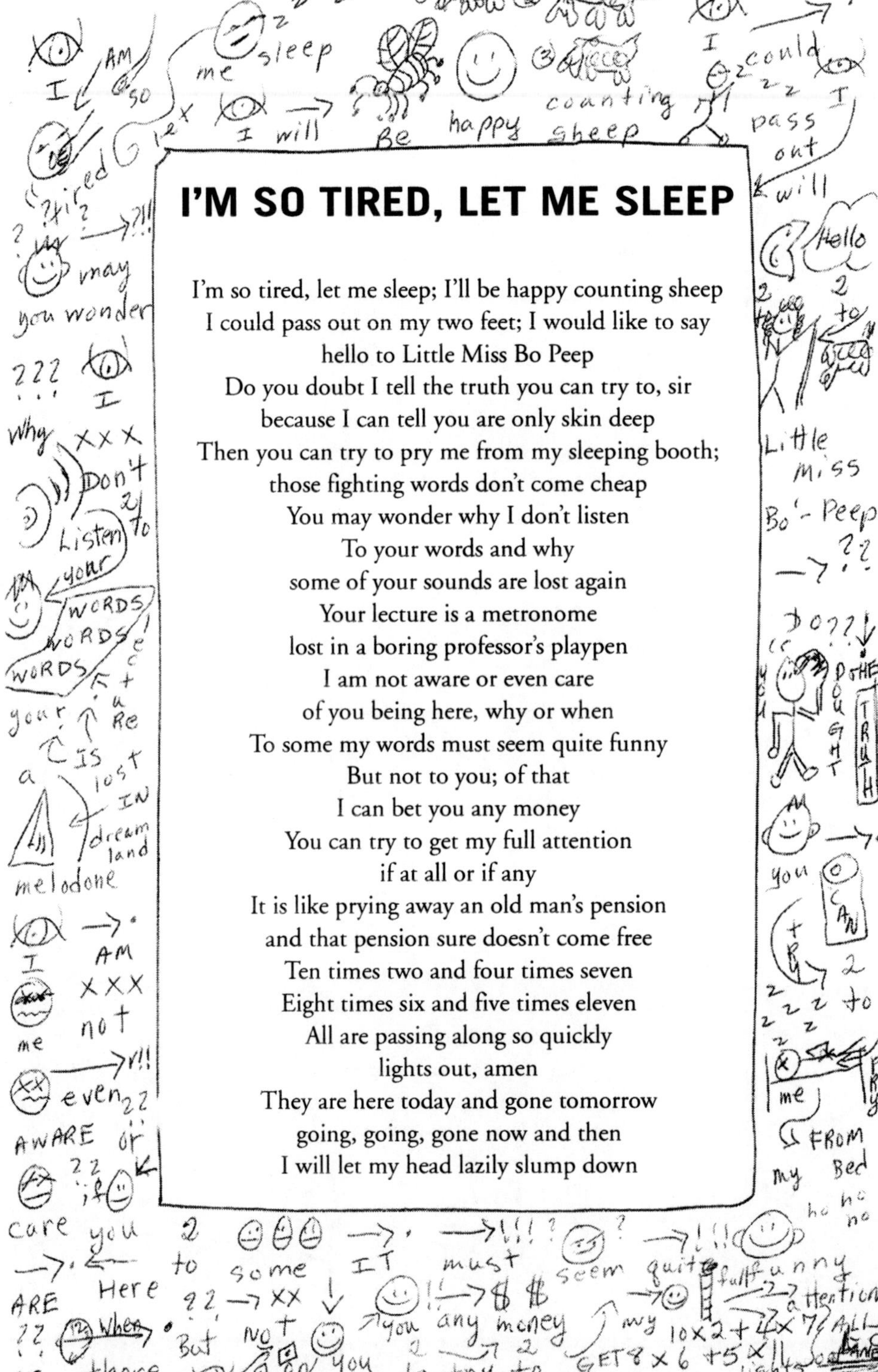

I'M SO TIRED, LET ME SLEEP

I'm so tired, let me sleep; I'll be happy counting sheep
I could pass out on my two feet; I would like to say
hello to Little Miss Bo Peep
Do you doubt I tell the truth you can try to, sir
because I can tell you are only skin deep
Then you can try to pry me from my sleeping booth;
those fighting words don't come cheap
You may wonder why I don't listen
To your words and why
some of your sounds are lost again
Your lecture is a metronome
lost in a boring professor's playpen
I am not aware or even care
of you being here, why or when
To some my words must seem quite funny
But not to you; of that
I can bet you any money
You can try to get my full attention
if at all or if any
It is like prying away an old man's pension
and that pension sure doesn't come free
Ten times two and four times seven
Eight times six and five times eleven
All are passing along so quickly
lights out, amen
They are here today and gone tomorrow
going, going, gone now and then
I will let my head lazily slump down

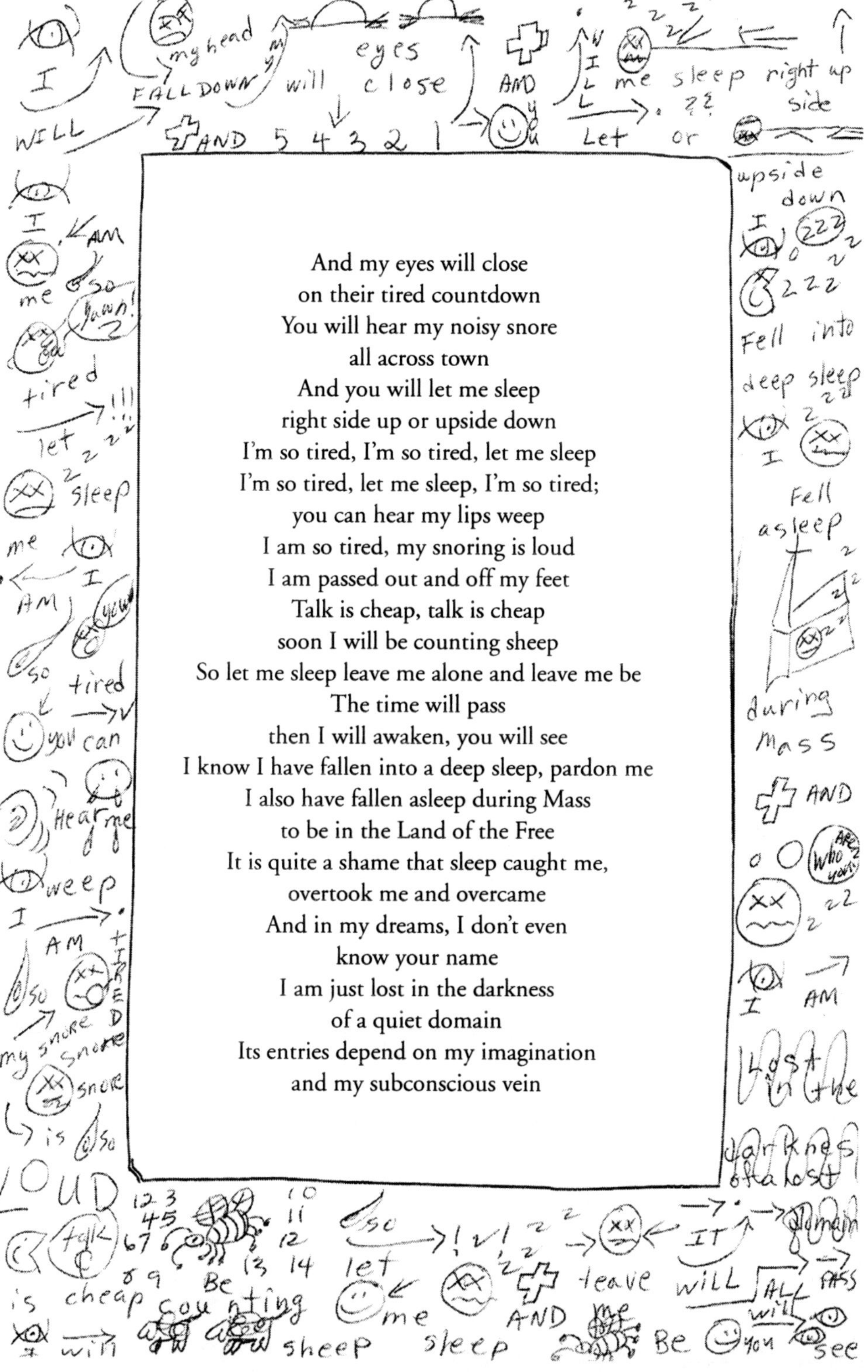

And my eyes will close
on their tired countdown
You will hear my noisy snore
all across town
And you will let me sleep
right side up or upside down
I'm so tired, I'm so tired, let me sleep
I'm so tired, let me sleep, I'm so tired;
you can hear my lips weep
I am so tired, my snoring is loud
I am passed out and off my feet
Talk is cheap, talk is cheap
soon I will be counting sheep
So let me sleep leave me alone and leave me be
The time will pass
then I will awaken, you will see
I know I have fallen into a deep sleep, pardon me
I also have fallen asleep during Mass
to be in the Land of the Free
It is quite a shame that sleep caught me,
overtook me and overcame
And in my dreams, I don't even
know your name
I am just lost in the darkness
of a quiet domain
Its entries depend on my imagination
and my subconscious vein

DEAN'S DOMAIN

Dean the mean machine
can't help but be seen
He is definitely
more than what he seems
He is wonderful,
if you know what I mean
Of my particular crop he is the cream
I must say in Dean's Domain
the real hint is in his name
This name will someday
bring him fortune and fame
You will be the one to gladly play at his game
And you will love him
all the while and all the same
Being great
just happens to be his fate
Someday,
he will find himself a fine mate
This wait for a mate
will definitely be worth his wait
He certainly will not be left at the gate
So jump to it, Dean
you know what I mean
You dare not sit; you must be sly and keen
You might like it all every bit;
that is to be seen
We will enjoy your wit, and
we know you are not really mean

You can't help but love him;
you will call him your friend
And you will want to perform
his every whim
Imagine something better
than Brothers Grimm
He will be the winner, on the outside rim
He will be gracious to your heart
And he will always
be the one to do his part
He will not be afraid
to be the one to start
And he will make computer
technology look like art
He never was one to brag or to flaunt
All his attributes he just acts
humble and nonchalant
He will probably never starve or want
Because he knows how to cook
just as good as any of his aunts
This young man, you can't help but love
Just because of everything
he is made of
He is as innocent and
as pure as a turtledove
But you cannot make him move when
he refuses to be shoved

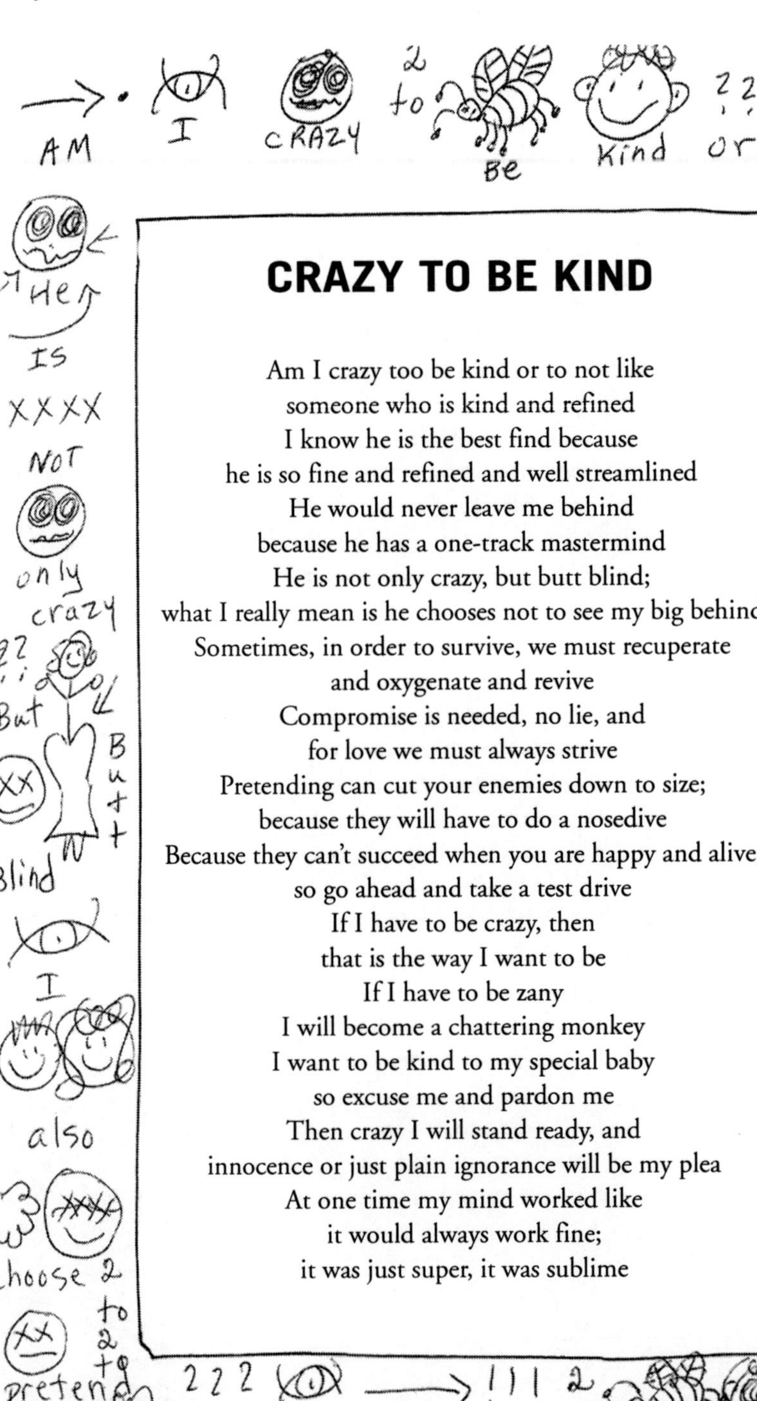

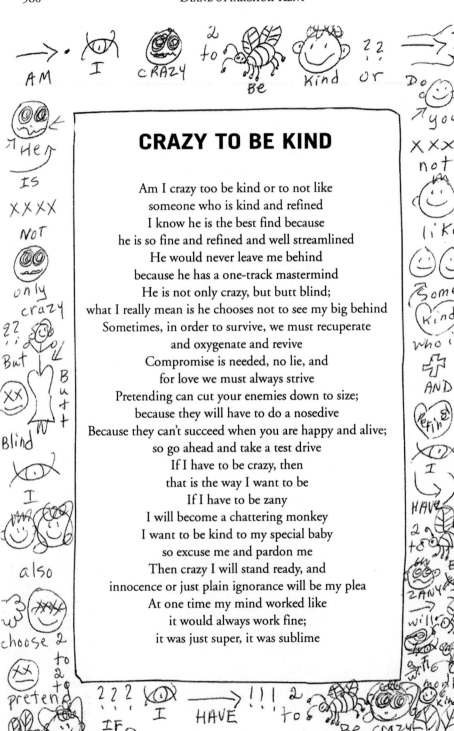

CRAZY TO BE KIND

Am I crazy too be kind or to not like
someone who is kind and refined
I know he is the best find because
he is so fine and refined and well streamlined
He would never leave me behind
because he has a one-track mastermind
He is not only crazy, but butt blind;
what I really mean is he chooses not to see my big behind
Sometimes, in order to survive, we must recuperate
and oxygenate and revive
Compromise is needed, no lie, and
for love we must always strive
Pretending can cut your enemies down to size;
because they will have to do a nosedive
Because they can't succeed when you are happy and alive;
so go ahead and take a test drive
If I have to be crazy, then
that is the way I want to be
If I have to be zany
I will become a chattering monkey
I want to be kind to my special baby
so excuse me and pardon me
Then crazy I will stand ready, and
innocence or just plain ignorance will be my plea
At one time my mind worked like
it would always work fine;
it was just super, it was sublime

Then I became crazy when I was in my early prime
and how my mind worked was nothing but a crime
At one time, I did not even own a dime
and life was one long, hard climb
I was an unlucky kind; I was the cast off of my peers
and all humankind
My life was not at an end entirely
or by any means
It started at the finish and came back
to the beginning; yes, it was quite keen
I started off fat and then became quite lean
That was the beginning and the middle
the end has yet to be seen
I knew it all along; my love was like a good folk song
it was where I was supposed to belong; especially
when I was innocent and young
It was like I would be the ugly duckling
going to do her swan song
I would be transformed before too long,
something like into a female King Kong
All I needed was blind faith, and lo and behold;
look what arrived, my future mate
I was the bait and I chose to wait and to hesitate
Let us get things right; let us get things straight;
I was not crazy to wait
I was in the hands of fate, and life wanted to
show me my prince, my loving candidate

Ah, victory is sweet; finally,
life has become a real treat
It was no small feat; it was definitely bittersweet
My body withstood all the heat;
and I proved I was not a deadbeat
And now I sit in the victory seat; I no longer
have to be discreet and my life is so complete

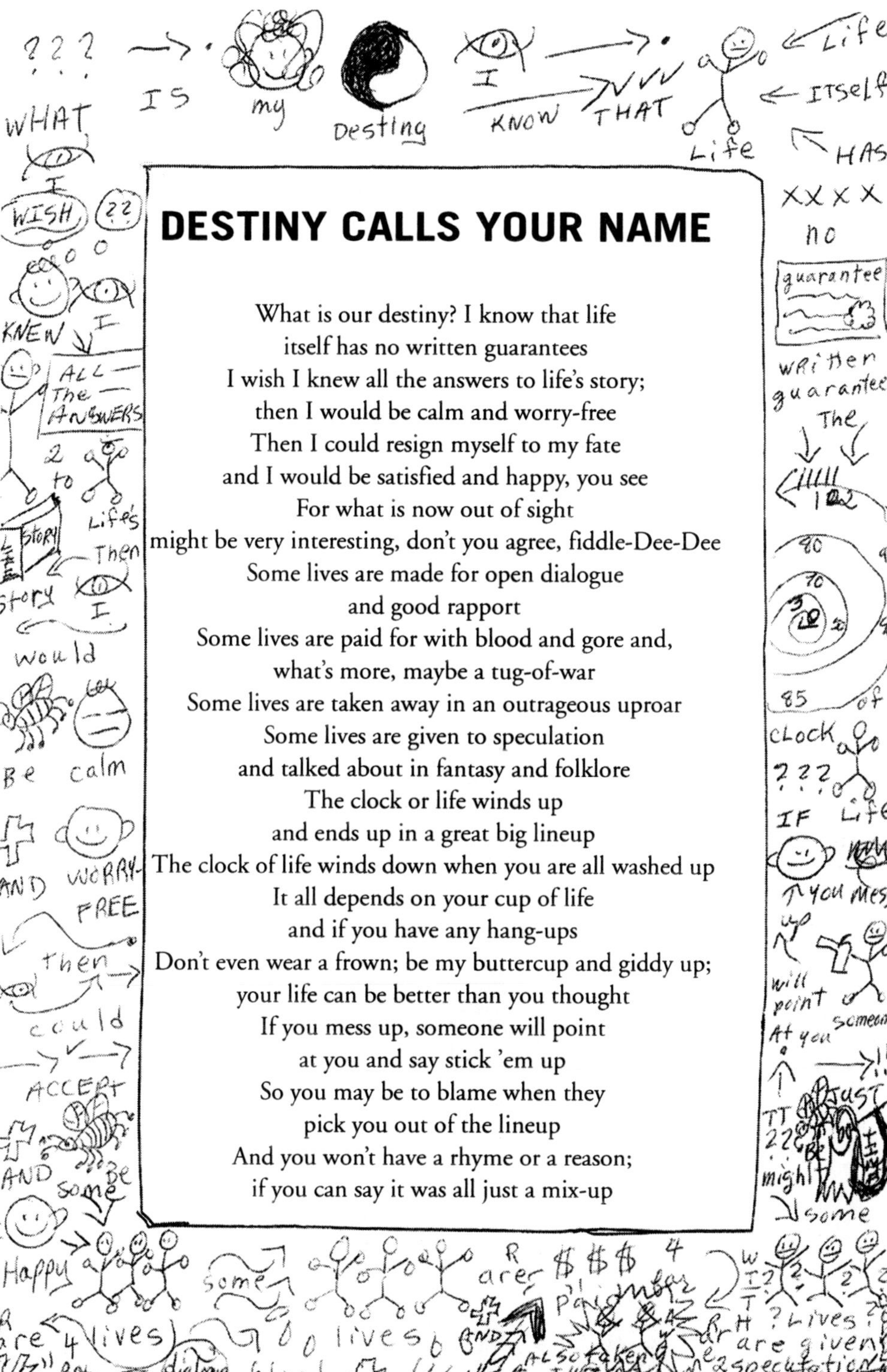

DESTINY CALLS YOUR NAME

What is our destiny? I know that life
itself has no written guarantees
I wish I knew all the answers to life's story;
then I would be calm and worry-free
Then I could resign myself to my fate
and I would be satisfied and happy, you see
For what is now out of sight
might be very interesting, don't you agree, fiddle-Dee-Dee
Some lives are made for open dialogue
and good rapport
Some lives are paid for with blood and gore and,
what's more, maybe a tug-of-war
Some lives are taken away in an outrageous uproar
Some lives are given to speculation
and talked about in fantasy and folklore
The clock or life winds up
and ends up in a great big lineup
The clock of life winds down when you are all washed up
It all depends on your cup of life
and if you have any hang-ups
Don't even wear a frown; be my buttercup and giddy up;
your life can be better than you thought
If you mess up, someone will point
at you and say stick 'em up
So you may be to blame when they
pick you out of the lineup
And you won't have a rhyme or a reason;
if you can say it was all just a mix-up

It might just happen all the same,
and then they will see you back at the big roundup
Glory is, I love life, and life loves me;
I feel like a busy bumblebee
Life is given and can be taken away; but it is best
when you participate and are not an absentee
It is surely fun to play along
and let it move you in a life spree, don't you agree?
Now can be the time in any old way
just to see what has been kept behind lock and key
Too much time has passed;
we must not let life stay at half mast
Life will go forward and face itself at full blast
Finally, we will fulfill our orders
and we will not again be downcast
We will go past all known borders
and we will no longer be known as outcasts
Don't let it pass; take your chance to tell the brass
You're not second class; in fact,
you can be at the head of your class
Make sure to go to Mass and learn some morality,
and you will not reach an impasse
You won't come in last
because you sir are full of sassafras
Destiny calls your name, come and say hello
It is not and will not be the same,
and it doesn't have to be a tale of woe
You may be pleasantly surprised and
you might end up at a fashion show
It may become even more than you hoped for
so get ready, set, go

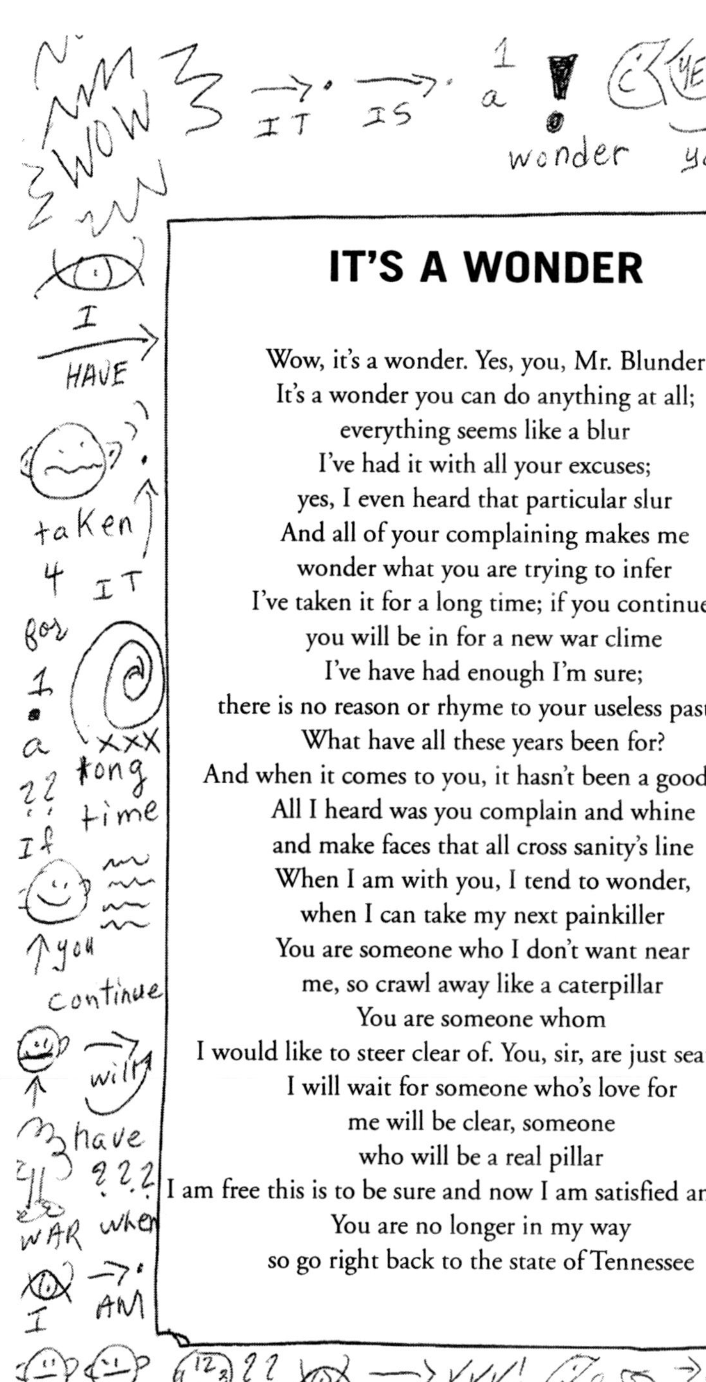

IT'S A WONDER

Wow, it's a wonder. Yes, you, Mr. Blunder
It's a wonder you can do anything at all;
everything seems like a blur
I've had it with all your excuses;
yes, I even heard that particular slur
And all of your complaining makes me
wonder what you are trying to infer
I've taken it for a long time; if you continue,
you will be in for a new war clime
I've have had enough I'm sure;
there is no reason or rhyme to your useless pastime
What have all these years been for?
And when it comes to you, it hasn't been a good time
All I heard was you complain and whine
and make faces that all cross sanity's line
When I am with you, I tend to wonder,
when I can take my next painkiller
You are someone who I don't want near
me, so crawl away like a caterpillar
You are someone whom
I would like to steer clear of. You, sir, are just seat filler
I will wait for someone who's love for
me will be clear, someone
who will be a real pillar
I am free this is to be sure and now I am satisfied and happy
You are no longer in my way
so go right back to the state of Tennessee

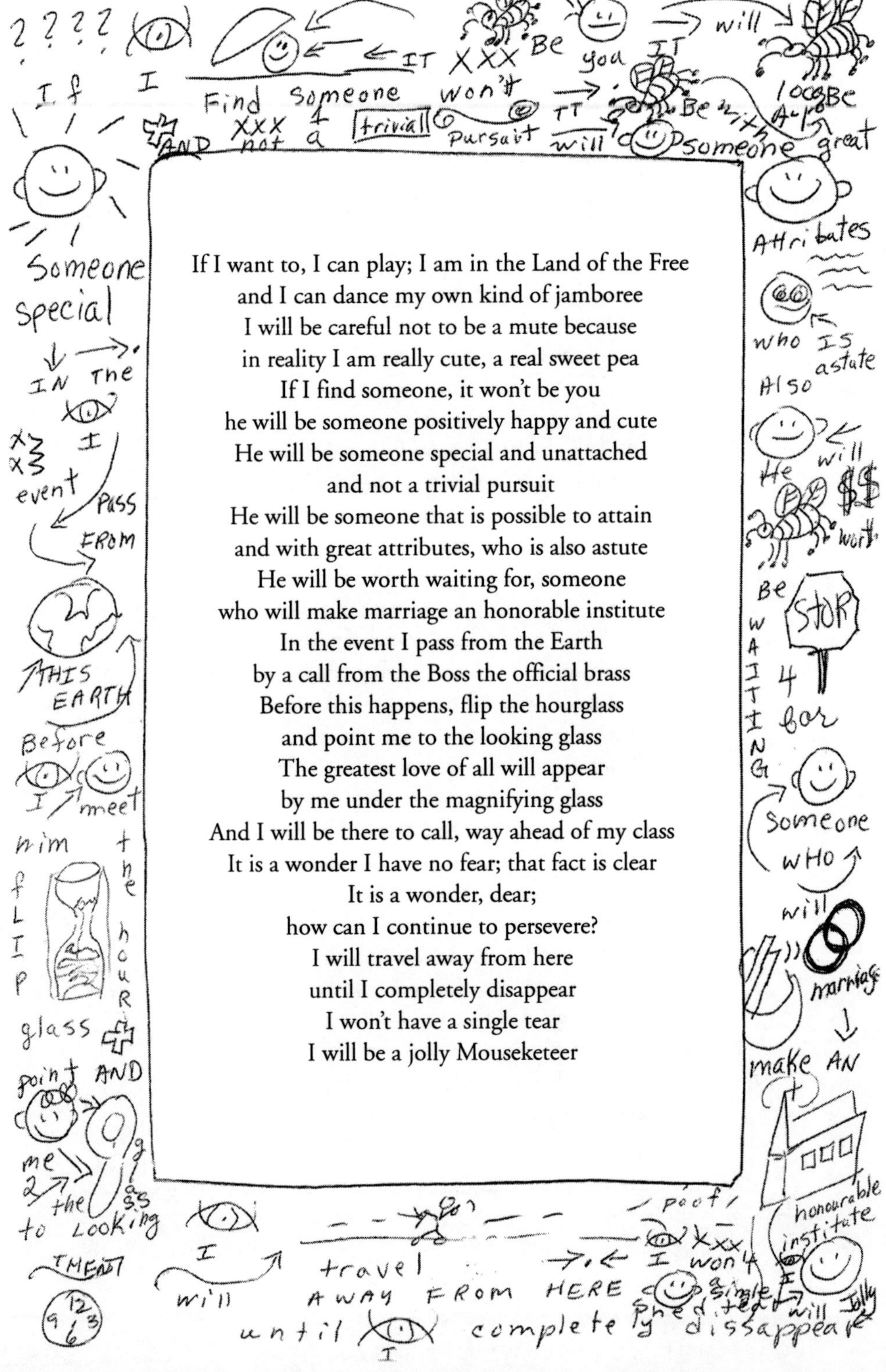

If I want to, I can play; I am in the Land of the Free
and I can dance my own kind of jamboree
I will be careful not to be a mute because
in reality I am really cute, a real sweet pea
If I find someone, it won't be you
he will be someone positively happy and cute
He will be someone special and unattached
and not a trivial pursuit
He will be someone that is possible to attain
and with great attributes, who is also astute
He will be worth waiting for, someone
who will make marriage an honorable institute
In the event I pass from the Earth
by a call from the Boss the official brass
Before this happens, flip the hourglass
and point me to the looking glass
The greatest love of all will appear
by me under the magnifying glass
And I will be there to call, way ahead of my class
It is a wonder I have no fear; that fact is clear
It is a wonder, dear;
how can I continue to persevere?
I will travel away from here
until I completely disappear
I won't have a single tear
I will be a jolly Mouseketeer

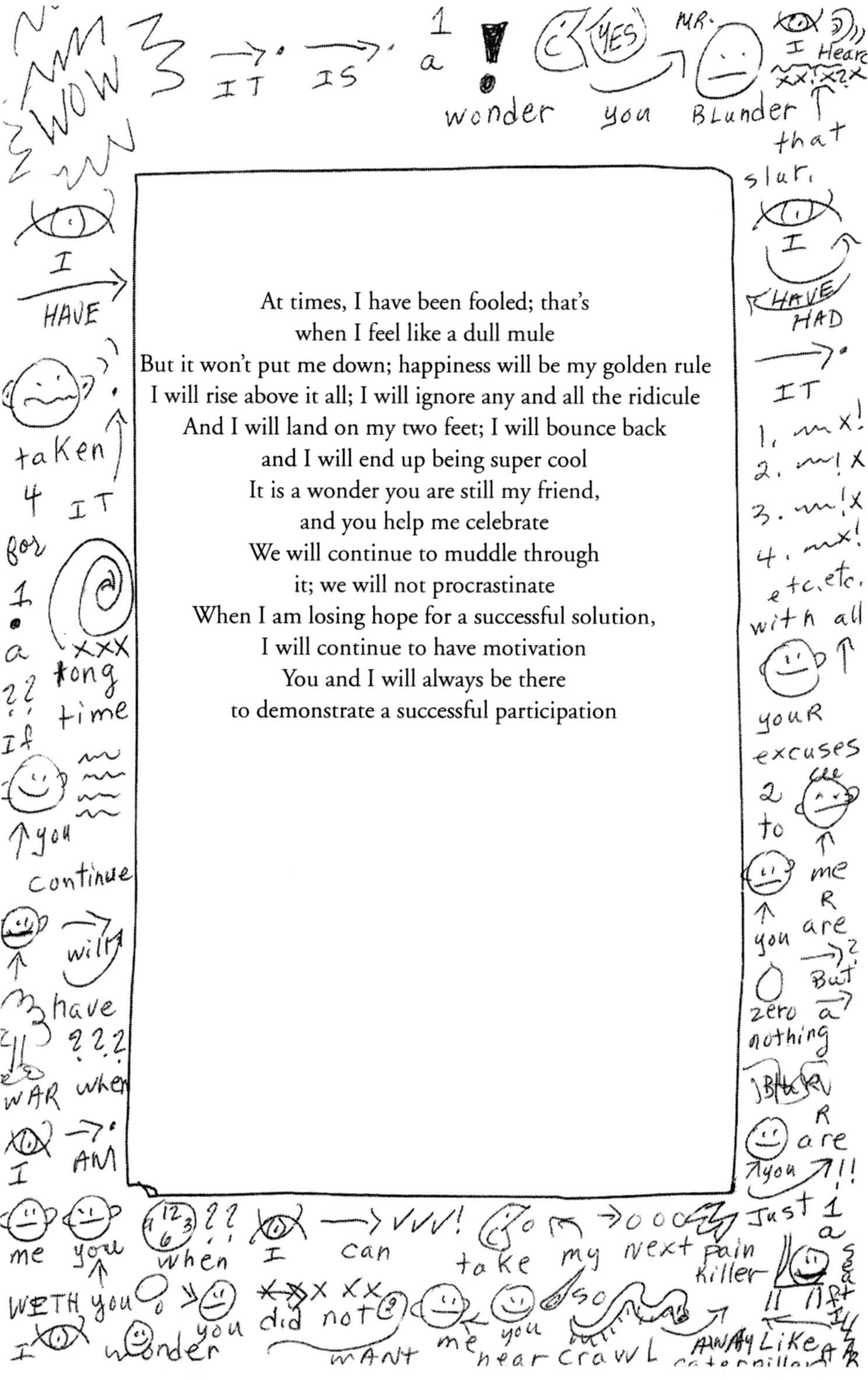

At times, I have been fooled; that's
when I feel like a dull mule
But it won't put me down; happiness will be my golden rule
I will rise above it all; I will ignore any and all the ridicule
And I will land on my two feet; I will bounce back
and I will end up being super cool
It is a wonder you are still my friend,
and you help me celebrate
We will continue to muddle through
it; we will not procrastinate
When I am losing hope for a successful solution,
I will continue to have motivation
You and I will always be there
to demonstrate a successful participation

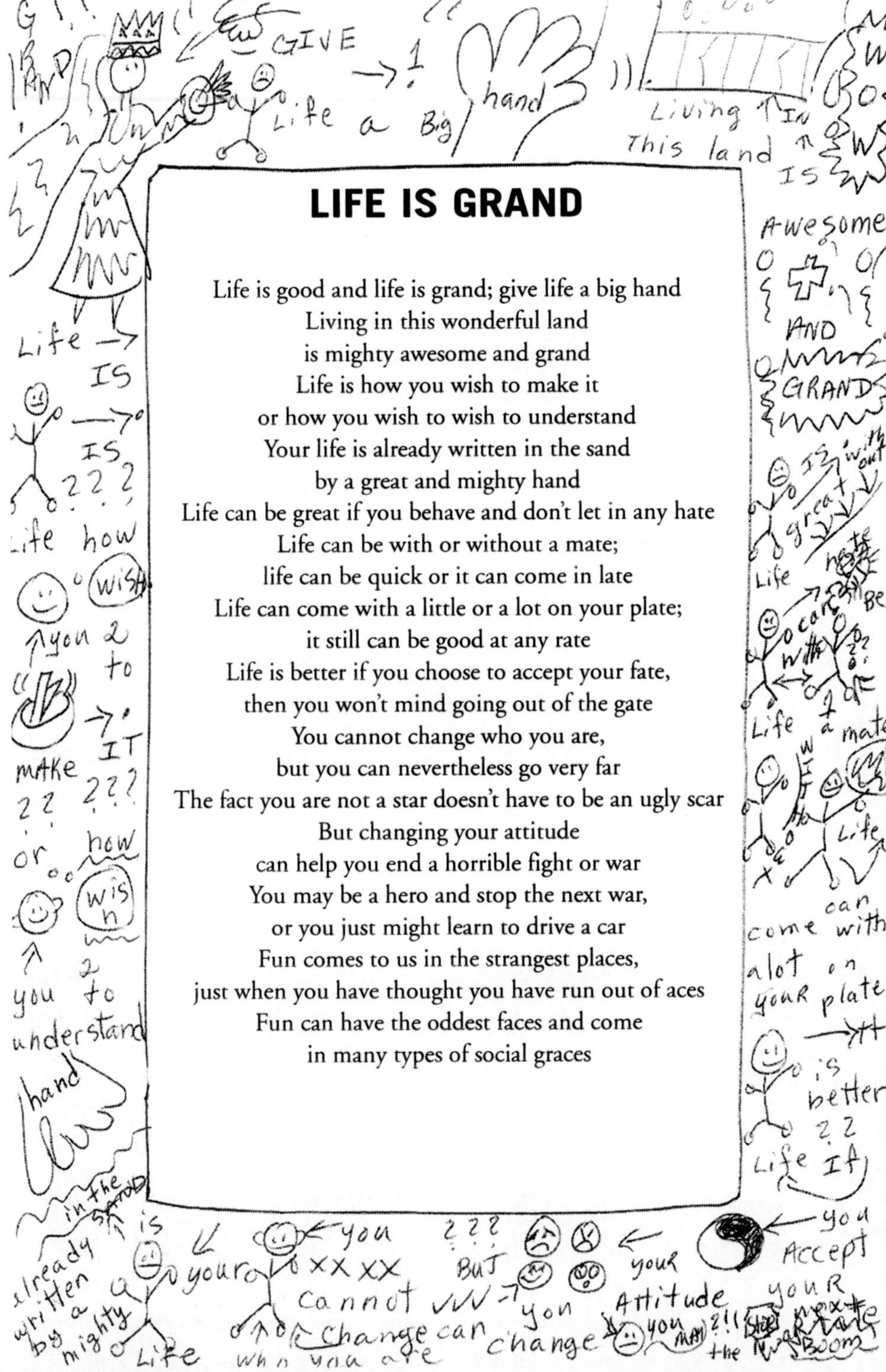

LIFE IS GRAND

Life is good and life is grand; give life a big hand
Living in this wonderful land
is mighty awesome and grand
Life is how you wish to make it
or how you wish to wish to understand
Your life is already written in the sand
by a great and mighty hand
Life can be great if you behave and don't let in any hate
Life can be with or without a mate;
life can be quick or it can come in late
Life can come with a little or a lot on your plate;
it still can be good at any rate
Life is better if you choose to accept your fate,
then you won't mind going out of the gate
You cannot change who you are,
but you can nevertheless go very far
The fact you are not a star doesn't have to be an ugly scar
But changing your attitude
can help you end a horrible fight or war
You may be a hero and stop the next war,
or you just might learn to drive a car
Fun comes to us in the strangest places,
just when you have thought you have run out of aces
Fun can have the oddest faces and come
in many types of social graces

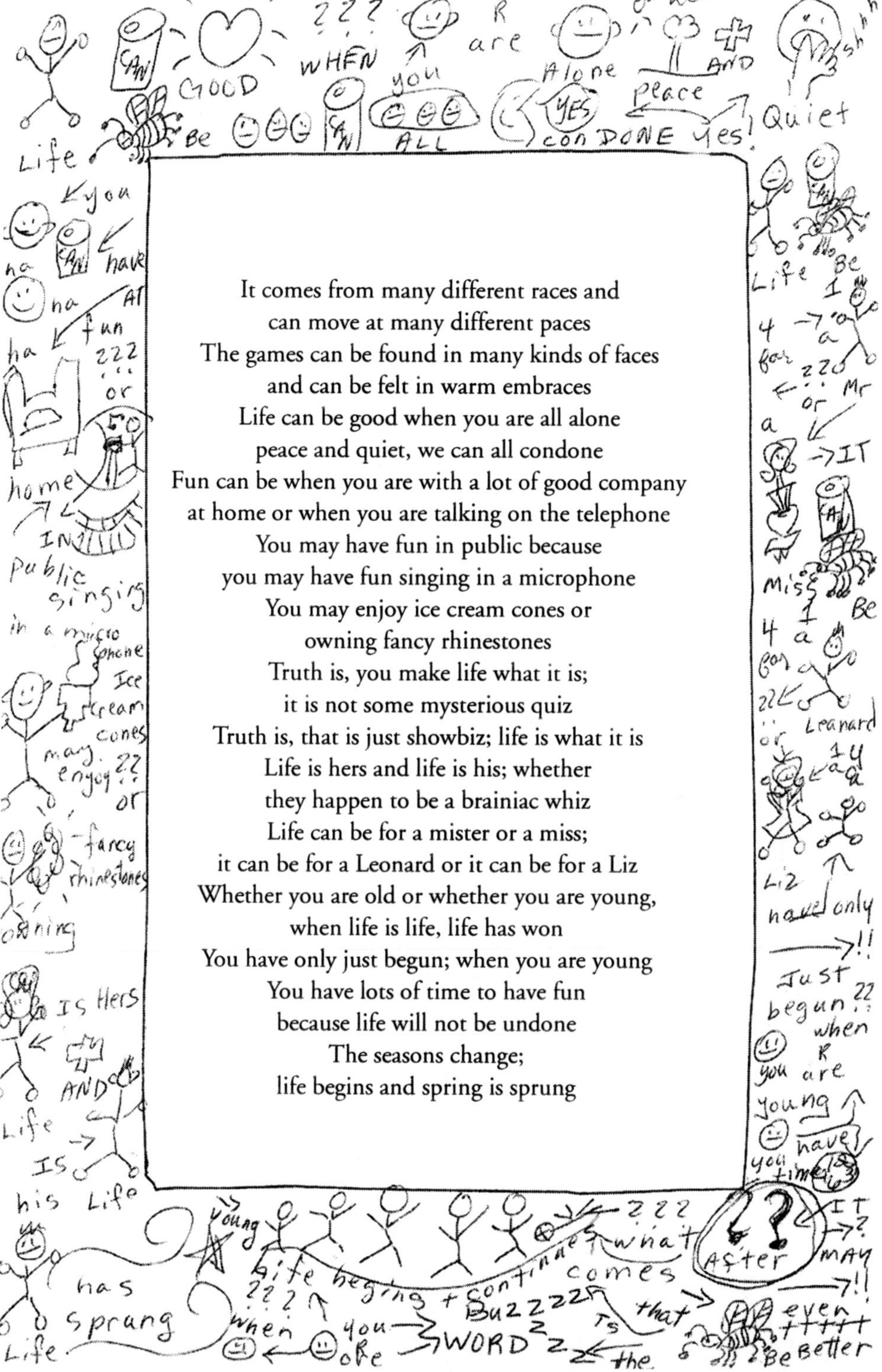

It comes from many different races and
can move at many different paces
The games can be found in many kinds of faces
and can be felt in warm embraces
Life can be good when you are all alone
peace and quiet, we can all condone
Fun can be when you are with a lot of good company
at home or when you are talking on the telephone
You may have fun in public because
you may have fun singing in a microphone
You may enjoy ice cream cones or
owning fancy rhinestones
Truth is, you make life what it is;
it is not some mysterious quiz
Truth is, that is just showbiz; life is what it is
Life is hers and life is his; whether
they happen to be a brainiac whiz
Life can be for a mister or a miss;
it can be for a Leonard or it can be for a Liz
Whether you are old or whether you are young,
when life is life, life has won
You have only just begun; when you are young
You have lots of time to have fun
because life will not be undone
The seasons change;
life begins and spring is sprung

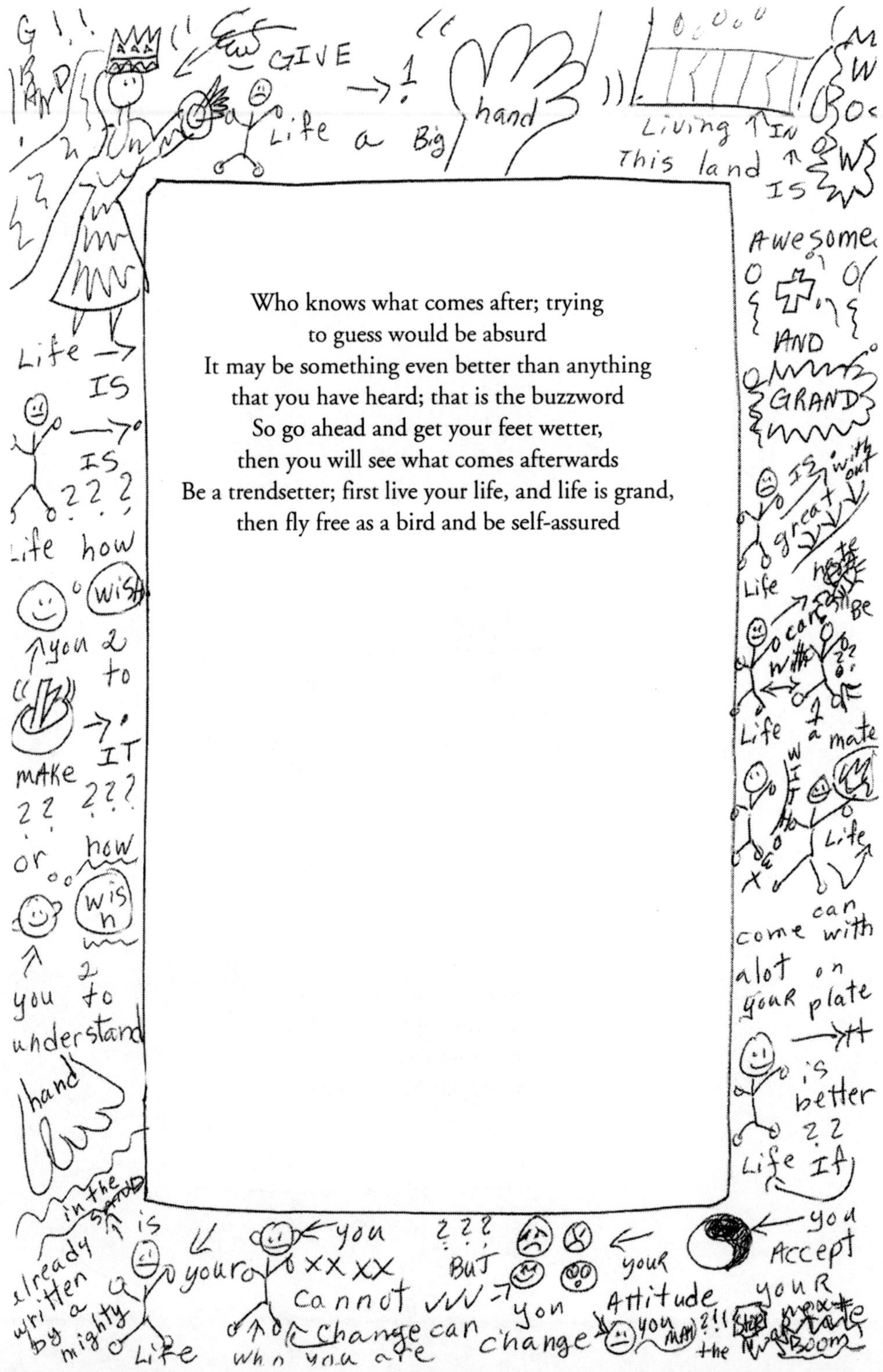

Who knows what comes after; trying
to guess would be absurd
It may be something even better than anything
that you have heard; that is the buzzword
So go ahead and get your feet wetter,
then you will see what comes afterwards
Be a trendsetter; first live your life, and life is grand,
then fly free as a bird and be self-assured

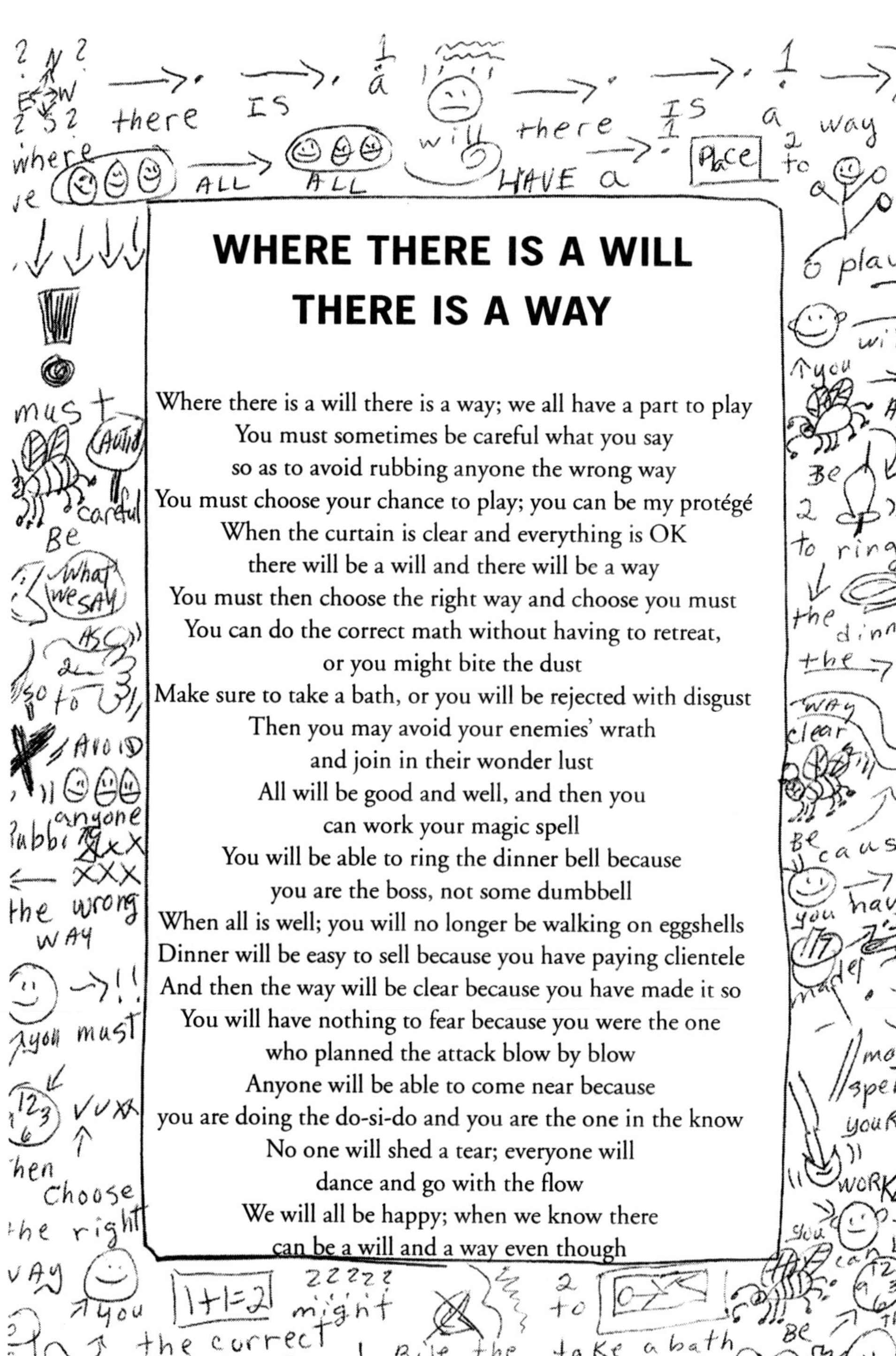

WHERE THERE IS A WILL THERE IS A WAY

Where there is a will there is a way; we all have a part to play
You must sometimes be careful what you say
so as to avoid rubbing anyone the wrong way
You must choose your chance to play; you can be my protégé
When the curtain is clear and everything is OK
there will be a will and there will be a way
You must then choose the right way and choose you must
You can do the correct math without having to retreat,
or you might bite the dust
Make sure to take a bath, or you will be rejected with disgust
Then you may avoid your enemies' wrath
and join in their wonder lust
All will be good and well, and then you
can work your magic spell
You will be able to ring the dinner bell because
you are the boss, not some dumbbell
When all is well; you will no longer be walking on eggshells
Dinner will be easy to sell because you have paying clientele
And then the way will be clear because you have made it so
You will have nothing to fear because you were the one
who planned the attack blow by blow
Anyone will be able to come near because
you are doing the do-si-do and you are the one in the know
No one will shed a tear; everyone will
dance and go with the flow
We will all be happy; when we know there
can be a will and a way even though

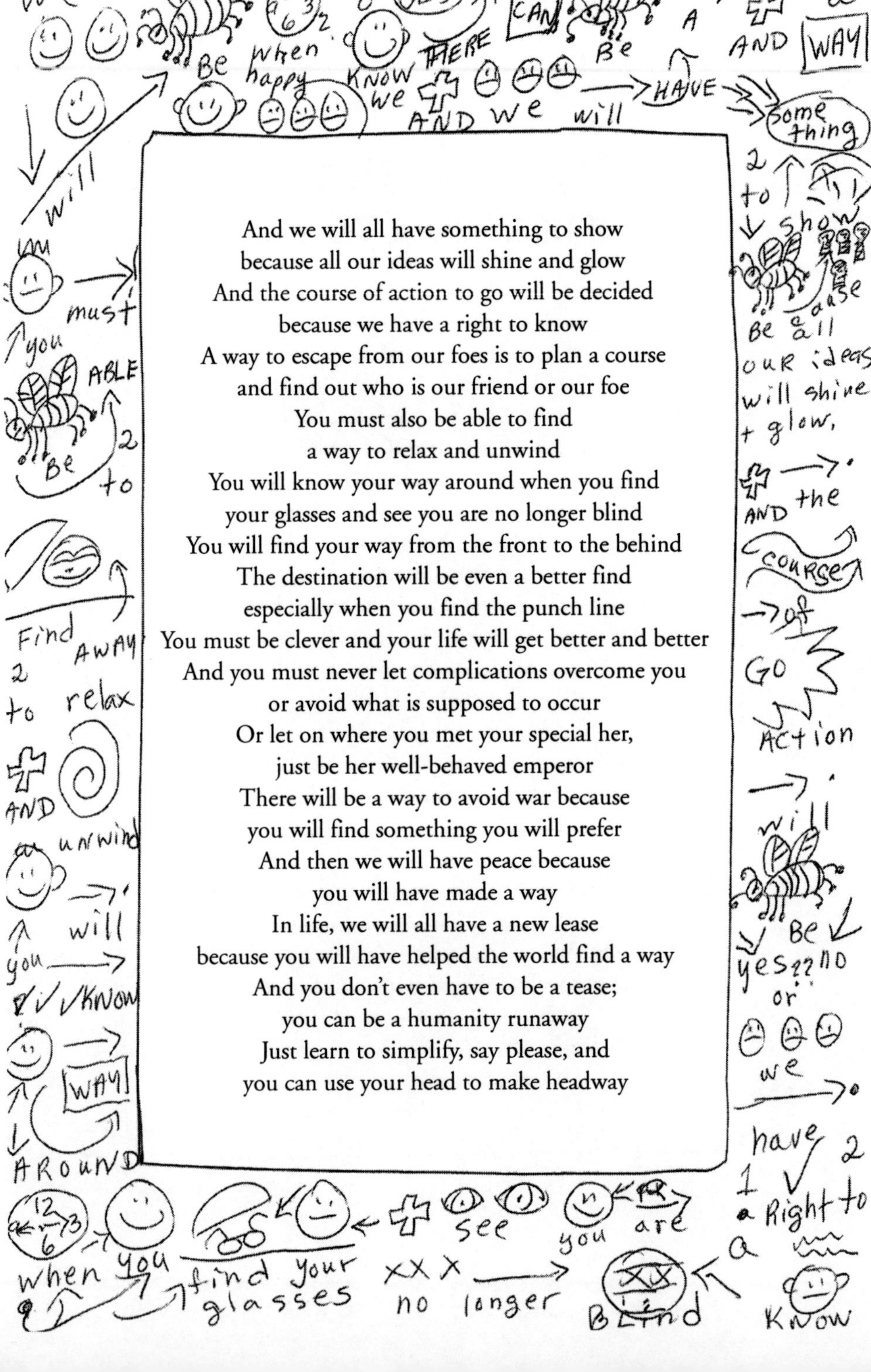

And we will all have something to show
because all our ideas will shine and glow
And the course of action to go will be decided
because we have a right to know
A way to escape from our foes is to plan a course
and find out who is our friend or our foe
You must also be able to find
a way to relax and unwind
You will know your way around when you find
your glasses and see you are no longer blind
You will find your way from the front to the behind
The destination will be even a better find
especially when you find the punch line
You must be clever and your life will get better and better
And you must never let complications overcome you
or avoid what is supposed to occur
Or let on where you met your special her,
just be her well-behaved emperor
There will be a way to avoid war because
you will find something you will prefer
And then we will have peace because
you will have made a way
In life, we will all have a new lease
because you will have helped the world find a way
And you don't even have to be a tease;
you can be a humanity runaway
Just learn to simplify, say please, and
you can use your head to make headway

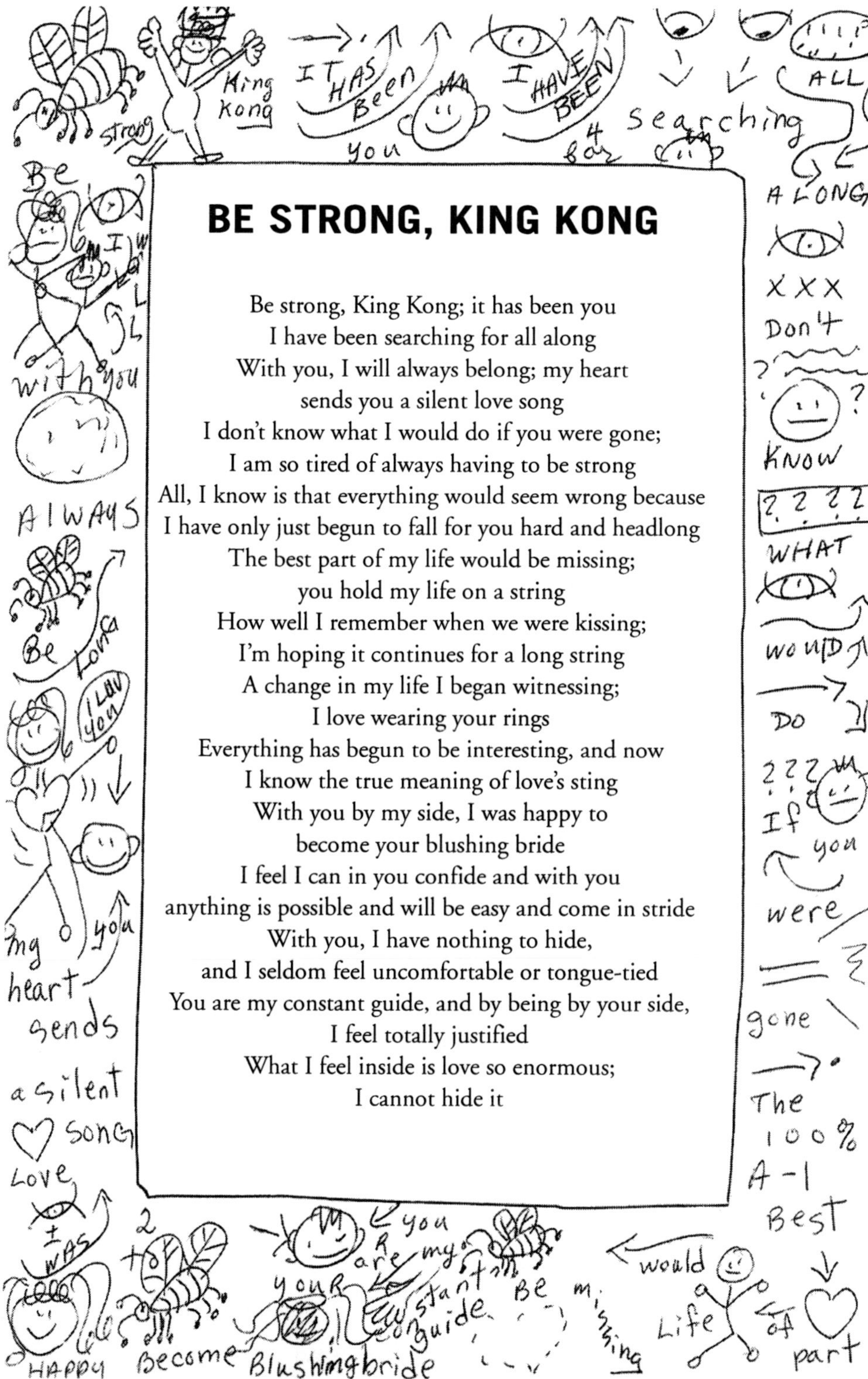

BE STRONG, KING KONG

Be strong, King Kong; it has been you
I have been searching for all along
With you, I will always belong; my heart
sends you a silent love song
I don't know what I would do if you were gone;
I am so tired of always having to be strong
All, I know is that everything would seem wrong because
I have only just begun to fall for you hard and headlong
The best part of my life would be missing;
you hold my life on a string
How well I remember when we were kissing;
I'm hoping it continues for a long string
A change in my life I began witnessing;
I love wearing your rings
Everything has begun to be interesting, and now
I know the true meaning of love's sting
With you by my side, I was happy to
become your blushing bride
I feel I can in you confide and with you
anything is possible and will be easy and come in stride
With you, I have nothing to hide,
and I seldom feel uncomfortable or tongue-tied
You are my constant guide, and by being by your side,
I feel totally justified
What I feel inside is love so enormous;
I cannot hide it

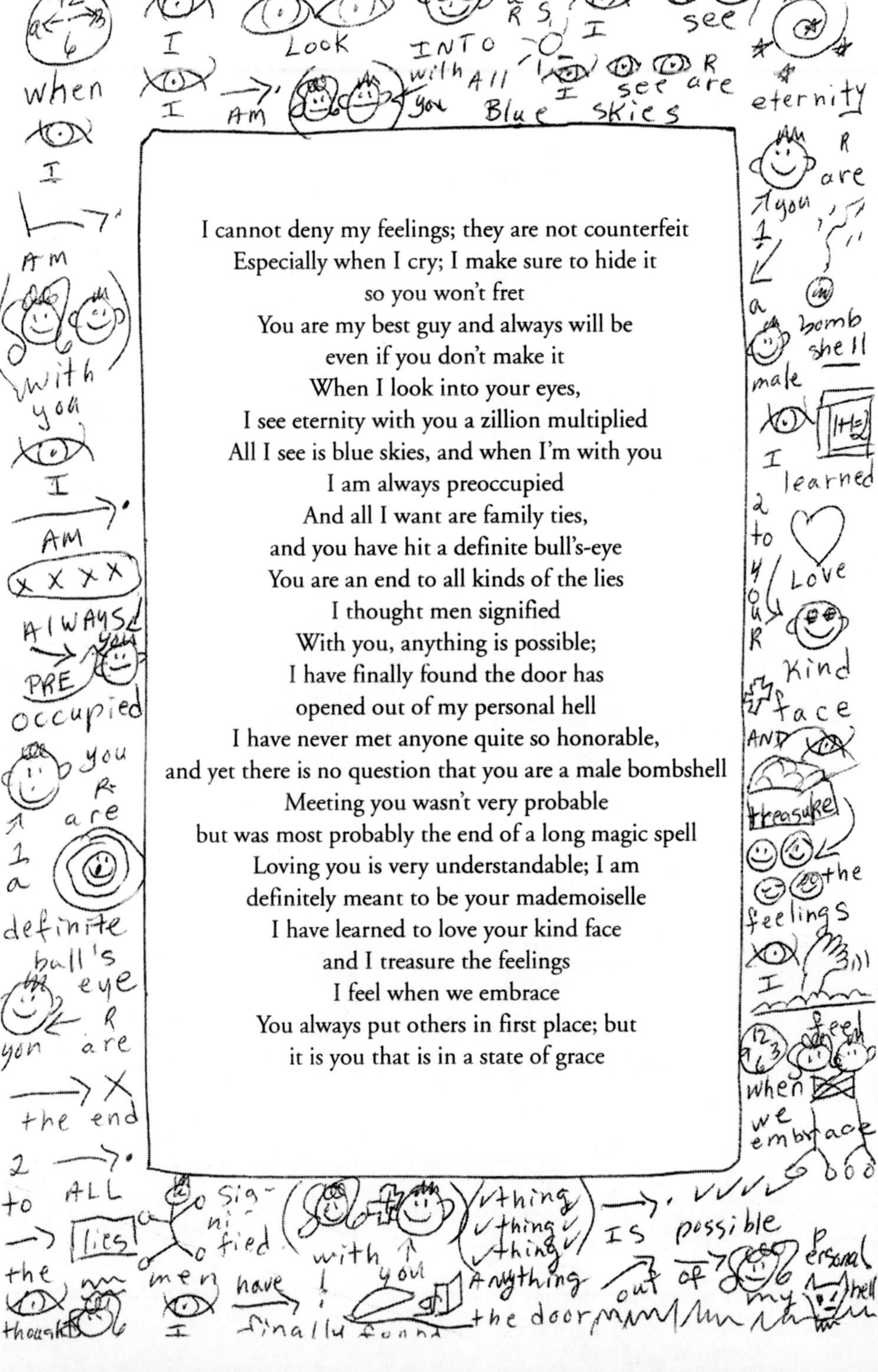

I cannot deny my feelings; they are not counterfeit
Especially when I cry; I make sure to hide it
so you won't fret
You are my best guy and always will be
even if you don't make it
When I look into your eyes,
I see eternity with you a zillion multiplied
All I see is blue skies, and when I'm with you
I am always preoccupied
And all I want are family ties,
and you have hit a definite bull's-eye
You are an end to all kinds of the lies
I thought men signified
With you, anything is possible;
I have finally found the door has
opened out of my personal hell
I have never met anyone quite so honorable,
and yet there is no question that you are a male bombshell
Meeting you wasn't very probable
but was most probably the end of a long magic spell
Loving you is very understandable; I am
definitely meant to be your mademoiselle
I have learned to love your kind face
and I treasure the feelings
I feel when we embrace
You always put others in first place; but
it is you that is in a state of grace

All I know is when I am with you
I have had a taste of living in the
universe in the winner's space
I have no time to waste;
I will keep you close as much as possible just in case
Please be strong; I want you to live long, my King Kong
You have done nothing wrong; you have always belonged
Listen to my song; I will be your little Din Din, your
ding-a-ling ding-dong
I have loved you all along; that is my life song, and
with you my heart will always sing along

A ROCK AND ROLL CHRISTMAS

Ding, ding, jingle ring a ling Christmas is the thing
Who needs summertime,
and what's so great about spring
When you can celebrate
the middle of winter and sing, sing
About Christmas and celebrate life and get into the swing
I can't wait until I get you
under the mistletoe
Because you are no ordinary, plain Joe
And when I shook you there,
you will be the first one to know
What it feels like
to be kissed by a raging inferno
When we get together, we will give
a new meaning to a rock and roll Christmas
Because we will rock and roll
until we run out of gas
Our kind of rock and roll will have a lot of class
We will rock, rock, roll, roll,
and make a lot of razzmatazz
Ring, ring a ling, let's sing
Rock, rock, rock that thing
Ding, ding
I'll be your ding-a-ling
Roll, roll, and roll
we can't help but win

Let's hear it for the Christmas class
Let's shake, shake,
and shake our sassafras
Let's rock and roll
the old-fashioned middle class
Let's roll and rock and rock and rock
and let's make it fast
Tick-tock, rock a ling rock rolls
Walk, run, rock, soar, fly, roll
Sip, drink, rock, taste, gobble, roll
Talk, yell, rock, whistle, roar, and roll
When we send Christmas packing
It will be with all wheels
rolling, rolling, and rolling
And we will be
rock, rock, rock, rocking
And there will be
no regrets or hesitating
So go ahead; you can
talk, talk, and talk
But me, I think I will
Rock, rock, rock
And even, if it is freezing
cold, cold, cold
I am going to continue to roll, roll, and roll

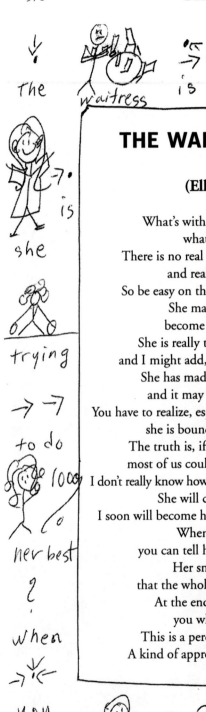

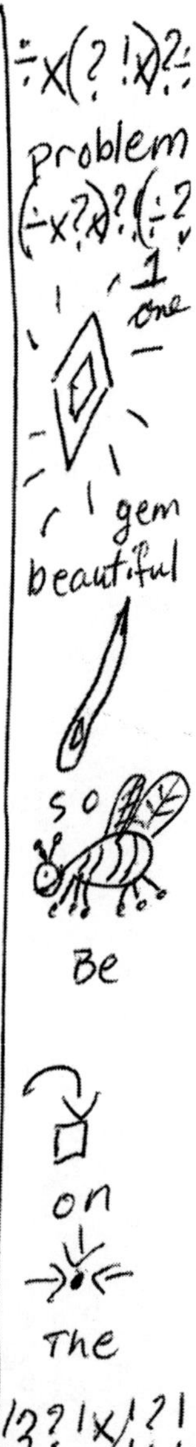

THE WAITRESS IS NEW

(Elle EST Nouveau)

What's with her, what is the problem
what a mistake again?
There is no real problem, she is just beautiful
and really a brand-new gem
So be easy on the insults, try not to condemn
She may, after all, someday,
become your very best friend
She is really trying her utmost and best
and I might add, with a lot of enthusiastic zest
She has made this job her latest quest,
and it may turn out to be a real test
You have to realize, especially when she is working alone,
she is bound to be busy and stressed
The truth is, if we could do as good as her,
most of us could not help but be impressed
I don't really know how she does it; to me, she is a smash hit
She will convince me bit by bit;
I soon will become her staunch protector and advocate
When you see her smile;
you can tell her smile is not counterfeit
Her smile is so contagious
that the whole room becomes lit with it
At the end of the day, we will say
you who and give her due
This is a percentage of her spoils, a tip
A kind of appreciative monetary thank-you

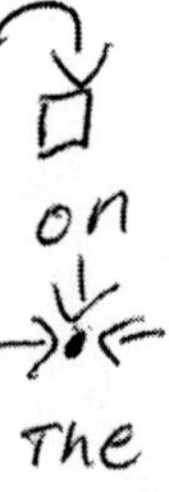

We must make her aware we appreciate
her through and through
We like her because she usually works
until the rooster goes cock-a-doodle-doo
To be realistic, being a waitress will be most girls' occupation
Sometimes, they will do this while they attend school
or just after they are all done
They may just need extra money or
are giving work a trial run
The fact that they are working
means their victory has been won
Being a waitress is a profession that is
not only meant for women, but also for men
In this case, they are dubbed waiters
in that working ballpark or rather bull pen
These men need special skills
like how to present a poison signature pen
Any which way; they prove they are
wonderful, again and again
We must try to be patient with these beautiful people
and show a good example of the golden rule
by showing them how to be super cool
We must avoid showing any ridicule,
no matter how tiny or miniscule
We will then show that politeness is the best tool
and has the majority rule
Yes, I know very well, that waiter or waitress is new

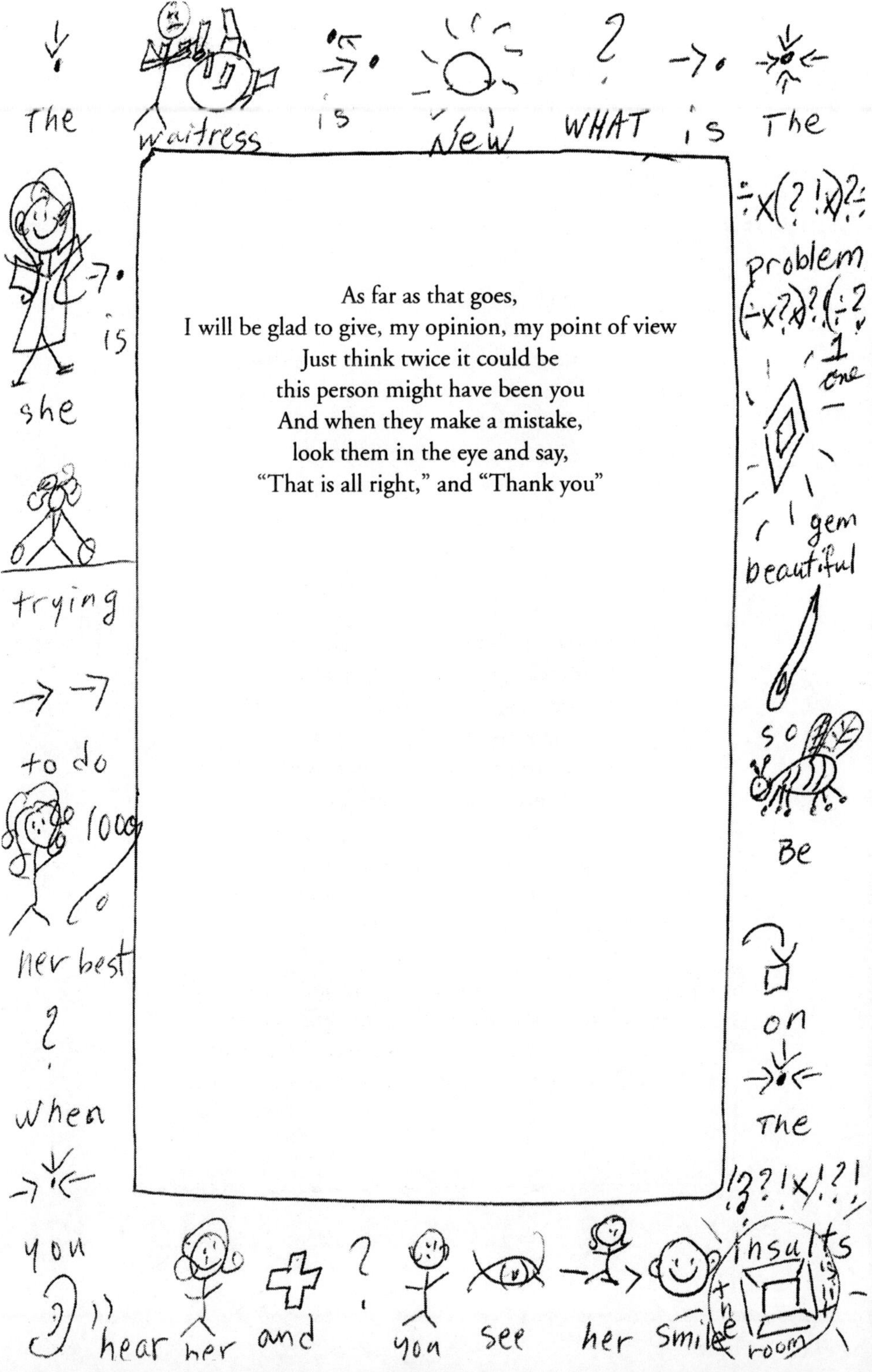

As far as that goes,
I will be glad to give, my opinion, my point of view
Just think twice it could be
this person might have been you
And when they make a mistake,
look them in the eye and say,
“That is all right,” and “Thank you”

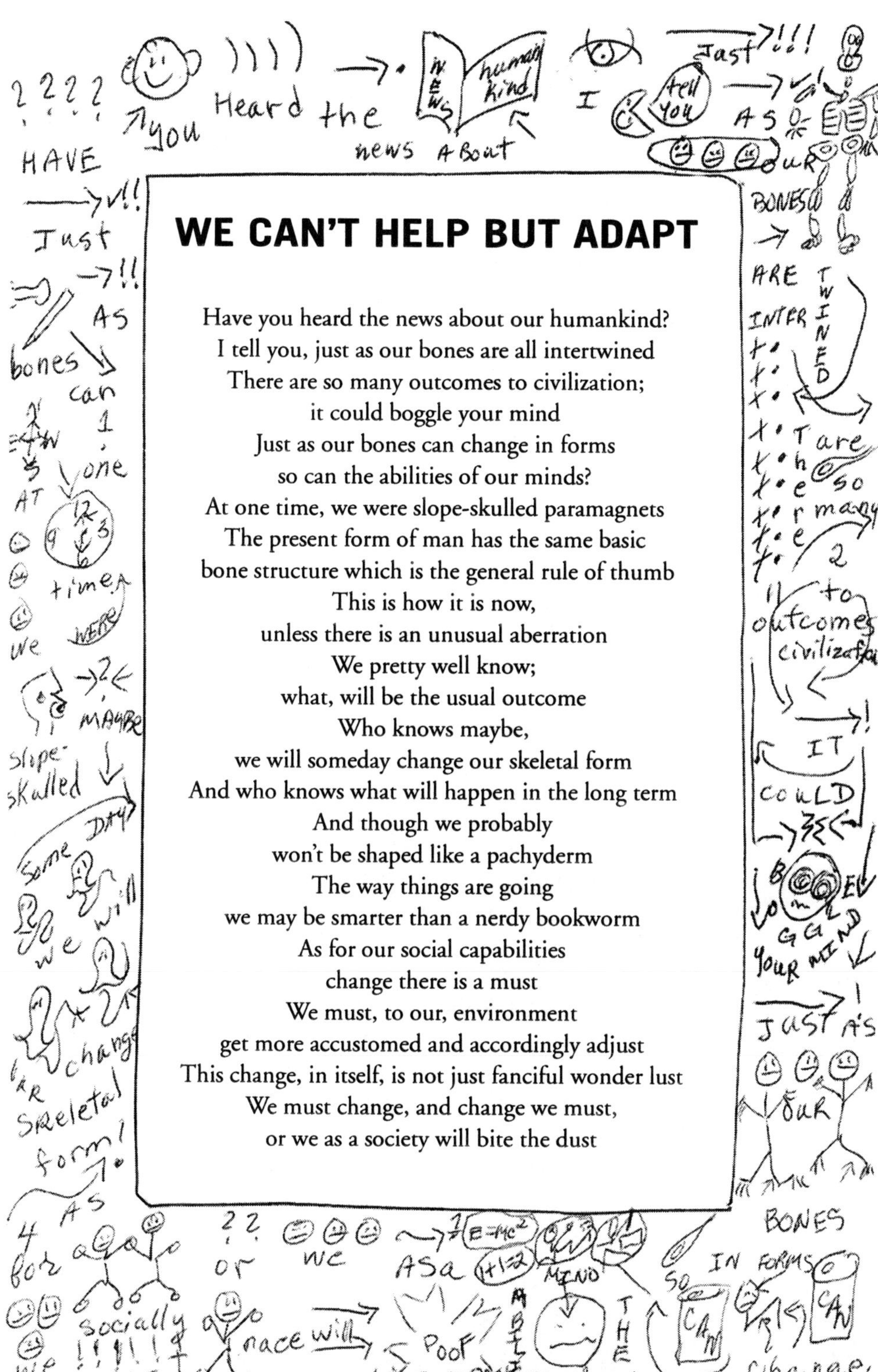

WE CAN'T HELP BUT ADAPT

Have you heard the news about our humankind?
I tell you, just as our bones are all intertwined
There are so many outcomes to civilization;
it could boggle your mind
Just as our bones can change in forms
so can the abilities of our minds?
At one time, we were slope-skulled paramagnets
The present form of man has the same basic
bone structure which is the general rule of thumb
This is how it is now,
unless there is an unusual aberration
We pretty well know;
what, will be the usual outcome
Who knows maybe,
we will someday change our skeletal form
And who knows what will happen in the long term
And though we probably
won't be shaped like a pachyderm
The way things are going
we may be smarter than a nerdy bookworm
As for our social capabilities
change there is a must
We must, to our, environment
get more accustomed and accordingly adjust
This change, in itself, is not just fanciful wonder lust
We must change, and change we must,
or we as a society will bite the dust

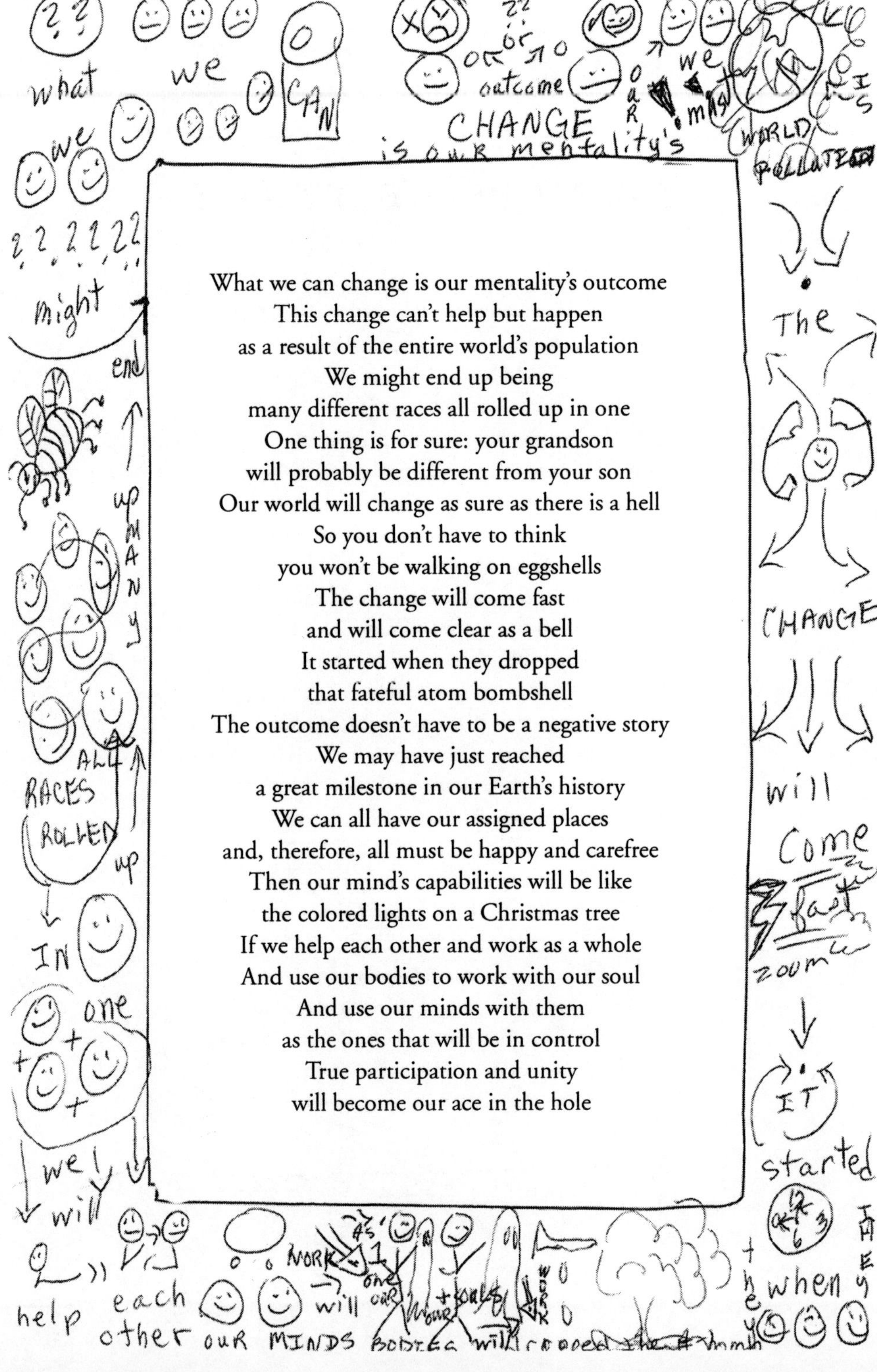

What we can change is our mentality's outcome
This change can't help but happen
as a result of the entire world's population
We might end up being
many different races all rolled up in one
One thing is for sure: your grandson
will probably be different from your son
Our world will change as sure as there is a hell
So you don't have to think
you won't be walking on eggshells
The change will come fast
and will come clear as a bell
It started when they dropped
that fateful atom bombshell
The outcome doesn't have to be a negative story
We may have just reached
a great milestone in our Earth's history
We can all have our assigned places
and, therefore, all must be happy and carefree
Then our mind's capabilities will be like
the colored lights on a Christmas tree
If we help each other and work as a whole
And use our bodies to work with our soul
And use our minds with them
as the ones that will be in control
True participation and unity
will become our ace in the hole

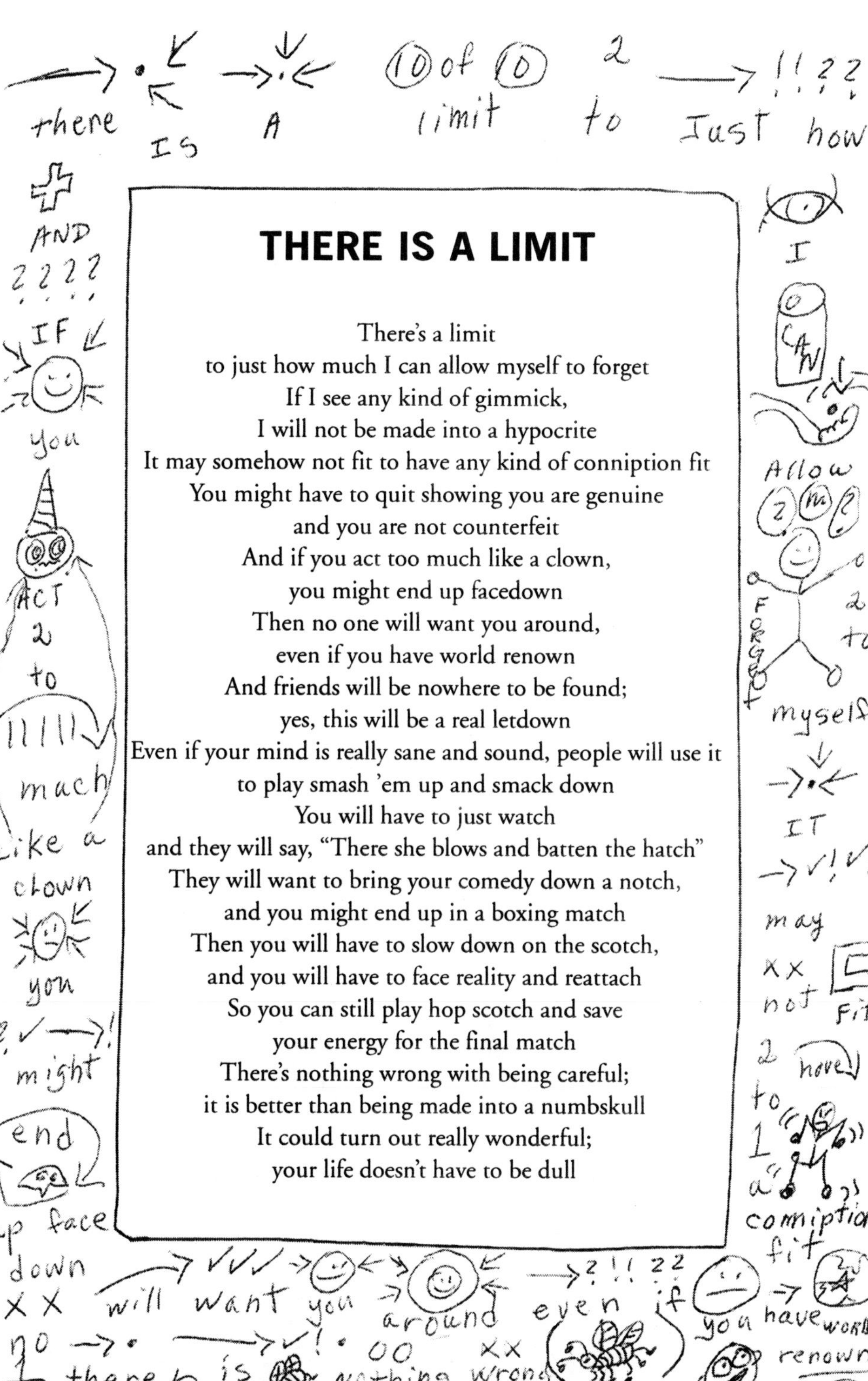

THERE IS A LIMIT

There's a limit
to just how much I can allow myself to forget
If I see any kind of gimmick,
I will not be made into a hypocrite
It may somehow not fit to have any kind of conniption fit
You might have to quit showing you are genuine
and you are not counterfeit
And if you act too much like a clown,
you might end up facedown
Then no one will want you around,
even if you have world renown
And friends will be nowhere to be found;
yes, this will be a real letdown
Even if your mind is really sane and sound, people will use it
to play smash 'em up and smack down
You will have to just watch
and they will say, "There she blows and batten the hatch"
They will want to bring your comedy down a notch,
and you might end up in a boxing match
Then you will have to slow down on the scotch,
and you will have to face reality and reattach
So you can still play hop scotch and save
your energy for the final match
There's nothing wrong with being careful;
it is better than being made into a numbskull
It could turn out really wonderful;
your life doesn't have to be dull

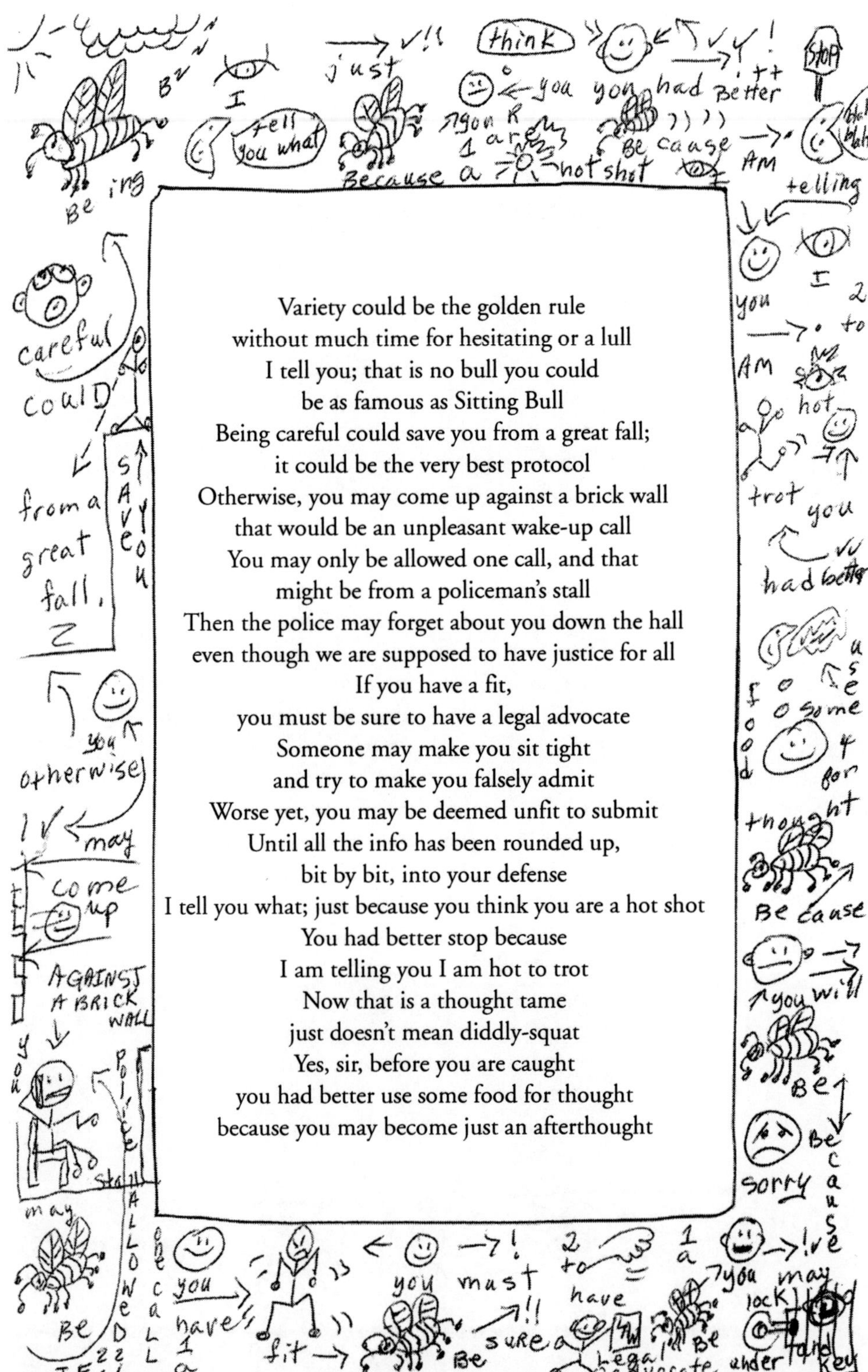

Variety could be the golden rule
without much time for hesitating or a lull
I tell you; that is no bull you could
be as famous as Sitting Bull
Being careful could save you from a great fall;
it could be the very best protocol
Otherwise, you may come up against a brick wall
that would be an unpleasant wake-up call
You may only be allowed one call, and that
might be from a policeman's stall
Then the police may forget about you down the hall
even though we are supposed to have justice for all
If you have a fit,
you must be sure to have a legal advocate
Someone may make you sit tight
and try to make you falsely admit
Worse yet, you may be deemed unfit to submit
Until all the info has been rounded up,
bit by bit, into your defense
I tell you what; just because you think you are a hot shot
You had better stop because
I am telling you I am hot to trot
Now that is a thought tame
just doesn't mean diddly-squat
Yes, sir, before you are caught
you had better use some food for thought
because you may become just an afterthought

If you don't, you will be sorry because
you might be the one under lock and key
Things may get messy, especially if they ask for your ID
It will happen in a sudden flurry when
they find the whole rest of the story
It will be a sad, sad situation
and you will be the one with all the worries

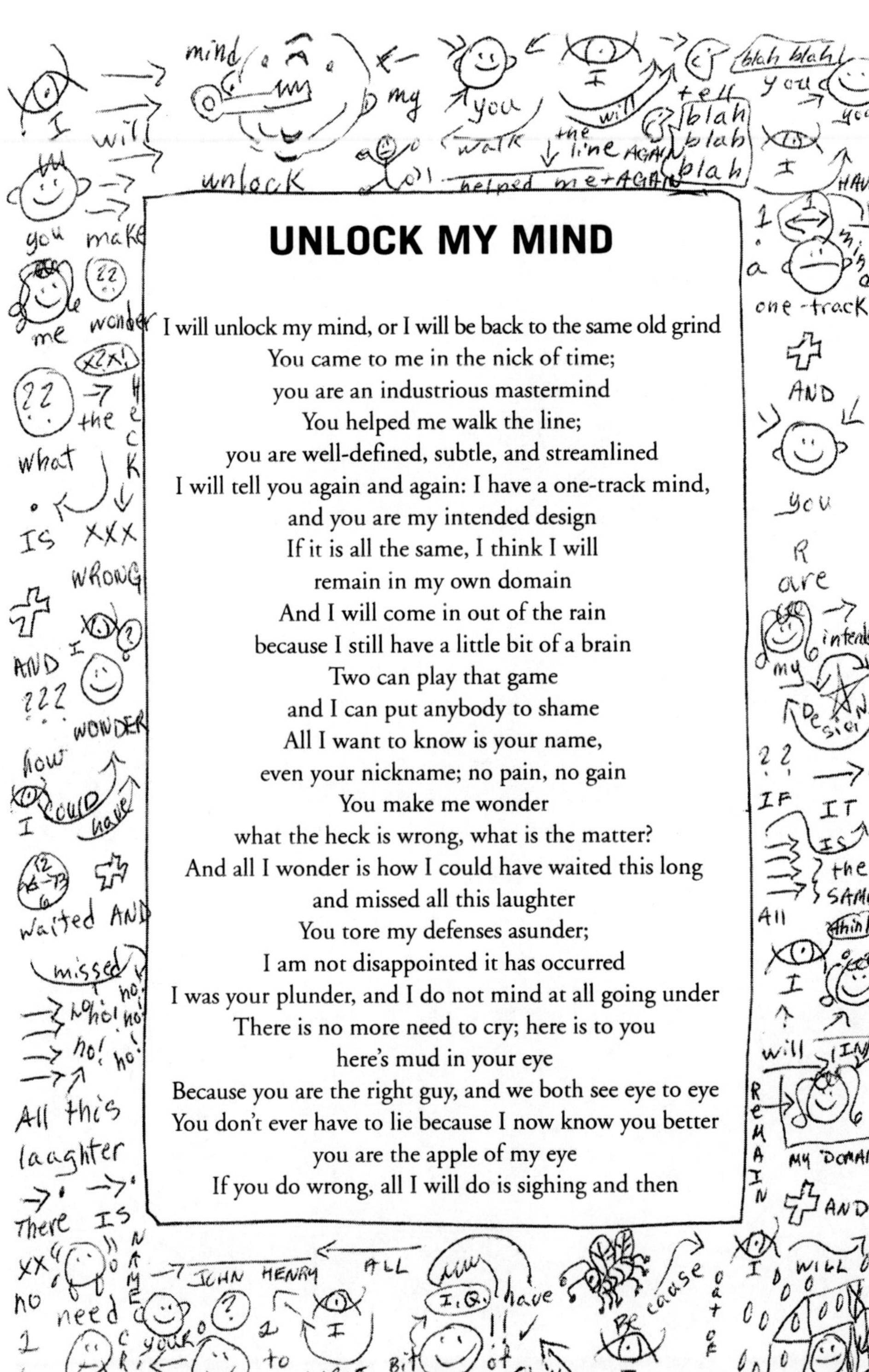

UNLOCK MY MIND

I will unlock my mind, or I will be back to the same old grind
You came to me in the nick of time;
you are an industrious mastermind
You helped me walk the line;
you are well-defined, subtle, and streamlined
I will tell you again and again: I have a one-track mind,
and you are my intended design
If it is all the same, I think I will
remain in my own domain
And I will come in out of the rain
because I still have a little bit of a brain
Two can play that game
and I can put anybody to shame
All I want to know is your name,
even your nickname; no pain, no gain
You make me wonder
what the heck is wrong, what is the matter?
And all I wonder is how I could have waited this long
and missed all this laughter
You tore my defenses asunder;
I am not disappointed it has occurred
I was your plunder, and I do not mind at all going under
There is no more need to cry; here is to you
here's mud in your eye
Because you are the right guy, and we both see eye to eye
You don't ever have to lie because I now know you better
you are the apple of my eye
If you do wrong, all I will do is sighing and then

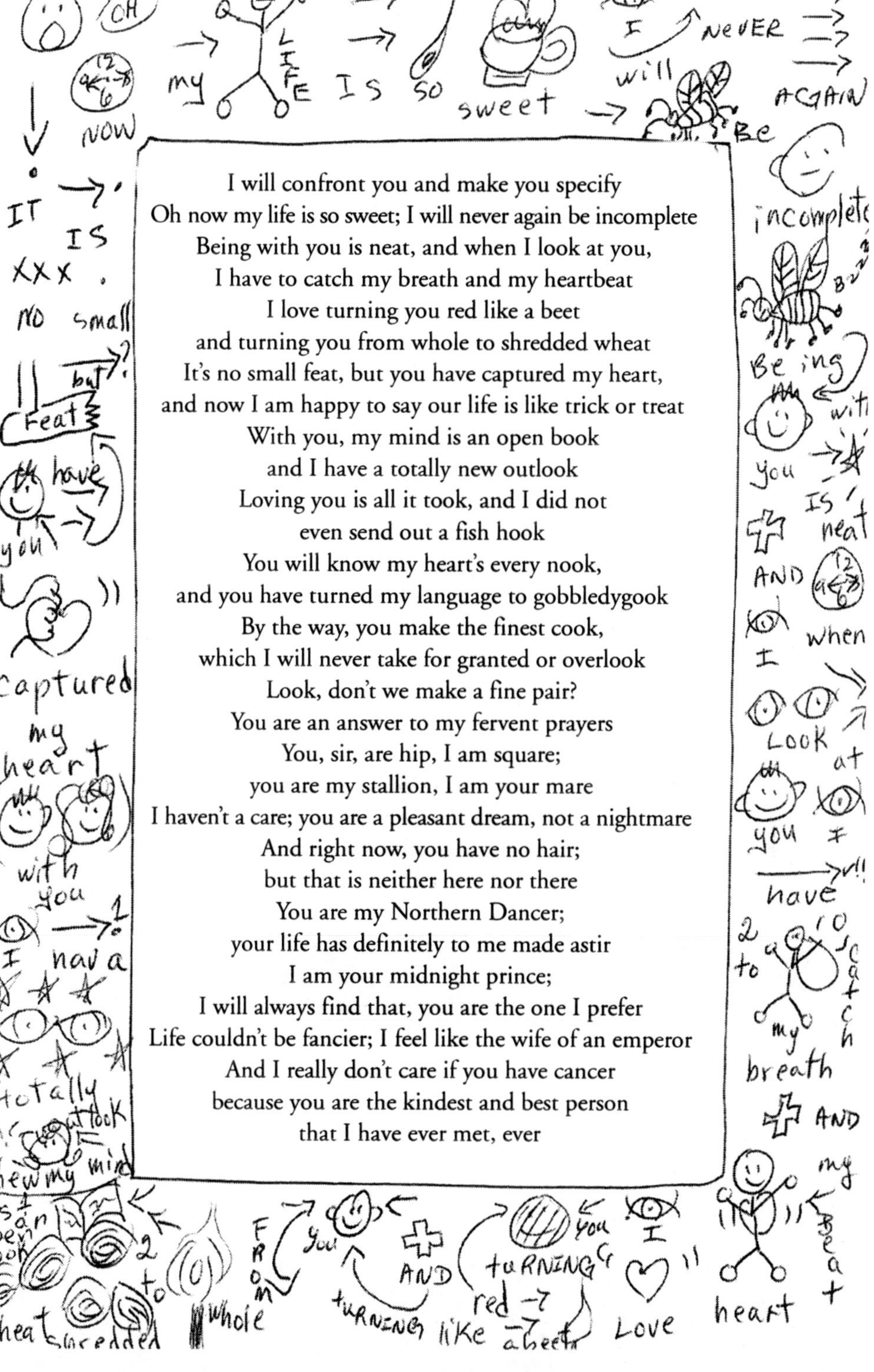

I will confront you and make you specify
Oh now my life is so sweet; I will never again be incomplete
Being with you is neat, and when I look at you,
I have to catch my breath and my heartbeat
I love turning you red like a beet
and turning you from whole to shredded wheat
It's no small feat, but you have captured my heart,
and now I am happy to say our life is like trick or treat
With you, my mind is an open book
and I have a totally new outlook
Loving you is all it took, and I did not
even send out a fish hook
You will know my heart's every nook,
and you have turned my language to gobbledygook
By the way, you make the finest cook,
which I will never take for granted or overlook
Look, don't we make a fine pair?
You are an answer to my fervent prayers
You, sir, are hip, I am square;
you are my stallion, I am your mare
I haven't a care; you are a pleasant dream, not a nightmare
And right now, you have no hair;
but that is neither here nor there
You are my Northern Dancer;
your life has definitely to me made astir
I am your midnight prince;
I will always find that, you are the one I prefer
Life couldn't be fancier; I feel like the wife of an emperor
And I really don't care if you have cancer
because you are the kindest and best person
that I have ever met, ever

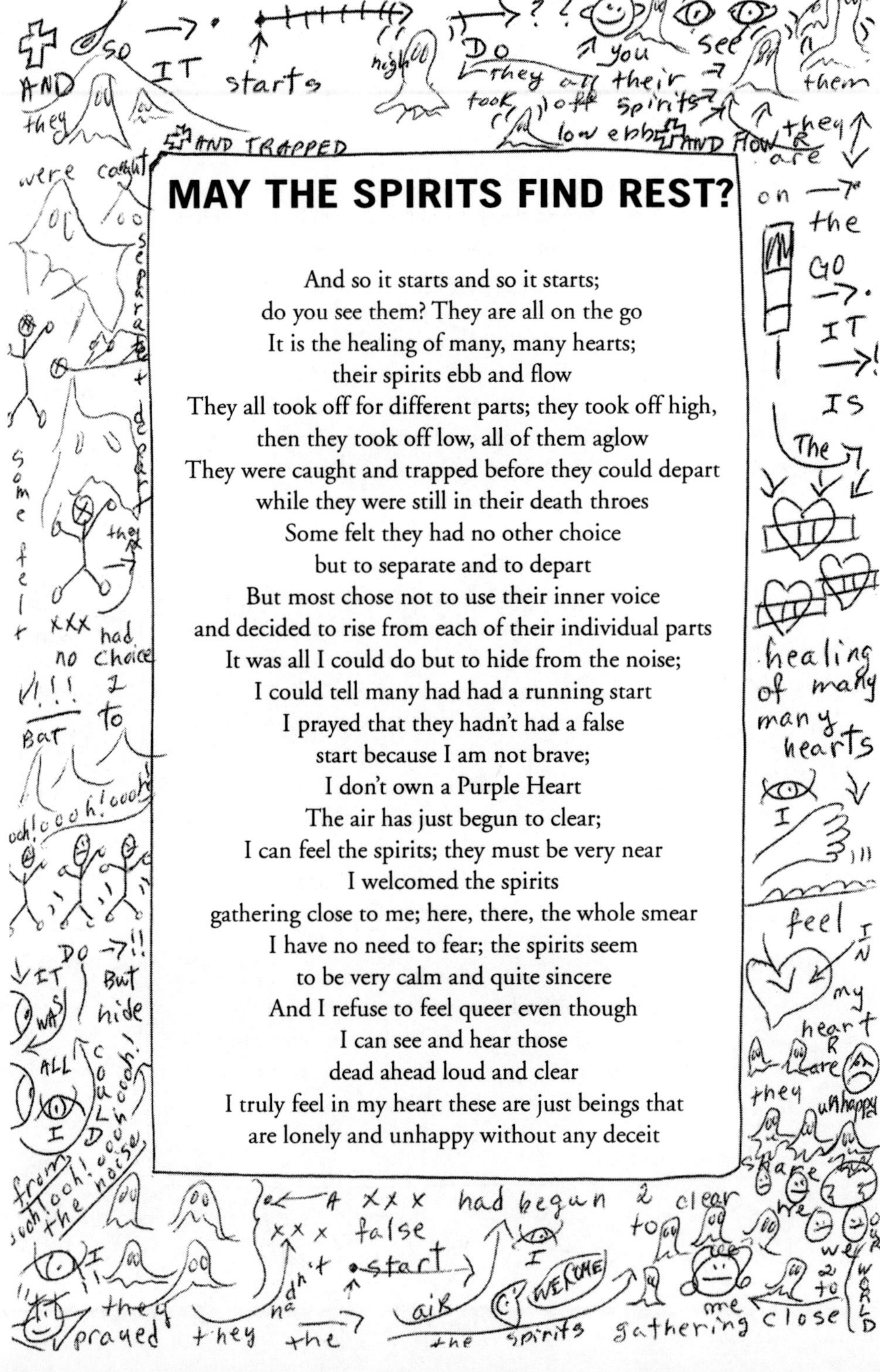

MAY THE SPIRITS FIND REST?

And so it starts and so it starts;
do you see them? They are all on the go
It is the healing of many, many hearts;
their spirits ebb and flow
They all took off for different parts; they took off high,
then they took off low, all of them aglow
They were caught and trapped before they could depart
while they were still in their death throes
Some felt they had no other choice
but to separate and to depart
But most chose not to use their inner voice
and decided to rise from each of their individual parts
It was all I could do but to hide from the noise;
I could tell many had had a running start
I prayed that they hadn't had a false
start because I am not brave;
I don't own a Purple Heart
The air has just begun to clear;
I can feel the spirits; they must be very near
I welcomed the spirits
gathering close to me; here, there, the whole smear
I have no need to fear; the spirits seem
to be very calm and quite sincere
And I refuse to feel queer even though
I can see and hear those
dead ahead loud and clear
I truly feel in my heart these are just beings that
are lonely and unhappy without any deceit

And if we welcome those spirits, we will do our part,
and the help we therefore contribute will be concrete
Because then we can prove we are smart
by helping all those that are unfulfilled or incomplete
And when we can admit we share our
world, with them for a start
and by not asking them to go away and retreat
Then maybe they will find rest
and they will no longer be distressed
So if we help them find their final intended destinations
to each of their quests,
then they may no longer wander and be distressed
If we will welcome the worst with the best,
these spirits may finally find their beauty rest
We will then welcome them to be our honored guests
When we open our minds instead of being fearful
we may even end up being impressed
instead of being spirit and color blind
We will be surprised what we find
right here, as well as on cloud nine
If we just take time to be kind, the spirits might toe the line
Then our eyes would be opened
and we would no longer be blind and
our understanding would be the new guideline
The spirits have been here all along, even if we did not know
They have been begging for us to hear their song
to show us that they are really our friends, not our foes

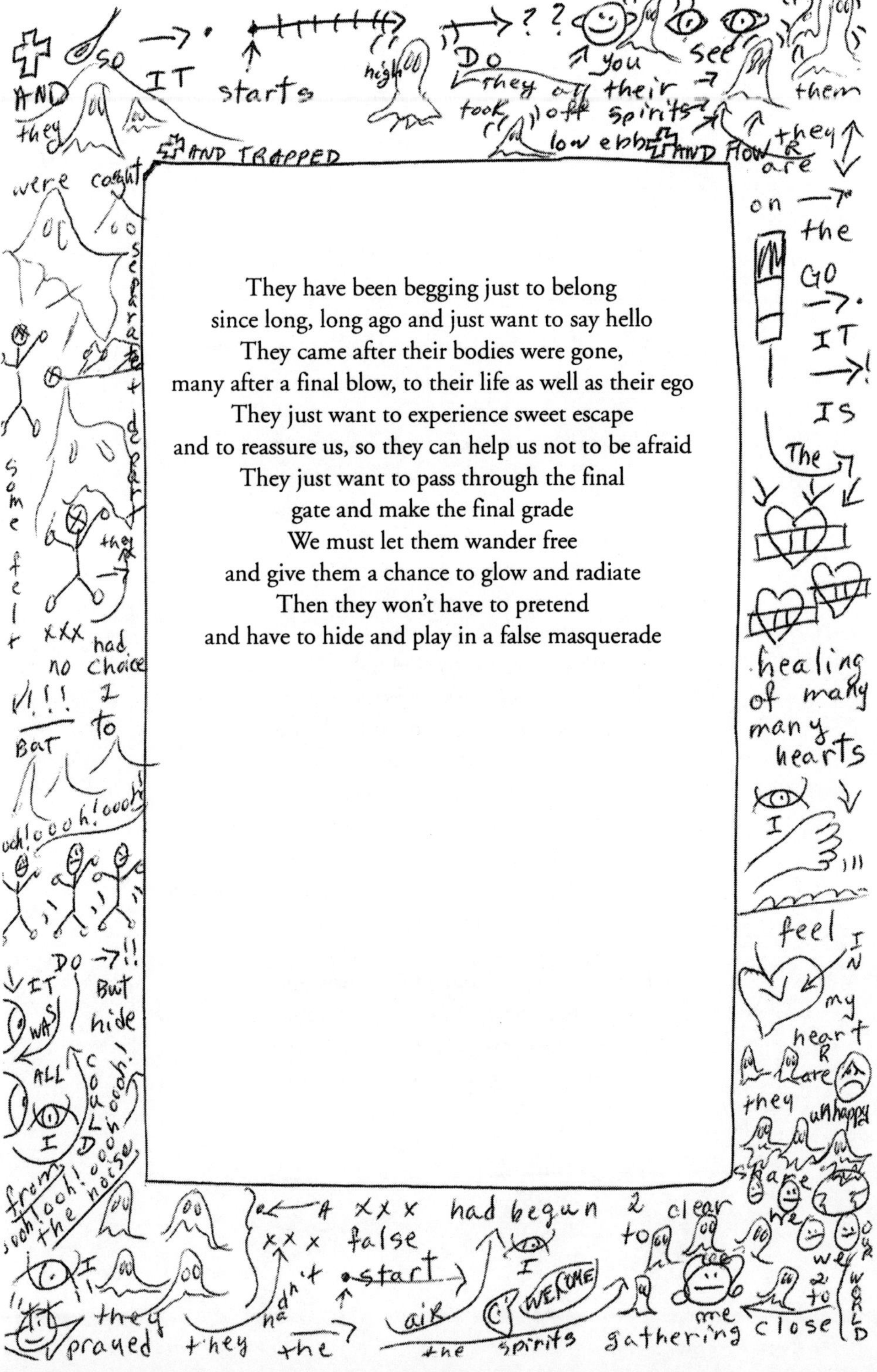

They have been begging just to belong
since long, long ago and just want to say hello
They came after their bodies were gone,
many after a final blow, to their life as well as their ego
They just want to experience sweet escape
and to reassure us, so they can help us not to be afraid
They just want to pass through the final
gate and make the final grade
We must let them wander free
and give them a chance to glow and radiate
Then they won't have to pretend
and have to hide and play in a false masquerade

LEST WE FORGET

We must find a way, to remember lest we forget
To remember, all the wonderful heroes we've met
And remember all the everyday heroes
who inspired us to be better yet
And all the heroes who helped us to enjoy
the quality of life they have let us get
We must be reminded and always remember
All the way from January
and through to December
Including all the letters from the
A letter to the Z letter
We must always remember that everyone
is important, whether it be a him
or whether it be a her
It would be an unfortunate and a crying shame
If we missed out someone
in our life's hall of fame
We must treat all people in our lives like
they are important pieces in our lives' game
Then they will no longer seem strange, rather
their names will be reclaimed
from inside of our brains
How about all the heroes in our lives that are unsung,
the everyday players, anyone and everyone
The ones we don't notice might be our
long-lost relatives and sons
They also deserve credit for all our fun because
they are the ones who are really homespun

We wouldn't want, them to be undone because
they are the ones who really deserve
all the credit for our fun
They are the ones who led us to be patient
enough to enjoy even the worst killjoy
They helped us to use all the powers we have to employ
and always smiled and said hello and ahoy
They helped us to use our minds, like they were our toys,
by finding the right combination of spices and soy
These heroes are one of the girls or one of the boys;
they were never coy; they let us be their pride and joy
It would be a real crime
for them to be unrecognized and
forgotten with the passage of time
If we forget to honor them who would be
there to remind us how to climb
And all the people who were here before and are now here
and who will be here with Father Time
They must all be recognized because they
make up our world's enzymes
Just let me say, if we as a people are to make any headway
And if I may continue to express my opinion,
in as best as I can, in this meager poetic essay
We must let our children grow and teach them to grow
on their own, and in their best possible way
And help our world see better solutions and peace,
better ways and better days

Then there will be telltale signs of change in our world
whether there is rain or whether it shines
When we find a universal way to get
along and we all toe the line
Then we can concentrate on working
on a real and great harmonious time line
And we can see all the warning signs
and fix them according to the great, grand design

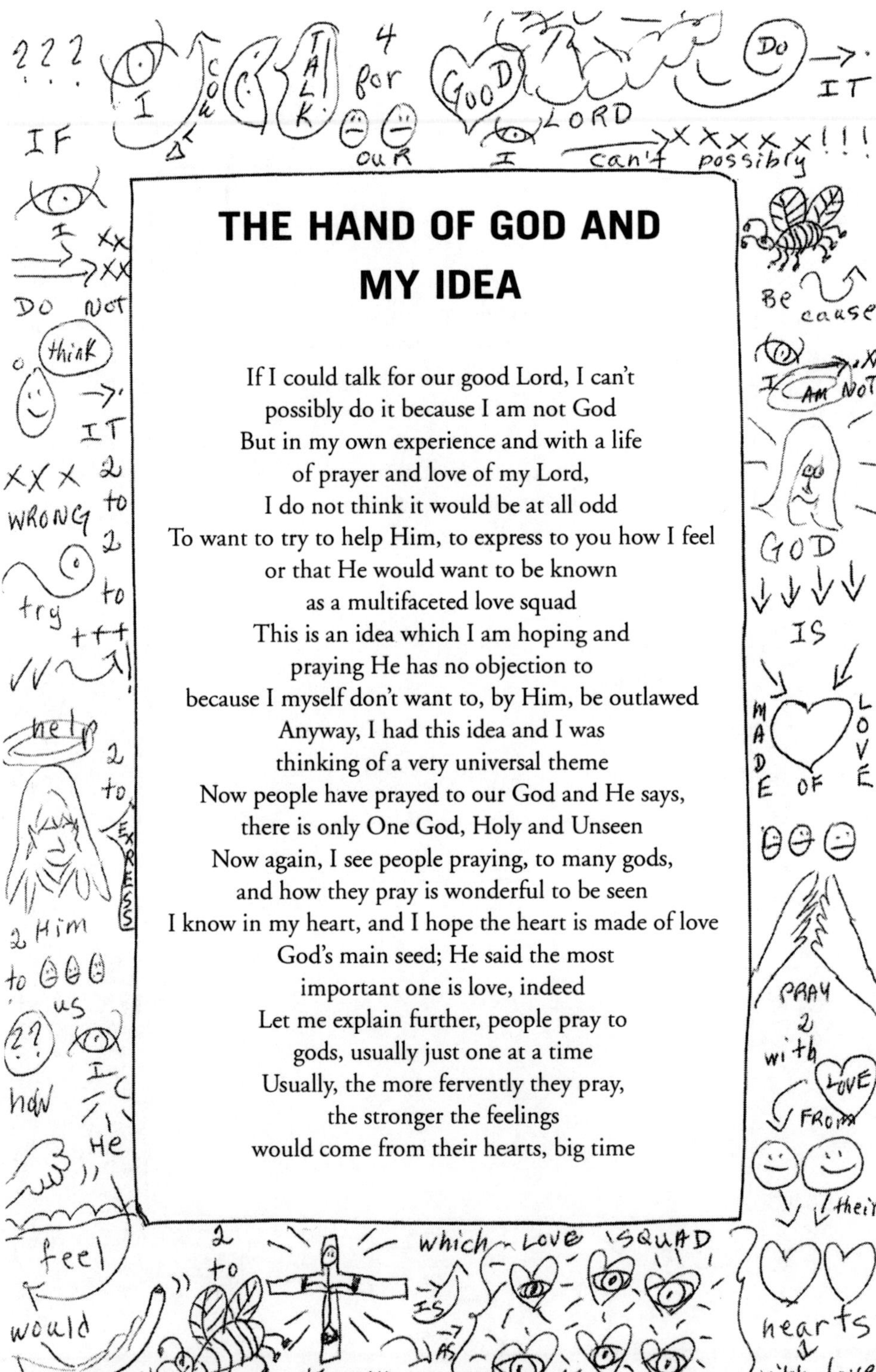

THE HAND OF GOD AND MY IDEA

If I could talk for our good Lord, I can't
possibly do it because I am not God
But in my own experience and with a life
of prayer and love of my Lord,
I do not think it would be at all odd
To want to try to help Him, to express to you how I feel
or that He would want to be known
as a multifaceted love squad
This is an idea which I am hoping and
praying He has no objection to
because I myself don't want to, by Him, be outlawed
Anyway, I had this idea and I was
thinking of a very universal theme
Now people have prayed to our God and He says,
there is only One God, Holy and Unseen
Now again, I see people praying, to many gods,
and how they pray is wonderful to be seen
I know in my heart, and I hope the heart is made of love
God's main seed; He said the most
important one is love, indeed
Let me explain further, people pray to
gods, usually just one at a time
Usually, the more fervently they pray,
the stronger the feelings
would come from their hearts, big time

Now if love in its goodness comes from the heart;
people must be praying with love to
their God all their lifetimes
Our God could then actually be their God because they
are using our God's main commandment which is love
and believing in their one true God, sublime
Our God loves all people, and if all people pray
for good qualifies and for strength and hope
In other words, the better and more we pray with our heart,
which is the seat of love, the more we
will be able to accomplish;
the greater the success of all peoples, the greater the scope
He has said in His good book He loves all peoples
if they live love's good life, on life's rope
So their prayers to their gods will turn
into prayers to our God
because our God has heard them like
through His love-healing stethoscope
Again, as an example, I had a beautiful dream and at first
I wondered what the dream meant; also if
there was a reason for it and why
Well, to understand, you must know what the dream was;
it was a beautiful vision of a pillar shaped like an arm
with a hand attached at the bottom, and
all this was coming out of the sky
This enormous ghostly pillar of an
arm was gentle as it was large
and rested on a figure lying still in
slumber where the figure lies

I was amazed and happy at the same
time for it was I who was resting,
and it was so pleasant I couldn't help but
awaken from my slumber and rise
I do truly love God, and when I had this pleasant
dream, I wanted to somehow thank Him
I wanted desperately to somehow
give back a little to Him,
so I decided I would write a poem
and go way out on a limb
In my thinking, as a tribute, I would
like to spread a little love
as my contribution before my life
force goes completely dim
So this is my best and only way to convey and thank Him
because in His love I like to swim
To all the people, I love and hold dear to my heart
I know He is looking on them;
when they do and did their part
He is surrounding them with a cloud of love
a wonderful work of art
And He will bring them closer to Him
when from this life they depart
For all those of you who yet do not believe in Him
and think it is not possible for Him to really be there
I say and pray that they will realize if they
acknowledge to anyone that He is not there,
they already believe there is a God, and that
God still loves them and, for them, cares

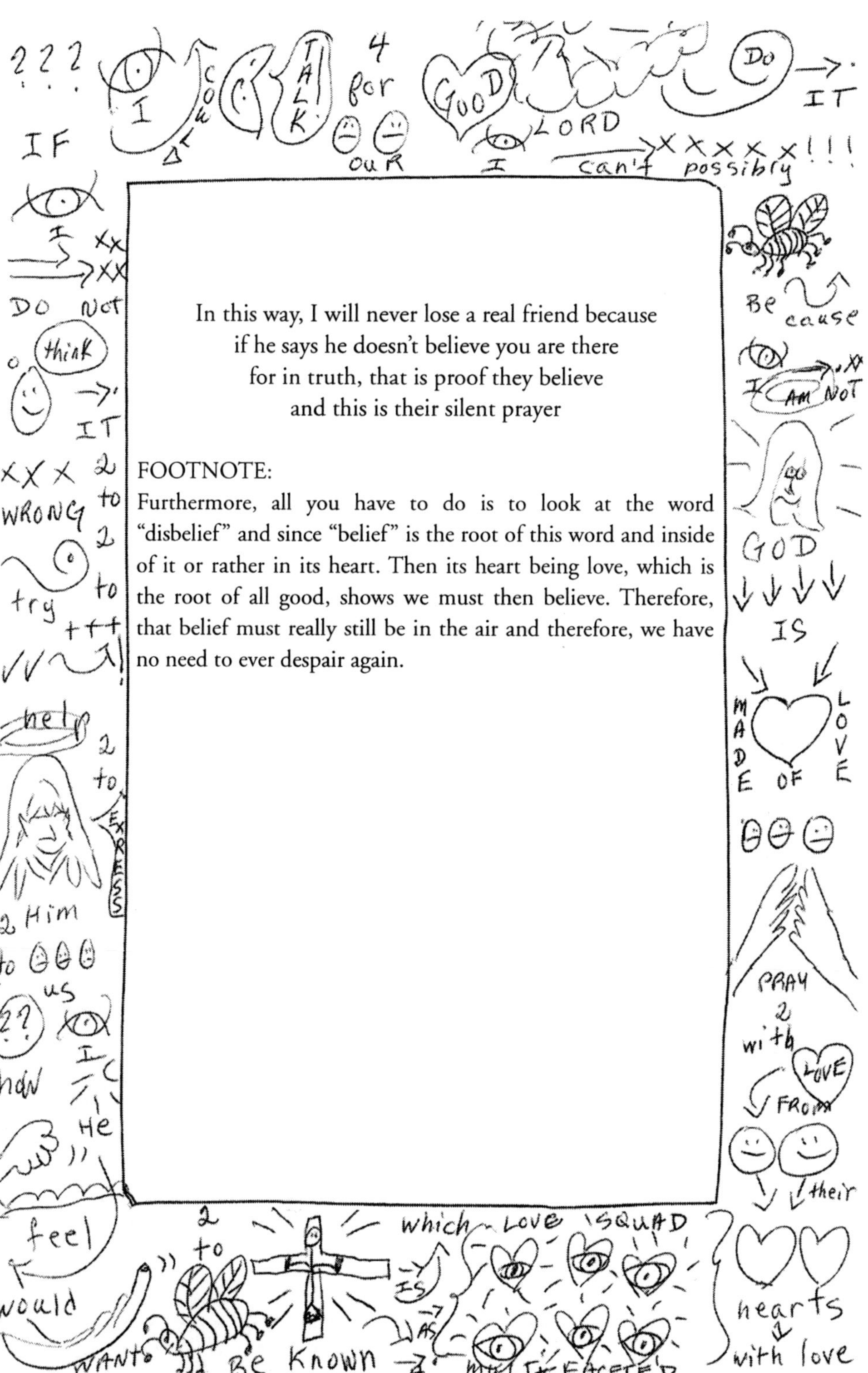

In this way, I will never lose a real friend because
if he says he doesn't believe you are there
for in truth, that is proof they believe
and this is their silent prayer

FOOTNOTE:
Furthermore, all you have to do is to look at the word "disbelief" and since "belief" is the root of this word and inside of it or rather in its heart. Then its heart being love, which is the root of all good, shows we must then believe. Therefore, that belief must really still be in the air and therefore, we have no need to ever despair again.

LIFE IN THE CLOSET

Living life in here
in the safety of my closet
For me, wasn't always or at all quiet
In fact, it turned out to be quite a riot
Why, don't you come in and see
it might be a smash hit
It taught me a lot about cheap shots
It taught me how not to get caught
and how to get caught when
my life was getting too hot
It taught me mostly by being self-taught,
which is, in itself, food for thought
It taught me a lot, especially that
the best things in life cannot be bought
Still, it taught me it was a safe place;
when and where I had to stay
And while in there
I still found many ways to play
My dreams still stayed,
and eventually they found their way
I always secretly thought I would still be OK
Sometimes life in the closet
was very lonely
And sometimes, I felt ugly, and homely
Still, I managed to find
my one and only
I still managed to find
my soul mate, my true honey

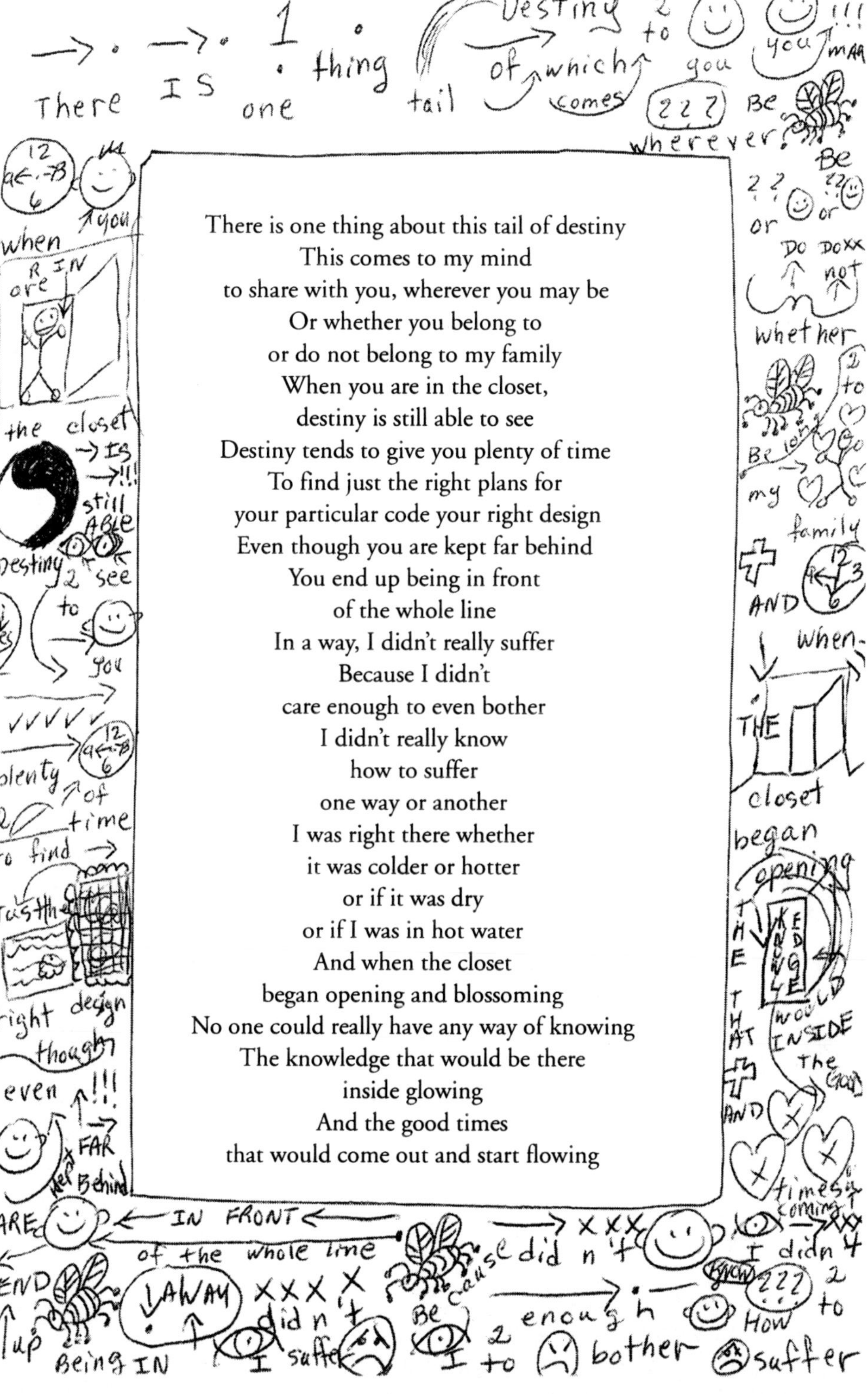

There is one thing about this tail of destiny
This comes to my mind
to share with you, wherever you may be
Or whether you belong to
or do not belong to my family
When you are in the closet,
destiny is still able to see
Destiny tends to give you plenty of time
To find just the right plans for
your particular code your right design
Even though you are kept far behind
You end up being in front
of the whole line
In a way, I didn't really suffer
Because I didn't
care enough to even bother
I didn't really know
how to suffer
one way or another
I was right there whether
it was colder or hotter
or if it was dry
or if I was in hot water
And when the closet
began opening and blossoming
No one could really have any way of knowing
The knowledge that would be there
inside glowing
And the good times
that would come out and start flowing

TRUE LOVE

What is it this time?
I see it now
it sparkles, it shines
It is an idea
one so sublime
It is so bright you can
see it during the day
as well as during the night
It is better than a double-header
It is a jewel; no, it is much better
Let us let her go
let us loosen her fetters
By the way, you will wish
that, you had met her
OK
the idea is called pure love
This idea you will want more of
Did pure love come from above?
Let us see more over
it will show you
No, you don't have to shove
You'll see true love
coming in from all over in different colors
Its brilliance will sparkle brighter and much, much sharper
The brilliance of true love
will shine like multicolored, pure crystal waters
True love has enough energy to burn through your mind
with a flame that gets hotter and hotter

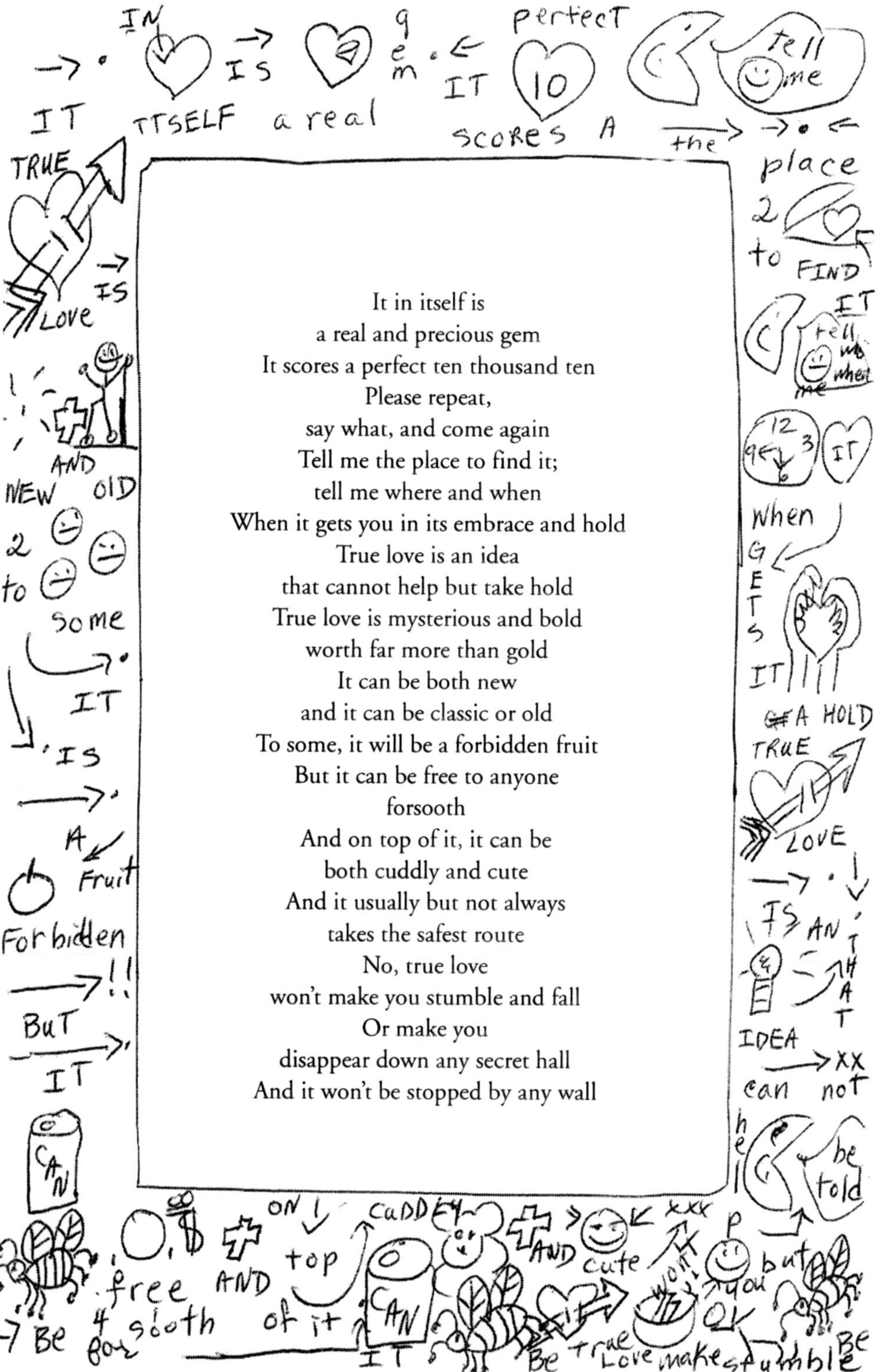

It in itself is
a real and precious gem
It scores a perfect ten thousand ten
Please repeat,
say what, and come again
Tell me the place to find it;
tell me where and when
When it gets you in its embrace and hold
True love is an idea
that cannot help but take hold
True love is mysterious and bold
worth far more than gold
It can be both new
and it can be classic or old
To some, it will be a forbidden fruit
But it can be free to anyone
forsooth
And on top of it, it can be
both cuddly and cute
And it usually but not always
takes the safest route
No, true love
won't make you stumble and fall
Or make you
disappear down any secret hall
And it won't be stopped by any wall

Also, it won't need
any special extension,
after you connect your call
True love is there waiting for everyone
Whether it be a she or a he,
be it a woman or a man,
or be it a daughter or a son
No, it cannot and will never be undone
And it will always be the best of fun

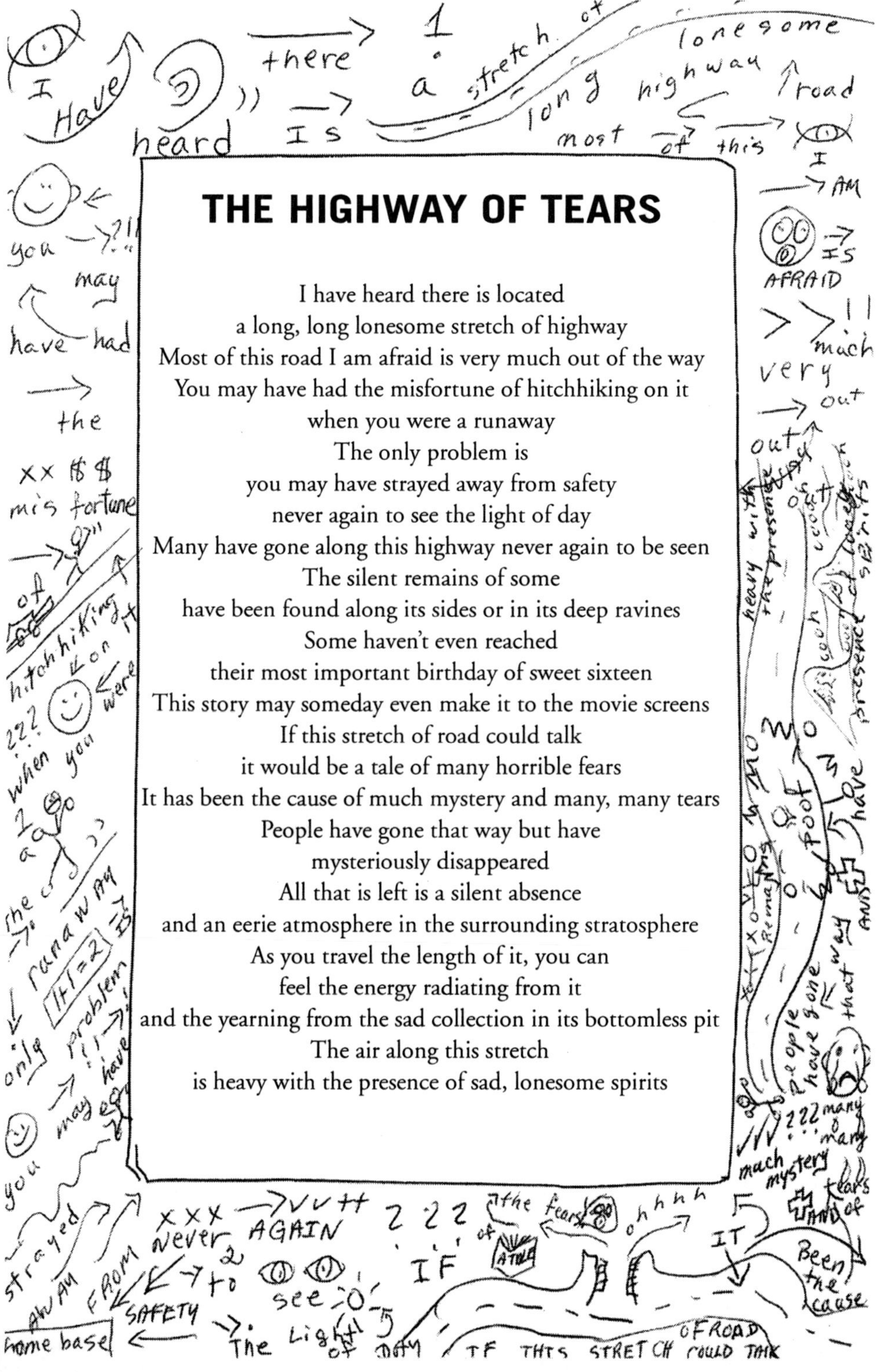

THE HIGHWAY OF TEARS

I have heard there is located
a long, long lonesome stretch of highway
Most of this road I am afraid is very much out of the way
You may have had the misfortune of hitchhiking on it
when you were a runaway
The only problem is
you may have strayed away from safety
never again to see the light of day
Many have gone along this highway never again to be seen
The silent remains of some
have been found along its sides or in its deep ravines
Some haven't even reached
their most important birthday of sweet sixteen
This story may someday even make it to the movie screens
If this stretch of road could talk
it would be a tale of many horrible fears
It has been the cause of much mystery and many, many tears
People have gone that way but have
mysteriously disappeared
All that is left is a silent absence
and an eerie atmosphere in the surrounding stratosphere
As you travel the length of it, you can
feel the energy radiating from it
and the yearning from the sad collection in its bottomless pit
The air along this stretch
is heavy with the presence of sad, lonesome spirits

It is surely not the road you want your
vehicle to go on the fritz or
you might go out of your wits
To travel this way it takes a lion's
heart and real true grit
plus a heavy dose of determination bit by bit
If you were even to travel this road,
you should make sure
you don't only have to go for a test drive
You must try to just plain survive and chances
are you might not ever even be seen again alive
The ditches of the road are filled with
enough forgotten tears
that, we would be able to, in them, swim and dive
One thing, for sure, you may have a chance to
arrive, but you may end up going into a nosedive
The older the road becomes, the greater is its mystery
And returning back from it is chancy
there is no real guarantee
so if you have just come traveling or just to sightsee
When you don't come back, the authorities will say,
"What did we say" and "Pardon me"
You can go that way if you want to,
but I will warn you it is taboo
My personal choice
will be to stay far, far away from there and say adieu
But if by some chance
I have to go there, or with it, make a rendezvous
I will make sure to be careful and
provide myself with a panoramic view

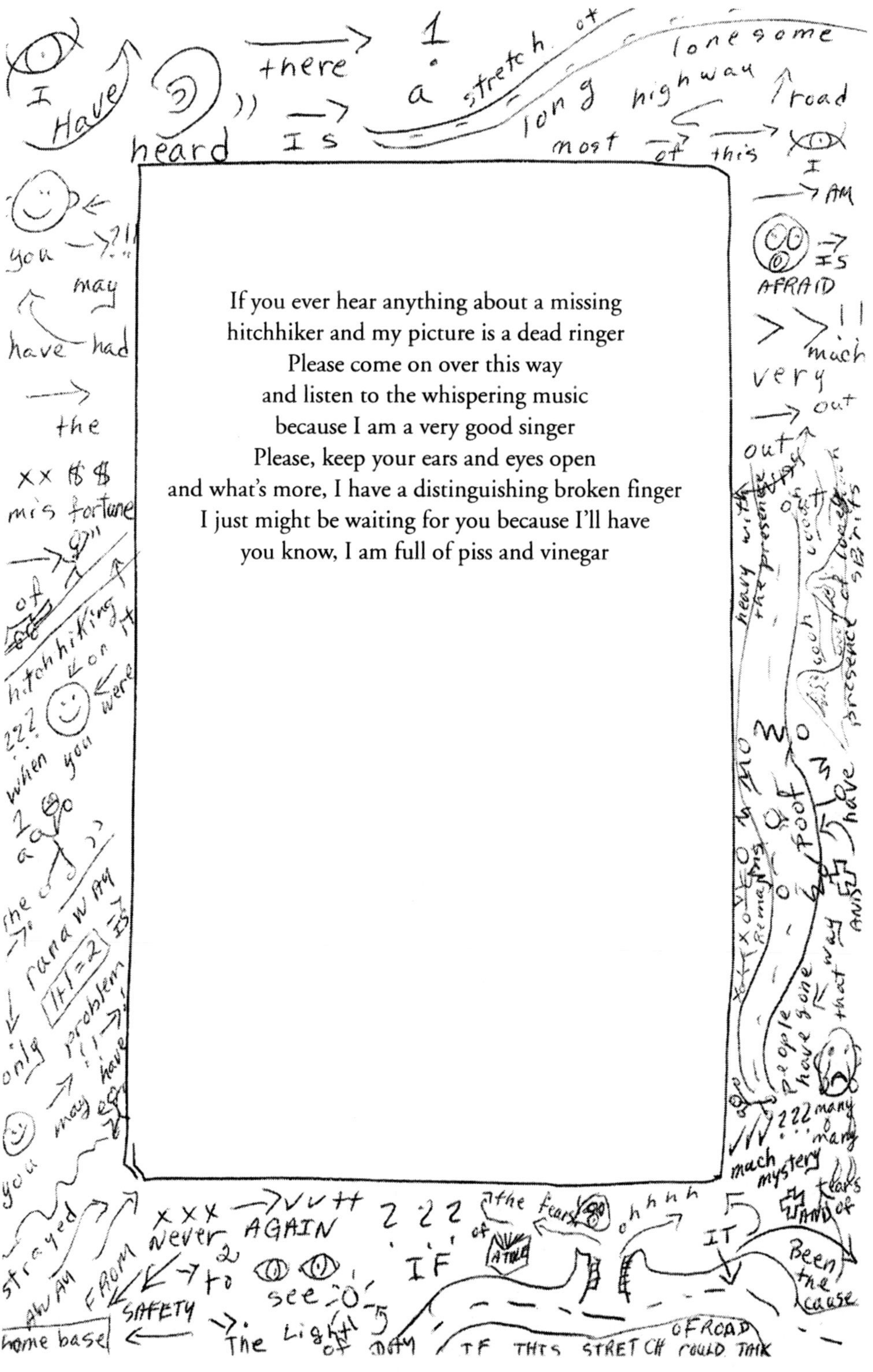

If you ever hear anything about a missing
hitchhiker and my picture is a dead ringer
Please come on over this way
and listen to the whispering music
because I am a very good singer
Please, keep your ears and eyes open
and what's more, I have a distinguishing broken finger
I just might be waiting for you because I'll have
you know, I am full of piss and vinegar

MY SLEEPING BEAUTY

My Sleeping Beauty
How beautiful she is even when her hair is all a frizz
No, this is not a quiz, even though she may be a whiz
She's better looking than Liz
although she has never been in showbiz
She is a cultivated miss and has no children;
all I can say to that is gee whiz
Where did she get all her good looks from?
You would think she is some kind of a crook
Can you learn that from books? It is
innocence that is all it took
Can you get that recipe from a cookbook
maybe it is just from her good outlook?
You can't find her hiding in a nook
even the greatest insult, she will overlook
You may find her here or you may find her there;
so you had better not be caught out in the cold
She doesn't always know what to wear,
but I do know she's in my heart and in my soul
She would never leave me in the cold;
in fact, she is my ace in the hole
A place in my heart she will always hold;
to me, she's more precious than the most precious gold
Her work ethics are the best;
especially when she gets her beauty rest
For her, this is always a constant quest
put that in your hope chest

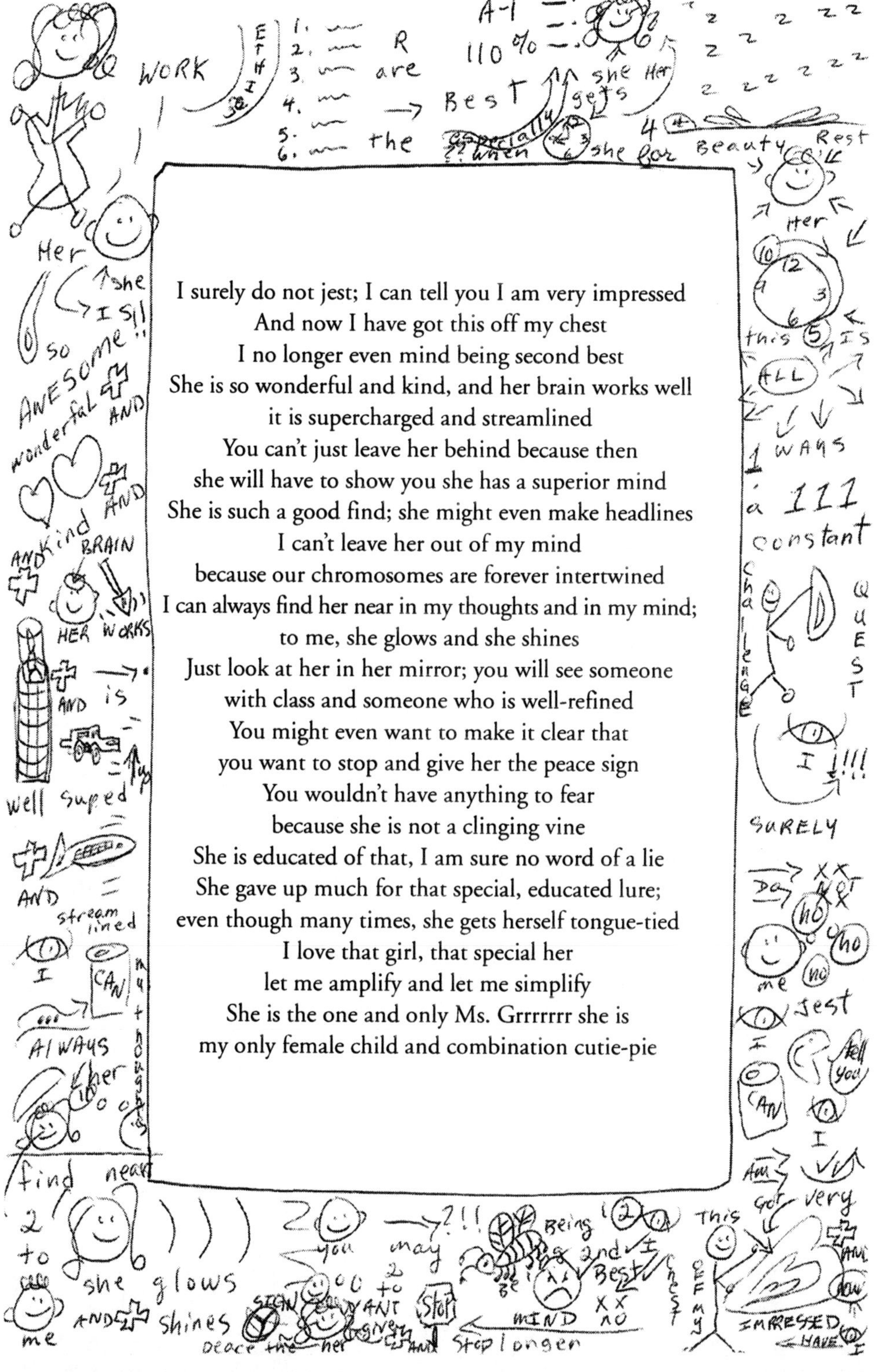

I surely do not jest; I can tell you I am very impressed
And now I have got this off my chest
I no longer even mind being second best
She is so wonderful and kind, and her brain works well
it is supercharged and streamlined
You can't just leave her behind because then
she will have to show you she has a superior mind
She is such a good find; she might even make headlines
I can't leave her out of my mind
because our chromosomes are forever intertwined
I can always find her near in my thoughts and in my mind;
to me, she glows and she shines
Just look at her in her mirror; you will see someone
with class and someone who is well-refined
You might even want to make it clear that
you want to stop and give her the peace sign
You wouldn't have anything to fear
because she is not a clinging vine
She is educated of that, I am sure no word of a lie
She gave up much for that special, educated lure;
even though many times, she gets herself tongue-tied
I love that girl, that special her
let me amplify and let me simplify
She is the one and only Ms. Grrrrrrr she is
my only female child and combination cutie-pie

MR. YIN AND MR. YANG

Mr. Yin meet Mr. Yang
bang, clang a Lang
Mr. Yin likes opera, Mr. Yang likes to twang
Mr. Yin is positively innocent
Yang belongs to a gang
Mr. Yin believes in quiet
and Yang lets it all hang
When Mr. Yin is happy
Mr. Yang feels crappy
When Mr. Yin is full
Mr. Yang is running on empty
When Mr. Yin is empty
Mr. Yang has plenty
When Mr. Yin fails Mr. Yang is happy
When Mr. Yin succeeds
Mr. Yang has a cow
When Mr. Yin hides
Mr. Yang is here and right now
When Mr. Yin ends, Mr. Yang begins to sew
When Mr. Yin forgets
Mr. Yang begins to know
When Mr. Yin is gracious
Mr. Yang is just plain mean
When Mr. Yin is plain to be seen
Mr. Yang is nowhere to be seen
When Mr. Yin tries hard
Mr. Yang is not at all keen

When Mr. Yin is keen, Mr. Yang is a has-been
Hip, hip, hip, hooray Yin met Yang halfway
Mr. Yin wants to play
Mr. Yang would rather lay
What do you say
Yin, don't rub Yang the wrong way
Mr. Yang wants to go away
he doesn't want to be Yin's protégé
So they can never agree
and most often they sing off-key
But believe you me
together they fit sure as can be
One on top of the other or beside the other you see
Because without one or the other,
the remaining one would be quite lost you see
It has to be this way
one cannot from the other run away
Together, they just like to play, they form a fine bouquet
They fit like a puzzle that way,
just like dark and light or night and day
Depending on how they decide to lay
you could say they like to do a little role-play
Mr. Yin is straight and Mr. Yang is gay
Mr. Yin has a steady walk
Mr. Yang swings and sways
Mr. Yin says to Mr. Yang, "Man, go away
I will meet up with you another day, OK?"

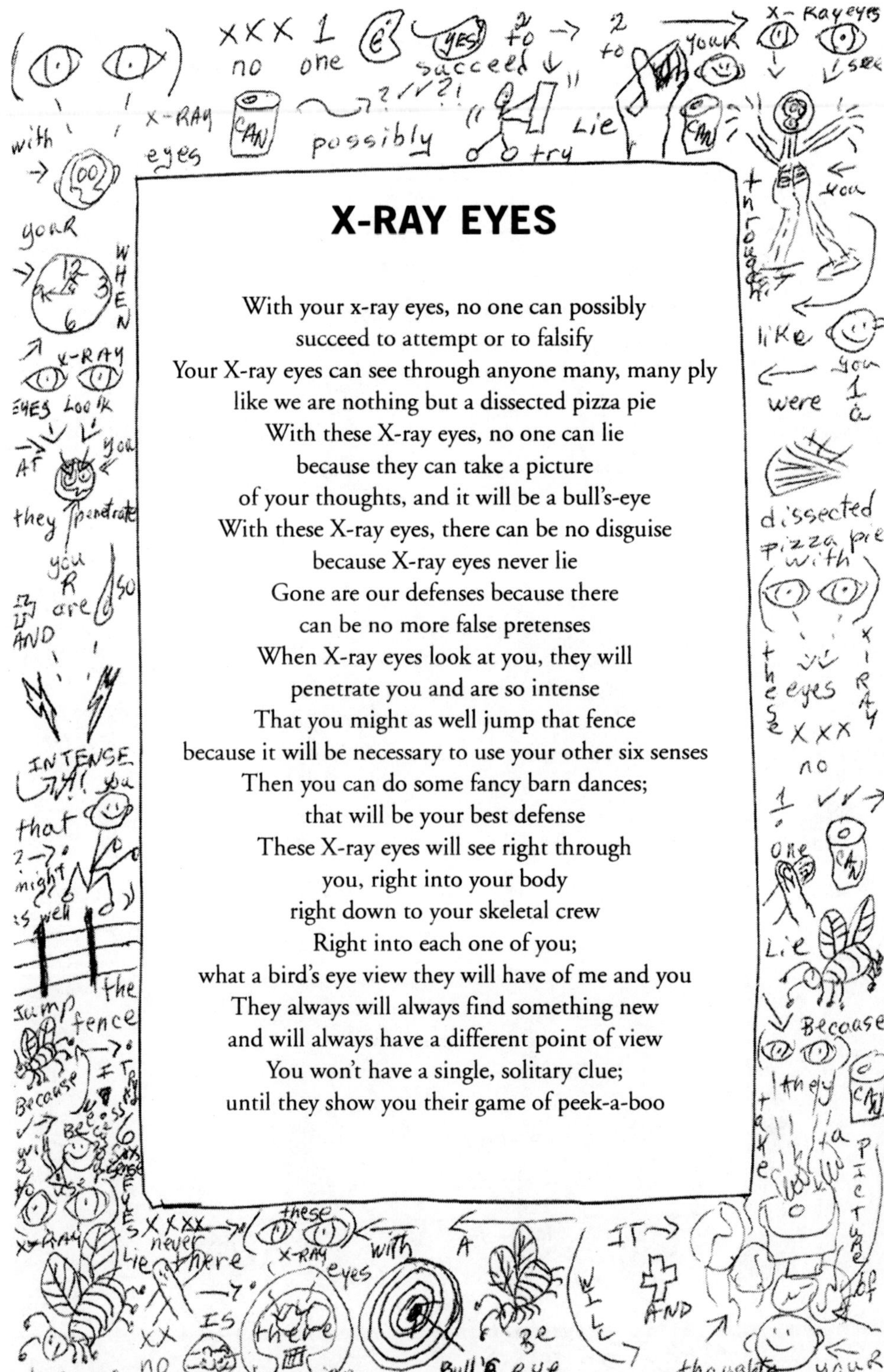

X-RAY EYES

With your x-ray eyes, no one can possibly
succeed to attempt or to falsify
Your X-ray eyes can see through anyone many, many ply
like we are nothing but a dissected pizza pie
With these X-ray eyes, no one can lie
because they can take a picture
of your thoughts, and it will be a bull's-eye
With these X-ray eyes, there can be no disguise
because X-ray eyes never lie
Gone are our defenses because there
can be no more false pretenses
When X-ray eyes look at you, they will
penetrate you and are so intense
That you might as well jump that fence
because it will be necessary to use your other six senses
Then you can do some fancy barn dances;
that will be your best defense
These X-ray eyes will see right through
you, right into your body
right down to your skeletal crew
Right into each one of you;
what a bird's eye view they will have of me and you
They always will always find something new
and will always have a different point of view
You won't have a single, solitary clue;
until they show you their game of peek-a-boo

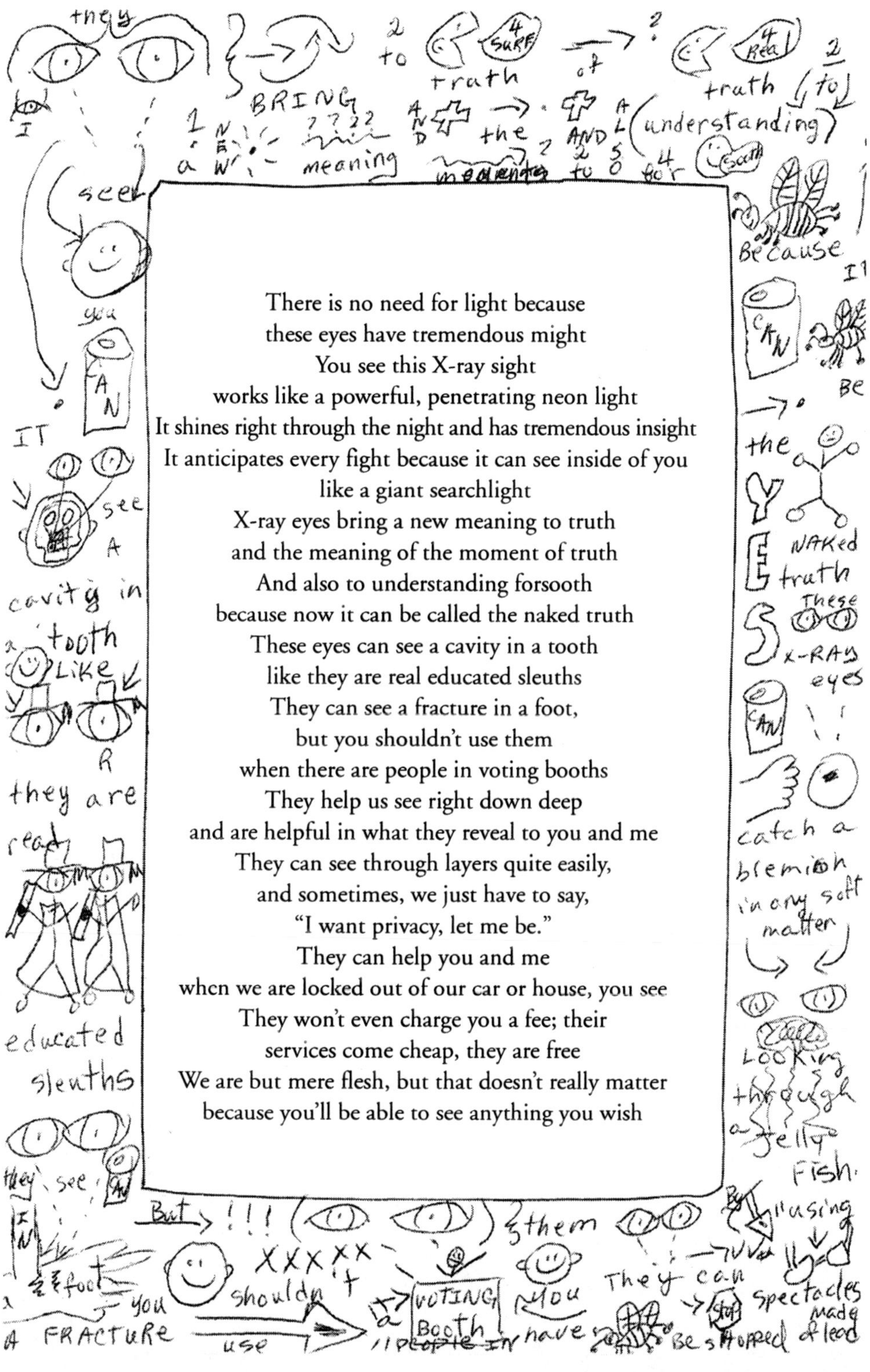

There is no need for light because
these eyes have tremendous might
You see this X-ray sight
works like a powerful, penetrating neon light
It shines right through the night and has tremendous insight
It anticipates every fight because it can see inside of you
like a giant searchlight
X-ray eyes bring a new meaning to truth
and the meaning of the moment of truth
And also to understanding forsooth
because now it can be called the naked truth
These eyes can see a cavity in a tooth
like they are real educated sleuths
They can see a fracture in a foot,
but you shouldn't use them
when there are people in voting booths
They help us see right down deep
and are helpful in what they reveal to you and me
They can see through layers quite easily,
and sometimes, we just have to say,
"I want privacy, let me be."
They can help you and me
when we are locked out of our car or house, you see
They won't even charge you a fee; their
services come cheap, they are free
We are but mere flesh, but that doesn't really matter
because you'll be able to see anything you wish

Because these X-ray eyes can catch a blemish
in any soft matter, just like looking through a jellyfish
And they can be the cause of an organized skirmish;
as a matter of fact, anything at all, anything you wish
which could be a prelude to exterminating the bad
right down to the finish or the cause
of someone's death wish
All in all, it will come to a good end;
when all is done and said
Because they were invented by mere mortal men
and shared by transplanting them into our heads
There is an important message that this sends; which is
they can be stopped from being able to fan out or spread
By using little spectacles made of
a simple thing called lead

TRACIE'S IN LOVE

The news came from way above
right from a beautiful turtledove
Tracie's in love and it is not puppy love
Love fits her like a glove;
she herself is a labor of love
Her love has a musical ring;
push comes to shove
she likes good fights
look at her in love boxing gloves
May she be happy and be blessed;
her love fills up a bottomless treasure chest
Let her get around to the rest; I wish
for her a bulletproof vest
She will be happy in her love nest;
I only want to give her a heavenly request
She will settle wherever she sees best;
I love her too, she has me totally impressed
She always has a smile on her face;
if you made her cry, surely you would be in disgrace
She will seldom be put in last place
because she has inward and outward heavenly grace
She is a good member of the human race;
she let me and my sick husband share an embrace
You will want to help her in haste; she
looks at death every day, face to face
She will make a beautiful belle;
when it comes to looks, she is a beautiful bombshell
Flowers will suit her well; she is as innocent as a baby gazelle

Everything will come together and gel;
she will be as beautiful as Tinker Bell
Her wedding guests will have good stories to tell;
when they get together, it will be like show and tell
If you knew her, you couldn't help but become impressed
You would agree with her new sir, that
she wins every kind of popularity and beauty contest
She should be dressed in furs
and she walks with grace and finesse
Say a word, and she'll open the door;
to help you, she will do her level best
She will serve you and always remember to say thank you
She doesn't deserve to be blue; she will be glad to meet you
Her love shines
shiny and new no matter what is your point of view
You got to love her too; she does
not need any kind of tattoo
She'll help you to understand;
when she is in town, you cannot help but be in dreamland
And she will make you feel grand;
her company will take you right to fantasy land
She is the best in all the land;
who needs to go all the way to Rio Grande?
Come on, give her a hand; help her see the answers firsthand
She's an angel in disguise;
all her attributes serve to mesmerize and to tantalize
That is all I can surmise;
and you cannot tell me anything otherwise
I wish her the best family ties and will take no compromise
I wish her a long life, let no one defy
then may her spirit take wings and fly

MIRACLE MANOR

Here we are on the top of the world, where
half of the time it is very cold
We can do nothing but be nice to each other to pass the time
and to keep ourselves under control
The nice thing is that
bugs and poisonous creatures have less time to take hold
Sometimes, nature takes a stranglehold,
but we must be satisfied
to look for our imaginary pot of gold
In this sparsely populated place,
there is a town with a church in it called Miracle Manor
Here, there is great love and Mass is said
in a respectful, fervent manner
You may see people like Richard, Caroline, or Phyllis
saying a humble Mass here
There may not be many people,
but our spirits are lifted high and we are sure we are heard
There is great amount of rooted faith
and fellowship and love
There is great faith in the Lord from all over
that fits these people like a glove
Many a testimony has been heard here of miracles
and healing and more of that sort of
Music also is heard lifting to the rafters
on the wings of a turtledove

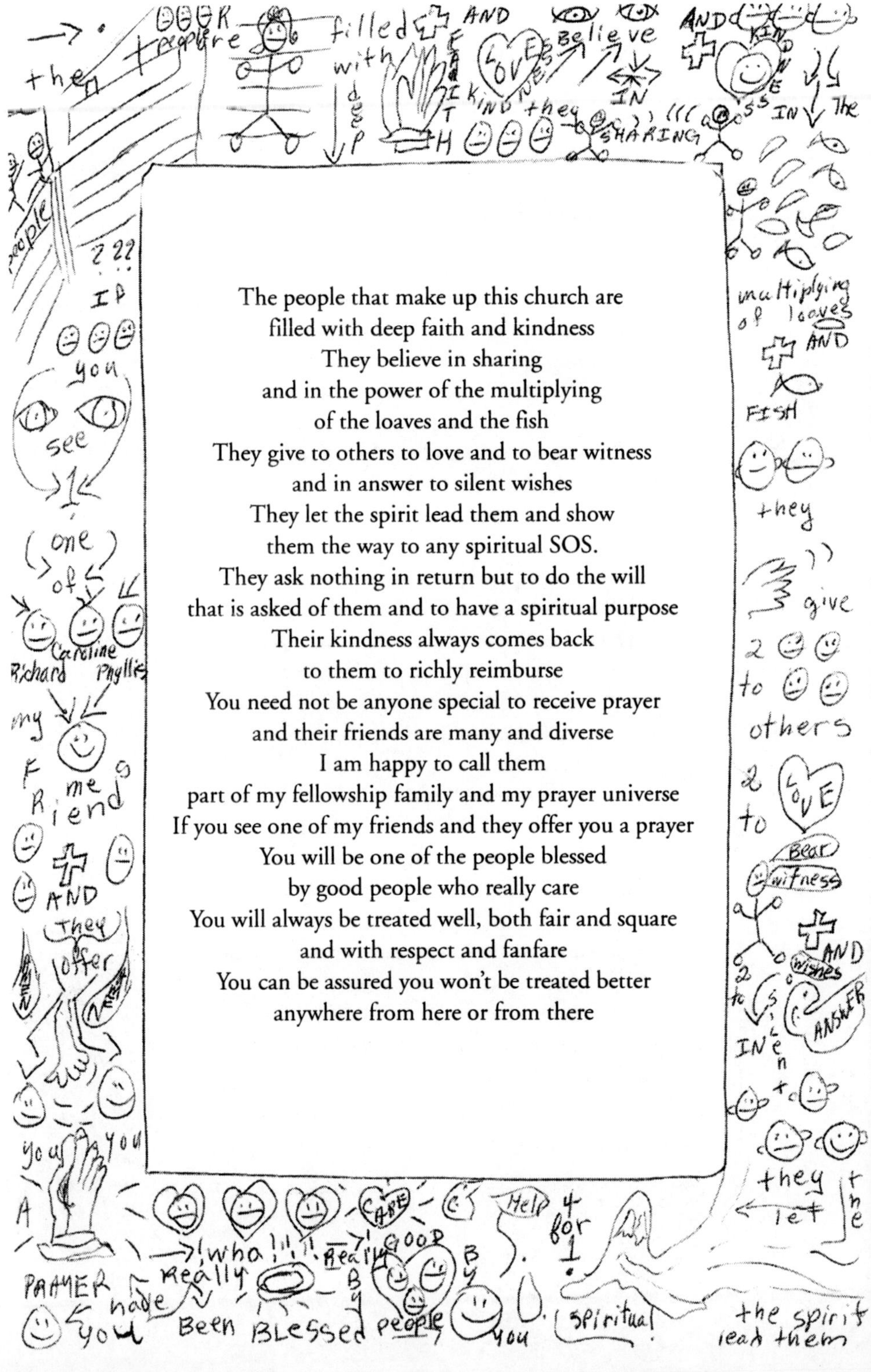

The people that make up this church are
filled with deep faith and kindness
They believe in sharing
and in the power of the multiplying
of the loaves and the fish
They give to others to love and to bear witness
and in answer to silent wishes
They let the spirit lead them and show
them the way to any spiritual SOS.
They ask nothing in return but to do the will
that is asked of them and to have a spiritual purpose
Their kindness always comes back
to them to richly reimburse
You need not be anyone special to receive prayer
and their friends are many and diverse
I am happy to call them
part of my fellowship family and my prayer universe
If you see one of my friends and they offer you a prayer
You will be one of the people blessed
by good people who really care
You will always be treated well, both fair and square
and with respect and fanfare
You can be assured you won't be treated better
anywhere from here or from there

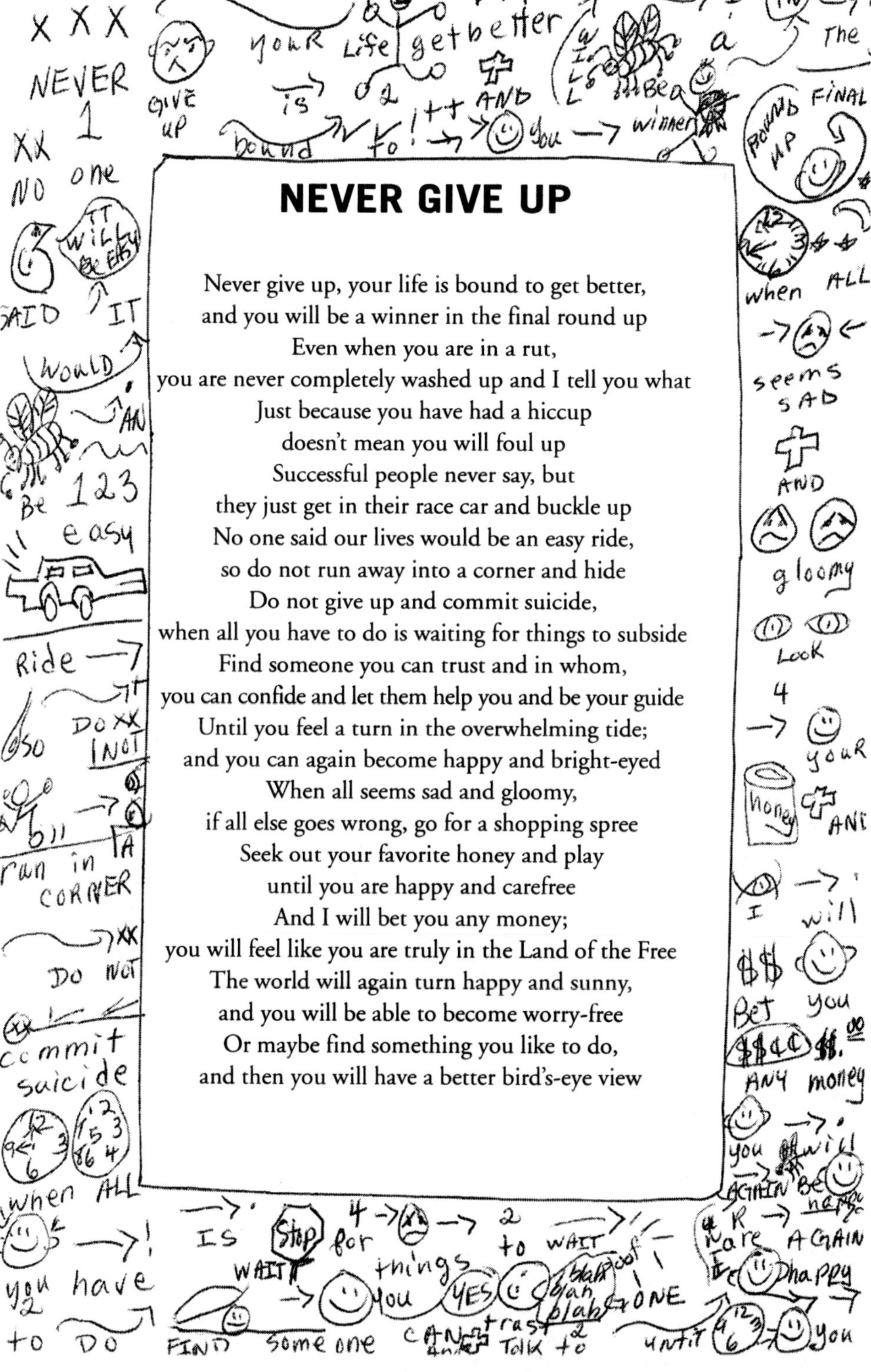

NEVER GIVE UP

Never give up, your life is bound to get better,
and you will be a winner in the final round up
Even when you are in a rut,
you are never completely washed up and I tell you what
Just because you have had a hiccup
doesn't mean you will foul up
Successful people never say, but
they just get in their race car and buckle up
No one said our lives would be an easy ride,
so do not run away into a corner and hide
Do not give up and commit suicide,
when all you have to do is waiting for things to subside
Find someone you can trust and in whom,
you can confide and let them help you and be your guide
Until you feel a turn in the overwhelming tide;
and you can again become happy and bright-eyed
When all seems sad and gloomy,
if all else goes wrong, go for a shopping spree
Seek out your favorite honey and play
until you are happy and carefree
And I will bet you any money;
you will feel like you are truly in the Land of the Free
The world will again turn happy and sunny,
and you will be able to become worry-free
Or maybe find something you like to do,
and then you will have a better bird's-eye view

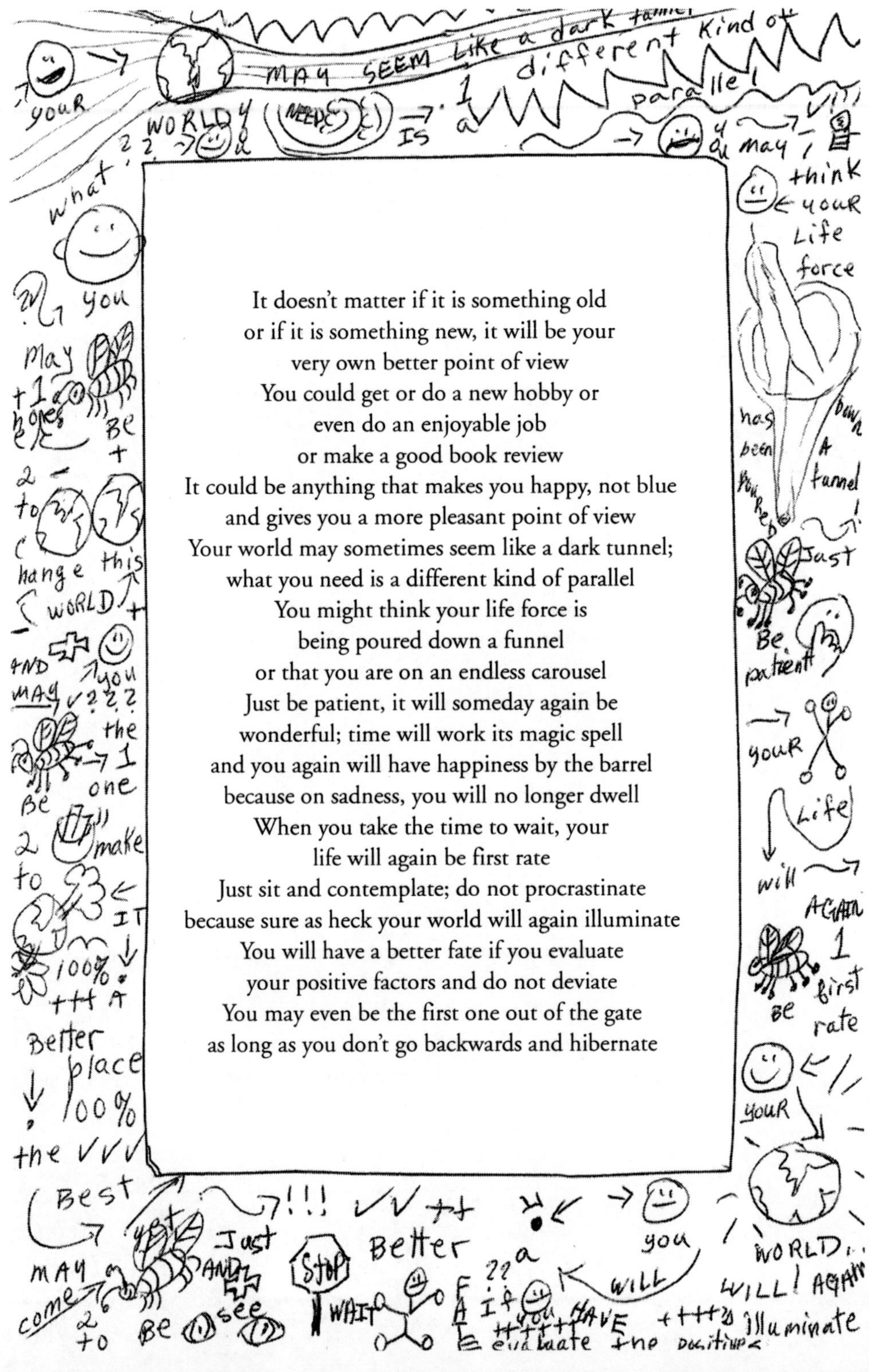

It doesn't matter if it is something old
or if it is something new, it will be your
very own better point of view
You could get or do a new hobby or
even do an enjoyable job
or make a good book review
It could be anything that makes you happy, not blue
and gives you a more pleasant point of view
Your world may sometimes seem like a dark tunnel;
what you need is a different kind of parallel
You might think your life force is
being poured down a funnel
or that you are on an endless carousel
Just be patient, it will someday again be
wonderful; time will work its magic spell
and you again will have happiness by the barrel
because on sadness, you will no longer dwell
When you take the time to wait, your
life will again be first rate
Just sit and contemplate; do not procrastinate
because sure as heck your world will again illuminate
You will have a better fate if you evaluate
your positive factors and do not deviate
You may even be the first one out of the gate
as long as you don't go backwards and hibernate

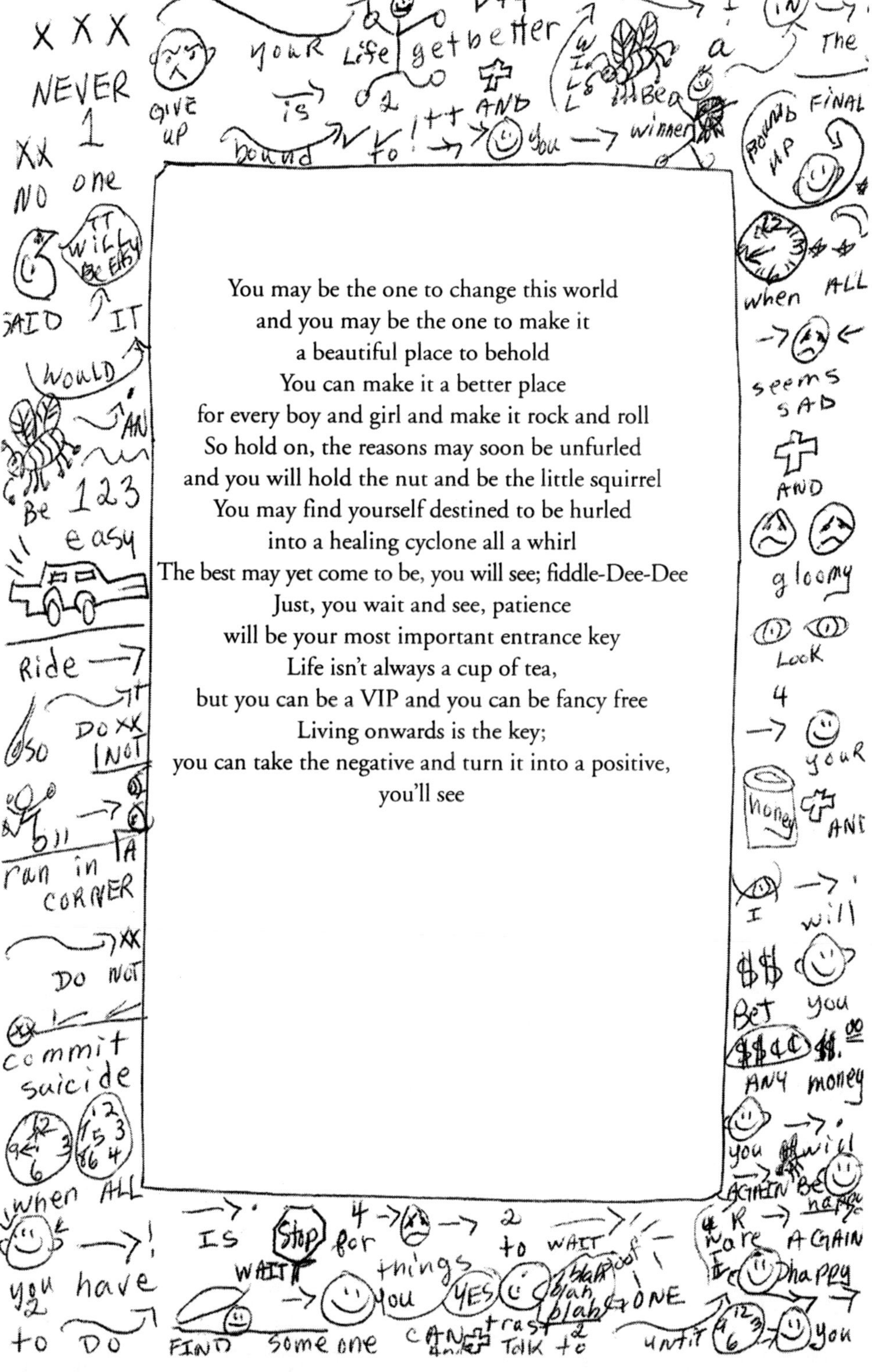

You may be the one to change this world
and you may be the one to make it
a beautiful place to behold
You can make it a better place
for every boy and girl and make it rock and roll
So hold on, the reasons may soon be unfurled
and you will hold the nut and be the little squirrel
You may find yourself destined to be hurled
into a healing cyclone all a whirl
The best may yet come to be, you will see; fiddle-Dee-Dee
Just, you wait and see, patience
will be your most important entrance key
Life isn't always a cup of tea,
but you can be a VIP and you can be fancy free
Living onwards is the key;
you can take the negative and turn it into a positive,
you'll see

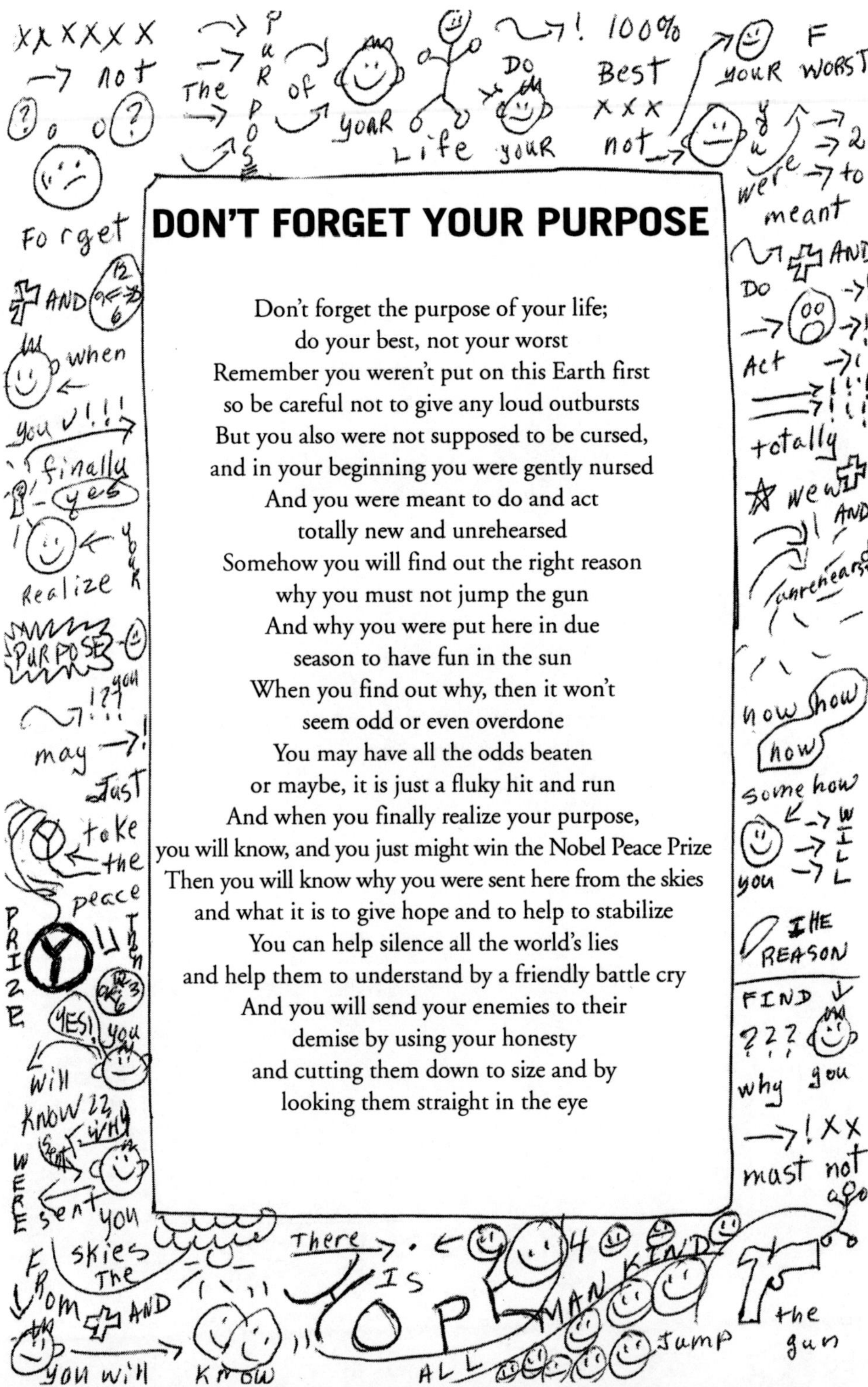

DON'T FORGET YOUR PURPOSE

Don't forget the purpose of your life;
do your best, not your worst
Remember you weren't put on this Earth first
so be careful not to give any loud outbursts
But you also were not supposed to be cursed,
and in your beginning you were gently nursed
And you were meant to do and act
totally new and unrehearsed
Somehow you will find out the right reason
why you must not jump the gun
And why you were put here in due
season to have fun in the sun
When you find out why, then it won't
seem odd or even overdone
You may have all the odds beaten
or maybe, it is just a fluky hit and run
And when you finally realize your purpose,
you will know, and you just might win the Nobel Peace Prize
Then you will know why you were sent here from the skies
and what it is to give hope and to help to stabilize
You can help silence all the world's lies
and help them to understand by a friendly battle cry
And you will send your enemies to their
demise by using your honesty
and cutting them down to size and by
looking them straight in the eye

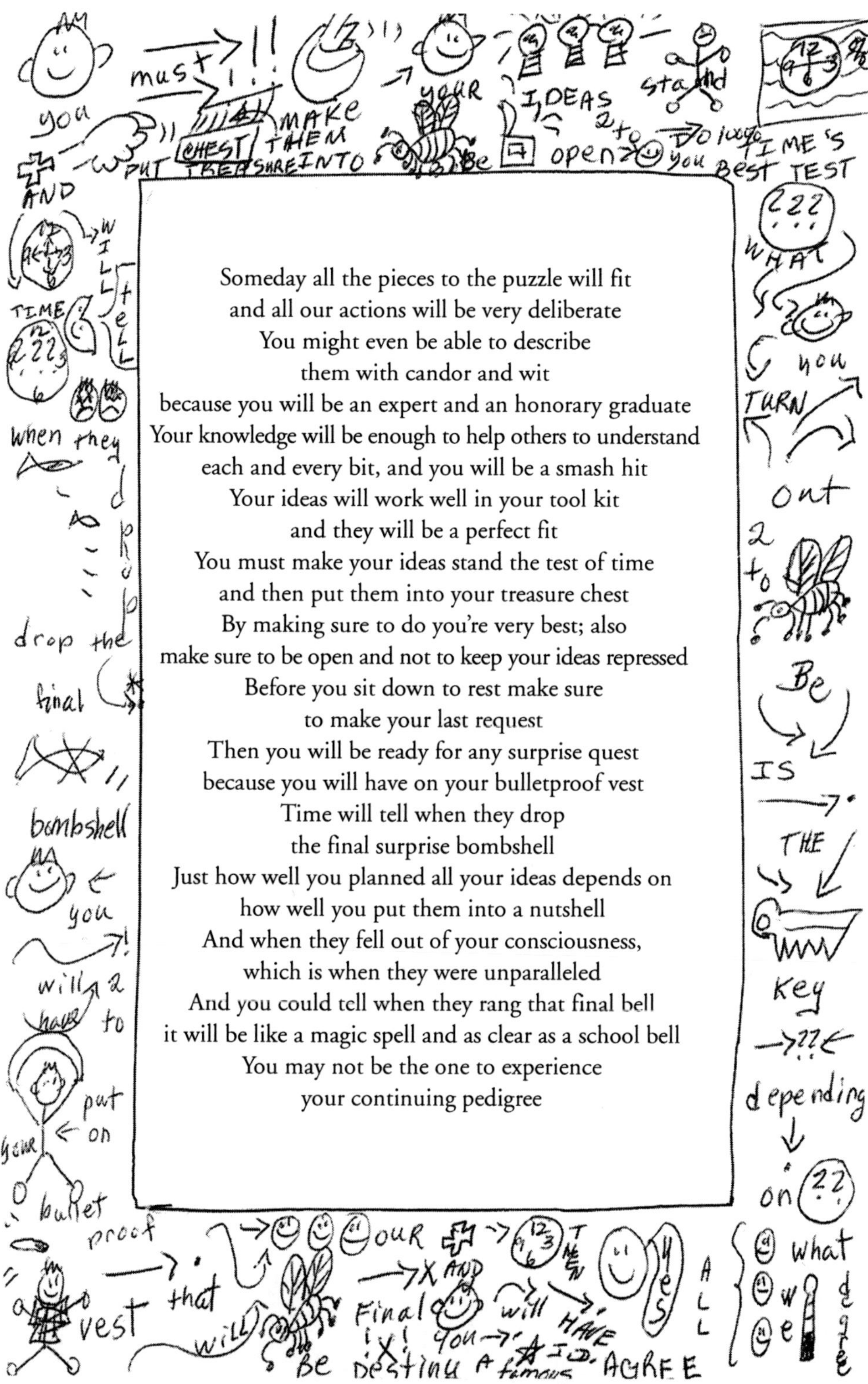

Someday all the pieces to the puzzle will fit
and all our actions will be very deliberate
You might even be able to describe
them with candor and wit
because you will be an expert and an honorary graduate
Your knowledge will be enough to help others to understand
each and every bit, and you will be a smash hit
Your ideas will work well in your tool kit
and they will be a perfect fit
You must make your ideas stand the test of time
and then put them into your treasure chest
By making sure to do you're very best; also
make sure to be open and not to keep your ideas repressed
Before you sit down to rest make sure
to make your last request
Then you will be ready for any surprise quest
because you will have on your bulletproof vest
Time will tell when they drop
the final surprise bombshell
Just how well you planned all your ideas depends on
how well you put them into a nutshell
And when they fell out of your consciousness,
which is when they were unparalleled
And you could tell when they rang that final bell
it will be like a magic spell and as clear as a school bell
You may not be the one to experience
your continuing pedigree

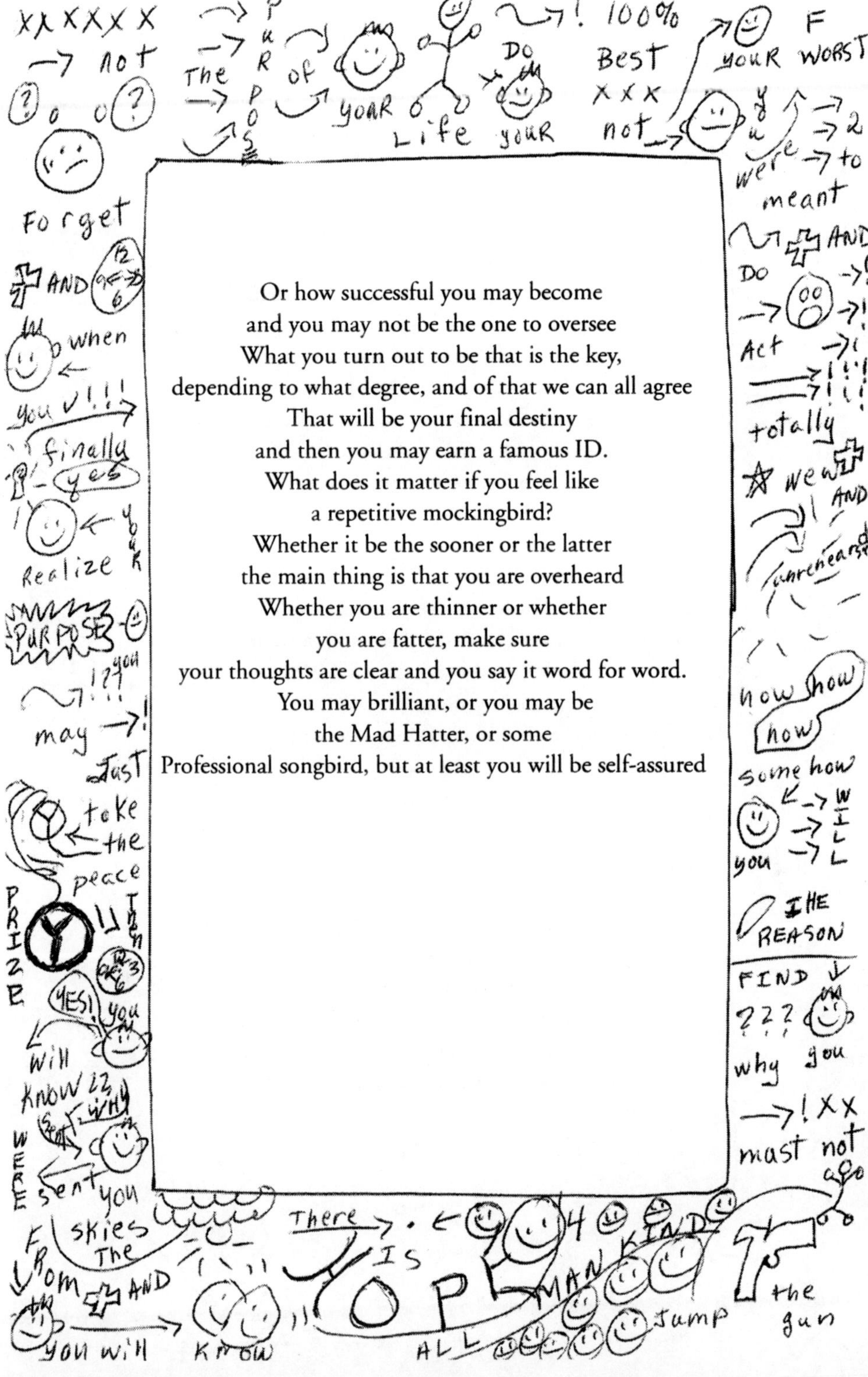

Or how successful you may become
and you may not be the one to oversee
What you turn out to be that is the key,
depending to what degree, and of that we can all agree
That will be your final destiny
and then you may earn a famous ID.
What does it matter if you feel like
a repetitive mockingbird?
Whether it be the sooner or the latter
the main thing is that you are overheard
Whether you are thinner or whether
you are fatter, make sure
your thoughts are clear and you say it word for word.
You may brilliant, or you may be
the Mad Hatter, or some
Professional songbird, but at least you will be self-assured

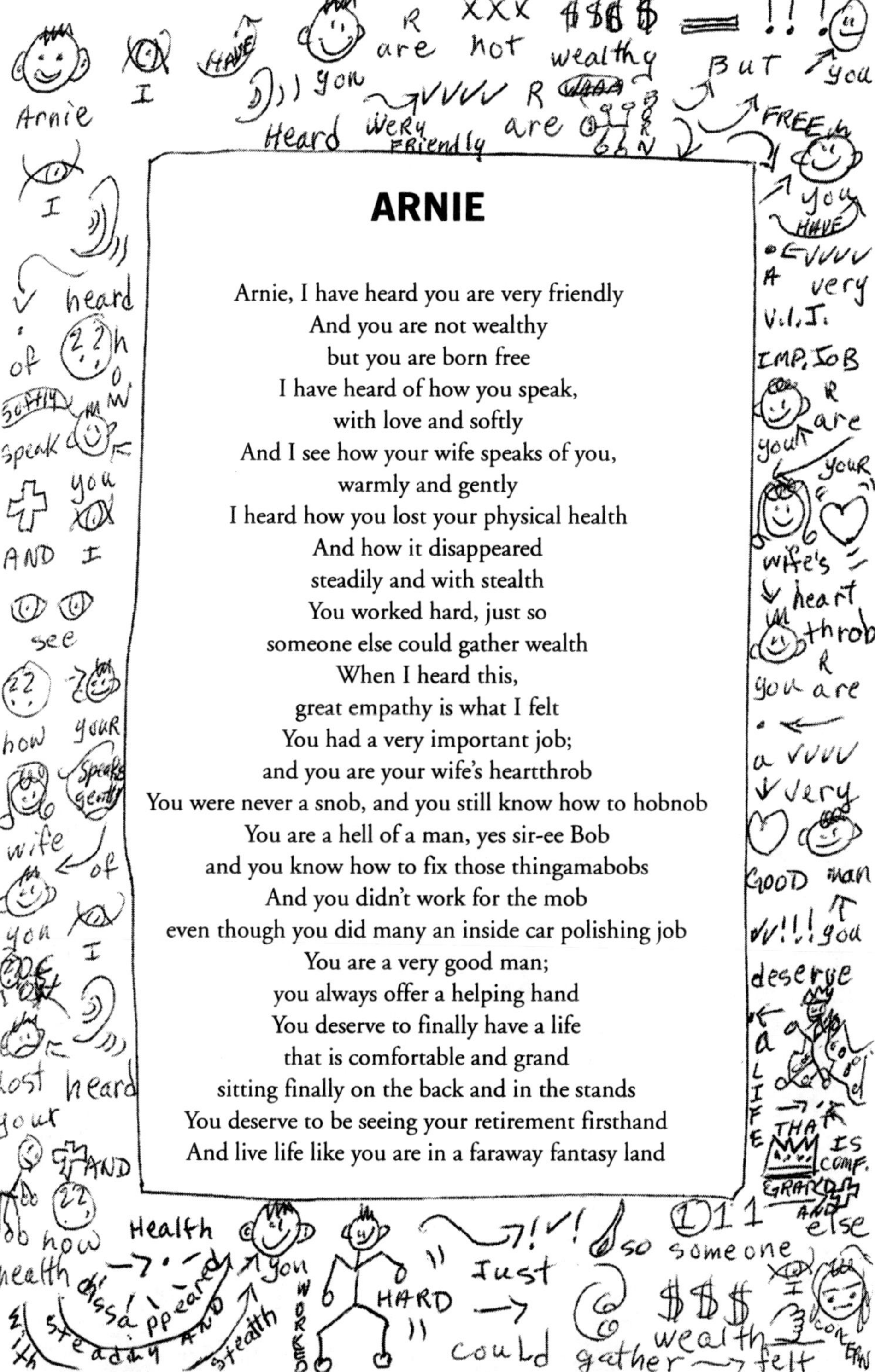

ARNIE

Arnie, I have heard you are very friendly
And you are not wealthy
but you are born free
I have heard of how you speak,
with love and softly
And I see how your wife speaks of you,
warmly and gently
I heard how you lost your physical health
And how it disappeared
steadily and with stealth
You worked hard, just so
someone else could gather wealth
When I heard this,
great empathy is what I felt
You had a very important job;
and you are your wife's heartthrob
You were never a snob, and you still know how to hobnob
You are a hell of a man, yes sir-ee Bob
and you know how to fix those thingamabobs
And you didn't work for the mob
even though you did many an inside car polishing job
You are a very good man;
you always offer a helping hand
You deserve to finally have a life
that is comfortable and grand
sitting finally on the back and in the stands
You deserve to be seeing your retirement firsthand
And live life like you are in a faraway fantasy land

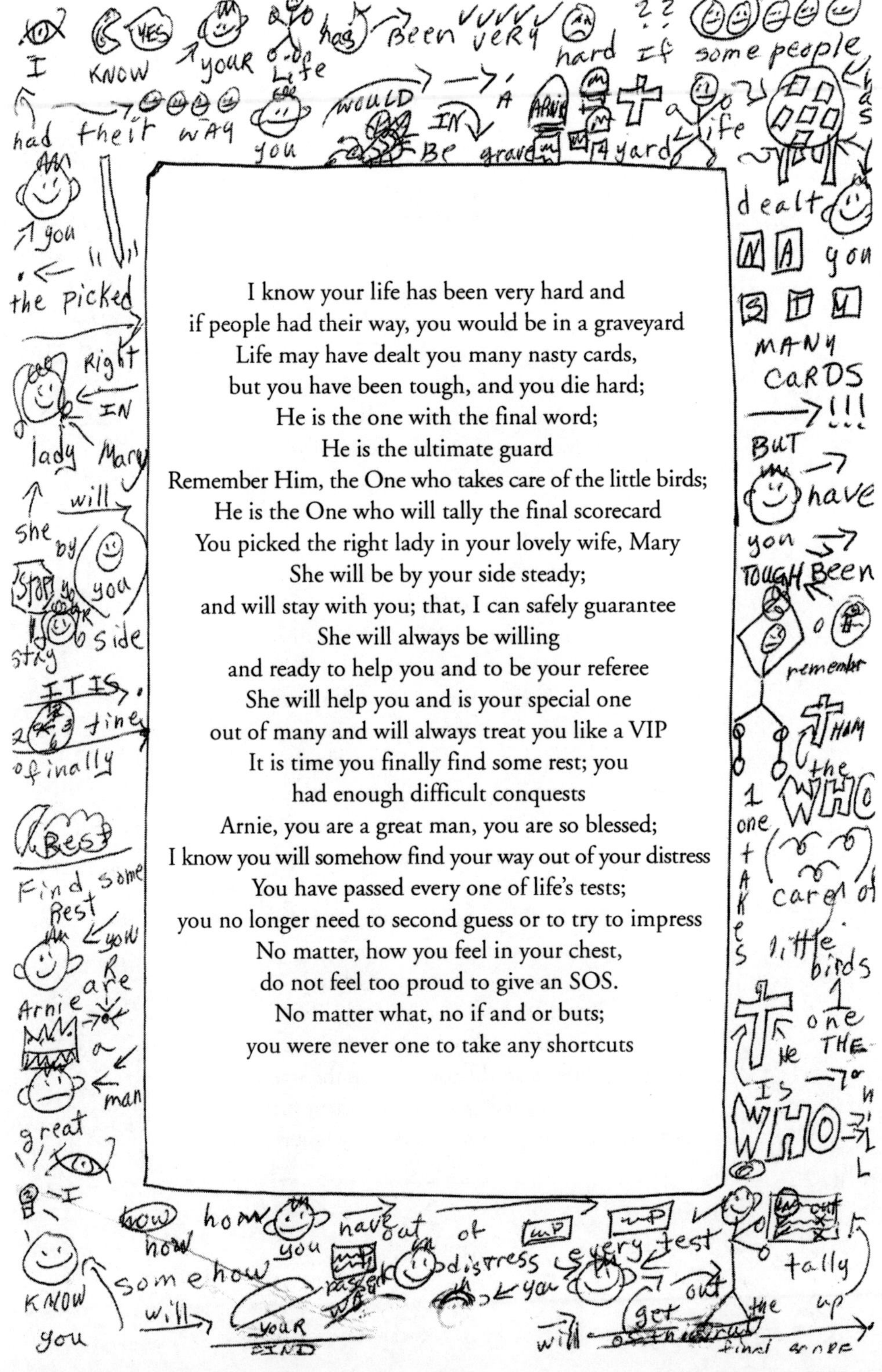

I know your life has been very hard and
if people had their way, you would be in a graveyard
Life may have dealt you many nasty cards,
but you have been tough, and you die hard;
He is the one with the final word;
He is the ultimate guard
Remember Him, the One who takes care of the little birds;
He is the One who will tally the final scorecard
You picked the right lady in your lovely wife, Mary
She will be by your side steady;
and will stay with you; that, I can safely guarantee
She will always be willing
and ready to help you and to be your referee
She will help you and is your special one
out of many and will always treat you like a VIP
It is time you finally find some rest; you
had enough difficult conquests
Arnie, you are a great man, you are so blessed;
I know you will somehow find your way out of your distress
You have passed every one of life's tests;
you no longer need to second guess or to try to impress
No matter, how you feel in your chest,
do not feel too proud to give an SOS.
No matter what, no if and or buts;
you were never one to take any shortcuts

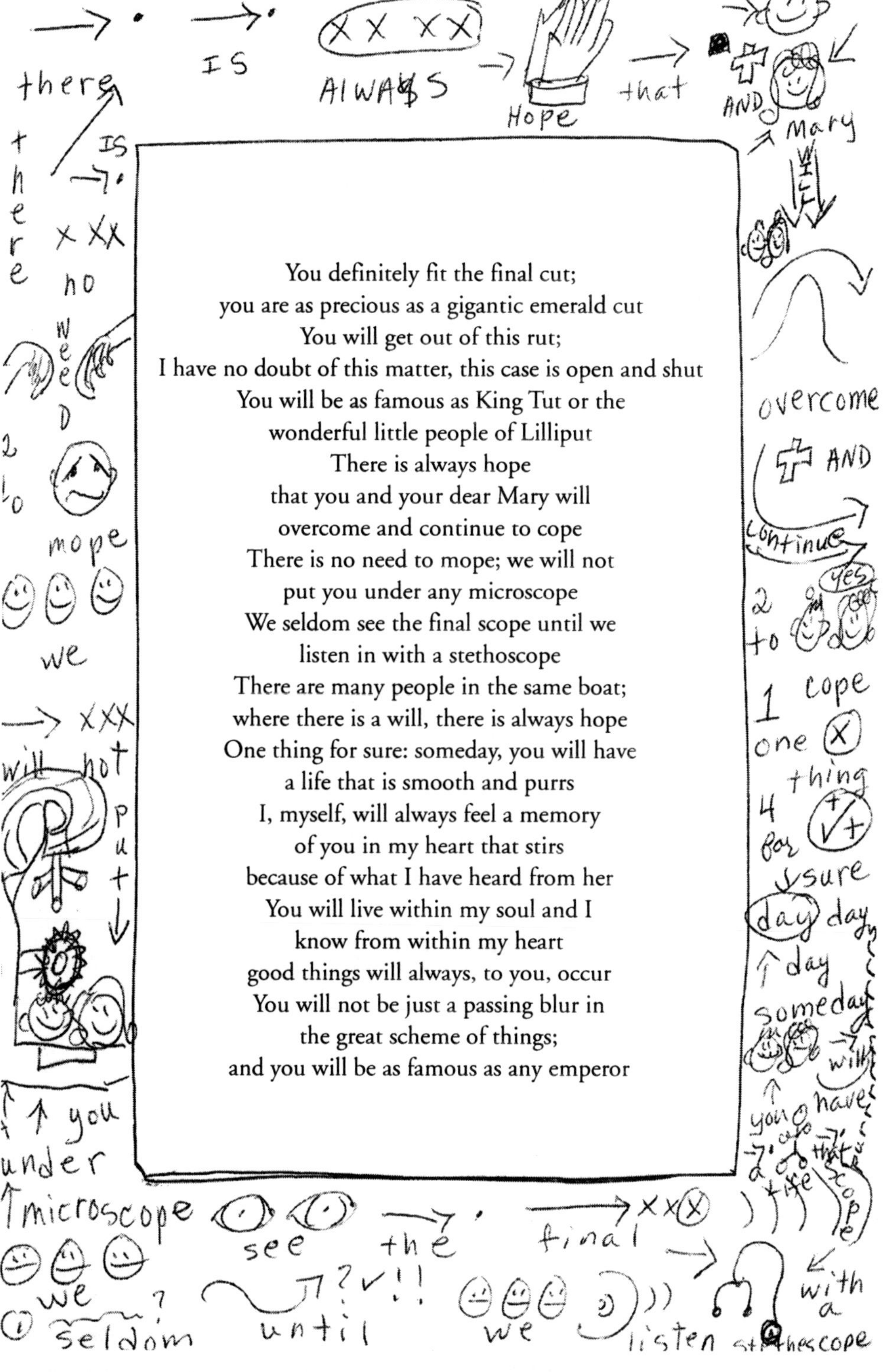

You definitely fit the final cut;
you are as precious as a gigantic emerald cut
You will get out of this rut;
I have no doubt of this matter, this case is open and shut
You will be as famous as King Tut or the
wonderful little people of Lilliput
There is always hope
that you and your dear Mary will
overcome and continue to cope
There is no need to mope; we will not
put you under any microscope
We seldom see the final scope until we
listen in with a stethoscope
There are many people in the same boat;
where there is a will, there is always hope
One thing for sure: someday, you will have
a life that is smooth and purrs
I, myself, will always feel a memory
of you in my heart that stirs
because of what I have heard from her
You will live within my soul and I
know from within my heart
good things will always, to you, occur
You will not be just a passing blur in
the great scheme of things;
and you will be as famous as any emperor

CAT WOMAN

There once was a cat woman
who was in great demand
She was a black beauty, the cutest in all the land
She was more beautiful than the pyramids
in the sand of a faraway land
You could swear that she was from a dreamland;
come on, give her some applause from the
bandstand where she stands

You would love what she wore;
it was guaranteed to be stylish evermore
When she walked through the door
cat men lined up in a cat tug-of-war
It was pure Halloween lore, leaving you
wanting more, more, more, and more
And leaving you wondering what was next in store
When it comes to the cat woman
there is more than meets the eye;
she can also be a big, soft, cuddly, cutie pie
She is not scared to meow you a comforting lullaby
Or to heave a sigh and travel to the great by and by
Look, she is saying hi
am I dreaming or have I hit the cat's-eye?

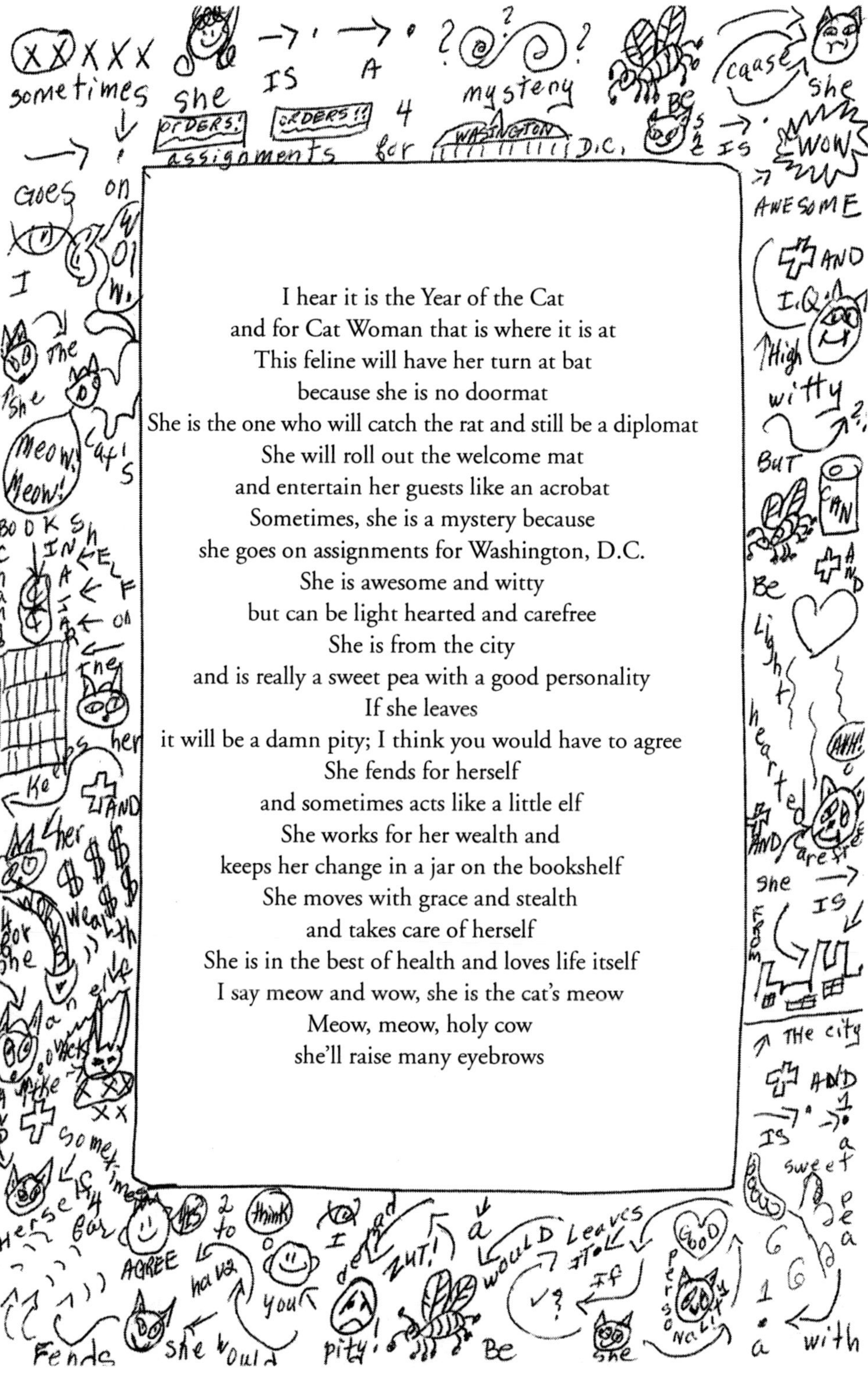

I hear it is the Year of the Cat
and for Cat Woman that is where it is at
This feline will have her turn at bat
because she is no doormat
She is the one who will catch the rat and still be a diplomat
She will roll out the welcome mat
and entertain her guests like an acrobat
Sometimes, she is a mystery because
she goes on assignments for Washington, D.C.
She is awesome and witty
but can be light hearted and carefree
She is from the city
and is really a sweet pea with a good personality
If she leaves
it will be a damn pity; I think you would have to agree
She fends for herself
and sometimes acts like a little elf
She works for her wealth and
keeps her change in a jar on the bookshelf
She moves with grace and stealth
and takes care of herself
She is in the best of health and loves life itself
I say meow and wow, she is the cat's meow
Meow, meow, holy cow
she'll raise many eyebrows

Bing bang paw, bow-wow, meow, meow
Cat Woman, come here now and take a bow
She can sure move and
she doesn't make any bad moves
I want her to approve
when I too am on the move so I will improve
Cat Woman's in the groove and no one disapproves
I want her to love me
and I dare anyone to disapprove

STRANGERS

Are you from out of town, or are you
just here from our hometown
Because I haven't seen you around this place
I will take a head count and do a knockdown
Your music seems to be sound
so come on, let us have a hoedown
Could it be you are glory bound or are
you headed for world renown?
You may be a newcomer, but I still
think you are no pushover
I think you are still an old timer,
but I think you should run fast for cover
Still there will be no one finer
once you are given the once-over
You will be the king of the one-liners
you must own a four-leaf clover
You are very welcome here;
we will give you a great big cheer
Have no fear, everything is A-OK, and it is all clear
You do not have to feel queer
even though you have a pierced ear
We do not mind you being near;
we all live in the same atmosphere
Don't let anyone push you away
you are entitled to the same right of way
Now you are here to stay; we can get introduced by the way
You are welcome in our town to play
just try not to rub anyone the wrong way

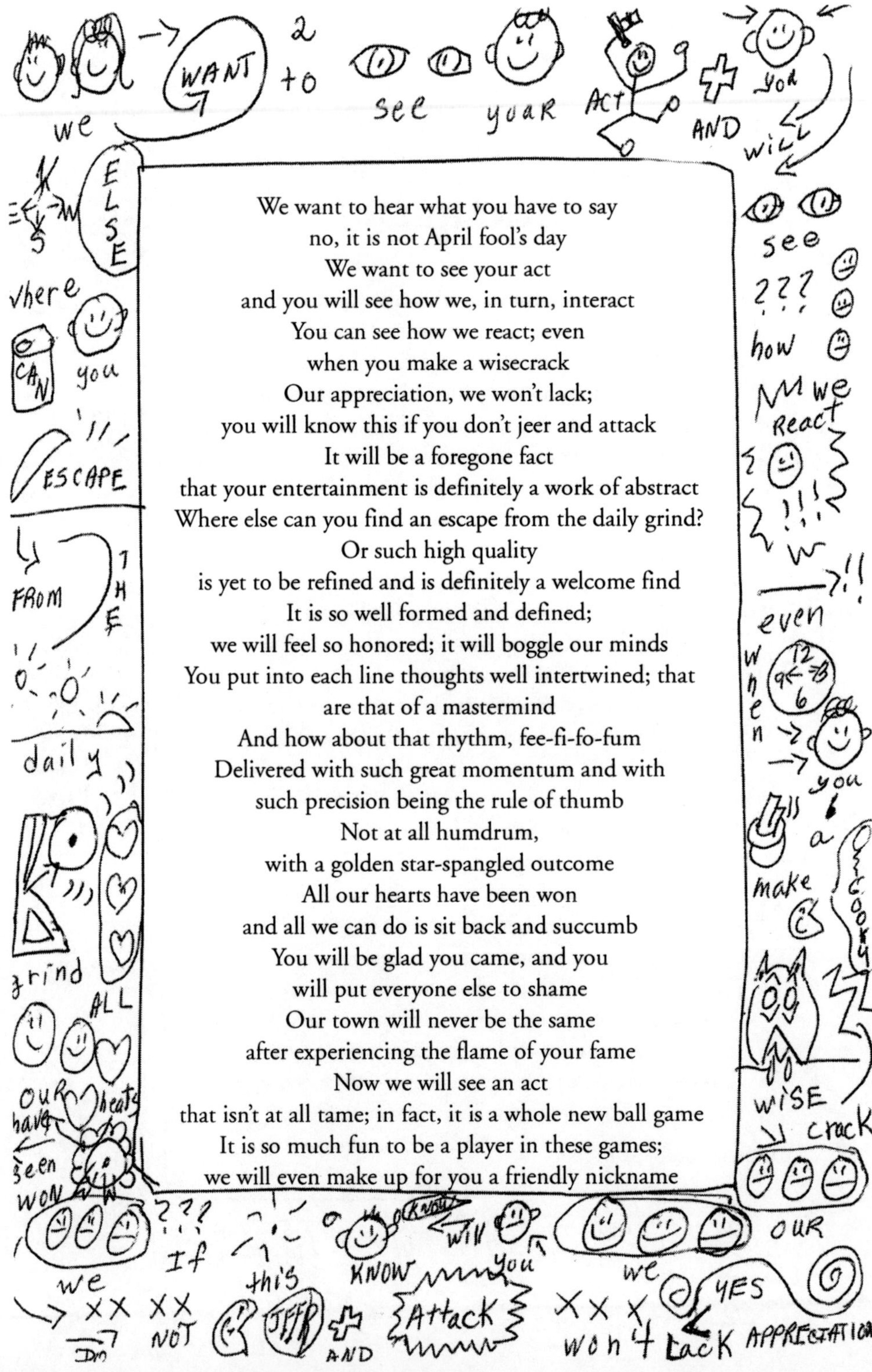

We want to hear what you have to say
no, it is not April fool's day
We want to see your act
and you will see how we, in turn, interact
You can see how we react; even
when you make a wisecrack
Our appreciation, we won't lack;
you will know this if you don't jeer and attack
It will be a foregone fact
that your entertainment is definitely a work of abstract
Where else can you find an escape from the daily grind?
Or such high quality
is yet to be refined and is definitely a welcome find
It is so well formed and defined;
we will feel so honored; it will boggle our minds
You put into each line thoughts well intertwined; that
are that of a mastermind
And how about that rhythm, fee-fi-fo-fum
Delivered with such great momentum and with
such precision being the rule of thumb
Not at all humdrum,
with a golden star-spangled outcome
All our hearts have been won
and all we can do is sit back and succumb
You will be glad you came, and you
will put everyone else to shame
Our town will never be the same
after experiencing the flame of your fame
Now we will see an act
that isn't at all tame; in fact, it is a whole new ball game
It is so much fun to be a player in these games;
we will even make up for you a friendly nickname

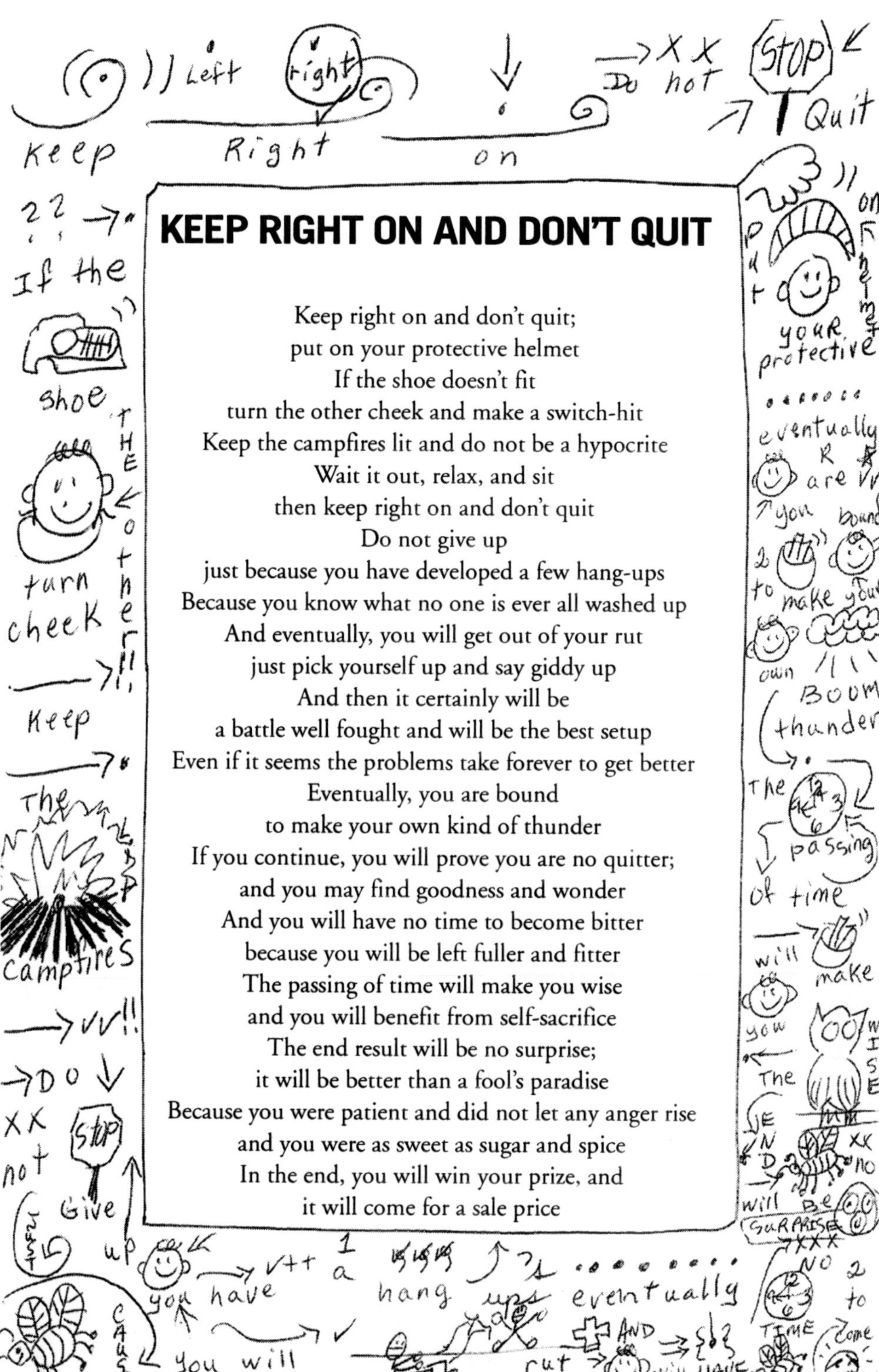

KEEP RIGHT ON AND DON'T QUIT

Keep right on and don't quit;
put on your protective helmet
If the shoe doesn't fit
turn the other cheek and make a switch-hit
Keep the campfires lit and do not be a hypocrite
Wait it out, relax, and sit
then keep right on and don't quit
Do not give up
just because you have developed a few hang-ups
Because you know what no one is ever all washed up
And eventually, you will get out of your rut
just pick yourself up and say giddy up
And then it certainly will be
a battle well fought and will be the best setup
Even if it seems the problems take forever to get better
Eventually, you are bound
to make your own kind of thunder
If you continue, you will prove you are no quitter;
and you may find goodness and wonder
And you will have no time to become bitter
because you will be left fuller and fitter
The passing of time will make you wise
and you will benefit from self-sacrifice
The end result will be no surprise;
it will be better than a fool's paradise
Because you were patient and did not let any anger rise
and you were as sweet as sugar and spice
In the end, you will win your prize, and
it will come for a sale price

It pays to be tenacious with no fuss and no muss
Being stubborn is very precious;
it has its own special place and purpose
It is a commodity, not a wish;
on these things you might want to discuss
It is also something we must learn to begin to have
in surplus because it works better, thus
It is like putting up a good fight
and it can become your birthright
If you continue to practice
you will get it right much to everyone's delight
Do not lose sight, and go when you get the green light
Hang on to your goals and hang tight
keep your end goal in sight
Even if the road is long and hard,
continue to keep a scorecard
If you continue on, you will be the main character
and you will have the last word
This may sometimes seem absurd,
but everyone has a good fairy or a heavenly guard
Your way will be eventually heard
even if your life is treacherous and battle-scarred
The reason people are so successful
even if they seem slow and dull
Is because they don't take any bull
and they don't let anyone pull, on them, the wool
They keep right on, even when
they get an earful and keep many
ideas in their heads chock-full
don't quit until you are at a lull
and until, they are as peaceful as Sitting Bull

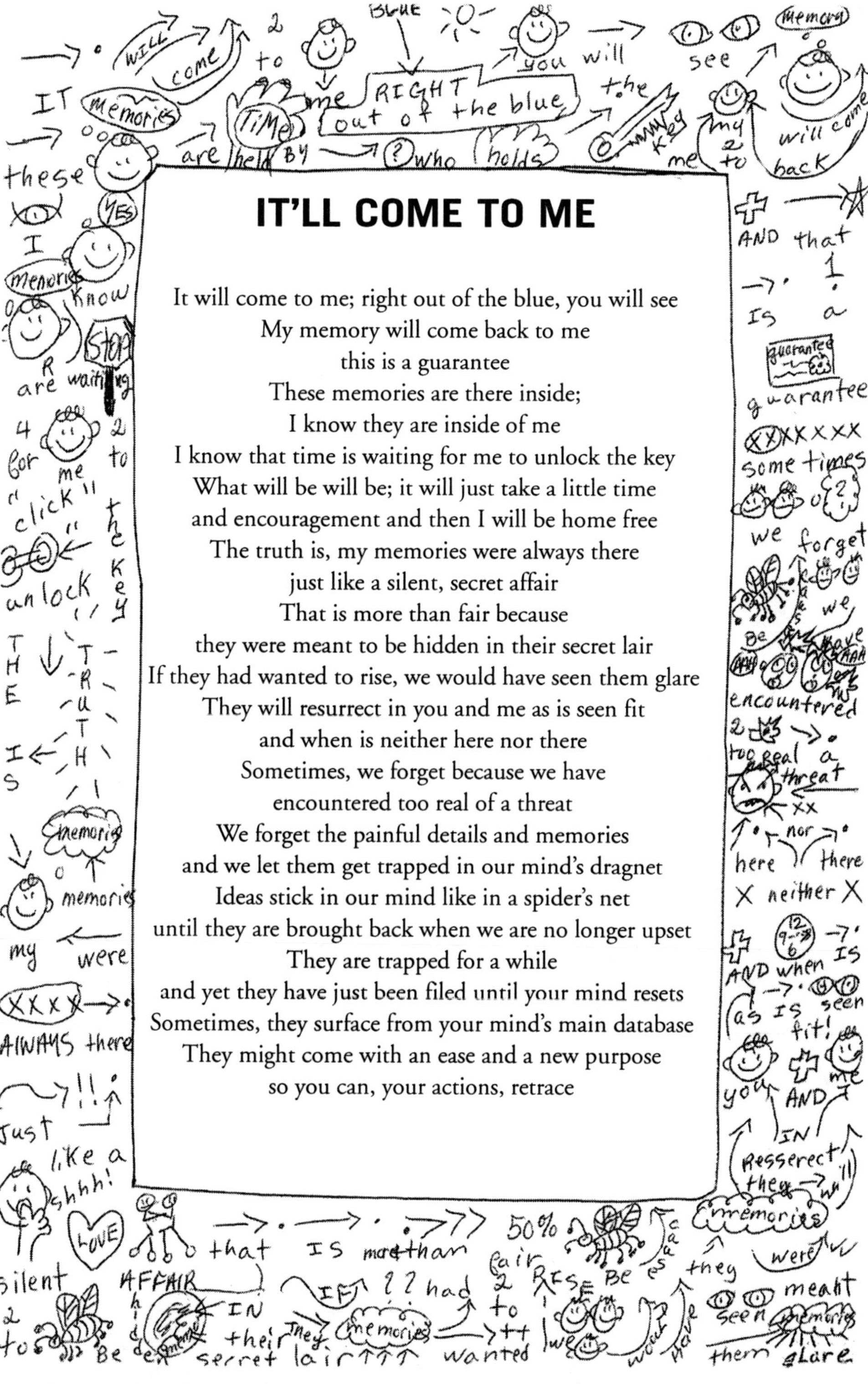

IT'LL COME TO ME

It will come to me; right out of the blue, you will see
My memory will come back to me
this is a guarantee
These memories are there inside;
I know they are inside of me
I know that time is waiting for me to unlock the key
What will be will be; it will just take a little time
and encouragement and then I will be home free
The truth is, my memories were always there
just like a silent, secret affair
That is more than fair because
they were meant to be hidden in their secret lair
If they had wanted to rise, we would have seen them glare
They will resurrect in you and me as is seen fit
and when is neither here nor there
Sometimes, we forget because we have
encountered too real of a threat
We forget the painful details and memories
and we let them get trapped in our mind's dragnet
Ideas stick in our mind like in a spider's net
until they are brought back when we are no longer upset
They are trapped for a while
and yet they have just been filed until your mind resets
Sometimes, they surface from your mind's main database
They might come with an ease and a new purpose
so you can, your actions, retrace

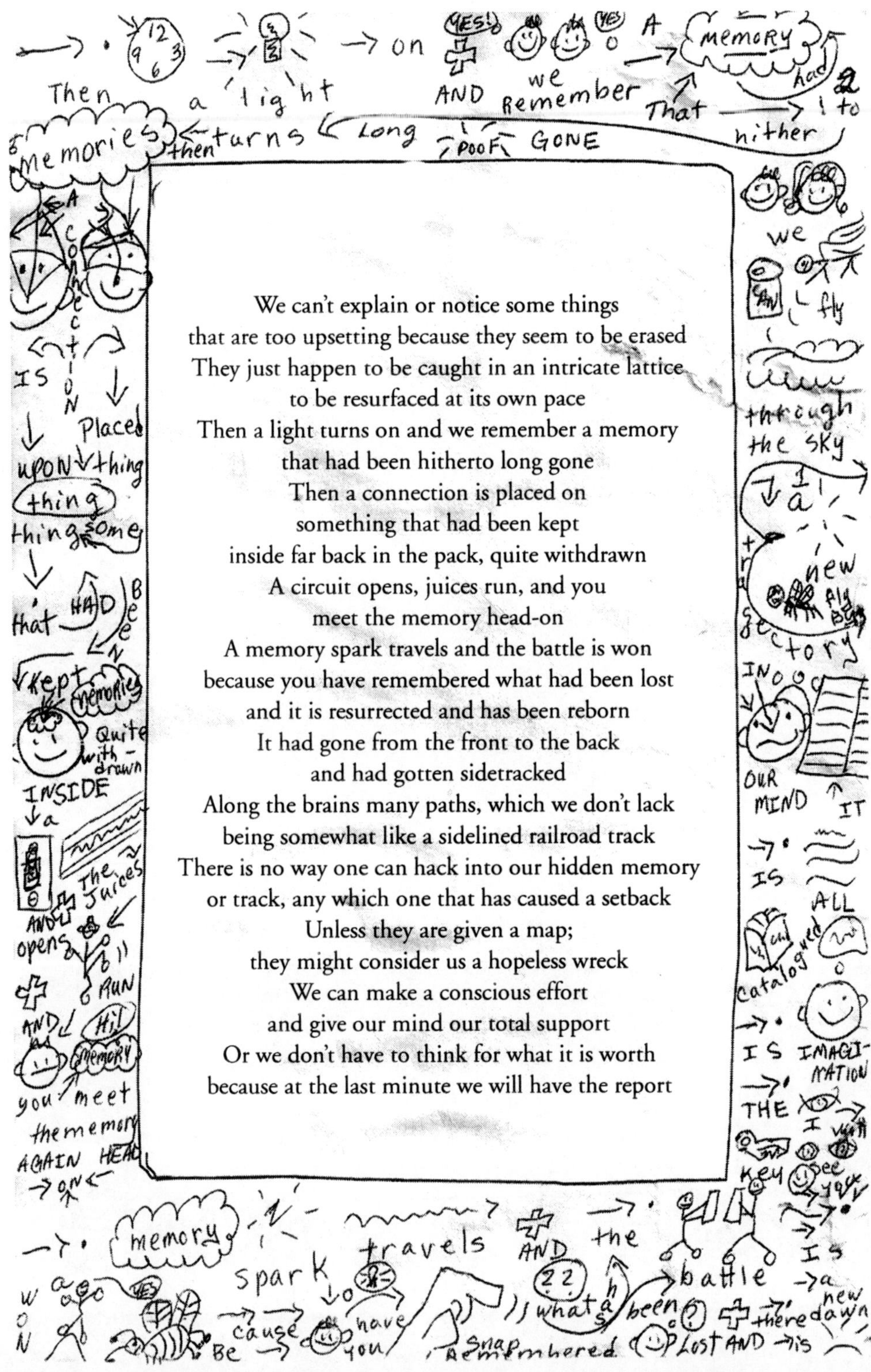

We can't explain or notice some things
that are too upsetting because they seem to be erased
They just happen to be caught in an intricate lattice
to be resurfaced at its own pace
Then a light turns on and we remember a memory
that had been hitherto long gone
Then a connection is placed on
something that had been kept
inside far back in the pack, quite withdrawn
A circuit opens, juices run, and you
meet the memory head-on
A memory spark travels and the battle is won
because you have remembered what had been lost
and it is resurrected and has been reborn
It had gone from the front to the back
and had gotten sidetracked
Along the brains many paths, which we don't lack
being somewhat like a sidelined railroad track
There is no way one can hack into our hidden memory
or track, any which one that has caused a setback
Unless they are given a map;
they might consider us a hopeless wreck
We can make a conscious effort
and give our mind our total support
Or we don't have to think for what it is worth
because at the last minute we will have the report

It can be the new birth of an idea
that was supposed to be used as a last resort
Or we could use a route, as traveled, as one around the Earth
from our side of the world to a new seaport
We can also travel through the sky in a
new ambitious trajectory fly-by
We can travel anywhere here or there, no lie
and it will all be cataloged up here in
our mind, neatly classified
There is no need for effort, just letting the time go by and by
at any time or place just like sci-fi
Imagination is the key vessel for this guy;
so I will see you and here is mud in your eye

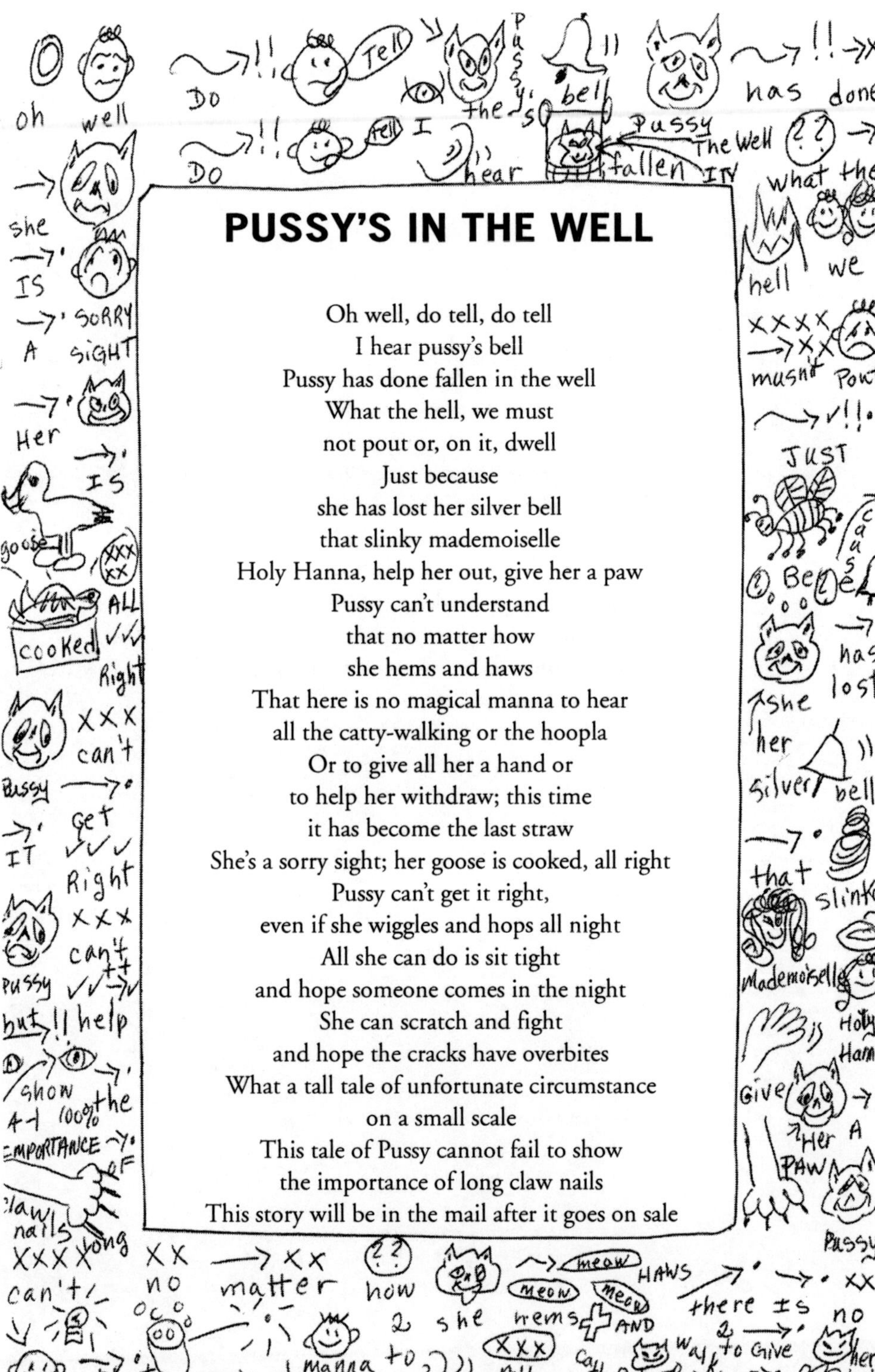

PUSSY'S IN THE WELL

Oh well, do tell, do tell
I hear pussy's bell
Pussy has done fallen in the well
What the hell, we must
not pout or, on it, dwell
Just because
she has lost her silver bell
that slinky mademoiselle
Holy Hanna, help her out, give her a paw
Pussy can't understand
that no matter how
she hems and haws
That here is no magical manna to hear
all the catty-walking or the hoopla
Or to give all her a hand or
to help her withdraw; this time
it has become the last straw
She's a sorry sight; her goose is cooked, all right
Pussy can't get it right,
even if she wiggles and hops all night
All she can do is sit tight
and hope someone comes in the night
She can scratch and fight
and hope the cracks have overbites
What a tall tale of unfortunate circumstance
on a small scale
This tale of Pussy cannot fail to show
the importance of long claw nails
This story will be in the mail after it goes on sale

This poor cat has an eerie wail
and is bound to prevail in this short tale
The pussy had some gall
not to see her unfortunate pitfall
She will climb the wall
like a professional cannonball
Then she will fall,
and we will all be appalled
She'll fall first in the well like a rag doll
Then we will step in
and we will help her out like good Boy Scouts
Yes, we will go that route and help Pussy
when she is down and out
We too know what it is all about to be down and out
We will not even have to shout
because there was never any real doubt
There will be a hot time tonight and a real wild party
Somehow, we will get it right, and we will give Pussy
a new bell engraved with the letters VIP.
Yes, the case is locked tight
and we can throw away the key
We have success, if you might
and the pussy has a new reason to be
Yes, the pussy's hot and no longer distraught
We love her a lot because when it
comes to her we have a blind spot
Was this life number 9 or maybe not
that was a tight spot, so we thought
I love what she's got;
her beauty cannot be store bought

HUSH NOW, DON'T TALK

Hush now, they say. Don't cry, don't talk
Hush now, how now, brown cow don't talk
Hush now and relax and go to sleep, don't talk
Hush now, sleep on sweet dreams, and don't talk
Hush now, swing low sweet chariot, and don't talk
Hush now, holy cow and bow wow, don't talk
Hush now; it's a cat's meow, all saucy and sweet
Hush now, bough after bough, row on row
Hush now, go ahead and take a bow, don't be shy
Hush now; make a solemn vow, that's good advice

Hush now, you are here and now morning follows night
Hush now, we made it from the beginning to the end
Hush now, bang, bang, boom, boom, paw, paw, the end
Hush now, go to sleep and don't make a peep
Thank you kindly, you are so sweet; you are a real treat
Thank you, I am really beat and I have flat feet
Thanks for trying to take the heat,
you certainly are no deadbeat
And try to be quiet, but if you can't, it is no sweat
It would be a real riot to go riding in your red Corvette
Can we just try it I promise you will not have any regrets
You won't have a fit because we will not pose you any threat
Everything will go in planned succession, and your
car will be safe because we will not accelerate
It will serve a good lesson in friends being able to cooperate

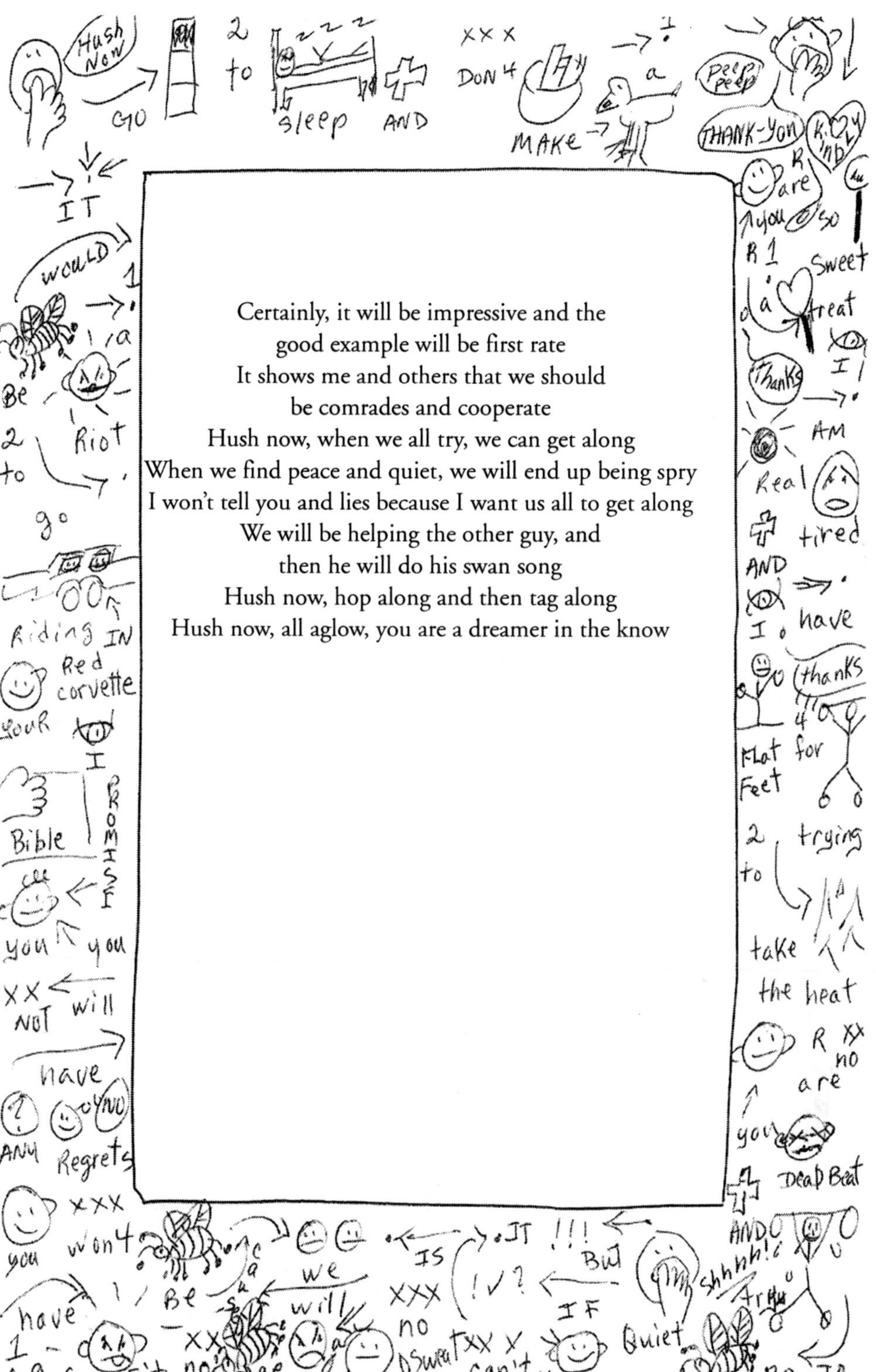

Certainly, it will be impressive and the
good example will be first rate
It shows me and others that we should
be comrades and cooperate
Hush now, when we all try, we can get along
When we find peace and quiet, we will end up being spry
I won't tell you and lies because I want us all to get along
We will be helping the other guy, and
then he will do his swan song
Hush now, hop along and then tag along
Hush now, all aglow, you are a dreamer in the know

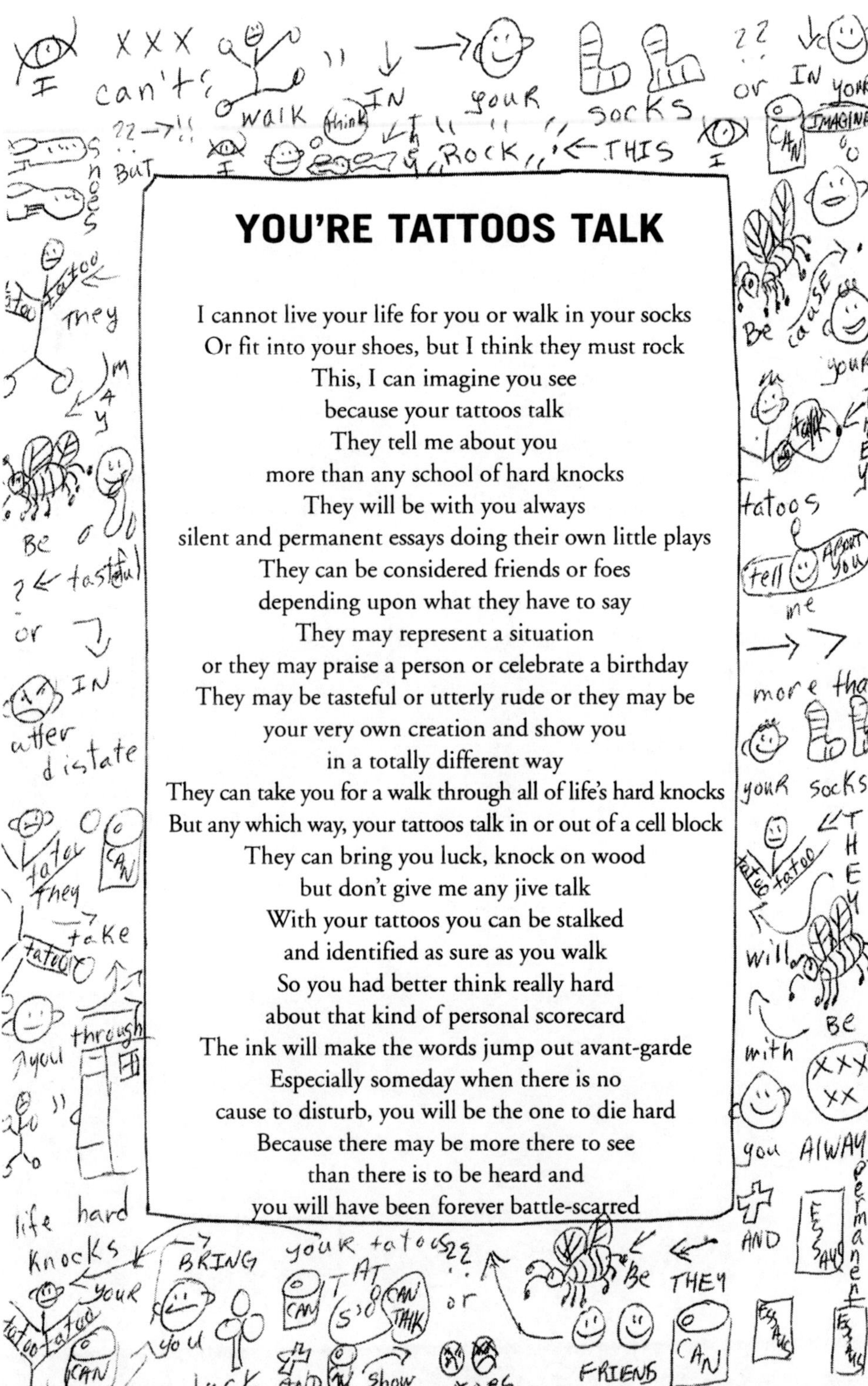

YOU'RE TATTOOS TALK

I cannot live your life for you or walk in your socks
Or fit into your shoes, but I think they must rock
This, I can imagine you see
because your tattoos talk
They tell me about you
more than any school of hard knocks
They will be with you always
silent and permanent essays doing their own little plays
They can be considered friends or foes
depending upon what they have to say
They may represent a situation
or they may praise a person or celebrate a birthday
They may be tasteful or utterly rude or they may be
your very own creation and show you
in a totally different way
They can take you for a walk through all of life's hard knocks
But any which way, your tattoos talk in or out of a cell block
They can bring you luck, knock on wood
but don't give me any jive talk
With your tattoos you can be stalked
and identified as sure as you walk
So you had better think really hard
about that kind of personal scorecard
The ink will make the words jump out avant-garde
Especially someday when there is no
cause to disturb, you will be the one to die hard
Because there may be more there to see
than there is to be heard and
you will have been forever battle-scarred

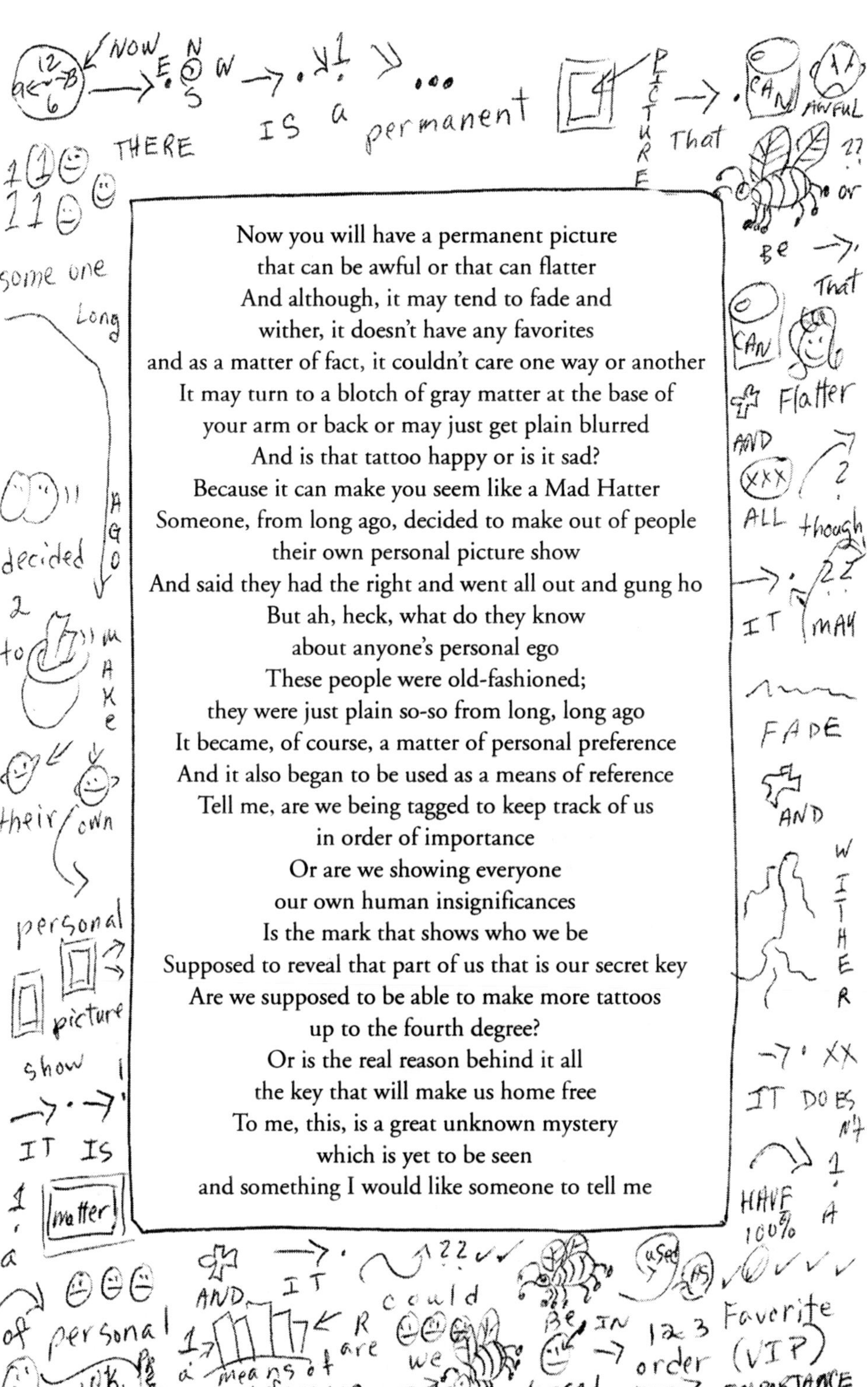

Now you will have a permanent picture
that can be awful or that can flatter
And although, it may tend to fade and
wither, it doesn't have any favorites
and as a matter of fact, it couldn't care one way or another
It may turn to a blotch of gray matter at the base of
your arm or back or may just get plain blurred
And is that tattoo happy or is it sad?
Because it can make you seem like a Mad Hatter
Someone, from long ago, decided to make out of people
their own personal picture show
And said they had the right and went all out and gung ho
But ah, heck, what do they know
about anyone's personal ego
These people were old-fashioned;
they were just plain so-so from long, long ago
It became, of course, a matter of personal preference
And it also began to be used as a means of reference
Tell me, are we being tagged to keep track of us
in order of importance
Or are we showing everyone
our own human insignificances
Is the mark that shows who we be
Supposed to reveal that part of us that is our secret key
Are we supposed to be able to make more tattoos
up to the fourth degree?
Or is the real reason behind it all
the key that will make us home free
To me, this, is a great unknown mystery
which is yet to be seen
and something I would like someone to tell me

POWER TO THE PEOPLE

You say I'm crazy, I say I'm brilliant
You say I'm stupid
I say I'm empathic
You say I'm slow
I say I'm so rapid, I'm graphic
You say I'm way out there
I say I have arrived

Power to the people; may they have a powerful spell
Here's to my fellow human people
may they all be happy and well
They are the true clan
my related friends and personnel
They are the greatest ones, Man they are the ones
that help me to be creative and ring my bells
We are true to form
and there is no need for alarm
And we will someday rule
all together arm in arm
The whole planet Earth will be safe from harm
We will all have peace and brotherly love
and see each other's charm
We will go outward and to the outer zest
but still be blessed
Out to the farthest, beyond the beyond and all the rest
All the places I am really fond of
because they make me impressed

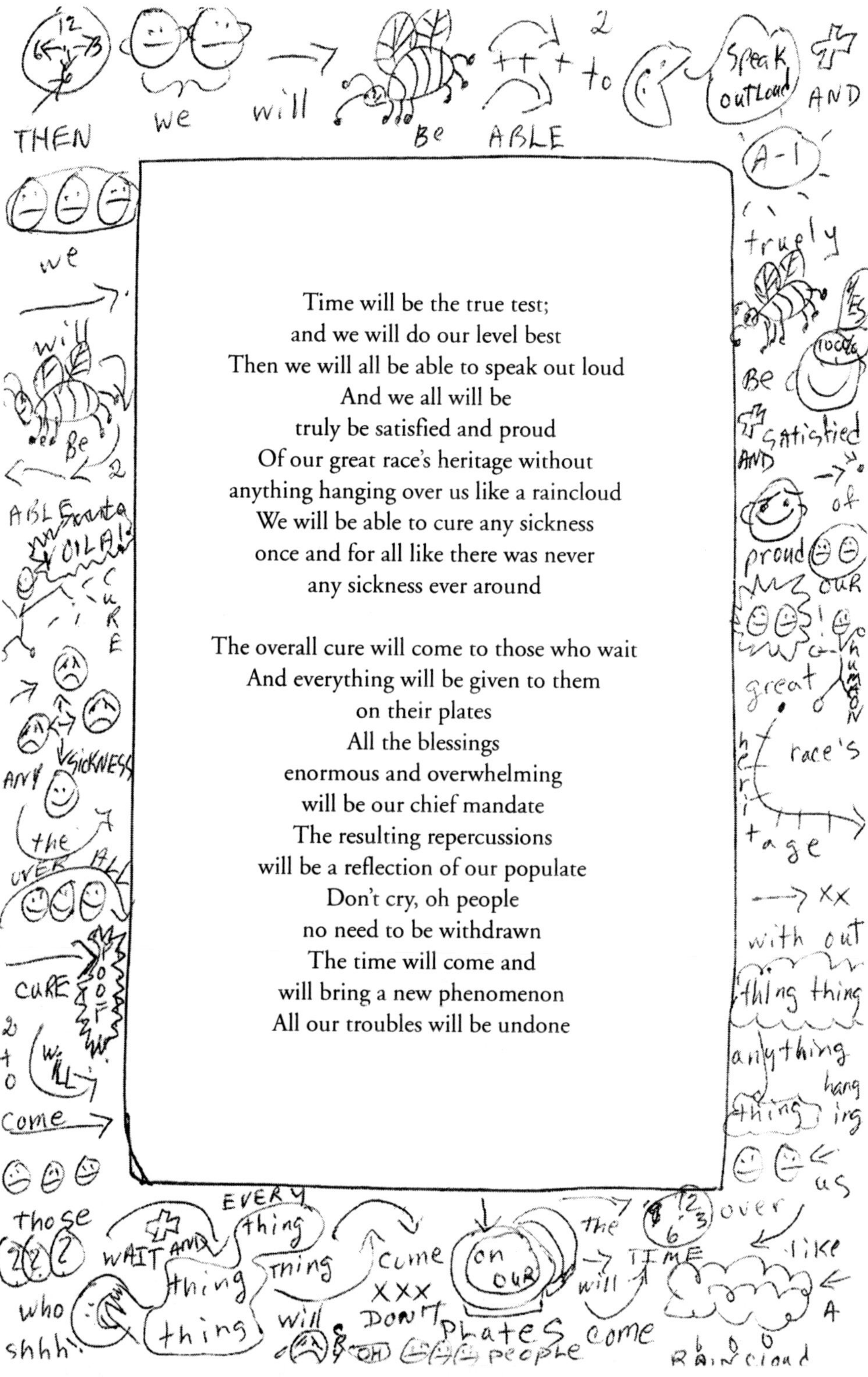

Time will be the true test;
and we will do our level best
Then we will all be able to speak out loud
And we all will be
truly be satisfied and proud
Of our great race's heritage without
anything hanging over us like a raincloud
We will be able to cure any sickness
once and for all like there was never
any sickness ever around

The overall cure will come to those who wait
And everything will be given to them
on their plates
All the blessings
enormous and overwhelming
will be our chief mandate
The resulting repercussions
will be a reflection of our populate
Don't cry, oh people
no need to be withdrawn
The time will come and
will bring a new phenomenon
All our troubles will be undone

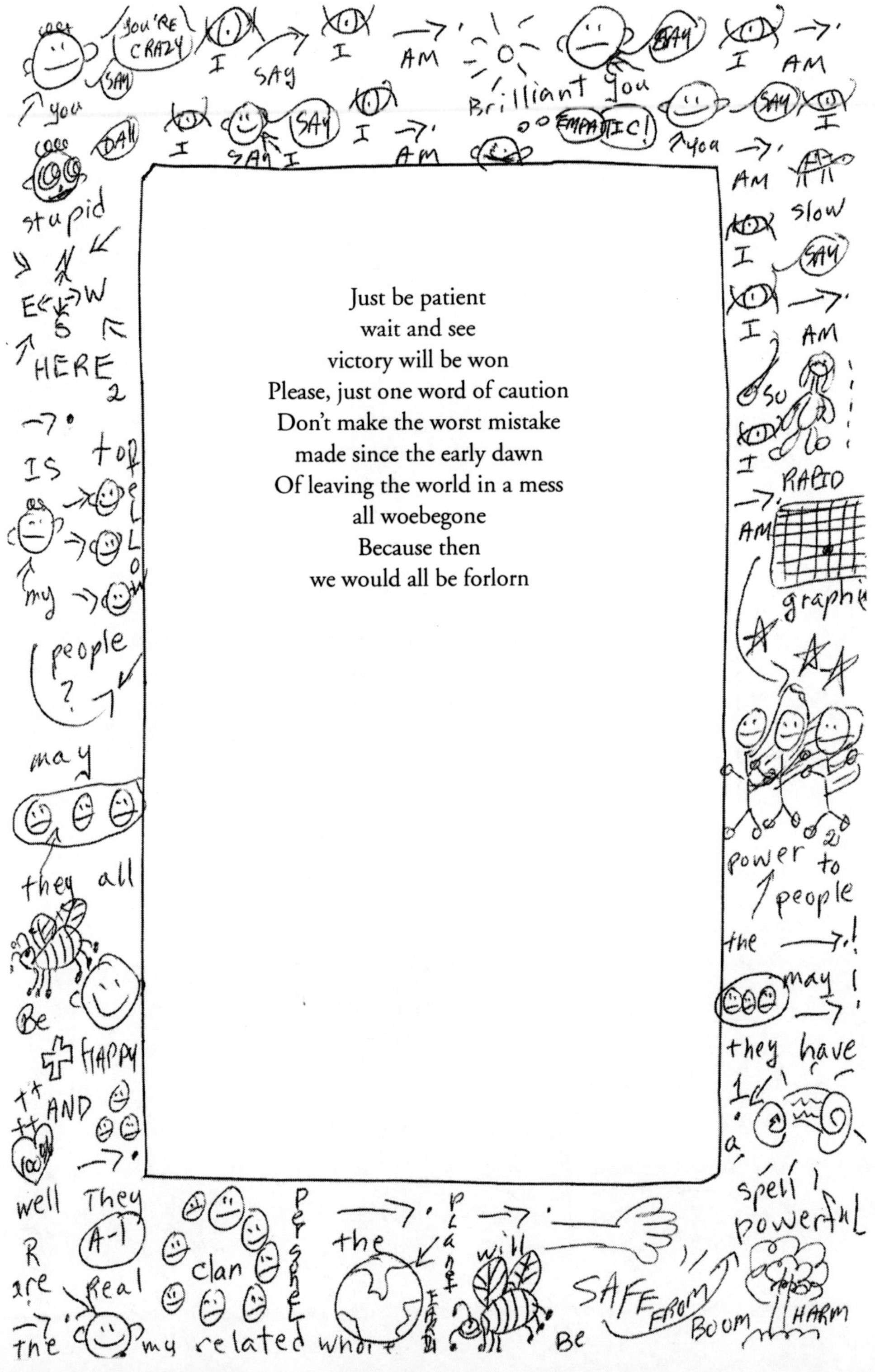

Just be patient
wait and see
victory will be won
Please, just one word of caution
Don't make the worst mistake
made since the early dawn
Of leaving the world in a mess
all woebegone
Because then
we would all be forlorn

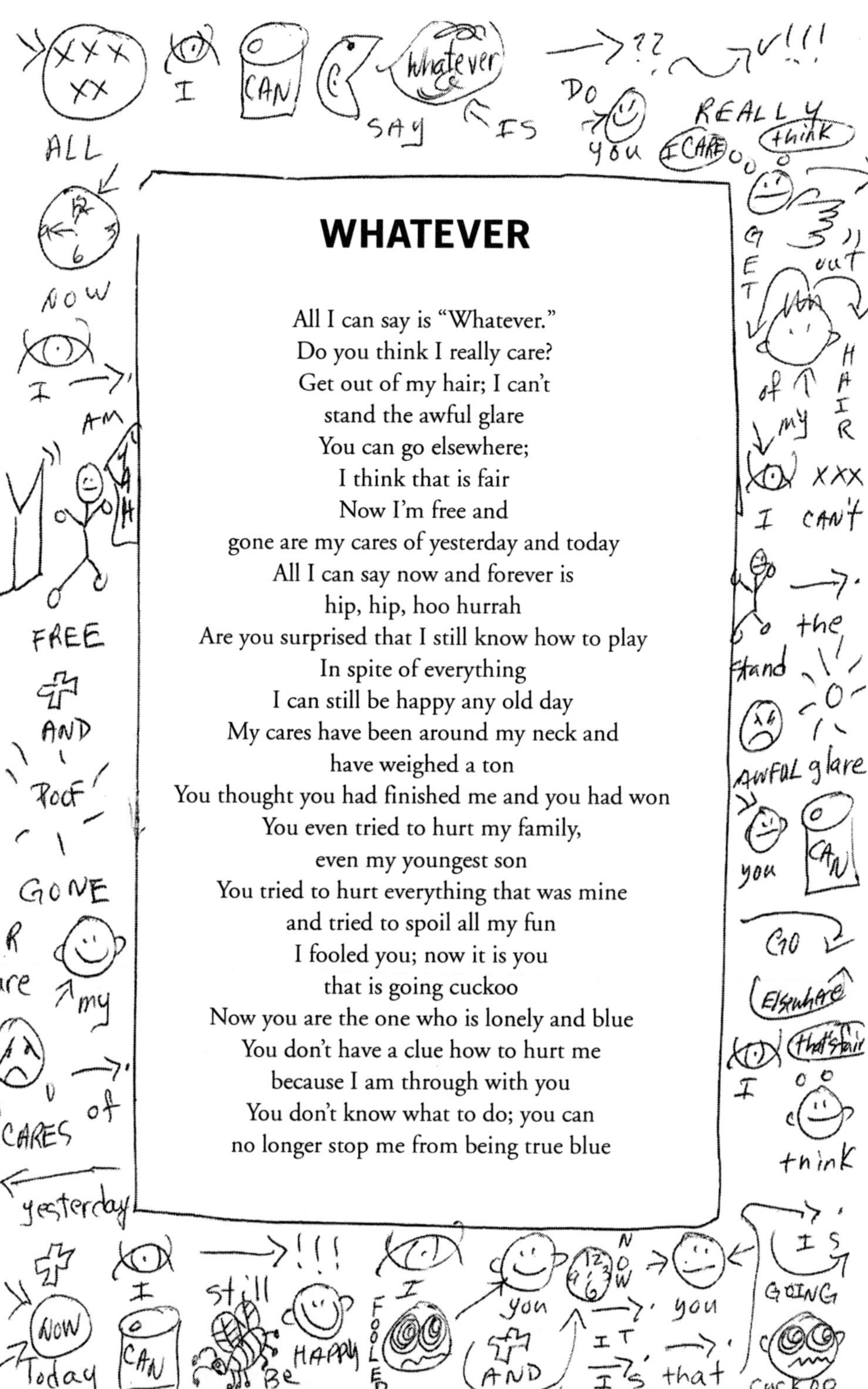

WHATEVER

All I can say is "Whatever."
Do you think I really care?
Get out of my hair; I can't
stand the awful glare
You can go elsewhere;
I think that is fair
Now I'm free and
gone are my cares of yesterday and today
All I can say now and forever is
hip, hip, hoo hurrah
Are you surprised that I still know how to play
In spite of everything
I can still be happy any old day
My cares have been around my neck and
have weighed a ton
You thought you had finished me and you had won
You even tried to hurt my family,
even my youngest son
You tried to hurt everything that was mine
and tried to spoil all my fun
I fooled you; now it is you
that is going cuckoo
Now you are the one who is lonely and blue
You don't have a clue how to hurt me
because I am through with you
You don't know what to do; you can
no longer stop me from being true blue

You can't even find me; I am now safe and home free
You claim ignorance; that is your plea
there are many that would disagree
You'll never be able to see the truth because
in order to do this, you must be truthful; you see
You'll go on with your evil spree;
but you will really be nothing but a refugee
You'll never know the difference between friend and foe
Or how you hurt me so, but that is in the past
that was long, long ago
My anger has gone with the winds that blow
because my character has continued to grow
You'll never again step on my toes because I am
now grown up, and with the prayers
that my mother taught me,
I will parry injury blow for blow
The longer I stay away, the better my case will run
on good's side and in my favor weigh
I and my loved ones will be able to play without fear;
there will never, ever be a need to run away
Each and every day, I've awoken to a brighter day because
I have always faced my problems head-on,
both at night and in the day
You'll never again get in my way because
the world is a large place, and now I am part of life's ballet
I may see you one last time or maybe not, but now

I have a voice that can be heard big time
You are now way past your prime;
you, as well as all of us, has to face Father Time
I'm afraid, this time; you'll be the one with
a long, long mountain to climb
in what's left of your lifetime
Myself, I choose to be a forgiving kind,
but be not mistaken;
you are nothing but a father and that's all you ever were.
Know that, hear my rhyme

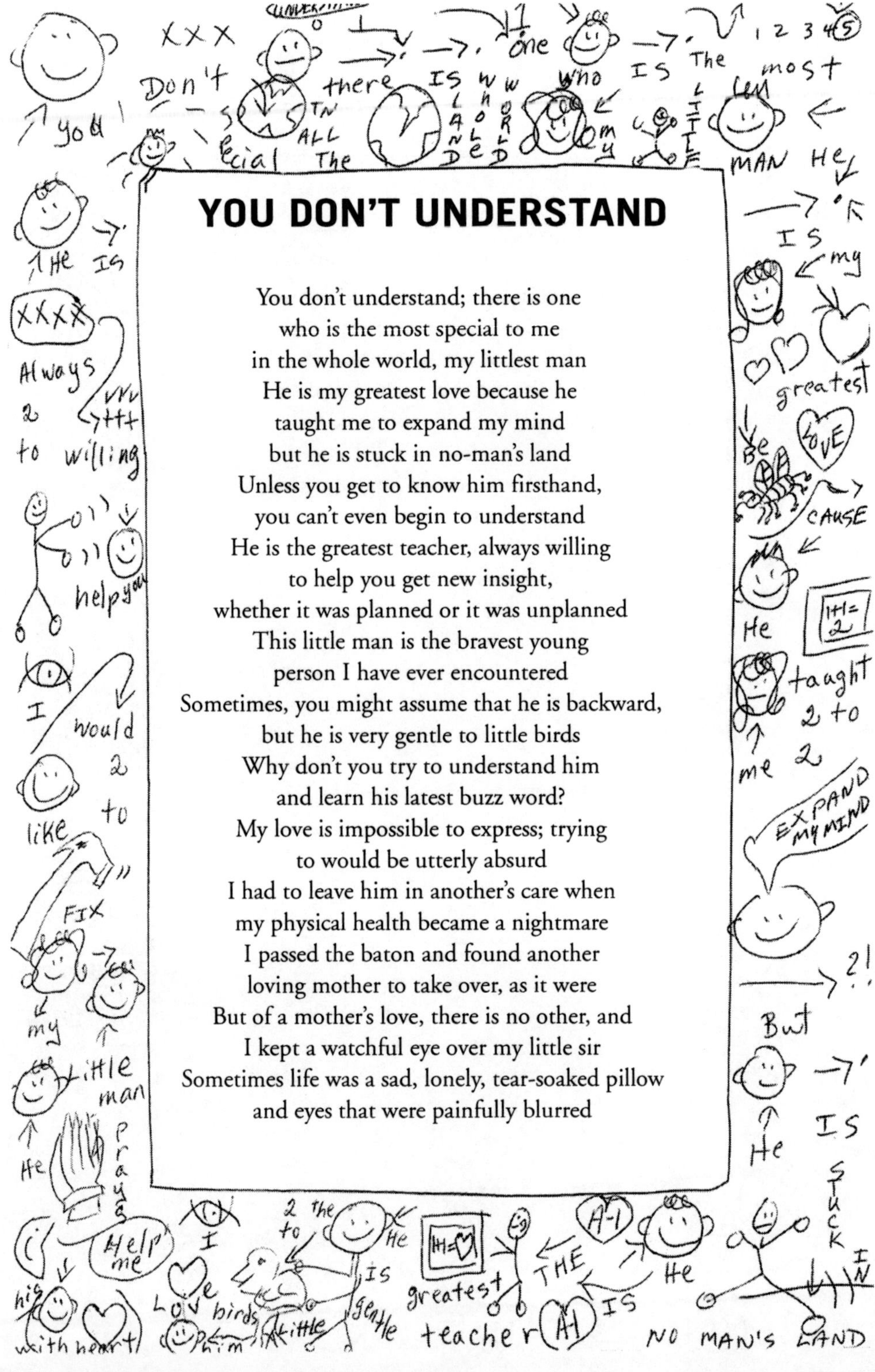

YOU DON'T UNDERSTAND

You don't understand; there is one
who is the most special to me
in the whole world, my littlest man
He is my greatest love because he
taught me to expand my mind
but he is stuck in no-man's land
Unless you get to know him firsthand,
you can't even begin to understand
He is the greatest teacher, always willing
to help you get new insight,
whether it was planned or it was unplanned
This little man is the bravest young
person I have ever encountered
Sometimes, you might assume that he is backward,
but he is very gentle to little birds
Why don't you try to understand him
and learn his latest buzz word?
My love is impossible to express; trying
to would be utterly absurd
I had to leave him in another's care when
my physical health became a nightmare
I passed the baton and found another
loving mother to take over, as it were
But of a mother's love, there is no other, and
I kept a watchful eye over my little sir
Sometimes life was a sad, lonely, tear-soaked pillow
and eyes that were painfully blurred

When will his suffering end? I don't mind,
except I would like to cure my precious little friend
Will a cure come around the bend;
that is not for me to be able to comprehend?
But before his life mends, I will be there
always to protect him and to defend
He prays, "Oh, please help me and be my friend,"
his hands show what his heart recommends
If you only knew how my heart bleeds for him every day
I know the misery he has and is going through
I can only hope and pray
That his ailments will somehow go completely away
And he will finally be able to hear and understand us
when we thank him for making that our very best day
Why must my little man be shown the worst side of life;
his suffering cuts into me like a knife
Why must he suffer this injustice,
this agony, this continual strife?
He does not want to be a bother
or be trouble in anyone's life
But still he is forced through no choice of his own
to be a person larger than life
It truly breaks my heart that he has to suffer
because he is really such a sweetheart
And when he says sorry when it is not
his part; it just tears me apart

He can't help it from the start
that he got a false start compared to his counterparts
This does not mean a thing, but
I'm hoping he will someday show
he is as smart as Mozart
How can a mother explain that
when he is in pain, my grief drives me insane?
When he comes rolling by like a freight
train, all our efforts may be in vain
But my love for him, is as plain as drops make up rain
and as clear as tears that I do not feign
And I have him to thank
for helping me to regain all of my mind's lost terrain

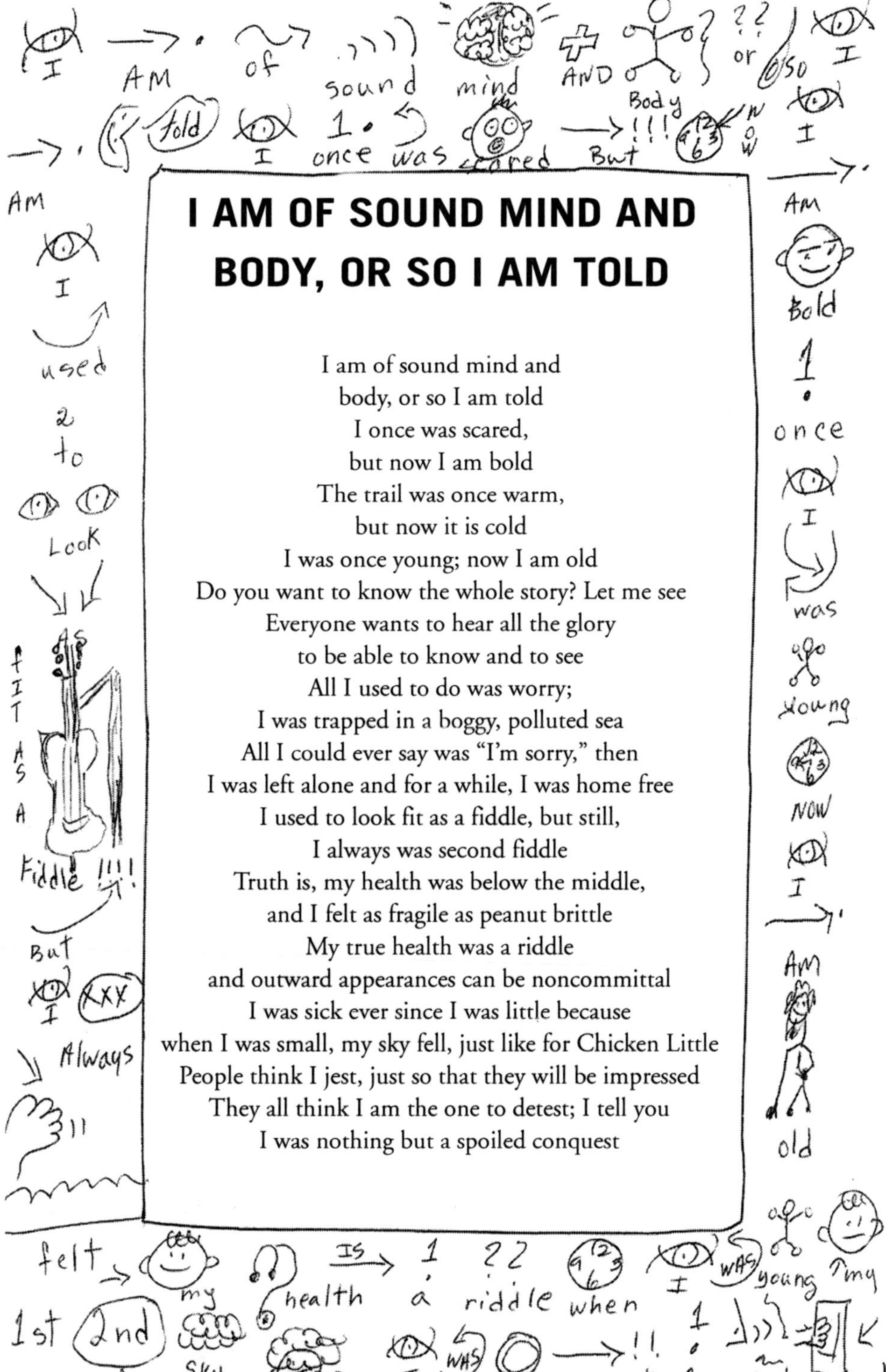

I AM OF SOUND MIND AND BODY, OR SO I AM TOLD

I am of sound mind and
body, or so I am told
I once was scared,
but now I am bold
The trail was once warm,
but now it is cold
I was once young; now I am old
Do you want to know the whole story? Let me see
Everyone wants to hear all the glory
to be able to know and to see
All I used to do was worry;
I was trapped in a boggy, polluted sea
All I could ever say was "I'm sorry," then
I was left alone and for a while, I was home free
I used to look fit as a fiddle, but still,
I always was second fiddle
Truth is, my health was below the middle,
and I felt as fragile as peanut brittle
My true health was a riddle
and outward appearances can be noncommittal
I was sick ever since I was little because
when I was small, my sky fell, just like for Chicken Little
People think I jest, just so that they will be impressed
They all think I am the one to detest; I tell you
I was nothing but a spoiled conquest

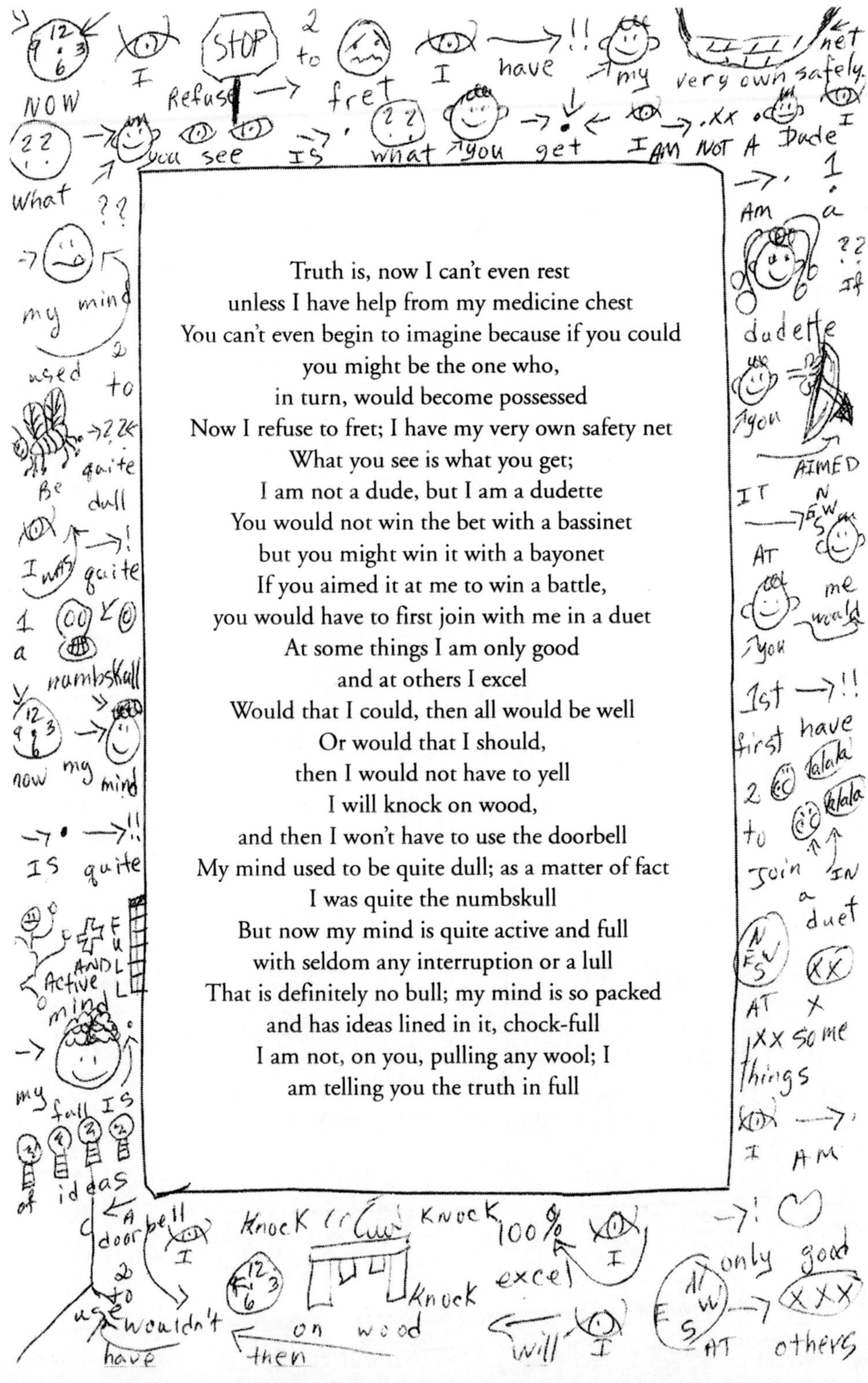

Truth is, now I can't even rest
unless I have help from my medicine chest
You can't even begin to imagine because if you could
you might be the one who,
in turn, would become possessed
Now I refuse to fret; I have my very own safety net
What you see is what you get;
I am not a dude, but I am a dudette
You would not win the bet with a bassinet
but you might win it with a bayonet
If you aimed it at me to win a battle,
you would have to first join with me in a duet
At some things I am only good
and at others I excel
Would that I could, then all would be well
Or would that I should,
then I would not have to yell
I will knock on wood,
and then I won't have to use the doorbell
My mind used to be quite dull; as a matter of fact
I was quite the numbskull
But now my mind is quite active and full
with seldom any interruption or a lull
That is definitely no bull; my mind is so packed
and has ideas lined in it, chock-full
I am not, on you, pulling any wool; I
am telling you the truth in full

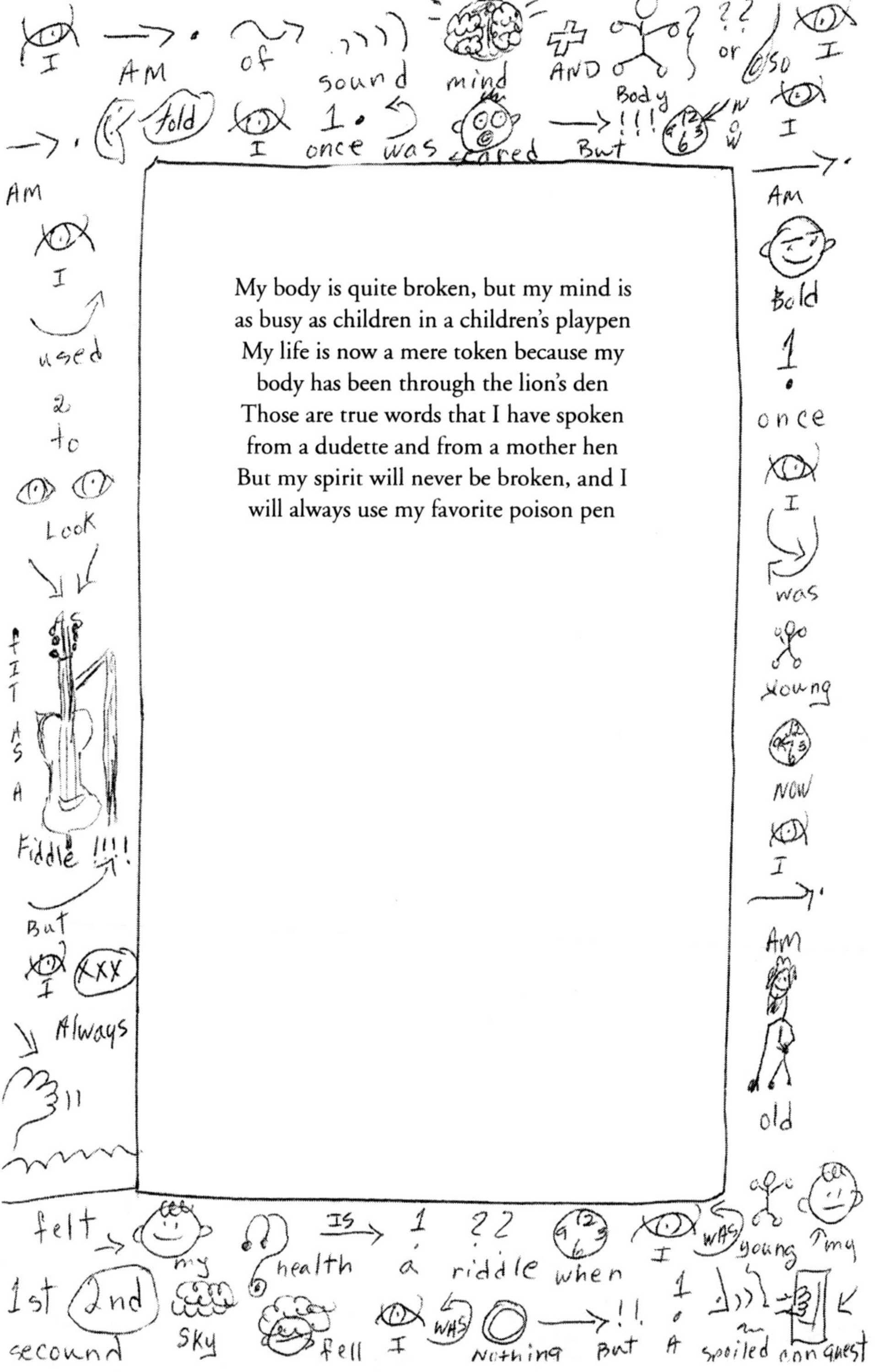

My body is quite broken, but my mind is
as busy as children in a children's playpen
My life is now a mere token because my
body has been through the lion's den
Those are true words that I have spoken
from a dudette and from a mother hen
But my spirit will never be broken, and I
will always use my favorite poison pen

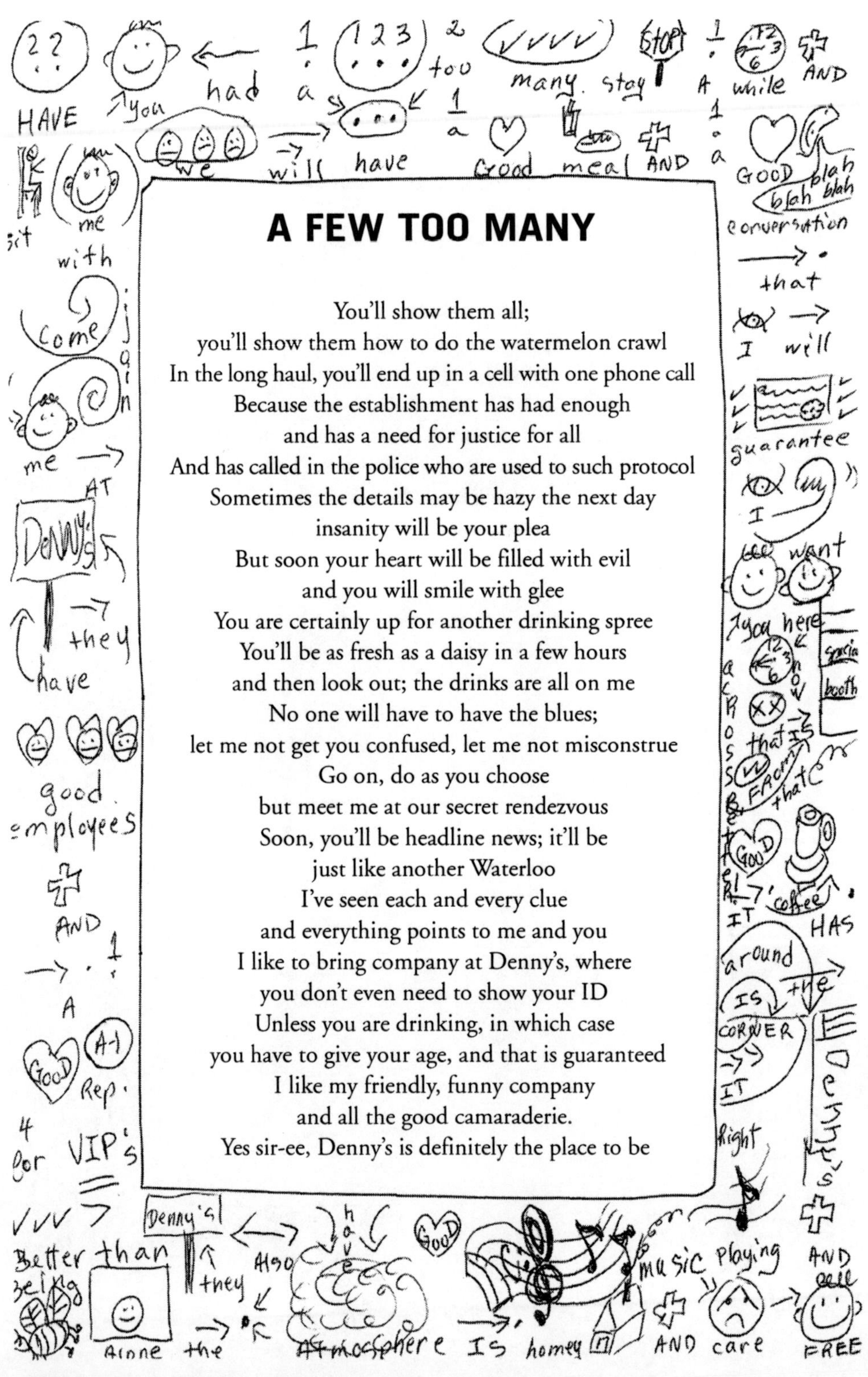

A FEW TOO MANY

You'll show them all;
you'll show them how to do the watermelon crawl
In the long haul, you'll end up in a cell with one phone call
Because the establishment has had enough
and has a need for justice for all
And has called in the police who are used to such protocol
Sometimes the details may be hazy the next day
insanity will be your plea
But soon your heart will be filled with evil
and you will smile with glee
You are certainly up for another drinking spree
You'll be as fresh as a daisy in a few hours
and then look out; the drinks are all on me
No one will have to have the blues;
let me not get you confused, let me not misconstrue
Go on, do as you choose
but meet me at our secret rendezvous
Soon, you'll be headline news; it'll be
just like another Waterloo
I've seen each and every clue
and everything points to me and you
I like to bring company at Denny's, where
you don't even need to show your ID
Unless you are drinking, in which case
you have to give your age, and that is guaranteed
I like my friendly, funny company
and all the good camaraderie.
Yes sir-ee, Denny's is definitely the place to be

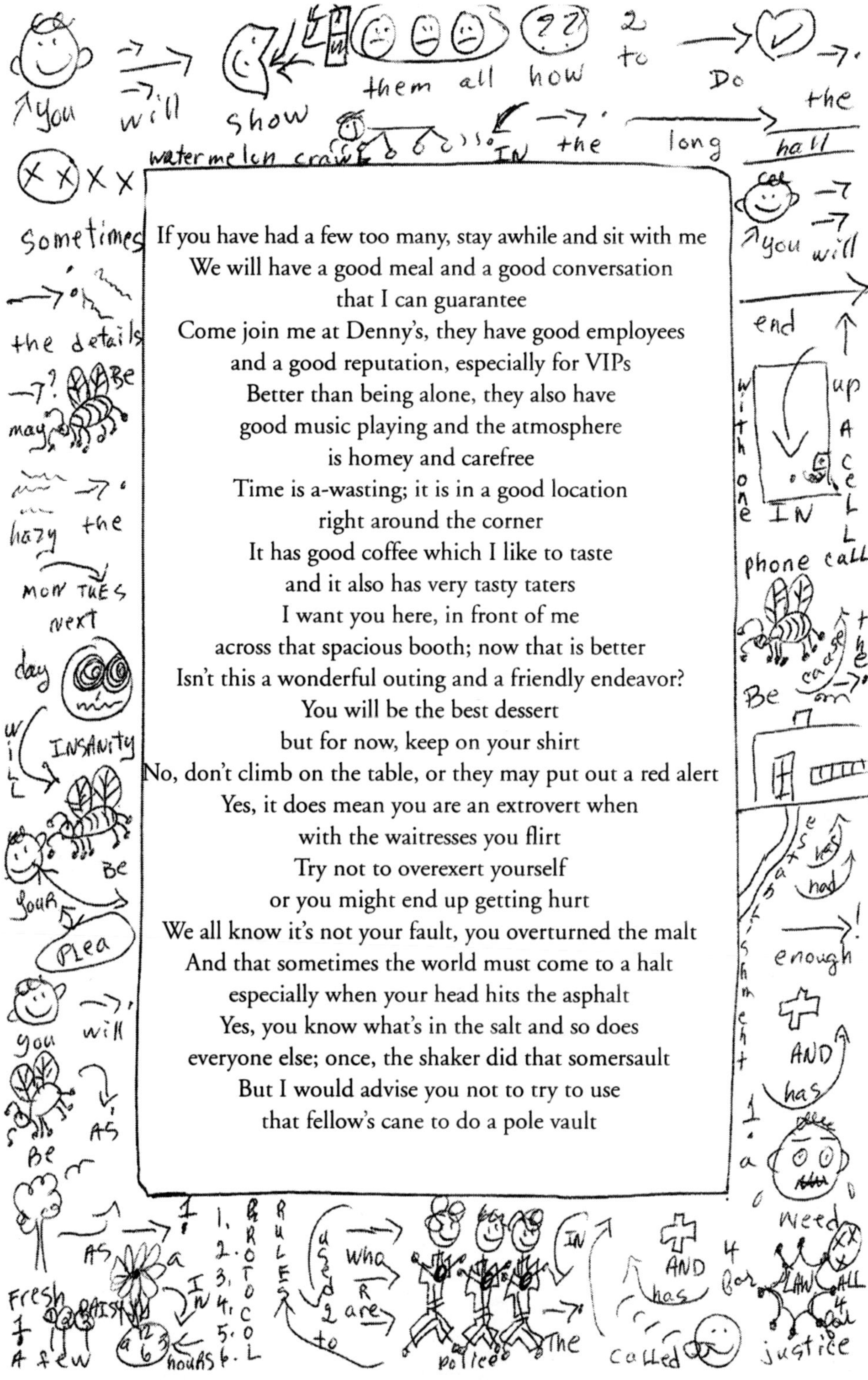

If you have had a few too many, stay awhile and sit with me
We will have a good meal and a good conversation
that I can guarantee
Come join me at Denny's, they have good employees
and a good reputation, especially for VIPs
Better than being alone, they also have
good music playing and the atmosphere
is homey and carefree
Time is a-wasting; it is in a good location
right around the corner
It has good coffee which I like to taste
and it also has very tasty taters
I want you here, in front of me
across that spacious booth; now that is better
Isn't this a wonderful outing and a friendly endeavor?
You will be the best dessert
but for now, keep on your shirt
No, don't climb on the table, or they may put out a red alert
Yes, it does mean you are an extrovert when
with the waitresses you flirt
Try not to overexert yourself
or you might end up getting hurt
We all know it's not your fault, you overturned the malt
And that sometimes the world must come to a halt
especially when your head hits the asphalt
Yes, you know what's in the salt and so does
everyone else; once, the shaker did that somersault
But I would advise you not to try to use
that fellow's cane to do a pole vault

APHRODISIAC

Aphrodisiac; he doesn't lack. He even has part of a six-pack
Come on; bring him back
he is my soccer player and my quarterback
I don't have any idea what he lacks because when
I see him, all I want to do is attack
He is the best pill for me; he fixes me when
I get on the wrong track
What could it be,
this strange allure, this strange attraction
Don't you see; he gives me his good-hearted attention
And with him
I can be totally free, without any intervention
What can I say,
but coffee, tea, or me? I am a foregone conclusion
All things aside; I fought many away to become his bride
In this, I take immense pride
and when I am with him, I can't help but be bright-eyed
Some consider it a free ride
but with him, I love to share and to divide
He puts me up on the crest of a tide of feelings
I cannot and do not want to hide
Now I do understand about God's great "love" command
Sometimes, I'll give him a hand
because he deserves the best in all the land
He takes me to never-never land
and living with him feels like living in fantasy land
He'll be the happiest man in all the land because
I'll give to him according to supply and demand

You and I both know he is a living dynamo
He knows just how fast to go and when
things are just reaching touch and go
He sings high and he sings low in karaoke
that is when his true talent glows
When he tries, he has a lot of get-up-and-go
and plenty of do-si-do
The greatest thing about him is his
tremendous attractive zing
He can take my bell and ring it
until I am a puppet on his string
He can pluck my line from his fishing line
and pull me in anytime on his drawstring
Join with us and lift your voice and sing
and you will complete our rites of spring
We will be innocent and pure
and as we learn we will both purr
We will have a clear vision
and there will be no confusion and no blur
The story will be of a happy him and a happy her
We will experience blue fire
and together we will be live wires, as it were
Everyone who we meet
will be able to tell what we have is pure spitfire
They will see we have built a love spire
and lit a love bonfire
We have a love that is hot-wired, and
we will conspire to fulfill each other's desire
Our happy music could easily fill a church choir

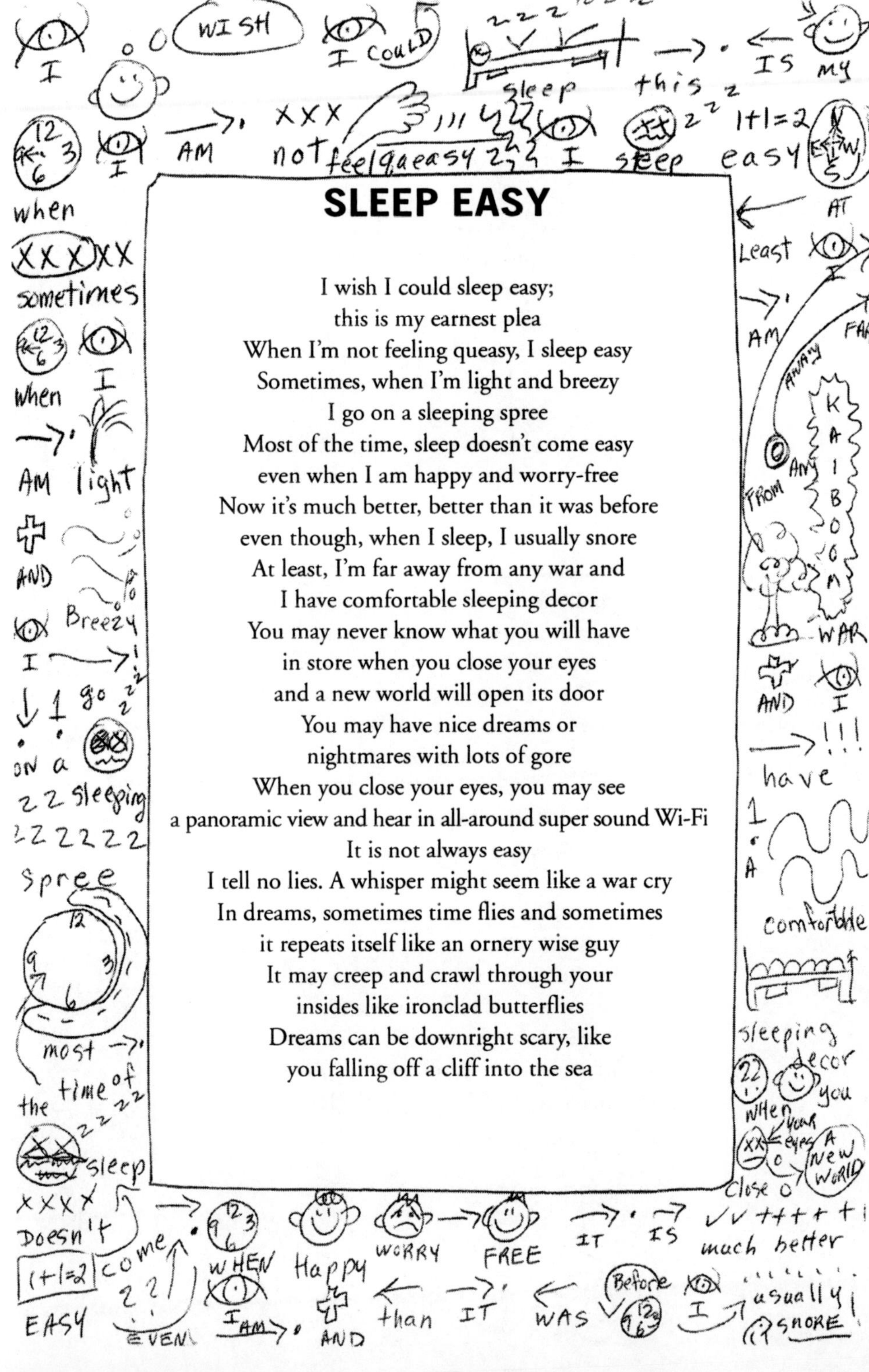

SLEEP EASY

I wish I could sleep easy;
this is my earnest plea
When I'm not feeling queasy, I sleep easy
Sometimes, when I'm light and breezy
I go on a sleeping spree
Most of the time, sleep doesn't come easy
even when I am happy and worry-free
Now it's much better, better than it was before
even though, when I sleep, I usually snore
At least, I'm far away from any war and
I have comfortable sleeping decor
You may never know what you will have
in store when you close your eyes
and a new world will open its door
You may have nice dreams or
nightmares with lots of gore
When you close your eyes, you may see
a panoramic view and hear in all-around super sound Wi-Fi
It is not always easy
I tell no lies. A whisper might seem like a war cry
In dreams, sometimes time flies and sometimes
it repeats itself like an ornery wise guy
It may creep and crawl through your
insides like ironclad butterflies
Dreams can be downright scary, like
you falling off a cliff into the sea

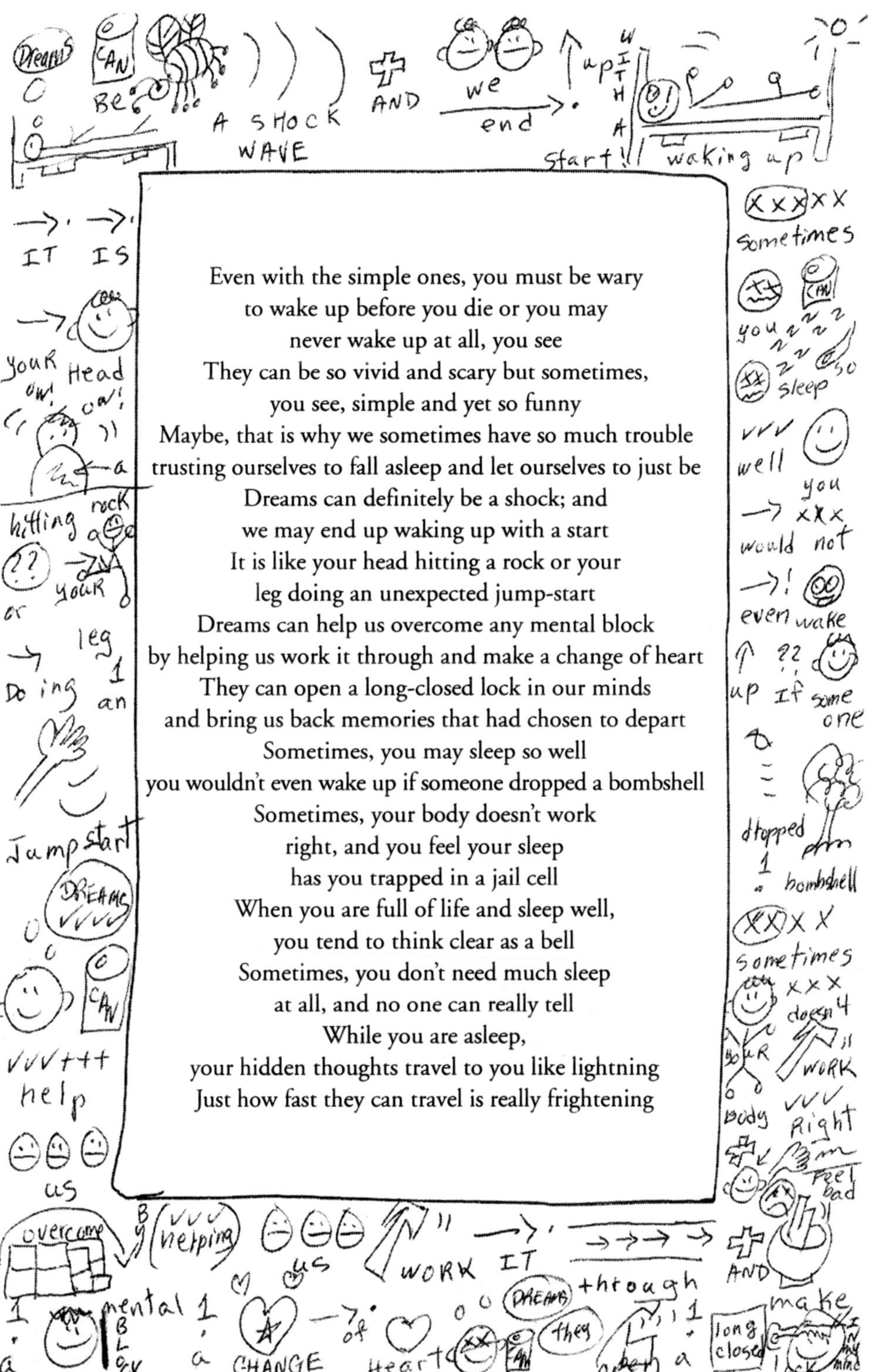

Even with the simple ones, you must be wary
to wake up before you die or you may
never wake up at all, you see
They can be so vivid and scary but sometimes,
you see, simple and yet so funny
Maybe, that is why we sometimes have so much trouble
trusting ourselves to fall asleep and let ourselves to just be
Dreams can definitely be a shock; and
we may end up waking up with a start
It is like your head hitting a rock or your
leg doing an unexpected jump-start
Dreams can help us overcome any mental block
by helping us work it through and make a change of heart
They can open a long-closed lock in our minds
and bring us back memories that had chosen to depart
Sometimes, you may sleep so well
you wouldn't even wake up if someone dropped a bombshell
Sometimes, your body doesn't work
right, and you feel your sleep
has you trapped in a jail cell
When you are full of life and sleep well,
you tend to think clear as a bell
Sometimes, you don't need much sleep
at all, and no one can really tell
While you are asleep,
your hidden thoughts travel to you like lightning
Just how fast they can travel is really frightening

They can give a new enlightening idea
or bring on an awakening
They can also give an insight
into your world's hidden working things
When I sleep, I never know what to expect
It could be a slow-running stream or
it could be a fast-running shipwreck
Any which way, I don't care, as long
as I do not become an insomniac
With this in mind, I will be happy
with almost any future prospect

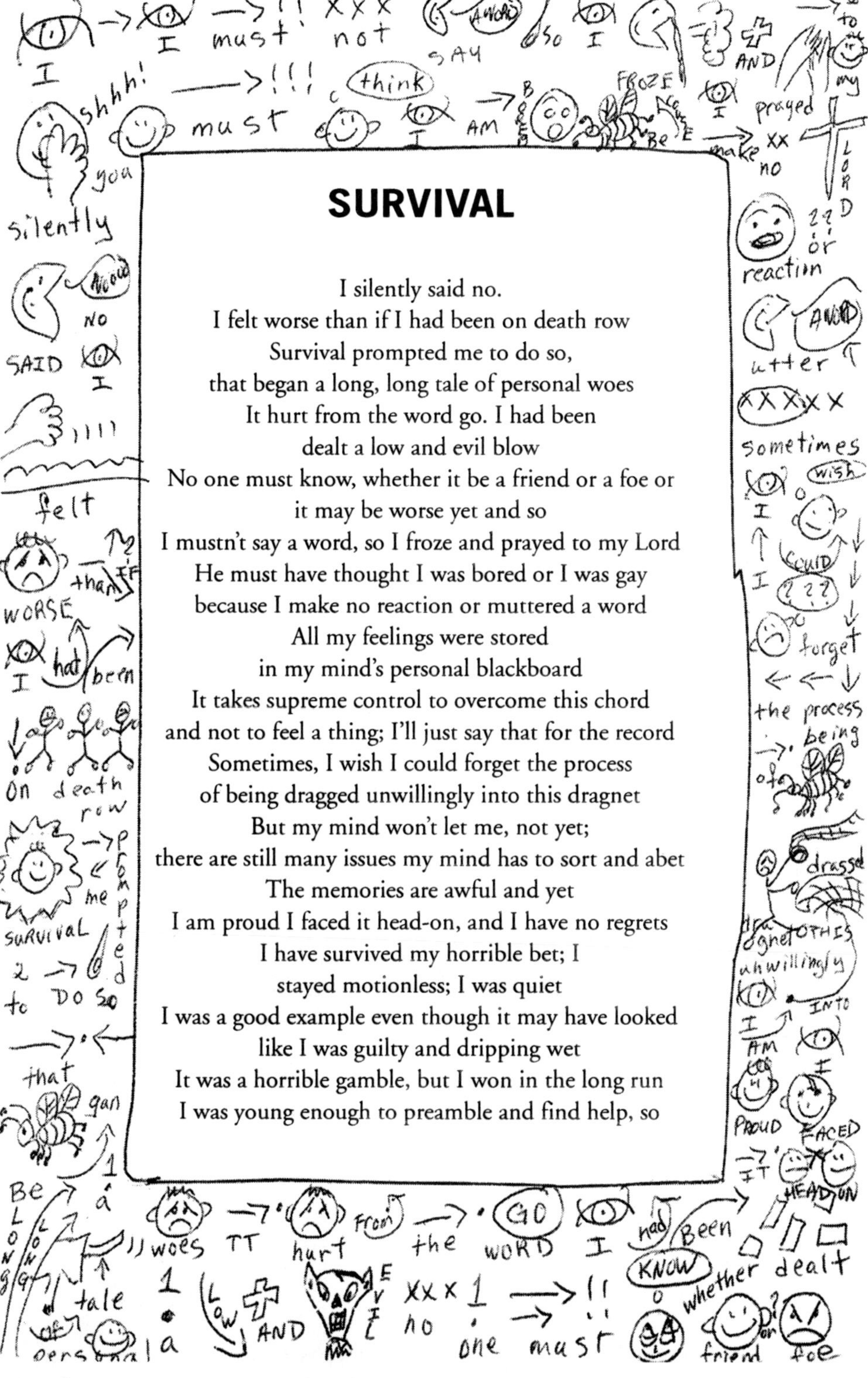

SURVIVAL

I silently said no.
I felt worse than if I had been on death row
Survival prompted me to do so,
that began a long, long tale of personal woes
It hurt from the word go. I had been
dealt a low and evil blow
No one must know, whether it be a friend or a foe or
it may be worse yet and so
I mustn't say a word, so I froze and prayed to my Lord
He must have thought I was bored or I was gay
because I make no reaction or muttered a word
All my feelings were stored
in my mind's personal blackboard
It takes supreme control to overcome this chord
and not to feel a thing; I'll just say that for the record
Sometimes, I wish I could forget the process
of being dragged unwillingly into this dragnet
But my mind won't let me, not yet;
there are still many issues my mind has to sort and abet
The memories are awful and yet
I am proud I faced it head-on, and I have no regrets
I have survived my horrible bet; I
stayed motionless; I was quiet
I was a good example even though it may have looked
like I was guilty and dripping wet
It was a horrible gamble, but I won in the long run
I was young enough to preamble and find help, so

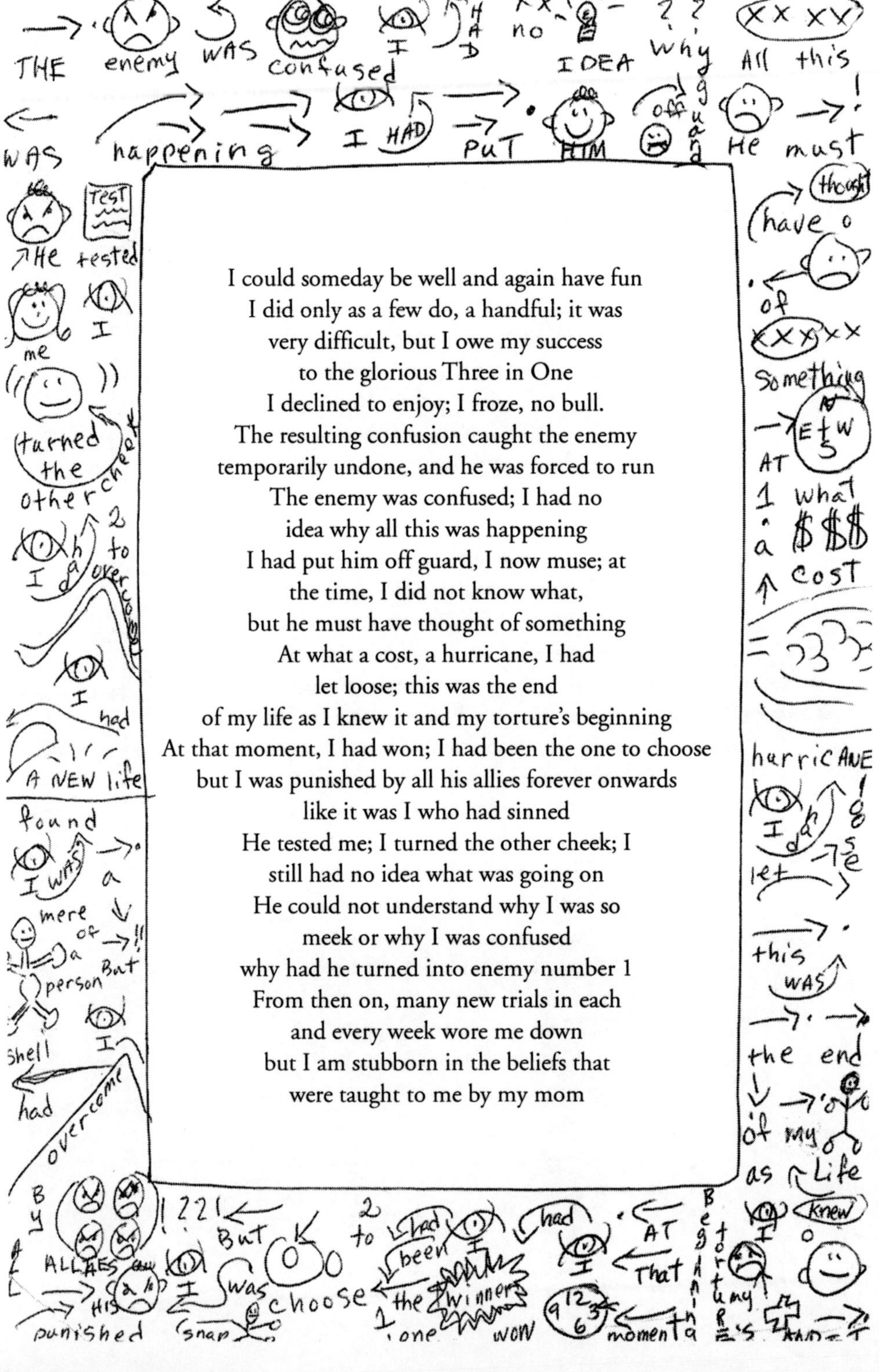

I could someday be well and again have fun
I did only as a few do, a handful; it was
very difficult, but I owe my success
to the glorious Three in One
I declined to enjoy; I froze, no bull.
The resulting confusion caught the enemy
temporarily undone, and he was forced to run
The enemy was confused; I had no
idea why all this was happening
I had put him off guard, I now muse; at
the time, I did not know what,
but he must have thought of something
At what a cost, a hurricane, I had
let loose; this was the end
of my life as I knew it and my torture's beginning
At that moment, I had won; I had been the one to choose
but I was punished by all his allies forever onwards
like it was I who had sinned
He tested me; I turned the other cheek; I
still had no idea what was going on
He could not understand why I was so
meek or why I was confused
why had he turned into enemy number 1
From then on, many new trials in each
and every week wore me down
but I am stubborn in the beliefs that
were taught to me by my mom

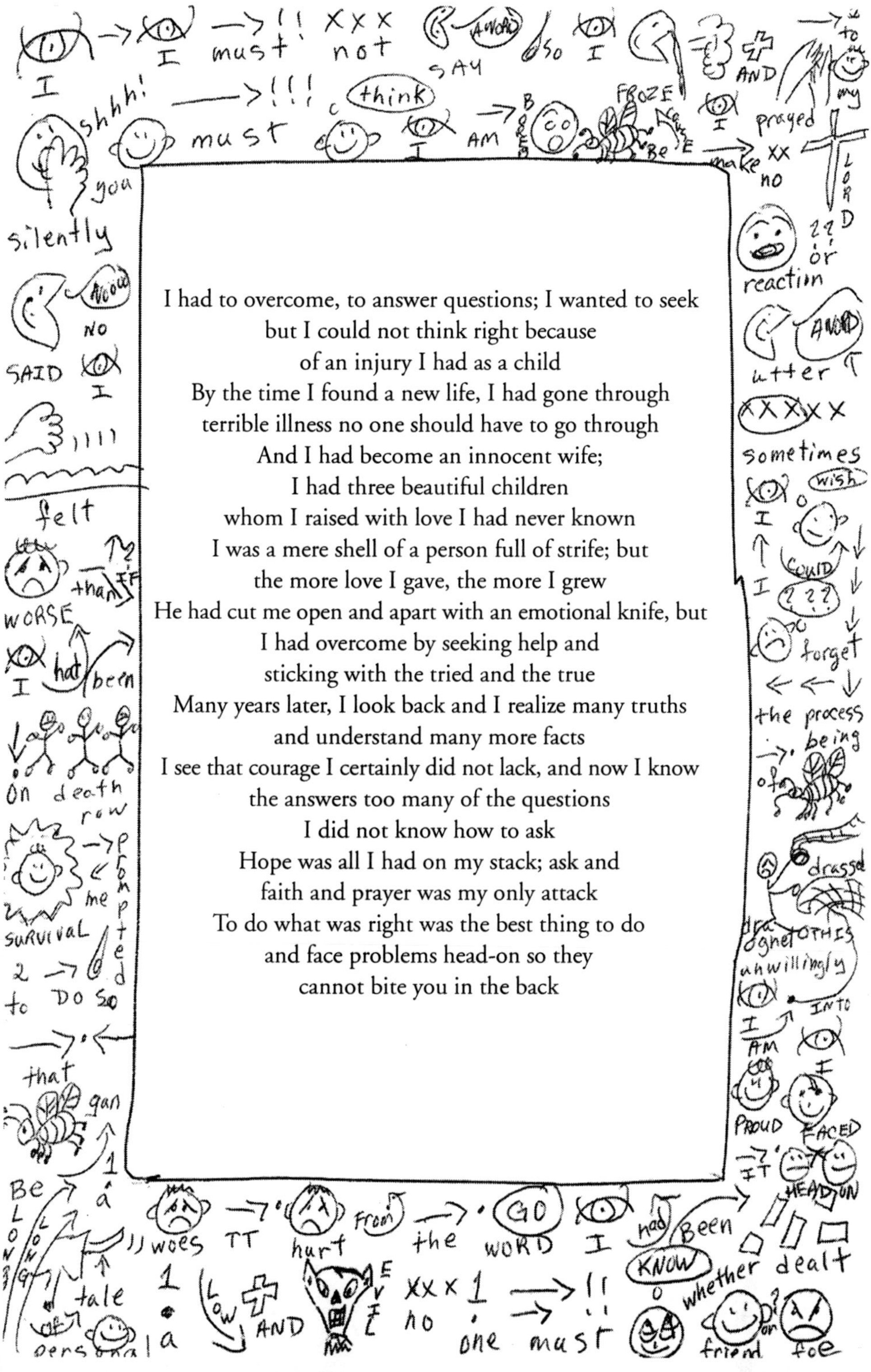

I had to overcome, to answer questions; I wanted to seek
but I could not think right because
of an injury I had as a child
By the time I found a new life, I had gone through
terrible illness no one should have to go through
And I had become an innocent wife;
I had three beautiful children
whom I raised with love I had never known
I was a mere shell of a person full of strife; but
the more love I gave, the more I grew
He had cut me open and apart with an emotional knife, but
I had overcome by seeking help and
sticking with the tried and the true
Many years later, I look back and I realize many truths
and understand many more facts
I see that courage I certainly did not lack, and now I know
the answers too many of the questions
I did not know how to ask
Hope was all I had on my stack; ask and
faith and prayer was my only attack
To do what was right was the best thing to do
and face problems head-on so they
cannot bite you in the back

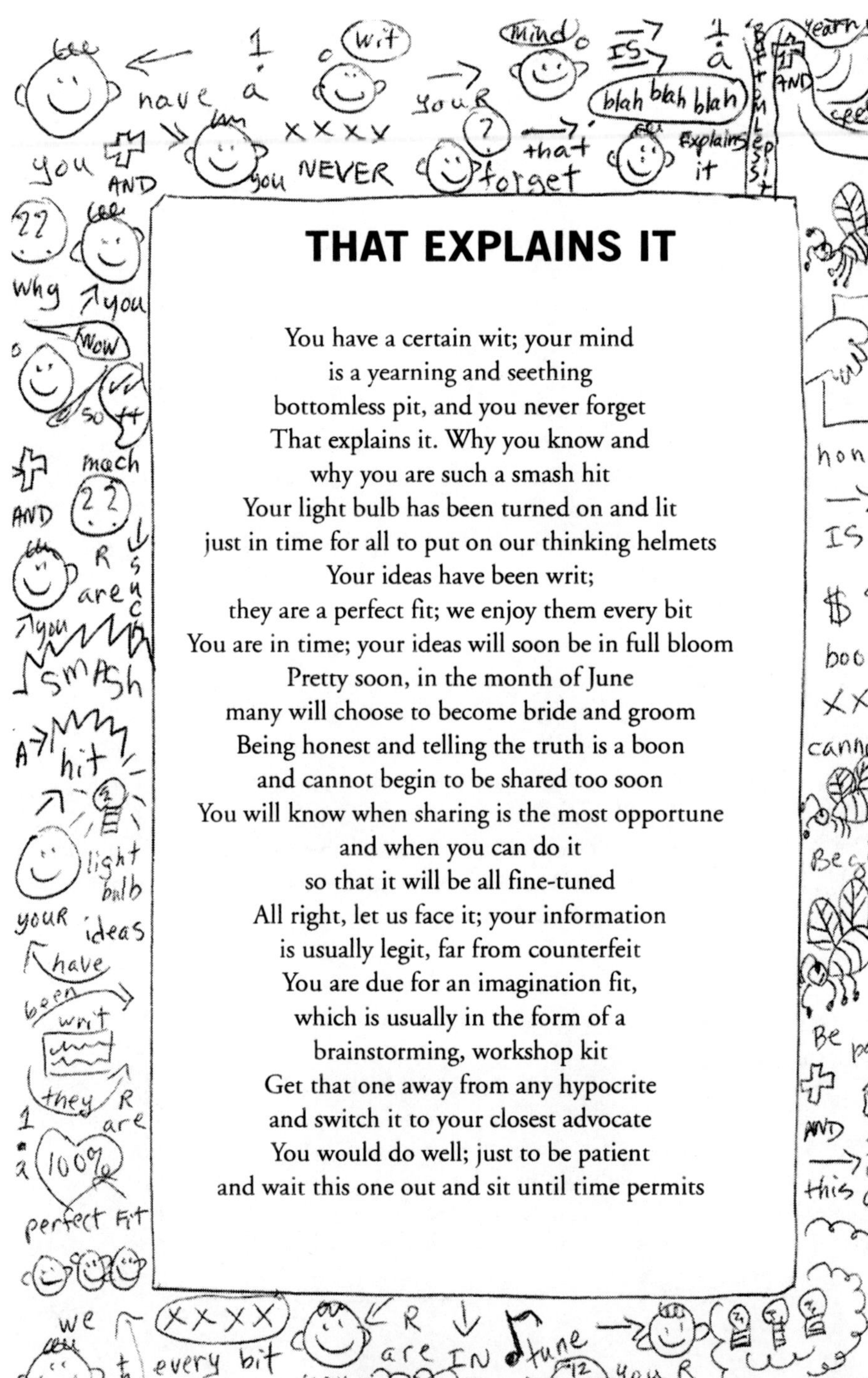

THAT EXPLAINS IT

You have a certain wit; your mind
is a yearning and seething
bottomless pit, and you never forget
That explains it. Why you know and
why you are such a smash hit
Your light bulb has been turned on and lit
just in time for all to put on our thinking helmets
Your ideas have been writ;
they are a perfect fit; we enjoy them every bit
You are in time; your ideas will soon be in full bloom
Pretty soon, in the month of June
many will choose to become bride and groom
Being honest and telling the truth is a boon
and cannot begin to be shared too soon
You will know when sharing is the most opportune
and when you can do it
so that it will be all fine-tuned
All right, let us face it; your information
is usually legit, far from counterfeit
You are due for an imagination fit,
which is usually in the form of a
brainstorming, workshop kit
Get that one away from any hypocrite
and switch it to your closest advocate
You would do well; just to be patient
and wait this one out and sit until time permits

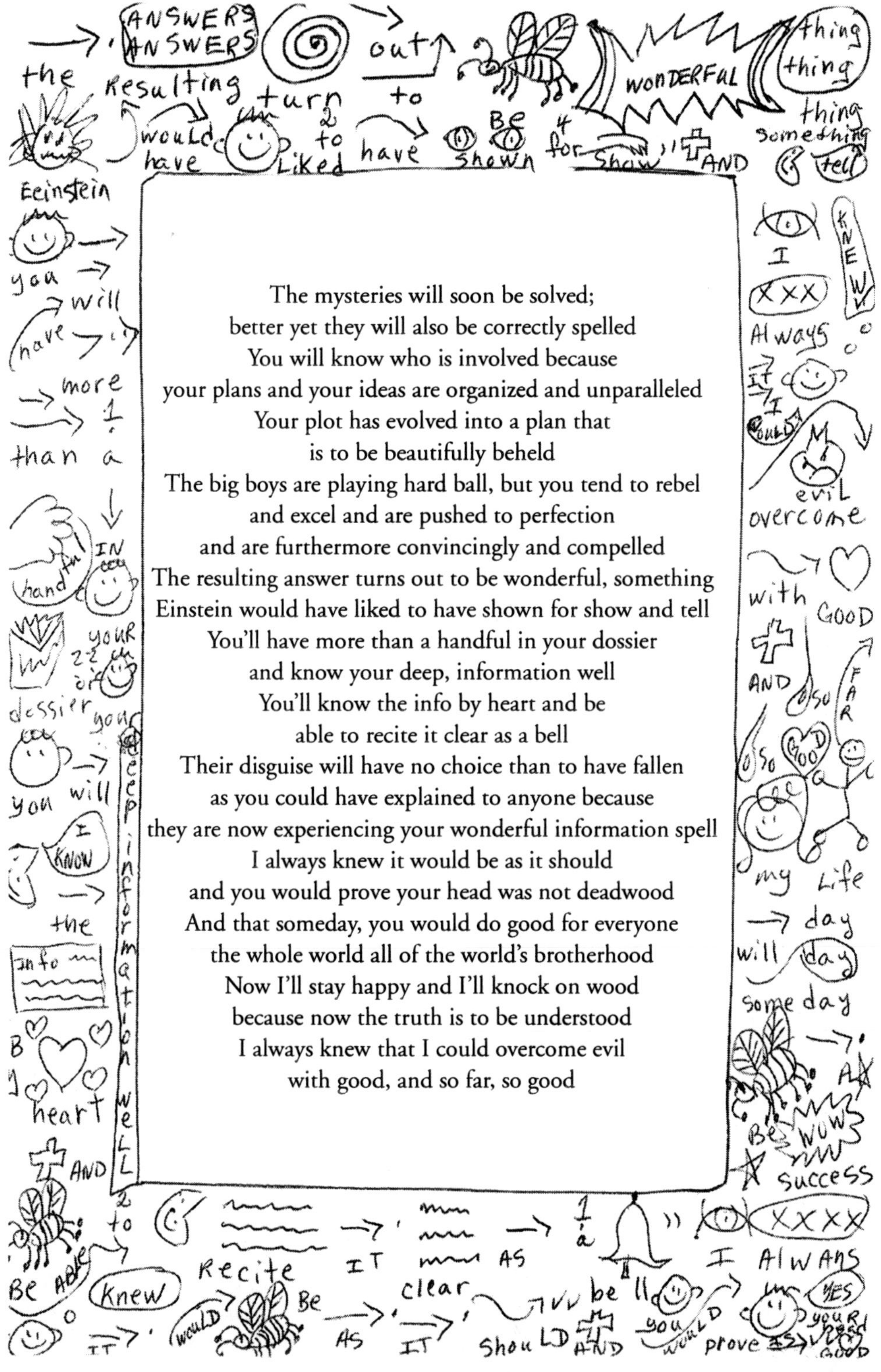

The mysteries will soon be solved;
better yet they will also be correctly spelled
You will know who is involved because
your plans and your ideas are organized and unparalleled
Your plot has evolved into a plan that
is to be beautifully beheld
The big boys are playing hard ball, but you tend to rebel
and excel and are pushed to perfection
and are furthermore convincingly and compelled
The resulting answer turns out to be wonderful, something
Einstein would have liked to have shown for show and tell
You'll have more than a handful in your dossier
and know your deep, information well
You'll know the info by heart and be
able to recite it clear as a bell
Their disguise will have no choice than to have fallen
as you could have explained to anyone because
they are now experiencing your wonderful information spell
I always knew it would be as it should
and you would prove your head was not deadwood
And that someday, you would do good for everyone
the whole world all of the world's brotherhood
Now I'll stay happy and I'll knock on wood
because now the truth is to be understood
I always knew that I could overcome evil
with good, and so far, so good

My life will someday be a success
because mainly I was able to share and to express
And it will no longer be a mess; my life's journey
has been my character's printing press
I will pass all my own tests and continue to progress
into a full-fledged peacock's headdress
I will invite the right guests; these will
be my self-claimed friends.
Who they are is anyone's guess

FOR THE NAME OF HUMANITY

Who are we? What is this thing called "humanity"?
Could it be we started off like our cousins,
the chimpanzees or the monkeys?
How many times have we been altered genetically?
We know we have a very large family
When did our species alter course,
and at what times in our history
The change, no matter how it came, had
some drastic reason for us to change
But the human race, as a species, did change
when all our chromosomes began to rearrange
We had no choice and had no ability to choose
which ways we would change in the short or long range
We barely noticed at first, but soon the changes
became more and more of a higher perceived interchange
There was no reason to fear anything
except the thought of fear itself
We were still come from the same genetic stuff
Better yet, we always improved
into a better version of our selves
Our new version was better able to live
in our new world and was an even more
intelligent version of our old selves
We learned, through experience, that change
even in ourselves was inevitable
So eventually, we accepted this new learned twist
and began to ready for what
we received in our humanity stables

Sometimes, we had to accept
when our lives became very unstable
But as a whole, humanity
continued on willing and able
Through the eons, we have overcome adversity
to survive and to flourish
We have survived whatever was put on our life's dish
We have continued to improve ourselves
as much as we could possibly wish
Even though sometimes
humans seem to have a death wish
Most likely, *Homo sapiens* will stay here on Earth
or some version of us will stay on this world
We, as a race, most likely will adapt,
no matter what kind of story unfolds
We may think we are the boss, but
nature is wiser and much older
Truth is, it is probably nature that will develop
a totally different version of us with results
that will be something spectacular to behold
But if we abuse our Mother Nature
she may decide to turn around and get nasty
She might decide to make our lives
far from worry-free and go on a killing spree
We, as a race, may never recover and may not
have time to flee our planet, you see

That would be the end of our brand
our particular family tree
So you see,
we must all band together and find a way to survive
Because if we cooperate with each other
we will then live and thrive
We must be nicer to our Mother Nature
in order to stay alive
And to give our human chapter time to adapt and to revive

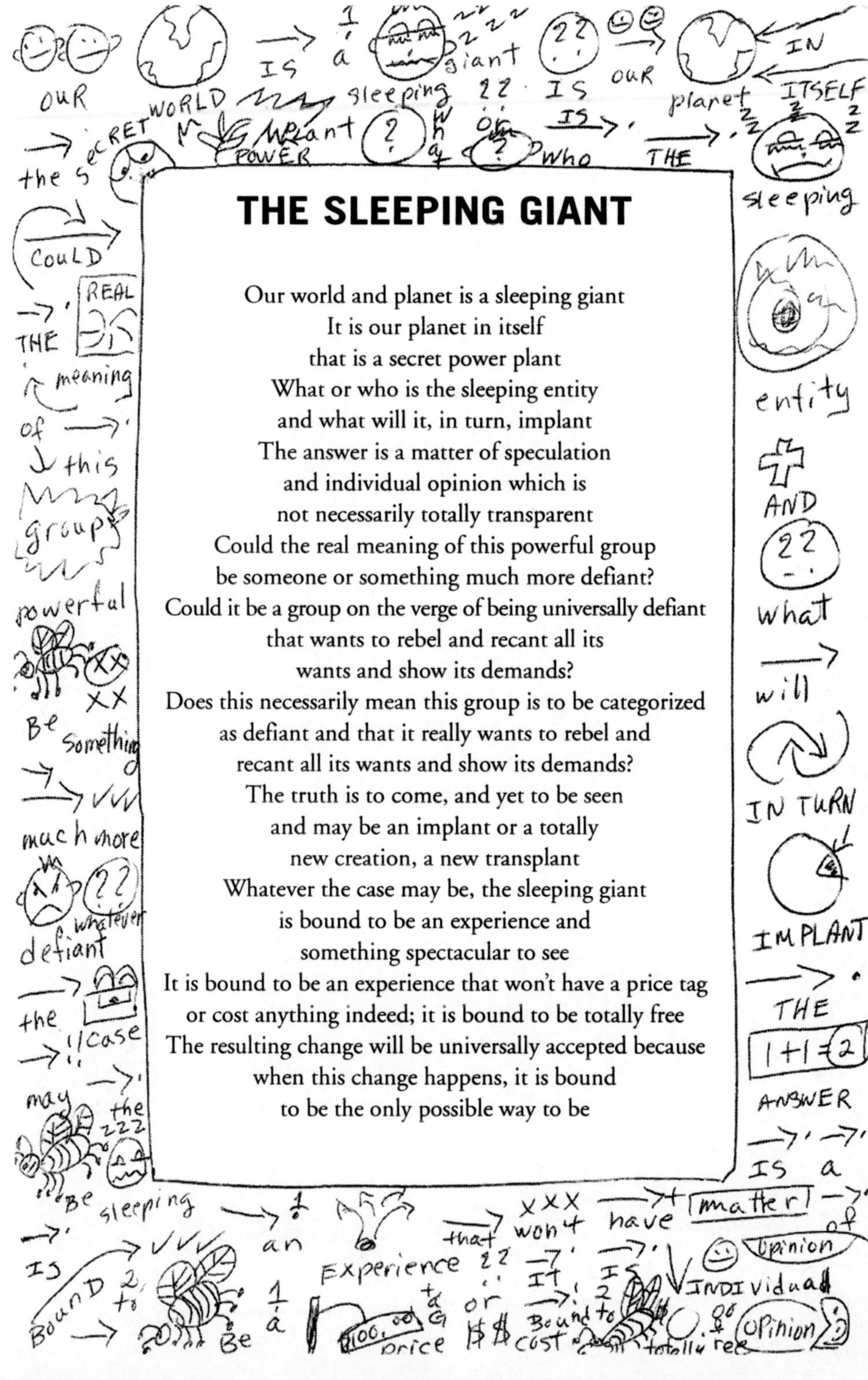

THE SLEEPING GIANT

Our world and planet is a sleeping giant
It is our planet in itself
that is a secret power plant
What or who is the sleeping entity
and what will it, in turn, implant
The answer is a matter of speculation
and individual opinion which is
not necessarily totally transparent
Could the real meaning of this powerful group
be someone or something much more defiant?
Could it be a group on the verge of being universally defiant
that wants to rebel and recant all its
wants and show its demands?
Does this necessarily mean this group is to be categorized
as defiant and that it really wants to rebel and
recant all its wants and show its demands?
The truth is to come, and yet to be seen
and may be an implant or a totally
new creation, a new transplant
Whatever the case may be, the sleeping giant
is bound to be an experience and
something spectacular to see
It is bound to be an experience that won't have a price tag
or cost anything indeed; it is bound to be totally free
The resulting change will be universally accepted because
when this change happens, it is bound
to be the only possible way to be

What we all make of it will be something
we will all be able to relate to
and something we will, as a race, accept
and something, with which, we all choose to agree
The people of the world may rise of one
accord and decide to all get along
This is something that will help us all be as one
and the result will exponentially be
freedom and being strong
We will all want this to be a united whole, as one,
and we will all agree to sing the same song
All peoples will get over our grievances and
we will all be on par and see eye to
eye and do no more wrongs
That is when true progress will be made and if we think
we have already accomplished miracles
we won't even begin to know what we are capable to do
We will then blossom into the greatest
hybrid flower, something brand new
Our people will be at peace with each other
and no one will again be sad or blue
Our world will again be a paradise
and we will all have a reason to rejoice and to be happy too
I can't even begin to understand what the
changes will be or the resulting scope
All I know is that I have always, in
our world and in our people
kept up my unending hope

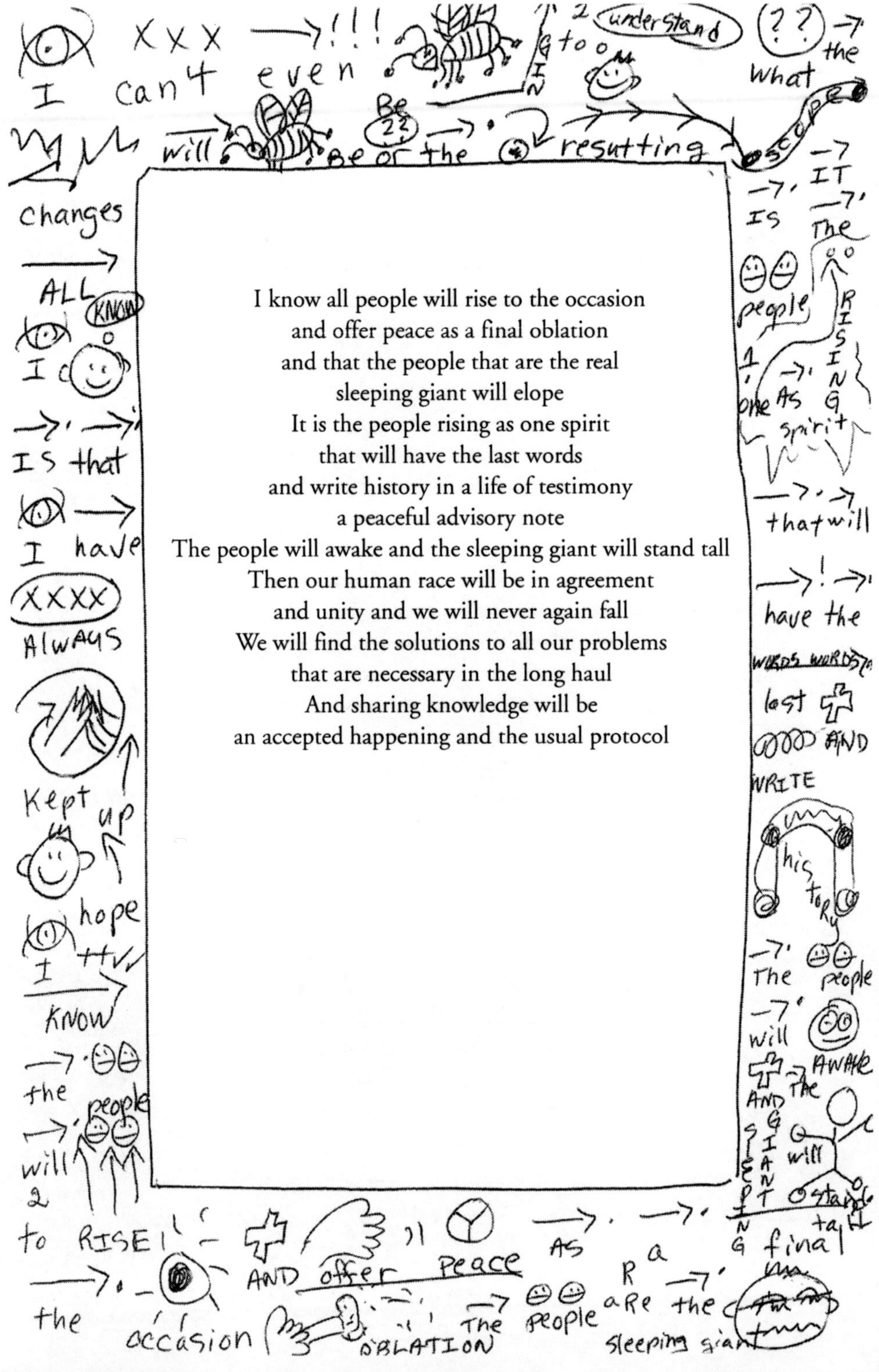

I know all people will rise to the occasion
and offer peace as a final oblation
and that the people that are the real
sleeping giant will elope
It is the people rising as one spirit
that will have the last words
and write history in a life of testimony
a peaceful advisory note
The people will awake and the sleeping giant will stand tall
Then our human race will be in agreement
and unity and we will never again fall
We will find the solutions to all our problems
that are necessary in the long haul
And sharing knowledge will be
an accepted happening and the usual protocol

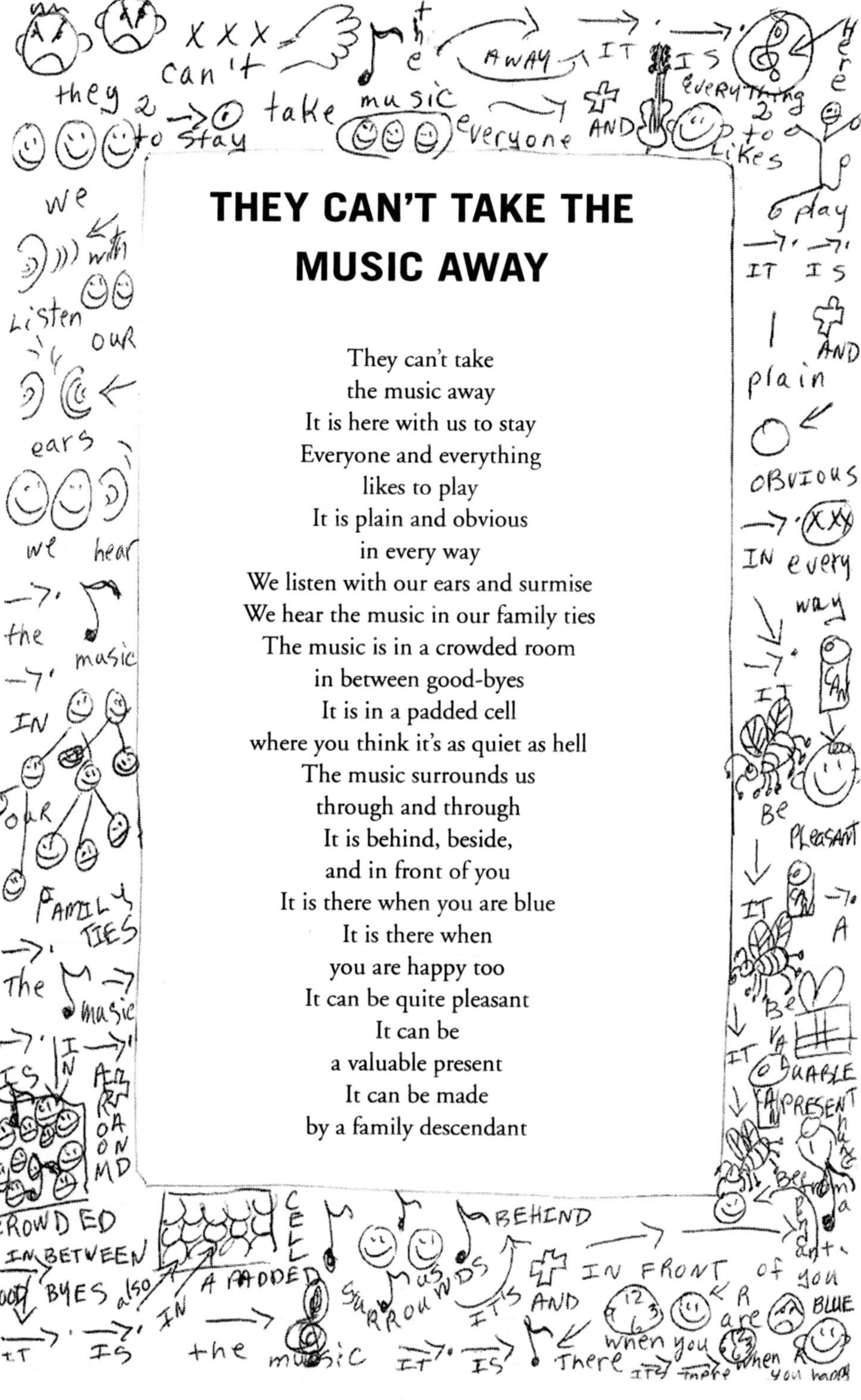

THEY CAN'T TAKE THE MUSIC AWAY

They can't take
the music away
It is here with us to stay
Everyone and everything
likes to play
It is plain and obvious
in every way
We listen with our ears and surmise
We hear the music in our family ties
The music is in a crowded room
in between good-byes
It is in a padded cell
where you think it's as quiet as hell
The music surrounds us
through and through
It is behind, beside,
and in front of you
It is there when you are blue
It is there when
you are happy too
It can be quite pleasant
It can be
a valuable present
It can be made
by a family descendant

It can be hung
from a pendant
The sounds will rise to the sky
They'll travel two- and three-ply
Even if they escape
and pass you by
The effect they have
will never die
It could have been worse
They could have been
put totally off course
Or have been cut
off at their source
Or could have blown up
with tremendous force
Every single solitary note
Is happier
when recorded and wrote
Then it no longer
has a disguise, just hope
Simple and pure—it will
take off its overcoat
The energy music will bring
Will make us all
yell out and sing
The notes will fly up,
down and around
They will surround us
and make us go for a fling

INDEX

J

K

L

M

N

O

CPSIA information can be obtained at www.ICGtesting.com
Printed in the USA
LVOW12s0021190714

395015LV00001B/18/P